THE
ROTHMAN
SCANDAL

STEPHEN
BIRMINGHAM

BERKLEY BOOKS, NEW YORK

THE ROTHMAN SCANDAL

A Berkley Book / published by arrangement with
Little, Brown and Company, Inc.

PRINTING HISTORY
Little, Brown and Company edition published 1991
Berkley edition / November 1993

ISBN: 0-425-13977-8

BERKLEY®
Berkley Books are published by
The Berkley Publishing Group, 200 Madison Avenue,
New York, New York 10016.
BERKLEY and the "B" design are trademarks of
Berkley Publishing Corporation

PRINTED IN THE UNITED STATES OF AMERICA

10 9 8 7 6 5 4 3 2

For Fredrica S. Friedman

Prologue

In those days, they all lived in Tarrytown, at "Rothmere," one big happy family. There were seven of them then: Ho Rothman and his wife, Anna Lily; their son, Herbert, and his wife, Pegeen; Herbert and Pegeen's son, Steven, and his young wife, Alexandra, and their infant son, Joel. Four generations of Rothmans lived under one capacious and many-gabled roof in a house that was considered one of the finest in the East, a Palladian jewel covering a hilltop that overlooked the mighty river, the graceful curves of the Tappan Zee Bridge, and the twinkling lights of Nyack on the opposite shore where some ancient volcanic event had created a break in the Palisades.

Of course, after the scandal and the tragedy that followed it, no one wanted to live at "Rothmere" anymore. The locals claimed that the place was haunted, or at least that it brought bad luck to anyone who lived there. Its previous owner, the man who built it in 1920, had died a broken and ruined man, whose wife walked out on him and was never seen or heard from again. Ho Rothman put it on the market, but it didn't sell. There were no offers even close to its worth. Then Ho tried to give the house away. He offered it to the federal government as a guest residence for visiting dignitaries, and then to the state of New York, for the same purpose, but neither Washington nor Albany wanted it, citing the high cost of maintenance. For a while, "Rothmere" was rented to the Reverend Sun Myung Moon and his Unification Church, and Lily Rothman's famous formal gardens with their elaborate parterres became a parking lot. But the Moonies neglected the place, made no repairs, and in 1980 the house was vandalized, and one wing burned, leaving the ballroom without a roof. Weeds grew up in the cracks of the parquet ballroom floor, where Lily Rothman had given her grand entertainments, where a secretary of state had dined, and where the Duke and Duchess of Windsor had danced, and moss covered the rusted pipes of the giant Wurlitzer.

In 1983, the house was razed, and the property was sold to a developer who divided it into quarter-acre lots and built five hundred cracker-box houses, which sold for up to $750,000 apiece. Only the name of the development, Rosemere Estates—the developer's wife's name was Rose— carried the faint hint of what was once "Rothmere." None of the family ever came back to view this real estate travesty.

It was at "Rothmere" that this letter was penned in a sharply pointed longhand:

ROTHMERE
Old Post Road
Tarrytown-on-Hudson, New York 10591

September 10, 1973

Dear Sir,

I address you as "sir" because I have no notion of what your real name is, nor have I ever had. I do not address you as "sir" to imply that you are even in the remotest sense a gentleman. No gentleman would threaten to do to a woman what you have threatened to do to me. I regard you as the lowest of the low, lower than the lowest species of earthworm, to threaten to destroy my family, my marriage, my child's future, my career, my whole life, as you have done. To think that I ever believed in you . . . that I ever believed I loved you . . .

However, I have discussed your threats with the senior members of this family in a perfectly businesslike way, and we have agreed to accede to your demands. If you will come to this house on Thursday, September

20, at three P.M., I will see to it that your demands are met. It is agreed that you will come alone, and you can be sure that I will be quite alone when you arrive, as you requested. No other family members will be present, and the servants will have been given the afternoon off. There will be no guard at the gate. You can drive straight to the boathouse.

Sincerely,
A.L.R.

Since 1973, the letter, along with the envelope in which it had been mailed, had been kept in a secure place. Clipped to the envelope was a short note, typewritten:

TO WHOM IT MAY CONCERN:

If the lessor of this Safe Deposit box is ever found dead under suspicious or other than natural circumstances, this letter will offer sufficient evidence as to the reasons why.

Lessor of Box No. 369
Manufacturers Hanover Trust
Fifth Avenue Office

I am the lessor of that safe-deposit box.

PART ONE

FIREWORKS OVER HELL GATE

Chapter 1

"René Bouché painted that of me in nineteen seventy-three," Alexandra Rothman said.

"Nineteen seventy-three. The year everything happened," Lucille said.

"Or the year after everything else happened. Whichever way you choose to look at it, I guess," Alexandra said.

"Any regrets?"

"No. Only—"

"Only what?"

"Only I wish he hadn't made me pose with the little dog. Not that I have anything against dogs. I *like* dogs. But it wasn't even my dog. It was Bouché's dog. Its name was Bonbon."

"I wasn't talking about the portrait," Lucille said.

They were sitting in Alexandra Rothman's green library at 10 Gracie Square—Alex Rothman and her old friend Lucille Withers, Lucille who had been Alex's first boss, really— the room where Alex's portrait hung over the green marble mantel, against the green paneling, the only artwork in a room of book-lined walls, books from floor to ceiling, even above the door and window frames, all bound in leather colors of gold and rose and blue and brown, books-of-a-color shelved together the way birds are supposed to flock. "I must say you don't look a day older, Lexy," Lucille said. "Only richer."

Alex Rothman laughed her throaty laugh. "Richer? What in the world do you mean by that?"

"You just do. Rich people develop a special set of worries. They develop special little worry-lines."

"That's just a nice way of saying wrinkles," Alex said.

"Character lines, I call them. How old were you then? Twenty-nine?"

Alex counted backward on her fingers. "*Just,*" she replied.

"I see you still wear his ring," Lucille Withers said, pointing to the ring on Alex's finger, and glancing at the ring finger of the hand in the portrait.

"Of course."

"Did you love him, Lexy?"

Alex spread the fingers of her left hand. "Sapphires are among the heaviest of all precious stones," she said. "Did you know that? Emeralds are among the lightest. Kashmiri sapphires are supposed to be the best. This is a Kashmiri sapphire."

"Of course I didn't expect you to answer that question," Lucille said.

"Certainly not. You know me, Lulu. Ask me a personal question, and I'll give you a gemology lesson. Ask me another, Lulu."

"What did you two do on your wedding night, honey?"

"A sapphire's specific weight is—"

Now they were both grinning at each other like happy conspirators, the only two women in the world who knew the whereabouts of the key to the king's countinghouse, and the secret schedule of the night watchman's rounds.

They had always been something of an odd couple, these two old friends who had known each other for nearly thirty years—Alex Rothman, the legendary Manhattan fashion editor, and Lucille Withers, the spinster Kansas City businesswoman who was at least twenty years Alex's senior. They appeared to have nothing in common, aside from the commonality of their sex. Alex was small-boned, almost dainty, still a perfect size four. Lucille was immensely tall for a woman, easily six feet, with large bony hands and feet that were always encased in sensible walking shoes. Her face was long and thin, with a high forehead and an aquiline nose, and her jet-black hair was always pulled back tightly from her face and secured in a bun that possibly concealed a rat or even a chignon; no one had ever seen Lucille with that black hair down but, if it was all her own, it would have reached to her waist. She dressed her long and lanky frame in high-necked Gibson Girl blouses with puffed sleeves and ribbon bows, and long, boxy, pleated skirts, usually black. "When you find a style that suits you, stick to it," Lucille often said, which of course was not bad fashion advice. But whether or not Lucille's style suited her, it was certainly distinctive. Lucille, on the street, did not go unnoticed, which was doubtless her intention. To a stranger, seeing Lucille's tall figure striding along the sidewalk, swinging her long arms—usually with an oversize briefcase in one hand—she suggested one's notion of a nineteenth-century high-school principal—she even affected a pair of wire-rimmed pince-nez spectacles slung from a cord around her neck—or, just possibly, a matador in drag. "Who *is* that woman?" people would whisper, spotting her for the first time. And this, of course, reflected the advice she always gave her girls: "Stand up, stand straight, walk tall, be noticed. Make people ask themselves who you are."

As a young girl, she had once told Alex, she had thought, because of her height, of becoming a fashion model. Instead, she had settled on being the proprietress of what would become one of the most important modeling agencies in the Midwest—not, she would quickly point out, that this was any big deal. The Midwest was hardly a Mecca for modeling agents.

And yet, despite the difference in their ages and sense of style, Lucille and Alexandra had become friends from the moment they first met, which was in 1960, when Alex was just sixteen, and the friendship proved to be a lasting one. In Kansas City they had been called Mutt and Jeff, but they were Lexy and Lulu—names no others were permitted to call them by—and whenever Lucille was in New York she always dropped by to see Alexandra, always unannounced, as she had done this afternoon, always with a portfolio of composite photos of new model clients for Alex to consider for the magazine. The photos were spread out on the sofa between the two women now, and Alex had placed check marks on certain of the prints with a yellow grease pencil. The advantage—to Alex—of using models from the Withers Agency was that the girls were fresh faces, newcomers, unknowns. And the advantage to Herbert Rothman, *Mode*'s publisher, was that newcomers and unknowns worked for less than models who were familiar and famous, which made Herb happier when he reviewed *Mode*'s production budget.

"Well, you've certainly come a long way, baby," Lucille said now. "But like you always said, you was gonna see you some big towns, hear you some big talk. You sure done it, honey."

"Damn right! Just 'cause I'se a li'l gal from a li'l ole pissant town in the Show-Me State don't mean I ain't got no brains!"

"Sure don't!" It amused them to drawl in the accents and elisions of the Missouri backcountry.

"But it's all thanks to you, Lulu," Alex said. "You got me started."

"Oh, bullets, honey," Lulu said. "Bullets to that one. I had nothing to do with it. You caught the brass ring, Lexy. Or the platinum ring. And it just happened to have a li'l ole Kashmiri sapphire planted on it."

"But you put me on this merry-go-round in the first place, Lulu. You put me on that carousel horse where I could reach for the ring."

"Bullets, honey." Her long hawk's nose pointed high in the air.

Coleman, Alex's butler, appeared at the library door. "Excuse me, Alex," he said. "The florist is here. I showed them how you wanted the little porcelain birds arranged around the centerpieces. Is there anything else?"

"Can't think of anythin', darlin'," Alex said. "I'll be out in a bit to check the tables."

"I wish," Lucille muttered when Coleman had departed, "that I had a butler I could call darlin'. I wish I even had a butler." Then she slapped her thigh. "But I've got to go. You've got a party to host, and a million things to do." She began stuffing the composites back in her big black portfolio.

"Remember the little blonde," Alex said. "Send me a few more shots of her."

"That's Melissa. She's okay if you shoot her straight on, and from the waist up. But she's got a rear end you could land a helicopter on. Full length, she goes to hell in a handbasket."

"I liked her face. She's got a foxy look. She looks like she's going to go to the party. And when she gets to the party, she'll have a good time. I'm working on a party issue."

"Okay," Lucille Withers said, standing up, and when Alex Rothman also rose the top of her head reached roughly the height of Lucille's shoulder.

"And I wish you'd come to my party tonight," Alex said. "All sorts of people are going to be here. The Kissingers. Richard Avedon. Dina Merrill. Won't you change your mind?"

"Hell, no, honey. You don't want an old belle like me at your party. You're going to be having all the Beautiful People. I'll read about it in *Women's Wear*. Besides, I don't have a party dress. Never did have one, in fact." They moved together toward the door and out into the entrance gallery.

"I'd like to introduce you as the woman who discovered me," Alex said.

"Bullets. I didn't discover you. You discovered yourself, Lexy."

"Please come, Lulu. Wear just what you're wearing now. In New York these days, it's pretty much anything goes."

"No, no. I've got to get back to my hotel. Got some phone calls to make."

"Where are you staying this time, Lulu?"

"Say, I've found a swell little place," she said. "It's called the Arnold Arms—on Adam Clayton Powell Junior Boulevard, at One Hundred and Sixteenth Street. Thirty-five dollars a night. Not bad, I say."

Alex giggled. "But Lulu, that's in *Harlem*," she said.

"That so? Now you mention it, I did see a few darky dudes hanging around the lobby this morning. But don't worry. No Nigra is gonna mess with Lulu." She brandished her large case to demonstrate how she would deal with an attacker. It was another of their private jokes. Though Lucille made plenty of money, she refused to pay what she considered to be New York's outrageous hotel and restaurant prices, and on each trip she searched for a hotel that would be less expensive than the last, and for the kind of diner where you could get a decent hamburger for $1.49.

At the elevator, which opened directly into the apartment, Alex pressed the button, and the giantess lowered her huge hawk-shaped head to give Alex a peck on the cheek. "I'll send you some more Melissas," she said. "But don't forget the helicopter pad."

Alex looked down at Lucille's feet. "You and your orthopedic shoes," she said, and giggled again.

"They're Red Cross. They're the best. My mother used to say that high heels made a girl's uterus tip—not that my uterus is much use to me anymore. But you wouldn't put high heels on a girl my height, would you?"

The elevator door slid open. "Say, now you-all take care, ya hear?" Lucille said, while Frank, the elevator man, held the door.

Alex squeezed her hand. "And you-all come back real soon, ya hear?" As the elevator door was closing, Lulu threw her a wink.

"Love ya, Lulu!"

"Love ya too, Lexy! Bye!" came the disembodied voice from the descending elevator car.

Chapter 2

On Alex Rothman's terrace, twenty stories above the East River, the florist's people were setting out the centerpieces on each of the twenty-five round, pink-draped caterers' tables, and the banquet manager from Glorious Food was delivering his instructions to the two dozen waiters, still in their shirtsleeves, who were lined up in front of him like soldiers on a parade field. "This will be a seated dinner for two hundred and fifty people," he was saying, "with music and dancing. Guests are expected to start arriving at eight o'clock, and between eight and nine you will be alternately passing hors d'oeuvre trays and taking drink orders. The bar is over there"—he pointed to the white wrought-iron gazebo—"and the bartenders are Buddy, here, and Jerry. There will be ten hors d'oeuvre trays, and when you pick up a new tray from the kitchen try not to offer it to the same group of guests you've just passed it to. Keep circulating from group to group. There are some important people coming tonight, and I don't want any glitches. At approximately nine o'clock, start suggesting that guests go to the tables. There will be no place cards. Mrs. Rothman likes her guests to sit wherever they like. The first course will be a lobster bisque . . ."

Other people, on stepladders, were attaching clusters of pink and white balloons to the awning posts and to the top of the gazebo, and a willowy young man wearing a golden ponytail and a turtleneck to match was wielding an electric hair dryer on a long cord to force open the tulip buds in the centerpieces.

"Why not just open the white ones, and leave the pink ones in the bud?" Alex suggested.

The young man with the dryer looked skeptical. "Think anybody'll notice?" he said.

"Some people will. Not everybody will, but in this group some people will."

"Who is this dame, anyway?" she heard one waiter ask another.

"The *dame* happens to be the lady standing right behind you, beanhead."

Alex turned and flashed a smile at both of them. "Dot's-a me," she said. Coleman followed her about the terrace with a pad and pencil, taking notes, for Coleman was more than Alex's butler and majordomo. He was her part-time social secretary, friend, and, tonight at least, almost her cohost. "That tablecloth is a little crooked," she pointed, and he made a note.

"I just called the weather report," he said. "Zero chance of rain. Zip precip, but it may get a little breezy after the sun goes down."

"Breezy? Do we have clothespins for the—"

"Clothespins are ready if we need them. And did you know there'll be a full moon tonight—rising at eight forty-seven? That should make it pretty out here."

"Is it true that people do crazy things on nights with a full moon?"

"This full moon was ordered especially for your party. It took some doing, but when I explained to the moon people the nature of the occasion, they agreed to rearrange their schedule."

"That waiter needs a shave. Can you tell him so politely? Maybe let him borrow your razor, and use your bathroom."

Coleman made another note. "The NBC television crew is on its way. They need a little time to set up their equipment."

"Anything else?"

"Cindy Adams called. She has the flu, but she's going to do the story anyway. She wants to know what you'll be wearing. I told her I'd call her back."

"This is Bill Blass—cotton challis pants and top with a cowl neck. Three-quarter sleeves, and an Old Pawn belt.

She may not know what that is. Old Pawn is silver and turquoise jewelry that the Navajo Indians used to make and pawn at trading posts out west. They pawned it for booze." She touched the heavy belt. "Can you imagine pawning this beautiful stuff for booze? This one has a squash flower design. It dates from about eighteen sixty."

He jotted down all this information. "Shoes?"

She extended one small foot. "Turquoise slingbacks. Perry Ellis. Oh, and I have a turquoise cashmere shawl that I may throw over my shoulders if it gets chilly."

"Turquoise—to match your turquoise eyes?"

She laughed. "Please don't tell her that, darlin'," she said. "What about the fireworks?"

"Everything's set. You give the signal to the band, the band moves to the north corner of the terrace and starts to play 'Happy Days.' That's my cue to push the button that will signal the fireworks barge on the river."

"Have we thought of everything, darlin'?" Planning a party like this one was like laying out a military campaign—at least when Alex Rothman planned a party.

"I think so." He consulted his watch. "Six fifty-eight," he said. "You have over an hour until launch time. Why don't you go into the library and relax? There's champagne on ice in the cooler."

"You know I can't relax before I give a party."

"Don't worry. I'll take care of everything. Tonight your only job is to be the most famous woman in New York."

"Like Andy Warhol said—famous for fifteen minutes."

"Just one thing," he said. With one hand, he reached up and lifted one small strand of hair that had fallen across her forehead. Then, holding the hair in place with one hand, he reached in his jacket pocket with the other and produced a can of Spray-Net, and quickly sprayed the errant strand into place. "Now you're perfect," he said. Among other things, Coleman was her part-time hair and makeup stylist.

He had been with her for fifteen years. Sometimes she noticed him gazing at her with a look of such soulfulness and longing that she wondered whether he was in love with her.

As she moved across the terrace toward the glass doors, she saw one of the waiters struggling to tie his black bow tie. "Need help?" she asked him.

"I can never learn to tie these damn things," he said. "And the boss said absolutely no clip-ons."

"Here." She took the two ends of the tie. "You—tie—this—exactly as you would—a shoelace," she said, straightening the knot and flattening the bow into place against his white shirtfront.

"My old lady won't believe this," he said. "The great Alexandra Rothman having to tie her waiter's bow tie."

"You tell your old lady that this old lady did it," she said.

In the library, she drew the curtains closed, and the room was dark, except for the museum light above her portrait, and the house was silent except, from the distant terrace, for the faint sound of the musicians as they began to bring their instruments into tune in a series of F-sharps. She stepped to the cooler, lifted the bottle from the ice, and poured herself a glass of champagne—liquid courage. "A person always needs a little liquid courage before a party," her husband Steven used to say. Steven's problem was remembering names. "I can't even remember my best friends' names when I see them in the middle of a mob of people," he used to say. Alex's problem was different. She would have no difficulty remembering the names of her two hundred and fifty guests tonight because she would be seeing them all in their proper *context*. It was when she encountered familiar faces *out* of context that she was thrown off guard. A year ago, for instance, she spent nearly six months seeing her dentist twice a week while he performed some extensive crown and inlay work. Week after week, this young man had spent hours with his boyish face bent over her open mouth while she familiarized herself with every contour of that face. Yet, when she encountered him one day at the small leather goods counter at Saks, and he greeted her warmly and by her first name, she had absolutely no idea who he was. She had mumbled something about how well he was looking, only to realize later that she had spent two hours with him just the day before! How do you account for that?

She found herself studying the Bouché portrait, asking herself that question. It had been a long time since she had really looked at the portrait, and she wished again that she had stood firm against Bonbon. M. Bouché's tiny white toy poodle. For one thing, Bonbon lent an aura of artifice, or sentimentality, to the painting. For another, it dated the portrait, time-freezing it in the early 1970s. Dogs, like everything else, go in and out of fashion. Since those days, entire breeds appear to have vanished from the animal kingdom. Who ever sees a cocker spaniel anymore? Whatever became of chow-chows, Saint Bernards, Boston bulls, even collies? Scotties are similarly extinct, while the noble Bedlingtons and Afghan hounds are decidedly endangered species, destroyed by popular acclaim as surely as if by acid rain. Toy French poodles, particularly the itsy-bitsy white ones, are a rather special case. One still sees them, Lord knows, but in all the wrong places—in the Indiana couple's farmhouse, on your cleaning lady's Christmas card, or being walked on West 49th Street after dark by ladies of easy virtue. In their place, where women of fashion walk their dogs, have come Shi-tzus, Yorkies, and maybe corgies. Was there an idea for a *Mode* story in this phenomenon? Alexandra quickly dismissed it as frivolous. That was the way Bonbon made her look in the portrait—frivolous.

But Bouché had insisted. He often included Bonbon in his portraits of beautiful women, and Bonbon was more than a cute prop. The dog, he explained, provided a crucial compositional element in the painting. Look how the animal's triangular shape, with its rear legs tucked under its chin, and curled under Alexandra's right arm, echoed the corresponding triangle of Alexandra's left elbow as it rested on the arm of her chair, her slender fingers curved upward to touch her cheek, the fingers forming another triangle. The composition was based on a subtle series of interrelated triangles, he explained. The triangle of her right shoulder, crooked to hold the dog, was balanced by the triangle of her right knee as it crossed her left, and then there was the triangle of the delicate cleavage of her breasts, answered by the triangular shape of the subject's face. And the significance of the triangle? Ah, but didn't Mrs. Rothman know? The triangle is the simplest, strongest geometric form in nature, as the Egyptians knew when they built the Pyramids, as the Indians knew when they carved their arrowheads, as Bucky Fuller knew when he designed his domes! What is the shape of a feather, or a bird's wing? Examine a fly's wing under a microscope, and what will you see? Triangles within triangles.

"My darling Mrs. Rothman, I assure you that Bonbon is *essential*," he said. "Look how his pearl-colored eyes echo your earrings! Now erase that little frown for me, and look beautiful for me again, my darling lady." And he picked up his brush again.

She hadn't argued with him. After all, he was charging her nothing for her portrait. He was painting it out of gratitude for the commission she had given him to illustrate some fashion pages for the magazine. In those days, he was not well known in America, and was eager for the exposure. And, she thought now a little guiltily, she had used him only once again. Such are the penalties of becoming fashionable. She remembered when she had been the first to introduce her readers to the hairstyles of Vidal Sassoon, and where is Vidal Sassoon today? Rich, but his hair products sell at K Mart, and are giveaways in hotels. Ralph Lauren will be the next to go that way, just wait and see. *Look beautiful for me again!*

Beauty is in the eye of the beholder, but what is in the eye that the beholder beholds? That was the trouble. Alexandra Rothman could never really see herself from those wide, unblinking albuminous tempera eyes. What had Bouché said when she asked him if she really looked like that? "Mirrors lie. My portraits don't." Alex had never thought of herself as beautiful, had never permitted herself to think of herself as beautiful. The woman who thinks she is beautiful is in deep trouble. The woman who believes she is beautiful is a real danger to herself because she begins to think of herself as God, whereas the man who thinks he's handsome is just a pain in the neck. Oh, yes.

Still, as she looked at the portrait now she decided it was probably an honest one—at least as honest as could be expected from such a romantically inclined artist as Bouché. At least Steven had told her she was beautiful. At least he had admired the portrait, which was why she had hung it here, in the library, his favorite room in the house. At least that was the way I looked to Steven, she thought. At least that was how young I was. And Bouché had not tried to play down her face's flaws. Her nose was long and straight and thin—"aristocratic," Bouché called it—though Alex herself had always thought it was too long and thin, since it tended to cheat her out of a certain amount of upper lip. Her chin was small and a bit too pointed—"My horrible, pointy chin," she often muttered to herself when she put on her makeup in front of her mirror.

But the dispassionate observer might have insisted that these were minor imperfections. He had certainly captured her best features—the eyes which were large, widely spaced, and luminous, and of an odd shade that seemed blue-green in some lights and hazel in others—her "tricolor eyes," the Frenchman had called them—and the thin, delicately arched eyebrows, slightly raised as though she was about to ask a question.

The expression on her face? "Too serious," some friends had told her, since Alexandra Rothman was famous for her throaty laugh. Others said that she looked haughty, and still others said that she looked sulky, remonstrative—even fierce, feral, almost angry. Her friend Lenny Liebling once told her that her expression was one of not-quite-amused skepticism, as though someone had just told her a story, or offered her a flimsy excuse, that she could not quite believe, or told her an off-color joke that she hadn't found funny. "You look the way you look every time Herb Rothman tells us we should get out there and try to sell more ad pages," he said.

And not a few people had commented that in this portrait she looked sad. Alex herself said she thought she looked as though she had a lot on her mind, which she certainly did that first year after Joel's birth—a lot on her mind, and very little in her pocketbook.

Still, Bouché had chosen an antique silk chiffon dress by Poiret for her to wear—pale pumpkin-colored, with thin spaghetti straps—borrowed from the Metropolitan Museum's costume collection. He had had to use safety pins at the back of the bodice to make it fit—Poiret must have designed it for a woman with a more ample figure than Alex's—but what would the museum have said if it had known that its precious dress was being pierced with pins! Alex could still feel the icy pressure of those pins against her skin. Then he had arranged a fichu, of a slightly darker pumpkin shade, over her bare shoulders. The colors, he explained, were subtly planned to draw the beholder's eye upward to the subject's crown of fluffy, feather-cut, reddish-blonde hair with its triangular widow's peak at the hairline, and of course the folds of the fichu fell in other loose, lazy triangles, into the folds of the Poiret as they fell to the floor about her feet.

"I want you to look like a duchess," he said.

"Ha—the Duchess of Paradise."

"Paradise?"

"Paradise, Missouri, the town where I was born. We called it Paradise, Misery."

"Ah, *ma petite zuzu* . . ."

He had even suggested a tiara—another triangle—but she had drawn the line at that. "Me—Miss Hick—in a *tiara?*" she had laughed. ("Heek? What is heek?" he wanted to know.)

Studying the portrait now, she wondered whether she should have let him paint in a tiara. Perhaps, seventeen years later, I have earned my little crown, she thought.

But instead she had worn the triple strand of twelve-millimeter pearls that Steven gave her when they became engaged in 1967. She was wearing these tonight, for the pearls had become something of a personal signature for her. In her ears—there on the wall, and here in the room—were the pearl earclips he had given her on their first anniversary. And on the third finger of her left hand, the hand that grazed her cheek in the painting, was the Kashmiri sapphire with its narrow girdle of diamonds, his engagement ring which, of course, she still wore. But there were few other reminders that the wary woman in the portrait, and the triumphant woman of tonight, were the same person.

"Did you love him?" Lulu had asked tonight.

"Do you love him?" Lulu had asked her in 1967, when she first showed her the ring.

"We're quite crazy about each other," she said.

"But are you truly, deeply in love with him? Or is it just the money and the power that attracts you to him? There's nothing wrong with wanting money and power. I *love* money, and I *love* power, honey, as much as the next one. But that's not the same as falling deeply in love with someone, and remember you heard it here."

"We know what we're doing, Lulu."

"Do you? Sometimes you seem so young, honey."

"I'm twenty-three."

"Marrying a rich dude isn't always as easy as it sounds. And the Rothmans? They have a reputation for being tough customers, I guess you know that."

"He's taking me to meet his parents next week."

Lucille Withers's look was dubious. "I just wish I could make this sound like a love story, Lexy. Do you really know what it's like to be in love?"

"Of course I do! Do you?"

The dark-haired hawk-shaped head inclined slightly, and her smile was wan. "Oh, yes," she said.

"Then why didn't you ever marry? Why didn't you have children? That's one of the first things we want to do—have children."

"Children. To feed the dynasty. Bullets."

"No! Children to raise and love. Didn't you ever want to have children to raise and love?"

Her smile was still wan, and the look on her face was faraway. "I'm like Mr. Chips," she said at last. "Running this agency, I've had hundreds of children. And all of them girls."

Later, Alex would wonder whether, perhaps, very discreetly, Lucille Withers was a Lesbian.

Lulu always wanted to talk about love. But no one knew better than Alex, even then, that if you fell too deeply in love, or even very much in love, or even if you fell in love at all, you risked losing all your happiness and peace of mind forever, and was it worth that precious candle? When love ended, you were left with nothing but a tiny splinter of ice in your heart. That was the only way love penetrated the dominion of the heart: when it ended, as a splinter of ice. But it was that icy shard that gave you strength, the ice-cold strength to survive in a business as reef-strewn and treacherous as this one, and in a family such as the House of Rothman. And remember, you heard that here. Alex learned that long ago.

She turned away from the portrait, which was beginning to have a hypnotic effect on her.

Here, right in this room, right on these library shelves, was the truest measure of her accomplishment, her success. Here, in a special section in the center of the book-lined walls, bound in lipstick-red morocco and embossed in gold lettering, were issues of *Mode* since it had become hers and hers alone—seventeen volumes, one volume for each year. That translated into more than two hundred individual issues, and it was impossible not to notice how the volumes grew fatter as the years went by—fatter, more prosperous and healthy, like a growing child. Partly, this was an indication of her advertisers' growing faith in her. But, even more, it was an indication of her readers' growing faith in her magazine, because a magazine's advertising pages—and revenues—do not increase unless readership grows first. But at the same time, a careful balance must be struck between editorial content, which draws the readers, and advertising pages, which make the money. A magazine editor cannot let her book become overwhelmed with advertising, tempting though that notion often is. There is no exact science involved here, no set formula for how to strike that delicate, perfect balance, though each editor may adopt a loose formula of her own. No amount of market research will tell you what makes a magazine appeal to readers. Only an editor's instinct can be counted on to provide that answer, issue by issue. *Taste* and *judgment* are words you often hear used to account for editorial success, but it is more like instinct, hunch, blind guesswork, and a gambler's idiot willingness to take the big plunge and throw all the chips on double-zero. Each new issue of a magazine goes out to face a public firing squad, with its editor saying the hell with the blindfold. Each issue of a magazine is a fragile, perishable vessel, as fragile and perishable as a human life. In those red-bound volumes on Alexandra Rothman's bookshelves were arrayed exactly two hundred and four separate lives. Rather like children, she often thought.

Years ago, in another library—at the house in Tarrytown—there had been a family meeting, a council of war, after Steven died. The mood was electric, tense. His will had just been read, in which he requested—not bequeathed, but requested, since the magazine was not his to bequeath—that Alex be given full editorial control of *Mode* "because she loves it so."

"What the hell makes you think you can run a magazine?" Ho Rothman, Steven's grandfather, the family patriarch and the head of everything, had asked her.

"Because I've been helping Steven run it for the last six years, in case you haven't noticed!"

"What's in it for us? The sheet's a loser. We're not in this business for charity, you know."

"I'm going to make it a winner."

"How? Tell me how."

"By doing more of what I've already started doing. By turning it into a magazine that isn't just about what women *wear*—but about what women *think*, or what they should be thinking. And about what women do, or could be doing!" She had never spoken to the great Ho Rothman so sharply before.

He stared at her, unblinking. Ho Rothman was a small man, but in that brocaded, high-backed antique Spanish chair that served him almost as a throne, he looked enormous, all the Rothman millions and the power that went with them contained compactly in that small frame in the big chair. Then he shrugged his narrow shoulders. "Hell, I suppose any damn fool can run a silly little fashion sheet like *Mode*," he said.

"But I'll show you I'm not any damn fool, and *Mode* isn't going to be a silly little fashion sheet," she shot back at him.

He pointed a skinny finger at her. "Tell you what I'll do," he said. "I'll give you a year. No, I take that back. You just heard Ho Rothman take something back. I'll give you *six months*. If the *meshugge* sheet isn't showing me black ink in six months' time, out you go and you don't come back."

"It's a deal, Ho!"

"Don't do it, Pop," Herbert Rothman, Steven's father, cried. "She'll fail! She'll fail!"

"Shut up, Herbert," the old man said. "I've made my decision."

Later, in an upstairs hallway, Herb Rothman accosted her, seizing her by the front of her blouse. "You humiliated me," he said. "You humiliated me in front of my wife, in front of my brother, in front of my entire family. You knew I'd promised the magazine to Mona Potter. You've humiliated me in front of Mona. I'll never forgive you for this, Alex. You'll fail. I'm going to watch you fail. I'm going to see to it that you fail. You've humiliated me once too often, Alex."

She pushed his hand roughly away. *"Don't touch me!"* she said. That night she packed and moved back into the New York apartment, even though she knew she would be confronted by Steven's ghost there, at every turn, in every room, and never spent another night under her in-laws' roof again.

*   *   *

But, you see, I didn't fail, she told herself now. I didn't fail, did I, Herbert. In fact, I succeeded beyond everybody's wildest dreams.

It didn't take six months for the black ink to begin to appear. It took only four, and from that point onward, Ho Rothman was her ally, her mainstay in the company, her trump card in this disputatious family. In any equation within the company, or within the family—and of course the company and the family were one and the same—the Ho Factor tipped the scales her way, balanced the solution in her favor. At least when it came to editing *Mode*.

She turned once more to the portrait above the mantel. Yes, she thought, Lulu was quite right. You *have* come a long way, baby. A mighty distance separated that frightened young woman on the wall, who knew from the beginning that she was facing an uphill battle in the company, doomed to fight her late husband's father every step of the way, and the woman of forty-six tonight who was celebrating her magazine's biggest milestone yet. You can never touch me now, Herb Rothman, she whispered to herself. You can never threaten to hurt me again. Our long and bitter sparring match is over, and look who's in the winner's corner. Me. She lifted her champagne glass in a little toast to the woman in the oval frame. "Here's to me," she said aloud, and winked at the young woman with the white poodle.

"Boo!" a man's voice said behind her, and she turned, startled, to see Lenny Liebling standing in the doorway.

"It's only me," he said, stepping quickly into the room. "And did I surprise the great editor saluting the same great editor when she was in her prime?"

"Ha," she said and laughed her throaty, bubbly laugh. "I'm still in my prime, you stinker."

"Or were you simply congratulating yourself on the eve of your greatest personal triumph?"

"How did you get up here without being announced?"

"Ah," he said, "I'm glad you asked that question. It was an arduous adventure, rather like that which my Russian-Polish ancestors underwent when they fled the pogroms of the czar. Border patrols with armed guards and savage dogs had to be outfoxed. Outrageous bribes had to be paid to loutish Cossack noncoms whose only aim was to rob me of my chastity.

Thank God for the belt my Yiddishe mama had locked about my tender loins. Finally, there was that last desperate dash through the frozen Ukraine night, with aurora borealis crackling overhead, and a pack of rabid wolves leaping at the wheels of our troika, to where a small but leaky launch was supposed to await us at Odessa, but where, alas, instead we found—" He stepped quickly toward her and kissed her on both cheeks. "Actually, it was quite easy," he said. "Your doorman was busy in the street—chasing down a cab for, I must say, the most *extraordinary*-looking young, bronzed Adonis—with a pair of buns, my dear, to *die* over—and so I simply slipped into the most secured building in Manhattan, got into the elevator, found your front door off the latch, and here I am! Had I been a cat burglar, instead of dear old Lenny, I could have made off with the family jewels. At first, I thought your house was empty, but then I saw that your entire staff is scurrying about the terrace, preparing for your party. Then I thought I might be able to surprise you in your bath, but now I find you here—bathed and ready for the evening. And aren't you pleased as punch to see me?"

"Dear old Lenny," she said. "You and your famous verbal concertos."

"Please—*oratorios*. We must be musically correct." He lifted his nose into the air and sniffed. "Wait," he said. "Do I detect the distinct odor of brilliantine? Does that mean that our Miss Lucille Withers has just been here?"

"Lenny, you are amazing. Can you really smell that Lulu was just here? Because she *was*."

"Well, you know how I love to lie, Alex dear," he said. "But actually, I saw the lady leaving as I was trying to sneak in. At first, I thought it was someone masquerading as Olive Oyl, or possibly Gertrude Stein after Weight Watchers. Then I realized that it was only the Bob Goulet of model agents."

"Lenny, you are very naughty."

"Thank you," he said, holding her by the shoulders at arm's length. "And may I say that you're looking particularly ravishing tonight, my darling Alex?"

"And you're also very early. My party doesn't start till eight."

"But aren't you going to offer dear old Lenny a drink, my love? I see you've already begun to fortify yourself for the night ahead—the night when we cheer you for pulling off publishing's grand slam."

"There's champagne in the cooler, darlin'. You're not getting anything stronger till the bartenders finish setting up."

He literally skipped toward the drinks cart. "Champagne!" he cried. "Plasma. Just in the nick of time! Just as I was about to expire from lack of liquid sustenance! *Olé!*" He threw his hands in the air, snapped his fingers as though they held castanets, and did a foot-stomping flamenco step in front of the drinks cart. "Blessed Alex! You are the Saint Bernard who has found the half-frozen mountaineer trapped in the glacial crevasse . . ."

He poured himself a glass. Then he turned to her and, in a more serious voice, said, "Actually, I wanted to be a few minutes early. I wanted to talk to you. My spies—you know I have spies throughout the Rothman organization—have been very active today. While you've been up here all afternoon, getting ready for your party, the thirtieth floor has been rife with rumors. Something's up, Alex, and I don't like the looks of it."

"Oh?" she said in a tone that was almost bored. "What's our darling little Herbert up to now?"

He started to speak, but suddenly his finger flew to his lips. Coleman had appeared at the library door. "Seven forty, Alex," Coleman said.

"Thank you, darlin'."

When Coleman disappeared, Lenny went on in a whisper. "No one knows what's up, but something definitely is. He's been closeted in his office with Miss Lincoln all afternoon. That means that he's dictating something—some sort of memorandum, or policy statement. My spies are very apprehensive and, frankly, so am I."

"Nonsense," she said. "Herb can't touch us now. Herb is only interested in the bottom line, and our bottom line has never been better."

"I know, I know. But—"

"In fact, we're now the number-one money-maker of all his magazines—five million circulation ad-rate base. Which happens to be what this little party of mine is all about."

"I know, but—"

"He told me I could never make five million, and I made it—with a few thousand to spare."

"I know. You proved him wrong. But Herb Rothman isn't a man who enjoys being proven wrong. You can be *right*, but he *can't be wrong*. When Herb is proven wrong, he gets very—unhappy, Alex. He gets very—vindictive. And he is our publisher, after all."

"Dammit, I wish there had been some way I could have avoided inviting him to the party. But of course I had to ask him."

"Of course. And of course he's coming. So—I hope you are prepared for fireworks, Alex."

"Dammit, Lenny—how did you know I was having fireworks tonight? Nobody was supposed to know that. The fireworks are supposed to be my big surprise."

"Hmm? Oh, you mean you're having real fireworks tonight? I didn't know that. I meant fireworks of the management variety—of the Herbert Rothman variety."

"Look," she said quickly, "there is no way Herb Rothman is going to mess with us, Lenny. We've got a winner. You don't shoot a Derby winner. You send him on to the Preakness and the Belmont. Herb Rothman isn't going to mess with the goose that's laying him all these golden eggs. Herb may be an arrogant bastard, but he's not a damn fool. Besides, Ho isn't going to let him stick any fingers in our little pie."

Lenny's sigh was audible. "That's another thing," he said. "How long has it been since you've talked to the White House?" The White House was what Lenny called the apartment at 720 Park Avenue, where Ho Rothman and his wife, known to all as Aunt Lily, lived.

"Three, four weeks."

"Yes," he said. "I thought perhaps not. But I spoke with Aunt Lily today. There's been a sudden change in the situation there."

"What sort of change?"

"Ho has become incommunicado. The little pin strokes he's been having. Apparently he had one on Saturday morning that was more severe. Aunt Lily blames the IRS—that huge suit they're bringing against the company for back taxes—you know about all that. But now the doctors say he can see no one, and receive no telephone calls, that anything like that would send his blood pressure shooting up."

"No one?"

"Not you, not me, not anybody except the doctors, the duty nurses, and of course Aunt Lily. Alex, remember that Ho is ninety-four years old."

She frowned. "But he's still—" She broke off, biting her lip.

"Do you have insurance, Alex?"

"Insurance? What are you talking about?"

"Nothing. Just thinking aloud. Let me put it this way. Do you know the terms of Ho Rothman's will?"

"I don't think anybody knows that, except Ho himself."

"And possibly Aunt Lily. But look at it this way. Under New York state law, the widow is required to receive at least one-third of the estate. The remaining two-thirds could be divided any way Ho wished—between Herbert, and Arthur, and Arthur's children, and you, and your son, Joel . . ."

"Arthur was always Ho's favorite. Ho and Herbert never got along. I'm sure he'd leave a bigger share to Arthur than he would to Herb."

"Yes. Little Arthur, his ewe lamb. Which was why Arthur was placed in charge of the radio and telecommunications arm of the company, while Herb was given the newspapers and magazines, which show a somewhat smaller amount of black ink at the bottom line. Yes, I, too, figured that Arthur would be favored in any will of Ho's. On the other hand, you yourself possess an asset that Ho wants very much to keep under his control. Or perhaps I should say used to want."

"Joel, you mean."

"Exactly. The only male heir in the fourth generation. So you see, there are many variables to take into consideration when we speculate about Ho's will. That is, of course, if there's a will at all."

"Oh? You mean you think there isn't one?"

"Dear Alex, I have no idea. But I do mean that men like Ho Rothman, who have come to believe in the myth of their infallibility, also begin to believe that they're immortal, and never make a will because the very thought of making a will reminds them of life's cruelest reality. It's utter idiocy, of course, but it's been known to happen. If Ho should die intestate, the situation would change considerably. His widow would still receive one-third, but the remainder would be divided equally between his living children, Arthur and Herbert. The estate of a person who dies intestate cannot provide anything to the deceased's grandchildren, or great-grandchildren. That means—"

"Me. And Joel."

"Yes. I see you are following my train of thought, Alex. If there is no will, and we have no way of knowing whether there is one or not, the Rothman fortune, and the companies, will be inherited by a threesome—Aunt Lily, Herbert, and Arthur. A troika—a vehicle which, if my Yiddishe mama was to be believed, was always a damnably difficult thing to control. And one to which, alas, neither you nor Joel would be given a single pair of reins."

"But what about Steven's trust? There was a trust fund that Steven left that was to take care of Joel and me."

"Ah, the elusive so-called Steven trust," he said.

"Elusive? Why do you say that?"

"Have you ever seen it, Alex? Have you ever seen this alleged trust instrument? Has it ever paid you any income?"

"I've left it untouched on purpose. As a matter of pride, and also so that it could go intact to Joel."

"I wonder if it really exists," he said. He took a sip of his drink. "Perhaps this is the moment to ask your lawyers to take a look at the terms of Steven's trust. It would be interesting to see what they turn up, if anything."

She shivered suddenly. "Lenny, you're frightening me," she said. "Of course the trust exists! They've talked about it for years."

His smile was quick and bright. "To frighten you was not my intention, Alex dear," he said. "My real point was simply this. In either scenario—whether Ho has a will, or hasn't— Aunt Lily is soon going to find herself with a much larger share of control of the company than she's ever had before. And if we do end up with a troika situation—remembering that Herbert and baby brother Arthur rarely agree on any-thing—Aunt Lily's could be the swing vote in any major decision. In other words, I think it is going to behoove us all to pay special attention to Aunt Lily from now on."

She said nothing for a moment. Then she said, "And I think you're also saying that there's a connection between Ho's declining health and what Herb and Miss Lincoln have been up to behind locked doors in his office today."

"Precisely, smart Alex. I think Herb may have decided that this is the moment to seize control of the company—before a

probate court steps in to tell everybody who gets what, and
who gets to tell whom what to do. I think the camel may be
trying to stick his nose into our little tent, Alex. Or, I should
say, *your* little tent."

In the silence that followed, Coleman appeared at the door
again. "Seven fifty-five, Alex," he said. "Everything is ready
on the terrace."

"Thank you, Coleman."

"Anyway," Lenny said when Coleman was gone, "I've
told you everything I know, everything that's been on my
mind, everything that's been worrying me. Meanwhile, my
spies will be busy—particularly in the corridors of executive
power, in the Ministry of Fear, on the thirtieth floor."

She drained her champagne glass quickly. "Well, we're not
going to let any of this spoil my little victory party, are we?"
she said.

He looked briefly doubtful. "I hope not," he said. Then
he brightened. "I mean, certainly not! *Mais non!* Meanwhile,
I'm quite cross with you, Alex. I've told you that *you* look
ravishing. But you haven't told me how *I* look tonight."

She laughed. "Dear old Lenny. You always look the same—
terrific."

"And speaking of bottom lines—" He did a quick little
dance kick-step and turn, flipped up the double vent of his
blue silk Brioni blazer, and wiggled his behind at her. "I may
be getting old," he said, "but I still have the cutest little ass
in the magazine biz, don't you agree?"

"Dear old Lenny. You may be getting older, but you'll
never grow up."

Once more Coleman was at the library door, and this time
his tone was urgent. "Four guests just announced from the
lobby, Alex!"

She tucked the fingers of her right hand into the crook of
Lenny's left elbow. "Come on," she said. "I want to greet
people on the terrace."

"I can never understand why you let your butler call you
by your first name," he whispered. "It sounds common."

"But I *am* common. Just as common as you are, Lenny
dear."

"You are not. You are *extraordinaire*. For instance, every
other hostess in New York, with her first guests arriving,
would right now be being zipped into her dress and checking

her makeup in the mirror. You look as though you've been ready for this party for at least an hour."

"Dot's-a me," she said cheerfully. "Dot's-a me," and she turned and steered him toward the terrace and the party.

Chapter 3

Now, in a light breeze that made flattering playthings of the women's dresses, the stream of party guests was flowing out through the open French doors and onto Alex Rothman's L-shaped terrace twenty floors above the East River. There was Lenny's friend Charlie Boxer, who was escorting Princess Irene of Greece. There was Bobby Short, flanked by Gloria Vanderbilt and Lee Radziwill. There was Elizabeth Taylor, recovered from her latest strange illness, in a voluminous pink caftan, with Bill Blass, and they were followed by Henry Kissinger and his towering wife, Nancy, and Henry Kravis and *his* towering wife, the glamorous Carolyne Roehm, who had started her extraordinary climb as plain Jane Smith, and then came Nan Kempner, Ann Slater in her trademark blue glasses, Saul and Gayfryd Steinberg, John and Susan Gutfreund, Leonard and Evelyn Lauder. Then there was a little murmured hush as *she* appeared—she being Jacqueline Onassis, still another woman who seemed to tower over her date, Mr. Tempelsman, in a dress of black and crimson. "Carolina Herrera," she whispered in response to someone's question, as the flashbulbs popped.

As each woman made her entrance, she paused, lifted her chin, and smiled her most radiant smile for the photographers and television cameras. There was nothing, Alex knew, that New Yorkers liked more than being photographed, especially for television. The presence of television cameras made a party an instant success. Of course there were also photographers there from the *News*, *Newsday*, and *Women's Wear*. No one knew how many of their pictures would be used in the next day's papers, but no one was taking any chances, and meanwhile the cameras were recording everything.

"To me, Alex Rothman is just one helluva great broad," Lauren Bacall was saying to the hand-held microphone in front of her.

"Only Betty could get away with that kind of language," Lenny whispered to Alex.

After each celebrity had affixed his or her smile into the cameras' lenses, and made his or her personal statement, they all moved toward Alex. "Alex darling . . . you look divine . . . congratulations . . . what a heavenly night for a party . . . you've never looked lovelier . . . congratulations . . . you look divine, Alex darling . . ."

"Here comes the great man now," said Lenny, as Herbert J. Rothman made his entrance, and the cameras and lights fell on him to record the moment, and the head of Rothman Publications, always unaccustomed to public smiling, smiled a tight smile.

"Who's the woman with him, I wonder?"

"I've no idea," Lenny said. "But she's borrowed Louise Brooks's old hair."

The woman in question was small and thin, all in black, in her middle twenties, perhaps, with a pale, heart-shaped face framed in a glossy helmet of black hair. She was wearing oversize dark glasses with black frames. Her smile, too, was nervous, uncertain.

"He certainly likes them young, our Herbert," Alex said.

"Young? Behind those perfectly ridiculous shades, it's hard to say. But the dress is either a Saint-Laurent or a very good knockoff."

"No, it's Yves. Look at the buttonholes. No one does buttonholes like Yves."

"She has a certain—shall we say surface chic? But until we meet her, I have a name for her. Anna Rexia."

"Bitchy, Lenny."

"Meanwhile, my dear, you have not just staged a party. You have not just staged an event. You have staged *une grande occasion. Une occasion du moment.* Everyone in New York is here. If a bomb fell on this building tonight, the entire city would go out of business."

"I just wish Ho and Aunt Lily could be here. I owe everything to them. If Herb had had his way, I'd have been back in Paradise long ago."

"No. You owe everything to *you*."

The occasion, of course, was simply this. It was Thursday, June 21, 1990, and the final circulation figures for the June issue of *Mode* had just come in, and circulation had passed the magical five-million mark. For a fashion magazine like *Mode*, five million in paid circulation had seemed all but unattainable—like reaching the top of Everest, or seeing the Dow-Jones hit three thousand. All spring, the circulation had been inching slowly upward—4,780,000 for April, 4,890,000 for May—and everyone at the magazine held their breath. But now the figures were in, and the June issue had broken the final barrier, and *Mode* had become not only the best-selling magazine in the Rothman chain, but the best-selling fashion magazine in the world. When Alexandra Rothman became editor-in-chief in 1973, circulation was just over 250,000.

How had Alex done it? She could not answer that question herself in any simple way. She could only say that it had taken her seventeen years to do it, with only grudging support from her father-in-law. She could say that she had tried to do what she promised Ho Rothman she would do— to make *Mode* more than just a fashion magazine. Though its focus was still on fashion, she had expanded that focus and made *Mode* more than a book that reported on what smart women were wearing, but that reported as well on what smart women were thinking and doing and talking about, or what smart women *might* be thinking and doing and talking about. She could say that she tried to avoid making *Mode* a book that told women what they *ought* to be thinking and doing and talking about, because she hated women's magazines—like *Ms.*, for instance, or even *Cosmo*—that so often seemed to be lecturing to their readers. She always assumed, she said, in planning each new issue, that her readers were at least as smart as she was, if not a good deal smarter.

"What was the secret of your success?" a reporter from the *Wall Street Journal* asked her the other day.

She thought a moment before answering. "Mainly, showing up."

"Showing up?"

"Isn't the basic secret of doing any job successfully: just
showing up every day to do it?"

"Would you describe yourself as a workaholic?"

"No—unless loving the work you do describes a workaholic."

"I've heard you described as a perfectionist."

"I think most people are perfectionists at heart. Wouldn't
it be wonderful if everything were perfect? But most people
are smart enough to know that nothing ever really is."

"I've heard you described as a completely driven woman."

She had laughed. "Well, I was driven to the airport the
other day," she said. "But I guess you could say that I can
be a little stubborn."

"They say the magazine is your entire life."

"It isn't. It's just the way I make my living."

She often wondered: What made reporters ask such silly
questions?

A reporter from *Women's Wear* had cornered her. "Now
that you've become a living myth, what next?" he asked
her.

"The main thing is not to begin to believe in one's
mythiness," she said. "Is that a word? Mythiness?"

"If you say it is, it is."

Coleman had appeared at her side. "The last important
guests have arrived," he said. "A few more of the working
press on their way."

"Forty-five minutes till the soup," she said. "You know I
hate a long cocktail hour."

"I guess *he's* the perfectionist," the *Women's Wear* reporter
said. "Knows the difference between 'important' and 'working press.' "

And now the full contingent of two hundred and fifty
guests was gathered on Alex Rothman's penthouse terrace—
guests that swirled together into little groups, groups that
quickly broke apart and re-formed into other groups. Alex's
terrace was a perfect setting for a party like tonight's which,
after all, was more of a theatrical production than a social

gathering. It was show business, and the terrace was a prop.
It covered nearly two thousand square feet, and faced north
and east, paved with flagstone. It was a real roof garden,
and solid stone planter boxes contained flowering cherry
and crab apple trees, even dogwoods, which the people at
Terrestris had assured Alex could not survive at this exposure in the city. There were even twin magnolia trees. The
terrace was bounded by a four-foot-high stone parapet and,
along the wide ledge of the parapet were more stone planters
filled, for tonight's party, with pink and white azaleas. For
the party, the garden furniture had been removed, and the
terrace had been set up with twenty-five round tables for
ten, covered with alternating pink and white cloths, with
centerpieces of English ivy and pink and white tulips. The
white wrought-iron gazebo, at the elbow of the L, where, on
good mornings, Alex liked to have breakfast, had been decorated with pink and white ribbons and balloons, and had been
put to use tonight as the bar, from which pink-coated waiters
radiated outward through the ever re-forming groups and the
flashbulbs.

Tonight's production was all about publicity, everyone
knew that. The socialites and celebrities were merely set-
dressing, interchangeable extras in the performance. More
important were the editors, writers, artists, photographers,
members of the fashion press, designers, models, the agency people, the retailers from Fifth and Madison avenues, the
wholesalers from Seventh, the advertisers and their reps. And
as her guests glided by, they blew their breathless kisses in
her direction, and murmured their congratulations: "Fabulous, darling . . . so exciting . . . what a thrill . . . it *had* to
happen . . . darling, just think, five *million*. . . ." And so on.
It was all meaningless and meaningful at the same time—
these elegant, splendidly coiffed carnivores, predators, syco-
phants, and parasites.

Because it would be naïve to suppose that all these people showering Alex with air kisses and affectionate greetings
actually loved and admired Alex Rothman, and no one knew
this better than Alex herself—surely she knew it. This was
New York, after all, and this was the fashion industry. Some
of these people were more than Alex's competitors. They
were her arch-rivals, would-be usurpers of her special throne.
There was fierce jealousy here on this terrace—bitterness,

anger, disappointment, rage, and all-consuming, outrageous, mindless envy. Because this was a party for *Mode*, every woman here tonight had arrived with but a single goal in mind—to outdress all the others—and, in terms of the designers represented here, and the amounts of money spent, it was almost possible to conclude that they had all succeeded. And yet, with her apparent instinct that the woman who dressed most simply was also the most chic, Alex—in her white Bill Blass, with the turquoise and silver Old Pawn belt cinched at her waist—had managed to outdress them all, and this fact did not go unnoticed, nor did Alex go unhated for it.

Turquoise was the color of her eyes and, as the astute could not have failed to notice, it was also the exact blue-green of the English ivy leaves in her centerpieces—no accident, of course, all planned with devilish cleverness to show the hostess off, and many women silently vowed never to use Renny the florist again. The evening breeze was rising, flipping up the corners of the pink and white tablecloths, while some women prayed for a hurricane, a tornado, a full-fledged monsoon to descend and ruin everything. Meanwhile, the waiters moved efficiently about, securing the tablecloths with clothespins. Alex had prepared for this contingency, and even the clothespins were pink and white. The women, especially, noticed this and made a mental note. *Who else but Alex?* they thought, hatefully.

Because there were some women on this terrace—and some men, too—who actively hated Alex Rothman, and hate was not too strong a word, who ardently wished that her June issue, with its daring cover, had fallen flat on its face, who cringed at the news that the press run of *Mode* had sold out in Nebraska. The fashion business was symbiotic, parasitic. Relationships here were like those between orchids in a rain forest and the trees to whose bark these exotic plants affixed themselves, and whose sap they sucked. These people all preyed on one another, yet they needed each other. The magazine could not live without the designers, nor could the designers survive without the magazine, yet they all despised each other unreservedly. Where would the fashion models be without photographers and the art directors, or the art directors without the photographers and models and designers? Yet they constantly derided each other's talents, each other's singular powers. Still, in the evening light high above the East River, they blew their air kisses at one another, told each other how marvelous they looked—beautiful, deadly moths in the jungle, scavenging for vulnerable quarry.

Tonight, their quarry of choice was clearly Alex Rothman. The person at the top, in this world, seemed to be asking to be toppled—her position was so exposed. Tonight, Alex was the brightest star in the fashion firmament, and she had managed to eclipse all the other stars on the horizon, who would remain eclipsed until she began to fall. At the top of her career, Alex Rothman stood out as an easy target, a sitting duck. Tonight, an open season had been declared on Alex.

Lenny Liebling moved about the terrace, smiling his bland and somewhat condescending party smile, from group to group, receiving and bestowing kisses, saying not much of anything, but listening, always listening, gathering bits and pieces that might be woven into something resembling solid information.

"I don't care what you say. No model on earth is worth two thousand an hour, regardless of her pelvic bones."

"Fucking her must be like fucking a venetian blind."

"Actually, she's not a bad lay."

"There's Betty Zimmerman. Her husband got a year in the state pen."

"It's more like a country club, really. Minimum security. I hear they can even have girls in. Besides, he's getting a book out of it. I hear Doubleday has offered a million five, and there's talk of a miniseries."

"Look who the cat dragged in. Dolores Blearman. God, she looks awful. Tom left her, you know."

"Oh? Another woman?"

"No, darling. Another *man*."

"Well, it's either one or the other, isn't it? Dolores! How marvelous you look. . . ."

"Him? I forget his name. He's really nothing but a gofer for Helmut Newton, but they say that in the darkroom he can salvage some of Helmut's worst shots."

"Darling, you can *imagine* what else goes on in Helmut's darkroom, can't you?"

"Photographed her through *gauze*? It had to be more like burlap, darling, or linoleum—to block out all her stretch marks. Look at that neck. It's one *solid* stretch mark. She looks like a turtle."

"Well, if she had as many dicks sticking out of her as she's had stuck into her, she'd look like a porcupine."

"There's Dodie Applegate, getting drunk again. The *Washington Post* trashed her last novel. They called it 'clitorature.' Don't you love it?"

"Alex's June cover? I hear it was a desperation move, darling—desperation city. Herb Rothman told her, 'Get me five million, or you're finished. *Finished.*'"

"Speaking of finished, there's Portia Perlman. . . ."

"Well, none of us are getting any younger, darling, including our hostess. Oh, Alex! *Darling!* You're looking marvelous tonight!"

Lenny moved slowly about the terrace, listening here, listening there, as the noise of the party rose, as the pink-coated waiters scurried about, as a few pale stars began to appear in the evening sky, as the lights of the city began to come on, and the clothes-pinned tablecloths swelled and billowed and slapped in the breeze like spinnakers. Lighted candles guttered from the centerpieces.

In the northeast corner of the terrace, Lenny overheard an interesting conversation.

"Has Alex Rothman had her face lifted? I'd say yes."

"Hmm. How old *is* she, anyway? Forty-six? Forty-seven?"

"Let's just say she's a few years older than her friend Mel Jorgenson, darling."

"Doesn't she look pleased with herself tonight? No wonder her husband killed himself."

"She actually did kill a man once, you know. With a gun. Bang-bang. It was years ago, but it was in all the papers."

"Oh? Was it a lover?"

"No one knows, exactly. But there were the usual rumors."

"Is it true that if a woman wants to get ahead at Rothman Publications, she has to fuck Herb Rothman?"

"What a ghastly thought, darling. But it's certainly not true of Alex. She and Herb loathe each other."

"Well, perhaps that's why?"

"I always assumed it was *Ho* Rothman she was fucking. She's always been Ho's little pet."

"But now they say Ho's a complete vegetable. Herb's getting ready to take over everything."

"Well, one thing's certain—she slept her way to the top one way or the other. She *must* have, considering her background, which is from Nowheresville."

"They say before she met Steve Rothman she was a disc jockey in Kansas City."

"Worse, darling. She read the weather."

"Still, you've got to admit she looks—*all right*."

"You'd look all right, too, darling, if every designer in the world gave you free clothes."

"Are you implying that I *don't* look all right—darling?"

"Well, one thing I happen to know. She's in deep trouble— in spite of all this nonsense about five million circulation, and the ridiculous ad in this morning's *Times*. As everybody in this business knows, circulation can be *bought*. But meanwhile, Vinnie, who does my hair, also does Pegeen Rothman's hair, and Vinnie told *me* that Pegeen told *him* that Herb was absolutely furious with what Alex did with the June cover. He was also furious about the ad in this morning's *Times*."

"Oh? I didn't know that Herb and Pegeen spoke to each other anymore."

"Oh, they speak. It's just that they don't have much to say to one another."

"That's a big difference, of course."

"Anyhoo, Herb hated the June cover. He said it was just another of Alex's gimmicks. He says Alex is getting to be just too gimmicky an editor, and all her gimmicks are beginning to seem old hat. He's definitely looking around for someone younger."

"Well, I think that's only fair. Alex has been in that spot for much too long. It's high time she moved over in favor of someone else. I always thought Mona Potter should have that job. She was promised it, you know, until Ho and Alex jewed her out of it."

"My dear, I said someone *younger*. Someone younger wouldn't be Mona Potter."

"I don't care what you say about Mona. Mona's always been very nice to me."

"Hmm . . ."

"She'd be nice to you, if you treated her properly—if you know what I mean, darling."

"Anyhoo, things are going to change around here when

Herb gets in the saddle, wait and see."

"How old is Herb, anyway?"

"Let's just say he's past the company's mandatory retire-ment age. But of course if you own the joint, I guess you can change the rules any way you want."

"They've certainly changed the rules when it comes to Lenny Liebling. What's his secret, d'you suppose?"

In a lowered voice: "I've heard he's Herb Rothman's gay lover."

"Herb? Gay? With all his women?"

"Beards, darling, nothing but beards. To protect the fami-ly's reputation."

"So it's Herb and—Lenny."

"Shhh, darling! He's standing right over *there. . . .*"

Wearing his bemused, supercilious smile, Lenny moved away from this pair.

In the corner of the terrace, he spotted young Joel Rothman in conversation with the young woman in dark glasses and the glossy helmet of short, jet-black hair, who had just identified herself as "a visitor from England." Joel was the only other blood Rothman at the party. Joel was Alexandra Rothman's son, soon to be eighteen and fresh out of Exeter. Though his horn-rimmed glasses gave him a slightly owlish look, he was a good-looking boy—tall and slim, with thick blond, slightly windblown hair.

"I know all about you from your grandfather," Lenny heard the young woman say. "I know you're the apple of his eye. Some day, you're going to take over the whole Rothman empire."

Joel ran his index finger around the inside of the collar of his white shirt. "I wish people wouldn't call it an empire," he said. "It's just a family business like any other."

"Your grandfather says you have the makings of a fine journalist."

"He just means I have certain pet peeves about the way the English language is used nowadays. I wrote my senior paper on this at school."

"Oh? Tell me about that."

"For instance, just the other day in the *New York Times*, Paul Goldberger, in his architecture column, wrote, 'This building is quite different than other buildings this architect has designed.' Doesn't Goldberger—doesn't anybody editing the *Times*—know that it should be 'different *from*'? And it annoys me to read, also in the *Times*, that the Helmsleys live in 'a twenty-one-room estate.' Don't they know that estates have acres, not rooms? And if you listen to the radio, you'll hear all kinds of mistakes. 'Baby-sitting her grandchild,' instead of with, or for. A chaise longue called a chaise lounge. A bedroom suite called a bedroom suit. 'Upon graduating high school,' instead of *being graduated from*. The other day I heard an announcer say that some society woman had eloped with her male *masseuse*. A masseuse is female, of course. More and more I hear people saying they feel *nauseous*, when they mean nauseated. I also hate it when I hear people say, 'My sterling,' or 'real gold,' or that somebody has 'his very own private plane.' And, over and over again, if you listen to radio giveaway shows, you'll hear the announcer say, 'Con*grad*ulations!' I could go on and on about this, but I'm probably boring you stiff, aren't I?"

"No! It's fascinating—and true!"

Joel Rothman blushed easily, and he was blushing now. "Anyway, that's what I wrote my senior paper on."

"Fascinating."

Joel smiled. He had a nice smile, and his teeth were white and even. "I heard a good one the other day. Two women were talking in Bloomingdale's, and I heard one woman say, 'Well, the way prices are anymore, and for no more than you're going to use it, why buy it?' "

"Which should have been—?"

" 'The way prices are nowadays, and for as little as you're going to use it.' And I've almost given up on 'hopefully,' as when the weatherman says, 'Hopefully, it won't rain over the weekend.'"

She laughed—a light, merry, almost tinkly laugh. "Hopefully, you got an A on your paper," she said.

"I did—gratefully."

Now they were both laughing.

"Actually, I put my paper together from things I'd already put down in my journal," Joel said. "So it wasn't a lot of work."

"Ah. You keep a journal?"

"Oh, yes. I write in it whenever I have a little bit of private time—which isn't often these days."

"It seems unusual to me for a chap your age to keep a

journal. I should think a lad your age would spend his private time thinking of ways to conquer the fair sex—handsome fellow like you. Do you plan to be a writer?"

Joel's blush deepened. "Well, I come from a publishing family," he said.

"Oh, yes indeed, I know. And a very distinguished one it is. In fact, I feel a bit out of place here," she said.

"Out of place? Why?"

"All these famous people. I'm just a nobody. In fact, I wasn't even invited, and I really didn't want to come. But your grandfather insisted on bringing me."

"You're not a nobody," he said. "Nobody's a nobody."

Lenny turned to the man standing next to him and, with a raised eyebrow and a slight nod in the younger couple's direction, mouthed the words, "Does she have a name?"

"Name's Fiona Fenton," the man whispered. "*Lady* Fiona Fenton. Friend of Herb's. From London."

"I see."

"Is this chap a friend of yours?" Lenny heard her ask, indicating the big stocky man in the brown suit who stood just behind Joel, and Lenny cocked his ear to hear how Joel would handle this particular question.

Joel gestured with his thumb over his right shoulder. "That's just Otto," he said, blushing even more deeply.

The woman named Fiona Fenton extended her right hand in Otto's direction, but Otto did not return the gesture and simply stared impassively into space. Otto's job was not to socialize with the party guests. Otto's job was to keep his hands free at all times, for use on the beeper that was clipped to his belt or, if the need arose, for the service revolver that was strapped in a harness across his chest, and bulged under the buttoned jacket of his brown suit.

"I have a bodyguard," Lenny heard Joel mumble. "That's why I have no privacy." Lenny turned away now, and moved on to other conversations.

Joel and his mother had had words about Otto just that morning, before Alex left for the office. Four years earlier, Herbert Rothman had received a crudely written note in the mail demanding ten million dollars in return for the life of the youngest male Rothman heir. Normally such a note, and such a demand, would not be taken seriously. Men in Herbert

Rothman's position received such threats fairly routinely, and routinely turned them over to the FBI and forgot about them. But, it turned out, one of the grandsons of Henry Ford II had been similarly threatened and, from England, Buckingham Palace had reported the same threat to Prince William, the heir to the throne, demanding the same sum translated into British pounds. The FBI had decided to take the case very seriously, that an international kidnap or extortion ring was at work, and Interpol was brought into the case. Herbert Rothman was advised to hire someone for Joel's protection, and Otto Forsthoefel, a former Pinkerton man, was chosen for the job.

That morning, at the breakfast table, Alex had said to Joel, "Well, Buster, have you decided what you want for a birthday present?" Ever since he was a baby, Alex and Steven had called him Buster, and how that got started she no longer remembered.

"Yes," he answered darkly.

"Let me guess," she said, squeezing the last polyp of her grapefruit into her spoon. "A Porsche? A Mercedes? A BMW?"

"I want to get rid of effing Otto. That's *all* I want, Mom."

She frowned and put down her grapefruit spoon.

"Mom, do you know what it's been effing *like* with effing Otto following me around all the time? Do you have any *idea*? Do you know what it's been like at *school*? Do you know they kicked me off the effing soccer team? I was a quarterback, but in our big game with Andover a guy illegally body-checked me, and I ended up on my ass. Effing Otto ran out on the field and made them stop the *game*! And we were *winning*, for Chrissake! Do you know that I wanted to go out for hockey this winter, but I couldn't because effing Otto doesn't know how to effing *skate*? Do you know how the guys at school tease me about effing Otto? Do you know what the *girls* call me? 'The Boy in the Bubble!' Dammit, Mom, nobody's going to kidnap me, nobody's going to murder me. Nobody's even *tried*. If you ask me, Mom, those effing letters were nothing but an effing hoax to begin with, until the effing FBI got into the act. But I'll tell you this, Mom. I'm not going to effing Harvard with effing Otto following me around, and that's effing final!"

"Enough of this effing business, Buster," she said. "Is that the way they teach you to talk at Exeter?"

"Dammit, Mom, have you heard a single effing word I've *said*?"

She bit her lip. "But I do worry about you," she said. "You're the only real family I have left. You're really the man of the house here. You're—"

"Dammit, Mom, if I'm the man of the house, why do I have to have an effing bodyguard?"

"But what if something should—?"

"Nothing's going to *happen* to me, Mom. Look, I'm going to be eighteen years *old*. I'm old enough to drive. I'm going to be old enough to vote. If there's a war, and they have an effing draft, I'll be old enough to be effing drafted, for Chrissakes. What're you going to do? Send me off to the army with effing Otto on my tail?"

"But there isn't any war, and there isn't any draft."

"But what I'm saying is that I'm going to be an effing legal *adult*!"

"You're right, of course," she said. "But don't forget that Otto was your grandfather's idea, not mine."

"Dammit, Mom, do we have to do *every*thing Gramps says? Does Gramps *own* us, or something?"

"Of course not. Nobody owns anybody."

"But this much is final. If I have to go to Harvard with effing Otto on my tail, I—just—won't—go!"

"What do you mean you just won't go? You've been accepted and—"

He tossed his mane of blond hair. "How can I not go? Easy! When I get to Harvard, I won't do any of the work. I'll see to it that I flunk every test! By the end of the first semester, I'll have flunked out of Harvard. What do you think of that?"

She laughed her throaty laugh. "Buster, you're turning into a true Rothman," she said. "You're as manipulative as the rest of them. Okay, it's a deal. Otto goes. And I agree with you—this Otto business has gotten ridiculous. I'll speak to Herb first chance I get."

"And do me another favor," he said.

"Sure. What's that?"

"Quit calling me Buster."

She looked at him. "All right," she said quietly. "All right, Joel." And then, "Hey, we're still pals, aren't we?"

He shrugged. "Yeah, I guess so," he said.

But of course Alex had not yet had a chance to speak to Herb about the Otto matter, and so, tonight, Otto was still on the job.

Now Mona Potter had approached Joel on the terrace— the same Mona Potter who had once expected to be named *Mode*'s editor, and who now wrote a syndicated column called "The Fashion Scene" for the *Daily News*. Famously nearsighted, Mona peered closely at Fiona Fenton's face and, realizing that this was someone she did not recognize, and that this therefore was a person of no consequence whatever, she ignored her and turned to Joel with her steno pad and pencil. "Your mother says you're a genius," she said.

"Well, that's nice," he said pleasantly.

"Okay, so say something genius for my column. Gimme a genius quote. You're the heir apparent. Wanna say something heir apparent?"

"Hmm—ah—"

"Your mother says you got an original mind. Say something original."

"I think she means I like word games," he said.

"Yeah? Like what?" Her pencil was poised over her steno pad.

"Can you think of a nine-letter word that has only one vowel?"

"No. What?"

"Strengths," Joel said. "I've only been able to discover one other word like it in the English language."

"Huh. What's that?"

"It's a proper name, so maybe it doesn't count. But it's still a word."

"Huh!"

"I'll give you a hint. It used to be the name of a chain of restaurants in New York."

"Huh!"

"Schrafft's," he said.

"Aw, you're pulling my leg," Mona said, and moved away from him in search of more quotable grist for her journalistic mill.

"Dear me, what a perfectly dreadful woman," the young Englishwoman said to him.

*   *   *

The orchestra was playing "You're the Top," changing the lyric slightly to suit the occasion:

> *You're the top,*
> *You're the Park Pavilion,*
> *You're the top,*
> *Now you've hit five million . . .*

And one or two couples were actually dancing, which was becoming a rare thing to see at a New York party these days, where there were too many important business matters, and people, to talk about. Lenny strolled among the party players, those fashionable savages, listening to their voices rising against the music, fueled by cocktails and champagne.

"She photographs okay if you shoot her in profile. Shoot her from any other angle, and she looks like Noriega in drag."

"Speaking of horrors, there's Molly Zumwalt. She must be on furlough from Silver Hill."

"Molly Zumwalt has a certain sense of style, but no taste. You know what I mean. Blue Rigaud candles."

"Her husband had a penile implant. Then he had a vasectomy. What's he *want*, anyway . . . ?"

Was it always this awful? Lenny sometimes asked himself. Was there always such cruelty, such venom, so much anger and envy and greed? "The East Side Razor Blades" was what Lenny called these women, who were for the most part thin and for the most part streaked blondes. At a certain age, in New York, every woman became a streaked blonde. He had christened them the Razor Blades, furthermore, long before Tom Wolfe called them X-rays in that book. His was a more apt description, Lenny thought. An X-ray was transparent, black-and-white, and flat. But a Razor Blade could cut, and nick, and slash, and kill. There were male Razor Blades too, of course, equally dangerous, and never satisfied until there was blood all over the floor.

And the answer to his question was no, it had not always been like this. When Lenny first came to New York in the early thirties, it had been quite a different place. The city had been vital, and pulsing, and fun, and everyone went everywhere. Those had been hard times, of course, but they were getting better, and everyone was simply glad to be alive and in the city together, helping things get better. Then had come the war years, and those had been the best of all. Having made sure that he was ineligible for the draft—that quite absurd incident back in Onward took care of that—Lenny had flung himself, yes flung, into the joy of those years when everyone was rooting together for the city, the country, the world.

There were real stores in the city then, not glitzy show-biz emporiums like Bloomingdale's, but *real* stores like Best's and DePinna, which everyone knew was better than Brooks Brothers, and Altman's, which always had the best of everything, including that wonderful bakery shop, and Bergdorf's, before Andrew Goodman sold it to a chain. And W&J Sloane—you never needed to hire an interior decorator in those days. Sloane's told you how to furnish your rooms, and you could be certain they were right.

And then there were the hotels and restaurants and nightclubs they all went to—the Marguery, with its extraordinary garden courtyard, the Ambassador, the old Ritz-Carlton, the Savoy-Plaza, and the pre-Trump Plaza when it really *was* the Plaza. No more. Those places were all, all gone. They had danced at places like Larue—those tiny blue sparkling, starlike lights in the ceiling—and the Monte Carlo and the Copa, and at the Persian Room they had listened to Hildegarde— the "Incomparable Hildegarde"—in her long white gloves sing "The Last Time I Saw Paris," and for her last number she always came out carrying a bunch of long-stemmed red roses in her arms as she would a baby. And they drank at places like the Stork Club and the old El Morocco with its zebra-striped banquettes and silver palm trees, and, oh, how innocent and free they had all been then! Lenny could remember ordering his very first martini—well under age, of course, but so sophisticated—and saying to the waiter, "Very dry, please—no water at all," and the laughter that order had provoked among his friends who all had names like Gloria and Bobo and Tommy and Dickie. When they were poor, they ate at the Automat or Childs, and when they were feeling a little richer they ate at Longchamps, or took tea at a wonderful little *bonbonnerie* on Fifth Avenue called Rosemarie de Paris, with its heavenly chocolate-peppermint smell, where waitresses in black uniforms with starched white lace caps and aprons passed the French pastry trays. It was here he learned that the only time it was polite to point was when it was at French pastry, and that it was considered rude and gluttonish to point at more than two, though Lenny could have eaten the entire tray because he was often hungry then, even though he smoked expensive Murad cigarettes. Nobody had any money then, and yet they went to all these places. There was a spirit of tomorrow-we-may-die during those war years, and so everyone wanted restlessly to live and love to the fullest, to the hilt, and relish life while it lasted. At the glamorous Cotillion Room, the cover charge was one dollar, considered steep, but if you tipped the captain another dollar he gave you a ringside table, which was worth it. And at the Stork Club drinks were fifty cents, unless you knew Sherm Billingsley, in which case they were often free. After a night at the Stork, you grabbed for Walter Winchell's column to see if your name was in it, and it sometimes was. The Ritz-Carlton was the most expensive hotel in town—seven dollars a night for a room! No wonder they went everywhere, and Lenny could remember many a rollicking, squandered night at the Ritz, and waking up at dawn, luxuriously hung over. Or, for the night, they might all go downtown for jazz at Eddie Condon's, or uptown because, in those days, you really could go to Harlem in ermine and pearls. And there was one little club up there, Lenny remembered, the Tic-Toc Club, where the most beautiful black boys danced naked on the stage. And, at the end of the night, you might all take the subway down to the Staten Island Ferry—over and back for a nickel—and watch the sun rise over Brooklyn Heights, and as the sun's first rays caught the windowpanes of the houses on Brooklyn Heights, there was such a sense of harmony and lyricism, modulated chords of domesticity and care and love, as windows opened and white curtains fluttered out. Gone, all gone, *le temps perdu*. But there was kindness then, and civility, and gentleness, and people you hardly knew would lend you a dollar for your cabfare home, long ago when the world was young and green and full of promises and hope.

Lenny had grown used to the way it had all changed. He had become hardened to the new cruelty that had replaced the old kindness, and he had learned to play by the tough new rules that had been imposed on this once-graceful business they were all in. Grace was out. Greed was in, and it

was Wall Street that had changed it all. Wall Street, and
the gnomes who determined interest rates, governed the city
now. It was Wall Street that had silenced the church bells
on Sunday mornings, and replaced them with the scream of
ambulance and police sirens. But Lenny had grown used to
it, taken it all in his stride, and if the new rules meant that
only Number One was going to look out for Number One,
so be it. He was a veteran now. He was used to being
resented and envied for the mysterious power he wielded
with the Rothmans. After all, he had survived in the company longer than anyone on that terrace tonight, and so Dear
Old Lenny was accustomed to being hated. He could view it
all with the icy cynicism that was required to step over the
dead bodies as they fell. But he often wondered about Alex.
Did she really understand the viciousness of the monsters
who were toasting her tonight with her own Dom Perignon
champagne, and dishing her behind her back? Sometimes he
guessed she did, but at other times he was not so sure. Under
that easy, confident demeanor, behind the secure smile, the
contralto laugh, the shoulder-length caramel hair, behind the
carelessly dropped final g's, there was surely another woman—innocent, vulnerable, too trusting—too long protected
by old Ho Rothman—who could never be cynical enough
to suspect the danger that she might be in. He decided to
find her in the crowd and warn her one more time.

As he glided through the elegant crowd, pressing his own
elegant backside against the elegant backside of Jacqueline
Onassis, he heard a conversation that struck him as particularly sinister and bitchy.

"When you're over forty in this business, you're over the
hill," he heard a man's voice say. "And she's over the hill—
five million or no five million."

He recognized the Very Important head of a New York
advertising agency, one of whose clients was a Semi-Very
Important Seventh Avenue designer.

"My client has spent over a million bucks on advertising in
her book," he heard the man say. "And I've spent thousands
of dollars taking her to lunch at Le Cirque and Côte Basque.
But has Alexandra the Great ever put one of my client's gar-
ments on her cover? We get zip. Instead, she puts this *dreck*,"
and he gestured to the cover of one of the copies of the June
issue that lay on a nearby tabletop. "I call that grand larceny.

But I'll tell you this, Myron. When Herb Rothman takes over, I'm going to tell him, 'Give us editorial support in the book, or forget about my client's account.' "

Lenny found Alex in a little group, and took her aside.

"What is it, darlin'?"

"My spies have been busy," he said. "They have learned a couple of things. I have learned, first, that our friend Herbert did not at all care for your June cover—as, if you recall, I warned you he might not."

"He's said nothin' to me about it."

"And I've learned, second, that he was not amused by this morning's ad in the *Times*."

"We hit five million. We had to announce it, didn't we? Did he want us to keep it a secret that we've got a new ad-rate base?"

He reached out and touched her hand with his fingertips. "I'm just warning you, my love," he said. "Ho is apparently very sick, and he may be dying. As I said before, I think the camel may be trying to push his way into the tent. There's a girl here from England, the one I called Miss Anna Rexia, who appears to be on *very* good terms with your father-in-law. In putting two and two together, as I said earlier, I think there may be fireworks here tonight."

She withdrew her hand quickly. "Don't talk like that, Lenny," she said. "You're frightening me. There's nothing that Herb could possibly do now that would hurt us—is there?"

"Us?" he said, almost automatically. "I'm not talking about us. I'm talking about you."

The band was playing "Somethin' Stupid," and the waiters were moving about the terrace, tapping little silver triangles—*ping, ping, ping*—to signal that it was time for Alex's guests to move to the tables.

> *Why'd I have to spoil it all*
> *By sayin' somethin' stupid like I love you . . . ?*

Lenny took Alex's arm to escort her to her table.

Chapter 4

If anyone had troubled to ask Lenny Liebling for the answers to the questions about Alex Rothman that the Razor Blades and their Eraserhead husbands, lovers, and walkers were gossiping about, and speculating about, that night on Alex Rothman's terrace, he could easily have supplied them. Her age, for example. Alex was born September 30, 1944, which made her nearly forty-six. A face-lift? Never, nor had she ever contemplated one, nor, in the opinion of most people who were able to look at her objectively, did she need one. "Wait until you're fifty-five before you even begin to think about it, Lexy, honey," her friend Lucille Withers told her once. "Fifty-five is an age when a woman's face begins to need a little tightening. Meanwhile, men between the ages of forty and seventy hardly seem to age at all. Don't you hate 'em? Men?"

It was only the women who had had their faces lifted who speculated about other women's face-lifts, and peered behind their ears for the little telltale signs.

And that business, the subject of much speculation over the years, about Alex and Ho Rothman, the company's founder, having been lovers—that was quite absurd. Ho Rothman was Alex's husband's *grand*father, for heaven's sake, Lenny thought. Alex and Ho's relationship was based on mutual respect—and, of course, the fact that Alex had made *Mode* display the black ink at the bottom of the balance sheet that

Ho Rothman so dearly loved to see. Meanwhile, Ho and Aunt Lily Rothman had been happily married—oh, they had their ups and downs like everyone else—for sixty-eight years, something of an accomplishment in this day and age.

And as for the difference between Alex's age and that of Mel Jorgenson, who had been her beau for the past two years, Mel was forty-three—hardly a significant age gap between a man and a woman in the Year of Our Lord 1990, Lenny thought.

Lenny could have pointed out the truths behind all these silly canards about Alex Rothman, but it was not in his nature to do so. Besides, the Razor Blades and their Eraserheads enjoyed their nasty little speculations too much for him to take the trouble to disillusion them; it would leave them with nothing to carp and prattle about, which would be too cruel and easy, like snatching pennies from a blind man's cup. Let them stew in their own Jews, he often said and, being Jewish, he could say that. And Lenny was not a stewer. Lenny saw himself as a *saucier*, a *gratinier*. He took the boring and the banal and added garnish. Lenny was not interested in gossip, and he was not interested in bedtime stories, either. But he was interested in secrets. Secrets were his weapons, the source of his power.

For instance, Lenny did nothing to quash the stories, which circulated in the trade, to the effect that Alex received free dresses from designers and manufacturers, though nothing could be farther from the truth. In an industry riddled with graft, bribery, greased palms, and under-the-desk payoffs, no one on *Mode*'s staff was permitted to accept gifts, or even discounts, from designers, manufacturers, advertisers, or other interested parties. Alex had made this an ironclad policy at the magazine and, like everyone else, she paid the full retail price for her clothes. The only exception to this rule was Carol Duffy, the beauty editor, who was powerless to curb the cosmetics industry's traditional practice of "sampling," and could not stem the flow of samples that poured into her office from Revlon, Estée Lauder, Arden, and the rest. Cartons, literally, of lipsticks, nail polishes, scrubs, scents, cleansers, moisturizers, and other elixirs and beauty panaceas arrived at poor Carol's desk daily—more beauty products than any woman could ever sample, much less use up, in a lifetime in front of a mirror. Alex's solution to this was simple. A bushel basket, decorated with red ribbons, was placed outside Carol's office door; the cosmetics samples were dumped there, and staffers were invited to help themselves to whatever they wanted. Whatever was left over at the end of each week was picked up by the Salvation Army.

But then there was always the problem—such as the complaint Lenny had overheard the agency head express tonight—of the advertiser who felt, rightly or wrongly, that he or she was not being sufficiently paid back, editorially, for the advertising dollars spent in the magazine. Advertisers were constantly threatening to "pull out of the book"—or even to pull their ads out of every one of the Rothman publications—because their products were insufficiently plugged in the editorial pages, or if they felt a competitor's line was being unfairly favored. If Ralph Lauren, a major advertiser, picked up an issue of *Mode* with a design by his arch-rival, Calvin Klein, on the cover, Lauren's fury was predictable. Fashion designers were a notoriously touchy and temperamental lot, and they always felt cheated out of the recognition they thought they deserved. But part of an editor's job was to play favorites, and obviously Alex Rothman had hers. If she had overheard that complaint tonight, she would have said, "Look, we're grateful for your advertising dollars, and we're proud to have you advertise in *Mode*. But I have to assume that you advertise in *Mode* because you want to reach our readers, and I have to assume that reaching our readers must pay off for you, or else you wouldn't advertise. What more can I say?"

Lenny could have said the same thing, if he had felt like it. He could also have said that, unlike some editors whom he could name, Alex did not believe in running around town begging for advertising. He could have said that, unlike some magazines, *Mode* did not offer substantial discounts to big advertisers. He could have said that the great Ho Rothman himself had disagreed—violently—with Alex when she had outlined her let-them-come-to-me policy about advertisers, and he could have added that, whether advertisers liked it or not, that policy seemed to have worked, thus far, for Alex.

And as for the Semi-Very Important Seventh Avenue designer whom the agency man represented, Lenny knew that this chap was not one of Alex's special favorites at the moment. The fellow was young, still growing, and had a way to go. He was certainly not ready for a cover of *Mode*. Should Alex, then, not accept his agency's invitations to lunch at Le Cirque and La Côte Basque? There was perhaps a gray area here, but not much of a one in Lenny's opinion. Alex was in the business of fashion news-gathering. Let her have her lunches with designers' reps. It was one way of keeping up with what was happening, and what might be on the designers' minds. Besides, it was a dog-eat-dog world, this whole business. The dogs were still dogs, even when they invited editors to French restaurants, and, naturally, when they didn't get exactly what they wanted, they tried to bite back.

Integrity was a word not high on the list in Lenny's lexicon of human virtues, but he was willing to recognize it in others, and he had to admit that Alex maintained her integrity better than most people in the howling, canine pack around her. It took guts to accept an advertiser's hundred-dollar lunch, and give him nothing in return.

But it was Herb Rothman's assertion—if he had indeed said such a thing—that Alex had become a "gimmicky" editor that disturbed Lenny the most. That was an aspersion on his own work for the magazine, in Lenny's opinion. Alex was an editor who believed in strong visual images and, as special projects editor, Lenny had had a hand in staging some of those images. Lenny was not the magazine's art director— that job belonged to a somewhat crass (in Lenny's opinion) but perfectly likable Irishman named Bob Shaw whose best work (Lenny happened to know) was accomplished in the morning, before Bob had washed down his lunch with several Scotches. Lenny knew why Bob Shaw's office door was often closed during the afternoon: Bob Shaw was sleeping off his lunch. Also, Lenny knew of a certain little blonde in the Art Department, who was eager to climb the masthead, who often slept off Bob Shaw's lunches with him, and about whom Lenny was sure Bob Shaw's wife had no knowledge, but that was neither here nor there. That item, for the moment, was one of Lenny's not-very-useful secrets, though who knew what might prove useful later on? The oddest things sometimes turned out to be useful.

Lenny saw himself as a stylist. Let Bob Shaw do his overall layouts for a picture feature, which were usually very good, but when it came time for a photo shooting session, it was Lenny who kept an eye on the little details, the little touches—a girl's scarf not quite tied properly, for instance, or a model's foot extended at an awkward angle, her chin tilted upward when it would look prettier tilted down, a speck of lint on her skirt—Lenny was good at catching things like that. In a famous Mary Poppins spread, for instance, which had involved huge wind machines and photographing the models flying through the air on invisible wires in the middle of Hyde Park, Lenny had spotted a leaf caught in one of the wires. "We'll airbrush it out," Bob Shaw had said. No, Lenny insisted. Airbrushing always looked like airbrushing, he said, and Alex agreed. And so they reshot the whole elaborate, expensive photograph. Lenny's ability to spot little details like that was one reason why he and Alex were a good team.

Were visual ideas like the Mary Poppins spread gimmicky? Lenny didn't think so, and neither did readers, who stopped to study the photograph and wonder how it had been done. And the wind did wonders for the flying models' clothes—one of whom, of course, was dressed as a nanny, wheeling a pram through the air. The issue was a sell-out at the news-stands, which provided the true barometer of a magazine's popularity.

For another story, titled "Is the Paris Couture Dead?" Alex had had the idea of photographing her models in the misty lanes and pathways of Père Lachaise Cemetery, among the elaborate tombs of Frédéric Chopin, Oscar Wilde, Edith Piaf, and Coco Chanel. For a story on architecture in fashion, Alex had posed her models on scaffolding, and in the baskets of cherry pickers, and on the I-beams of a rising skyscraper. Then there was her famous Seraglio issue, at a time when Middle Eastern influences were creeping into fashion, when all the models were posed as though they were members of a desert sultan's harem. One shot, showing a model holding up a bunch of purple grapes before the sultan's open mouth, was positively erotic. Issues like these became collectors' items, and Alex discovered that readers were saving old issues of *Mode*, the way some people refused to throw out copies of the *National Geographic*.

Sometimes Alex's visual ideas for the magazine turned out to have real social impact. During a season that had been characterized by a certain *fin de siécle* decadence, she had asked Richard Avedon to pose her models against the grotesque background of a mountainous, rusting automobile graveyard in Southern California—a risky notion, since it took the chance of offending advertisers in Detroit, who might see it as a reminder of how quickly their products became obsolete. Instead, something quite different happened. The vivid setting did more than dramatize the Decadent Look from Paris. The photographs so incensed readers in Encino, who recognized the mountain of twisted steel that had been rising in their own backyards, that they campaigned—successfully— to have their local eyesore bulldozed underground.

All this went into building up five million circulation and the ad announcing it in this morning's *Times*, which, apparently, Herb Rothman had not cared for, though Lenny had thought it rather clever. The ad, which filled the entire back page of the paper, had been prepared by the magazine's agency, and the idea for it had been theirs, not Alex's. The illustration, by the cartoonist Roz Chast, showed a pert and saucy whale breaching the water and blowing a tall spray of foam into the air, and the headline was simply:

THAR SHE BLOWS!
CIRCULATION OVER 5,000,000!

The only other visual element was a small photo of *Mode*'s June cover in the lower lefthand corner of the page. Originally, Chast had shown a tiny whaling vessel in the distance, with a sailor, holding a spyglass, pointing from the ship's crow's nest. But even on her magazine's promotional advertising, Alex Rothman managed to place her own personal stamp. When the agency's account executive had first shown Alex the paste-up of the ad, she immediately covered up the image of the small boat with the palm of her hand. "We're the whale—right?" she said. "We don't want it to look as though we're about to be harpooned out of the water, do we? Save the whale. Leave out the little boat." Then she took a grease pencil, and gave the whale long, curling eyelashes. "We're a woman's magazine—right?" she said. "Let's make our whale more of a lady. And we're a stylish magazine, so we should have a stylish whale. And suggest to Mrs. Chast that she might have the whale wink at the reader with one eye. That tells the industry that, while we're pleased, we don't take it all *too* seriously. We knew it would happen all along—right?" And so, somewhat grumpily, Chast had gone back to her drawing board, though even she admitted that Alex was right in terms of the message the ad was intended to convey. "Sure she's right, dammit!" Roz Chast said.

And the agency was so pleased with the finished ad that it immediately submitted it to the Clio Awards committee. Why should Herb have objected to that? That mystified Lenny. A pattern was emerging, a plot was unfolding, but Lenny was not yet certain what it was.

The controversial June cover was quite another matter. Lenny had been sure that Herb would object to it, and had told Alex so. Bob Shaw had also been against it but, as usually happened, Alex had her way. "The magazine's been around for nearly a hundred and twenty years," she said. "Isn't it time we did something really bold and different with the cover?" Then a delightful coincidence had occurred. The June cover had been photographed months before, but when it made its appearance, nothing really newsworthy was happening in either Washington or New York or Moscow, or in Tokyo or in Tiananmen Square. For lack of anything better to report on, it seemed, the nation's newspapers and news magazines were headlining a relatively bush-league squabble over what constituted art and what was pornography, set off by an exhibit of the photographs of Robert Mapplethorpe in some Midwest city. *Mode*'s June cover became part of the controversy, and there were stories in the *Times* and the *Washington Post* and *Time* and the *Wall Street Journal*. *Newsweek* even ran a photo of *Mode*'s cover. Not even Alex had counted on so much free publicity, which had certainly helped boost newsstand sales. It was just luck that it turned out that way. But this was a business in which you always had to gamble, and be willing to be lucky.

There were no place cards at the tables, but Lenny was able to work it out so that he seated himself next to Mona Potter. Though not always reliable, Mona was often a source of little tidbits. Lenny did not really like Mona Potter; neither did Alex Rothman. (Nor did Mona like Alex, who she continued to believe had cheated her out of the editorship of *Mode* seventeen years ago.) In fact, it would be safe to say that no one in New York really liked Mona Potter, but, with her three-times-a-week column, Mona had become a force in the city and had to be reckoned with, and had to be included on the invitation list of any party such as Alex's tonight. It was said that the social status of any woman in New York could be measured by how often she was mentioned in "The Fashion Scene" each month. Some people actually kept running scores of Mona's mentions. Mona's mentions of Alex Rothman were invariably snide and catty—referring to Alex as "the venerable editor of *Mode*," or "*Mode*'s vintage editor," "*Mode*'s veteran editor," "*Mode*'s perennial editor," "*Mode*'s longtime editor," "*Mode*'s durable editor," "*Mode*'s forever-young editor," or, when Mona was feeling particularly spiteful, "the well-seasoned fashion maven." These sly little barbs were intended to enrage Alex Rothman but, if they did, Alex was careful not to let it show, and she had greeted Mona as warmly tonight as she had all her other guests.

Mona's column was mostly about the fashionable world, with the celebrities' names set in boldface type, and it was notorious for its inaccuracies—names spelled wrong, quotes misattributed or simply made up—and when she tried to write about clothes she frequently lapsed into atrocious French. A peignoir became a "paisnoire," a chemise was a "chamoix," and once, trying to describe Kitty Miller in a gown of peau de soie, Mona had written that Kitty was "swathed in pas de soleil." But she had a wide readership in the city and elsewhere among people who apparently didn't know the difference, and she maintained a high profile.

Also, at a party, Mona was hard to miss. If the young Englishwoman named Fiona Fenton had borrowed her hairstyle from Louise Brooks, Mona had borrowed hers from Lucille Ball. It was an improbable tangerine shade, piled high on top of her head, teased to the limit, and rigid with hair spray. In tonight's breeze, Mona's metallic coiffure was as indestructible as Gibraltar. Mona had two other personal trademarks. One was her fondness for rubies, which, she felt, set off her orange hair. The other was her spectacles with magnifying lenses as thick as the bottoms of Coca-Cola bottles. Alex often wondered how a woman who was almost certifiably blind could claim to report on fashion. Mona had difficulty navigating her way about a party like this one, particularly after she had had a few glasses of wine, but that didn't matter. The people who wanted to be mentioned in her column, and who wanted to see their names in boldface type, made their way to her. Of all the gossip columnists in New York, "Mother Mona," as she was called, was the undisputed queen.

Now Mona was fixing her myopic gaze on Lenny. "Tell me, sweetie," she said, "now that the mag has reached five mil, the rumor is that Alex'll be taking early retirement. Any truth to that?"

Lenny smiled his noncommittal smile. "I hadn't heard that rumor," he said. "But there's no truth to it, Mona darling."

"But how can she top herself now, sweetie? Isn't five mil what Herb wanted? Now that he's got that out of her, what else can she do for him? He can't get blood out of a turnip. That's the rumor."

"Really? Where do these rumors come from, I wonder. Do you simply make them up?"

"Listen, I hear something very top secret's been going on on the thirtieth floor of the Rothman Building. How come Herb Rothman canceled a lunch date today at the Four Seasons, and had a pastrami on rye sent up to his office instead? What's the hot poop?"

"Interesting how you learn these things, Mona," Lenny said. "I assume that Emilio at the Four Seasons is one of the little people you take care of. But how did you learn about the pastrami on rye? Interesting. Where was this sandwich sent up from, do you know?"

"Ha! I don't have to tell you my sources. Ever hear of something called the First Amendment? Come on. Take the cork out of your mouth, sweetie. Give me a little scoopie-poo."

"How about a little scoopie-poo of lobster bisque?" Lenny said, reaching out and guiding Mona's blindly groping hand toward the soup spoon at the right of her plate.

But he realized that she was actually groping for the stem of her wineglass, which she found and gripped with ruby-encrusted fingers, and of course this was not her first glass of wine tonight.

Now Mona turned to the man on her left, Gregory Kittredge, who was Alex's young secretary-assistant. For some reason, Lenny had never quite trusted Gregory, though he had no real basis for his distrust. It was all vague and intuitive, visceral. For one thing, Gregory was quite disturbingly beautiful—too beautiful, really, for a man of twenty-five to deserve to be. Gregory Kittredge looked like a young Tyrone Power, an actor on whom Lenny had had a violent boyhood crush back home in Onward, where he kept a collection of Tyrone Power photographs under his mattress. He had written a letter to Tyrone Power—"Mr. Tyrone Power, Metro-Goldwyn-Mayer Pictures, Inc., 3459 La Cienega Boulevard, Los Angeles, California"—asking for his autograph, and never heard a word. Lenny assumed that Gregory was gay, but he could not be sure of that, either. He knew nothing about Gregory's private life, but wasn't it a little odd for a man named Gregory to insist on being called "Gregory," and not Greg, or some other shortcut? Gregory was such a stilted-sounding, three-syllable name, like Percival or Archibald. Gregory was a very preppyish young man, Brooks Brothers from top to bottom, almost too preppy-perfect. Sometimes he brought his squash racquet to the office. He had come to the magazine right out of Princeton, had worked his way up from the mail room, through Production as a Production mole, and had been Alex's assistant—screening her telephone calls and mail, typing her letters at eighty-perfect-words a minute, keeping her appointment book, handling her travel arrangements, balancing her checkbook—for the better part of the past three years. Alex found him conscientious, efficient, discreet, and bright. Across the vest of his dark blue three-piece suit, on a gold chain, there dangled a gold Phi Beta Kappa key, which Lenny found just a tad pretentious. "Gregory." Or Manfred Goldbogen, or whatever Tyrone Power's name had been before.

With Gregory, Mona was trying a somewhat different journalistic approach. "Who'll replace Alex when she retires, sweetie?" Mona asked him.

"I didn't know Mrs. Rothman was thinking of retiring," Gregory said.

"That's the rumor. They say Herb Rothman would like to ease Alex out, now that she's got him his five mil circulation, which was all he ever wanted out of her. They say he's looking for someone younger. It could be you, I suppose."

"Hmm," Gregory said, spooning his soup.

"Or then again, it could be me. It was me Herb wanted in the first place, you know. Think I might have another shot at the top spot? What do you think? Has Herb Rothman said anything to you about me lately?"

"No, I don't believe he has, actually."

"What's on the big boy's mind, d'you know?"

"Mr. Rothman is sitting right over there. Why don't you ask him?"

"Ha! I know Herb Rothman too well. He plays it too close to the vest. He won't say boo till he's good and ready. But what about your boss's love life? Think she'll marry whatsisname, the TV news guy, that Merv Jorgenson?"

"I think you mean Mr. *Mel* Jorgenson?"

"Merv, Mel—what the hell? Think they'll make it to the altar?"

"Really, Mrs. Potter, I have no idea," Gregory said, as a waiter refilled Mona's wineglass.

In another corner of the terrace, Mel Jorgenson had just approached Alex at her table. Bending over her shoulder, he whispered, "I hate to leave early, darling, and before your big show, but I've got to get to the studio."

"I know, darling."

"I'll watch the whole thing on our NBC monitor. Think you'll still be propped up after I do the news? If I'm back around midnight?"

"Absolutely, darling. I'll have Coleman fix us chicken sandwiches, and we'll have a nightcap and a nice schmooz."

"Terrific party," he whispered. "Congratulations. You're wonderful. I love you." He kissed her quickly on the top of the head, and was gone.

Now Herbert Rothman approached Alex's table. Herb was not usually a demonstrative man, but now he pressed Alex's hand between his palms. "Alex," he said. "Alex, I just wanted you to know how proud I am of you."

"Why, thank you, Herb," she said.

"You and I have had our differences in the past, I know. Some of that's been my fault, perhaps. But tonight—well, tonight I just wanted to tell you that this is your finest hour, your finest hour."

"Thank you, Papa Bear," she said, using a term for him that she had not used in years, not since Tarrytown, when they had all lived together under one roof, trying—trying—to be one big happy family, and she had tried—tried so hard—to make her father-in-law become her friend. Under that chilly exterior, she decided, there really was a sweet side, and every now and then he let it show and, after all, he had not led the happiest of lives. She smiled up at him. "Give me a kiss," she said, "to show me we've made up. Besides, it's a great photo op."

Flushing slightly, he bent and kissed her lightly on the cheek, and the television and newspaper cameras recorded this moment.

Back at her table, Mona Potter was still trying to dredge information from Gregory Kittredge as the main course was being served. When Mona was with the wine, she often became maudlin or belligerent, or sometimes both, and Lenny was enjoying watching Gregory's obvious discomfiture. Mona's soup bowl had been removed untouched, and now she was ignoring her main course. In fact, Lenny realized, he had never actually seen Mona eat, in all the years he had known her. Probably this was because she could not see what was on her plate. At home, she no doubt lapped up her meals out of a bowl, like a dog. When drinking, she had another habit, a kind of nervous tic, or compulsion. In her lap, she carried a large gold compact, and she kept flipping this open and looking down at her image in the mirror. The mirror, Lenny had noticed, was magnified, and so she was continually checking her magnified appearance through the further magnification of her corrective lenses. The face she saw in her compact mirror, Lenny imagined, must seem the size of Brazil. Opening and closing her compact in her lap, peering downward, she was saying to Gregory, "I gotta do something on this party for my column. Gimme something for my column. What about you? Don't forget, I could help your career if I plugged you in my column. So let's talk about you. What turns you on? What's kicks for you?"

"Delicious dinner," Gregory murmured, slicing carefully into his veal chop. "You can always count on Glorious Food."

"C'mon, you can talk to me. You can level with me. Don't forget, I could have been where she is right now—right up there at the top. You could have been working for me instead of her, ever think about that? I could have been your boss instead of her, ever think about that? I could have been sitting where she is, right at the top, handing out the orders, calling out the orders loud and strong, instead of sitting in a lousy little office at the *News*, pounding out copy for a column deadline three times a week. I could have been Miss Mode. I could of! I was that close—*that close*—" and she indicated the minute distance between a rubied forefinger and her thumb—"to having her job, until she kicked the ladder out from under me."

Gregory picked up a baby asparagus spear with his fork, and chewed it thoughtfully.

"And now she's up there at the top, instead of me. Well, I'll tell you this. She'd better be very, *very* careful. It's not easy being at the top. You know why? They say it's lonely at the top, but there's more to it than that. The person at the top has to keep topping herself, which ain't easy. And now she's got a new man. Think she'll marry him?"

"Really, Mrs. Potter, I wouldn't know."

"Funny thing about her, isn't it? She's always had a man. She's always had to have a man, even at her age. What's her secret, d'ya think?"

"Really, Mrs. Potter, I wouldn't know."

She opened and closed her compact, opened it and closed it again. "I've got a lousy marriage. I guess everybody knows that. And d'you know why? Partly I blame her for that. Yes I do! Potter has no respect for me. If I was a big-time fashion magazine editor, like I could have been, and not pounding out a column on a deadline three times a week, Potter would show me some respect, but he doesn't. But do I care what Potter thinks of me?"

"I'm sure you do, Mrs. Potter," Gregory said.

"Hell, no! I don't care. Potter can go to hell. Potter sells insurance. I've interviewed Nancy Reagan, Pat Nixon, Fawn Hall, all the big ones. So. D'ya think she'll marry whatsisname? I say no. My sources say that Merv Whatsisname doesn't want a career woman–type wife. They say he wants a little housewifey-type wife who'll sit in a little rose-covered cottage in Scarsdale or someplace and darn his socks and cook him chicken soup. Whadda you think?"

"Really, I just wouldn't know."

"And I don't have to tell you who my sources are. Ever hear of something called the First Amendment? But I guess everybody knows she's sleeping with him. D'you think that's gonna be the extent of it, or what?"

Gregory Kittredge put down his knife and fork. "Really, Mrs. Potter," he said, very carefully, "I do not wish to discuss Mrs. Rothman's private life with you."

"Well, fuck you, sweetie," Mona Potter said. "See what I have to say about you in Monday's column." She turned immediately to Lenny on her right. "How long have you and Charlie Boxer been lovers, sweetie?" she said. "Don't you two ever worry about AIDS? Or do you figure you're both too old for that?"

Lenny Liebling smiled his brightest, most beatific smile, the smile he reserved for only the most tinglingly rapturous moments. "Darling Mona," he said. "Tell me. Where did you learn to make such utterly charming dinner-table conversation?"

Chapter 5

Now the pink-coated waiters were clearing the dessert course—Alex's famous chocolate mousse served in individual terra-cotta flowerpots, with a fresh pink geranium sprouting from the center of each, looking as though it was growing there, a confection the caterer prepared only for Alex—and the orchestra had just finished a set. Alex stepped over to the bandleader. "As soon as the waiters have finished clearing," she said, "play about eight bars of 'Happy Days.' That will be Coleman's cue to signal the fireworks barge in the river. Then you can go to the mike, and say, 'Ladies and gentlemen, if you'll all please stand and face in the direction of Riker's Island, we have a short show for you,' or something like that. Then give us a quick fanfare, and the fireworks should start—okay, darlin'?"

The bandleader nodded. "Got it, Mrs. Rothman," he said.

Alex returned to her table, where Lenny, who had escaped from Mona Potter, had joined her. "Cross your fingers," she whispered. "I hope this all works."

But now Herbert Rothman stepped to the microphone. "Ladies and gentlemen," he began. "Ladies and gentlemen—good friends—dear friends—If I may just say a few words—" And slowly the crowd grew silent. The lighting engineer from NBC turned his floods on Herb Rothman, and the cameraman hoisted his Port-O-Cam to his shoulder and trained it on Herb to capture whatever the president of Rothman Publications, and the publisher of *Mode*, would have to say.

"Ladies and gentlemen," he said, as the camera rolled and the flashbulbs popped, "we all know why we're gathered here tonight—to celebrate the remarkable circulation break-through of *Mode*, a breakthrough none of us at Rothman thought possible, and to toast the editorial triumph of *Mode*'s editor, Alexandra Rothman, my favorite daughter-in-law. . . ." The camera panned briefly to Alex's face, and her smile was automatic as she mouthed the words, "Thank you, Herb." There was a polite round of applause.

"He only has *one* daughter-in-law," someone whispered.

Herb Rothman raised his wineglass. "Here's to Alex," he said. "As I told you earlier, Alex, this is your finest hour."

Responses of "Hear, hear" echoed across the terrace.

"Now I can't let this historic moment pass without com-ment," he continued. "As we enter a new decade, the decade of the nineties, we will be entering a period of profound change, which will be felt in the world of fashion as well as on other fronts. We must be prepared for these changes. At Rothman Publications, we are already preparing for these changes. Here at *Mode*, we are addressing the future, not the past. . . ."

Several members of the fashion press were already reach-ing for their pencils and note pads. "Dammit, he's turning my party into a press conference," Alex whispered.

"I'm not a social historian," he went on, "but let us exam-ine these changes. In the nineteen seventies, when Alexandra Rothman first came to us—and how long ago that seems!—there was a settling down and a seriousness that, in the beginning of it, the magazine really caught. This coincided with the rise of women in the work force. This is one of the themes we've been involved with, and that was impor-tant to our readers. However, in many ways, the ideological, political side of that has softened. Coming cultural changes will be profound. They will include increasing informality, and a blurring of the rigid guidelines of what is high art and kitsch, all of which will be manifested in fashion. There have been clear lines of what was high fashion and casual fashion. . . ."

"Do you have any idea what he's talking about?" someone whispered from a corner of the terrace.

Alex Rothman turned to whisper to the deposed bandleader. "Sorry, but I didn't know there were going to be speeches. As soon as he finishes, go right into 'Happy Days.' "

He nodded.

In his bedroom at 720 Park Avenue, many blocks away, the old man lay flat on his back on his hospital bed, breathing evenly. In one corner of the room, the night duty nurse, Evelyn Roemer, sat in front of her television set, with the picture tube aglow but with the sound turned off. Though she glanced occasionally at the screen, she was also reading a romance novel in which the heroine, who had been brutally raped, now found herself madly in love with her assailant, and Mrs. Roemer had just come to the conclusion that it might not be all that bad to be raped. In fact, it might be kind of exciting.

Suddenly her patient pushed himself up on his elbows and shouted, "Goddammit, turn up the sound!"

"Sure, hon," she said, and turned up the volume. "It's about some party they're having on the East Side. It's pretty boring."

From the screen, the voice said, " . . . clear lines of what was high fashion and casual fashion. I think those lines are less apparent now. I think the change in the nineteen nineties, when we look back, will be as decisive as . . ."

"That's my son!" the old man said. "That's Herbie! Get the missus!"

"Now, hon, you know Mrs. Rothman has went to bed. Let's just us settle back and get ourselves a good night's sleep."

" . . . the shift from the sixties to the seventies. There's been a . . ."

"Get the missus! Like I tell you! Now!" He was sitting straight up in bed now.

"Now, hon, let's have our blood-pressure pill."

"Get the missus! Like I tell you, *meshugge* woman! Is my order! *Get the missus!*"

"All *right*, Mr. Rothman, all *right*," she said, rising and slamming down her book, then padding on her crepe soles to the door.

" . . . recognition of that in magazine publishing. I think. . . ."

* * *

"I think," Herbert Rothman continued into the camera's lens from Alex's terrace, "at the midpoint of the seventies there was a very decisive change in the way we all lived, and in people's attitudes toward fashion, culture, and health. It was a change from the headlines of the sixties, and the whole eroticism from Britain . . ."

"From Britain? *Eroticism?*" Lenny whispered in Alex's ear.

"Excuse me, I meant *ex*oticism," Herb corrected himself, and there was light, nervous laughter from his audience. "In many ways, the British are fashion's bellwethers. In many ways, the British entered the nineteen nineties years before we did. . . ."

"Neatest trick of the week," Lenny whispered.

"In many ways, the British entered the nineties back in the seventies and eighties, and the best way to perceive this is to study the facts. And the facts are that we are now in the nineties, and we are in the nineties and here to stay, at least for the next decade, and we are prepared for the soon-to-be-realized eventualities that will be reflected in fashion in the nineties, and even beyond, for the foreseeable future, as the experts foresee it, and even beyond that, and, believe me, I have consulted all the experts, and I have even become something of an expert on it myself."

"Beyond the beyond," Lenny murmured dreamily.

"But to return to the present, which is where we are right now, and to the future of *Mode*, which is where we are headed, and to throw off the shackles of the past, which was where we were before we got to where we are today, we know we are here to celebrate and extol and praise the fine work of a great fashion editor, which is what Alexandra Rothman has been, who has shown us all how far she can go, how greatly a great publication can grow—grow in power, prestige, and influence, not to mention circulation. And the very process of that growth, and all those long, long years of toil, have taken an enormous toll on Alexandra Rothman. She may not admit it, but we all know the toll those years have taken on her because, as the enormity of Alexandra's responsibilities, tasks, and duties at the magazine have grown, they have grown too enormous to be enormities that one mere woman can handle alone."

There was a small collective gasp from his audience at

these last remarks and, briefly, Lenny Liebling closed his eyes and, with the little finger of his right hand, he reached out and circled the little finger of Alex's left, which she quickly withdrew, sitting forward in her chair and staring at Herb intently.

"And so," Herb said, turning again to Alex, "Alexandra Rothman, you will not go unrewarded for all those years of toil. Tonight, I am announcing your reward for those years of toil. Your reward, which I know will please you, will be a good right hand. I have today created a new spot on *Mode*'s masthead—that of co-editor-in-chief, to provide you with the good right hand you so desperately need. The young woman I have chosen to fill this spot comes to us with splendid credentials—from brilliant editorial work for one of Britain's leading fashion magazines to, more recently, the proprietress of one of London's most fashionable custom design studios, in the heart of the West End's fashionable Sloane Street, where she has overseen the fashion needs of all of Britain's most fashionable women, up to and including Diana, the Princess of Wales, who, I am told, rarely makes a fashion decision without consulting this special lady, who will join our staff on July the first. Ladies and gentlemen, may I present the new co-editor-in-chief of *Mode*, Miss Fiona Fenton." And the tiny woman in the oversize sunglasses and the oval of glossy black hair stepped forward and, with just the slightest trace of a curtsy, smiled nervously for the cameras. Herb Rothman remained at the microphone, apparently expecting applause, but there was none. Instead, the terrace immediately became abuzz with excited, astonished conversation, while Alex sat rigidly in her chair. In the confusion, Lenny spotted Fiona's Chanel bag sitting unattended at her table. He stepped quickly toward it.

In the semidarkened bedroom at 720 Park Avenue, where Ho Rothman's wife, Aunt Lily, had joined him in her nightie, her face creamed, wearing her chin strap, her ash-blonde hair in rollers—the two stared at the television screen.

Aunt Lily was the first to speak. "I warned you the damned fool might try to pull something like this," she said.

Nurse Roemer puttered in the background. "Time for our blood-pressure pill," she said.

"Shut up," Aunt Lily said. "Just you shut up."

* * *

Yes, there might have been some people on Alexandra's terrace that night who had actively hated her, who had longed for her downfall, uttered prayers that she would fail, and who knew in their heart of hearts that any one of them could have done her job as well as, or even better than, she had, but what they had just heard and witnessed from Herbert Rothman was too much for any of them. One of their own had just been publicly humiliated, and in the most awful of ways. In front of two hundred and fifty people, she had been told that she could no longer manage her job by herself. A great wave of sympathy—sympathy, the last thing Alex wanted—poured out for her now, as voices rose in shock and consternation.

"Poor Alex—what a way to be told that you're finished."

"Did you hear him? 'A mere woman'?"

"Typical Herbert Rothman. His father may have been a son-of-a-bitch, but he'd never do something like this!"

"Who is this new woman? Has anyone ever heard of her?"

"Mona Potter's been screwed again."

"Poor Gregory—I wonder what will become of him?" Gregory Kittredge's too-handsome face was a mask.

"Poor Alex—did she have so much as an inkling?"

"Shocking . . . awful . . . in the worst possible taste . . ."

"In my book, Herb Rothman is a bastard."

"It's ageism, is all it is. If I were Alex, I'd sue."

Alex could hear some of these whispered comments and, though her eyes might be blue-green in some lights, and hazel in others, when she became angry they became black as coals. She sat rigidly in her chair with her fists tightly clenched, her knuckles white, her face frozen in a dreadful parody of a smile that she was sure convinced no one. Beside her, Lenny whispered, "It's worse than I thought. The whole camel is *in* the tent. But don't let it show, Smart Alex. Keep your famous cool, Smart Alex. Remember who you are. . . ."

Meanwhile, there was indeed a great difference between the important guests and the members of the working press. It was not just that the general-assignment reporters and photographers were not, for the most part, wearing dinner jackets, and instead wore blue or gray pinstripe suits, white shirts, and

neckties. They also wore furtive, hunted looks, expressions
of discomfiture that revealed that these were men and wom-
en who were unaccustomed to appearing in such perfumed,
opulent surroundings. Had they been wearing creased fedo-
ras with "PRESS" cards tucked in their hatbands, they could
not have looked more conspicuously out of place. These were
not just people from the large metropolitan dailies, the weekly news magazines, and from *Spy* and *Vanity Fair*. There
were also reporters and photographers from suburban papers
on Long Island, Westchester, Connecticut, and New Jersey,
as well as stringers from other cities—Boston, Washington,
Baltimore, and Philadelphia. These people knew that they
had been invited to—or in some cases merely assigned to
attend—the party simply because their hostess wanted to
generate as much publicity for her magazine as possible.
The evening, after all, was all about ink for *Mode*.

The *grandes dames* of the press—women like Bernadine
Morris, Enid Nemy, Aileen Mehle, Mona Potter, and Liz
Smith, who, for some reason, had come dressed in a cow-
girl outfit—comported themselves like the giant celebrities
they knew themselves to be, letting Dr. Kissinger envelop
them in his bear hugs, blowing kisses to Brooke Astor,
calling each other darling. But the others, whose names no
one really knew, or would probably ever know, or would
ever really care to know, had spent most of the evening
trying to be inconspicuous, hovering mousily in the background, scribbling in their notebooks the names of famous
guests that were attachable to famous faces, noting designer
dresses, and guessing at the caratage of large gems, knowing (at least they knew that much) that the question, "How
many carats in that ruby?" would be answered with a frosty
stare. Instead, they tended to interview each other. Those
not bold enough to ask Jackie Onassis who had designed
her dress asked others from the little fraternity. A reporter
from a South Norwalk paper who had missed Brooke Astor's
entrance kept trying to find out, from his fellows, where the
great lady was. And when dinner was served, all these press
people gravitated toward a few tables at the east-facing end
of Alex's L-shaped terrace so they could be close to one
another.

But the moment Herbert J. Rothman stepped away from
the microphone, these members of the so-called working

press knew at once they were on to something they understood, something they had never expected to come away
from this evening with—*a story*. All at once they were
on their feet, pushing, shoving, elbowing their way toward
the publisher and the new editor. All at once they were
transformed from little gray wrens, pecking quietly at the
sidelines for little scraps of this and that, into a braying pack
of newshounds on the scent of a Major Development, even a
front-page by-line. Pencils poised and cameras at the ready,
they pushed their way forward toward the pair in the center
of the circle of the television cameras' floodlights, shouting
questions, all at once on a first-name basis with the principals
in the drama.

"Hey, Herbie! Look over here, Herbie! Does this mean
Alex Rothman will be retiring?"

"No comment."

"Hey, Fiona—over here, Fiona! Smile, Fiona—*big* smile!
Take off those damn shades, Fiona, so we can see you!"

"How old are you, Fiona? How much do you weigh?
Who designed your dress, Fiona? Are you married? Any
boyfriend? What's your love life?"

"Herb, does this mean you are finally taking over the reins
of Rothman Communications?" the reporter from *Women's
Wear Daily* asked him.

The question clearly annoyed him. It was the word *finally*,
which reminded him that close to seven decades of his life
had passed before he had been given any control, or any real
power, at all. "Mr. H. O. Rothman is a very old man, and
very ill," he replied stiffly.

"How about the IRS lawsuit against Rothman Communications?" the same reporter wanted to know. "How has your
father responded to that?"

"I doubt my father is even aware of it," Herb said.
"Besides, I'm not at liberty to discuss the lawsuit at this
point in time."

"We've heard the figure eight hundred million dollars.
With penalties and interest, that could amount to—"

"I'm not at liberty to—"

"Herb, you said you had consulted experts who have
foreseen the future of the magazine. Specifically, could you
give us the names of these experts, and explain a bit more
fully why they have some sort of crystal ball?"

"Herb, why did you choose not to promote someone from within the organization to this new post? Why an outsider? Why an unknown?"

"Yes, why a Brit, Herb? Why not an American?"

"Fiona, what's the name of that Brit fashion magazine you worked for? *Lady Fair*? Never heard of it. Who publishes it? Who owns it? *Who*? Never heard of 'em!"

"Fiona, what was the name of your shop in Sloane Street?"

"Who does your hair, Fiona?"

"Fiona, does this mean you're being groomed as Alex Rothman's successor? What makes you think you can fill her shoes?"

"Fiona, do you have a particular fashion philosophy?"

"Take off the shades, Fiona, so we can get a shot of you."

"How do you spell 'Fiona'?" Mona Potter called from the periphery of the crowd, and then, more loudly, "What's she look like? Is she pretty? I can't see her from here."

"Skinny. No tits," someone yelled back.

Meanwhile, when Herb Rothman stepped away from the microphone, the bandleader, as instructed, struck up the opening chords of "Happy Days." No one, not even Alex, heard him, of course, except Coleman, inside the apartment, who was waiting for his cue. "Ladies and gentlemen . . . ladies and gentlemen," the bandleader shouted into the microphone, "if you'll all please rise and face Riker's Island, we have a very special little show . . ."

And Coleman pressed the button that was the signal to the fireworks barge in the river.

"Oh, my God, the fireworks," Alex said, jumping to her feet.

Lenny also sprang to his feet. "Fireworks!" he shouted. "Fireworks! Look this way, everybody!"

But still only a handful of Alex's guests saw the first flare that shot up, burst, and cascaded down through the night sky in a fountain of colored light, exploding and popping.

"Fireworks! Fireworks!" Lenny shouted, as Alex gazed in dismay at the shambles of her party.

"How old did you say you were, Fiona? What's your cup size? Is that your real hair or a wig?"

The second flare shot upward from the barge, exploded, and hung in the air as the sparkling lights gathered and coalesced to form the word *MODE*, before the letters tumbled apart and fell to the river.

A third flare went up, and the words *THAR SHE BLOWS!* were spelled out.

A fourth and final flare then went up with an almost earsplitting bang, and the figures 5,000,000 arranged themselves across the sky.

This last explosive blast drew a few more onlookers to the edge of the terrace, but the questions to Fiona Fenton continued, and her whispery, all-but-unintelligible replies seemed to make the reporters' questions even more hostile and intrusive.

"Hey, Fiona—who's your favorite designer?"

"Who's your favorite *Limey* designer, Fiona?"

"How much is Rothman payin' ya, Fiona?"

"Fiona, will you take those Goddamned glasses *off*?"

"Do you sleep in the nude, Fiona baby? Look this way, Fiona."

Suddenly a television cameraman roughly shoved a news reporter out of his way. "Move, fuck-face! You're blockin' my frame!"

"Fuck your frame!" And now fists were flying. The reporter's body was flung against the side of the gazebo bar, and there was the sound of shattering glass as a waiter's serving table was overturned. There were screams as women, seated close to the fray, tried to duck under tables to protect themselves, and one tall gentleman, resplendent in evening dress, rose to his feet and lifted a gilded caterer's chair over his head, in a Statue of Liberty pose, as though to defend himself from all attackers, while a young woman in a scarlet Scaasi evening suit was trying to crawl, on her hands and knees, among flying fists and kicking feet, across the terrace toward the French doors that led into the apartment. Meanwhile, the orchestra, doing its best to prevent Alex's party from turning into a well-dressed riot, had launched into a noisy, upbeat version of "Ain't She Sweet?"

Fiona Fenton had managed to make her way through the jostling, pushing, shouting crowd to where Alex stood watching it all with helpless horror. Alex saw that there were tears streaming down the young woman's face, and suddenly she was filled with a great wave of pity for this poor, benighted girl—surely no more than twenty-three or twenty-four—who had certainly not meant to cause all this. It was Herbert—Herbert alone—who had done it, and now he was nowhere to be seen.

"Please, Mrs. Rothman," the girl sobbed. "I begged Mr. Rothman not to announce it like this—not here, at your party. He insisted that it would come as a nice surprise for you, but it didn't, did it? It didn't come as a nice surprise at all!"

Alex started to say that nothing Herbert Rothman did would ever surprise her, but instead she said, "Don't worry about that. The first thing we've got to do is get this crowd under control."

"He says he thinks you and I can work well together. He says you and I can be a team, but I can't be a part of a team unless you want me too! He says it can work, and I want to believe it will work, because I admire your work so much. Please tell me you believe we can at least try to work together. I'll try—I'll try so hard—to learn—"

Once again Alex started to say something angry. She could have said that there were three things in life she had learned never to believe in: the tooth fairy, no-run panty hose, and Herbert Rothman. But the girl was so clearly distraught that she simply said, "If we're going to be a team, help me think of a way to stop this fighting! This party's being televised, for God's sake." Because it was getting worse. One of the principal reporter combatants had managed to step on Carolyne Roehm's foot. She had screamed in pain, and already her diminutive husband, Henry, was shedding his jacket and rolling up his sleeves, preparing to join the fray. Now there was another crash, as one of the round pink-draped tables was overturned, sending crockery, glassware, hurricane lamps, a pair of Chelseaware porcelain birds, and one of Renny's floral centerpieces shattering across the flagstones.

"Oh, *please!*" Alex cried, stooping to pick up a white dove's broken wing. "*Please stop all this!*"

But all at once help, as if by divine intervention, came from an unexpected direction.

The guests who were seated on the north-facing arm of the L-shaped terrace were largely unaware of the free-for-all that was developing around the corner of the building,

on the east-facing arm, and around the gazebo bar. Beyond
wondering why the music had become suddenly so loud and
spirited, these guests had found another diversion. Just before
the fireworks began, a small pleasure boat had appeared on
the river, moving briskly downstream. It was a snappy little
cruiser, and as it zipped along, slapping the waves with its
fiberglass hull, it sent up twin white feathers of spume, and
left a wide trail of foam in its wake. As the little boat
approached the northern tip of Roosevelt Island, the fireworks started, and the boat paused to watch the display
from the barge. Then, apparently sensing that there was a
connection between the fireworks they had just seen and
the music and noise from the terrace high above Gracie
Square, the skipper of the boat had steered his (or her—
it was never clear who was at the wheel) craft closer to
the Manhattan side of the river, for a better look at the
party.

One didn't often see pleasure speedboats on the East River; in fact, they were discouraged, and often challenged,
though not banned, by the Coast Guard, since they tended
to interfere with the commercial barge traffic on the river.
So the appearance of the little speedboat was an unusual,
and cheering, sight. It seemed to be all about innocence and
love and youth and fun and irresponsibility, and to the celebrated guests on Alex's terrace it was a reminder of the
days when they, too, had been young and foolish, and as it
approached the towers of 10 Gracie Square, one of Alex's
guests at the parapet identified it as a Regal Runabout, about
eighteen feet long, and someone else later claimed to have
made out the red-white-and-blue burgee of the American
Yacht Club in Rye, which meant it was about twenty-five
nautical miles from home, though it was difficult to make
out much else in the dark, and from twenty floors above.
As the little boat slapped and spanked its way through the
water below, its passengers—who appeared to be three, or
possibly four, young people because, later, accounts would
differ—seemed to be lifting toasts with cans of beer to the
people leaning on the parapet, and the people at the parapet
waved back and returned the toasts with their champagne
glasses.

But then, all at once, something was terribly wrong. The
small boat suddenly listed sharply to one side, then instantly

to the other. Its passengers gripped their seats and handrails, and their cries could be heard twenty floors above,
as the skipper struggled with the wheel to bring his craft
under control. Now the prow of the runabout made a violent
swing to the right, and the boat was spinning, spinning in
circles, faster and faster circles, as though caught in a mael-
strom. There were screams from the terrace now, and cries of
"Oh, my God! Somebody help them! They're sinking! Call
nine-one-one! Call the Coast Guard!" And all were straining
over the parapet, pointing toward the dark river below, while
the television crew, aware of some new calamity, rushed to
the scene.

What they saw was the speedboat being literally sucked
into the river. The surface of the river seemed to swell up,
then open into a whirling eddy, with the small boat spinning
at the center of a deepening hole. The whirling hole in the
water opened wider and deeper and blacker, as the helpless
boat was drawn into it like a toy into a huge and churning
drain, and disappeared from sight. As quickly as it began, it
was over. The river seemed to swell again, then flatten, and
its surface was the same as before.

"I got it!" the TV cameraman cried triumphantly. "Got
it all!"

"Oh, my God, help them!" someone said. "Help them!"

"Call nine-one-one!"

"No, call the Coast Guard!"

"Call the police!"

"How do you call the Coast Guard?"

"For God's sake, just call the police! Somebody—just call
the police. . . ."

Later that night, on the eleven o'clock news, Mel Jorgenson
would describe the accident. It became the lead story on all
the New York stations.

"A rare, but by no means unheard-of, freak of nature
appears to have claimed the lives of three, or possibly four,
young boaters in a small pleasure craft on New York's East
River earlier this evening. The phenomenon, known as a tidal
bore, is caused by a sudden confluence of tides from opposite directions, particularly at phases of a full moon, which
we have in New York tonight. It is particularly apt to occur
in narrow stretches of water, such as that at the foot of East

Eighty-fourth Street in Manhattan, where tonight's tragedy occurred. Tidal bores, or whirlpools, can be extremely hazardous to shipping, and especially hazardous to small craft. Tidal bores have been observed in the East River before, but this is the first known to have claimed human lives. . . .

"The East River, of course, is not a river at all, but a tidal estuary connecting Long Island Sound and Upper New York Bay. . . .

"No survivors of tonight's tragedy have been reported, nor have bodies been recovered, nor are the identities, or exact number, of the victims known. . . .

"I might add that tonight's accident occurred in a section of the river known, since Colonial times, as Hell Gate—well named, it would seem, in light of tonight's tragedy. . . ."

At that point in the telecast, Mel Jorgenson pressed his thumb and forefinger across the bridge of his nose and said, "As it happens, I was a guest at a gathering this evening at an apartment just above the site where the tragedy occurred. I left the building not long before it happened. Conceivably, I could have been an eyewitness to it. . . ."

Two weeks later, two bodies of teenage brothers would be recovered from the sea just off the Battery. No other bodies were ever found. The Regal Runabout was never recovered.

But meanwhile, in the aftermath of what they had just seen, Alex's guests were crowded along the length of the parapet, frozen in silent horror now, staring down into the dark water, hoping—even praying, perhaps—for the sight of bodies popping to the surface, while the television cameras continued to roll in order to capture such an occurrence. But there was nothing to record, and the river remained as smooth as glass. From the drive below, police sirens were screaming now, and presently police divers could be seen lowering themselves into the water.

As two hundred and fifty people pressed against the parapet, straining for a better look at what was happening twenty floors beneath them, somehow someone (or, more probably, it was the pressure of several bodies) managed to push against one of the stone planter boxes filled with azaleas, and to dislodge it from its pedestal base. The stone box tilted, tipped, and began to fall, spinning almost lazily downward with its cargo of pink and white flowering shrubbery, toward the river. Now there were more screams, and several people turned away and covered their faces with a long collective groan, for it seemed almost certain that the plunging planter would crash upon one of the bobbing heads of the wet-suited frogmen in the river, and the evening's disaster would be complete. But, miraculously, this did not happen. The masked heads of the frogmen surfaced as the stone planter plummeted into the water harmlessly. Then their heads disappeared again to investigate this new occurrence.

Otto Forsthoefel, the former detective, seemed to have placed himself in charge of crowd control as well as in charge of Joel Rothman's safety, and as the throng of guests pushed and elbowed their way for a better view of what was happening in the river, Otto was barking commands. "Stand back! There's nothing to see! Stand back! Don't shove! Disperse! Go back to your tables! Let the police officers do their work! Stand back . . . !"

Now Joel found himself looking down into the tearful face of the young Englishwoman. "Help me," she sobbed. "Get me out of here. This is a nightmare. I can't find your grandfather. Please take me home. Now."

"How?" he said miserably, rolling his eyes in Otto's direction. "He's in charge of me."

Quickly, she turned and seized the lapels of Otto's brown jacket. "Conspiracy," Joel heard her saying. "It's a plot—to draw our attention away from what's going on. There's a man on the roof."

"*Where?*"

"Up there—on the roof." She pointed. "Look—he saw us! He just ducked behind that ledge. He had a gun."

Immediately Otto pulled his service revolver from his shoulder holster. "Don't anybody move!" he roared, brandishing the pistol in the air. "Stay right where you are. If anybody moves, you're all under arrest," and, waving the gun in front of him, he charged through the crowd toward the French doors that led into the apartment, and the stairs that led to the roof, and now—with an armed gunman in their midst—if anything resembling mass hysteria could be said to exist, it existed on Alex Rothman's terrace, with black-tied men throwing their hands in the air, and shrieking women clutching at their jewelry.

"Now, we run," the Englishwoman said to Joel.

"Run?"

She grabbed his hand. "Run! Through the kitchen—the service elevator. *Run!* You lead the way."

Alex Rothman had seated herself in a little gold chair in the farthest corner of the terrace she could find, which was where Lenny Liebling discovered her, an almost dreamy expression on her face. "Could anything else go wrong?" she asked him quietly. "Could anything else *possibly* go wrong with my party? Can you think of just one little thing, darlin'?"

"Yes," he said, and nodded toward the French doors, through which four uniformed New York policemen had just emerged.

Alex began to laugh. Soon she was laughing so hard it seemed she might never stop. She laughed so hard that hiccups came and, after hiccups, finally tears. "Dear old Lenny," was all she managed to say, at first, and then savagely, "I'm going to kill him!"

Chapter 6

The last limousine had pulled away from the entrance to 10 Gracie Square, and Alex Rothman and Lenny Liebling were alone in her book-lined library, where her Bouché portrait gazed down from above the fireplace, and where Alex was now furiously pacing up and down the room, her arms clasped around her shoulders, a slim, white, moving exclamation-point of a woman. "Did you know this was going to happen, Lenny?" she said. "Tell me the truth."

He raised his right hand. "I had no idea," he said. "I had no idea that this woman was involved. Of course, since this last stroke of Ho's, I've been worried that *some*thing like this might happen. And I did try to warn you."

"I'm going to speak to Ho. He won't allow this. Ho and I may have had our ups and downs in the past, but he's always respected me."

"My dear Alex," he said with a sigh, "I hate to speak of the great Ho Rothman in the past tense, but that is what we're going to have to do. Ho Rothman *used* to respect you. He's beyond respecting anyone now. We must accept the fact that the Ho era has ended. Tonight we saw the dawning of the era of the son. The son also rises."

"What about Aunt Lily? She's an officer in the corporation. Herbert isn't."

"I agree," Lenny said carefully, "that this is a very good time for all of us to be especially nice to Aunt Lily. Just this afternoon, in fact, I sent a lovely flower arrangement over to her from Renny's. But the only trouble is—"

"She wouldn't let that little snake son of hers take over the company. She knows what a snake he is."

"But don't forget that Herbert is *her* snake. She is a woman, Alex, and she is his mother. If forced to choose between what you want and what he wants, she might choose—"

"What the little snake wants."

"Lily has always been a weak link in the chain. Often useful, but weak."

"She can be tough as nails when she wants to be!"

"*Could* be. Could be. We must use the past tense again. She could be tough as nails when Ho was behind her. But Aunt Lily is not another Ho. There will never be another Ho."

"What about—?" But she broke the question off, biting her lip. She had been about to ask: *What about you, Lenny? You've always seemed to have some strange influence over the Rothmans, all the Rothmans, including Herbert.* But she was not about to ask any favors of Lenny Liebling. She knew this world, and this town, too well. One did not ask favors of anyone to whom one couldn't offer favors in return. This was a world in which no one could be trusted, not even Lenny with his secrets, whatever they were.

"You were about to say, What about me? Let me just say that, from the very beginning, I have planned very carefully for my future. I asked you earlier this evening if you had any insurance. From the very outset of my association with the family, I recognized the need for insurance—against a very painful affliction known as Rothmanitis. Another word for Rothmanitis is abuse of power. The Rothmans have become rich through the abuse of power, at which they are world-class experts. But I have taken out insurance, over the years, to be sure they could never use their power to abuse dear old Lenny."

"Blackmail, you mean."

He sighed again. "Blackmail is such an ugly word," he said. "Blackmail, I believe, is against the law. I prefer the word leverage. I have developed leverage with the Rothmans. Leverage is what one uses to move an object from here to there. With a large enough lever, one could move the world. Of course my levers are very small, though they have been effective enough to suit my simple needs. Do you have any special leverage with the family?"

"Not the sort you're talking about."

"And of course, years ago, you may remember, I gave you a piece of advice about dealing with Herbert Rothman. It was advice you chose to ignore. I hate to say I told you so, my dear, but I did."

"I'm sorry. I couldn't go that route."

He sighed once more, and sat back in the big leather chair and stared at the ceiling. "And so here we are," he said. And then, "Would you like me to use my leverage in your behalf?" he asked. "I'm not promising it would work, but I could try. And if you want me to try it, all you need to do is ask."

Her eyes flashed. "No," she said. "And do you know why? Because I don't trust you, Lenny. I never have. I love you, but I don't trust you. You're one of my dearest friends, but you're devious and conniving. Lenny is only interested in what Lenny wants."

"And Alex is only interested in what Alex wants—or do I mistake the subject of this conversation? My dear, I see no real difference between the two of us. Each of us wants what each of us wants."

"But I have a better way to get it."

"Oh?" he said, still gazing absently at the ceiling. "And what is that, pray?"

"I'm going to sue the little bastard. He's not going to get away with this. I happen to have a contract with Rothman Publications, which he happens to have signed, and which happens to run for two more years. That contract states that I am to be editor-in-chief of *Mode*. It says nothing about being co-editor-in-chief. He's not going to get away with this."

"Oh, Alex, Alex," he said wearily. "That's not the way to deal with Herbert. He has fifty lawyers working with him right now on the IRS case. They're not going to tolerate another lawsuit over your silly little contract. They'll wipe the floor with you."

"A contract is a contract!"

"They'll find a paper clip in your purse, and claim you stole it from the company supply room. He'll fire you for pilferage. No, no, Alex, that is not the way. No, as I see it, there are two things you can do."

"What? What are they?"

"One, you can resign. He's certainly given you reason enough tonight. If you resigned tomorrow, everybody in the business would understand. In fact, I rather imagine that's what he's hoping you'll do—resign."

"And forfeit the balance of my contract?"

"Oh, the hell with your contract, my darling child. Surely you don't need the money. Surely you're quite rich. And with your reputation, there isn't a magazine in town—a publisher in town—a designer in town—a company or ad agency in town—that wouldn't snap you up in a minute, at twice what he pays you. Or television. Any one of the networks would kill to have you. Or you could do what Vreeland did, and become a museum director. There isn't a glamour industry in this town that wouldn't want the glamorous Alex Rothman in some glamorous position. If you resign, you'll hardly be out on the street. Remember who you are, Alex. You are *Alex Rothman*—a high priestess of fashion. A legend. Resign, and your phone will be ringing off the wall with offers."

"But, Lenny," she said, "I just can't do that. I just *can't*. Don't you understand? Herb is a horse's ass! He'll destroy *Mode*. I can't let him do that. I can't let that horse's ass undo everything I've done. It's seventeen *years*, Lenny. Look—" She pointed to the bound volumes in the shelves. "Seventeen years—more than two hundred issues, each one bigger and better than the last. That's *me* in those pages, Lenny. That's me. If I let him destroy *Mode*, he'll be destroying *me*."

"Well, then," he said quietly, "the only other thing you can do is not resign. You'll just have to realize that we both now have a new boss, that Ho Rothman is finally sailing off into his final sunset, and that Herbert Rothman is now at the helm of this little ship. And if you stay on, you'll just have to play by the new rules, swallow your famous pride, and hope for the best. Who knows? Little Miss Louise Brooks Hair may fall flat on her face."

"No," she said, pounding her fist against the mantelpiece. "I've always run this magazine by my rules. I'm not going to run it by his rules. I'm going to call my lawyer in the morning. I'm going to sue. The little midget bastard can't do this to me. I made *Mode* what it is. *Mode* is mine. *Mode* would be nothing without me, and he knows it, and everybody else knows it. Did you hear what the little midget bastard said about me tonight? 'Responsibilities too enormous for one *mere woman* to handle . . . the terrible toll those years have taken on her.' He called me a used-up has-been. I'm not going to take that, Lenny. And of course it was typical— typical of Herb—typical of the little snake—to wait until his father's practically on his deathbed before even *daring* to make any sort of move. Waiting till his father's too weak to stop him. And then, after making his little announcement, what became of him? He simply disappeared—too cowardly to face what he knew I'd have to say to him. Well, he'll find out soon enough when he hears from my lawyer!"

Lenny shook his head wearily, but said nothing.

"And who is she, anyway? I've never heard of her, and neither has anyone else. And this 'leading British fashion magazine' she supposedly worked for. Something called *Lady Fair.* Ever hear of it? I never have, and every fashion magazine that's published in the world comes into my office. I have a detective friend, and I'm going to call him in the morning and have him run a background check on her. She's obviously some little slut he's sleeping with, and this is her payoff."

"If that's the case, take comfort," he said. "None of Herb's girlfriends ever lasts very long. There'll be a new one in another week or so."

"Actually, she seemed rather sweet," she said. "She seemed genuinely shocked by the way Herb handled things tonight. But I know what he was saying. I could read the subtext, couldn't you? He was saying that she's next in line for *my job.* She's going to be my replacement—that's what he was saying. Well, I'm not about to be replaced."

"Your name would still be at the top of the masthead," he said.

"But I'm not going to share it with *her*—whoever she is. I'm not going to let him do this to me! I'm not going to let him destroy my magazine. Herb Rothman is a *fool.* Anyone who heard that speech tonight knew he was listening to a fool. Even his own father knew he was a fool. Ho fought Herb every step of the way. Well, I'm a fighter too. I'll fight him now."

"But, unfortunately, Herb seems to hold all the trump cards now."

Tears were standing in her eyes again. "Little midget bastard! Oh, I know—he's been waiting for years to do this to me. He's always hated me."

"*Why* has he always hated you, Alex? I know it's true—but why?"

"Oh, you know why. I was never good enough for Steven. He and Pegeen never thought I was good enough for their son."

"I've always thought," Lenny said carefully, "that there must be more to it than that."

"And jealousy. Because Ho listened to me, and not to him. Because Herb wanted Mona Potter to have the job, and Ho gave it to me."

"Herb was sleeping with Mona at the time, you know."

"Which makes her *eminently* qualified to run a magazine! Ho saw through all of that."

"I still think there must be more to it than that," Lenny said, "to have caused all these years of bitterness, when, if you recall, I advised you—" He broke off. "Are you sure there isn't another reason, Alex?"

She shook her head. There was silence in the room now, and finally Lenny said, "Think, Alex. Think hard."

"No," she said. "There was nothing else. It's just Herb's vindictiveness."

He still looked doubtful. "Then what about Tarrytown?" he said.

"What about it?"

"What about what happened there September twentieth, nineteen seventy-three? Is there something that could provide you with a bit of leverage in that?"

She stared at him. "Why?" she said. "Everybody knows what happened. It was in all the newspapers at the time."

"I'm talking about what *really* happened. The part that wasn't in the papers."

"I don't know what you're talking about," she said sharply.

"I think you do. But I gather you don't want to talk about that. I gather also that you're not interested in possible ways to apply leverage."

"No, I'm not."

"Even though leverage may provide the easiest solution to this little problem. Ah, well."

"I've told you what I'm going to do," she said. "I'm going to show him that he can't do this to me."

Lenny said nothing, but stared down at his feet in their crocodile Gucci loafers, and at the square of dark green carpet between them. What was Lenny thinking? Alex knew what he was thinking. He was thinking: *He can't do this to you. But, in fact, he already has.*

Now Lenny was gone, and Alex was alone in the library with her angry thoughts. *Tarrytown*, she thought. That was typically Lenny. Lenny was always dropping little hints that he knew more about what had happened that afternoon in Tarrytown than any of the others knew, but how could he possibly? The only people who knew the truth were the ones who were there, and one of these was dead, and the other two had never spoken of it to any other living soul. It was their shared secret, and of what possible use could that secret be to anyone else? If, say, Alex were to go to Aunt Lily and say, "I've decided to tell the truth about what happened that afternoon in Tarrytown," what would that accomplish? Alex would simply lose Aunt Lily as her friend, and that would certainly do nothing to help the present situation. Alex unclasped her silver Navajo belt and tossed it in a chair, and ran her fingers through her hair. She glanced briefly at the portrait in the oval frame. *You are not me*, she thought.

You are me, and she moved to the bookshelves that held the bound morocco volumes, and ran the tip of her index finger along the spines, the embossed lettering in gold— *Mode*: 1973, *Mode*: 1974—feeling the volumes grow fatter as her finger moved; and now he was trying to take that *me* away from me. On the bottom shelf were the card catalogues—the table of contents of every issue, indexed and cross-indexed according to date, subject, writer, photographer, production cost, subscription and newsstand sales, revenues, reader response, and other facts and figures about each issue, and each story, so arcane that only an editor would find them meaningful—cryptic notations such as "10/84 prod. 1,680,000; n/s. ret 32,164; sub. refs. 106, ltrs pro 240, ltrs neg, 987." Which could be translated to mean that for the October 1984 issue, there was a production run of 1,680,000 copies; newsstands had returned 32,164 copies unsold; 106

subscribers, for whatever reasons, asked for refunds after that issue; 240 readers wrote favorable letters about that issue, while 987 wrote negatively. In the beginning, it had worried her that the negative letters always outnumbered the positive. Then she realized that readers usually took pen in hand only when they were angry. When they were happy, they said nothing.

"When did you publish that Robert Graves profile of Ava Gardner?" someone might ask her, and a quick glance at the card file would tell her everything: the date, the page numbers, how much Graves had been paid for the story, how many photographs had been used, the photographer's name, how much he had been paid, the word length, the column inches, the reader response, and on and on. Of course, at her office, computers could supply the same data, but Alex had started her card-file system before the magazine had been able to afford computers, and she still liked her system best. Using her card catalogue, she could reconstruct an issue of a magazine more quickly than if she were running it off on a spool of microfiche.

Of course what neither her card catalogue nor the computers could contain were the feelings and the memories—the disputes, the disappointments, the fits of artistic temperament, the photographers who walked off the sets, the art directors who threatened to quit, the wheedlings, the cajolings, the bargaining, the pleas, the tears, the raging storms, the stamped feet, the curses, the prayers, the threats and teapot tempests—and, oh yes, the laughter and the joy—that went into assembling each issue of the magazine, piece by piece, word by word. All these were locked in Alex's head and heart. Because editing a magazine was like a love affair—passionate, forgiving, hurting, healing, angry and orgiastic, all-consuming and all-rewarding. Her magazine, she often thought, had become the last great love of her life. This was no exaggeration. The love was not as overpowering and terrifying as that first love, perhaps. But wasn't the last love supposed to be the most stable and enduring? And, like any love, it grew more precious when someone threatened to take it away.

She thought: *Every impulse I ever had, every feeling I ever felt, has somehow spilled over into these volumes. I am all here. I am not a high priestess, I am not a legend, I am simply a woman who worked hard for something I loved. I am just a woman who wanted to make her ailing lover healthy, and I did, and this is it, and this is me. This is what I created. This is what created me.*

"Make your peace with your father-in-law," Lenny had told her years ago. "Make this first on your list of priorities. You have Ho and Lily on your side already. That's all very well and good. But now you must engineer some sort of peace with Herbert. It won't be easy. But you must do it, Alex."

But how could any woman make peace with a man like that?

"An heir. A male heir. That's the only other thing the family wants from you," Herbert had said to her that day in Tarrytown.

It sounded so pompous, so Old World, so old-fashioned— the whole idea of a *dynasty*—that she had laughed at him.

"I'm quite serious," he said, and seized her wrist. "If you are having trouble doing this with Steven, I could help you."

"How? How could you help me? Please let go of my arm. You're hurting me."

But he had not let go. "How?" he said. "Don't you know where babies come from? Let me show you how."

How—*how*—could a woman make peace with a man like that?

And would anything have been any different if she had let him do what he wanted? Ah, that, of course, was the sixty-four-million-dollar question.

From the entrance hall, she heard the lock turn as Mel let himself in with his own key.

He walked into the library and went immediately to her and took her in his arms. "Oh, my darling," he said. "What a helluva night you've had!"

"You heard?"

"Heard. Watched. Saw everything on the monitor."

"Herb's speech? They aired that too?"

"Everything. And then the boating accident. It was their full 'This Is New York' segment. Well, if that's New York, let's get out of this cesspool. I mean it, Alex. Marry me, and let's get the hell out of this Rothman shit. I'm not going to let you put up with any more of it."

"I realized tonight that Herb has been waiting a long time to do this to me."

"Well, he chose a helluva time to do it, didn't he? As usual, his timing was perfect." He released her and went to the drinks cart, dropped ice cubes in a glass, and poured himself a stiff Scotch, filling the glass to the top. "I mean, I couldn't *believe* what I was seeing," he said, still with his back to her. "I couldn't believe what those ungrateful bastards were doing to you. I mean, thank God the station didn't send me to cover your party. I think I'd have thrown the camera in the little son-of-a-bitch's face, rammed the microphone down his throat." He turned to her now, and his face was livid. "Goddammit, Alex, aren't you mad? Aren't you furious? Aren't you ready to kill those Rothman bastards?"

"Oh, I'm mad all right. But I'm also—kind of numb."

"Little son-of-a-bitch comes to *your* party, the party that was supposed to celebrate what *you'd* done for *him* and his magazine, and right in *your* house he stands up in front of *your* guests, including people who work *for* you and *with* you, plus half the Goddamn media in this town, and tells everybody that you can't do your job anymore—that it's gotten too big for you, and that he's taken on some Brit bimbo to give you a hand. I mean, that's the way the Rothmans show their gratitude for everything you've done for them— a kick in the face! And in public! On television! Oh, I know why the ungrateful bastards did it the way they did—because they're too fucking cowardly to tell you to your face. They need a crowd of extras around to protect them. May I tell you something about your in-laws, Alex—something I've been wanting to tell you for a long, long time? They're all *loathsome*. Marry me, and I'll give you some in-laws who are at least decent people, for God's sake! They're *all* loathsome—every last Jack-shit one of them, and that includes that old fake Ho, and sweet old Aunt Lily who has a cash register for a heart, and that bastard Herb and his Jack-shit brother Arthur—all of them. Do you realize how much the Rothmans are hated in this town, Alex? I mean really *hated*? It's a lucky thing Arthur Rothman doesn't run a TV station in New York—that the closest Rothman station is as far away as Memphis—or he'd have been strung up by his testicles long before now. How you've put up with that family for as long as you have is a mystery to me, Alex. They've never given you sweet fuckoff, and you know it—and now *this!* The insult! The humiliation! Well, the only thing you can do now is resign, Alex. He's finally done you a favor—given you a golden opportunity to do what you should've done a long time ago, and get yourself out of this chickenshit Rothman operation, and into something where your talents are finally appreciated—out of the Rothman snake pit. Out of this hellhole world of drunks and faggots and shit-kickers and ass-kissers. Did you hear how the NBC announcer introduced their segment on your party? 'Welcome to the fashionable world of Alexandra Rothman, where, tonight, the cream of New York's fashion elite has gathered.' Fashion *elite?* Drunks! Faggots! Shit-kickers! Ass-kissers! That's all they are," he said, and paused to catch his breath. "There. I've said it. Of course, in some ways it was kind of great—watching that lowdown, loathsome little fart showing off his loathsomeness in front of eight million television households in the Tristate Area! That was the greatest part—watching him stand there, showing eight million viewers what a loathsome lowlife he really is. There. Okay, I've let off my head of steam."

He smiled now and raised his glass. "Cheers," he said. "Welcome to your new freedom. You are now emancipated from the Rothmans—the whole damn pack of them. Marry me. We'll fly off somewhere and celebrate. We'll lie in the sun and turn brown as berries, and make love in the sand."

She sat very still, arms crossed over her bosom, her hands hugging her shoulders. "I have a contract," she whispered.

"A *contract?* Are you out of your mind, sweetheart? Are you going to honor a contract with some little prick who tells you—in the most insulting, public way possible—that you can't do your job anymore? Who is this British bimbo, anyway?"

"I have no idea."

"Some money-grubbing Brit bimbo who's been kissing Herb Rothman's ass, and probably sucking his dick as well. No, you're well out of it, darling. *Well* out of it. If you ask me, this is the luckiest day of your life."

She shivered. "Somehow, I can't think of it that way—yet," she said.

"And I only say that because I love you," he said. "Hell, if I didn't love you, I wouldn't give a damn. But after all, you're Alexandra Rothman. You're the greatest fashion editor in the country, and everybody knows it. You took a lousy little fashion sheet that was practically brain dead in the seventies, and made a success of it, turned it completely around, made a winner out of a loser. Has anyone else in publishing ever done that?"

"Yes. Helen Gurley Brown."

"But you're bigger than she is! Five million circulation! You're number one! So—you did it, darling. You proved it to the world. Now it's time to move on to something else. Fuck the Rothmans!"

"I could always work with Ho."

"Yeah, and where was Ho tonight? Ho had to be behind this. Ho Rothman never lets that little shit son of his go out the door alone without knowing what his instructions are. Ho was behind this. He just let Herbie do his dirty work for him. Typical Rothman."

"No, you don't understand, Mel. Ho is really much sicker than we thought. He's had another stroke. He can't see anybody anymore."

"He's probably faking it, if I know the old bastard."

"Darling, remember that Ho is ninety-four years old."

"So now he's brain dead, too."

"Apparently. It's hard to believe, but Lenny says it's true."

"And so it's new-broom time at Rothmans. Some new broom they've got, I must say—worse than the old worn-out one. But what the hell difference does it make? It's still the same old ball game, but with meaner rules, and a crookeder umpire. Anyway, it's time for you to shake hands with the whole Rothman *mishpachah,* and get out of the ring. Matter of fact, it might be kind of fun for you to watch—from the sidelines—and see what happens next." He was grinning now. "Think of that, darling! It really could be fun."

"Fun?"

"Sure. Look—everybody in town knows that Herb Rothman doesn't know sweet fuckoff about publishing. Maybe his old man was some kind of media genius—maybe. Maybe I'll grant him that. But this is his *son*, and his son ain't his old man. So it might be kind of fun to sit back and watch Herb Rothman, and his Brit bimbo, take *Mode* down the tubes."

She gestured vaguely in the direction of the bound copies of the magazine. "About as much fun as watching your child die," she said.

"Look," he said earnestly, "I know how much *Mode* means to you—don't get me wrong. But, in the end, it's only a *job*, isn't it? Just as my job is only a job. My job is to work in front of a television camera, but it's only a television camera, and it's not the only television camera in the world. Putting out a magazine is putting words and pictures on paper, but *Mode* isn't the only magazine in the world—it's not your last chance to prove that you do what you do brilliantly, that you're a brilliant editor." He put down his drink and moved toward her and put his hands on her shoulders. "But listen, I know you've been through a hell of an evening, and you're still in a state of shock. Maybe we shouldn't even be talking about things like this tonight. We're both too upset." He kissed her lowered forehead. "I love you, Alex," he said. "Meanwhile, I've had no dinner. I'm hungry—hungry for food, and hungry for you. Know what my Jewish grandmother used to say? 'If it's a problem that can be solved with either a little love or a little money, *bubeleh*, it isn't a problem.' Just think—it's not every man in the world who gets to make love to a high priestess."

She stood up. "I forgot to tell Coleman to fix us chicken sandwiches," she said miserably. "But let's see what we can find in the refrigerator. There must be something left over from the party."

In the kitchen, they sat side by side on stools at the long butcherblock counter.

"You really think I should resign?" she said.

"Absolutely," he said, munching on a veal chop. "Absolutely. It's the only way you can come out of this with a shred of dignity, with a shred of pride."

"I'd like to fight him, you know."

"Don't. Too undignified. You're a classy dame. Fighting Herb Rothman would be about as dignified as mud wrestling."

"Maybe I'm not so proud," she said. "Remember, this is my entire life."

He put down his chop. "Your entire life? Then where do I fit in, I wonder?"

"Oh, you know what I mean. My entire professional life."

His gaze at her was even. "I'll tell you this," he said, "if you get into a mud-wrestling match with that little *putz*, you'll lose a hell of a lot of respect from me."

Later, in bed, she said to him, "Please, darling. Not tonight. I just can't make myself be in the mood."

He rolled away from her, across the bed, and pretended to go to sleep, but she knew he was only pretending.

"I'm sorry," she said.

"I think you're still in love with Steven," he said.

She said nothing, merely stared up at the dark ceiling, and the only sound in the room was the low moan of a tugboat's horn from the river below. She felt really terrible now, because she loved their lovemaking. It was so even, so smooth, so perfectly timed and cadenced. Not like that first love long ago that overpowered her with its vastness, but more sharing. When she and Mel made love, they were like one soul.

You blew it, darlin', the tugboat's horn seemed to say.

Chapter 7

Alex had learned how to deal with her husband's grandfather, Herbert Oscar Rothman—or "Ho," as he was usually called, an acronym of his first two initials—and she had learned early on. There was nothing particularly complicated about Ho, once you discovered what drove him, impelled him, stimulated him, inspired him, which could be summed up in a single word: Power. There was no particularly fine-tuned intelligence here, she had discovered. There was no "fingertip on the pulse-beat of America," as his hired publicists boasted. There was no sophistication, no sensitivity, and not even very much in the way of education. Ho, she soon realized, understood very little about communications, or publishing, though he headed what was usually described as "a Communications/Publishing Empire." But he understood Power, and how to use it and abuse it. Lenny was right.

He was a diminutive, almost frail-seeming man who had stood, in his prime, at no more than five-feet-five and, over the years, had seemed to shrink. When Alex met him, he could have weighed no more than 120 pounds. But Power was tangible in the huge, sprawling signature, "H. O. Rothman," which was attached to the directives that came down from his office on the thirtieth floor of the Rothman Building at 530 Fifth Avenue. Power was apparent in the size of his office itself, which was as big as a squash court (the offices of other Rothman executives were for the most part half-walled cubicles), and in the dimensions of his oversized antique walnut partners' desk, behind which he sat in a chair on a raised platform, usually with an unlighted cigar clamped between his teeth.

In front of this desk were two low, black-leather sofas, so deep that, once a visitor had settled into one of them, he usually had difficulty rising. And the sofas seemed to have been strategically placed so that sunlight from the tall south- and east-facing windows blazed directly into the visitor's eyes, making it hard for the visitor to get a good look at the president and chief executive officer of Rothman Communications who gazed down upon him.

Covering the entire north wall of the office was an enormous map of the United States of America—Texas alone was nearly five feet wide—and this map was dotted with large gold stars, indicating the cities where Rothman owned newspapers, radio and television stations, or otherwise maintained offices. When Alex first met her new husband's grandfather, there were 119 of these gold stars. Today, there were 171. The country, the map not very subtly implied, was Ho Rothman's domain; to each of these cities and towns, his Power extended.

It was true that many people in the communications industry hated Ho Rothman. Like many men who sit in seats of absolute Power, Ho Rothman had made his share of enemies. The great Moe Markarian, the other communications czar and Ho's chief rival during the years of his rise, had written a famous will. After directing that he be cremated, Markarian had instructed his executors "to take my ashes, place them in an open box, carry them to Ho Rothman's office, and blow them in Ho Rothman's face." Needless to say, this directive was never actually carried out.

It was Moe Markarian who had labeled Ho Rothman "the chameleon," and while Alex would agree that Ho had many lizardlike qualities, she had decided that he was not really a bad fellow, simply because his deviousness was so obvious as to be almost reassuring, almost endearing.

She had had her first experience with the way Ho operated at a luncheon at "Rothmere," the Tarrytown house, not long after she married Steven. The principal guest at the table was a young editor whom Ho had just hired to run a newspaper he had acquired in Taunton, Massachusetts, and the subject under discussion, for some reason, was the late President Franklin D. Roosevelt. Pounding on the tabletop with his fist for emphasis, and jabbing his skinny finger angrily at the young editor as though accusing him of feeling otherwise, Ho Rothman was depicting Roosevelt as a traitor, an apostate, a Judas.

"He was Communist!" Ho was saying. "He sold out million pipple to Stalin! He was Russian agent, Russian spy! He should have been hung for treason! He sold out his country!"

"He was worse than that," the young editor agreed. "He was a bastard, a son-of-a-bitch adulterer!"

"He was a liar, cheat! In his own country, he sold out to unions and Mafia. In Russia, he sold his own country to Stalin!" And he pounded the table so hard that the stemware trembled.

"He was a disgrace," the young editor said. "The country will never recover from what Roosevelt did. I could tell you stories—"

"In nineteen thirty-five, he saved this country from revolution," Ho continued, without missing a beat. "You don't remember nineteen thirty-five, but in this country would have been revolution if not for Roosevelt. He saved America! Thank God for Roosevelt. Without him, the whole world would be Communist. He was a saint."

"You're right, Mr. Rothman," the young editor said, nodding enthusiastically, in agreement. "No doubt about it, he was the greatest president America ever had."

"The greatest!" Ho said, pounding his fist on the table again.

At first, Alex had wondered whether Ho's sudden reversal in midargument might be intended as a subtle lesson to editors—that they should be able to back, with strong words, whichever side of a political discussion they happened to believe in. Then she realized that it was simply a performance designed to remind all who witnessed it—including, no doubt, herself—that Ho's power was so vast that he could completely contradict himself in front of anyone without losing one shred of his dominance, and that whichever side of an argument he chose to take was the right one, even when he took both sides at once.

This childlike faith in his power she found almost charming, and having discovered this fact about Ho Rothman, she was able to maneuver him from one position to another with relative ease.

Over the years, she and Ho had had any number of spirited arguments, which Alex had learned to relish, and even look forward to—if not actually predict. Most of their arguments had to do with the kind of advertising her magazine would accept. Selling advertising, after all, was what Ho understood best. Selling advertising had made him rich. Alex often supposed that Ho would advertise raincoats in the Gobi Desert, bikinis in Antarctica, condoms to a convent, if he could find advertisers to foot the bills. "I make a rule for you," he used to say. "I make a lesson for you. All advertisers is *momzers*. Each is *momzer*, each is liar, each is crook. But if the *momzer* will pay your page rate, and his check clears bank, the *momzer* is a *mensch*."

But *Mode* was a specialty magazine, with a specialty audience, and it was necessary for Alex to bring Ho around to her point of view, and persuade him that certain advertisers, despite their ability to pay her page rate, were not suited to her special breed of women readers, or to the special image her magazine was trying to project. She refused, for instance, to accept advertising for feminine hygiene products, or laxatives, and she had turned down an ad depicting an implicitly incontinent June Allyson cavorting on the deck of a cruise ship, implicitly wearing Depend adult diapers. She would not accept cigarette advertising, a lucrative category for many magazines. She would accept ads from Armani, Calvin Klein, and Bulgari, but not ads for Jaclyn Smith's designs for K Mart clothes. She accepted Calvin Klein's mysteriously erotic advertising for Obsession, featuring elaborately intertwined nude bodies, but when Avon Products submitted a moisturizer ad depicting a nude female, she turned it down. She scrutinized the copy for painkiller advertising carefully, and would not accept anything with the words "pain," "inflammation," "suffer," "hurt," "ache," or "flare-up."

Naturally, Ho Rothman disagreed vociferously with all of these decisions, seeing them simply as a needless loss of revenue. When Ho disagreed with you, he became an outraged prima donna, screaming imprecations, tugging wildly at the wispy fringes of his hair, pounding his fists on his desk top, even hurling breakable objects across the room. "How can you talk this craziness?" he would wail. "You a crazy woman, Alex? Why you trying to ruin me? Why you trying to make me crazy? I think you a candidate for nuthouse!" And he would cast his eyes heavenward, and throw his clasped hands in the air, as though beseeching the Old Testament deity for the gift of sanity. "I am surrounded by lunatics!" he would cry.

She had tried explaining that she did not see herself as putting out a magazine that would advertise only expensive products to expensive people. Her own demographic studies showed that many of her readers were far from wealthy. It had more to do with what she called her magazine's "chin-line." "We're a chin-up publication," she would say to him. "We try to come to our readers saying we're proud of who we are, and we want our readers to come away from us feeling a little prouder of who *they* are. No publication is worth its salt if it doesn't boost its readers' self-esteem." Needless to say, this argument made no sense at all to Ho.

She had also tried to point out that advertising money that might be lost in certain advertising categories was more than made up for in others—automotive advertising, for instance. It used to be an article of faith in Detroit that the purchase of the family car was a man's decision, and Detroit refused to advertise in publications that could not deliver a large male readership. Alex had managed to change all that. She produced studies that showed that even in households where the man completely controlled the purse strings, the woman had a great deal to say when it came to choosing a car's make, size, color, and styling. She also showed a study indicating that women were seventy-five percent more willing to finance the purchase of an automobile than men were—an important factor in new car sales. "We women have a reputation for liking to run up bills," she had told a meeting of potential advertisers at the Detroit Athletic Club, with a wink. "But since, in eighty percent of American households, the wife balances the checkbook, we don't run up bills that we can't pay." She produced a now-familiar statistic showing that the majority of America's personal wealth was in women's hands—and, finally, a survey showing that American women actually drove more automobile miles than men did, running errands, delivering and picking up children at school, collecting their husbands at commuter trains, and so on. As a result, *Mode* had become a primary medium for automobile advertising. But none of this impressed Ho Rothman, who saw rejected advertising only in terms of disappearing dollars.

Cool, well-reasoned logic got you nowhere with Ho. Neither did carefully fact-supported argument. On the other hand, you could often play successfully on his own irrational fears, prejudices, and superstitions. And it was always important to remember that, in order to sell any idea to Ho Rothman, he had to be persuaded that the idea actually had been his own to begin with.

When he had exploded over her wish to ban cigarette advertising from *Mode*, Alex remembered that Ho was almost obsessive in his dislike of what he called "colletch boys"— or, indeed, of anyone who appeared to be better educated than he was. "Look," she had said, "cigarette advertising is for college kids. It's for the back pages of college humor magazines, where the tobacco industry hopes it can hook 'em when they're young."

"Colletch boys," he fumed. "Is all *momzers*, smart-alecks, wisenheimers. But is millions dollars you are throwing out the window, Alex. Millions dollars!"

Then she remembered how virulently he distrusted doctors, and she pointed to the mandatory surgeon general's warning that had to be displayed prominently in every cigarette ad. "Then we'll have to include that," she said. "It's a federal regulation." He read the line slowly, moving his lips.

His fist crashed down on his desk. "Surgeon general!" he shouted. "Who is this surgeon general? Why we plugging him in my book? Why we give him free plug? Doctors is rich enough already, and if this *momzer* was elected surgeon general, he is richest *momzer* of them all! I make a rule for you. No doctors get free plugs in my book. Doctors get rich enough from killing sick pipple."

Later, when she had rejected an ad for a product that claimed it was "prescribed by most doctors for relief from painful swelling and itching of hemorrhoidal tissue," he had called her on the carpet again.

"But, Ho," she said. "You made a rule. No doctors get plugged in our ad pages."

"Right," he said. "I just wanted to make sure you remembered it."

Alex accepted most liquor advertising, but she had decided to draw the line at beers that were sold in long-necked bottles, and wines that were sold with screw-tops rather than corks. This had produced one of Ho's most violent outbursts. "You are *meshugge*, Alex!" he had roared. "That's the most *meshuggeneh* idea I hear from you! You trying to kill me, or what else?" And he tore at his fringe of hair as though trying to pull it from its roots. "Long necks! Screw-tops! Beer is beer, wine is wine. What is difference in neck, if long neck, short neck, or no neck, or if in cork or no cork? I think you are the screw-top talking long necks and corks. I am hearing true craziness now!"

"Now listen, Ho," she said. "Beer in long-necked bottles is what hillbillies drink in Appalachia. Wine with screw-caps is what winos drink out of paper bags down on Skid Row— because they don't want to push a cork in and out every time they take a slug. Look at yourself, Ho. Look at yourself and Aunt Lily. You are both ladies and gentlemen. You are people of taste and refinement. You like the finer things of life. Would you ever serve a wine with a screw-top at *your* table? Would you ever offer a guest a beer in a long-necked bottle? Never! You'd be considered crude and uncultivated. Would you even want a magazine that showed pictures of such things in your house?"

"Look," he shouted immediately. "I make a rule for you. I make a lesson for you. No beer in long-neck bottles. No wines in crew-cut tops. You think we advertise to hillbillies? You think we advertise to Skid Row winos? Not in *my* magazine, you don't! Never! We advertise only to the best!"

There was something in the business world called "factoring," which was a little like trying to sell postdated checks. A piece of paper, such as an IOU, might be worth nothing today but worth a lot next week. Still, it might be sellable today, if you could find the right buyer, and offered him the right discount, kept sweetening your sales pitch with little concessions and giveaways. Dealing with Ho was a little like that. You had to haggle with his pride, and bargain with his power. Alex called it dealing with the Ho Factor. Oh, Lenny was absolutely right. There would never be another Ho.

There was another thing she had learned about Ho Rothman over the years. His Russian accent came and went. At first,

she had thought that his English became fractured—full of
Yiddishisms and dropped articles—only when he was angry
or excited. Then she saw that he was able to turn the fractured English on and off at will. He used it to befuddle an
adversary, to confuse an opponent in an argument or in a
deal, to put his opponent at a linguistic disadvantage, and to
lure the unsuspecting adversary into supposing that he was
dealing with an innocent, a naïf, or a scatterbrain—until Ho
Rothman was ready to pounce.

Dealing with his elder son, Herbert Joseph Rothman, was
an entirely different matter. The trouble with Herb, Alex
decided long ago, was that Herb had hated too many things
for too long. He hated being his father's son, hated having
to grow up, and live so long, in his tiny father's powerful
shadow. His father was always called Ho, but Herb hated the
nickname "Ho-Jo" he had been given at college, and flew into
a rage whenever a reporter used that name in print.

He hated his height—like his father, he was short in stature, for height had not entered the Rothman family until the
third generation, with Steven, and Herb hated watching his
son grow seven inches taller than himself. He tried to com-
pensate for the shortness by working on his physique, and
there was a fully equipped gym in his apartment at River
House. He was proud, at sixty-seven, of his hard, flat belly, and his well-muscled arms, shoulders, and pectorals. His
body, he hoped, made him physically attractive to women,
but secretly he seemed to know it didn't, and Herb was no
Don Juan.

Having gone to Yale, Herb was embarrassed by his parents. He hated his father's fractured, heavily Russian-accented
English, and he visibly winced every time either of his parents used a Yiddish word. He hated being Jewish, and once—
Steven had told her this—had wanted to change his name,
either by dropping the "th" to make it "Roman," or else changing it to Ross. This proposal had provoked one of his father's
most furious tirades. "Change it! Change it!" Ho Rothman had
bellowed. "Why don't you change it to Shmuck!"

At Yale, he was very athletic. He coxed on the crew, was
on the golf team, and even played polo—six goals, it was
said, before he gave up the sport—but he was not tapped for
Skull and Bones, Scroll and Key, or any of the other senior

societies which he considered his due, and for this slight he blamed anti-Semitism, though there were other obvious reasons. Because of this, he hated Yale and, though he was one of the university's richest alumni, and despite numerous entreaties and inducements, he had never given a penny to his alma mater. He had purposely sent his son to Princeton as the most effective way he could conceive of getting back at Yale.

He was a man totally consumed by hate. He even hated being rich because of the time and trouble it took to turn down endless requests for philanthropy. For the last dozen or so years, for reasons Alex refused to become involved with, Herb also seemed to hate his wife, and he and Pegeen kept separate bedrooms at opposite ends of River House, with separate elevator entrances so that neither would have to encounter the other when they came and went.

He hated his younger brother, Arthur. He hated black people. He probably hated women. And of course he hated Alex. She knew why.

"Let me make a baby for you," he had said. "My sperm count is exceptionally high. My baby would have the Rothman genes, which is all the family really wants. And after all, Steven is impotent."

Somehow, if he had tried to seduce her the idea would have seemed more palatable. Even rape would have seemed a lesser violation. Instead, he had offered her a deposit from the Rothman sperm bank. He had offered to empty his seminal vesicle into her. Her refusal—with a roar of angry laughter—was certainly the real reason why he hated her, but she saw no reason to tell Lenny any of that. Hell had no fury like Herb Rothman scorned, she thought.

"Make your peace with him," Lenny had told her. "Someday that will be very important, Alex."

Now, apparently, that day had come.

But she would like to ask Lenny this: How—how in the world—how could any woman, any woman in the world—make her peace with a man like that? Was there anything at all you could do with a man like that?

A magazine. What was it, after all? she asked herself as she lay, unable to sleep, in her dark bedroom, listening to the distant river sounds. Of course Mel was right, it was only words and pictures printed on glossy paper. She was under no illusions about what her creation was. *Mode* was not the Sistine ceiling. It was not immortal, it was not even art. Readers might save back issues for a while, but eventually they were thrown out, out with the garbage, out with the dusty and mildewed contents of attics, cellars, and garages. A magazine was nothing but a piece of show business. Like a Broadway musical, it had its run, then closed, and was replaced by something else. After a while, you even forgot the words to the songs.

But words were living things created by living people, and so were pictures, and the words and pictures had to be gathered and assembled and arranged with faith and love. That's it! Bingo! And she was back to love again. A magazine must enter into a long-distance love affair—millions of love affairs—with its readers. Like a clever lover, it must flirt. It must seduce. It must conspire and share little special secrets. It must whisper, stroke, inspire, thrill, and amuse, at exactly the right times and places. Like the perfect lover, it must feel needed. Like the perfect lover or perfect love affair, it should never seem boring, or settle into a routine, or be predictable, or take itself for granted. Like the perfect lover, it should never be cold, or unresponsive, or forgetful, or unfaithful. The perfect lover should always be surprising. The perfect lover should never grow old or fretful or cranky and complaining. On the other hand, the perfect lover should never be complacent. The perfect lover is strong, with a point of view, and a willingness to argue that point of view, defend it—even fight for it—for love is no lotus land, no Capri, but a stern landscape of precipices and perilous mountain steeps. Love was work, perhaps the hardest work of all, but between the lover and her beloved there always had to be, at the very bottom of everything, a profound and enduring respect and trust.

Of course there were no perfect lovers, and no perfect love affairs, and there were no perfect magazines—never would be, Alex Rothman would be the first to admit—but one had to keep pushing, striving, climbing, working toward that impossible goal.

And how many people truly loved the work they did? Damned few, Alex would reckon. That would make a good subject for a survey, a good question for a Harris Poll: How many people truly loved their work? Sometimes it seemed as though there were no more than one or two.

And what was the editor's role in sponsoring, abetting, and keeping alive all those long-distance love affairs? She was a kind of marriage broker between the people who contributed the words and pictures, and the readers who turned the pages of glossy paper. "I'm a kind of procurer," she once said, "or, as the French say, *une maquerelle*. But I've tried to be an honest one."

At a seminar for college students interested in careers in journalism, Lenny Liebling once said, "Putting out a magazine like *Mode* is like having a new baby every month."

Alex had disagreed with him. "Having a baby is easy," she said. "Putting out a magazine like ours is more like reinventing the wheel every month."

But even that hardly said it all. In the end, there was no definition for love.

Chapter 8

The telephone beside her bed was ringing and, from the little flashing red light on the panel, she saw that someone was calling her on her private line. Though Mel groaned unhappily from his side of the bed, she picked up the receiver and said, "Hello?"

Lily Rothman was one of those New York women who, when placing a telephone call, never troubled to identify themselves to the person being called, but just immediately began talking, and who, when they had finished saying what they had to say, simply replaced the receiver without troubling to say goodbye. "Alex," she was saying, "I watched it all on television. I know how you must be feeling, and I know what you must be thinking. But don't resign."

"He hasn't given me much choice," she said.

"But don't. Don't do it. That's what he wants you to do, don't you see? Don't play into his hand. Make him fire you."

"I don't particularly like the idea of being fired, Aunt Lily!"

"I mean make him think he's going to *have* to fire you. Because he can't fire you—not now, anyway."

"Why can't he?"

"Profit sharing. Don't you remember profit sharing? Do you realize how much you have in your profit-sharing plan? Nearly three million dollars! If he fires you, he'll have to give you all of that—in cash—right now. But he can't afford to do that. Not now. Everything is tied up in the IRS case, and as treasurer of the company, I can't release funds like that. The lawyers won't let me. But if you resign, he doesn't have to pay you a penny. That's why he's hoping you'll resign. So don't do that."

"But Lily, I—"

"Listen to me. You mustn't. You're too valuable to us. You're too valuable to me. You're too valuable to Ho."

"How is Ho, Lily?"

"Oh, dear. Don't ask. Ho is just—a vegetable now, Alex. The doctors say he has the heart of a teenage boy, and the constitution of an ox. But it's his mind that's gone. I'm not even sure he recognizes me anymore, Alex."

"I'd like to come to see him."

"No, don't. Visitors just make his blood pressure go up. The doctors say it's because of frustration—frustration and anger because he can't speak anymore, because he can't recognize people anymore. You wouldn't want to see him the way he is now, Alex. Just remember him the way he was, when he was strong and alert and on top of everything. Remember him when he was the Ho we both loved, not the way he is now, old and angry and frustrated, and just a vegetable. It's the IRS business that did this to him, you know. It was the last straw. The man who advised presidents! And now having the government turn on him like this! It's shocking, that's what it is. If Ho dies because of this, I'm thinking of suing the IRS for manslaughter. Don't laugh. They're looking into it, the lawyers."

"I'm very sorry, Aunt Lily."

"So don't resign. Promise me you won't resign. Make Herbie sweat it out for a while, because he knows he can't fire you, and meanwhile I'll think of something."

"I've pretty much made up my mind—"

"Don't. Don't make a single move. Do nothing. Promise me. Remember, you owe me a lot, Alex. And I owe you a lot, too. We both owe each other a lot. We're in this together, which is why we've got to make this work, *bubeleh*."

"Would you be in a position to fire Herbert, Lily?"

There was a brief silence, and then she said, "Not right now, I can't. Right now, we need Herbie, too. It's this IRS business, again, and it's all too complicated to explain to you now. Just take my word—we need him. But we also need you. So promise me you won't resign, and meanwhile I'll think of something. *Just don't resign.* Remember, you owe me." And the line went dead, and Alex realized that Aunt Lily had terminated the conversation.

In the apartment at the Gainsborough, Lenny Liebling lay in his tanning bed listening to a Mozart tape through his stereo headset. It was a nightly ritual, twenty minutes in the tanning bed just before bedtime, a time when Dear Old Lenny ministered to the special needs of Dear Old Lenny. The physical, and spiritual, needs.

Dear Old Lenny. Everybody had always called him that, even when they didn't mean it. Dear Old Lenny Liebling was not universally loved, nor did he for one minute expect to be.

How old was dear old Lenny? "He must be seventy-five, at *least*," they said. But naturally Lenny would never divulge that statistic. He was certainly older than Herbert Joseph Rothman, because Lenny sometimes dropped hints about Herbert's teenage escapades. Still, with his carefully dyed and marcelled champagne-colored hair—*all his own*—styled weekly by Jerry at Bergdorf's, and after at least two face-lifts, and in his corset, Lenny managed to look considerably (twenty years?) younger than Herb. And how many titles and positions had Lenny Liebling held at Rothman Publications over the years? Lenny himself had trouble keeping track of them all. Right now, his title was special projects editor for *Mode*, a job that could be described as loosely and imprecisely as one wished. What where the duties of a special projects editor? That depended. At Rothman, they said, there always had to be some sort of a job found for Lenny Liebling. Always. They said he must know where some significant corporate bodies were buried—how else would one explain it?

Over the years, Lenny had worked, in some capacity or other, for nearly every one of the Rothman publications, the newspapers as well as the magazines. His titles had included features editor, managing editor, art editor, fashion editor, beauty editor, antiques editor, design editor, deputy editor, food & wine editor, roving editor, assistant editor, associate editor, society editor, contributing editor, and editor-at-large. For a while, he was even executive editor of *Wanderlust*, the

Rothman travel magazine, and, for an even briefer period, he was given the editor-in-chiefship of *Mirror, Mirror*, that ill-fated celebrity magazine that was the Rothmans' attempt to challenge *People* and *Us* at the newsstands. In each of his capacities, furthermore, Lenny always commanded a corner office (not the largest corner office, to be sure, but always a corner), with his choice of drapes, furnishings, and carpet, and a secretary. The secretaries came and went, complaining that all they were asked to do was run personal errands for Lenny—to and from his tailor and his dry cleaner, fetching his regular luncheon hamburger from "21" (returning it if it was overdone), ordering his theater tickets, setting up the table in his office for the thrice-weekly visits from his masseur, making appointments with his hairstylist, misting and watering his plants. So many secretaries had come and gone that he no longer bothered to learn their names, and called them all "secretary."

From all the positions Lenny had held with the Rothmans, one might credit him with a certain versatility. Durability would be the better word. A mysterious survivability.

Still, Lenny had not done badly for a little boy from Onward, Mississippi (pop. 512 and growing smaller by the day), who came to New York almost sixty years ago, knowing no one, without so much as a high-school diploma, with no more than fifteen dollars in his pocket and a hole in his shoe, where he suddenly became the darling of the Rothmans, and where—overnight, it seemed—he was transformed into the elegant, poised, sophisticated, witty, worldly, and polished Lenny Liebling whose name popped up regularly in Liz Smith's, Cindy Adams's, and Mona Potter's columns. None of these ladies knew a thing about Lenny Liebling's past, and by now it no longer mattered.

Wasn't it odd, people often said, that both Lenny Liebling and his boss, Alexandra Rothman, came from tiny midwestern and southern towns that almost no one had ever heard of. But it was a fact that many of New York's most successful people came originally from obscure places. Was there something about small towns that spurred the clever and ambitious to set their sights on the big city, where one had to be willing to be lucky? The very smallness of the towns, and the openness of the open country, seemed to force the clever and ambitious into the claustrophobia of crowded sidewalks and jostling skyscrapers, where they seemed to thrive. Or at least the lucky ones did.

Of course everyone knew how Alex Rothman had done it. She had married a Rothman. She had started out as a small-time model, had won some sort of contest, and had wound up on the cover of *Mode*, where her beauty had caught young Steven Rothman's eye. But then she had done even more than that. She had not just settled, as so many young women of that sort do, for being a rich man's wife, a part of his domestic decor. She had gone on to take over the editorship of her husband's magazine, which meant that she had been lucky, *and* clever, *and* ambitious. No wonder certain women hated her.

But how had Lenny Liebling done it? No one knew, and so naturally along the gossipy grapevine of the Rothman organization the rumors flew.

He was Ho Rothman's illegitimate son.

He was Aunt Lily Rothman's illegitimate son.

He was Herb Rothman's secret homosexual lover.

He was Alexandra Rothman's secret heterosexual lover.

He was Joel Rothman's father. Joel was blond, wasn't he? Steven had been dark.

And so on. Lenny was aware of all these rumors, did nothing to discourage or disprove them—rather enjoyed them, in fact. When people tried to excavate the truth, he was deliberately vague. A reporter once asked him how he spent his days at Rothman Publications.

"Climbing," he replied with a wave of his hand.

"Climbing?"

"Just climbing. Aren't we all climbers, actually? Don't *you* want to be better off tomorrow than you are today?"

That was as far as he would go. Lenny Liebling didn't mind being in the gossip columns. But when reporters tried to do "in-depth" stories, he was very clever at sending them down blind alleys, and leaving them with nothing but loose ends.

And so, all that anyone knew for sure was that Lenny Liebling was the darling of the Rothmans, but even this was not quite true. He was not the darling of *all* the Rothmans. Herb Rothman, for one, barely tolerated him. On the other hand, both Ho and Lily Rothman appeared to find Lenny useful, and Alexandra Rothman clearly liked him. A better word than *darling* would be *force*. Lenny Liebling had become a force within the Rothman family, a power, a controlling influence in their lives—inescapable and indispensable—a force and a fixture in the Rothman family firmament.

But it was not really true that Lenny knew where certain corporate bodies were buried, though there were one or two human resting places whose whereabouts he knew.

What, then, was Lenny's special usefulness? For one thing, he was an invaluable—and usually reliable—source of inside company information. His ear was always to the ground and, as he said, he had his spies. Who were Lenny's spies? No one knew, exactly, but there were certain obvious suspects. The mail-room boys were one. Nearly every new male employee at Rothman Publications started in the mail room, and the mail-room boys were as eager to get ahead as anyone else. To keep track of who was who, and who was telling what to whom, the mail-room boys read all the mail and memoranda—even, and especially, those items marked "PERSONAL" and "CONFIDENTIAL"—before placing them in In boxes. (Lenny himself had started at Rothman as a mail-room boy, so he knew how it worked.) The mail-room boys knew all about those foreign magazines that arrived, in plain brown wrappers, addressed to Herbert J. Rothman and even spent time giggling over the pictures before slipping the publications back into their envelopes.

Then there was Wally, the shoe-shine boy who made daily rounds of the executive offices. Most people paid no attention at all to Wally as he squatted on his bootblack's box tending to their uptipped toes, and went right on with their business conversations as though Wally weren't there. But Lenny had discovered that Wally not only liked to listen, but that he also liked to talk, and enjoyed an audience, and it was quite amazing what significant scraps of corporate news Wally was able to pick up, and which Lenny was able to fit together into a larger picture.

There were also the people Lenny called "the Production moles"—the solemn-faced kids who came out of Yale and Princeton, Smith and Wellesley, who had made it out of the mail room to the next step up, the Production Department, but who were still willing to work for next to nothing because, after all, this was considered a glamour industry, and the Production moles were able to tell their friends that they had glamorous jobs "in publishing." Lenny had managed to skip that particular stage in the scramble up the masthead—where the names of the Production moles were listed, in tiniest print, at the very bottom—and so Lenny had no idea what the Production moles actually did. Some of them seemed to spend their days crouched over computer consoles, staring at moving lines of green print. Others seemed to occupy themselves with pots of glue. The moles spoke a strange and incomprehensible lingo all their own. At times they spoke of headers and footers, flats and column-inches, which sounded as though they were in the construction business. They also talked of plants and inserts and tip-ins and slugs and mice, as if they were landscape gardeners. At times, the instructions from the Production chief sounded like instructions for a space launching: "Bring your ruler bar up to the foreground, and click the mouse button when your cursor is on it, and set your tab stop." When they spoke of serifs and fonts, it sounded as though they were part of a religious cult. Lenny comprehended none of their mysterious language, beyond knowing that a "typesetter's widow" was not the surviving spouse of a deceased typesetter, and only when the moles talked about paste-ups, proofs, galleys, and tear-sheets did Lenny realize that the moles were involved in the grubbiest, mechanical part of putting a magazine together. In fact, the final printed-up, pasted-together page was called a mechanical. The moles were mechanics. Their fingernails were even dirty.

But Lenny felt deep pity for the moles. They all worked together in one large, windowless room over messy desks, where the floor was always strewn with discarded scraps of paper and computer printouts, where the rows of bright fluorescent lights overhead bathed the bespectacled faces of the moles in a kind of prison pallor, and where they breathed the fumes of rubber cement. The moles were universally unpopular with their higher-ups. "Production has a problem with this piece" meant that an editor had to go back and cut a story or—even worse—had to add to it to fill the necessary column inches, which meant that everything had to be cleared with Alex Rothman all over again. Nobody ever thanked the moles for what they did—except Lenny, even

though he didn't understand what it was. No one offered
a sympathetic ear to the moles as they recited, unbidden,
their litanies of the woes inflicted upon them by those higher on the masthead whose jobs they naturally one day hoped
to have—except Lenny, even though he could be mentally
planning an entire month's itinerary in Europe while they
talked. Still, the moles occasionally picked up an interesting
tidbit or two, and when that happened Lenny quickly pricked
up his ears. It was from one of the moles, for instance, that
Lenny had first learned that Herbert Rothman had called Alex
Rothman's offbeat June cover "a piece of shit."

How did Lenny repay his spies for what they passed along
to him? With promises, mostly. "You seem like a bright lad,"
he might say to one of them. "I'll put in a word for you with
Ho Rothman when I speak to him next." And everyone knew
that Lenny Liebling had special access to the Rothmans—all
the Rothmans, including Herbert, who hated him.

He could never have repaid his spies with cash, even if
he'd wanted to. Because it was a sad fact of Lenny's existence that, despite his long years of loyal service to the
Rothmans, and despite his apparent power in the family
company, Lenny had never earned much in the way of salary.
Rothman Communications, Inc. was a notoriously tightfisted
organization. Even Alex Rothman, *Mode*'s editor-in-chief,
called the High Priestess of American Fashion, earned only
slightly more than $200,000 a year—low by industry stan-
dards—and it had taken her seventeen years to reach that
level. The Oracle at Delphi, Lenny assumed, earned more
than that. At Rothman, bonuses were rare, and always grudg-
ingly given. Ho Rothman's idea of a promotion had always
been to give a favored employee a slightly more exalted title,
perhaps a slightly larger office with, perhaps, a nameplate on
the door, or an extra chair. Higher-ups also got chrome-plated
Thermos jugs for their desks. But salary increases rarely
accompanied these lagniappes. And the fact was that Lenny
Liebling, in any of his positions in the company, had never
earned more than $55,000 a year. And, as Lenny often com-
plained to his longtime companion, Charlie Boxer, "In New
York, in nineteen ninety, fifty-five thousand is hardly enough
to keep Bridget in birdseed." Bridget was their canary.

It was certainly not enough to keep Lenny and Charlie
in their apartment at the Gainsborough, not enough to pay

for Lenny's silk Turnbull & Asser shirts, his Patek Philippe watch, his Louis Vuitton luggage, his Baccarat wineglasses, his Porsche sunglasses, his silk pajamas and robes from Sulka, his Brioni suits, his Guerlain toilet water, his Plisson badger-hair shaving brushes, his Caswell-Massey soaps and talcum powders, his collection of alligator belts and Gucci loafers, not to mention the bills for face-lifts, hamburgers from "21," hairstylists, and a masseur three times a week. It was nowhere near enough to support Lenny and Charlie in the style in which they chose to live, which demanded Porthault sheets and towels, as well as that sweeping north-ward view of Central Park. Oh, Charlie helped as best he could, of course, but it had for many years been necessary for Lenny to supplement his salary from other sources.

In England, this was called "the fiddle." In England, vir-tually everyone who worked for wages was on the fiddle. In England, the fiddle was so commonplace that employers figured it into their overhead. In England, where the fiddle was understood, it was easy to accomplish. In America, it was slightly more difficult, but not impossible.

A special projects editor, for example, must do a certain amount of traveling to research his special projects and, for years, Lenny had charged the company for first class tickets while flying in economy. But then Aunt Lily, who had started in the company as its bookkeeper, and was still its treasurer, had begun asking for receipted ticket stubs. This had proven awkward, and the airline companies stubbornly refused to doctor their tickets, and so that was the end of that, alas.

But, as the saying goes, there is more than one way to skin a cat. In fact, there are several ways. Hotels, for example. When Lenny went to Paris, as he did twice a year to view the collections (Alex covered the *couture*, and he covered the *pret-à-porter*), he was expected to stay at one of three hotels—the Georges Cinq, the Plaza Athenée, or the Bris-tol—where other members of the fashion press routinely stayed. But Lenny had been able to make a little arrange-ment with the Georges Cinq. For a modest tip, the concierge there would take his telephone messages and collect his mail, and otherwise treat him as though he were a registered guest. When Lenny was ready to leave the city, this same gentleman would prepare a delightfully large bill for him to attach to his expense account. Meanwhile, Lenny had found perfectly comfortable digs for himself in the rue de la Chapelle, near the Gare du Nord. Not the best neighborhood, of course, but the room could be had for thirty francs a night.

He had a similar arrangement with Claridge's in London. The British were particularly understanding, having invented the fiddle. But hotels in Rome, Milan, and Tokyo could also be persuaded.

Restaurants, too, were cooperative—even some of the finest dining establishments in the world. In return for a small consideration, the captain would inflate the check, Lenny would charge it all on the company's credit card, and Lenny would pocket the difference, though some captains made him split it with them. Then there was the matter of conference room lunches. From time to time, when meetings in the conference room ran over into the lunch hour, meals were ordered up from outside. There was a coffee shop around the corner where the company maintained a charge account for such occasions, and Lenny had been able to make an arrangement with the coffee shop's proprietor. Every month, a few extra conference room lunches made their way onto the company's bill. The proprietor of the coffee shop kept ten percent of these bogus charges, and Lenny got the balance for having set the system up. Every now and then the proprietor, one Mr. Bogardus, got greedy, and asked for a bigger cut. "You're not the only coffee shop in town," Lenny would politely remind Bogardus. There were certain advertisers and agency people who liked a drink before lunch, and the conference room contained a well-stocked bar. Lenny had made a similar arrangement with the neighborhood liquor store.

But the easiest fiddle of all was with taxicabs and livery companies. Not all cruising New York taxicabs were equipped with meters that printed out receipts for their fares, and so Lenny was always able to fill out a few extra petty cash slips for taxis every week, while he walked or took the bus or subway. Aunt Lily never bothered to go over the petty cash account, but that part of it amounted to peanuts.

The livery company fiddle was much more lucrative. Like many large New York corporations, Rothman Communications, Inc. maintained a commercial charge account with one of several private livery services that operated a fleet of radio-dispatched cabs, and every Rothman executive and department head was given a book of trip vouchers with this company. The passenger then kept one copy of the voucher, and the second went back to the livery company, which once a month submitted its bill to Rothman's Accounting Department, itemizing the various trips it had supplied to Rothman personnel. The Accounting Department then paid this bill with one company check.

It was all supposed to be foolproof, and would have been unless, as in Lenny's case, one had a special little arrangement with the owner of the livery company. The owner, whom Lenny knew only as Jocko, was most obliging. All month long Lenny filled out vouchers for Jocko, using various employees' names, and making sure that they all worked in different departments, sending Rothman employees on fictitious trips to different points in the city on fictitious bits of company business. Lenny's vouchers were marked with his special code. His "Driver's initials" were J.D., and his was "Cab #13." Needless to say, there was no driver with the initials J.D., and no driver wanted to be given the number thirteen. But Lenny was not superstitious.

Jocko ran a special tab on the receipts that came in on vouchers charged to Cab #13. After skimming ten percent off the top for himself, Jocko turned over the balance to Lenny. This could amount to between two and three thousand dollars a month, and it was all tax free!

But even these measures were not sufficient to permit Lenny and Charlie Boxer to live in the style in which they chose to live. Charlie had always longed to own a summer weekend place in the Hamptons and, Lord knows, at today's real estate prices out there, where nothing decent could be had for under a million dollars, that dream was still far beyond their financial reach. But lately Lenny had been working on another plan to supplement the couple's income. The idea had been suggested by a small sidebar item in the *New York Times* following the paper's report on the multimillion-dollar art theft from the Isabella Stewart Gardner Museum in Boston.

The item had been headlined:

The Social Hierarchy
of Thieves

In the netherworld of thievery, there is a social hierarchy as strict, and as strictly observed, as in the world of High Society.

Lowest in the social pecking order of thieves are the muggers and purse-snatchers. House burglars enjoy a social status only slightly higher than the muggers.

Higher up on the social scale of thievery are the jewel thieves. Since most jewelry is small and pocketable, most jewel thefts are relatively easy to pull off. On the other hand, since jewelry is often insured, it is difficult to fence unless pieces are broken up, or unless important gems are cut up into smaller stones, which can be sold for only a fraction of the value of the original stones.

Close to the top of the social ladder of thieves are those who steal antique furniture and home furnishings. Many dealers, galleries, and auction houses will accept without question a stolen antique.

And at the very pinnacle of thievery's social status are the thieves of great art masterpieces, such as those removed from the Gardner Museum yesterday. Enormous skill and planning are required to execute a successful art theft, and thieves of this caliber are held almost in awe by lesser thieves. A famous painting is extraordinarily difficult to fence. On the other hand, great art can be held for ransom, and insurance companies, though reluctant to advertise this fact, have been known to pay ransom for the return of stolen art. But the art of collecting ransom is in itself a complex science, not to be undertaken by the amateur or by the unsophisticated.

Meanwhile, the paintings stolen from the Gardner were not insured, adding to the deepening mystery as to the motive behind this particular theft. . . .

Lenny had been particularly interested in the next-to-highest category of this hierarchy. "Close to the top of the social ladder" described Lenny and Charlie rather nicely. They might not be at the very top, but they were certainly close to it. And he was also struck by the notion that "Many dealers, galleries, and auction houses will accept without question a stolen antique." "Without question" was a tantalizing phrase.

He was thinking, in particular, of a seventeenth-century rug, an Isfahan, very nice, measuring about thirty by forty feet, with unusual shadings of blues, purples, golds, cherry-red, and a background that was almost face-powder pink. He was also thinking of a little Armenian fellow he knew, in TriBeCa, who had told him he could make a more than passable copy of this. He was thinking, too, of a matched pair of Boulle commodes, elaborately scrolled and inlaid with marquetry of ebony, tortoiseshell, chased copper, and white gold. A matched pair of Boulle commodes was in itself unusually rare. Burned into the back of each was the signature of André Charles Boulle himself, and the date, 1672. Also, each bore the familiar royal floral circlet, topped by a crown, and the words *Palais du Versailles*. It seemed certain—"without question"—that Louis XIV himself had feasted his eyes on both these pieces.

At the moment, Lenny knew of no one who could copy Boulle's cabinetwork, but that did not mean that someone could not be found. In any case, these were all projects for the future, with many small details that would have to be worked out.

Back to Onward, Mississippi, where it all began! The name of that little town could serve as a metaphor for Lenny's life. Did a kindly deity look down on that lonely, restless youth in Onward, and select him to be a force, a power? ("If you've never heard of Onward," he often said, "it's roughly thirty-five miles from Yazoo City. And surely you've heard of Yazoo City. It's the nearest big town.") In Onward, Lenny's mother ran the general store, which meant she was also the postmistress, while his father read the Talmud. It was said that, as a child on his mother's knee while she sorted the mail, Lenny fell in love with postmarks from faraway places. Lenny's parents were dead now, of course, and Lenny never spoke of them, nor of the brothers and sisters who stayed behind there, because from Onward the seventeen-year-old Lenny's ambitions were to go—onward! When he suddenly appeared in New York, never mind the year, with his astonishingly golden hair (more astonishingly golden than it would be appropriate for his hairstylist to maintain today), and his golden Mississippi Delta tan, people said that he looked just like a jar of honey. He was that beautiful. Lenny's aim, he said then, was simply to become America's best-kept boy. It could be said that he achieved that goal. A best-kept Jewish boy from Mississippi!

"My father did me a wonderful favor when I was a boy," he once said. "He threw me out of the house. I had to leave Onward. I've been eternally grateful to him ever since."

Of course that old Lenny was gone now—gone with the thick, muddy accent and the bumpkin manners and the chewed-down fingernails—gone with the wind. That boy had been replaced by the completed Lenny, world traveler, bon vivant, man about town, always in demand by hostesses of the best parties, perennially on the best-dressed lists. This was Lenny of the monogrammed Sulka undershorts. This was the Lenny who, though he had never bothered to register to vote, dined at the White House under three U.S. presidents. This was the Lenny who was master of ceremonies at Bob Hope's last birthday party. This was the finished Lenny Liebling, Lenny at climax, whose musical accent now combined the soft elisions of Charleston and the flattened vowels of what Scott Fitzgerald called the St. Midas schools. This was Lenny at his self-destined rainbow's end—gone onward, and outward, and upward, from Onward.

This was Lenny who lived with Charlie Boxer at the Gainsborough Studios high above the park—one of Manhattan's finest pre–World War I buildings, and Lenny would never live in a building that was not pre–World War I. Lenny and Charlie's apartment was featured in *Architectural Digest* in 1986. The article spoke of their regular Sunday afternoon salons, which had become something of a New York institution. No invitations were ever issued for these soirees. Anyone who wished to could drop in, though Peter, their doorman, had certain discretionary powers, and those who were not welcome knew who they were. Those who were welcome were a glittering array. Last Sunday's guests included Gloria Vanderbilt and Bobby Short, Walter and Betsey Cronkite, Ivana Trump, Melina Mercouri, Rex Reed, Bobby Zarem, Doris Duke, Barbara Walters, Roger Mudd, and Walter and Lee Annenberg. Over in one corner, Candace Bergen and Rudolf Nureyev played backgammon, while the others shared in their hosts' wealth of amusing anecdotes, and pretended to enjoy their not-very-distinguished nouveau Beaujolais, which was all Lenny and Charlie ever served.

Charming Lenny, they said. Delightful Lenny, witty Lenny. This was the Lenny who always knew the inside story of the latest scandal, who always knew the juiciest gossip, particularly when it dealt with the Rothman clan, who always knew who was trying to stab whom in the back, and who just might be going to get away with it.

This was the Lenny who, just that morning, had decided, from bits and pieces of information that he had fitted together, that it might be a good time to pay a little extra attention to Aunt Lily Rothman.

"Secretary! Secretary!" he had called out from his office, clapping his hands, just before leaving to dress for Alex's supper dance. When the latest girl appeared, he said, "Ring up Renny the florist on Sixty-fourth Street, and have him send a *really* nice arrangement to Mrs. H. O. Rothman at seven twenty Park. Tell her on the card that everyone at the office is terribly concerned about Ho's latest illness, and that she's in all our thoughts and prayers. Just sign my name. No, wait—I have a *much* better idea. I'll tell you how to do this, secretary. I know we've got some old Renny boxes lying around, so find one of them. Then go over to West Twenty-seventh Street and the wholesale flower market, pick out some flowers, and arrange them in a Renny box. Then deliver them to Mrs. Rothman—yourself."

Looking pained, the young woman departed, and Lenny made a little note to put the price of the flowers on one of his radio cab vouchers.

The best place to find a helping hand is at the end of your own arm.

The timer on the tanning bed ticked quietly away, while Lenny Liebling's thoughts swirled to the strains of Mozart. He was listening to *Mitridate, Rè di Ponto*, marveling at Mozart's genius, marveling at the noble pathos of the recitative, and marveling that Mozart was only fourteen when he composed this opera—already a genius composer, singer, master of the harpsichord, organ, and violin, his head already in the heavens of melody, orchestration, vocal and choral style. If only Lenny had been possessed of such genius, who knew to what heights in life he might have climbed. Still, he had climbed far enough with his own particular genius, which was the genius of survival. Aunt Lily had called tonight. There had been a message waiting for him on his answering machine. That meant that Aunt Lily wanted something, and that was good. It was always good when one of them wanted something. Aunt Lily would not have called at midnight to thank him for his flowers. No, she definitely wanted something, and that was another aspect of Lenny's genius, the genius to be wanted.

It might not be the genius of a Mozart, perhaps, or of an André Charles Boulle, inspired cabinetmaker to kings, but it was a genius nonetheless. And, with the thrilling music pounding in his ears, he let his thoughts drift blissfully off to the Isfahan, thirty by forty feet, so marvelously colored, and to the genius of half-naked Persian peasants crouched in the desert sun by the banks of Zaindeh Rud, going blind over their looms tying six hundred knots to the square inch. In his mind, the gnarled brown fingers knotted the bright threads as the music rose. Genius.

The Mozart was just reaching a particularly exciting arpeggio when he realized that Charlie Boxer was trying to say something to him. He removed the earphones and lifted the lid of the tanning bed a fraction of an inch. "Yes, dovey?" he said, mildly annoyed at the interruption.

Charlie was standing by the bed in his pajamas, Mark Cross slippers, and his red silk Sulka robe, looking worried. "I was just saying," Charlie said, "that if Alex leaves the company, won't that mean that our principal insurance policy will become almost worthless?"

"I had thought about that," Lenny said. "And I admit there is some risk. But then there is always risk where insurance is involved. Insurance is a business about risks. It is a gamble. You are always betting against the underwriters, who have the statistics in their favor. With insurance, you are always betting against the odds. But, if things work out the way I think they will, our insurance policy may turn out to be worth more than we ever imagined in our very wildest dreams. So don't worry your pretty head about it, dovey-pie. Leave everything to Daddy." And he replaced the earphones, lowered the lid of the tanning bed, and returned to Mozart and the vision of peasant weavers squatting in the dusty sun. You underestimate the vasty deeps of Herb's bitterness toward her, he thought. So does she. . . .

Chapter 9

Once again the telephone at her bedside was ringing, and she reached to pick it up.

"For God's sake, turn that damned thing off," Mel muttered. "People will be calling you all night if you let them."

"I'd better see who this is," she said. "Hello?"

"Lexy!" she heard Lucille Withers's voice exclaim. "I watched it all on television. You know, this Arnold Arms really is a nifty little ole hotel. For two dollars a day extra, they'll let you rent a TV set. Not bad, huh? Anyway, you looked terrific. When ole Herb Rothman let you have it, you had just the right expression on your face—mad, but *tough*. It was the old chin-up look I taught you on the runway. You really did old Lulu proud tonight. So—how's it feel to be the most-sought-after woman in New York?"

"Right now, I feel like the most-shat-upon woman in New York," she said.

"Oh, but what golden shit! He shat on you with shit of twenty-four-karat gold! Every big shot in this town is going to be after you now, Lexy, and all you have to do is sit back and name your price. Head-hunters' holiday begins at the opening bell tomorrow morning. I can just see them all lining up outside your door, dangling their offers. Well, you just let 'em dangle for a few days, honey, and let the offers get bigger and bigger. Then snap at the biggest one of all. Honey, you-all have got this town by the *balls*!"

"Actually, I haven't quite decided what to do," she said.

There was a shocked silence at the other end of the connection. Then Lucille Withers said, "Well, you're going to *quit*, aren't you? My God, you've *got* to quit!"

"I haven't decided yet, Lulu."

"Come *on*, honey. If you don't quit after this, you'll look like a damned *fool*. Right now, Herbert Rothman looks like the damned fool. He's the one out there with shit all over his face."

"There are other considerations, Lulu. There's a contract, and—"

"Contract, shmontract. Take his contract, and shove it down the little shit's throat. You're about to move into the big time, honey, and I mean the *really* big time. To hell with the chickenshit Rothmans, who never paid you a tenth of what you're worth. Guess—for one—who's after you right now."

"Who?"

"Rodney McCulloch, that's who. How does that grab ya? You know who he is, I guess."

"Yes," she said. "I've never met him, but I know who he is."

"We're talking *billions*," Lucille Withers said. "With Rodney McCulloch, we're talking *really* big bucks. Next to Rodney, the Rothmans look like two-bit pikers. This is Big League, honey, and compared with him the Rothmans are out in the sandlots somewhere. Anyway, Rodney is an old pal of mine from way back, and he knows I know you. And fifteen minutes after that TV show was over, he managed to track me down here at the Arnold Arms, and wanted your private number. He wanted to call you *right now*—tonight—at *midnight!* But of course I wouldn't give it to him. I told him to call you at your office in the morning."

"Thank you, Lulu. I don't think I could have dealt with Rodney McCulloch tonight."

"Oh, bullets, honey, don't thank me. I wouldn't give out your private number if it was the Queen of England calling. Don't you think, running a modeling agency, I've had plenty of experience saying no to mashers who want a girl's private number? But, boy, that made him mad! He was so mad at me he slammed the phone down in my ear. But, boy, that really made me feel good, Lexy—saying no to a man like Rodney McCulloch."

"Thank you, Lulu."

"Anyway, I thought I'd better warn you. You're going to be hearing from Rodney in the morning. He wants to be the first in the line that's going to be forming on the left outside your door with offers tomorrow morning. Just one word of warning when dealing with Rodney, honey. Don't accept his first offer. Don't even accept his second. Keep him dangling, play hard to get. Believe it or not, Rodney *likes* to be kept dangling. He *likes* people who play hard to get. That's part of the game for him. That's how he gets his jollies. Aw, honey, I'm just so excited for you!"

"But, Lulu," she said, "you seem to be assuming that I'm going to be leaving *Mode*."

There was another shocked silence at the other end of the line. "Aw, honey, talk sense to Lulu," she said finally. "Of *course* you're gonna quit. You gotta quit! But what a way to go! Talk about golden parachutes!"

"I'm considering my options," she said quietly.

"Yeah, well, let me just tell you one final thing, Lexy honey. There's a lot of women in this town who're gonna be pretty jealous of you, 'cause you're sitting in the catbird seat. But I'm not jealous of you, Lexy. I'm *proud* of you, I really, truly am. You said tonight you wanted to introduce me around as the old belle who discovered you, and I said bullets to that. But when I saw your face on the TV screen tonight when the little shit was trying to dump on you— looking so proud, so *tough*, and I mean the *good* kind of tough—I said to myself: 'Hey, I'm gonna go around town from now on, and I don't just mean this town, and I don't just mean Kansas City, I mean *every* town, just crowing— shoutin' it from the rooftops—sayin', Hey, I *discovered* that li'l ole gal!' "

"Thank you, Lulu."

"And give Rodney McCulloch a big kiss for me. Actually, you won't want to give him a kiss—he's the ugliest-looking man you ever met. But when you think of those deep, deep pockets of his, he's Tom Cruise. 'Night, now, honey. Love ya. And congratulations."

"Love ya too, Lulu," she said, and replaced the receiver with a sigh.

She lay back against the cool pillows, and pulled the cool sheet up around her neck. "What am I going to do?" she whispered.

But Mel had rolled over on his right shoulder, and was fast asleep. She reached out with one bare arm and turned off the telephone.

In another darkened bedroom not far away, the young woman raised herself on one elbow and whispered, "I shouldn't have let you do this."

"Do what?" the young man said.

"Let you seduce me."

"But it was wonderful for me, my darling. I loved it. I love making love to you, and I want to do it all the time. Wasn't it just as wonderful for you?"

"Yes, but . . . but it was wrong. I know it was wrong. I didn't intend this to happen, but I was so upset. Never in my life—never in my life have I felt so much open hostility from a whole terraceful of people. So much anger, so much envy. So much hatred. I just had to get out of there. And you were kind enough to take me home."

"And you were clever enough to think of a way for us to do it. Didn't you love it when old Otto whipped out his gun? His piece, he calls it. I loved that. Ha-ha . . . tra-la . . . tra-la." He was laughing, and singing a little tuneless, wordless song at the same time.

"You have a beautiful body," she said, and with one finger she stroked the light hairs on his chest, and caressed his nipples.

"Now look what you're doing to me again," he said, and he threw the sheet back and lowered her moving hand to show her what he meant.

"Oh-oh-oh-oh," she said.

"You are so lovely," he said.

"Your mother hates me too."

"She won't when she sees how sweet you are. . . ."

From Joel Rothman's journal:

6/22/90
4:16 A.M.
Tra-la . . . tra-la. Life is full of unexpected wonderments, isn't it? No one would ever guess what I've

been doing half the night. F---ing my brains out is what! Whoopee and hallelujah, free at last! There was a nurse I used to have who wanted me to call her "Mamzell," even though she wasn't French, but Irish— thought "Mamzell" sounded a little "tonier," she said— who told me that if I touched myself it would drain the fluids out of my brain cavity. Well, shit—surprise, surprise—tonight I spent half the night just f---ing my brains out, and look, my brain's still here, fluids and all! The Boy in the Bubble is out of the Bubble at last—ta-ra-ra-boom-dee-ay! And this was so different from the other time, the time I've already written about, when old Otto took me to see that whore in Concord— a "hoor," he called her—the one with the dirty under- wear who only pretended (I'm sure of it) to come. An experience like that one could turn a guy off sex for the rest of his life, I guess, but thank God it didn't. But this was entirely different. This was the real thing. This was the real turtle soup, not merely the mock. This was Granada I've seen, not just Asbury Park! And I think I'm in love. Her name is Fiona—isn't that a lovely name? And she is so sweet—so sweet, and so clev- er. It was so clever the way she got rid of old Otto, I'm still laughing about that—pretending she'd seen a man on the roof (my would-be killer!) with a gun, so she and I could make our escape together. Old Otto's probably still tearing around the city looking for me! He wasn't in the lobby when I got home a few minutes ago, and I'm sure he wouldn't dare tell Mom he lost me! Well, old Otto's days are numbered anyway, thank God. Christ, a guy couldn't have any social life, much less a sex life, with old Otto tagging along. I couldn't even jack off in bed at night, with old Otto sleeping in the same room! Know where I had to go to jack off? In the shit-house stall in the dorm, and even that wasn't all that private because someone could always come in and take the stall next to mine. But anyway, those days are gone forever, and back to Fiona. Took her home in a taxi—she lives at the Westbury—and she asked me up to her apartment for a nightcap, in return for the favor, and when I started to go she asked to kiss me goodnight, and when I kissed her she stuck her tongue

*between my teeth, and the next thing I knew we were
f---ing! We were f---ing our brains out, right in her
living room on her big white sofa. But that was just
for starters. After it was over, the first time, we got to
talking a bit, and she told me a little about herself. She
has no real friends in New York, she told me, having
come here from London not long ago. She told me she
felt like an alien in a strange land. She finds New York
to be kind of an unfriendly city. I told her I wanted to
be her friend, and she told me quite a lot about herself
then. She comes from a really good family in England,
where she even has a title—"Her Ladyship," but she
hates the whole idea of titles. And, title and all, she
has really had a pretty unhappy life. Good family or
not, her father abused her. She didn't say how exactly,
and I could tell she didn't want to talk about that, so I
guess she was abused in some really awful way. Then,
when she was six, her mother ran off with another man,
and she's never seen or heard from her mother since.
She was left to be raised by the abusive father—like me,
she was raised by a single parent—but she really hates
her father, and she's actually afraid her father might do
something to try to bring her back, even though she's
a grown woman. Incidentally, I didn't ask her how old
she is. I guess she's a few years older than I am, but
whatthehell. Mom's dating a guy who's a few years
younger than she is, and she's probably going to marry Mel one of these days. Besides, I've always kind of
been attracted to older women, haven't I? I'm thinking
in particular of K.G., and all that stuff at St. Bernard's.
Anyway, she said, "Bertie rescued me." Bertie is what
she calls Gramps. I never heard the Great Herbert J.
Rothman called Bertie, but I guess that's the English
of it. Seems she met Gramps in London a couple of
months ago, and when she told him how bad the situation was with her father, Gramps offered to bring her
to this country and give her a job with the magazine.
I guess Gramps must have his sentimental side. (Funny, I've never seen it!) Anyway, Fiona said she doesn't
think Mom's too happy about the job he's given her. She
said she really wants to be Mom's friend, but doesn't
think Mom will let her be. I promised to help her any*

*way I could—with Mom. And then, as we were talking
like that, she did the cutest thing. We were lying there,
bare-assed on her sofa, and she suddenly took this crazy big pair of sunglasses she wears and wrapped them
around my limp cock, and made my pubic hair stand
out around the frames like a pair of bushy eyebrows,
and she said, "Oh, look at the little old man!" And
then she said, "Oh, look, his nose is getting bigger.
Are you Pinocchio? Have you been telling lies to me?"
And before I knew it, we were starting to f--- again. But
she said, "No, this time we're going to do it right," and
she got up and led me by the hand, just like a little girl,
into her bedroom, with her crazy sunglasses still hanging from my stiff cock, and she turned down the covers
of her big Hollywood king-size bed, and there were these
beautiful pale blue satin sheets, and I was so excited I
almost came again before I could get inside her! Oh, she
is a wild thing, wild and beautiful, and I think she loves
me, too. I would like to ask Mom what it's like for a
woman to be in love, how it feels, but I don't know if she
could even tell me, because I think it's so different for a
woman, being in love, from what it is for a man. But if
what I feel now is love, then it's a wild and wonderful
feeling that has nothing to do with f---ing, a feeling that
seems to creep up on you after the f---ing's over, a feeling of wanting to protect, and comfort. Because after it
was over, this time, she said she felt it was wrong, that
we shouldn't have f---ed, and she shouldn't have let me
because of her new relationship with Mom. I told her it
didn't matter because I would never tell Mom about it,
or anybody else in the world about it, for that matter.
And then she even got a little tearful, and said that she
thinks Mom hates her. And I tried to comfort her and
reassure her that Mom would never hate her, and that I
would take care of that because I loved her, and before
we knew it—well, we were f---ing again! So—what other words can I use to describe this lovely girl I've met?
Pert is one. She is pert, lively, spirited, bubbly (like
champagne), energetic, peppy, snappy, frisky, bouncy,
sparkly, as hard to pin down as quicksilver, but also
brave and strong and sad, and I want to make her
happy. But look, it is almost 5:30 in the morning, and*

*the sun is coming up, and I am f---ing tired! And I
haven't even bothered to make paragraphs for tonight's
entry, and this is probably the sloppiest piece of writing
I have ever done, but whatthehell—I'm in love. Tra-
la! Just one more item for my collection of misused
words in the public press. Headline in yesterday morning's* Times: *"DATA SHOWS CHINESE POPULATION
GROWTH IS STABILIZING." Of course "data" is a
plural word, and so it should be "DATA SHOW." Who
edits the* Times, *anyway? I could do a better job. And
one new vocabulary word: FIONA. Those three lovely
vowels, and just two consonants. All the loveliest, most
delicate words in the language have more vowels than
consonants.*

Enough for tonight.

It was one of those dreams which she knew was a dream
and, knowing that she was dreaming, she knew she could
rouse herself from it if she wanted to and yet, for some queer
reason, she chose not to, and made the dreaming, conscious
choice to let the dream spin itself out. In the dream, she was
leaning over the parapet of her terrace, staring down at the
dark river below, and at the little boat, spinning crazily, being
sucked into the tidal bore. There were cries from the boat, and
the woman's voice was familiar. Murderer! she was crying.
This is my life you are taking, and this is my blood in the
water. And down there in the darkness, she was able to make
out the woman's upturned face as one she knew. The eyes
blazed up at her with terrible accusation, and it was her own
frightened face from the Bouché portrait. The woman held
up the little white dog, as if offering it for sacrifice, as if to
say, If you won't spare me, at least spare this helpless animal, but her open mouth kept screaming the word *Murderer!
Murderer!*

She forced herself awake, and out of the dream, and, groping for a cool corner of her pillow, tried to sleep again.

PART TWO

THE HO FACTOR

Chapter 10

ROTHMAN DYNASTY COULD OWE
$900,000,000 IN UNPAID TAXES,
IRS CLAIMS
With Penalties, Interest,
Figure Could Top $1 Billion
—The *New York Times*, May 1, 1990

To Alex Rothman, there was something almost surrealistic about figures like these. It was impossible to take them seriously. At that level, it all became Monopoly money. She had been in Ho Rothman's office, in fact, the day his lawyers had telephoned him with the bad news that a major Treasury Department audit was under way. He had uttered just one word: *"Momzers!"* Then he seized the telephone cord, ripped it from the wall, and flung the instrument against his map of the United States, where it dislodged several gold stars from the tip of the state of Florida before crashing to the floor in several pieces. So much, he seemed to imply, for that.

Later, she was reassured that there was nothing to worry about. The Rothman lawyers had the situation well in hand. The IRS, she was told, often zeroed in on prominent taxpayers just to reassure the general public that the agency was doing its job, going after the fat cats. In due course, the case would be settled for a tiny fraction of the amount claimed. It was nothing but bluster, nothing but stagecraft, on the part of the feds. It was all part of George Bush's promise not to raise taxes. His administration would show that it had other ways of balancing the budget. And, a week later, when a telegram arrived from the White House on Ho's ninety-fourth birthday, reading BIRTHDAY FELICITATIONS FROM GEORGE AND BARBARA, Ho waved the telegram triumphantly in front of his staff. "See?" he cried. "He is wishing me Happy Birthday, while his pipple are saying they're going to kill me!"

At the same time, it amused Alex whenever the newspapers referred to the Rothman clan as a "dynasty," as though they were of the same ilk as the Rothschilds, or the Hapsburgs, or the great Imperial families of China, when in fact it had all started as recently as 1910, in Newark, New Jersey, when Ho Rothman was an ill-educated immigrant lad of fourteen who could not even remember his original name.

The man who became Herbert Oscar Rothman had only the vaguest memories of his parents, who died when he was five years old. There was a woman who used to sing to him. Could that have been his mother? Perhaps. His most vivid childhood memory was of being carried away from a burning house, of flames filling all the windows and doorways and bursting through the rooftop with the sound of thunder and towering into the sky. Of course the flames could not have been that towering, for it could not have been that much of a house, but to a child's eye the flames seemed to vault for miles up into the night sky. He was told that this had happened on a Christmas Eve, when the Russian soldiers were given extra rations of vodka, and were encouraged to run loose in the Jewish quarter of wherever it was. He assumed that his parents perished together in that fire. Were there other children, brothers and sisters? He never knew. Was the house torched as part of a pogrom, or was it an isolated incident? He never knew that, either.

For the next year or so he was cared for by a couple who must have been relatives, for he was told that he could call them "Mother" and "Father." They lived in a village called Volnitskya, or at least that was the way it was pronounced— he never saw it spelled out—which no longer appears on any map of Poland, for apparently it disappeared during the Revolution. He could remember a muddy river, and a muddy road that ran down to it, where women did their washing and where he and other children launched sailboats made of leaves and twigs and swam naked in the summer. It was here that he first noticed that little girls had no little *putz*, but when he asked his new mother why, she slapped his face and sent him to bed without his supper. He remembered their little house, with walls of brick that seemed to have been fashioned from the same river mud, and that, in winter, he could reach out and touch the wall beside his bed, and that the wall was covered with a thin layer of ice. He remembered drawing frost-pictures on the icy walls.

He remembered the woman he was told to call Mother, though she was not his mother, sitting at a spinning wheel by candlelight. He remembered her telling stories of her ancestors, who were huge, fierce men who lived in the mountains and wrestled lions singlehanded, and of whom even the Cossack soldiers were terrified. "They bit the heads off live chickens, my people," she told him proudly. He remembered the dirt floor of the little house, and a rug in a pattern of bright flowers laid down carefully in the center of the floor. The woman he was told to call Mother was inordinately proud of this little rug. It had great value, he was given to understand. It was a rug worthy of the czars themselves, and the children—how many were there?—were not permitted to walk on it, but had to step carefully around it. His new mother always rolled this rug up and hid it under a mattress whenever a stranger knocked at the door. Other treasures were hidden under this lumpy mattress: a menorah, a silver teapot, six silver spoons, and a *chuppa* that was being saved for a daughter's wedding, but the rug was the most precious possession of them all. Ho Rothman used to dream of one day going back to Poland to search for the lost village of Volnitskya, where he would try to retrieve this special rug. Of course, he never did.

Sometimes, in the old days at "Rothmere," when he was in a mellow mood, Ho Rothman would sit after dinner with a brandy and a cigar, and recall his scattered memories of the Old Country.

He was called Itzhak in those days, and if the family used any special surname, he had forgotten what it was. But he remembered that it was as Itzhak that he was told, when he was eight years old, with much weeping, that the family had grown too large for the little house—there seemed to be a new baby born every year—and that he must be sent somewhere else to live. Where did the babies come from? he used to wonder. "From the river," his new mother would tell him. Periodically, it seemed, she would go down to the river and scoop out a new baby. He remembered asking her why, if there were too many babies, "too many mouths to feed," as she put it, she kept going down to the river to add to the oversupply. Later, he would wonder how, in that crowded household where everyone slept in the same room, and many to a bed, this pair ever found moments intimate enough in which to conceive a child. Perhaps, at night, when all the children were asleep, they slipped off to the riverbank and found a place to couple under the willow trees.

He was told that his new home was to be in London, where some distant cousins had agreed to take him in. Of the long trip across the face of Europe, which involved many changes of trains in crowded stations, crossing borders, and paying bribes to border guards at each, he remembered very little. He was too frightened of the unknown world that lay ahead to do more than show his ticket, which was pinned to his overcoat, and to be pointed in one direction or another. In his memory, there were soldiers everywhere, soldiers with machine guns pointed at the crowds, and everywhere there was talk of war—war, terrorism, riots, strikes, killings, bloodshed, and the "Black Hundreds," whose mission was solely to kill Jews. Somehow, though, he made it to Dieppe, where he crossed on a Channel ferry, and found his way to the cousins' flat in Whitechapel.

The cousins were named Belsky, and for the next two years he used the name Itzhak Belsky. The Belskys' neighborhood was almost entirely Yiddish-speaking, but it was in London that the future Ho Rothman learned to read and speak rudimentary English.

It was likely that he had already become a difficult, willful child, hard to manage or control. There were signs that this may have been the case. Certainly no one seemed to want to hold on to him for long. In just two years the Belskys told him, again, that there were too many mouths to feed, and that he must move on. Even more distant cousins had been found, he was told, in America, and his next home would be in a place the Belskys called Manhattan Island City. How these long-distance custody arrangements—which must have involved months of letter-writing back and forth across the Atlantic—were made, Ho Rothman never knew. But, trying to put the best face on things, the Belskys told him that in Manhattan Island City the streets were paved with gold. Practically all one had to do, they assured him, was reach down and pick up the gold that lay in the cracks of sidewalks; the riches were strewn about everywhere. "Soon you'll be wearing a red coat and a purple feather in your cap," he remembered Mrs. Belsky telling him. The Belskys were apparently kindly, generous folk. In addition to his steerage ticket from Southampton, they gave him a five-pound note, which seemed to him a huge fortune at the time. They also reminded him that, since he owned only one pair of shoes, he must take special care of those shoes because, when he got to America, he would have to go to work as a foot-peddler, as everyone else did at first, before the riches started to come in. As a result of this injunction, Ho Rothman crossed the Atlantic barefoot, with his only pair of shoes tied together by their laces and slung across his shoulders.

When he told this story to visitors at "Rothmere" years later, as he often did, he usually rose at this point in the rendition of it, and offered to show his guest the famous shoes. They would then mount the curved marble double staircase with its burgundy carpet and velvet-swagged handrails to the landing, where a bronze casting of Rodin's "Thinker" stood, and where the staircase branched again, and on up to the second floor of the house, where Ho and Lily had connecting apartments. Ho would then lead his visitor into his walnut-paneled dressing room, and begin opening the mirrored doors of closets. The closets displayed, on row after row of brass hanging bars and tier after tier of glass shelves, his collection of bespoke suits from Savile Row, his collection of overcoats, hats, gloves, and walking sticks, the soft piles of custom-made shirts from Jermyn Street, his socks, handkerchiefs, underwear, pajamas, and robes. He flung open door after door until he finally came to the shoe closet, where hundreds of pairs of gleaming shoes were displayed on trees in shiny brass racks. There he kept the shoes he came to America with. Ho's feet were small, size-fives, but in comparison those first shoes seemed tiny—more like a child's pair of black lace-up booties. His valet, he explained, polished these little shoes daily, just as he did every other pair.

His new parents, those exceedingly distant cousins, were named Sam and Sadye Rothman, and they lived in a third-floor walk-up at 45 Henry Street. The Rothmans were far from rich, but they were not exactly poor, either, though Sadye Rothman complained about what was happening to the neighborhood, which, she claimed, was "filling up with Chinamen." Chinamen lived on the floor above, and on the floor below. The food the Chinamen cooked gave the building its exotic, gingery odor. Still, the Rothmans were, as Sadye often pointed out, much better off than their neighbors, and their two-bedroom railroad flat with its huge cast-iron bathtub in the center of the kitchen and a semiprivate toilet down the hall, which they shared with only one other family, seemed absolutely spacious to the ten-year-old Ho. Also, the Rothmans had no children of their own, which meant that for the first time in his life the little boy had a room of his own, the room Sadye Rothman rather grandly called "the guest room." The reason for the Rothmans' relative prosperity was that Sadye Rothman was an independent businesswoman. Downstairs, on the ground floor of 45 Henry Street, she had a little store, where she sold candy, cigars and cigarettes, the Yiddish newspapers, and what she called "my special line," items of costume jewelry in a glass display case lighted with a small electric light. Ho used to study those rings and necklaces and bracelets, pasted with bits of colored glass, and suppose that these were emeralds and diamonds, rubies, sapphires, and pearls.

Sometimes Sadye's husband helped her in the store, when he was not upstairs studying the holy texts, scribbling petulant questions in the margins of the Talmud in his tiny, pointed European hand, busy, as his wife sneeringly put it, "arguing with God."

Sadye's other specialty was giving enemas, which she did with great proficiency and dispatch. Her word for enemas was "constitutionals," and she administered a constitutional for the slightest of reasons—a cough, the hiccups, a runny nose, or what she called "the mullygrubs," when anyone's facial expression didn't look to her quite right. She gave frequent enemas to her husband, to herself, and presently she was giving them to Ho. Ho often told of the threatening sight of Sadye Rothman looming around the corner with her enema bag in her hand.

The name Itzhak Belsky, the boy was told, was not a "good" name. It was not "American" enough. In America, his new guardian explained to him, there were good names and bad names, and Itzhak Belsky happened to be of the latter variety. The importance of a good name was that it helped you obtain something called "credit," and Sadye Rothman's lectures on the value of credit were his first lessons on how the American capitalist system worked. Credit was to free enterprise what enemas were to a healthy body. If you wanted to "make a name for yourself" in America, you had to establish credit, and this notion left Ho with the distinct impression that the phrase "making a name for yourself" meant that you could go by whatever name you chose—an idea that would stand him in good stead later on.

His new American name, it was decided, would be Herbert Oscar Rothman. Where the Herbert came from, Ho Rothman never knew, but he was fairly sure where Sadye had got the Oscar. Sadye considered herself vaguely "musical," and, on periodic trips uptown on Sundays on the streetcar, she was always careful to point out to her young charge the magnificent Harlem Opera House that the great theatrical impresario Oscar Hammerstein had built on 125th Street. He also learned that, thanks to the Rothmans' comparative affluence, he would not, after all, have to go to work as a foot-peddler, as other boys did. Instead, Herbert Oscar Rothman was enrolled at a school on Rivington Street, in the first grade, where he was several years older, though not much bigger, than most of his classmates.

As the boy entered his teens, he grew increasingly restless and impatient, increasingly independent-minded and difficult for Sam and Sadye to handle. Already he seemed determined to lead his life on a broader landscape than the narrow one defined by Rivington and Henry streets. He began refusing his enemas. Also, Sadye began noticing shortages in her cash box—nothing much, but ten cents one day, and a quarter the next—and Sadye began to have her suspicions. One day a zircon ring was missing from her little display case. Ho was supposed to come home directly after school, but he often tarried and found himself involved in other pleasures and pastimes. He was fourteen years old when a green-eyed, red-haired girl named Rachel winked at him and beckoned him to follow her into a shadowy alley that led between two

Rivington Street buildings. The alley took a right-hand turn, and ended in a cul-de-sac, and here, across a bed of barrel staves, lay someone's discarded mattress. Rachel tossed herself down on this, hiked up her skirts to reveal that she was wearing nothing underneath, and proceeded to instruct her neophyte lover, step by exciting step, on what must happen next, guiding him with experienced hands and covering his mouth with kisses as she did so. Unquestionably, he enjoyed this initial encounter, and soon there were almost daily afternoon sessions in the alley where the old mattress had been so obligingly tossed. Soon, also, Ho Rothman was rewarding Rachel for the pleasures she afforded him with candy bars and other items filched from Sadye Rothman's store.

Then, one afternoon in the early spring of 1910, Rachel greeted him with a smug and knowing expression on her face. "Guess what? I'm pregnant," she informed him. "What does that mean?" her bewildered lover, who still somewhat vaguely believed that babies were fetched out of a river, wanted to know. "It means there's gonna be a Blessed Event," she told him saucily, "and that you're the father of it. It means you're gonna have to marry me." "But I can't," he protested. "I've got to finish school." "You got to," she said. "There's no two ways. You gimme this Tiffany diamond ring, din'tcha? That means we're engaged, in case you didn't know it, greenhorn. If you don't marry me, then I'll tell your folks you got me in a family way," she said with a toss of her red hair. "Then they'll make you marry me 'cause I got the proof, and I know your folks are rich."

It was the young man's first lesson in the cold connivingness and duplicity of women, and one he never forgot. It never occurred to Ho Rothman that the scheming girl routinely offered her favors, and the convenience of her secret mattress, to dozens of other partners, and usually in return for more than purloined candy bars or zircon rings, or that she had chosen him to be her victim simply because of the supposedly elevated financial status of his foster parents. Thoroughly frightened, he promised to meet her at the usual place the following afternoon, to take her to City Hall, where she told him they would find a justice of the peace to marry them.

That very night, Sadye Rothman had decided to confront the boy about the missing ring. But she never got the chance.

That night, after waiting until Sadye had closed her store so he could empty her cash box, he ran away from home.

He never saw Sam and Sadye Rothman again, nor did he know what became of them. Nor did he know what became of the calculating girl called Rachel, or of his child by her—if indeed it was his child, or whether there was actually to be any child at all. Needless to say, the Rachel episode was not a part of Ho Rothman's usual repertoire of tales of his early days in New York, nor was how pivotal this episode would become included in the story of how he founded Rothman Communications, Inc.—the stories he liked to tell around the family dinner table while August, the butler, in white gloves, poured the claret into Cristofle goblets. But at times, after long evenings of gin rummy with his male cronies—Jake Auerbach, Adolph Meyerson, and the rest—he told the tale, omitting the cash box part, and it always produced roars of raucous laughter. "If wasn't for that *trayfeneh*, I not be here today!" he would shout, pounding on the card table with his fist, shuddering the brandy snifters. "If wasn't for that little piece of dreck, I never get to Newark!"

Oh, Rachel, Rachel, wherever you may be in one of life's dark alleyways of perfidy, if you read of yourself here, think how different it might have been for you if you had been able to play your hand just a bit more cleverly.

Chapter 11

Go West, young man! Of course those weren't Horace Greeley's exact words. What he actually said to Aspiring Young Men was, "Turn your face to the great west, and there build up a home and fortune." But young Ho Rothman had heard of Greeley's advice, and it was westward that he headed that night—west across the Hudson on the ferry to Newark, figuring, sensibly enough, that crossing a state line would place him handily out of Rachel's reach. He spent that first night on a bench in the ferry terminal, as what a later generation would call a homeless person, alternately sleeping and trying to figure out what to do next. His only experience, he decided, was in the jewelry business, and he guessed he might be able to pass himself off as having been previously employed by the Sadye Rothman Jewelry Store in Manhattan. In the morning he bought a newspaper, and studied the Help Wanted ads. He was in luck! A jewelry store on Passaic Avenue was advertising for a delivery boy.

He set off on foot through the unfamiliar city looking for the address. He never found it. Instead, he found himself turning a corner and facing a line of rough and angry-looking men carrying placards on long sticks that announced "TIMES-UNION UNFAIR TO LABOR!" The men eyed him menacingly, and as he tried to dart through their line they began swinging at him with their placards, and shouting, "Scab! Scab! Scab!" To escape them, Ho pushed himself

through a swinging door, where an older man immediately
seized him by the collar and said, "Get in here! Those guys
could kill you for crossing their line! What can you do? Can
you set type trays?"

"Delivery—" Ho began. "Jewelry. Sadye Rothman—"

"Okay, we can use you in the mail room," the man said.
"But remember, you'll have to sleep here at the plant till
those guys either give up and go home, or decide to come
back to work. Five bucks a week."

And so that was how H. O. Rothman got his start in the
newspaper business, as a strikebreaker for the old *Newark
Times-Union*.

The mail room! It was absolutely the most auspicious place
for a bright young man to start in any business. Where else
but in the mail room did such famous hosts and bon vivants
as Lenny Liebling, the frequent dinner guest of U.S. presidents, get their start? And what better time to get started than
during a strike, when the typesetters' union had walked out,
and management was pitching in to keep the paper running?
In no time at all, Ho learned who all the important people in
the organization were, what each one did, who counted for
more and who counted for less, and who told whom what to
do. As a strikebreaker, he was working shoulder to shoulder
with executives and editors and reporters whom, under ordinary circumstances, it would have taken him months to meet.
He had also found himself a place to sleep, even though it
was across bales of newsprint on the mail-room floor.

The work was hard, and the hours were long, but within
two weeks' time—which was how long the strike lasted,
before the typesetters grumblingly returned to work, with
none of their demands met—young Ho Rothman knew, or
thought he knew, all there was to know about the *Times-
Union*'s operations. After all, the smart mail-room messenger
also got to read all the mail, all the interoffice memos and
even the letters marked "CONFIDENTIAL." The confidential correspondence made particularly interesting reading, and
Ho had not been at the paper for more than six months before
he felt he had a clear grasp of the publication's considerable
strengths, and its even more considerable weaknesses.

It was at the *Times-Union*, too, that he first acquired the
nickname "Ho" that was to stick with him for a lifetime. He
had been given a name badge with "H. O. Rothman" printed

on it, and, as he scurried about the newspaper offices on his daily rounds, he found himself being greeted with calls of "Ho, ho, ho—here comes Ho!" He took this teasing in good spirit because he knew he was an excellent messenger. At the same time, he had assumed for himself certain perquisites. During the strike, when they had all been pulling together in the face of the union's demands, and when all the nonstriking employees had been pitching in to do whatever they could to get the paper off the presses every day, there was a spirit of relaxed camaraderie, and everyone got to know everybody else on a first-name basis. Even the newspaper's owner and publisher, James Meister III, who had always been "Mr. Meister" or "J.M." to his staff, became, for the duration of the strike, "Jim." Once the strike was over, most employees resumed the more formal style of address for the scion of one of Newark's oldest and wealthiest families. But to Ho this seemed both awkward and unnecessary. And so now, when the mighty James Meister III encountered Ho Rothman in a corridor, and greeted him with a cheerful "Hi-ho, Ho!," Ho Rothman returned the greeting with an equally jaunty "Hi-ho, Jim!"

Of course some of the senior employees were somewhat taken aback by such temerity on the part of the company's most junior employee. But there was nothing they could do about it, and James Meister III didn't seem to mind, and even seemed mildly amused by such forwardness. Besides, Ho Rothman was known as the spunky lad who had dared to cross the picket line.

The *Times-Union*'s greatest strength, Ho had decided, was its gleaming new physical plant, where all the most modern—for those times—linotype and printing equipment had been installed. James Meister III had modeled his printing plant on Mr. Henry Ford's assembly-line innovations in Detroit, and the *Times-Union* was able to turn out newspapers, from final-edited copy to newsprint, faster than any paper in the East. But this great strength had caused, ironically, the paper's greatest weakness. To finance all these improvements in the printing process, Mr. Meister seemed to have seriously overextended himself. Remember that 1910 was a year of severe economic recession. Wall Street had suffered one of its periodic "Panics," and advertisers had cut back their schedules. At the *Times-Union*, the costly strike had not helped matters at all. A number of bankers, young Ho learned from some of the confidential letters and memos, were already beginning to call in, or demand more collateral for, funds that had been borrowed by Mr. Meister.

As his months of employment wore on, Ho realized that the *Newark Times-Union* was sinking into deeper and deeper financial trouble. The bankers, and their law firms, were writing increasingly sternly worded letters. What, they demanded to know, did Mr. Meister intend to do about his continued indebtedness? When might the bank expect an interest payment on notes he had signed? Mr. Meister, who was now spending more and more time on mysterious missions outside the office, seemed to have no ready answer. The messenger boy could not help but notice the stack of unanswered telephone messages that was mounting on the publisher's desk. When he encountered his boss in the corridors now, the expression on Jim Meister's handsome face was grim and preoccupied.

Ho Rothman felt sorry for his friend and his predicament. And, Ho happened to know, Meister's state of mind was not being improved by the state of his romantic life, which appeared to be in some real disarray. A woman named Eloise had been writing him angry and importunate letters. Ho knew that this Eloise should not be writing to him at his office, and he also knew from hard-earned experience the amount of trouble that a woman was capable of causing. "I know you've been seeing that blonde floozy again," Eloise had written, "and I know that she's nothing but a chorine from Mr. Ziegfeld's *Follies*. Really, Jimmy, I thought you had better *taste!* How would you like it if I slapped a breach of promise suit on you? Daddy says I could, and Daddy says if *I* don't *he* will! And if you continue to refuse to answer my letters, and don't return my telephone calls, I'm going to march right down to that office of yours and make a scene the likes of which you won't soon forget! Daddy says . . ."

Ho Rothman had developed an intense disliking of this Eloise, and her daddy.

The other great weakness of the newspaper, in Ho's opinion, had to do with its content. Out of budgetary considerations, no doubt, the paper had made it a policy to report primarily local news and, in those days, Newark was far from the exciting, vibrant city that it is today. Today, Newark boasts one of the highest crime rates of any city in the world, and scarcely a day goes by without a murder, or a drug bust, or a prostitution ring exposed that will make for an attention-grabbing headline. But in 1910 and 1911, Newark was a sleepy little place where very little of interest happened. The news of Newark, as reported by the *Times-Union*, reflected the town's uncompromising dullness. A shoplifter apprehended at the lingerie counter at Bamberger's might make a feature story. The fire department called in to rescue a cat out of a tree could easily make the front page. Church potluck suppers filled the society pages. A photograph of the mayor of Newark, headed "Ouch! That hurts!" might reveal in the accompanying story that the mayor had recently visited his dentist.

News of the big city across the Hudson was left to the Manhattan dailies to report. The *Times-Union* had no foreign bureaus, and any news of international import was lifted from other newspapers and reported in the *Times-Union* a day later. Subscriptions to the various wire services had been dropped, and even the syndicated comic strips had been abandoned, and a single strip called "Beanie," drawn by a local artist, had been substituted for the funnies page. (The local artist turned out to be an eighteen-year-old nephew of James Meister III.) The astrology column was written—which was to say made up—by James Meister's secretary. Roughly once a month, a *Times-Union* reporter took the train down to Trenton, to see what the state legislature might be up to, but nothing much of interest seemed to happen in the capital, either. Probably the best-read feature was the advice-to-the-lovelorn column. Readership of the paper had been declining for several years before Ho joined the staff, and as readership declined so did advertising revenues. In fact, the entire enterprise seemed to be in an inexorable spiral of decline.

At night, in the tiny boardinghouse cell that Ho had been able to rent for a dollar a week, with kitchen privileges, the young messenger boy used to compose imaginary banner headlines describing fictitious events—schoolchildren disemboweled by rabid dogs, headless torsos fished out of the Passaic River, earthquakes, tidal waves, shipwrecks off Sandy Hook—that might make the readers of the *Times-Union* sit up and take notice, that might lift Newarkers out of their increasing torpor, that might make them snatch papers from the newsstands.

The first really disturbing news to reach the paper's staff appeared in a general memorandum in early June of 1911— a memorandum which, of course, Ho Rothman was among the very first to read. It was going to be necessary, the publisher announced, to "trim" the staff somewhat. Ho read this with a sinking feeling because, as one of the paper's newest employees, he was certain that he would be among the very first to be let go. But when the actual trimmings were made official, and the names of those dismissed were posted on the bulletin board, his name was not among them. The trimming, in fact, seemed to be from the top, with the senior, best-seasoned, and highest-paid staff members being the first to go. From now on, this bulletin explained, certain duties at the paper would be "telescoped." The woman who wrote the popular advice-to-the-lovelorn column would also cover society news, write the pet-health column, and cover the daily police blotter. The sports editor would additionally cover cultural events, edit the business page, handle obituaries, and prepare the church calendar. James Meister's secretary would write the "You and Your Doctor" column in addition to the horoscopes. And so on. But a messenger, it seemed, would always be a messenger.

The next blow fell nearly six months later, in December. In another memorandum, the publisher announced that "due to certain bookkeeping problems," employees' paychecks would be delayed "for a few days." One can well imagine how an already demoralized staff reacted to the news that, within weeks of Christmas, their salaries had been placed in a state of suspension. The editorial caliber of the newspaper grew palpably more flaccid and careless during the anxious days that followed. The "few days" turned into two weeks, but then, to everyone's profound relief, the payroll was somehow met. A line formed at the bank as *Times-Union* employees rushed out to turn their paychecks into hard cash.

But the worst news of all came a month later, on January 23, 1912. Ho would always remember that date, and he would always remember his horoscope in that morning's paper, not that he took much stock in such things: "Opportunity knocks for you today. Tell others what you think, and you will be rewarded." That morning, a heavy brown manila envelope was hand-delivered to the mail room by a messenger from City Hall. Naturally, the mail-room boy was the first to learn its contents. The envelope was sealed, but as Ho entered the publisher's empty office—his office was nearly always empty now—the brown envelope itself looked so official and forbidding that Ho decided to moisten its flap and open it.

Inside was a notification from the City of Newark's Department of Taxation and Finance. Though the document was filled with elaborate "whereases" and "henceforwards" and "heretofores," its message was clear. Unless grievously delinquent property taxes, owed to the City of Newark by the Times-Union Company, were paid within ten business days, the *Times-Union*'s properties would be put up for sale at a public sealed-bid auction "to satisfy the city."

That afternoon, Ho Rothman had a telephone call from James Meister's secretary. "J.M. would like two black coffees and one regular coffee, and three sweet rolls for a meeting in his office," she said.

Ho scurried out, without even putting on his coat against the icy winter weather, to the delicatessen around the corner, sensing that a real crisis was at hand. He placed the order, and then, on an impulse, decided to buy something extra for his friend, which he paid for with his own money.

When he returned to the publisher's office, he found James Meister seated behind his desk facing two other stern-looking men in business suits who were seated opposite him. Ho immediately noticed how tired and drawn Jim Meister looked—his eyes bloodshot, his jaw slack— and Ho wondered briefly whether Jim had been drinking. He distributed the coffee and sweet rolls to the three men. Then he said, "I brought something special for you, Jim."

"Oh? What is it?"

He handed the paper container to his boss. "It's an egg cream," he said.

Jim Meister lifted the lid of the container, and sniffed. "Hmm. An egg cream," he said. "What's in it? Eggs and cream, I suppose."

"No eggs, and no cream. But an egg cream is what it's called."

"What's it taste like?" He took a sip. "Hmm. It tastes like—well, it doesn't taste like much of anything, does it. Kind of fizzy."

"We Jews say that egg creams are good for the soul."

He smiled a thin smile. "Good for the soul," he repeated. "Well, in a way that's rather appropriate, considering the business at hand. Ho, these gentlemen are my attorneys, and we are in the cheery process of preparing my last will and testament."

The two men rose a little stiffly and uncomfortably, and shook Ho's hand.

"Ho," Jim Meister said, "to whom would you bequeath an estate that is totally bankrupt? To whom would you leave an estate that is way over the Plimsoll line with debt? Not to your worst enemy, I suppose. And yet, if I am going to declare bankruptcy, it is apparently advisable that I prepare a last will and testament and leave all my bad debts to some-body, or so these boys tell me. Whom would you leave it all to, Ho?"

Ho shook his head. He didn't know.

"And yet a man must have a last will and testament," he said. "I have no wife. I have no children. I have only a few nieces and nephews, who are already quite rich, and who would hardly be overjoyed at inheriting my IOUs." He passed his hand across his face. "What if I were to leave it to you, Ho? What if I left all my debts to you? Would you accept them?"

"Yes."

He was smiling the same thin smile. "No," he said. "I was only making a joke, and not a very funny one at that. No, Ho, I wouldn't do a thing like that to you." He took another sip of his egg cream, and made a face. "Egg cream," he said.

"There's things I could do with the paper, Jim."

"Things? What things?"

"Things. Lots of things."

Meister was smiling again. Then he said, "Well, gentle-men, why not? What's there to lose? Let's leave my entire, worthless estate to Ho Rothman here."

There was a silence. Then, clearing his throat, one of the lawyers said, "Surely you're not serious, James."

"Oh, but I surely am. Quite serious. Absolutely serious. Deadly serious. That's supposed to be a joke too, considering

the fact that we're drawing up my last will and testament."
He laughed harshly.

"James, once we get this bankruptcy matter out of the way,
you'll be able to get this company back on its feet in no time."

"Will I? I wonder," he said.

"Of course you will. You're a young man, in your prime,
James."

"I wonder," he said again. "But, for the time being, let's
leave everything to Ho."

"James, your will is merely a technicality. But it is a technicality that should not be undertaken frivolously. This is a
serious matter, James."

"But I *am* serious."

"James, we cannot permit you to make this young and—
excuse me, Rothman—ignorant young boy your heir."

"But it's *my will*, isn't it?" he almost shouted.

"Of course, James, but—"

"And—ignorant? I'm not so sure." His eyes were fixed
hard on Ho now. "I see something in this young boy's face
that I used to see in my own face when I looked in the mirror
when I was his age. Courage, and intelligence, and determination, and—things. Other things. Or things I used to think
I saw in my own face. Or maybe just things I wanted to see,
and perhaps they weren't really there, after all—who knows?
Ho—are you sure you want to inherit this can of worms?"

"James, we—"

"Shut up! Let him answer!"

"Yes," Ho said.

Jim Meister pressed his palms on his desktop. "Very well,
gentlemen," he said. "That's the way I want my will to read.
'I bequeath my entire estate to Ho Rothman, who crossed the
picket line.' No—wait. Change that wording to read 'To Ho
Rothman, who bought me an egg cream.' "

And that was the way the will was written, and witnessed
by the lawyers, that afternoon.

That night, James Meister III, the grandson of the paper's
founder whose bronze bust loomed imperially over the
entrance lobby above the legend "Through truth and integrity, there is light"—words the senior Meister certainly never
uttered—locked himself in the library of his great graystone
mansion in East Orange, the house in which he had been born
forty-two years earlier, and put a bullet through his head.

*   *   *

As the sole heir to the debt-ravaged Meister estate, there were two things Ho knew he must do. He must put the East Orange mansion up for sale; but the house itself was heavily mortgaged, and Ho was certain that a house of that size would not sell quickly for anything close to what the property was worth. More pressing was the problem of saving the newspaper from being sold at public auction for back taxes in ten days' time. How he accomplished this became one of his favorites of the stories he liked to tell around the family dinner table at "Rothmere."

What he did was this. On the first morning of his inheritance he marched down the street to Newark's City Hall and submitted his sealed bid for the Times-Union Company properties. His bid was for ten thousand dollars. Later he would say that he was certain he had no chance of winning the company with a bid that low. But somewhere, in the back of Ho's mind, there must have been a hunch that he might win it. And win it he did. He received a notification in the mail that the *Times-Union* was his, the plant and the adjacent office building. He was given the usual "ten business days" to come up with the cash in the form of a certified check. Otherwise, the property would go to the next-highest bidder.

But—ten thousand dollars! He had worked for the paper for a little less than two years, and had saved less than two hundred dollars. For doing odd jobs around her house and yard, his landlady had reduced his rent to fifty cents a week, and that had helped. But still, two hundred dollars was a far cry from ten thousand. How, in ten days, could he possibly come up with the difference?

The answer was simple. He stole it. He robbed banks.

At this point in his story, he always paused for dramatic effect, and his audience, no matter how many times they had heard it before, was expected to gasp. "I was not Bonnie Clyde," he would say with a chuckle. "But was close!" He had had one experience with a bank, it seemed, that impressed him. At a bank teller's window, a few months earlier, he had asked to have a twenty-dollar bill changed into smaller denominations. With wide-eyed amazement, he had watched as the careless girl placed the twenty-dollar bill on the counter in front of her, counted out twenty singles on top of it, and then pushed the entire sum across the counter to him. He had walked into that bank with twenty dollars, and walked out with forty—doubled his money! Banks, he had learned, could make mistakes.

At first, he thought he would try this bill-changing technique again, using increasingly larger bills. But, after a few tries, and finding tellers more attentive than the one who had given him his twenty-dollar bonus, he gave up on this, and decided on another tactic.

Sadye Rothman had always stressed the importance of establishing credit. Credit, she said, meant—first of all—having a bank account. And so Ho Rothman, with his two hundred dollars, went to a Newark bank and opened a checking account. With his fresh book of checks in his pocket, he hopped on the ferry for Manhattan—crossing state lines, he figured, might make the mechanics of his scheme a bit less easy to detect, and he was right—where, in a New York bank, he wrote out a check on the Newark bank for two hundred dollars, and opened a second checking account, with a new book of checks. Now, as far as the two banks were concerned, he had four hundred dollars—double his money—at least until his checks were processed by the central clearinghouse, which, in those days, could take as much as a week.

Next, it was back to the first bank, where he cashed out his first account, then back to the second bank to cash out the second. Back and forth he went, always using different banks and, of course, different names and addresses because, in America, it didn't really matter what name you used, and there were no such things as Social Security numbers. In a little notebook, he jotted down the names he was using, and the names of the different banks, as back and forth across the river he went, doubling his money with each trip. Four hundred became eight hundred, eight hundred became sixteen hundred, sixteen hundred became thirty-two hundred . . .

"Was not Ponzi scheme," Ho Rothman would crow when he told this story. "Was Rothman scheme!"

Of course in this age of computers a Rothman scheme would probably not work so smoothly, even if it could be made to work at all, but those were older, more naïve and trusting, forgotten times. And, using the Rothman scheme, it took less than half a dozen ferry crossings of ten minutes' duration each before Ho Rothman had his certified check for ten thousand dollars and a few hundred dollars in cash to spare.

When he told of all this, as he often did, Ho was always careful to add that, when he became rich, he used his little notebook to write to all the banks he had defrauded that week, giving the names he had used to defraud them, and offering to repay them all, with full interest. To be sure, some of his dinner guests looked a little skeptical when he came to the paying-the-banks-back part of his story. But no one ever dared suggest that he was not telling the truth. "What a wonderful story, Ho," they would say.

"Was better than Bonnie Clyde, eh? No guns!"

By the time he became the legal owner of the *Newark Times-Union*, the paper had been shut down. Still, it must have been quite a moment when Ho walked down Bergen Street to look at his new property—a defunct newspaper, an empty office building, and a silent printing press. He must have wondered what to do next. "I was scaredest boy in Jersey!" he would tell his listeners. He was not quite seventeen years old.

And now, in the vast floor-through apartment at 720 Park Avenue, the ninety-four-year-old Ho Rothman lay quietly in his narrow hospital bed. His eyes were closed, and his breathing was gentle, but regular. Periodically, using her big watch, his private-duty nurse—today's eight-to-four was named Agnes O'Sullivan—checked his pulse. She did so in a desultory way, indifferently. It was always the same. Now she was sitting in Ho's old Barca-Lounger, with her knitting. She was knitting a sweater for her niece, the nun in Florida. Knit one, purl two, knit one, purl two. It was a black sweater. Agnes O'Sullivan hated black, but her niece's order banned bright colors. A yellow would have been pretty, but this sweater wasn't going to be pretty. It wasn't supposed to be. Simultaneously, as she knitted, she was reading a copy of the *Reader's Digest*, an article on how to test yourself for frigidity, and as she knitted and read, the television set was also going. "The Gong Show" was on.

In the gilt drawing room, Ho's wife, Aunt Lily, had just fixed her first martini. She needed a little something at this time of the day to dispel "that little sinking feeling" she experienced in midmorning, and besides, Lenny Liebling was coming by in half an hour or so, and there was important business to discuss. Already, after the first sip of the martini, she was feeling a good deal better.

In the kitchen, the butler was polishing the silver, which, even though it was rarely used these days, Aunt Lily insisted be polished daily. Farther down the hall, the cook was taking a nap. It was too early to think about fixing Mr. Rothman's luncheon tray. Except in the room where the television was going, the house was quiet. This apartment, like "Rothmere," was full of memories—parties, dinner dances, weddings, deaths—and these memories were all in Aunt Lily's head and, perhaps, in Ho Rothman's dreaming.

Agnes O'Sullivan was bored now with her knitting, bored with her *Reader's Digest* story, even bored with "The Gong Show." Hers was the most boring job in the world, she often thought, just highly paid baby-sitting, sitting with an old man who should by rights be dead by now, but wasn't.

"It's an adv Alz case," her rep at the agency had told her that morning before giving her the assignment. Adv Alz was nursing shorthand for advanced Alzheimer's. "And the file's marked 'Difficult.' "

"What's difficult about him?" Agnes O'Sullivan had wanted to know.

"Well, they're R.P.A.J.s," her rep had told her.

Agnes O'Sullivan hadn't known the meaning of this term.

"Rich Park Avenue Jews, and you know what that means. Just slap him with a Xanax if he gets obstrep."

She put down her magazine now, and got to her feet. She probably ought to crank the old man's bed up now. The doctor's instructions had said that it was better for his circulation if he spent a certain amount of time in an upright position. But she didn't feel like cranking up his bed. That seemed too much like work, and what did they expect for a hundred and twenty dollars a day, fifteen percent to the agency? Instead, she began moving around the room, quietly opening and closing dresser drawers. Shirts, socks, handkerchiefs, underwear, the usual stuff. In one drawer she found what appeared to be his jewelry case, and she opened this. In it she saw, among more ordinary pieces, a pair of diamond and sapphire cuff links, and a matching set of studs. She tucked these quickly in the breast pocket of her starched white uniform.

"*Stop, thief!*"

Ho Rothman was sitting straight up in his bed now, his eyes wide open, pointing at her with one scrawny finger. "Stop, thief!" he screamed again. "Put those back! Lily! Lily! Pipple is robbing from us! *Lily!* Come quick! Get this *treyfeneh* out of here!"

Chapter 12

Every magazine has what is called its "lead time," which is to say the time between when the contents of a particular issue are decided upon, and story assignments are handed out, and the actual date of publication. Weekly magazines naturally have very short lead times, and often the final contents of a weekly are not determined until within hours of publication. The editor of a news weekly, for example, may have as many as three or four cover stories set in type and ready to print before deciding, at the last minute, which one to use.

The editor of a monthly magazine like *Mode* enjoyed a much more relaxed and leisurely lead time. In fact, Alex Rothman liked to begin planning each issue of her magazine, in a general sort of way, at least six months in advance. And so, over the years, the twice-monthly meetings with her editorial staff had evolved into a certain pattern. The first meeting to discuss an upcoming issue was called a "What-If" meeting. In format, the "What-If" meetings were loosely based on the custom of "brainstorming" that had enjoyed a certain vogue in businesses in the 1960s. At brainstorming meetings, all sorts of wild and woolly ideas were tossed onto the table, on the theory that somebody's hare-brained notion might spark someone else's brilliant idea. That, at least, was the theory. In practice, it rarely worked out that way, and Alex Rothman considered brainstorming a waste of time and talent, since the crazy ideas nearly always outnumbered the useful ones. And so Alex's "What-If" meetings always started out with what she called "a track," or theme. If the theme of the issue was to be, say, Paris, then Paris would immediately become the focus of the meeting. ("What if we put the Eiffel Tower on the cover?" someone might say. Audible groans from around the conference room.)

Then, two weeks after the "What-If" meeting, when the proposals brought forth at the meeting had been sorted out, explored, and at least partway developed, there was what was called a "Let's-Go" meeting, when the general shape and format of the issue would be roughed out, and the preliminary table of contents would be drawn up, with editors assigned to specific projects, to which the Production moles would give job numbers.

This morning's meeting was to be a "What-If" meeting for the January issue of the coming year.

Meanwhile, Alex had already spent a busy morning. Coleman, as usual, brought the morning papers in to her with her breakfast tray, and she had scanned them. The freakish boating accident on the river last night had made the front page of the *Times* but, she was pleased to see, her father-in-law's announcement at the party had been relegated to a small item in the Advertising column of the Business section.

In a surprise move Thursday, *Mode* publisher Herbert J. Rothman announced that Alexandra Rothman, 46, will be joined at the top of *Mode*'s editorial masthead by the relatively unknown Ms. Fiona Fenton, 28, a London fashion figure. Mr. Rothman left the impression that Ms. Rothman, who has been editor-in-chief of the fashion publication since 1973, will be relieved of some of her editorial responsibilities, possibly in preparation for her retirement. Ms. Rothman could not be reached for comment, and Ms. Fenton did not return messages left on her answering machine.

Ms. Rothman is Mr. Rothman's daughter-in-law, the widow of Mr. Rothman's son, Steven. . . .

"Joel isn't up yet, Alex," Coleman said. "Should I wake him?"

"No, let him sleep, darlin'," she said, sipping her coffee. "He had to get up early enough at that school of his. Let him catch up on his sleep."

Mona Potter's column in the *News*, "The Fashion Scene by Mona," was predictably more fulsome and chatty.

> Well, ya coulda knocked over Mother Mona with a feather, kiddies, when *Mode*'s Big Boss, handsome Herb Rothman, took to the microphone at Alexandra Rothman's fashionable East Side digs, and told a slew of fashion VIPs that the venerable editor will now share the top rung of *Mode*'s ladder with petite and glamorous Lady Fiona Hesketh-Fenton, the London fashion biggie. Though teensy in size, Fiona has big fashion clout in Merrie Olde Englande, Mother's informants tell her.
>
> What's up? Is Ageless Alex being e-e-e-eased out of *Mode*? That's Mother Mona's best guess, 'cause they say Handsome Herb's been scouting for younger blood, and Old Man Ho Rothman, who's 90-something, is now too sick to call the shots. So make way for Herb, kiddies. And if you've been reading Mother as you oughta, kiddies, you knew that Herb and Alex never really got along all these long, long years while Old Man Ho let her do whatever diddlysquat she wanted.
>
> And—buzz, buzz, buzz—they say that Handsome Herb literally foamed at the mouth when he saw Alex's oh-so-naughty June cover. Alex's cute sidekick, Gregory Kittredge, confirmed all this to Mother. . . .

Reading this, Alex was certain that Gregory had done no such thing.

> . . . Meanwhile, the reason for the bash at Alex's digs was that *Mode* has just made some big circulation breakthrough. Don't ask Mother Mona what the figures are. If you know Mother, she's a dummy at numbers— and too busy keeping track of the scuttlebutt on the Fashion Scene for her kiddies! The party featured fireworks, which caused a boat to sink, and a coupla people drowned, don't ask me how. Kinda put a "damper" on the party, huh? Oh, well, say la vee!
>
> Stay tuned for more developments at *Mode*. Ta-ta.

COMING SOON: AN "EXCLUSIVE" INTERVIEW
WITH LADY FIONA HESKETH-FENTON

Alex Rothman tossed the newspaper aside with disgust. She should never have invited Mona to the party. On the other hand, if Mona hadn't been invited she would have written something even worse.

Now she picked up the telephone beside her bed, and called her lawyer, Henry Coker; she made an appointment with him for the following morning. Then she placed a call to her friend Mark Rinsky.

She and Mark were telephone friends, since they had never actually met. Mark ran a private investigative agency, and Alex had used his services over the years—mostly to do background checks on models she was considering using in the magazine, and whose résumés sounded questionable. It had all started with a memorable cover girl in 1982 who, it turned out, had a second career as an Eighth Avenue hooker, and had a criminal record. The supermarket tabloids had had a field day with that one:

MODE COVER GIRL CHARGES $100 A THROW,
$1,000 FOR ALL NIGHT!

After that episode, Alex had been much more careful.

"Mark," she said now, "her name is Fiona Fenton. She's English, and she also calls herself Lady Fiona Hesketh-Fenton. I'd like you to find out everything you can about her, as well as about this magazine she claims to have worked for, called *Lady Fair*."

"Yes, I was just reading about her," he said.

"Oh. Then you saw the item in the *Times*."

"No, I saw it in Mona's column," he said.

"Mark," she said, "do you mean to say that private detectives read Mona's column? Big, macho private eyes read *her?*"

He chuckled. "It's kinda like junk food," he said. "You get addicted. And I'm not a big, macho private eye. I'm a nebbishy little Jewish guy from the Bronx."

"Another illusion shattered," she said. "Well, see what you can find out about Her Ladyship."

Smiling contentedly, feeling that she was once more on

top of the situation, she set her breakfast tray aside and rose
to bathe and dress for the office.

On her way out of the apartment, she peeked briefly into
Joel's room. He lay sprawled across the bed, sleeping sound-
ly, covered only by the top sheet, and for a moment she
was tempted to step inside and kiss the top of his tousled
blond head, but she decided not to disturb him and continued
toward the elevator.

In the elevator foyer, Otto sat, stiffly, in one of the straight-
backed Chippendale chairs that flanked the elevator door,
waiting for Joel.

"Oh, Otto," she said. "I've been meaning to speak to you.
After this weekend, we won't be needing you anymore."

Otto sprang to his feet. "It's because of last night, isn't it?
It's because of what happened last night!"

"No, it has nothing to do with last night. It's just—"

"They tricked me!" he said. "Him and she, they both
tricked me!"

"I really don't know what you're talking about, Otto,
but—"

"It was her—that woman. She said there was a man on the
roof, but there wasn't no man on the roof!"

"I'm sorry, Otto, it has nothing to do with you. You've
done a wonderful job, and I'm prepared to—"

"I went up to the roof! There was no man! It was a
lie!"

"—prepared to give you excellent references. It's just that I
feel Joel doesn't need you any longer. And he really doesn't.
And I think you know that too, Otto." With her finger, she
pressed the button to call the elevator.

He looked at her narrowly. "Does Mr. Herbert J. Rothman
know about this?" he asked.

"This is my decision, Otto."

"I was hired by Mr. Herbert J. Rothman," he said. "Only
Mr. Herbert J. Rothman can fire me. Not you! I ain't takin'
no orders from no woman!"

She stared at him coolly. "Your arrangements with Herbert
Rothman are between you and him," she said. "If he wishes
to employ you in some other capacity, that will be up to
him. But meanwhile Joel is my son, and this is my house.
In fact, I would like you to be out of here before I get home
tonight."

"It's because of what happened last night. Well, you won't get away with this!"

"We'll see," she said.

The elevator door slid open.

"Frank," she said to the elevator operator, "please be of any assistance you can to Mr.—" and for a moment she could not for the life of her think of Otto's last name—"to Mr. Otto, and help him gather whatever belongings he has here and see that he is out of here by five o'clock tonight."

"Yes, ma'am."

She stepped into the car, the door closed, and the car began its descent.

There was a loud thud from above, as Otto apparently kicked at the door.

"He'd better not have left a mark on my mahogany door," Frank said. "Them's solid mahogany, solid Philippine mahogany, all these doors. Germans. I was in the war, ma'am, and they're all alike, those Germans. Except maybe Mr. Kissinger. I brought Mr. Kissinger and his wife up to your party last night, and he struck me as a gentleman, not like the others. But don't worry, ma'am. I'll see that that one is out of here by five P.M., ma'am."

"If he gives you any trouble, call Security."

"And that thing in this morning's paper, ma'am, does that mean you'll be retiring from the magazine, like Miss Mona said?"

"No."

"It's a wonderful thing, retirement. Sure wish I could do it. Fort Myers, Florida, is where I'd go. That's God's country, Fort Myers, Florida. Needlefishing. Well, here we are, ma'am. Now you have a nice day, you hear?"

"Thank you, Frank." And Alex Rothman stepped out of the elevator into the glory and brilliance of a whole new day.

Immediately, she noticed that the company limousine, which always waited for her at the curb, was not there.

Charlie, the doorman, looked anxious. "Your car didn't show up today, Mrs. Rothman," he said.

"That's all right, Charlie. I'll take a taxi," she said, and he stepped into the street with his whistle.

She had decided to treat this day like any other. There was no other way to treat it. She was certain that her staff would be full of nervous questions but, since she didn't have the answers to any of them, she decided not to address them. She would go through this day—and yes, thank God, it was a Friday—as though precisely nothing at all had happened. It would take some doing, it would take some stagecraft, but she knew she could pull it off. "Walk tall, Lexy," her friend Lucille Withers had told her when she was training her to model clothes on the runway. "Walk tall, think tall and straight. Remember the chin line. Chin up, toes pointed slightly outward when you walk. No, don't wiggle your ass as though you had a fifty-cent piece pressed between your cheeks—it's *not* sexy, Lexy. Just remember that the shoulders and the hips should be on the same plane, like a skier's. Think of yourself as a skier. Take slightly longer steps. Pleasant expression on your face, not a big smile. This is *acting*, honey, and the clothes you're wearing are your lines. . . . *There*, that's *better*. . . . In that black dress, you're not a woman now. You're a panther stalking its prey. . . ."

She was wearing a black silk suit by Ungaro today, this panther.

She also knew that Herb Rothman would be expecting a call from her, demanding an explanation, or clarification, of what he was trying to do. Well, if that was what he was expecting, she was not going to give him the satisfaction of having his expectations fulfilled. If he wanted a confrontation scene, he would have to set the stage himself and write the script—for the time being, at least. He had said that Fiona would join the staff on the first of July, and that left some time for plans to be made and strategies laid. In the meantime, she would treat this day, and the next, and the next, and the next, exactly like any other. It was called playing it cool.

From the moment she stepped off the elevator on the fourteenth floor—from the receptionist onward through the long corridor of offices—the tension in the air was palpable. Everyone here, of course, had read Mona Potter's column. The responses to Alex's customary, cheery "Good morning" were lowered eyelids and nervous smiles. *Click, click, click* went the sounds of the heels of Alex's Susan Bennis pumps on the vinyl tile as she made her way down the corridor toward her office, chin up.

The greeting smile of Gregory Kittredge, her assistant, was also nervous. "Good morning, Gregory!" she said brightly.

There was a stack of pink telephone-message slips on her desk, taller than usual. She flipped through them. The *New York Times* had called. *Women's Wear* had called. The *Washington Post* had called.

"Most of those calls are from Mr. Rodney McCulloch," Gregory said. "He's been calling every ten minutes since before nine o'clock, leaving a different number where he could be reached every time." He consulted his watch. "Right now, we should be able to reach him at five-five-five-oh-two-oh-two, until ten fifteen. Want me to get him for you? He says it's extremely urgent."

"No, no," she said with a wave of her hand. "I don't have time to talk to Mr. McCulloch now."

Gregory's dark eyes widened. "You don't have time to talk to Rodney *McCulloch?* Do you know who he *is*, Alex?"

"Of course I know who Rodney McCulloch is. I just don't have time to talk to him right now. I wouldn't have time to talk to the Queen of England if she were calling," she added, remembering Lulu's line.

Gregory looked crestfallen, and Alex suspected she had hurt his feelings. "It's just that we have a planning meeting at ten thirty, remember?" she said. "I want to prepare for that, Gregory."

"Alex—" he began.

"Yes?"

"I hope you don't think I said anything to Mona Potter last night. In spite of what she wrote in her column. She kept pumping me, but I told her absolutely nothing. You believe me, don't you?"

"Of course I believe you," she said. "Everybody knows that if Mona can't get a quote, she just makes one up."

The light on one of Alex's telephone lines was blinking, and Gregory pressed the button and picked up the receiver. "Mrs. Rothman's office," he said. "One moment, sir. Let me check." He pressed the Hold button. "It's Rodney McCulloch!" he said. "Himself!"

She shook her head. "No calls."

"I'm sorry, sir, she's still in a meeting. . . . Yes, yes, let me take those numbers. . . ." Gregory stood there, scribbling, scribbling numbers on pink message slips. "My God," he said, replacing the phone, "he's given me his entire schedule for the whole *day*. That guy really moves around town, doesn't he?"

She smiled. "He has that reputation," she said.

"He says that he's to be brought out of whatever meeting he's in to take your call. It's that important." And he added, "Whatever it is."

"I have no idea what he wants."

He hesitated. "I think I know what he wants," he said.

"Oh? What's that?"

"I think he wants to know what everybody else wants to know. What's going on around here? What's Mr. Rothman up to? What's going to happen? Frankly, Alex, everybody here is very, very worried."

"Worried about what?"

"Their jobs, for one thing. With this new—woman."

"Now, darlin'," she said. "There's nothing really to worry about. Everything's under control. Nobody's job is in any danger. Everything's going to be just fine." Of course she didn't know whether she meant any of this, or whether anything she was saying meant anything at all. She touched her triple strand of pearls. Get through this day, she told herself. Put one foot in front of the other, toes out, chin up. "Now, shoo, darlin'," she said. "I really do have to go over my notes for today's meeting."

Alex sat alone at her desk, looking at the walls. She touched her pearls again, for luck, for courage. In the little town of Paradise, Missouri, where Alex grew up, no one had ever seen pearls like these. No one had ever dreamed of pearls like these, Steven's pearls, or the Kashmiri sapphire ring with its girdle of diamonds. "Is this your *office?*" her mother had said, disappointed, on one of her increasingly rare visits to New York from that place where she lived now, that place that was known as a "facility." "But it's so small, Alex. I thought the Rothmans were supposed to be so rich."

She had laughed. "This is a very cost-conscious company," she said. "Every square inch of space has a price tag on it. All the offices are small—except for Mr. Ho Rothman's office, which is very, very large."

It *was* a small office. She was sure her mother had expected to find her in a kind of Donald Oenslager stage setting for

Lady in the Dark, with Louis Quinze furniture and a gilded French phone on her desk and great swagged Fortuny
hangings at the windows—and Alex in a huge picture hat,
looking like Gertrude Lawrence—instead of a very ordinary-
looking office, with one window and venetian blinds, and
industrial-grade carpet on the floor and Alex herself, that
day, in tweeds and flats and a pencil stuck behind her ear.
Still, she had managed to imbue her small office with a certain theatricality.

At first, the walls had been painted flat white, and for a
long time she had studied those bare, white-painted walls,
wondering how she could brighten them up a bit. Then, all
at once, a solution had presented itself. Strolling down the
corridor one day, she had encountered a maintenance man
wheeling stacks of old magazines on his dolly. Files, it
seemed, were being cleaned out, and back issues of *Mode*,
from the date of its first issue in 1874 onward, were being
thrown out. They had all been committed to microfiche, and
the actual magazines were being discarded to create valuable
space. Alex had salvaged the magazines, and had her walls
papered with a collage of nineteenth- and early-twentieth-
century *Mode* covers, some of which were extraordinary.
They had featured fashion paintings by such artists as Edward
Penfield, Paul Helleu, Grace Wiederseim, Harrison Fisher,
Kate Greenway, Sir John Millais, and John Singer Sargent.
She then had the walls covered with a lustrous clear lacquer.
As a result, though she might not have the largest office in
the building, hers was easily the most distinctive and color-
ful. Herb Rothman frowned when he first stepped into the
redecorated office. It smacked of the kind of extravagance
for which Rothman Communications, Inc. was not noted. But
he couldn't really complain. The job had cost the company
nothing, and all the materials had been bound for the incinerator anyway.

"Damn," Lenny Liebling said when he first saw what
would become known as "Alex's little jewel box"—"I wish
I'd thought of that."

"You could still do it," Alex said. "There are hundreds of
more covers."

"I can't do it now that *you've* done it," he said, pouting.
"It wouldn't be original. It would be just copycat. After all,
I have a certain reputation for originality to uphold."

Hundreds of more covers, she had thought at the time, and immediately had the idea of papering the ceiling with more *Mode* covers, and her little jewel box was complete.

She gazed about her jewel box now. All those covers represented nearly twelve decades of work, of an editor's work and thought and imagination. Over the years, there had been a baker's dozen of *Mode* editors. Some had been brilliant, some had been dull. Some had been extravagant, some had been penny-pinching. Some had been innovators, some had been copycats. Some had lasted for just a few months, and others had stayed in their posts for years. There had been editors who had worn huge picture hats in the office, editors who wore turbans, an editor who affected a monocle on a pink satin ribbon, and an editor who always wore white opera-length gloves while she worked. There had been eccentric editors, autocratic editors, despotic editors, and there was even a tale—possibly apocryphal—of a *Mode* editor who had succeeded in making a Philadelphia-bound passenger train back up into Pennsylvania Station because she had forgotten a layout she needed for a meeting. There was the editor who had declared that the bikini was "mankind's greatest invention since the atomic bomb," and who devoted an entire issue of the magazine to huaraches. And there was the editor who, one afternoon for no apparent reason, put on her Lilly Daché hat and coat, and stepped out on the window ledge of this very office and jumped to her death on the Fifth Avenue sidewalk a hundred and twenty feet below. This room, Alex thought now, was not only filled with the tastes and imaginations of editors. It was also filled with ghosts. And all those editors, with the exception of Steven Rothman, had been women like herself.

But there had never been such a thing as a co-editor of *Mode*. And, she reminded herself, there was not going to be one now.

She walked into the conference room, a slim Hermès briefcase under her arm, chin up, smiling at everyone, greeting everyone, and took her place at the head of the table. Looking around the room, she said, "Where's Lenny?"

"He had a dental emergency," someone said. "I think he lost a crown."

"Well, we'll just have to do without him."

Bob Shaw, the art director, looked up from his usual chair and said, "You haven't lost *your* crown, have you, Alex?"

There was brief, uneasy, and decidedly embarrassed laughter at this not very funny joke, and Alex gave Bob a quick look and wondered if he'd been drinking again. She sat forward in her chair, unsnapped her briefcase, and took out a pad of legal cap and a handful of ballpoints. "I've been thinking about picnics," she began. "I've been thinking about everything a picnic can be." She was setting her "What-If" meeting on its track, suggesting a theme.

"Picnics—for a January issue?" someone asked.

"January is a blah month," she said. "I'm thinking about something upbeat for January, like picnics. And I'm not just thinking about outdoor picnics, though we might do a Caribbean picnic. I'm thinking about picnics as a whole lifestyle for the 'nineties. It seems to me that people aren't cooking elaborate dinners these days. They're picnicking, right in their apartments on the Upper West Side. Have you looked at your supermarket shelves lately? They're full of stuff that's essentially for picnicking. I'm not talking about old-fashioned TV dinners, where you get a slab of meat and gravy, mashed potatoes, and buttered peas in a compartmented tray. I'm talking about really wonderful-looking prepared dishes you can find in supermarkets now—lobster salad en brioche, skewered shrimp, soufflés of all sorts, galantines of beef, duck, even quail and pheasant. Picnic food. I think fashion's in a picnic mood, too—elegant, pretty, but easy and fun—quick, impromptu. I see picnic as a mood, a spirit. The word is from the French *pique-nique*, which means pick-and-choose, suit yourself, and I think we could have a lot of fun with this. Does anyone remember that wonderful scene in *Citizen Kane*, when Kane's second wife complains that she's bored, and so Kane decides to treat everybody to a picnic? They all set off for their picnic in a long string of chauffeur-driven limousines. I imagine we could get a still shot of that, and use it in a fun way in the issue. Any more thoughts on a picnic issue?"

There was a silence. Then someone said, "Ants. It wouldn't be a picnic without ants."

Alex wrinkled her nose. "I don't think ants are much fun, indoors or out." She could see that her meeting was starting out badly, and that she was going to have to expend more than her normal amount of energy to keep things on track this morning.

"Speaking of insects," someone else said, "I remember a summer picnic at my grandmother's house by the lake. We were all sitting around on the lawn, and suddenly my grandmother began to scream. A big spider was crawling toward her. My grandfather, who always carried a pistol, whipped out his pistol and shot the spider. 'So much for Little Miss Muffet,' he said."

There was no response to this story, which did not seem to lead them anywhere.

Then Gregory Kittredge spoke up. "That reminds me of a picnic when I was a kid," he said. "We'd been swimming in the river, and my mother, who had long, dark hair, was sitting on the riverbank, drying her hair. Suddenly a bee landed in her hair, then another, and another, and presently a whole swarm of bees was hanging in her long hair."

"My God, how horrible!" someone said. "Why wasn't she stung to death?"

He smiled. "My mother is a woman possessed of odd bits of information," he said. "She explained that bees in swarm will never sting if you don't disturb the swarm. She stayed very calm, and told us all to stay very calm, and in about fifteen minutes they all flew away. 'They're just choosing their new queen,' she said. Later, she said that having bees swarm in her hair was the closest she had ever come to having a religious experience."

Alex's eyes were bright. "What a wonderful image!" she said. "You know how pictorial my mind is. Wouldn't that make a great photograph? Bees swarming in a model's hair?"

"You'd never find a girl who'd agree to do it."

"I have just the girl in mind. Her name's Melissa. She's a beauty, and she's a honey blonde. Doesn't that sound perfect? Honey bees swarming in a honey blonde's hair? I have one of her composites at home, and I've asked her agency in Kansas City to send me more shots."

"You and your Kansas City models," someone said.

"I like that Midwest look. They look fresh—"

"And they're cheap."

"And hungry. Hungry enough to let bees swarm in their hair."

"But first we've got to find out what makes bees swarm, so we can set up the shot," Alex said. She turned to Bob Shaw. "Bob, find out what makes bees swarm. If we can pull this off, we could have an unforgettable cover, Bob."

"Jesus," Bob Shaw said. "Here I am, the art director of the greatest fashion magazine in the world. And what's my assignment? Find out what makes *bees* swarm!"

"I still can't quite reconcile picnics with January, Alex," someone said.

"But we'll be showing resort wear. Resorts are picnics in themselves. Life is a picnic, a movable—"

"*No!*" It was Carol Duffy, the beauty editor, who had said nothing at all so far. "No!" she cried again, and pounded her fist on the conference table. "I don't want to talk about any of this, Alex! I want you to tell us what's going to happen. I want to know what Herb Rothman is trying to do." There were tears in her eyes.

Alex's returning gaze was steady. "We're here to plan our January issue, Carol," she said. "And the theme is picnics."

"I really don't want to cry. I'm not going to let you make me cry," she had said to him years ago in Tarrytown, in the boathouse.

"I don't want to make you cry. I love you," he had replied.

Chapter 13

Of course there had been very little publicity about the dispute between the IRS and Ho Rothman so far. And, since the case had not yet come to trial, there was no way of knowing what the government might be planning to introduce as evidence. The case was still in what was called the discovery phase.

But, as Lenny understood it, it boiled down to this:

Rothman Communications, Inc. had always been a tightly held, privately owned family corporation. As a result, it had always enjoyed a high degree of secrecy in terms of its bookkeeping operations. Indeed, Lily Rothman, who started with the company as its bookkeeper, still bore the title of vice-president and secretary-treasurer. There was nothing wrong with any of this. But the government's contention was that, since the company's inception, H. O. Rothman had been its sole proprietor and owner, and that all corporate decisions had always been, and still were, handed down by him unilaterally. The company, the government charged, had been Ho Rothman's personal dictatorship. Therefore, they were claiming that the company's entire annual earnings should have been reported as individual income by Ho Rothman. Any disbursements of cash to other members of the family, the government said, were made in the form of gifts, the way a benevolent patriarch might hand out allowances to his children and grandchildren.

The cynicism of the government's timing was obvious. If it could prove, at this advanced stage of Ho's life, that no one but Ho had ever owned or controlled the company, it could move in, at the time of his death, and tax his estate at the full book value of the company. The Rothman lawyers even suspected that the government was conducting its case in such a manner that the case would not even come to trial until after Ho's death, so that it could claim not only back taxes, but also huge estate taxes.

The Rothman lawyers—and there were presently a battery of 126 attorneys from the firm of Waxman, Holloway, Goldsmith & McCarthy working on the case—were taking a very different stand. Rothman Communications, Inc., they claimed, was not now and never had been a one-man operation. The company was owned, they countered, by a consortium of family shareholders. The lawyers contended that the company was not run like a monarchy, but like a democracy, with shareholders meeting regularly, and making decisions by majority vote. Decisions concerning acquisitions, sales, and so forth were not handed down from on high, but were reached after lively—often heated—discussion and debate among the stockholders. Obviously, the question of whether Ho Rothman owned his entire company, or only a share of it, was an important one. If the government pursued its case successfully, it could expect to collect some $600,000,000 in back income taxes, plus a possible additional $450,000,000 in fines, penalties, and interest. The government was not after chickenfeed. Lenny Liebling was sitting with Aunt Lily Rothman right now, in her red-and-gold drawing room—red damask walls and window hangings and upholstery coverings, gilt frames on all the furniture—at 720 Park Avenue, balancing a Sèvres teacup on his knee.

"Yes, people say I'm remarkable," she was saying. "Remarkable specimen for a woman my age, and I guess they must be right. Look at me. Perfect eyesight, perfect hearing, all my own teeth, still a perfect size six. This is my natural hair color." She touched her ash-blonde curls. "Oh, I won't say that I don't give it a little help from a bottle now and then, but it's still my natural *color*, and that's the important part. It isn't fair, is it, that I should be in perfect health, while poor Ho is in there just wasting away . . . wasting away. It just isn't fair, but then life's not fair, is it."

"It certainly isn't," Lenny said.

"Of course you remember him when he was in his prime. The drive, the power, the personal magnetism he had, the intellect of that little man! The energy he had! The wisdom, the creativity! It was all there, and now it's gone. And yet this is the man the IRS is now accusing of being the singlehanded mastermind of the entire corporation, when everyone knows there are lots of stockholders, who all have votes. I said to our lawyers just this morning, I said, 'If it were possible to move him, we should take this man—this vegetable—down to that Federal Court House in Foley Square. We should carry him in on a stretcher, and say to the IRS—"Here's the man you're calling a press lord, a communications czar, the sole power behind the Rothman empire! Take a look at your czar, lying there like that day after day—his mind gone, a vegetable." ' The lawyers thought that was a pretty good idea."

"Would he be up to that, Lily?"

"No. It would probably kill him. But then we could sue the IRS for murder."

"Oh? I didn't know it was possible to sue the federal government," Lenny murmured.

"Well, we'll see. It's only an idea, and the lawyers liked it. We'd only do that if worse came to worst. His doctors say he has the constitution of an ox. The heart of a teenage boy, and the constitution of an ox. But it's his mind that's gone, totally gone."

"I'd like to step in and see him," Lenny said.

"No, no. Doctors' orders. No visitors. Nobody can see him anymore except the doctors, the duty nurses, and me. Anybody else, and his blood pressure shoots up."

"Interesting that a man with the heart of a teenage boy should be having blood-pressure problems," Lenny said.

"Doctors' orders," she said again. "Anyway, it's not his heart that's involved, as I told you. It's his arteries. They're completely hardened. It's the arteries that cause the blood pressure, and arteries have nothing to do with the heart. They're not even connected."

"Hm," Lenny said. "Interesting case, from a medical standpoint."

"Well, I didn't ask you here to discuss Ho's health, which you know all about anyway. There's something I want you to do, Lenny."

"Ah," he said, setting down his teacup. "Now we get to the point of this meeting."

"Ex*act*ly," she said. "Now, as I said before, there have always been lots of stockholders of this company. But the thing is, we never got around to issuing any actual stock. We were always—just too busy to do it, I guess. But now, with this IRS business, I think it's high time we did it. If we can show the IRS the actual stock certificates, we can prove that there were individual stockholders all along. They'll have no case."

"I see," Lenny said.

"So. Here's what I need you to do. I want you to get lots of stock certificates printed up. The certificates should bear various dates, to reflect splits, et cetera, et cetera, over the years, dating back to nineteen twenty-three, the year Herbie was born. Have them printed up in different colors—you know what stock certificates look like—some in yellow, some in green, some in blue, and so on. And in different amounts. Also, I want some of them to look really old. Have some of them printed on distressed paper, the kind that looks old."

"I believe that papers, and inks, can be tested for age," Lenny said.

"Ha! The bozos at the IRS won't know about any of that. At least that's what I'm betting on. Once they see these certificates, they'll call off their dogs."

"Hm," Lenny said. "Have you discussed this with your lawyers, Lily?"

"Of course not! This is my idea. You know what Ho always said about lawyers. 'The more you tell a lawyer, the more it costs you.' To hell with the lawyers."

"I see," Lenny said. "I believe there's a word for what you have in mind, Lily, or rather two words. It's called stock fraud."

"No. It's called estate planning. It's something Ho should probably have done long ago, but didn't get around to. Now he's getting around to it, but the IRS doesn't need to know any of that. This is just between you and I."

"I see," Lenny said.

"Now here's the way I want everything divided up," she said, and withdrew a slip of paper from the front of her dress. "I've got it all written down, who's going to get what. Twenty percent of the company will belong to Herbert Oscar

Rothman, that's Ho. Fifteen percent of the stock will belong to Anna Lily Rothman, that's me. Herbie will be given fifteen percent, and his wife, that Pegeen, will get ten percent, though it kills me to give the bitch that much. Arthur will get another fifteen. We'll put twenty percent into the estate of Steven Rothman, to be held in trust for Alex and Joel, and a final five percent in a separate trust for Joel, to be his when he reaches age thirty, but to be voted by his mother until then. Got that? That will prove to the IRS that nobody in this family has ever owned more than twenty percent of this company, which is what our lawyers have been claiming all along. That's the beauty part."

"I see," Lenny said. "But I wonder, Lily, why you have chosen me to carry out this bit of—creative paperwork?"

"Because you're someone I can trust," she said.

"Or," he said, "is it because if, as we say, someone has to take the fall for all this, the fall won't be taken by a member of the Rothman family? The fall will be taken by Dear Old Lenny. Isn't that it? If someone ends up having to sit for this—and, if your scheme is discovered, someone will—the person who sits will be me."

"What a way to talk! Nobody's going to take a fall. Nobody's going to have to *sit*. I've got it all worked out. Besides, if you did get caught—which you won't—they'd let you off easy. You have no record. Whereas Herbie, as you know—"

"Yes," he said quickly. "So you do know that what you're proposing is quite against the law."

"It's just estate planning! Just estate planning that should have been done years ago."

"And I take it Herbert knows nothing about this—estate planning?"

"Absolutely not! This is strictly between you and I, Lenny."

"Well, I just don't think I want to become *engagé* with this, Lily," he said. "I'm sorry, but it's just too risky. Not for you, perhaps, but for me. After all, I have a certain reputation for integrity to uphold."

"Oh?" She sat forward in her chair and eyed him narrowly. "Cab number thirteen has been awfully busy these last few months."

"Honestly, Lily, I have no idea what you're talking about.

What in the world is cab thirteen?"

"Just thinking aloud," she said. "Cab number thirteen has been the busiest car in the fleet. Isn't it funny? It's just one of those little things a bookkeeper notices."

There was a long silence, and he made a mental note to call his friend Jocko and arrange for a new code number, or perhaps several numbers.

"Oh, look," she said, and lifted one hand and pointed. "Look at how the sun has just hit that crystal obelisk on the table there, and thrown colored lights all around the room. Every day, there's a certain hour when the sunlight hits that obelisk, and makes a rainbow in the room. So many aspects of things, aren't there, like the sides of a prism in the sun. 'How far that little candle throws his beams! So shines a good deed in a naughty world!' You owe us a few good deeds, Lenny."

"Yes, but—"

"And the liquor store on Forty-sixth Street. The bar in our conference room seems to need replenishing so often nowadays. Funny, isn't it?"

"Really, Lily, I'm not following your train of thought."

"Just woolgathering," she said. "Just woolgathering. And the little sandwich shop on Forty-fourth. So many conference room lunches sent up from there lately. And so many people who seem to order turkey club sandwiches. Doesn't that strike you as odd?"

"Perhaps. I suppose. But HoBo's is famous for their turkey club sandwiches." He touched a bead of perspiration on his upper lip.

"Yes, well I suppose that's it. Our lawyers are trying to stay on very good terms with the people at the IRS right now. No point being hard-nosed with the feds, they say. That just gets their back up. Failure to report income—that's the big no-no, you know. That's Fort Leavenworth time. Thank goodness they're not accusing *us* of failure to report income. They're just challenging our accounting system. But if we could offer them somebody else who had really failed to report income—who knows? It might be a little bargaining chip. It certainly wouldn't hurt our side. Might even help."

Lenny cleared his throat. "You say your lawyers know nothing about this stock-printing plan?"

"Nothing. Nada. Zip."

"And how do you suppose they'll react to the sudden appearance of these—certificates?"

"I'll handle that. Don't forget, I've been cooking the books for this company for over sixty years. I'll just dump the certificates on them and say, 'Here—you want proof of multiple ownership? Here's proof.' They're not going to question the treasurer of this company—the one who's paying their bills! Then they can dump the certificates on the IRS. That's why I want lots and lots of certificates, Lenny, dated from way, way back. I want huge bundles of certificates, enough to fill a couple of wheelbarrows, at least. That's the way to deal with bureaucrats—bury them in paper!"

"And how would I go about this stock-printing operation, I wonder?" he said.

"We own printing presses, don't we? That's the easy part."

"Certain palms may have to be greased."

"Certain palms are already being greased. I think you know how to go about that."

He nodded, a little absently.

"And I want these certificates printed up as quickly as possible," she said. "And you're just the man for the job."

He nodded again. "Funny," he said quietly, "when you said you wanted to see me, I thought it must be about this new woman Herb's putting on *Mode*'s masthead—the new co-editor."

"Ha!" she said. "Herb's new chippie, you mean? That's what she is, isn't it—his new chippie? You see, Herbie thinks that now his father's a vegetable he can take over the company. But I'm not going to let him. He thinks he can force Alex to quit, without having to fire her, and give the job to this new chippie. That's what he's trying to do—force her to walk out of her contract."

"He's certainly making life very unpleasant for her right now."

"But I'm not going to let him do that, either."

"You've always been very fond of Alex, haven't you, Lily."

"She's made a lot of money for us. If you've got a winning team, you don't get rid of your star player. You don't kill the goose that keeps laying golden eggs, and I'm not going to let him."

"I warn you, Lily, Herb's playing hardball now."

"I can play hardball, too!" She rose now to her full height of five-feet-two and faced him. "That's the *second* beauty part of these stock certificates you're going to have printed up for me. Look at the percentages." She tapped her slip of paper with a fingertip. "Once we get certificates showing who owns what, we'll have a stockholders' meeting on the subject of this chippie. The lawyers have made me Ho's conservator, which means I can vote Ho's shares. That means that Ho and I and Alex and Joel will own sixty percent of the company, and Herb will be voted down—all perfectly businesslike and legal! Why, even if Arthur and Pegeen voted on Herb's side—which I'm damn sure they wouldn't do— he'd *still* be voted down! See? See what I mean? It's called killing two birds with one stone."

Lenny also rose. "You are—remarkable, Aunt Lily," he said, a trifle wearily.

"Damn right I am. Perfect eyesight, perfect hearing, perfect size six, all my own teeth, my natural hair color—and all my marbles, Lenny. That's the best beauty part of me. I may be eighty-five years old, but I've got all my marbles!"

"Just one thing," he said. "How much does Herb know about Tarrytown?"

"Nothing! Zip!"

"You're sure?"

"Absolutely!"

"Well, then—" His eyes traveled slowly around the room. "I've always loved this room," he said. "Your gold-and-red room. It's so very *you*, Lily, and this lovely rug sets everything off so perfectly. Beautiful rug."

"Damn right it is. It's an Isfahan. Sixteen thirty-nine."

"Well, perhaps it is and perhaps it isn't," he murmured. "When I was antiques editor, I became something of an expert, and—"

"Of course it is. I've got its papers. I've got its whatchamacallit, its pedigree from Sotheby's."

"Well, even Sotheby's—I mean, even Shakespeare nodded. But I couldn't help noticing as we were sitting here that it needs cleaning, Lily. You really should send it out to have it cleaned professionally."

"It looks clean to me."

"But look, there's a spot—there." He pointed. "And another over there." He considered mentioning, too, that the legs of the two Boulle commodes were badly scuffed, from where her stupid maids had banged them with their vacuum cleaners. But he decided to let that wait for a later date. First things first.

"I don't see any spot."

"Right there, Lily dear."

"That's part of the pattern."

"No, Lily dear. It looks like coffee, or perhaps red wine. You see, remarkable though you are, one of the sad things that happen to people when they get older is that they let things slide a bit. In terms of maintaining their possessions. My own dear mother, in her later years, took to covering up her priceless antiques with sheets of plastic, rather than having them recovered. So sad. I'd hate to see you show any of those little signs of—aging, Lily dear."

"I still don't see any spots." She moved about the room, peering down at the rug.

"And this one here. I expect that was where your little Fluff may have had a little accident. Remember your little Fluff? I do. What an adorable little creature she was! Well, she gave you fifteen wonderful years of companionship."

"Well, perhaps that was from Fluff. I guess it could have been."

"You were so wise not to replace her. There never could have been another Fluff. Look," he said brightly, "I have a wonderful little man in TriBeCa who does wonders with orientals. He does work for the Metropolitan Museum. Let me send him around to you first thing Monday morning, and have him take this up and clean it for you."

"Will it take long? I hate bare floors."

"Just a few days. And it will come back to you looking like a brand-new rug, I promise you!"

"Well, I don't think so," she said.

"Have you *ever* had it cleaned?"

"I guess not."

"See? So let me send my little man around."

"Oh, all right," she said. "But meanwhile you've got a much more important job to do."

In her husband's room, after Lenny had gone, Aunt Lily Rothman said to the new eight-to-four who had replaced Agnes O'Sullivan, and who had been on the job for only a few hours, "Nurse, why don't you run down to the kitchen and fix yourself a cup of coffee? I'll sit with Mr. Rothman for a while."

When the nurse had gone, Ho pushed himself on his elbows and said, "Well, what did the *schnorrer* say? He gonna do it?"

"Of course," Aunt Lily said. "Lenny knows what side his bread is buttered on."

"Good," he said. He adjusted the pillows behind his back. "Goddammit to hell, Lily, I getting sick of these Goddamn nurses. Thieving pipple! Got to watch them like Hawkeye, Goddamn to hell."

"Now, now," she said. "You know it's just till we establish that you're too far gone to testify. You know what the lawyers said about perjury. Perjury's a felony charge, and we can't have them slapping us with a felony charge on top of everything else now, can we?"

"Goddamn bed," he said, pounding the mattress with his fist. "Hate this Goddamn bed. Bed with bars, like baby's crib. Want to get back into my own bed." He winked at her. "With you."

She patted his hand. "Now, now," she said. "As soon as the IRS calls off its dogs, you're going to have a miraculous recovery. And it's going to happen sooner than you think."

His eyes were bright. "My darling Lilykins," he said. "Have I ever told you what a wonderful wife you've been to me? How could I ever have lived all these years without you, Lilykins? Do you know that there are still some *pipple* who think I can't say *people?*"

"I know, I know," she said.

In the kitchen, the new eight-to-four, whose name was Irene Zabriskie, was staring into the open refrigerator under the baleful gaze of Richardetta, Lily Rothman's black cook. This was Richardetta's kitchen, and this was Richardetta's refrigerator, and this large white woman in her large starched white uniform had no business being there, poking around in the refrigerator's contents, opening jars and plastic containers, unwrapping Saran- and foil-wrapped packages, peering and sniffing at what was inside them.

"What's for my lunch?" Irene Zabriskie said.

"Miz Rothman, she be having half an alligator pear. That

be all she ever have for lunch," Richardetta said.

"That won't be enough for me. Got any tuna?"

"Nope!"

"Got any crabmeat?"

"Nope!"

"You've got to give me lunch, you know. It's in my contract."

"For you I got fried chicken."

"I can't eat that. I'm allergic to chicken."

"Fried chicken be all I got."

"Got a little strip sirloin? You could pan-fry it in polyunsaturated vegetable oil."

"Nope!"

"What's this?" Mrs. Zabriskie said, unscrewing the lid of a Mason jar.

"That be Miz Rothman's martinis."

"She a drinking woman? They didn't tell me at the agency I'd be working for a drinking woman."

"They be her martinis. She like 'em well *chilled*."

Mrs. Zabriskie replaced the cap. "Wait a minute," she said, removing a Saran-wrapped plate. "What's this?"

"That be Mr. Rothman's lunch."

"What is it?"

"That be lox and potato salad."

"Hm! I'll take that."

"I tol' you that be Mr. Rothman's lunch! And that's the last of the lox."

"Hm! Last adv Alz case I had would only eat mushy peas. Had to spoon 'em into him like a baby. Choked on 'em in the end, but it wasn't on my shift." She sounded vaguely disappointed.

"Never heard of no mushy peas."

"What else have you got?"

"I could fry a couple eggs."

"Can't eat that. I've got high cholesterol. What's this?"

"That be lamb chops from last night. That be *my* lunch."

"Can't eat that, either. What else have you got?"

"For you I got fried chicken. . . ."

Chapter 14

The first thing that the not-quite-seventeen-year-old Ho Rothman decided as he walked through his new property—the empty office building and the silent printing plant with its gleaming, unpaid-for new equipment that now belonged to him, unencumbered—was that, if he was going to run a newspaper, he was going to have to do it all by himself. This, he felt—with that wonderful self-confidence of youth—he knew enough about newspapering to do. He would have to write all the stories, set them in type, sell all the subscriptions, all the advertising, and deliver the papers personally to the subscribers' doors, for a nickel a copy. It would not be an easy job, but the few hundred dollars that remained from his bank-fleecing operation ruled out the hiring of any employees. His would be a one-man operation.

And he could do it all by himself, he decided, if he made his paper a weekly instead of a daily. He also decided that, since the now-defunct *Times-Union* had a bland and stodgy reputation, he would give his new weekly enterprise a new name. He decided to call it the *Newark Explorer*. The word *Explorer* had all sorts of exciting, adventurous connotations in Ho's mind. It suggested exploration into new worlds, a new journalistic universe. It suggested the Beyond, the Great Unknown, vast uncharted seas, unanswered questions, mysteries, fantastic happenings. Ho Rothman had read the popular fantasy-tales of H. G. Wells—*The Time Machine*,

The War of the Worlds, and so on—and why, he asked himself, should a newspaper like his new *Explorer* refrain from exploring the possibility that there were men on the moon, that the Loch Ness Monster existed, that Abominable Snowmen patrolled the Himalayas, that Sasquatch and Bigfoot lived in the Wild West, and that the dead came back to haunt the living? He would, in other words, put out a newspaper like no other at the time, a newspaper that not only reported facts but also might-be facts and could-be facts. His newspaper would carry his readers far beyond the dreary confines of the city of Newark, New Jersey.

On the shelves of the Newark Public Library, Ho had discovered a volume called *Tales of Monsters and Madness*, by the little-known nineteenth-century author C. E. Lahniers. Some of the "tales" were loosely based on factual evidence. Others were based on legend or hearsay, and still others seemed patently fictitious, such as an English widow's nightmarish account of how she had been transported, by way of a cave in Tunbridge Wells, to Hell, where she had been sexually assaulted by the Devil himself, whose sexual instrument "was the size of an eighteen-pound halibut, and covered with scales." With glee, Ho noticed that *Tales* was no longer in copyright. Each issue of his weekly, he decided, would contain at least one tale of monsters or madness, which he could lift, virtually intact, from the Lahniers work, and he would splash that tale in a giant headline across the front page.

Thus, as he planned and laid out his issues, he came up with headlines such as this:

MOTHER GIVES BIRTH TO THREE-HEADED BABY!

Then Sells It to Circus for One Dollar

Readers of this tale were not deceived, exactly. They were told, in copy that was cleverly tucked well inside the paper, that the freakish birth took place in Rumania in 1801. But there was no doubt that headlines like these were eye-catching and, from its first issue, which appeared in March 1912, the *Explorer* did well at newsstands, and presently Ho was pleased to see orders for subscriptions begin trickling in.

Sex was one of the staples of the *Explorer*'s content during those early days, as evidenced by the following front-page screamer headlines:

GIRL, 14, IS PREGNANT
BY APE IN ZOO!

FATHER BOILS ILLEGITIMATE
SON IN OIL!

ARCHBISHOP ADMITS HE IS
WHITE SLAVER!

So was religion:

BALLOONIST SEES GOD!
TALKS TO HIM!

And so on. Most of these stories were picked up, word for word, from *Tales of Monsters and Madness*.

But, with Ho's fondness for H. G. Wells, there was also some pseudoscientific material, such as:

SCIENTISTS DESCRIBE
MARTIAN MEN!

If there are men on Mars, leading scientists told the EXPLORER today, their bodies will consist almost entirely of a pair of lungs, due to the thinness of the red planet's atmosphere. . . .

Needless to say, the "leading scientists" were Ho Rothman himself. And it should be noted that, though Ho's spoken English was in those days still actually a bit rough and heavily Russian-accented, he nonetheless wrote serviceable journalistic prose, with hardly any syntactical lapses.

He was also adept at taking small, relatively insignificant items that had appeared in other newspapers, and blowing them up into front-page stories for his weekly tabloid. The death of an elderly resident of Des Moines, who had apparently choked on his shaving cream, became, on the *Explorer*'s front page:

SHAVING-CREAM DROWNING
BAFFLES POLICE!

He was even able to get a follow-up story out of this event for the front page of his next week's issue:

MEDICAL EXPERTS DESCRIBE HORRORS
OF SHAVING-CREAM DROWNING!

Once again, the "medical experts" were none other than the youthful editor.

And, when no tale that seemed lurid enough for his front page presented itself, Ho Rothman was not above making something up. Thus he was able to use the headline he had imagined in his boardinghouse cell, about mad dogs disemboweling schoolchildren. By changing the venue of this fictitious event to a nonexistent hamlet in faraway California, "high in the wild ranges of the Sierra Madre," and the dogs to coyotes, he was able to come up with:

CHILDREN DEVOURED BY
RABID COYOTE PACK!

But, to give him credit, he also gradually began adding elements to the *Explorer*'s pages that were both innovative and helpful. He had begun to think of a newspaper that not only reported news events, but that also provided a "service" to its readers. Up to that point, American newspapers were considered a male medium. They were largely written by men, for male readers. The typical reader, American publishers assumed, was the man of the house who read his paper while his wife cooked and served his breakfast, and who then took the paper with him to read further on the train or streetcar that bore him to his place of business. Except for the inevitable advice-to-the-lovelorn column, or perhaps the church calendar, nothing in American newspapers of the day was designed to appeal to women readers. Women readers were expected to be served by the relatively small handful of ladies' magazines, including a venerable fashion magazine called *Mode*.

Ho Rothman had begun seeing, with some regularity, a

pretty young lady of his own age named Sophie Litsky. Sophie was a far cry from the perfidious Rachel. A rabbi's daughter, Sophie Litsky had been gently bred and gently raised. Sophie's mother, Bella Litsky, had taken a liking to young Ho and, since he appeared to have no family, often invited him to the Litskys' table for dinner, a gesture that was much appreciated. Sophie's mother, he soon learned, had a well-deserved reputation in her neighborhood as a cook and Bella Litsky once boasted that she could go into anyone's ice-box or larder and, with whatever ingredients she happened to find there, could come up with a tasty and hearty dish. To tease her, more than anything else, Ho dared her to do this. With the cooperation of an agreeable neighbor, Bella Litsky said she would take him up on the challenge. Bella marched into her neighbor's kitchen, where she found a couple of onions, a carrot, two tomatoes, a potato, a gill of sour cream, a bit of cheese, and half a roasted chicken, and proceeded to create—to Ho's taste, at least—a simply ambrosial casserole. Bella even gave it a clever name: Hopalong Casserole.

Ho decided to make use of Mrs. Litsky's cooking talents for the *Explorer*, and presently a recipe column called "From Mrs. L's Kitchen" became a regular weekly feature. Circulation jumped—from women readers who mailed in their subscription money. Quickly retitled "Exploring Mrs. L's Kitchen," and expanded to include not only recipes but also housekeeping, shopping, and budgeting hints, and given a full page in the paper, the "Mrs. L Page," seemed to be drawing more readers than any other. And Ho Rothman was hinting that he might make Bella Litsky his first paid outside contributor. But he was not quite ready to take such a drastic step, and for the time being Bella Litsky was satisfied with her photograph in the upper left-hand corner of the page, and a certain amount of local celebrity.

Today, of course, nearly every American newspaper has its so-called Women's Page. But Ho Rothman's paper was the very first to have one.

The only part of the paper to bear Ho Rothman's name was the editorial page, which appeared under the general banner:

EXPLORING THE ISSUES!
by

H. O. Rothman
EDITOR & PUBLISHER

The general tone of the editorial page was one of indignation, though here Ho had to walk a thin and careful line. The
people involved in the issues that the *Explorer* explored were
actual, living human beings, and Ho was aware of American
libel laws. He could, however, with reasonable impunity,
question the propriety of a building contract for a new city
hospital that was awarded to the mayor's brother-in-law. He
could safely inveigh against the United States Congress for
shortening the working day of all government employees
to eight hours while, in private industry, most workers still
labored ten to twelve hours a day, six days a week.

But he was most comfortable taking to task individuals and
institutions that were far away, beyond the law's long reach.
By the spring of 1912, Ho Rothman, who read the "real"
newspapers regularly, was becoming increasingly annoyed
by the boastful publicity coming out of England concerning a new luxury liner that Britain's White Star line was
planning to launch in mid-April. Everything about the under-
taking seemed to him to be grossly overblown. In addition to
being the world's most luxurious, the passenger ship would
be the world's largest and heaviest, 882 feet in length, and
weighing 46,328 tons. With what struck Ho as outrageous
chutzpah, the new liner was being billed as "unsinkable."
Even the new liner's name—the *Titanic*—struck Ho Rothman
as preposterously grandiose.

In a series of *Explorer* editorials, Ho Rothman wrote scathingly of the White Star venture, which he called "the Rich
Man's Liner," and "White Star's Folly." He noted that the
British company had high-handedly provided only enough
lifeboats to accommodate the ship's first class passengers.
Should the unsinkable vessel ever sink, passengers in cabin
class, tourist, and steerage would have to fend for themselves. The entire enterprise, he wrote, struck him as an act
of arrogant defiance against God and Nature. From his own
experience crossing the stormy North Atlantic, he doubted
that any ship that ever sailed the seas could proclaim itself
unsinkable. He wrote of how he personally had been aboard a
mighty ship as it pitched and rolled, as forty-foot-high waves
crashed across its decks, how its planks and beams shuddered

and groaned as its hull seemed about to fly asunder beneath the impact of tons of water. He wrote of his own terror. He wrote of the threat of icebergs, whose giant, ghostly tips he had himself seen looming above the waves, and of his knowledge that, below these tips, huge and invisible hazards lurked that were impossible to estimate. He even noted that the *Titanic*'s departure date—midnight, April 12—was an unlucky Friday, and that when the ship entered the Channel it would be an unlucky 13, a congruence of dates that struck him as a sign of ill omen.

He even, out of wishful thinking, perhaps, that his pessimism would prove justified, had a banner front-page headline set in type for the *Explorer*:

TITANIC SINKS!
Thousands Feared Lost

He set this rack of type aside for possible future use.

Meanwhile, Ho Rothman had needed to find another job in order to give himself some steady income until, with luck, his fledgling newspaper began to show a steady profit. He had taken a position at Bamberger's department store, as a general clerk and errand boy, for seven dollars a week, and his days were now spent scurrying back and forth between his paper and the store. If other Americans were then working ten to twelve hours a day for six days a week, Ho Rothman was working eighteen to twenty hours a day, seven days a week.

The principal items of overhead in running a newspaper were three: the cost of newsprint, the cost of electricity to run the presses, and the cost of water needed to mix the inks. In terms of the first item, Ho was in luck. He had inherited some two tons of newsprint from the late Mr. Meister. But paying for his electric and water supply was another matter. For a while, he had toyed with the idea of somehow connecting his electric supply line to a neighbor's meter. But that seemed risky and, besides, he knew too little about electricity to carry out such an operation. Then he had another idea. If banks made mistakes, couldn't utilities companies make mistakes as well? And, since he had bought his plant from the city, didn't that mean that the city had been its previous legal owner? He placed a call to the service manager of the Newark Light & Power Company.

"This is J. D. Sasser at City Hall," Ho said in the best brusque American accent he could muster. "Why have not we received a bill for service at the three-oh-five Bergen Avenue property?"

"One moment, sir. I'll check." When the manager came back on the line, he said, "We were notified, Mr. Sasser, that title to that property was assumed last month by a Mr. Rothman."

"Not at all," said Ho authoritatively. "Not at all. Now please see to it that the bill gets sent to the city right away."

"Yes, sir!" said the manager.

"We have a city to run, you know, and a budget to balance, my good man."

"Yes, sir!" said the manager.

"Give me your badge number, for our records."

"Sir, we don't wear badges."

"I just don't want you to get into any trouble over this, my good man."

"No, sir!"

It might be months, Ho figured, before the respective bureaucracies of the city government and the power company discovered what was going on, and then someone else would be blamed.

The same tactic worked with the water company.

Meanwhile, his duties at Bamberger's turned out to be somewhat loosely defined. Some days he would be asked to sweep out the store's offices and empty the wastebaskets before the executives arrived for work. On others, he might be asked to help the window dressers set up their displays and dress their mannequins. One day he might be assigned to the store's sign shop, where the in-store signs and notices were printed, and the next day might find him running ad copy between the advertising department and the buyers' offices for the buyers' approval. As a result, he soon felt he knew as much about running a department store as he did about running a newspaper.

The buyers, he quickly realized, even though they worked out of tiny, cluttered, windowless cubbyholes, were the real kingpins of the store's operations. In theory, the buyers

reported to a smaller number of higher-ups called merchandise managers. But, in actual practice—at least as long as
the buyer's figures appeared in the Gains column of each
day's sales sheet—the buyer was given carte blanche to
do whatever he chose. The activities of the major buyers
were rarely questioned, unless the figures from a buyer's
department showed a trace of red ink. Then he would be
summoned by his merchandise manager and asked to account
for himself.

Young Ho also noticed that some buyers were definitely more important than others. At the top of the pecking
order stood Mr. Gossage, the furniture buyer. When the great
Eldridge J. Gossage strode through his department, under-
lings bowed and stepped out of his way, and otherwise tried
to look busy. Next in rank came Mr. Rubin, the buyer for
Major Appliances. The eminence of these two men was based
on two factors: their merchandise was among the highest-
priced in the store, and the square-footage their departments
required comprised the store's two largest selling areas—
Mr. Gossage's Furniture took up the entire seventh floor.
The buyer for Furs, even though he dealt with expensive,
luxury goods, ranked far below Furniture and Major Appliances on the status ladder. This was because his business was
mostly seasonal, and furs were considered "impulse items."
But regardless of the time of year, customers still bought furniture and new kitchen stoves.

Ho Rothman also couldn't help noticing another oddity
about the buyers. Physically, they called to mind the merchandise they dealt with. Mr. Gossage and Mr. Rubin were
as massive and solidly put together as the overstuffed sofas
and refrigerators that filled their respective departments. The
fur buyer was a rabbity little man with a Persian lamb beard.
The toy buyer was a jolly Santa Claus. The bespectacled
book buyer looked like a librarian. The antiques buyer was
an elderly bachelor. The women's shoe buyer was a dainty,
effeminate little fellow whose slender back exhibited a curva-
ture that almost exactly echoed the arched insole of a lady's
pump. The fashion buyers were haughty, hatted, bejeweled
women who carried themselves with the air of models about
to pose for a cover of *Mode*. The faces of the cosmetics buyers were masked heavily with their products, while the faces
of the buyers of the low-priced Basement Store wore a kind

of prison pallor, as though they had never seen the light of day or been able to afford a decent meal. Even the window dressers were slender, willowy young men who, in conversation, often affected the exaggerated gestures and poses of the mannequins they dressed.

Miss Rabinowitz, the umbrella buyer, was important only on rainy days, when she was galvanized into action and seemed to commandeer the entire street floor as she repositioned her merchandise next to the store's entrances and exits. Only when it rained was Miss Rabinowitz ever seen to smile.

Ho observed other peculiarities about the way department stores were run. Once a year, for instance, in October, Bamberger's staged a storewide anniversary or birthday sale. But then so did every other department store in the New York metropolitan area. Did this mean that every department store in the Tristate region had come into being in the month of October? Or did it have more to do with the slow selling season that regularly occurred between back-to-school and Christmas?

As he carried sheets of advertising copy back and forth between the copywriters' and the buyers' offices, reading the copy as he went, he learned something about the advertising business that would stand him in good stead later on. He learned that much of the store's advertising was misleading, if not downright false. He would read: "This magnificent set of dining room chairs by Heritage will go on sale tomorrow—*for one day only*—for the amazingly low, low price of $129.95!" He was familiar with the chairs in question, having often passed them on his rounds. Their price tag had always been $129.95.

He had befriended a young copywriter named Chris, and he asked Chris about this. "Remember that buyer rhymes with liar," was his friend's reply. "The 'z' key on my typewriter is worn out from typing the word *amazing*."

Other things went on. In the Basement Store, during a sale of misses' blouses that had been advertised as "One Day Only—All Sales Final—No Returns," he had watched as the frantic misses' blouse buyer and her assistants changed the size labels on a stack of shirtwaists. The small sizes had all sold out, it seemed, and so they were relabeling the large and extra-large sizes "small."

The store's Giant Midwinter Furniture Sale was coming up. For some time, Ho had rather wistfully been eyeing, as he passed it, a Queen Anne–type chest-on-chest on the furniture floor. Someday, he thought, if he were able to afford a home of his own, he would like to have a chest-on-chest just like that one standing proudly in his front hall. (Later, when he became rich, Ho Rothman would not have put a piece like that in his maid's room!) Its price was $59.95, far beyond his humble reach, even if he used his employee's ten percent discount and the store's Lay-Away Plan, and even if he had a place to put it. On the opening day of the great sale, Ho made a special trip to the chest-on-chest, to see how much it had been marked down. Sure enough, there it was with a new price tag that read: "Sale priced just $59.95—formerly $259.95!"

He had occasion to encounter Mr. Eldridge J. Gossage that day, as the latter marched down the grand *allée* between his highboys and his breakfronts, looking important and pleased with himself, and Ho took the liberty of mentioning the matter of the Queen Anne chest-on-chest. Mr. Gossage looked pained, and mumbled something about comparable prices at other retailers. But, Ho wanted to know, what would happen if word of this sort of activity leaked out to the press—even to the humble newcomer, the *Newark Explorer*, that he himself was publishing? Would not the confidence of Bamberger's customers be eroded if they learned that Newark's leading department store was advertising phony sale prices? Particularly if the *Explorer* should decide to publish the news on its front page?

Eldridge J. Gossage looked very angry. "Why, you little kike whippersnapper," he said, "I'm going to see that you get exactly what you deserve!"

And Mr. Gossage was as good as his word. From that week onward, a full-page ad for Bamberger's furniture department appeared on the back page of Ho's tabloid. Bamberger's furniture department became his first regular paid advertiser.

And Ho was quick to show his gratitude, and began what would be a lifetime practice of editorial quid pro quo. He saw to it that, whenever possible, Bamberger's furniture got favorable mention in his paper. In a story on troglodyte witches in fifteenth-century Spain, for example, he wrote:

The witches' caves of Andalusia were dank, unhealthy holes—a far cry from what they might have been had they been furnished with the kind of taste and elegance shoppers are accustomed to finding at Bamberger's excellent furniture department, where quality at amazingly low prices is the rule.

Whether or not Mr. Gossage noticed these editorial pats on the back, Mr. Gossage never deigned to say. But Ho was fairly sure he did.

In 1912, radio was something very new—a novelty, a plaything, a toy. It had occurred to no one that radio could ever become a medium for transmitting news, music, sporting events, or other entertainment. It was a just a gadget. Ham operators used radio sets to gossip back and forth with one another. But such was the public interest in Mr. Marconi's invention that Bamberger's had decided to install a small, glass-enclosed radio studio on the store's top floor. Ostensibly, the purpose of the radio station was to transmit information between Bamberger's and its "sister" stores— Macy's in Manhattan, and Abraham & Straus in Brooklyn— without paying long-distance telephone rates. It was also used to broadcast news throughout the store: "Attention, Bamberger's shoppers . . . right now, in our third-floor lingerie department, and for a short time only, you will find luxurious stays and camisoles, marked down to *unbelievably* low prices. . . ." But its real purpose was to lure curious customers up through the store's upper floors, where shopping traffic was always lightest. Customers crowded around the little booth, their faces pressed against the glass, watching and listening to the operator sending and receiving messages over the miraculous new medium of the airwaves.

On the night of April 14, 1912, Ho Rothman was asked to man the radio station while the regular operator went down to the cafeteria to have his dinner. There was not much to it. It just meant putting on a headset, setting up the microphone, and operating a simple set of keys, buttons, and switches. It was in this glass booth that Ho Rothman was sitting when, by accident as he experimented with his switches and buttons, he picked up a faint but distinct signal from the

North Atlantic: "S.S. *Titanic* . . . ran into iceberg . . . Sinking fast. . . ."

He then did something he never in his life had done before. He walked off his job—walked, ran, *flew!*—to his newspaper printing press where the tray of type was already set up. Within twenty minutes, he had his cover story written and, within an hour, he was running down the streets of Newark, hawking his Extra edition, shouting, "Extra! Extra! *Titanic* sinks!"

Ho Rothman was always proud of the lead he wrote for that story in such record time:

As THE EXPLORER predicted three weeks ago, the S.S. *Titanic* has gone down, with great loss of lives, a victim of what the Greeks call *hubris*, or the sin of pride. Tonight's disaster, in which thousands have gone down to a watery end, proves that mere man, or any of the creations of man, dare not defy the mighty forces of Mother Nature, nor the cruel vengeance of a punishing ocean. The *Titanic* had the supreme audacity to proclaim herself "unsinkable." For this insult to Nature, she has paid at the cost of untold human suffering and agonizing death. . . .

Of course the details of the disaster that followed were wildly inaccurate—Ho simply made them up. But it didn't matter. In the weeks that followed, all the published reports of the tragedy were confused and garbled, full of errors, misinterpretations, guesswork, and Monday-morning quarterbacking. Even to this day, many details of what happened that night at sea are open to debate and speculation, and there are many questions that may never be answered properly.

Ho was always proud, too, of the last two lines of his story:

The officers and directors of White Star did not listen to THE EXPLORER'S warnings then. Perhaps—too late—they will listen now.

What mattered most was that Ho Rothman's little weekly tabloid had been the first newspaper in the world to report the sinking of the S.S. *Titanic*. What had really been only a warning very quickly became a "prediction" that the disaster would happen. And, in the days that followed, seventeen-year-old H. O. Rothman found himself the most famous newspaperman in the United States.

Chapter 15

Actually, her day had gone better than she had thought it would, considering its somewhat rocky start. Plans for the picnic issue had been roughed out, and it had been generally decided that all the fashion pages would be shot out of doors. It was the kind of subtle touch most readers wouldn't even notice, but it would add a certain continuity of texture and feel to the issue, as readers turned the pages. In terms of graphics, there would be conventional picnics—a picnic on the beach, a picnic on the deck of a sailboat, a tailgate picnic at a polo match—and also unconventional ones: a picnic in a greenhouse, an after-theater picnic in the back seat of a stretch limousine. In other words, the issue would have as its subtheme Getting Out of the House, Getting Away. . . .

"I want it to be our prettiest issue ever," she had said. "I want everything to be just—pretty. I want views. Views of oceans, views of mountains. What about a picnic in the warm-up hut at a ski resort?"

Yes, it had gone well. And from her father-in-law's office on the thirtieth floor, there had been not a word.

At four o'clock, Bob Shaw came by, flopped on her sofa, and said, "Well, believe it or not, I've found out what makes bees swarm. It's very simple, it turns out. They swarm when the hive is overcrowded. They swarm to found a new colony, and select a new queen, like Gregory said. All we got to do is find a beekeeper with an overcrowded hive, and we've got a potential swarm. Now *where* the bees will decide to swarm is another matter. Beekeepers can control this to some extent, but whether we can make the bees swarm in a model's hair is something I don't know yet, but I've got the library working on it. The bees that swarmed in Gregory's mom's hair were wild bees, and there's always a lead bee that guides the others to the swarming spot. Since Gregory's mom had been swimming in a river, there may have been some mineral in the river water that attracted that lead bee."

"Fascinating," she said. "Good work, Bob."

"Now all we have to do is find a model with nerves of steel who'll let a bunch of bees swarm in her hair."

"I'll take care of that," she said. "It's amazing what a girl will do to get herself on the cover of *Mode*."

"So much for bees," he said. "But speaking of those little critters, what are we all supposed to make of this new queen bee that's going to be joining you at the top of the masthead? A lot of people would sure like to know, Alex."

She winked at him. "No comment," she said.

He shook his head and stared at the backs of his hands. "I don't like it," he said. "I don't like it one bit. We've all been a team here, and now—"

"Don't get any more gray hairs about it," she said. "Promise me."

Four thirty passed, and there was still no word from the thirtieth floor. Obviously, Herb Rothman was expecting the next move to come from her, but she wasn't ready to make that move. Let him wonder what I'm up to, she thought. Let him sweat it out a bit.

Then she had taken a call from Mark Rinsky.

"This is just a prelim report," he said. "About the Brit broad."

"I'm not supposed to let you use words like broad," she said. "But in her case, perhaps I will."

"Yeah, well, here's what I've found out so far. She lives at the Westbury Hotel, in one of their fancier suites with a woodburning fireplace. She wanted a piano in her sitting room, and so the hotel moved in a Baldwin grand. She rented the place in May, on a two-year lease, first and last month paid, and this spread rents for twelve thou a month, so obviously the broad's got dough."

"Either that, or a rich sponsor."

"Yeah, I'll be looking into that. But meanwhile she seems to live very quietly. The hotel was a little worried about the piano—late-night parties, and all. But as far as they're concerned, so far she's been the perfect guest. No big demands. Hotel staff likes her, which I guess means she tips well. Oh, just one demand, besides the piano. She likes her bed made up with her own sheets—blue satin—but, what the hell, I guess a lot of rich broads do that. She doesn't go out much—coupla times. Sticks to herself. Not too many visitors."

"No particular—romantic life?"

"Not that anybody knows about. Young man brought her home last night, and went up with her. Night bell captain saw them. But then he went off duty, so he doesn't know how long the young man stayed. Nobody remembers seeing him leave."

"A *young* man?"

"Yeah. Her age or younger. Guy with glasses, the bell captain *thinks*. Obviously, we'll be keeping a closer watch on her from now on."

"It wasn't Herbert Rothman?"

"Herb Rothman's in his late sixties, isn't he? This guy was her age or younger, and she's—"

"The *Times* gave her age as twenty-eight."

"Yeah, but it's hard to judge a woman's age these days, isn't it? Particularly behind those big shades she wears. Let's see—what else? Like I say, she appears to be something of a loner. She hardly ever eats in the hotel dining room, and has most of her meals sent up by room service. She has the hotel screen her phone calls, but the switchboard says she doesn't get that many. Oh, and here's a kind of funny thing. She's also had a couple of private lines run in, both of them unlisted. But one line's for residential service, and the other's for business. She has an answering machine on the residential line, but not on the business one. Doesn't that strike you as funny?"

"I dunno, darlin'. Why?"

"If you were running a business of some kind, wouldn't you put your answering machine on your business line, and not on your residential one? Well, maybe it's nothing."

"What about England? Have you found out anything there?"

"It's nearly ten at night in London now. But I have an associate there, and I'll try to reach him early Monday morning. Be back to you as soon as I have anything."

"Thank you, Mark. . . ."

Now it was a little after five o'clock, and Alex was packing her briefcase with a few manuscripts she planned to read over the weekend. In the morning, she and Mel were driving out to the Island to spend the weekend at his house in Sagaponack. From the outer office, she heard the telephone ring as, indeed, it had been ringing all day long, and presently Gregory was standing at her door. His look was apprehensive. "It's Mr. Herbert Rothman," he said. "He wants to see you."

She started to say, "Tell him it'll have to wait till Monday." But then she thought: Well, if there's going to be a confrontation, it might as well be now, and so, in the jauntiest manner she could affect, she said, "Okay. Tell him I'll be right up, darlin'."

On her way up the elevator to the thirtieth floor, she reminded herself: chin up. Whatever happened now, she must not lose her temper. She was never at her most effective when she lost her temper and, besides, her temper had never been a match for Herb Rothman's. She entered his office with a breezy wave of her hand at his secretary, Miss Lincoln, who hardly looked at her, and then stepped into the inner sanctum, closing the door behind her.

Herb Rothman sat at his desk, moving pieces of paper about the top as though searching for some important document, and did not immediately look up at her. "Hi, Herb," she said pleasantly, and quickly settled herself in one of the two leather chairs that flanked his desk. He still did not look up at her, but continued shuttling papers back and forth across his desktop.

Herb Rothman's office was no bigger than her own— in fact, it occupied the same space in the building's floor plan—but it was much more Spartan in its furnishings. A glass case behind his desk displaying athletic trophies—polo, golf, tennis, and crew had been his sports—was the office's only decorative touch, a hard-edged one at that. As a young man, Herb Rothman had been considered good-looking and, in many ways, he still was. He still had a full head of short-cropped, steel-gray hair, and a hard, firm jawline. "Herbert J. Rothman is all corners," a writer had written about him once, referring to his tight, angular build and his sharply defined features. Though small in stature like his father, he had maintained his flat-bellied jockey's physique through rigid exercise in the private gym in his apartment. He was dressed now, as he often was at the office, for sport—in a sweat shirt, sweat pants, and Nike running shoes, a style of attire certainly calculated to astonish first-time visitors, and throw them off their guard. He still jogged the fifteen-odd blocks between 44th Street and home at River House. Alex was used to all this, of course, and was no longer even amused by these affectations of his. She knew her father-in-law too well. These were Herb's defenses—against his own father and a cruel world. She tucked her feet underneath her in the chair, touched her triple strand of pearls, and cupped her chin in her hand, waiting for him to acknowledge her. She even knew what his first words to her would be.

Then, still without looking up at her, he spoke them: "What time is it?" It was always the same.

She glanced at her watch. "Five fifteen," she said, and she added, "I hope this won't take too long, Herb. I was just on my way home, and I have to pack for the country tomorrow."

His answer was to press a buzzer on his desk. "Miss Lincoln," he said, "record this conversation."

This was called intimidation. Alex smiled. "Very nice," she said.

"What's very nice?"

"That you're going to record our meeting," she said. "I have no objection, Herb. It's just that it adds a certain—solemnity to the occasion, doesn't it?"

"I don't want there to be any misunderstanding, later on, about who said what," he said.

"I understand."

A copy of that morning's *Daily News* lay on his desk. He patted it with the palm of his hand. "Most unfortunate," he said.

"What's unfortunate?"

"The boating accident."

"Oh, yes. But what could anybody do?"

"Mona writes that the accident was caused by the fireworks display at your party."

"That's just your usual Mona—getting all her facts a little

wrong. *Mode* can do a lot of things, Herb, but we can't cause a tidal bore."

"Isn't it true that the boat came by to watch the fireworks?"

"Yes," she said carefully. "But look at it this way, Herb. If you hadn't decided to make your little speech, and the fireworks had gone off as scheduled, the boat would have been nowhere in the vicinity. So I suppose someone could say that *you* caused the boating accident."

He scowled. "Very funny," he said. "But it's most unfortunate publicity. Most unfortunate for us, at this particular juncture in time."

"I agree," she said quickly.

"Will Mona print a retraction of that statement?"

"I thought of that," she said. "But I decided that wouldn't be wise. When you get a journalist to print a retraction, all you do is get the misinformation printed again."

"I would like to see a retraction printed."

"Then you ask her to do it, Herb. I'm not going to."

He scowled again. "Fireworks," he said. "How much did that party of yours cost us, anyway?"

"It didn't cost *us* a thing," she said. "I paid for that party myself."

"Are you sure?"

"Of course I'm sure. If you like, I can show you the receipts."

"You have that kind of money? Of course I suppose you intend to write it off as a tax deduction."

"I hadn't really thought about it," she said. "But its purpose was to publicize the magazine, so I suppose I could."

He sat forward in his chair. "You see, Alex," he said, "this is what is so unfortunate—so unwise—about your party last night, at this particular juncture in time. We face a lawsuit by the IRS. And therefore any publicity involving the expenditure of large sums of money, extravagant spending on a lavish party that is obviously tax-deductible, sends exactly the wrong message to the IRS. Exactly the wrong message. I spoke to our lawyers this morning, and I must tell you that they are dismayed—absolutely dismayed—by the kind of publicity your party has received."

She was quite certain that this was a lie, but she decided to let it pass. Every publication in the country, when it had something important to announce, gave a party—including *Mode*. But she suddenly remembered, with a shiver, another *Mode* party, in 1971, that had ended in a tragedy. That had been Steven's party.

"I suppose everyone knows by now," he continued, "that you and I do not see eye to eye on many issues."

"That's true," she said. "But, by agreeing to disagree, we've managed to come up with a successful product— wouldn't you agree? Wouldn't you agree that, by agreeing to disagree, we've forged a successful partnership? You stay out of my hair, and I stay out of yours."

"Perhaps," he said. "But I must say I found your June cover disgusting."

She smiled. "Our readers didn't seem to think so. Newsstand sales were up twelve percent over May. That's a good barometer."

He sniffed. "Prurient interest, no doubt."

"Well, we got through the U.S. mails with no problem. Don't you find a woman's body beautiful? I do."

"That's beside the point."

"I suppose it is. The point is the box office, and the figures are in. What is it your father says? 'You don't take your money off a winning horse.' "

"I don't find your imitation of Mr. H. O. Rothman's accent amusing," he said. He always referred to his father as Mr. H. O. Rothman. "And I hope you're not implying that you intend to do the same thing again."

"Have I ever repeated myself, Herb?"

"Disgusting," he said again. "But never mind. That's water over the dam. I wish now to turn to another matter. This," and he picked up a second piece of paper. It was yesterday's edition of the *New York Times*. "This advertisement." He held up the whale ad.

"Like it?" she said brightly. "The agency's submitted it for a Clio Award. They think it might win."

"Whether I like it or not is beside the point," he said. "But since you ask me, I don't like it. I don't like it—again— because it sends entirely the wrong signals to the IRS. We are boasting of our bigness, of our financial success. The timing of this is all wrong. It is wrong at this juncture in time."

"We owe it to our advertisers to announce what they're

getting for their money. If they're getting something big, we need to announce it big."

"Perhaps," he said, putting down the newspaper with an expression of distaste. "Was this ad your idea, or the agency's?"

"We both worked on it."

"You know, of course, that an agency is only interested in generating commissions. But you haven't answered my question, Alex. Whose idea was it to run this ad?"

"It was mine."

"I see," he said. "Which brings me to this," and he picked up a third piece of paper. "I am holding in my hand *Mode*'s advertising promotion budget for fiscal nineteen ninety. I see no provision here for a full-page advertisement in the *New York Times* for Thursday, June twenty-first."

She bit her lip. "It seemed important," she said. "We had to announce. We thought—"

"Are you now making budgetary decisions, Alex? I thought budgetary decisions were made by the publisher, which I am. I believe an important step in the chain of command has been omitted. Or am I wrong?"

"I'm sorry," she began. "I suppose in the excitement—five million—I suppose we—"

"So you admit to making a mistake," he said. "And a very costly mistake. Do you know how much the back page of the *New York Times*—national edition—costs?"

"Of course I know."

"Thirty-five thousand dollars. Where is that money to come from in your publisher's advertising budget? Or are you taking it upon yourself to assume the duties and decisions of your publisher? Or do you admit that you seriously overstepped your authority?"

"Yes," she said. "I suppose, in the excitement of it all, I forgot to consult you on this one. But shouldn't the agency have—"

"Don't try to blame the agency. An agency is not to be trusted. All an agency is interested in doing is spending our money, and taking their fifteen percent off the top." He leaned toward her again, and suddenly his attitude was grandfatherly. "You see, Alex," he said, "you keep making these mistakes. First you run a cover with a girl exposing everything but her—never mind. Then you spend unauthorized advertising dollars. You look tired, Alex. You look tired, and you look overworked. I think you could use a long vacation, or perhaps a leave of absence. I would gladly give you an extended leave of absence, if that would help you through this midlife crisis. After all, none of us are getting any younger."

"I'm not tired, I'm not overworked, and I'm not going through any midlife crisis!"

"That's what they all say. But that's why I've brought in Lady Fiona Fenton, to give you a hand. She's young, she's vital, she's full of fresh ideas. Also, having worked in retailing, she's got good business sense, which you have admitted you lack. And she has good public-relations sense, which you lack. You haven't said, incidentally, what you think of my addition of Lady Fiona to our masthead."

"What do I think of it? I'm appalled, that's what I think of it." She could feel the edge of anger in her voice. Careful, she told herself. Anger is not the way to deal with this.

He had picked up a yellow pencil and was rolling it between the palms of his hands. "It's a move designed to provide a better balance between the publishing and editorial divisions of the magazine," he said. "Between the way the magazine is edited, and the way it is merchandised and sold—and advertised. She will be a much-needed liaison between the editors and the sales staff, who, incidentally, had no inkling about yesterday's promotional ad in the *New York Times*. As I say, she has highly developed, and much-needed, business skills. With her influential circle of acquaintances—"

Suddenly she realized he was reading from a press release. "And I can't imagine where you intend to *put* her. There isn't an inch of space left on the fourteenth floor," she said.

"What about whatsername, the beauty editor?"

"Carol Duffy."

"Is she really needed? I gather all she does is copy off the releases sent to her by cosmetics companies."

"Carol is a very valuable editor! She does much more than that."

"And your art director, Mr. Shaw. Drinks, doesn't he?"

"Bob Shaw is the best art director in New York!"

"Well, Fiona expects to find a good deal of dead wood down there. I expect we shall be doing a bit of pruning, a bit of streamlining, of the staff, thereby reducing the magazine's not-inconsiderable overhead. There are people down there who have just been at their jobs too long."

"I can't believe this," she said. "This woman hasn't even joined the company yet, and she's already messing with my staff. *My staff.*"

"Fiona has already proposed some much-needed cost-cutting measures."

"Like taking away my company car, for instance? It wasn't there to pick me up this morning. But that's all right. I can take a taxi, or the bus."

He dismissed this with a wave of his hand. "Meanwhile, you asked where Fiona will be sitting. For the time being, at least, I intend to let her use this office, which would be appropriate, since she will be working closely with the publisher. And I myself will shortly be moving into Mr. H. O. Rothman's old office, which is now just wasted space."

She stared at him. "So," she said, "you really are taking over Rothman Communications. Just like that!"

"The word *takeover* has unfortunate connotations in the nineteen nineties," he said. "Let us just say that I am assuming Mr. H. O. Rothman's mantle, now that he has let it fall. After all, someone has to. A company like ours cannot go on without a leader, like a riderless horse. So let us just say I am fulfilling my destiny—my destiny in this family, and in this company. My manifest destiny, if you will—just as, one day, your son will fulfill his manifest destiny in the family, and in the company. Someday"—he gestured around him—"this will all be his."

"My son has nothing to do with this. I have no idea whether or not Joel plans to join the company. And if he asks me for my advice, I'll certainly advise him against it."

"But that is Joel's destiny. There's nothing he can do about it. That is what Joel Rothman has always been for."

"That is not what Joel's *for*. People aren't *for* anything."

"Which brings me to another point," he said. "Joel is the only male Rothman heir. The company will one day be his. He must have protection. His life has been threatened. And yet I gather that you have taken it upon yourself to dismiss Lieutenant Otto Forsthoefel this morning."

"You're damn right I did!"

"Lieutenant Forsthoefel was hired for Joel's protection. He

was hired by me. I pay his salary. It is not up to you, Alex, to dismiss one of my salaried employees."

"Well, I don't care who pays his salary," she said. "Joel is *my son*. And Otto is not going to follow *my son* around any longer, and he's not hanging around *my house* any longer, and that's that."

"Well, we'll see," he said. "But you admit you had no authority to dismiss Lieutenant Forsthoefel. That's the third mistake you've admitted to this afternoon, Alex." He counted on his fingertips. "First, the objectionable June cover. Second, unauthorized advertising expenditure. Third, unauthorized dismissal of a Rothman corporate employee. You see, that's what worries me. You've been making these mistakes with increasing regularity, one after another. You're losing your grip, Alex."

That was it, she thought. That did it. There went her pressure valve. Now she could see why his wife no longer spoke to him, though why Pegeen stayed with him she could not imagine, unless it was for the money, which of course it was. If I had let you fuck me years ago, she thought, the way you wanted to, would it have been any different? She started to ask him this, but didn't. If I had had a secret son by you ("I've demonstrated that I can father male heirs, Alex"), would that have satisfied your stupid ego? She started to say this, too, but didn't. Because of course it wouldn't have been any different, it wouldn't have been any different at all. She jumped to her feet. "Now listen to me, you bastard," she said. "You're not going to get away with this. I have a contract with this company that calls for me to be editor-in-chief of this magazine. It does not call for me to be co-editor-in-chief, or anything else, and my contract has two more years to run, you bastard, and the next thing you hear from me will be from my lawyer, whose name is Henry Coker, you bastard!"

Now he too rose. Like his father's, Herbert Rothman's desk and chair were on a raised platform, and now, from his platform, even this small man towered over her. "You mean you intend to challenge me?" he said in a voice that was more like a snarl.

"You're damn right I do!"

"I warn you! Don't try it!"

"I damn well will try it! You've been busting for this fight for a long time, haven't you, Herbert? Well, now you're going to have it, darlin'!"

"Challenge me, and I'll ruin you, Alex Rothman!"

"You can't ruin me! Even if you fire me, you'll still have to pay me the balance of my contract—plus profit sharing. How will that sit with your IRS boys? How will that sit with your cost-cutting ladyfriend?"

"I'll also see to it that you never work in New York again."

"Nonsense. There isn't a publisher in town who wouldn't snap me up. In fact, there's one who's trying to already."

His eyes narrowed. "Tarrytown. What about Tarrytown?" he said.

"What about it? Everybody knows what happened there. Tarrytown was a closed book years ago."

"There is no statute of limitations on a murder case, Alex. That case could be reopened at any time."

"But there wasn't any murder. So to hell with your threats!"

"Oh, *wasn't* there?" His eyes had narrowed to tiny slits. "What if there were some new—evidence, Alex?"

"What sort of new evidence?"

"You'll see."

"Ha! You're bluffing, of course. There is no new evidence. If there were any new evidence, you'd be using it against me right now. I know you, Herb. You've always hated me. You've wanted me out of the magazine from the beginning, and if there'd been any legal way to do it—if there'd been any way you could overrule Ho—you'd have done it long before this. But now that Ho is old and sick, you think you can force me to resign with threats and bluffs and innuendoes, and garbage about new evidence. Well, it ain't gonna work, baby!"

"Watch what you say very carefully, Alex. Remember, this conversation is being recorded."

"Well, you can turn your damned recorder off, because this conversation is over." She started toward the door.

"I'm warning you, Alex," he said. "If you try to challenge me, you'll find yourself back in that miserable little pissant town you came from—what was it called? Paradise, Missouri! You'll find yourself back in Paradise, Missouri, so fast you won't know what the hell hit you! You'll find yourself headed back to Paradise, Missouri, in the back of a Greyhound bus! And without a pot to piss in!"

"And with Joel with me!"

"*Without* Joel! Joel belongs to us!"

"Fuck you!" And she was out the door, resisting the urge to slam it—hard, in his face—as she left.

Except for that last expletive, she was proud of herself—proud, exhilarated, happy even, although her heart was pounding wildly and her mouth was dry, and her hands were shaking and, as the elevator doors closed, she gasped for breath. Look—no tears! Years of frustration with that man, years of trying to remember that he was her husband's father, had been sloughed away, like loose and flaking skin, like unwanted weight, and she felt eighteen years old again—the way she had felt when she was first in love. Oh, wonderful, wonderful! On the fourteenth floor, the *Mode* offices were silent, wonderfully, emptily, peacefully silent, blessedly deserted and hers alone, for nearly all the staff had left for the weekend. Distantly there was the click of a copywriter's typewriter—working on a picture caption, perhaps, or perhaps moonlighting or using his machine to write a great romantic novel of passion and pursuit and heroism and betrayal. Most were gone, except for Gregory, who never left before his boss. Outside the anteroom to her office where Gregory would be waiting were a cleaning lady's squeegee mop and pail—so homey, so normal, with the healing, disinfectant smell of hot suds. She sent a message to her moonlighting copywriter: Put the cleaning lady's mop and pail into your novel as a signal of the basic orderliness of things. Take that simple signal with my blessing, and my love.

The expression on Gregory's too-handsome face was still anxious. Her meetings with the publisher seldom lasted for more than a minute or two. This one had lasted more than half an hour. Yes, Gregory's face was too handsome, handsomer than any young man's face had any right to be. And yet, behind that too-perfect face, behind those double-lashed dark eyes, weren't there deep glimmerings of intelligence and courage and kindness and love that had yet to be—were still waiting to be—expressed? She saw all this as their eyes briefly locked, and she knew he knew exactly what she was feeling then. Dear Gregory. "Oh, Gregory," she said suddenly, "you're such a nice guy. You really are."

The dark lashes lowered, and the eyes withdrew.

"If you can still reach him," she said, "I'll speak to Mr. Rodney McCulloch now."

She kicked off her shoes and sat down at her desk.

Chapter 16

In their apartment at the Gainsborough Studios on Central Park South, Lenny Liebling and his old friend Charlie Boxer were preparing for a quiet Friday evening at home. Friday and Saturday nights are not social nights in New York; everyone goes to the country. As a result, weekends are peaceful times in the city, and the peace begins to settle in as the Friday sun begins to set. This hush had already begun to fall as the first lights began to twinkle on in the park below. Charlie, who did most of the cooking, had prepared a ratatouille and that, with a bottle of nouveau Beaujolais, would be their dinner.

Both Charlie and Lenny watched their weight, but Lenny was more successful at it than Charlie was. This, Lenny suspected, was because Charlie snacked from the refrigerator during the day while Lenny was at the office. How else did one account for the steadily diminishing size of the Zabar's cheesecake? How else did one explain the empty peanut butter jars and Ritz cracker boxes in the garbage can? But Lenny had long ago stopped mentioning these matters to his friend. They had reached that point in their relationship where each accepted the other at face value, and where neither expected the other ever to change. Long ago, they had simultaneously made the unspoken discovery that people never really change. What you see is what you get. If psychiatrists admitted this, they would be out of business.

Charlie was a few years younger than Lenny—a few, not many—and Charlie was as short and round and plump as Lenny was tall and angular and elegant. *Cherubic* was a word that was sometimes used to describe Charlie. He was nearly bald—just a few wisps of fine hair brushed across his pink scalp—while Lenny, of course, had that magnificent head of wavy, champagne-colored hair, Danny Kaye hair. They had been called Mutt and Jeff, though naturally never to their faces. They had also been called Jack Sprat and his Wife, with Charlie being the wife. There were also some people who referred to them as the Sunshine Boys.

Charlie had had some money once. An ancient aunt in Boston had left him $200,000, which seemed like a fortune at the time, and so Charlie had never seen the need to work. The money was all gone now, of course, spent on this and that, not very wisely for the most part, and now Lenny supported Charlie—for the most part without rancor or recrimination. After all, to a man who has never worked, the whole idea of work is incomprehensible, and what could Charlie really do? And, also, Lenny had certainly helped Charlie spend the $200,000. Charlie was very skillful at stuffing the centers of pitted olives with cream cheese, and he had prepared a plate of these for their hors d'oeuvres. He popped one of these into his mouth now, as they sipped their wine.

Their apartment in the grand old pre–World War I building was full of comfortable clutter, which was the way they liked it, clutter that had been collected over years of poking about in antique and secondhand stores, here and abroad, and in obscure little pawn shops in unlikely reaches of the city. Nothing in the apartment was really very good, which was perhaps part of its charm, why it all came together in a haphazard, homey sort of way. A Donald Duck cream pitcher held some sprigs of dried baby's-breath, and stood next to some plated-brass candlesticks on a coffee table that also held an antique beaded purse, a threadbare teddy bear wearing a bib, a pair of opera glasses from the Rastro in Madrid, a toast rack from the Portobello Road, an ashtray pinched from the Paris Ritz and another designed to commemorate the coronation, which never came off, of Edward VIII (the Duchess had roared over that), the very first issue of *Flair* (with the hole in its cover), several snuffboxes, a cigar that had been presented to Lenny by Winston Churchill (or so he said), an old Baccarat inkwell that would have been quite nice if it hadn't been badly chipped, a *millefleur* paperweight that was not by Baccarat, a chambered nautilis shell from some Florida beach, a huge and battered-looking door key that Lenny's mother always claimed opened the door of *der alte Heim*, where she had been born in nineteenth-century Germany and, incredibly or not, a great many other objects, precious only to their owners.

In one corner of the apartment next to Bridget's cage sat a parlor grand piano draped in a comfortably motheaten cashmere Paisley shawl that Lenny often claimed "belonged to my great-grandmother, the Archduchess Louisa of Saxe-Coburg." Actually, he and Charlie had bought it on Second Avenue for fourteen dollars. Lenny often falsified and fancified his family's past. He often spoke of his late mother's "priceless collection of antiques," but how could the postmistress of Onward, Mississippi, have amassed a priceless antiques collection? He once remarked to Maria Callas, "My late, sainted mother had a pair of emerald earrings almost exactly like the ones you're wearing." But how could this same postmistress have afforded emeralds? Still, since nobody really believed any of Lenny's stories anyway, it didn't matter whether they were true or not. Charlie Boxer's lineage, meanwhile, was genteel. There had been Boxers in the Boston Social Register. But when, several years ago, the Social Registers of all U.S. cities were combined in one big volume, Charlie's name was inexplicably omitted. Try as he might, Charlie had never been able to get himself reinstated. He could only conclude that he had enemies on the Register's selection committee.

Arranged on top of the shawl, in plated-silver frames that could have stood polishing, were arrayed dozens of autographed photographs of some of Lenny's and Charlie's celebrated friends, many of them, alas, no longer living— Gloria Swanson, Garbo, Ava Gardner, Elizabeth Taylor, Hedy Lamar, Clare Boothe Luce, Lady Diana Cooper, Nancy Reagan, Greg and Veronique Peck, Bob and Dolores Hope, Edith Piaf, Bricktop, Duke Ellington, Larry Olivier as Richard III, Helen Hayes, Lily Pons, Barbara Hutton, the Duke and Duchess, Tony Snowdon, Gloria Guinness, Hermione Gingold, Babe Paley, Gloria Vanderbilt, Oona O'Neill, Monty Clift, Bianca Jagger, and on and on. Nearly all bore affectionate inscriptions to Lenny and Charlie.

On a long Spanish refectory table against the opposite wall was arranged what their friends referred to as The Shrine. It was a shrine to their late friend Adam Amado, and it was a shrine, in a very real sense, to failure, although Lenny and Charlie didn't choose to look at it that way. To them, Adam Amado would always be a great star whose time had never come.

Surrounded as they were by great stars and celebrities, it had long been Lenny's and Charlie's dream to create a star of their very own, and they were convinced that in Adam Amado they had found just such a potential luminary. Adam Amado was a street person, of sorts, though he had the looks of a Jon Whitcomb illustration come to life. He could have been so much more!

Adam Amado was not his real name, of course. Who remembered what his original name was? The name "Adam Amado" was created for him by Lenny and Charlie after much thought, and after many alliterative combinations of names had been proposed and discarded. The name Adam, of course, connoted "first man," and Amado, from rather loose Italian, suggested "loved one," and Lenny and Charlie were certain that, with this young man's striking good looks, combined with his appealing new name, they had the makings of a new screen or stage matinee idol. Had they succeeded, as Adam's agent-managers they would certainly have become very rich, and would not have needed the help of the Rothmans.

At first, they had begun working on their discovery in the greatest secrecy, since their plan was to spring Adam on the world as a full-blown creation. To friends, during this period, they alluded to Adam's existence mysteriously as "a certain project we're working on." Meanwhile, they were giving Adam speech and elocution lessons, acting lessons, singing lessons, dancing lessons, fencing lessons. He was even given karate lessons, and through this period they were also feeding and clothing him, for Adam had no money. They had his teeth straightened and capped to improve his smile line, they had a small bump on his nose surgically removed, and a slight cleft added to his chin, and they darkened his hair color and created a hairstyle for him that made him look like a blow-dried Rudolph Valentino. Though his body was in excellent shape, Lenny and Charlie supervised his daily exercise regimen. Soon Lenny and Charlie were telling themselves—and Adam—that they had discovered "the brunet Tab Hunter," and a new teenage heartthrob, forgetting, perhaps, that Tab Hunter was a creature of the 1950s—as Valentino had been a creature of the 1920s—and that by the late 1960s, when all this was going on, there were no more bobby-soxers with heartthrobs.

The trouble was, in retrospect, that Adam was too quick a learner, too impatient to see his name in lights on a marquee. Once he had improved his diction, his posture, his walk, learned how to use his hands effectively and how to smile for the camera without squinting his eyes, he didn't see why he should not be elevated immediately to the pantheon of great performers. He refused to listen to Lenny's careful counseling that these things took time, patience, and step-by-step planning. "I won't pose for a toothpaste ad!" he would storm. "And I certainly won't pose for it in jockey shorts."

"But you have a beautiful body, Adam. This is what's known as giving you exposure."

"And I'm not going to do a voice-over for a used-car commercial that's not even *national*."

"They'll pay you two thousand dollars, Adam."

"I wouldn't do it for less than twenty."

By the time Lenny and Charlie were ready to show Adam off to their influential friends—who could have done so much to help him—he had become arrogant, temperamental, demanding. And though everyone agreed that Adam looked great in the new clothes that Lenny and Charlie had bought for him, most people found him personally insufferable. Lenny tried enrolling Adam in a charm school, but later discovered that Adam had never attended the classes. Instead, he had asked for a refund on Lenny's tuition payment, and then apparently pocketed the money himself.

At the same time, Lenny and Charlie began to suspect that Adam had become dependent on certain prescription medicines. He took pills to wake himself up in the morning, pills to elevate his mood, and pills to help him sleep at night. Friends began to notice, though they did not immediately mention it, that when the boys brought Adam to their parties their medicine chests were raided—their Valium, lithium, and Dexedrine bottles emptied.

Adam had also begun drinking heavily. The boys noticed this when they saw how rapidly their liquor supplies in the apartment were dwindling. Soon it was necessary to hide the liquor, but one cannot really hide liquor from an alcoholic determined to find it. Secretly, the boys began to suspect that they had created a monster. And yet, at that point, they had already made a public commitment to Adam's success, and it seemed too humiliating to admit failure.

Meanwhile, he lived in their guest bedroom, and of course many people assumed that there was a sexual relationship there. But there really wasn't—not, at least, in any significant way, though it was clear that both Charlie and Lenny were devoted to Adam—hoping against desperate hope that something would change. As for Adam himself, he swung, as they say, both ways. Did that make him a bisexual? Lenny and Charlie simply knew that Adam Amado was a young man who was accustomed to taking sex wherever, and whenever, and with whomever, he found it.

There was more erratic behavior. He showed up late, or else failed to show up at all, for casting calls that Lenny had arranged for him. He showed up drunk on a nationally televised talk show, whose host Lenny had begged to use Adam as a guest. He urinated in the office fireplace of an important producer who had just offered him a part in an off-Broadway play. And there was more, much more, and much worse. And yet the boys persisted with their dream, their vision. . . .

Pity the Pygmalion who produces a flawed Galatea!

It was Mona Potter, of all people, who finally blew the whistle on Adam Amado. In a 1969 column reporting on a fashionable East Side party, Mona wrote:

> The evening's festivities were somewhat marred by a certain Manhattan freeloader who calls himself an actor, but who acts best as a drunken deadbeat, who circulated among the guests telling them he was the next Rock Hudson. Yuk!

Even though it was a blind item, with Adam's name not mentioned, everybody knew who Mona was talking about.

Overnight, Adam Amado became a social pariah—to everyone, that is, except Lenny and Charlie, who remained

loyal to him. Why? Well, for one thing, there was certainly
nothing boring about those Adam Years, as they often referred
to that period of their lives. In fact, the boys sometimes missed
the excitement of that time, when no one knew what awful
thing might happen next. They had become like two scientists,
committed to finding the cure for some obscure, incurable
disease through all disaster. They kept hoping that somehow,
somewhere along the way, it would appear—the magic formula—and all their labors would be vindicated. But they also
knew that their friends were laughing at them behind their
backs and calling them damned fools. It was Marlene Dietrich
who provided them with a rationale that enabled them to hold
their heads high in face of all the ridicule.

Dear Marlene. Lenny often thought that if she had not possessed the beauty to become a great film star she would have
entered the nursing profession. Marlene was drawn to sick
people like carborundum to a magnet. She actively sought out
the ill and the neurasthenic, and she thrilled at the prospect
of treating the dying. She was a walking medicine cabinet.
Her voluminous handbag was always filled with pills and
potions, herbal remedies and exotic lixiviums and panaceas
from around the world. She carried cures for everything from
whooping cough to gonorrhea.

"Dis is a very sick boy," she had told Lenny and Char-
lie. "He needs your help. De Almighty has given you dis
meesion, to care for dis sick boy. Ees a scared meesion.
Ees what God has put you on dis earth to do, Charles and
Lenny. You are like Albert Schweitzer in Africa! You are like
Father Damion among the lepers! You are saints, Charles and
Lenny. Both of you! Saints!"

Thus canonized by Marlene, Saint Lenny and Saint Charlie lifted their cross to their shoulders once more and carried
on their God-appointed mission with renewed diligence and
self-esteem.

And, basically, they loved Adam, and he could be amusing enough company, particularly when he wasn't drinking.

Unfortunately, the drinking periods far outnumbered the
nondrinking ones.

But, thanks to dear Marlene, Lenny and Charlie were able
to translate their continued tolerance of, and loyalty to, Adam
Amado as a kind of advertisement to the world at large of

their own grit and superior character. They would never, thanks to Marlene, be accused of being rats deserting the sinking U.S.S. Adam, the way the rest of New York was doing.

Of course, a certain amount of ego gratification was involved here. Sympathy was not an altogether bad commodity to elicit from your peers, and weren't the greatest tragic heroes in literature always those who suffered longest and with the least complaining? Lenny had even thought of having dear Marlene's words embroidered on a sampler.

For four more long, tortuous years the pair supported him. They had never known Adam's real age—he claimed not to know himself—but, in this period, he did not age well. Still, they continued to pay him an allowance, and loaned him extra money whenever they could. They took him out to dinner, and tried to keep him sober. They tried to soothe him during his drunken, hallucinatory rages. They held his head when he vomited in their toilet, and they nursed his hangovers. They tried to referee his increasingly violent battles with a series of increasingly inappropriate lovers. They put him into, and took him out of, a series of substance-abuse centers. When he was thrown in jail, they bailed him out. They gave him useful tips in dealing with the law: "If a squad car is chasing you, run the wrong way down a one-way street." When his driver's license was taken away, they served as his chauffeurs. Even when it turned out that he was stealing money from them, they forgave him. Right up until the time of his horrible and unnecessary death—his death on a mission they most certainly would have tried to stop, had they known he was going to undertake it—they defended him. Of course, the circumstances of his death, ugly as they were, turned out to have a not-unpleasant side benefit, as they would later discover. "Hold on to these papers for me," he had said, mysteriously, the last day Lenny saw Adam alive. "In case something should happen to me." And he handed Lenny a long, sealed manila envelope.

Then, what he had apparently feared might happen to him happened.

Still, Lenny and Charlie had continued to defend Adam Amado, and his memory, to this very day. Looking back, the Adam Years had been the best years of their lives.

Hence, The Shrine. Across the length of the Spanish refectory table were displayed mementos of their fallen idol—the pair of aviator-type sunglasses that he often wore, his silver-plated crucifix on a slender chain, his billfold that he had not carried with him on that fatal day, and what appeared to be his high-school class ring, though its date and legend had been rubbed away. Here too were the monogrammed gold Tiffany cuff links that Lenny had given him one Christmas and which, because of the embossed "A.A." monogram, he had been unable to pawn. Here, in a scrapbook, were collected all the little notes that Adam ever left for Lenny and Charlie, even notes of little consequence such as "*Be back in 1 hr.—A*," which meant he had gone out to cruise the bars, and laundry lists, and all the IOUs. Also displayed were posters, handbills, and programs from Adam's most memorable performance, as Claudio in a short-lived off-Broadway production of *Measure for Measure*, and copies of the generally positive reviews ("Newcomer Adam Amato [sic] breathes a little life into a thankless role"—*The Village Voice*.) There was the sword he carried as Claudio, and there was the muffler Claudio wore in the last scene, when he was presented to his sister, Isabella. Oddly, there were no photographs displayed of Adam. They were too painful to look at, Lenny said. Photographs existed, of course, many of them—including an extraordinary series of Adam in the nude—but they were hidden away, and no one, since Adam's death, had seen them except Lenny and Charlie.

Perhaps the most extraordinary objects standing on the long table, and propped up against the wall, were a pair of stained-glass windows, which might have come from some church in rural England, and which Adam, inscrutably, left them in his will. That will, along with other bits and pieces of paper, was found in the long manila envelope, as well as the storage receipt for the windows from a Brooklyn warehouse. It had cost Lenny and Charlie three hundred and fifty dollars in unpaid storage fees to retrieve the windows. But how had someone such as Adam, who appeared to have no home or family, come by a pair of stained-glass windows? It was another of the riddles and mysteries about their lost friend that Lenny and Charlie would never unravel.

*   *   *

Now, nibbling on a stuffed olive and staring into his wine-glass, Charlie Boxer said, a little wistfully, "Gus and Maggie Van Zuylen are having their big beach party in Southampton tomorrow night."

"I know, dovey, but we weren't invited."

"If we had a place in the Hamptons, we would have been."

"But we *don't* have a place in the Hamptons, dovey."

It was becoming a familiar plaint of Charlie's, particularly when summer began to roll around: What they really needed was a weekend place in the Hamptons.

"If we *did* have a place in the Hamptons, dovey," Lenny said, "what would happen to our Sunday-night salons here? We'd be spending Sunday evenings fighting the traffic home on the expressway. Incidentally, Betty Bacall said she might pop by this Sunday. It's always fun to see Betty."

"If we had a place in the Hamptons, we could have our salons out there on Saturday nights."

Lenny shook his head. "No, dovey. Saturday nights are cocktail-party nights in the Hamptons. Saturday nights in the Hamptons are strictly reserved for serious drinking, and the accompanying nonsense-talk, to be followed by a drunken roll in the hay. If you ask me, weekends in the Hamptons are becoming a cliché—like that Razor Blade Maggie Van Zuylen."

"Everybody else has a place in the Hamptons," Charlie said. "Everybody but us."

Lenny was finding Charlie's whining tone somewhat annoying. "And how would you expect us to pay for a place in the Hamptons?" he asked testily. "You can't even rent a decent place out there for less than fifty thousand, Memorial Day through Labor Day."

It was the only thing they ever argued about. Money—or the insufficiency of it—was the only source of friction between them. Charlie still sometimes spoke of "my inheritance." But that was spent long ago, much of it on the creation of Adam Amado. When Charlie was angry, he sometimes reminded Lenny of this, since Adam had been Lenny's original idea. If it weren't for Lenny, Charlie seemed to imply, he would still be rich, which was nonsense, because if Charlie hadn't spent his money on Adam he would have frittered it away on something else. Now, neither one of them was rich. They lived—well enough, to be sure—on what Lenny managed to bring in. But they were always just a little bit in debt.

"Of course I don't suppose it would ever occur to you to *work*," Lenny said with an edge to his voice. "Some people work for a living, dovey. I've just spent a particularly exhausting week at the office, and you talk about getting a place in the Hamptons."

"Work? I've got a full-time job just keeping house for you—Mary," Charlie said.

"And speaking of keeping house, those picture frames on the piano could do with some polishing—Mary."

"I've put through three loads of wash today—most of it yours, Mary!"

This could be dangerous, when they started calling each other Mary, and Lenny mentally groped for a change of subject. With a slight *frisson*, he thought: Was it possible that Charlie was becoming bored with him after all these years? He hardly ever talked with Charlie about what went on at the office. The fascinating office intrigues did not fascinate Charlie. They bored him. Having never worked in an office, Charlie didn't even understand them. Office politics were *terra incognita* to Charlie. Lenny could not discuss the Fiona threat with Charlie. He wouldn't grasp its significance. The news that Alex Rothman was under a state of siege would bore him. He could not tell Charlie about Aunt Lily's secret stock-cooking scheme. Charlie wouldn't understand it and, besides, when more than two people were in on it, a secret wasn't a secret any longer. And Charlie was a notorious blabbermouth. He couldn't even tell Charlie about his plans for the Isfahan, exciting though they were, or about what he planned to do next with two signed Boulle commodes.

Charlie was looking very pained and pouty now. And, suddenly in a mollifying mood, Lenny decided to drop just a little cheerful hint. "Actually, I'm working on something right now that may turn out to be a nice little thing for us," he said.

"Oh?" Charlie sat forward, looking interested. "What is it? Money?"

Lenny smiled a prim, sphinxlike smile. "Never you mind, dovey," he said. "But let me just say that if all goes well you might just get your precious house in the Hamptons. And you might get it sooner than you think. Just leave everything to dear old Lenny, dovey dear.''

At that very moment, not many blocks away, Joel Rothman was walking up Madison Avenue toward the Westbury, a spring in his step, his feet in their Paul Stuart loafers barely seeming to touch the pavement, on an adrenaline high. He was free! Mom had been as good as her word, and Otto was gone! Gone forever! There had been quite a scene, and Frank, the elevator man, had told him all about it. It had taken three security men from the building to subdue Otto and carry him out, kicking and screaming and cursing all the way, and brandishing his expired police officer's badge in their faces. Joel laughed at the picture of it, and wished he could have seen it. "Germans," Frank said. "I was in the war, and I killed my share of 'em. They're all alike, them Germans. Krauts, we used to call 'em.''

As he strode up Madison, he paused to appraise his reflection in a shop window. Not bad! He had spent the afternoon shopping. At Stuart's, he had bought a new light blue shirt with a rolled collar, a blue-and-green regimental striped tie, and a pair of color-coordinated blue-and-green-striped socks. She was the kind of girl who noticed these things, and he was wearing them now. He had been especially careful in his selection of underwear. He was also wearing his new double-breasted blue blazer and gray doeskin slacks from Sills of Cambridge. She had teased him about his "specs," as she called them, and so tonight he was wearing his contact lenses. He had also found time for a haircut at Jerry of Bergdorf's. Tonight was their first real date.

She had sounded overjoyed with the idea when he called her earlier in the day. "Pop by my place around seven," she said. "We'll have a bit of bubbly.''

"Then I'm taking you out to dinner," he said.

"Oh, super!" she said.

He glanced at his watch, and forced himself to slow his pace. It was quarter of seven, and he didn't want to be a minute too early or a minute too late. He had timetabled the evening very carefully in his head.

Seven o'clock, arrival.

Seven to seven twenty for the bit of bubbly.

Then he was allowing about an hour for serious fucking, on those blue satin sheets!

Then, allowing for time for them to shower and dress, he had made dinner reservations for half past nine, at Le Cirque. Le Cirque seemed like the perfect place to take a woman like Fiona for dinner. It was where the women in Mona Potter's column always seemed to eat, when it wasn't Mortimer's, and Le Cirque was so much grander than Mort's. And more expensive, of course, but that didn't matter. As a graduation present, his grandfather had given him his very own American Express Gold Card, with a five thousand credit balance. Tonight it would be put to use for the first time. Membership had its privileges.

And after dinner? Well, that would doubtless take care of itself. She might, or she might not, feel ready for a little more action, and after a dinner at Le Cirque she certainly might.

At the corner of 69th Street, Joel stepped into a drugstore and bought a packet of condoms. The night before he had been unprepared. A purchase like this was so much easier now than when you were a kid, and had to wait until no grown-ups were within earshot, and then had to whisper to the druggist to tell him what you wanted, and half the time he pretended not to hear you, to make you speak up louder so the whole damned store could hear, and then you had to hope that the druggist wouldn't roll his eyes (when all you wanted them for, for Chrissake, was to figure out how to put one on—the instructions were a little vague). Now they were all out on the counter, all makes and varieties, and all you had to do was make your selection and take it to the register. Like buying a pack of Life Savers. No, it was not even like that. Condoms had become the status symbol of the '90s. Buying them was more like strolling into Cartier's and picking out a gold tank watch, Joel thought.

At the checkout counter was a sample bottle of some new men's cologne. He spritzed some into the palm of his hand and rubbed it into his cheeks. Ah, yes, he was ready now! He gave the cute checkout girl a big wink. She knew!

That purchase made—thinking of that white-white face and those tiny, firm, pointy breasts—he continued up Madison Avenue. Yes, this was the real thing now. This wasn't going to be like the time with the whore in Concord, the one Otto had got for him—a forty-dollar whore with garlic breath.

That had been disgusting, actually—watching her pull off
her sweaty pink slip to expose the stretch marks on her fat
thighs, and hearing Otto the Hun pumping away on another
one in the next little cubicle . . . and then, when it was over,
watching her lick her thumb as she counted out the bills. It was
damned lucky, in fact, that that experience hadn't turned him
off sex altogether. He had heard of that happening—one disgusting experience like that one with a stretchmarked whore
in a water bed with semen-stained sheets could easily turn a
guy off sex altogether. But thank God that hadn't happened,
though it could have, disgusting as the whole thing was.

In the next block, he made one last stop, at a florist's
shop, where he picked up a dozen long-stemmed red roses.
He checked his watch again. Two minutes of seven, and he
pushed his way through the revolving doors of the Westbury,
his roses in one hand and his condoms in the lefthand pocket
of his Sills navy blazer. He made his way straight to the elevators. "Don't have them announce you. Just come straight
up," she had said. He pushed the button for the eighteenth
floor.

At the door to apartment 1815, he pressed the doorbell,
and waited for the sound of footsteps.

From inside the apartment, he could hear a telephone ringing. But no one was responding, and it continued to ring.
After a minute or two, he pressed the doorbell again.

Now a second phone was ringing, a different tone, and
now both telephones were ringing, their rings alternating. Joel counted the rings . . . ten . . . eleven . . . twelve . . .
He pressed the doorbell a third time, but there was no
response.

It was eerie, listening to those phones ringing. And all at
once a third phone in the apartment began to ring, and now
there were three different telephone lines ringing all at once.
Presently he heard a beep, as an answering machine picked
up on one of the lines, and then he heard a man's voice
delivering what seemed to be a long, complicated, urgent-
sounding—even angry-sounding—message. But even with
his ear pressed against the door, Joel could not make out
the words. One by one, the other telephones stopped ringing,
but the man's unpleasant voice continued from the answering
machine. Joel pressed the doorbell once more, then tried the
knob. The door was locked. Joel wondered all at once if she

might be in some sort of trouble. He knocked loudly on the door, and called, *"Fiona! Are you there?"*

Two middle-aged women in pants suits, laden with shopping bags, stepped off the elevator and started down the corridor in his direction. As they passed him, both seemed to give him peculiar looks. Was it because they had seen him with his ear to the door? Or because they had heard his loud banging or his yelling? Or was it the bunch of long-stemmed roses he was carrying? Or had they noticed the bulge of the packet of condoms in his jacket pocket, or another bulge, the beginning of an erection, in the silhouette of his doeskin slacks? He pressed the doorbell impatiently several more times, and the ladies in the pants suits glanced back at him from down the corridor, and one of them whispered something to the other.

Downstairs, he approached the receptionist's desk. "Is Miss Fenton in?" he asked.

"Miss Fenton? Oh, you mean Her Ladyship. No, Her Ladyship went out at about four o'clock, and I believe she may have gone for the weekend. She had luggage."

"Did she leave any sort of message for me—Mr. Rothman?"

The clerk looked at Joel over the rims of his horn-rimmed glasses, another look that struck Joel as peculiar. "No, sir, she did not."

From Joel Rothman's journal:

6/23/90
9:30 P.M.

I put the roses in Mom's room with a note thanking her for getting rid of Otto for me. No point in letting Fiona's roses go to waste. . . .

I'm sure she didn't mean to stand me up tonight. Something very important must have come up, some family emergency perhaps. After all, Fiona is a pretty important lady. She wouldn't have deliberately stood me up, and I know I'll hear from her soon with the explanation. . . . I'm sure she tried to call me this afternoon while I was out shopping, getting my haircut and all that shit, but she didn't leave a message because she didn't want Mom to find out about our date. But still the whole experience of tonight has kind of spooked me, because I was really horny for her, and she seemed to be looking forward to our evening, too. "I'd adore to see you tonight," she said. Oh, well. Came home. Jacked off. And now I feel really shitty about having done that. Funny thing happened after I left the hotel. I was walking down Madison, and as I was waiting for the light, I looked back and I swear to God I saw old Otto in the crowd on the sidewalk, about half a block behind me, as though he was still following me! But when I looked again, he was gone, so it must have been my imagination. It must have been because I was feeling so spooked about not having my date with Fiona. I'm sure that's it. Today's journalistic question: What about "tuna fish"? Recipe in today's N.Y. Times called for tuna fish. But isn't tuna the name of the fish? So isn't "tuna fish" a redundancy? We don't say "bass fish," "trout fish," "salmon fish," etc., etc., etc. Swordfish, cuttlefish, needlefish seem okay, since they're all one word. But tuna fish sounds wrong to me. Or am I being silly? Spooked.

Chapter 17

Henry Coker was one of the most buttoned-down men she had ever known. Even here on her sunny terrace, on a Saturday morning when he could not possibly be going to his Wall Street office, he was dressed for business, in a dark blue suit with the tiniest of pinstripes running through the fabric, a dark blue necktie and wingtip shoes. He was a tall, thin man whose prematurely white hair had the odd effect of making his not-unhandsome face appear more boyish. Henry, Alex guessed, was about her age. Alex, by contrast to Henry's buttoned-down look, was wearing faded blue jeans, rope-soled sandals, and one of Joel's old Brooks Brothers shirts, with the tails knotted at her waist. She had pulled her hair back into a loose ponytail, and tied it with a red scarf. She had dressed for the drive to Long Island.

Henry Coker put his coffee cup down, and snapped his briefcase closed. "Well, as I say, your contract is pretty cut and dried," he said. "Your title and duties are clearly defined. This contract is hardly of the boilerplate variety, if I do say so myself." He smiled slightly. "Since I helped work out the terms for you. So I don't anticipate any difficulties. I feel confident that I can persuade Herbert Rothman that what he proposes is in violation of the terms of this instrument, to which you are both signatories. And I trust I can settle this—ah, disagreement—with Mr. Rothman or his attorneys on amicable terms, without the threat of legal action on our part. At least this is what I hope to do, Alex."

"I warn you, Henry. My father-in-law is not in an amicable frame of mind toward me right now."

He sighed. "Family disputes," he said. "They're always the most painful kind, aren't they? So many little things that can divide a family. Little things like—"

"Money."

"Well, yes."

"And power."

"Well, yes, and that too. Well, let me see what I can do, Alex, at this initial stage of our negotiations."

"Tell me something, Henry," she said. "How rich am I?"

He looked startled by the question. "How rich? Well, I—"

"It's something I've never paid much attention to, but I know your office has made some investments for me, and of course you prepare my taxes. But I've been thinking that perhaps it would be a good thing if I knew where I stand, financially. I mean, if I do end up having to resign—which some people are saying I should do, and others are saying I shouldn't—I ought to know where I stand."

He scribbled a note on the pad of legal cap in front of him. "Let me ask our financial department to prepare a full statement of your assets," he said.

"For instance," she said, "there is supposed to be something called the Steven Rothman Trust. It was in Steven's will when he died—a trust fund that was set up for Joel and me. I've deliberately never touched a penny of that trust. Since I didn't need to, I didn't want to. But I have no idea how much is in it. Could you find out for me?"

He made another note. "I don't believe I've ever seen a copy of that instrument," he said.

"Neither have I," she said.

"Let me see what I can find out," he said. He looked around the terrace from the gazebo where they sat, at the flowering trees and shrubs, at the ilex hedge that framed the northeast corner of the L. "Of course, in terms of assets," he said, "surely one of the most important ones would be this apartment."

"The McPhersons, on fourteen, just sold theirs for three million five."

"And yours is higher up, with a better view."

"And nobody else has this terrace." She shrugged. "I don't suppose I need all this acreage now, do I?" she said. "Joel will be going off to college in the fall and, after college, he'll surely want to live somewhere else. I suppose I really should consider selling this apartment. But it's just that I'll miss this terrace. I've probably spent more time and thought and money on landscaping and maintaining this terrace than I have on the entire apartment. My mother."

"Your mother?"

"My mother's genes, I was thinking. My mother was an avid gardener. Used to be, when I was a little girl, growing up in a little town called Paradise. Then she gave up gardening."

"Let me check with our real estate department, and see if we can get some sort of valuation on this apartment. It wouldn't hurt to know." He made another note on his long pad.

"No, it wouldn't. Putting together a garden is like putting together a magazine, isn't it?" she said. "You start from scratch." Then she straightened her shoulders, and forced herself back into the reality of today, which was a conference with her lawyer who was probably charging her $750 an hour for horticultural woolgathering. "There's another thing, Henry," she said. "I may be getting married again."

He raised his eyebrows. "Oh?"

"Nothing definite. No date set, or anything like that. But I was wondering whether, if I were to remarry, that would have any effect on the status of Steven's trust fund."

"Good thinking," he said. "It might indeed. It might have a profound effect. But of course I'd have to study the trust instrument, and see how it's worded. It might well state that you would derive benefits from this trust only while you remained unmarried."

"And what about Joel? If I were to remarry, would Joel's benefits from the trust be affected?"

"Again, I'd have to study the trust instrument, Alex. There are so many ways these things can be worded."

"I wouldn't want to jeopardize Joel's share of the trust by remarrying."

"Of course not. I understand completely. Do you have any idea where the trust instrument might be located?"

"No, I don't."

He scribbled some more notes on his legal pad. "Well, let me see what I can find out," he said. "Of course, under the circumstances, it may be—"

"What?"

"Since I will have to be dealing with other members of the Rothman family, or their attorneys, and we are currently disputing the terms of their contract with you, they may be unwilling to cooperate with us on the matter of the trust instrument. Until the matter of your contract is resolved, that is."

"Yes, I thought of that, too."

"But I've had friendly dealings with the Waxman, Holloway people in the past. I don't anticipate any real problem."

"There's just one other thing, Henry."

"What's that?"

"What if Steven wasn't Joel's father?"

His gaze at her was long and cool, and he stretched his long legs. "What are you saying, Alex?"

"I'm saying—I'm asking—if someone was able to prove that Steven wasn't Joel's father, would that affect the trust fund?"

He was silent for a moment. "I assume Steven Rothman is listed as the father on your son's birth certificate," he said at last.

"Oh, yes."

"Then that's all I need to know. I don't want to know anything else. Years ago, in my first year at Yale Law School, one of the first things we were taught was 'Never let your client tell you too much.' So I have just forgotten that you asked that question. And I think that you have just forgotten that you asked it, too."

"Yes," she said quietly, "I guess I have."

"Good," he said. He snapped his briefcase open, dropped the legal pad inside, and snapped it closed again. He stood up. "Very well. I'll call you as soon as I have anything to report."

"Thank you, Henry."

As she walked him to the elevator entrance, Coleman, in his silver-polishing apron, appeared from the direction of the kitchen. "Mr. Jorgenson is downstairs with the car," he said.

"Thank you, darlin'. Tell him I'll be right down."

As she made her way back through the apartment to her bedroom to collect her garment bag, she noticed Joel's navy blue blazer lying across a bench in the hallway. It was where he often left things that he wanted sent out to be cleaned, and she routinely picked up the jacket and patted the pockets to be sure that they were empty. That was when she found the unopened packet of condoms in his lefthand pocket.

She experienced a sudden rush of heat to her face, and a pounding in her temples. Surely every mother experiences a queer rush of feeling like that, when she discovers what she surely knew all along, that her son is a grown man. Still, it was the queerest feeling—anger, bitterness, and jealousy were all involved in it, but what for? Her son was behaving like a responsible adult, she should be proud of him, so why should she feel this swell of rage? It made no sense at all, except that in some tiny but all-important way he had betrayed her by growing up without consulting her. He had taken some part of himself away from her, and she would never have it back again. She forced herself to laugh. There was nothing else to do but laugh. But she felt more like weeping.

She dropped the packet of condoms back into the lefthand pocket, and laid the jacket back across the bench as she had found it. "I've been a good mother," she pleaded to herself as she hurried on to her bedroom. "I've been a good mother, haven't I?" She slung her garment bag across her arm. For weekends in the Hamptons, she always traveled light.

A weekend in the Hamptons! It was every New Yorker's dream. Of course this weekend, she and Mel were getting a later start than usual. They usually left the city on Friday afternoon, but now it was eleven o'clock on Saturday morning, and who knew what they would encounter in terms of traffic on the expressway at this time of day? Out around Jones Beach, the traffic could be very problematical on a Saturday. That was the only trouble with the Hamptons—the traffic. People plotted their journeys to and from the Hamptons like military campaigns, trying to outwit the enemy, the traffic. Depending on traffic, the trip could take anywhere from two to six hours.

Downstairs, Mel was waiting in his bright red BMW convertible, whose name was Scarlett O'Hara. Charlie the doorman helped Alex spread her garment bag across the back seat, which was also shared by Mel's big English sheep dog, whose name was Walter Cronkite. Alex hopped into the front seat. Mel gave her a quick kiss, and, from behind, Cronkite licked her ponytail, and they were off.

"Well, how'd it go?" he asked.

"Good, I think. Henry says my contract is absolutely airtight."

"Good. Now remember our promise. We're not going to discuss this business at all this weekend. This weekend is just for relaxing and having fun, not worrying about anything, and"—he put his lips to her ear—"having some nice sex."

She giggled. "Ssh! Not in front of Cronkite."

"Cronkite knows," he said solemnly. "Cronkite knows all about us, darling." He squeezed her knee. "I love you," he said.

"I love you, too," she said, and they turned into the FDR Drive, heading downtown toward the Midtown Tunnel.

"Look, the traffic's a breeze," he said.

"A breeze," she echoed.

"Tunnel's a breeze," he said, as they entered the tunnel.

"A breeze." She let her right arm trail from the open window of the car, feeling happy just to be with him on this glorious day, leaving the city.

"I hope Buster will be all right, being left alone for the weekend," she said. "I mean Joel. He doesn't want to be called Buster anymore. I hope he'll be okay. But he insisted that this was what he wanted."

"He'll be fine. He's more grown up than you think."

"I mean without Otto," she said.

"Kid's too old for an Otto. Otto was an embarrassment to him."

"Still, he's all I've got."

He gave her a sideways glance. "You got me, babe," he said.

"I mean family—real flesh-and-blood family."

"Don't be too protective. You've got to give him his head at some point."

"I found a packet of condoms in his jacket pocket."

He chuckled. "Guy's obviously got a heavy date this week-end."

"Yes, but still—it gave me the queerest feeling."

"He's a big boy now."

"But he's still the baby whose diapers I used to change."

"Don't be overprotective, Alex. If you ask me, he's been overprotected most of his life. The time has come for Buster to head out on his own."

"You mean Joel."

"I mean Joel."

"Still—he seems so young."

They were approaching the end of the tunnel now, and Mel slowed the BMW for the tollbooths. He reached in the breast pocket of his green-and-white-checkered shirt and removed a twenty-dollar bill. "Got anything smaller?" he asked her.

"Sorry, I got five hundred dollars at the money machine last night, and it all came out in twenties."

He stopped at the booth, and handed the bill to the toll-taker, a woman in harlequin glasses with rhinestone-studded frames.

She counted out his change from the two-fifty toll, and was about to hand it over to him when she suddenly gave him a hard, searching look. He was wearing his favorite hunter-green snap-brim cap, and much of his face was obscured by wraparound Alain Mikli sunglasses, but apparently this inno-cent attempt at a disguise had failed him. The eyes behind the harlequin frames had penetrated it—recognizing, perhaps, the dark hair that curled out from under his cap, and the famous cleft chin. "Hey, I know who you are!" the toll collector cried almost indignantly. "You're that Mel Jorgenson from on the TV!"

He nodded, grinning his famous, telegenic grin.

"Wait till my sister-in-law Lucille hears about this one!" she said. "She'll never believe me! You're her favorite! Nine booths to pick from, and you went and picked mine. What a coincidence! Can I have your autograph to prove it?"

"Sure," he said, and then, after a pause, "Got something I can write it on?"

"Aren't celebrities supposed to supply their own pencil and paper? I got nothing to write on in here."

"Here," Alex said, a little crossly, opening the glove com-partment and fishing out the ballpoint pen and pad of note paper that he always carried there. "Use this," she said, passing the writing utensils to him.

He scribbled his signature on the pad, and handed the sheet of paper to the woman.

"My sister-in-law Lucille *still* won't believe it. Put the date on it to prove it."

"Let's see. Today's date is—"

"June twenty-third," Alex said, still crossly.

"And up there, on the top of the page, write 'To Marsha Bernice Apfelbaum, toll attendant, booth four, Queens-Midtown Tunnel, New York Bridge and Tunnel Authority.' No, no—it's M-A-R-S-H-A," she said, seeing that he had spelled it "Marcia." "No, you better start the whole thing over. Lucille will never believe you're who you are with my name spelled wrong."

"Oh, for heaven's *sake!*" Alex said.

The woman in the harlequin glasses scrutinized the redone autograph. "No, it's Apfelbaum, not Applebaum," she said. "There's an 'f' goes there, not a 'p.' Can you draw that second 'p' better, so it looks like an 'f'? Put a little tail on it."

"Oh, eff you," Alex whispered.

"There, that's more like it," said the woman, examining the final work. "Now you've finally got it right. Now tell me something, now I've got you here. You know Johnny Carson? What's he really like? Is he as funny off the television as he is on?"

"Wrong coast, wrong network," he said with a smile.

"Why's he keep having all those wives, I wonder?"

Still smiling, he said, "Have to ask him."

"Just thought I'd ask. Well, you have a nice day, Mel, you hear me? And I'll tell Lucille you said hi."

"You do that," he said.

"Say—is that a dog you got back there?" she said, peering into the car for a closer look.

"No, it's a fur lap robe," Alex said.

"What's its name?"

"Pudd'n Tane," said Alex.

"Is she a boy or a girl?"

Alex leaned across Mel's knees. "May we please have our *change?*" she said.

"Yipes! I almost forgot," she said. "What'd I do with it? Didn't I give it to you?"

"I saw you put it back in your drawer when you were getting his autograph," Alex said.

"Did I? You gave me a ten—right? Here you go—seven fifty."

"We gave you a twenty," Alex said.

The woman's eyes narrowed. "You gave me a ten," she said.

"Look," Mel said pleasantly, "I gave you a twenty, but it doesn't matter. If your drawer is ten dollars over at the end of your shift, you'll know who it belongs to. You can send it to me at the station."

"You gave me a ten," she said. "You rich celebrities are all alike. You're always trying to jew people out of money. If my drawer's short, it comes out of my pay. Ten dollars is nothing to *you*. To me, it's dinner."

"Mel, let's get out of here," Alex said.

"Who's *she?*" the woman said, glaring at Alex. "I never seen *her* on TV. It's you I'm talking to, not *her*. Don't look at me, bitch!"

"If you'll please raise your gate, we'll be on our way," he said.

"Rich celebrities! All alike! Don't give a rat's rear end about the little guy who has to work for a living!"

But the barrier gate went up, and Mel gunned the engine, and they were through.

"Good heavens!" Alex said, sinking back into the bucket seat.

He was humming a little tuneless tune, *toot-toot-te-toot-te-toot*, as they moved out onto the elevated section of the expressway. The experience with the toll collector seemed to have left him unperturbed, but for Alex, at least, the episode had taken some of the buoyancy out of her mood, and some of the splendor out of the day. Why did she resent intrusions like these? They happened often when she was out in public with him. Certainly it was not jealousy. The editor of a fashion magazine—even a fashion magazine that has just achieved a circulation of five million—did not expect her face to be recognized instantly, except in certain professional circles, and certainly not by a woman collecting tolls at the Midtown Tunnel. He, on the other hand, was a news anchorman whose face came into the homes of millions, night after night. He was a genuine media star. She should not resent that, and yet she did, in a funny way, and she resented her own resentment. Her resentment was ill-placed, illogical, and unbecoming.

"Well," she said at last, "I'm sure her sister-in-law Lucille still isn't going to believe her." But the remark wasn't funny, and she added, "Thank God that's the last tollbooth." And then, "Jackie always uses the exact-change lanes."

"Jackie?"

"Onassis. When she takes her car to New Jersey, she always uses an exact-change lane. She has one of those little change-gun gizmos that you load with quarters. You shoot the quarters—ping, ping, ping—into the hopper. If she didn't have that, toll collectors would be asking for her autograph all the time. I'll get you one for your birthday."

"Oh, hell, I don't mind," he said. "It probably made old Marsha's day. Besides, she didn't have anything else to do. As you can see, there's no traffic to speak of. She just wanted somebody to shoot the breeze with. Boring job."

"Perfect job for a sociopath," she said.

And that was another thing she tended to forget. He *enjoyed* his celebrity. He loved being famous, loved being recognized by all sorts of unlikely people. That was why, even when the fans turned ugly, as they occasionally did, he didn't really mind. The certain perils of celebrity didn't worry him. He never worried that what had happened to Jack and Bobby Kennedy and John Lennon could happen to him.

So—why shouldn't he enjoy his fame? He had worked hard enough to gain it, that recognition. He had told her all about the early days. His was an almost classic, almost Horatio Alger, American success story—the poor Jewish boy, a tailor's son, who from the time he reached high school was determined to rid himself of his Brooklyn accent. He practiced speaking with marbles in his mouth, practiced with a pencil clenched between his teeth, practiced with a tape-recorder, playing his voice back to monitor his progress, practiced speaking into a mirror to be sure the face muscles worked right, practiced by watching old movies and imitating the way the actors spoke. Practice, practice, practice, until he was perfect. What he wanted was an accent that was a kind of cross between Cary Grant's and Jimmy

Stewart's—Ivy League, but with a down-homey flavor. The best American accents for the airwaves, he had told her, came either—with much fixing—out of the Deep South, or from Nebraska. Nebraska? How had he learned this? Johnny Carson was from Nebraska. So was Dick Cavett. So were Henry Fonda and Marlon Brando, and many other distinguished voices of the stage and screen. The Nebraska accent, he explained, came closest to what linguists called Standard American Diction. And, in the end, Mel had mastered the kind of speech he wanted for himself: Cary Grant *cum* Jimmy Stewart. And with it had come his spectacular glass house in Sagaponack, where they were headed now, and the equally spectacular town house on Beekman Place, and the red BMW named Scarlett O'Hara, and a contract that paid two million a year, and much, much more. He had done it all by working hard and being a pro.

He was still whistling the little tuneless tune—*toot-toot-te-toot-te-toot*. "Can you be*lieve* this?" he said as they drove along. "No traffic at *all!*" She loved him, in such a comfortable, easy way. He was like a favorite old bathrobe. It was not a dangerous love, like that first one that had left her with a sliver of ice in her heart, or like Steven, which had been more of a practical thing. This was an entirely different sort of love. An old bathrobe, and a pair of comfy, flip-flop slippers. She tucked her hand into the crook of his elbow.

But she knew exactly why she resented intrusions such as the one from Miss Marsha Bernice Apfelbaum of the Bridge and Tunnel Authority. It was because when they happened—and they happened in restaurants, on street corners, in the waiting rooms of airports, strangers who came right up to him and started conversations as though they had known Mel all their lives—she herself was made to feel invisible. He was a star, but she became a cipher, anonymous, a nonperson. Marsha Bernice Apfelbaum, at first, had not even seen her sitting beside him in the front seat of the car. She had noticed the dog before she noticed her. Never mind that it was she, Alexandra Rothman, who provided the pen and paper for the celebrity's autograph. Never mind that it was she, Alex Rothman, who had fielded some of the woman's more impertinent questions. She had simply been ignored, made to feel even less than a nobody. She had been

dropped off the face of the earth, into oblivion. That was the
way his fans made her feel, nonexistent. Of course she didn't
expect him to introduce her to the intruders. That would be
neither necessary nor appropriate. He simply tried to handle
these situations as politely as possible. How else would she
have him handle them? But if there were only some way that
this star's fans could be made to treat her, Alex, as though
she were something more than a zero—but there wasn't. "Is
this your attractive wife?" they might say, but they wouldn't
because they all knew that Mel Jorgenson had no wife at the
moment. They had read all about his divorce in their supermarket tabloids. And so it was a problem without a solution.
But that was what lay at the core of it. That was the hard
kernel at the heart of her resentment. When she was with
him in public, she became zilch, zip, nothing, nada, as Aunt
Lily would say.

Did these sound like the thoughts of a jealous woman?
They came dangerously close to it, she thought. And she
couldn't even console herself with the notion that she was
jealous of people who meant nothing to him. They meant a
lot to him, the Marsha Bernice Apfelbaums of the world.

There was nothing that Alex held in lower esteem than
jealous women. There was nothing more unattractive, more
pathetic even, than a jealous woman unless, perhaps, it was
a drunken woman, and the jealous woman and the drunken
woman had a lot in common. Both did stupid, irrational, ugly,
and self-destructive things. The jealous woman will pester
her man at his place of business. She will eavesdrop on
his telephone calls, go through his wallet and credit-card
receipts, steam open his mail. She will detect another woman's perfume on him, even if it is his own after-shave. She
will spot the long blonde hair on the lapel of his jacket, and
refuse to believe that he could have acquired it in a crowded elevator. She will call him at home, and hang up if he
answers. Or, if he doesn't answer, she will stake out his
house and, when he appears, demand to know where he
has been, and with whom, even if he has just been around
the corner to the hardware store. Alex knew one jealous
woman who became convinced that her lover was secretly married. Using a bent wire coat hanger to unlock the
door—like a common thief—she had broken into his car
to look for evidence. What had she found in the creases of

the back seat? *Crayons*. Crayons! What did crayons mean? They meant that he not only had a wife, but children as well! When she tearfully accused him of lying to her, she refused to believe his innocent explanation—that he had recently driven two small nephews to the Bronx Zoo. "Nephews!" she screamed at him. "You never told me you had nephews! Why have you been hiding these nephews from me? How can we have a relationship when you hide these secret nephews from me?"

Alex's own magazine even ran a story on the disastrous side effects that the slimy green-eyed monster could have on a woman, emotionally and physically. Liquor might create bags under a woman's eyes, cause her chin to sag and her hips to thicken, but jealousy could do all those things as well, besides creating angry little pinched lines around the mouth and between the eyebrows. The anger-lines of jealousy were permanent, like scars. But besides being ugly and intolerable, the jealous woman was, worst of all, a bore.

Alex would not let herself be jealous of Mel's—of Mel's what? His fame? Just because he loved his fame?

She realized that she had experienced irrational rushes of jealousy twice today—first with Joel, now with Mel. The two men she loved the most. Stop it, she warned herself, and stop it now, bitch. That woman had called her a bitch.

"*Toot-toot-te-toot-te-toot*. Oh, Keeee-*rist*!" She had been wool-gathering again, paying no attention to the road or to the passing scenery, which for some time had seemed to consist of an endless series of drearily pompous cemeteries. Now she felt him apply the brake pedal and, looking up, she saw that suddenly all three lanes of traffic ahead of them had become a bobbing sea of red taillights stretching to infinity. The red BMW slowed to a complete stop. "Do you be*lieve* this?" he wailed. "What *hap*pened?"

"I guess we spoke too soon. Must be an accident ahead."

The mass of traffic that they were now a part of moved forward an inch or two, then stopped again.

"Damn," he said. "*Damn*."

Once more the traffic inched forward, then stopped.

Now, for the next twenty minutes, it was like this—an inch or two forward, then a five- or six-minute stop.

"Wanta hop out and see if you can tell how far ahead the trouble is?" he suggested.

She did this, and it was a signal for other passengers in their vicinity also to alight from their vehicles and stand, craning their necks and shielding their eyes from the sun, looking out across the glittering sea of automobile rooftops on the expressway that had now become a parking lot. She slumped back inside the car, and other passengers did the same. "It seems to go on for miles," she said.

In twenty-five minutes, they had traveled perhaps a hundred feet. "We could walk to the Hamptons faster," he said.

"Well, we're in no great hurry," she said, trying to sound cheerful. But it was no use.

A little later, he said, "Car could overheat like this." He was now talking largely to himself. And, sure enough, several motorists had already pulled off on the shoulder, raised their hoods, and were standing helplessly, arms akimbo, glaring hatefully at their vehicles' unlovely steaming insides. "Turn off the air conditioning," he said to himself, obeying his own instructions and flipping off the air-conditioner switch. "Top down? Okay?"

"Sure," she said, and he lowered the convertible top. The day was growing quite warm, and now, instead of air conditioning, they had automobile fumes and a relentless view of ugly, identical two-family Queens houses that lined the expressway. Everything about the day now seemed ugly.

Alex retied the red scarf in her hair to accommodate the breeze, but there was no breeze. *You'll find yourself back in Paradise, Missouri, without a pot to piss in*! Herb had said to her. But she had promised herself not to think about any of that. She would think about her picnic issue instead. Fashions in picnics. . . .

After a while, she said, "How about a little music? Or will playing the radio cause the car to overheat?"

"Of *course* the radio won't cause the car to overheat!" he snapped.

"What I know about cars . . ." She flipped on the radio, and managed to find the classical music station. The Cleveland Symphony Orchestra was playing Mozart's Piano Concerto Number Five in D Major. "Music hath charms to soothe the savage beast," she said.

"Breast," he said. "It's savage breast."

"Don't talk dirty," she said. But it wasn't very funny.

Once more, the little car inched forward, then stopped again. More motorists were pulling off the roadway now, with radiators aboil, as the sun beat down through a leaden sky.

He was stroking the steering column of the car now, and saying, "Good little Scarlett. You're not going to heat up on Daddy, are you? You wouldn't do that to Daddy, would you?"

The Mozart concerto ended to thundering applause, and the radio commentator had begun his scholarly dissertation on the composition's history and importance to the world of music. Alex played with the dial, trying to find something as pretty as the Mozart, but all she located were hard rock stations, and a woman interviewing an author who had written a book about French cathedral cities.

"And how would you describe a groin vault, Winston?" the woman interviewer asked.

"More dirty talk," Alex said, twisting the dial.

"See if you can find a traffic report," he said. "See if you can find out how much more of this we've got to face."

She tried, but failed, and flipped the radio off.

After a while, she said, "Look, what if we get off at the next exit, and try to make our way down to the Southern State? A lot of people swear by the Southern State."

"The Southern State is always *worse*," he said angrily. "Besides, have you noticed any exit signs lately? I sure as hell haven't."

She said nothing. When he was in a mood like this, she knew that the best policy was silence.

The car jerked sharply forward for a few feet, then stopped abruptly, and there was a sloshing sound from behind their seats. Mel turned in his seat to look and cried out, "Oh, Christ! Cronkite's tipped over his water dish! He can't sit out in this heat without any water! Cronkite will *die*!"

She did not point out that it was the driver's lurching acceleration of the car that caused the water dish to overturn, not anything that Cronkite did. Instead, she suggested, "Would it be cooler for him if we put the top back up?"

"No! It's always hotter with the top up!"

Once again she said nothing.

"We've got to be coming up to the scene of the accident soon," he said, though there was no evidence along the clogged expressway to support this assertion, and the mood between them now was thoroughly sour.

"Goddammit, find me a traffic report on the radio," he said.

"Find it yourself," she said. "It's your fucking radio. It's your fucking house in the Hamptons we're going to."

He turned to her. "You wanna go back?" he yelled. "All right, Goddammit, we'll turn around and go fucking back if that's what you want to do!" But, of course, reversing direction in the middle of a traffic jam on the Long Island Expressway was out of the question, and Mel merely wiped the perspiration from his forehead with the back of his hand, and added, "Shit!"

"Why are we quarreling?" she asked quietly. "I thought this weekend was for relaxing, having fun, not worrying about anything."

"Goddammit, I am *not quarreling!* You're the one who's being a pain in the ass!"

All at once there were tears in her eyes. She opened the glove compartment and groped inside. "Do you have any Kleenex in here?" she whispered.

"Now what's the matter?"

"Nothing . . . my sinuses . . . this heat . . . this air . . ." The red scarf was hot against the back of her neck, and she untied it to fluff up her hair.

"Now what are you going to do? Blow your nose in that scarf? That happens to be a Hermès scarf, and I happen to have bought it for you! Do you know how much that scarf cost me? Three hundred and fifty dollars!"

She hurled the scarf out the window.

"What the hell—?" The car was not moving, and Mel shifted into park, opened the door, and got out and crossed in front of the car to retrieve the scarf from where it lay on the highway, beneath the door on the passenger side. As he returned with the scarf, she remembered that she had chosen it that morning because he had given it to her, and because it matched the color of his car.

"What the hell's eating you, Alex?" he asked, as he climbed back into the car. "What the hell's eating you?" He placed the scarf almost tenderly in her lap. Then he said, "I'm sorry, darling. It's just this Goddamn traffic."

She felt two tears stream down her cheeks. "No. It was that Goddamn woman," she said.

"What Goddamn woman?"

You see? she told herself. He's already forgotten. "The woman in the tollbooth! If she hadn't kept gabbling with you, we'd be way past this accident, or whatever it is that's causing this mess up ahead."

"Aw, don't blame that stupid old bag," he said.

But she knew that it was more than Marsha Bernice Apfelbaum who was causing the tears. It was also Herbert, and Joel, and Otto, and Henry Coker, and Mark Rinsky, and Fiona Fenton, and Mona Potter, and the fiasco that her beautiful party had turned into, and even the people in the runabout who had been swallowed by the East River in front of her eyes, and everything else. *Every big shot in town is going to be after you now, Lexy,* Lucille Withers had told her, and she had a lunch date with Rodney McCulloch on Monday, and he was certainly after her for something. But she had taken over *Mode* when she was in her twenties, and now she was in her forties, and she all at once felt too old to move on to anything new.

Mel handed her his hanky. "Here, give your nose a good blow," he said. "I'm really sorry, darling. I really am. I didn't mean to yell at you. I love you, Alex."

"Well," she said, accepting his handkerchief, "I guess that's nice to know." She blew her nose noisily, and the car inched forward again.

Love, she thought. Love came in such a variety of sizes, shapes, and flavors. No two loves were alike. And, since love did not occur all that often in one's life, it was important to examine each specimen very carefully.

She and Mel Jorgenson didn't live together in the conventional sense, though some people assumed they did. True, he often spent the night at 10 Gracie Square, and kept some of his clothes and toilet articles there, and she often spent weekends with him at Sagaponack, and kept some of her things out there. They had often talked seriously about marriage. But it wasn't the idea of getting married that gave them pause. It was the idea of *being* married. Being married entailed so much sacrifice, so much compromise. Alex knew that she was independent-minded, headstrong, stubborn, and had a quick temper. She knew she had a low flashpoint. Throwing his silk scarf out of the window, for instance, had been a childish thing to do, and she had been immediately ashamed of herself for doing it. People who were married shouldn't behave like that.

And both of them, they often reminded each other, had been badly bruised by marriage—Alex by Steven's unhappy death, and Mel by that rancorous, well-publicized divorce. He was only permitted, by court decree, to visit his two children on certain court-specified Saturday afternoons and holidays and, under those rigidly imposed restrictions, he often said he would rather not see his children at all, would rather let them pass out of his life altogether, and relegate them to some previous, all-but-forgotten existence. Or best-forgotten existence, because who could really forget the bitterness of all that?

And, she sometimes wondered, did a man like Mel really want to be married to a woman who came home from an office every night with a briefcase filled with manuscripts to read, page proofs to correct, headers to rewrite, designer sketches to study, composite photos from modeling agents to pore through, advertising and circulation figures to compare against the competition?

Perhaps, in the end, he would be better off settling for one of those blondely beautiful, nubile, sexually artful, Hostess Twinkie types. Or a sleek, rich, postdebutante type who dabbled in helping her rich friends decorate their apartments—not a mature, forty-six-year-old widowed career woman, past childbearing years, with a grown son. Perhaps he should settle for something saucy and twisty with cute little boobs that were of just the size to be cupped in a man's two hands—something just the opposite of his first wife, the one he called The Mouse.

Some mouse. She turned out to be The Mouse That Roared when it came to the divorce. She demanded, and got, twenty thousand a month in alimony, plus child support and tuition, plus custody of the children, plus the court-ordered stipulation that he could spend no more than four hours with each child during any visitation period, plus the house, plus the car, plus the furniture, plus the paintings, the books, the silver, the china, the Steuben glass, the orientals, and the Saint

Bernard. Plus, plus, plus. So much for mice.

Yes, in the end, he would probably opt for a noncareer-type wife. Steven was different. Steven had needed a strong woman, a woman who would take his hand and help lead him along the way. Mel needed a woman who would find the traffic report on the radio when he wanted it. Mel needed . . .

Suddenly she guessed why he was in a foul mood. If she hadn't had her appointment with Henry Coker that morning, they could have left for the Island at least two hours earlier, and missed all this. It wasn't the woman in the tollbooth's fault. It was her career again, interfering with his life. He was still scowling through the windshield at the congestion of traffic ahead of them.

"I'm sorry," she said quickly. "I've been acting like a bitch. Forgive me?"

"I'm just worried the car will overheat. Then we'll really be stuck."

"I know."

"And Cronkite really needs his water in this heat."

"Of course he does. We'll get his bowl refilled first chance we get. I could use something cold to drink myself."

"Look," he said in a let's-get-down-to-business tone of voice. "It's now three thirty. We're still in—what do you call this neighborhood, anyway? Rego Park? We're still in Rego Park. The Van Zuylens want us at seven. What would you say if—I mean if we ever get out of this, and this jam-up's got to end *some*where, doesn't it? What if we go straight to Southampton, and to the Van Zuylens', without stopping at Sagaponack? It'd save us twenty minutes in each direction if we did it that way."

"Like this?" she said, fingering her shirt. "In jeans, and one of Joel's old shirts?"

"It's a beach party," he said. "Very casual. Swimsuits, T-shirts. Bare feet."

She started to say that, after the long, hot drive, she would be looking forward to a bath, but she said nothing. Then, as though he had read her thoughts, he said, "You could take a dip in the pool when you get there. Maggie always keeps her dressing rooms stocked with suits. All sizes."

"As a matter of fact, I tossed an extra suit in my bag."

"Besides, I thought that whatever the editor-in-chief of *Mode* wore, it automatically became a fashion statement."

"Co-editor-in-chief of *Mode*," she said.

"Now remember. We promised."

"What would you do with Cronkite?" she asked him. "Take him to the party? Remember that Maggie has a real thing about dogs."

"He could stay in the car, as long as we leave the windows partway open and he has his water dish. I'd check on him every hour or so."

"Well, we'll see."

"There'll be parkers at the party. They'll check on Cronkite, too, for a ten-buck tip."

Now, all at once, they seemed to be approaching the scene of what was causing the massive traffic tie-up. "My God!" he cried. "Will you look at that? Do you be*lieve* this?"

They had both expected an accident of colossal magnitude—dozens of automobiles piled up together or overturned, police cars with rotating bubble lights, fire engines, ambulances, sirens, roadside flares, lanes blocked off with orange cones. Instead, what they saw was a blue Toyota up on the median divider with a very obviously flat left-rear tire. Two dismayed-looking women—one older, one younger—stood outside the beached vehicle, and the younger woman was holding a baby in her arms. The baby was howling and waving its tiny clenched fists, obviously wanting its bottle. They appeared to be grandmother, mother, and three-month-old.

"So this was *it*!" Mel wailed, slamming the heel of his palm against the steering wheel. "Traffic slowed down for hours, so people could rubberneck two women *with a flat tire*! Of course nobody'd offer to help them. Think I should stop? I can change a tire in five minutes, if they've got a spare."

"Oh, darling, do you think so?" she said. "I mean, if word got out that Mel Jorgenson was changing a tire in the middle of the Long Island Expressway, you'd have people stopping for autographs. You'd have traffic backed up from here to New Jersey."

"Maybe you're right. But I'm gonna do *some*thing." He picked up his car phone and began punching numbers into the handset. Already, as the scene of the disaster fell behind them, traffic was beginning to resume its normal speed.

"Hello, Al?" he said, and she realized he was calling a garage he used. "Al, it's Mel Jorgenson—I'm out here on the L.I.E. about—yeah, I see an exit sign now—I'm a mile west of the Grand Avenue exit, Rego Park. There's a couple of women with a flat tire on the median, blue Toyota. Will you get somebody out here as fast as you can to take care of them? Yeah, give it everything you got—your siren, your flashing lights—and put it on my bill."

Now they were just speeding along. With the top down, and the wind blowing in their hair, Alex retied the red silk scarf, pulling her hair back in a tight ponytail again. They passed Jones Beach without delay—the beach crowd was beginning to leave by now, heading back in the opposite direction toward the city—and Alex felt her buoyant mood returning. All the problems that the city held for her were receding farther and farther behind her, and she could smell the ocean.

Soon they were off the expressway, on Route 27, heading for Riverhead and the various Hamptons. At a service station, they stopped, used the rest rooms, filled Cronkite's water bowl, and Mel brought out two cans of ice-cold Coke to the car.

"That was wonderful, what you did," she said.

"What'd I do?"

"Calling for help for those women. Nobody else would have done it."

"One of them had a *baby*, for Chrissakes!"

"When you do something like that, I fall in love with you all over again," she said. "Nothing seems wrong anymore."

He pulled out of the service station with one hand on the steering wheel, and the other cupping his can of Coke.

"Straight to the Van Zuylens'?" he asked.

"Straight to the Van Zuylens'. We're going to be a little late as it is."

They did not slow up again until they reached the Van Zuylens' entrance gate in Southampton, and joined the line of expensive automobiles that was proceeding down the long graveled drive toward the front door where the car-parking boys scurried efficiently about. It was seven fifteen. They had been on the road for more than eight hours, which was surely something of a record for a trip to the Hamptons.

Chapter 18

"Finisterra," the Van Zuylen estate on Gin Lane in Southampton, was one of the legendary residences on Long Island's South Shore. It had been much changed since Maggie Van Zuylen purchased the property in the 1960s, at a distress-sale price.

Maggie had started by completely gutting the interior of the main house, and adding the great double staircase that swept upward, with handrailings especially created for her by Steuben Glass, from the dramatic front entrance hall with its floor of polished chrome squares. Then she decided that she didn't care for the house's exterior, either. When the house was built in the 1920s, it had been in a vaguely Mediterranean style, with a façade of pink stucco. And so, as soon as the interior rooms were completed, the exterior façade was removed, and replaced, in a classic Georgian style, with geranium-colored brick that had been sun-baked in Siena, and six white marble columns were added across the front of the house. The windows of the house were custom-made in Belgium. The slate roofing tiles had come from a château outside Épernay.

She had done much more. In the basement, where the original owner's pistol range had been, she created an indoor tennis court. Outside, on the grounds, Maggie had supervised the construction of her English water garden, where a series of man-made streams, ponds, and waterfalls led down the terraced hillside on which the house stood, past the grass tennis court and a croquet lawn to the swimming pool, and the pool house, which Maggie also built. Beyond the pool house lay the ocean, and at the edge of the beach was Maggie's beach house, a sort of miniature version of the main house, with an arched loggia facing the sea. The beach house contained men's and women's changing rooms for the beach, and also doubled as a guest house, with two guest suites, each with a bedroom and bath, a sitting room, dining room, and kitchenette. Each time Alex Rothman visited "Finisterra," it amused her to remember that it had all been paid for from a fortune made with a popular brand of mouthwash, called Breath-o-Kleen.

Maggie had designed "Finisterra" for entertaining, and the entire estate had been laid out so that guests, entering for the first time, would make their way from one architectural or landscaping surprise to another, for Maggie expected an appreciative gasp at every turn in the house, at every new vista in the garden. Guests tonight approached the main house up the long gravel drive, where they were met by the parkers, then up the wide marble steps and between the white columns, into the entrance hall with its chrome-tiled floor and the Steuben staircase. "I didn't know Steuben made staircases," someone murmured. "Neither did they, till I ordered it!" Maggie Van Zuylen laughed her big laugh. Then they made their way through the principal rooms on the ground floor, where they could pause to admire some of the major paintings from Maggie's collection—the four Braque still lifes, Picasso's *Arlequin au Violon*, Modigliani's *Portrait of a Girl*, Seurat's *The Bathers*, Gauguin's *Ia Orana Maria*, Cézanne's *L'Éstaque*, Monet's *Grapes and Apples*, and, one of the many gems of the collection, which hung in the mauve-silk-covered dining room, the famous *Danseuse sur la Scène*, by Degas. The version that hung in the Louvre, Maggie liked to explain, was a copy.

Then they moved out into the garden, down the series of terraces with their accompanying waterway, past Maggie's collection of specimen rhododendrons and azaleas—now, of course, in full bloom—the hedges of hybrid hydrangeas, the parterres planted with boxwood and yew, through the trellised rose garden, past the grass tennis court and croquet lawn, past the pool and pool house, and on through the beach house to the beach, where tonight's party was being held. In the women's changing room, it was suggested that the women leave their purses and shoes, for dinner would be served out on the sand, under the stars.

On the beach, tables had been set up, lighted by Hawaiian torches. Under a white tent, a dance floor had been erected on the sand, and a five-piece jazz combo was playing, while strolling musicians in bright shirts moved among the guests with guitars and ukuleles playing Hawaiian tunes. "Look at that!" someone gasped, pointing to a spot, near the water's edge, where an elaborate sand castle had been built, complete with moat, towers, minarets, belvederes and battlements and flying buttresses, nearly twelve feet high. Toy soldiers, in full battle regalia, and in perfect scale with the castle, guarded the castle's ramparts and gates. Maggie had had the castle floodlighted, and more floodlights were beamed directly into the foaming surf.

"Who in the world built your sand castle for you, Maggie?" someone asked.

"I had my florist do it," Maggie said. "It took ten men."

"I didn't know florists built sand castles."

"Neither did he, till I ordered it. When the tide starts coming in at ten o'clock, it'll all be washed away, which should be fun to watch, shouldn't it?"

At one end of the beach, over a driftwood fire, a whole pig was being roasted, turned on a spit by barefoot, white-coated members of Maggie's staff. In another spot, a large pit had been dug in the sand. All day long, Maggie's staff had been heating stones over charcoal until the stones were white-hot. Now the hot stones were being placed across the bottom and along the sides of the pit, and the stones were being covered with fresh wet seaweed which sizzled on the hot stones and sent bursts of live steam into the air. Now, on top of the steaming seaweed, more barefoot, white-coated men were tossing live lobsters, handfuls of steamer clams and mussels, fresh corn on the cob, pieces of cut-up chicken, and new potatoes in their skins. Then came another layer of seaweed, and a final layer of hot stones to complete the clambake.

"Just a simple little picnic," someone commented.

"I hope it doesn't get too chilly later on," Maggie Van Zuylen said. "But in case it does, I've had this section of the dunes heated."

Alex saw that she wasn't kidding. Large electric brazi-
ers stood in readiness at the periphery of the party, to be
moved closer to the tables should the need arise. Alex was
making mental notes of all of this, for possible use in her
picnic issue.

"Alex, darling," Maggie Van Zuylen said, "I have a special
surprise for you this evening. But I seem to have lost her for
the moment. I'll see if I can find her."

More barefoot, white-coated men were circulating among
the guests, passing trays of hors d'oeuvres and taking drink
orders. Alex accepted a glass of champagne from one of
them.

"She's using her Baccarat on the beach!" she heard someone say and, through the crowd, she spotted the metallic cage
of orange curls that belonged to Mona Potter. Across one section of sand, a volleyball net had been set up, and a group of
bikini-clad young men had started a game, and Alex could
see why lifeguards referred to men's bikinis as banana hammocks. She made a mental note: No men in bikinis in my
picnic issue.

She was also, naturally, noticing what the women were
wearing. It was, as Mel had said, mostly shorts and cutoffs,
halters, cotton T-shirts, and tank tops. But she spotted one
young woman, who had the figure for it, wearing what was
obviously a white cashmere T-shirt, something new. She
made a mental note of that.

Maggie Van Zuylen had roped off her section of the
beach—from the waterline to her seawall—with velvet-
covered chains hooked to stanchions, like those used to
control crowds in a theater lobby. This was probably quite
illegal, since all American beaches technically belonged to
the public, at least as far up as the high-water mark. But
no one would have the temerity to cross Maggie's barriers
and crash such an elaborate party, though a small group of
onlookers had gathered on the other side of the stanchions
to watch the goings-on.

If these outsiders had joined the party, they would have
heard very different conversational gambits than one heard
at parties in Manhattan. In Manhattan, the talk was generally of divorces, love affairs, interior designers, and security
systems. In the Hamptons, it was usually about real estate.

Moving through the crowd, brushing lips with some of

the guests, squeezing the hands of others, Alex listened to them.

"They're asking fifty thousand for July first through Labor Day—*unfurnished.*"

"Memorial Day, I could see that much. But July *first?*"

"If it doesn't have an ocean view, I say forget it."

"Frankly, I'd rather be on a pond than on the ocean. The damned *salt spray.* Maggie has to have her windows washed twice a week."

"And what about Mel Jorgenson's house? He must have to have his windows washed every *day!*" Mel's glass house on the dunes in Sagaponack had caused much local comment ever since he built it.

"They'll never develop that property. It's zoned one-A residential."

"Well, his brother-in-law is on the zoning commission, so we'll see."

"The Allertons will sue if anybody tries to put condos there."

"Frank says let 'em sue. The publicity will help him sell his condos. . . . "

"They're asking four-point-nine? For that *dump?* They'll never get it. . . ."

"She paid eighty thousand for her pool, and it's only one-third filtered."

"She should sue the contractor."

"I don't care what you say. Keeping a pool at eighty degrees is one thing. But ninety is ridiculous."

"You think your taxes are bad. Mine are sixteen thousand a *month.*"

"There's Alex Rothman."

"Darling, she's about to be *history.*"

The sun was going down, and the smell of steaming seafood was in the air. Very carefully, the white-coated young men were scraping the hot stones away from the top of the clambake with long-handled rakes. Others were lighting the Hawaiian torches, while still others were turning the roasting pig on its spit, the fat hissing and flaming as it hit the live coals.

"I didn't know Zabar's would sell a whole boar," someone was saying.

"Neither did they, till I ordered it!" said the hostess in her farmerette's outfit of blue velvet coveralls and many gold chains. Alex had a thought: a story on outrageous picnics?

Mel touched Alex's arm. "I'm going up to check on Cronkite's water before we eat," he said. "I'll be right back."

"Who're *you*?" Mona Potter was saying, on her fourth glass of wine, peering myopically at a guest she did not immediately recognize. "Are you supposed to be anybody?"

Mel Jorgenson made his way back through the gardens carrying water in a large Baccarat highball glass. Floodlights lit some of the specimen rhododendron bushes, and low, invisible lighting illuminated the boxwood parterres, while other floodlights beamed up into the trunks and canopies of some of the larger trees. It was a far cry from the picnics of his youth—hard-cooked eggs on a paper plate, laid out on a sandy towel at Coney Island. He could still feel the sand in his teeth from the eggs. "You've got to eat a pound of dirt before you die," his mother said.

Even in the fading light, it was easy enough to pick out Scarlett O'Hara from the two hundred–odd cars in "Finisterra"'s parking lot, and he headed toward her with his water glass, and opened the door on the driver's side. "Ho, Cronkite," he said.

Then he jumped back with alarm, and dropped the glass, which shattered at his feet on the pavement. A pile of glittering fabric lay across his front seat, and it was moving.

Then he realized that it was a woman's body sprawled across the bucket seats, and that she was sobbing uncontrollably.

"I beg your pardon," he said. And then, "Can I help you?"

She gave a little startled cry, and looked up at him, her eyes streaming. Immediately she reached for a pair of oversize sunglasses that lay beside her on the seat, and put them on, and he recognized her. "Miss Fenton," he said.

"Oh, please," she sobbed. "Please forgive me! I didn't know where to go. Yours was the only car I could find that was unlocked, with the windows open. I just had to get away from that party. I didn't know where to go. I came here."

"What happened?"

"Look at me!" she sobbed, sitting up and gesturing to her

dress, which was full and floorlength and glistening with gold and silver embroidery. "*Just look at me!*"

"What's wrong with you?"

"It's my new Chanel. I bought it just for this party. And look at my shoes!" She lifted her long skirts to show him her shoes, which were gold pumps with high, thin stiletto heels. "Look at me! I'm supposed—supposed to be going to work for the—the leading fashion magazine in the *world*, and I came dressed like this. I look like a fool, I look like a clown!"

"It's a very pretty dress."

"But did you see what the others were wearing? Blue jeans. Swimsuits. Bare feet. I couldn't even take off my shoes because I'm wearing *hose!*" She sobbed again. "A beach party," she said. "I had no idea what she meant by a beach party. We don't have beach parties in Britain. And so I came dressed—like this!"

"I think you look just fine," he said.

"People were giggling about me behind my back. I just know they were. They had to have been. I just had to get out of there. The hostess—this Mrs. Van Zuylen—I don't even know her!" She dabbed at her eyes behind the big glasses. "It's just too humiliating," she said, and then, "Forgive me for carrying on like this. I shouldn't even be sitting here in your car."

"I just came back to see if my dog needed water," he said, looking back at Cronkite who lay sleeping peacefully across the back seat, his head between his front paws.

"Your pooch and I have become great friends," she said with a little sniffle. "His water dish was getting a little low, but I filled it from that little stream that runs through the garden."

"That was nice of you."

"Sheep dogs are my favorite breed. So lovable." She reached behind her and scratched Cronkite's nose. His eyes blinked open, then closed. "I must go," she said. "I need to call a taxi. But I don't know where to find a telephone. I don't want to go back into the house, dressed like this."

Mel looked briefly at his car phone. Then he said, "Would you like me to drive you home?"

"Oh, *would* you?" she said eagerly. "That would be terribly kind of you, Mr. Jorgenson! That would be just the kindest thing."

"Where're you staying?"

"It's a place called Gurney's Inn," she said. "It's on—I believe it's called the Montauk Road."

"I know Gurney's Inn," he said. He glanced at his watch. Gurney's Inn was at least a twenty-five-minute drive in each direction. "Okay, let's go," he said, and hopped into the car beside her.

"You really are too kind," she said.

"Don't mention it."

"You see," she said, as he pulled the car out of the lot and started down the Van Zuylens' long drive toward Gin Lane, "I really don't know Mr. and Mrs. Van Zuylen, and that's what makes it so much worse—to come to someone's house, someone you've never met, dressed all wrong. At least it does to me. To someone who's supposed to know a *little* about fashion, to come dressed all wrong to someone's house you've never met. Or does that seem like a terribly silly form of female vanity to you, Mr. Jorgenson? Can you understand a woman's vanity?"

"I guess I can," he said. "By the way, how'd you know my name?"

"My goodness, you're famous from the telly. I recognized you right away!"

"Aha!" he said.

"She called me yesterday out of the blue, this Mrs. Van Zuylen," she said. "And asked me to her party tonight. Out of the blue. I'd no idea who she was."

"That will happen in New York," he said. "Once your name is in Mona Potter's column, everybody in town wants to meet you. It doesn't matter whether they know you or not. They'll invite you to their parties to check you out."

"You see? That's what I meant. I knew I was to be checked out tonight, and that's why I couldn't bear to stay, dressed as I am. Anyway, I rang up my friend Mr. Herbert Rothman, and he told me that Mrs. Van Zuylen is one of your most important hostesses, and that I should by all means accept. He neglected, however, to tell me what I ought to wear for this 'party at my beach,' as she put it," she added with a little laugh. "Obviously."

"Herb Rothman wasn't invited?"

"In fact, he was. But Mr. Rothman is in San Francisco this weekend, on some sort of company business. He urged me to come alone. He recommended this hotel called Gurney's Inn, where I'm stopping."

He turned out onto the Montauk Highway, and she fell silent.

"Tell me about yourself, Miss Fenton," he said at last.

"Please call me Fiona."

"All right. Tell me about yourself, Fiona."

"Oh, you don't really want to hear about me, Mr. Jorgenson."

"And I'm Mel."

"You don't really want to hear about me, do you, Mel?"

"Yes, I do."

"Well—" She seemed to hesitate. "I had a fairly typical English girlhood, I suppose. Brought up, rather strictly, by nannies, in a picture-postcard little English village—nannies who kept me carefully protected from the facts of life. Two doting parents, and—*oh!*" And suddenly he realized she was weeping again.

"What's wrong?" he asked her.

"I can't—I just can't," she sobbed.

"Can't what?"

"I just can't go on telling all these lies, Mel!"

"Lies? What lies?"

"The lies I've told everyone . . . the lies I've told Mr. Rothman. The lie I've made of my whole life . . . I just can't go on. . ."

"Care to tell me about that?" he said, interested.

"If I tell you the truth—the real truth—the truth I've never told another living soul, will you promise not to tell anyone? Will you promise not to tell Mr. Rothman?"

"Promise," he said.

"Because it isn't a pretty story." She blew her nose into her hanky, and dabbed at her eyes. "How well do you know England, Mel?" she asked him then.

"I've been to London often. But the rest of England—not well at all."

"Have you heard of Viscount Hesketh?"

"No."

"Viscount Hesketh's name is known in England, but very little is known about the man himself. He is famously reclusive, and hardly ever leaves Hesketh Castle, where he lives. Few people outside his family have ever seen him. I guess you could describe him as one of our famous English eccentrics. There's a certain mystery about him."

"Hm," he said.

"Viscount Hesketh is my father."

"Oho," he said.

"My mother left him when I was a very little girl. I hardly have any memories of my mother, though I do have photographs of her. She was very beautiful. She left him—ran off—to Spain, we think, though we don't know. She disappeared, and no one has ever seen or heard from her again."

"Another man?"

"Perhaps. No one knows. But we think she left him because she found out what was going on."

"Oh? What was going on?"

"I have an older sister, Bridget. Two years older, who lives in Australia now. She escaped. I wasn't so lucky. It started with Bridget. Then it was my turn."

"What started?"

"It started when we were little girls—first Bridget, then me. I don't even remember when it started with me, I was that young. Three, perhaps. He would ask me to touch him in—intimate places. Then he would ask me to do other things, intimate things—things that were—degenerate."

"How awful," he said quietly.

"But no," she said. "No! It wasn't awful! I loved my father! I worshipped him! I adored him—I thought he was a god! I was raised by nannies, and they told me my father was a god! He was Viscount Hesketh, Earl of Langdon! He could do no wrong! Of course they never knew about the things we did together. That was our secret, Pater's and mine. And I loved the secret things we did together, loved them more and more as the years went by, and I'm sure Bridget loved them, too. I looked forward to our secret times together—I grew to crave them! I thought he was the most wonderful father a girl could ever have. I thought I was the luckiest girl in the world to have a father who loved me so much, and in that special, wonderful way! It wasn't until later—much later—that I learned that what we had done was considered evil, that it was called a sin against God and man, and that there was a word for it—incest. And that, in the eyes of every civilized society in the world, my beloved father was a degenerate, morally polluted, perverted in the most contemptible of human ways."

He glanced at her and, in the lights reflected from the dashboard, he saw that tears were standing in her eyes.

"That was when the guilt set in—guilt in knowing that I'd enjoyed my sin, enjoyed my willing share of his evil, encouraged the evil, helped bring the devil into our house. I felt I was going to explode with guilt! Can you understand how I felt?"

He nodded. "Yes, I suppose I can," he said.

"Bridget had already gone through the same thing. She had made her escape. I knew I had to escape from that evil house. I tried. I was seventeen, and I went to London, found a job, and tried to hide from him, from the past, from everything, but I knew he was still after me, with detectives hired to find me, and bring me back. Then—"

"Then?"

"Then, in London, I met the most wonderful young man. He was a soldier, stationed at Aldershot. We fell in love, and I thought—at last, escape! He asked to marry me, and we were married at the Post Office registry office. We were so much in love, and those few months we had together were the happiest of my life. But my father found out about it. Even though most people thought of him as a harmless old eccentric, he had friends high up in the War Office. He had influence. After all, he was Viscount Hesketh, Earl of Langdon, a Peer of the Realm! The Order of the Garter! All his mates from Eton were in the War Office. In Britain, the old school ties mean everything—more than human life itself, it sometimes seems. This was just before the Falklands War, and so, when the war started, my father saw to it that Eric was ordered there, and placed in the front lines. And so— and so—my beautiful young husband never came home from the Falkland Islands. He's buried there—and I—and I—they sent his uniform home to me in a box, wrapped in a British flag. It's all I have left of him, his uniform, and the flag they draped his coffin in."

"What a terribly sad story, Fiona," he said. "I'm—awfully sorry."

"His head was blown off by machine-gun fire. But why am I telling you all of this? I never even told Eric about my father and myself. I was certain, if I told him about any of that, he would stop loving me, that he would be repelled by me, that he would think me a less than worthless person, a piece of spoiled and damaged goods. And the guilt was still exploding inside me. It still is. Sometimes, when I think about it too much, I think my whole being will explode with guilt. And on top of that was my guilt over Eric's death, because if he hadn't married me he would still be alive."

"You mustn't think that, Fiona."

"But I do! I do. But why am I telling you all of this—you, almost a complete stranger?"

"Sometimes it helps to share your feelings with another person."

"Perhaps it's because you were kind enough to let me blubber in your car, and offered to drive me home," she said. "Anyway, after Eric died, I got another job. I worked for a little fashion publication called *Lady Fair*—just an advertising giveaway sheet, really, with offices in Maida Vale. Nothing at all like *Mode*. Then, for a while, I worked in a dress shop in Sloane Street, which was where I began to learn a little bit about fashion. Then, last December, I happened to meet Mr. Herbert Rothman in London, where he was on business, and he seemed to take a fancy to me— nothing romantic, of course, but he seemed interested in my fashion philosophy which, if I do say so myself, is a bit different from others, and he asked me if I would like to come to America to work for *Mode*. Of course I was thrilled! The chance to work with the great Alexandra Rothman, who is such a legend. Mr. Rothman seemed like my salvation at last—my savior. He arranged everything. I had no passport, no green card to work in America—he took care of all of that. Suddenly, it seemed as though I had a fairy godfather. At last I could escape. I thought if I put an ocean between myself and my guilt, perhaps it would go away. It hasn't."

"It will, in time, Fiona. You were just a child. What happened was wrong, but it wasn't your fault."

"You're Alexandra Rothman's fiancé, aren't you?" she said.

He laughed softly. "*Fiancé* is kind of a pompous word for a man my age," he said.

"Her beau, then. You know, I was so excited at the prospect of working with her that I didn't give much thought to the logistics of it. But now it doesn't look as though it's going to work out—at all. I know she's terribly upset—I could see it in her face at her party the other night. The whole thing was handled very badly. Sometimes, for all his good qualities, Herbert Rothman lacks a certain amount of—sensitivity."

"Yes," he said grimly.

"I begged him not to handle it that way, but he assured me she'd be pleased as punch. But she wasn't. And so, I guess, there it goes—my dream. And I'll be heading home for England soon."

He said nothing, but stared straight ahead at the path of his headlights on the Montauk Highway.

"I thought, perhaps if I saw her at the party tonight, I could talk to her, and explain to her how badly I feel about the whole thing, and the way it was handled, and perhaps we could work things out. But then—well, nothing seems to work out for me, does it?"

He still said nothing.

"I mean, it doesn't have to be co-editor-in-chief, or anything as grand as that, for me. Even if I were to be just a little editorial assistant, that would be thrill enough for me. Just to work for her, and learn from her, would be thrill enough to me."

"Let me talk to her," he said. "Maybe something can be worked out."

"Would you do that?" She touched his arm. "That would be most awfully kind of you. It would make me feel so much better about the whole thing—just to know she'd heard my side of it. You are a very kind man, Mel. Alexandra Rothman is very lucky to have a man like you."

He turned into the drive to Gurney's Inn. "Well, here we are," he said.

"Thank you so much, Mel."

He parked the car. "My room is just down that little board-walk there," she said.

"I'll walk you to your room," he said. "Those walks are pretty dark. . . ."

"And me, in my ridiculous high heels!"

They walked in silence down the boardwalk.

"I'd ask you in for a drink," she said, "but—"

"I've got to get back to the party."

"Of course." At her door, she fished in her large shoulder bag for her key. "Oh, my goodness!" she said.

"Lost your key?"

"No—here's the key. But my money's gone!"

"Your money?"

"I placed two twenty-dollar notes right here, in this pocket of my bag, in case I needed money for a taxi home. They're gone!"

"You're sure?"

"Absolutely! I always carry my money here."

"Do you need to borrow some money, Fiona?" he asked, feeling suddenly uncomfortable.

"Good heavens, no! I've lots of cash in the room. But it's just so strange! I've had my bag with me all evening, except—"

"Except when?"

"Except when I left it for a few minutes on the sofa in the women's changing room at the little beach house, before I went down to the beach. Do you suppose someone pinched my money out of it then? One of the servants, perhaps? I've never seen so many servants scurrying about."

"Well, perhaps," he said.

She laughed. "Well, it's certainly not enough to worry about is it—forty dollars? But thank heavens you came along. If you hadn't, I really would have been a damsel in distress! Thank you so much. And thank you for listening to me. I'll treasure what you said."

"What did I say?"

"You said sometimes it helps to share your feelings with another person. It's true. I shared mine with you, and it helped. You are a kind man, Mel, and I needed kindness tonight. Thank you." She reached up, touched his chin, and kissed him very lightly on the cheek, and he was suddenly conscious of the odor of gardenias from her perfume.

She opened the door quickly with her key, stepped inside, and closed the door behind her.

Mel walked slowly up the inclined boardwalk to his car.

When he got back to "Finisterra," and the beach, waiters were clearing the tables. Dinner was over, and he had missed it.

"There you are, darling," Alex said. "The McCutcheons

and the Moores have asked us to join them for a nightcap
at Bobby Van's after this is over. Shall we? It's on the way
home."

"Sure," he said, and wondered, briefly, whether she had
even noticed that he had been gone.

"Hurry, everybody!" cried Maggie Van Zuylen, who was
now a little drunk. "Hurry! Hurry! Down to the water! The
tide's coming in, and the sand castle's about to go!"

Some four hundred pairs of eyes turned toward the Atlantic
Ocean to watch as the first of the castle's crenellated turrets,
and the toy sentinel guarding it, sagged into the surf and were
washed away. "I hear the florist charged three thousand for
it," someone said.

Later, at Bobby Van's, the local bistro, Mel and Alex,
Mimi and Brad Moore, and Pussy and John McCutcheon
were finishing their drinks. "This is my treat," Alex said.

"No, let me get the drinks," John McCutcheon said.

"No. I insist."

"Why?"

"Because I feel like it. No arguments." She reached in her
Chanel bag. Then she said, "Oh, dear."

"What's wrong?"

"My wallet's gone." She looked at the others helplessly.
"Well, perhaps I won't treat."

Mel was looking at her strangely. "Cash?" he said.

"Cash—and credit cards."

"Pussy, check your purse," Mel said.

"What's the matter, Mel?"

"Pussy, check your purse," he said again.

Pussy McCutcheon opened her bag, and squealed with dismay. "Mine's gone, too!" she cried.

"Mimi, check yours," Mel said.

Slowly, Mimi Moore opened her clutch bag. "I only had
a few loose bills in here," she said. "But they're gone."

For a moment, they all looked at one another uneasily.

"We've all been ripped off!"

"We all left our bags on that long green sofa in the wom-
en's dressing room while we were on the beach. It must have
been then."

"It must have been one of Maggie's staff."

"But Maggie's used that same crew for years! I've used

them, too. I know most of those boys by their first names," Pussy McCutcheon said.

"Would a waiter go into the women's dressing room?"

"The women's dressing room wouldn't stop a determined thief, lover," Mimi Moore said to her husband. "Besides, I'm sure she had women in the clean-up crew."

"They all come from Goldman's—the best caterer in the Hamptons!"

"I wonder how many others—"

"There were dozens of purses lying on that sofa."

"Well, one thing we must all promise to do," Alex said. "We must not tell Maggie Van Zuylen about this. It would kill her to know that something like this might have happened at her party. Mel, you are looking at me in the strangest way. Are you all right?"

"Tell you later." He reached for his wallet. "I'll pay for drinks," he said.

Chapter 19

Mel Jorgenson's house in Sagaponack was his newest toy. He had designed it himself. It was low and large—ten thousand square feet—and sprawled across a beach-grass-tufted dune, facing the sea, and, at the rear, it overlooked three salt ponds. The walls of the house were almost entirely of glass, and the walls were uncurtained because—look for yourself, he would point out—there were no neighbors for as far as the eye could see. The levels of the house rose and fell in the pattern of the dune it was built on, and there were no interior doors at all, though sliding parchment panels could be opened and closed to shut off certain private areas. The house, as it climbed and descended Mel's private dune, could be treated as one enormous room.

Thick white rugs, so thick they were almost ankle-deep if you were standing in them barefoot, were scattered across the honey-colored polished hardwood floors, and the furniture—also designed by Mel and custom-built—was oversized, low slung, and deep. When he settled his tall, lanky frame into one of his white leather sofas, there was a kind of whooshing sound, and when he sank into one of these, and when Alex sat opposite him, his head seemed to sprout up from between his knees.

On the ocean side, a series of whitewashed decks led down to the pool, which was painted black to reflect the clouds and the sky, and, from the pool, another terraced series of decks led to the beach itself. The only sounds that ever approached this house were the *shuuuuu-shuuuu* sound of the surf as it broke and skittered across the sand, the moan of an occasional passing seagull, and the rustle of the wind in the beach grass.

A house like this had its drawbacks, of course, and the publicity it received when it was placed on the cover of *Architectural Digest* hadn't helped. Curious strollers from the beach sometimes made their way up the terraced decks and could be found with their noses pressed against the glass walls, hoping for a glimpse of their television idol. These intruders had to be politely shooed away. Also, as someone at the party had pointed out, the constant salt spray from the sea meant that the glass window-walls had to be washed at least once a week, if not oftener than that. Sand from the beach below blew into the black pool, which had to be regularly emptied and cleaned. Sand, like snow, drifted in the wind, and the contours of Mel's dunes were constantly changing and rearranging themselves. The house itself was stabilized—two dozen reinforced concrete pylons that supported the house extended down into the bedrock—but the earth around it was forever shifting. After a storm, or high winds, a maintenance crew had to be hired to shovel Mel's spectacular glass house out of the sand. Some sort of fencing, it had been pointed out to him, might prevent these periodic inundations, but Mel resisted the idea of fencing. After all, why should a man who had no neighbors surround himself with a fence?

No, no one could say that a house such as Mel's was exactly practical, or care-free, nor did honey-colored, highly polished hardwood floors take kindly to wet or sandy feet, nor to the comings and goings of Mel's dog, Cronkite. Still, Mel himself seemed oblivious to the shortcomings and headaches of beachfront living. In fact, the very impracticality of the house seemed to excite him. He loved the fact that the views through his glass walls were never exactly the same. "The wind does my landscaping for me," he liked to say. This was the sort of house he had always dreamed of owning and, he said, if ever he retired from broadcasting, he wanted to live year-round in his costly Sagaponack fish tank. It was to this house that he and Alex were headed now, down the mostly empty highway, with Cronkite in the back seat.

"It had to be one of the waiters," Alex was saying. "I can see how it would happen. Those poor guys don't get paid much, and probably some poor kid, who's never done anything dishonest before in his life, has got his girlfriend pregnant, and she's pressing him for money for an abortion, or pressing him to marry her, and she's otherwise driving him crazy. He goes out to serve this party, where all these rich people are, where people are talking about four-million-dollar houses and where the hostess has spent three thousand dollars on a sand castle, just to see it get washed away, and he thinks—why do they deserve all of this? Why don't I deserve a share of it? And he passes a room where two hundred women have just tossed their purses, and he thinks—why don't I just help myself to some of it? Poor kid. He's probably home right now, ridden with guilt, wishing he hadn't done it, but of course it's too late now to put the money back. I feel sorry for him, actually."

He chuckled softly. "Typical Alex," he said. "Always writing a scenario."

"Part of an editor's job, I guess. Trying to get the story to make some sort of sense. Still, it makes me mad. There's enough of the country girl in me to think that five hundred dollars is a lot of money—plus the nuisance of reporting all the stolen credit cards. Anyway, your weekend date is now penniless."

"Fiona Fenton also had money taken from her."

"What? Was she there? I didn't see her."

"She only stayed a few minutes. She felt she was dressed all wrong. She was wearing a long evening gown and high heels, and everybody else was in sneakers and jeans. She was embarrassed, and left."

"Huh! And this is the woman who has overseen the fashion needs of Britain's most fashionable women, or whatever it was Herb said about her the other night."

"She didn't know what 'beach party' meant. They don't have them in England."

"And that's what Maggie meant when she said she had a surprise for me. She invited us both, hoping to see some fur fly between us, the bitch."

"Now don't be too hard on Fiona," he said. "I drove her home, and she's really a sweet kid who's had a very unhappy life."

"Huh! Living in one of the biggest suites at the Westbury? Chauffeured limos? All paid for by Herb, of course. These titled Brits never have two nickels to squeeze together."

"Just don't be too hard on her," he said. "I drove her damn near all the way to Montauk, and we had a long talk. I think she may really need a friend."

"Well," she said. "She seems to have made quite an impression on you. Are you sure that's all you did with her? Drive her home?"

He glanced sideways at her. "Now that," he said, "was an unworthy comment for you to make, Alex. Truly unworthy. She's really not after your job, as you seem to think."

"Huh!"

"She's actually rather naïve. I don't think she had any idea what she was getting into with Herb. I think she feels quite out of her depth in this situation. She was appalled by the way Herb handled things the other night at your party. She knows how upset you are, and she feels very bad about that. She's even thinking about packing up and going back to England."

"Good. Tell her I'll pay for her ticket."

"Please, Alex. I've gotten to know the woman. You haven't."

"Go back to England? Why should she, with a sugar daddy like Herbert Rothman picking up her tab at the Westbury? No way."

"I don't think it's that kind of a relationship at all. She refers to him, very formally, as Mr. Rothman. I don't think they're even on a first-name basis."

"Mel, I think you're the one who's being naïve."

"She said to me, 'I don't want to be co-editor. I'd work as a little editorial assistant, just for the thrill of working with Alex Rothman.' She admires you so."

"Hah!"

"Don't be mean-spirited, Alex."

"But don't you see? It's too late. It's too late for her to be just a little editorial assistant. The fat's in the fire. Herb has already made his announcement. It was in the *New York Times*. It's official. Herb can't offer her a lesser position now without looking like a damned fool, and if there's one thing Herb Rothman doesn't want to look like, it's a damned fool, with egg all over his face."

"But will you just talk to her, darling? I think if you talk to her, you'll get an entirely different impression of this girl. She's no threat to you. What harm would there be in talking to her? Would you? I told her I'd ask you."

"Well, I guess I'll have to talk to her at some point," she said. "She's supposed to be coming to join the magazine on the first of July."

"Good," he said. "Have a talk with her between now and then. I think you'll see what I mean." He patted her knee.

They were turning into Mel's sandy driveway now, and the dark silhouette of Mel's house loomed ahead of them. The glass walls caught the twin reflections of Scarlett O'Hara's headlights.

"I thought we weren't going to discuss this business this weekend," she said.

"I know."

"You brought it up."

"I know," he said wearily.

He parked the car in the drive, and opened the door. Cronkite leaped out and headed for the nearest clump of beach grass, where he began relieving himself.

Mel and Alex started together up the oystershell path toward the dark house.

First, as always, there was a brief inspection tour of the glass house, to be sure that everything was as it had been left the week before. "Now, Cronkite," Mel said in a stern voice. "Tonight's lesson is—no sticky nose-marks on our glass walls. Last week, at nose level, these windows were one solid smear from wall to wall—from *your nose*, Cronkite!"

Obediently, as though Cronkite had caught the drift of at least part of the admonition, the big dog padded toward the window and pressed his wet, black nose against the glass.

"Bad Cronkite! Oh, what the hell." Mel immediately began tossing off his clothes, throwing his green cap on one of the huge white sofas, unbuttoning his shirt, kicking off his shoes and socks, slipping out of his trousers and jockey shorts. Naked, he headed for the glass doors leading to the beach. It was always the second thing he did after arriving in Sagaponack—his swim in the ocean.

She followed him out onto the deck and perched on the whitewashed railing, and watched as he bounded naked down the steps, two at a time, to where the white sand began, and watched as he ran down the slope of the wide beach to begin his swim—in that perfect Australian crawl that he had taught himself, the way he had taught himself to play tennis and golf, to ride and to speak—in the general direction of Portugal, with Cronkite lumbering behind him. There was a moon, and the sand glowed palely, and the man and his dog were slightly darker moving figures against this glow. She watched as he strode into the creaming surf, and saw his buttocks flinch as the first cold wave hit his midsection. He dove into the second wave, and Cronkite leaped into the surf after him. She rose and turned back into the house, closing the sliding glass door behind her.

He had accused her of being mean-spirited.

Against one expanse of white wall—the only interior wall in the house, really—leaned a large abstract oil painting, unframed. The painting had been sitting there, unhung, for the past two weeks.

They had named that stretch of wall the Wailing Wall, because they had been unable to agree on how to treat it. Alex felt strongly that this wall demanded, cried out for, an important piece of contemporary art. Mel disagreed. He said he liked that wall left dramatically bare. But he was wrong. She had spotted this particular painting—by a young Cambodian who now lived in France, and who signed himself simply Sam—in a Madison Avenue gallery, and had it shipped out to Sagaponack for Mel's approval. Everything about the painting was perfect—the size, the colors, everything—for that wall. But Mel's approval had not been forthcoming.

"Fifteen thousand seems like a lot to spend for some streaks of oil on a canvas," he said.

"But you're rich, darling," she said soothingly, though she knew that, in his heart of hearts, he would probably always think of himself as poor. "Think of it as an investment," she said. "This Mr. Sam is very young. He's just beginning to be discovered by important collectors. His work isn't going to do anything but increase in value. If you buy him now, you'll be in the vanguard."

"I don't want to be in the vanguard."

"But look how those golden browns would pick up the colors of the dunes. And there's the blue of the sky and ocean.

And look—those slashes of bright green with the palette knife echo the color of the beach grass. It's a landscape, really, and it's perfect for this room."

"Hmm," he said, frowning. "I don't see any landscape in it."

"You have to sit and look at it for a while. You have to get your eye in, as we say in the fashion business. You have to let a painting like this grow on you. Let's put a nail in the wall, and hang it up. You'll see how it'll bring this whole room to life."

"*What?*" he cried. "Drive a nail into my beautiful white plaster? Are you nuts? If I end up not buying the thing, I'll end up with a nail hole in my wall, for God's sake."

"A tiny little nail hole could be easily spackled over."

"I don't want my wall *spackled!*"

Or repainted, she had thought. Wasn't it amazing, she sometimes thought, how this man, who would spend God-knew-what amounts of money to have his fish-tank house shoveled periodically out of the shifting sand, and to have his walls constantly washed—from the salt-spray outside, and from Cronkite's nose-marks inside—would nonetheless dig in his heels at the thought of patching a tiny, almost invisible, nail hole in one wall?

"I'm not sure I want *any*thing on that wall," he said at last.

And so there they were, stalemated again on the subject of the Wailing Wall.

She curled herself in one of his deep white chairs, and gazed upward at the pale ceiling of the dimly moonlit room. The ceiling was full of shifting shadows reflected from the glass walls. His model for the house, he often explained, was what the Japanese called a compound house, where many different areas for different uses combined and flowed together. The Sam still leaned against the long white wall, unhung, its colors bleached by the light of the moon. Mel's house had a kind of buoyant beauty on a night like this—a great glass ship floating in a moonlit sea.

But the room demanded this painting! Even in the colorless moonlight, its colors haunted the room. With this, and only this, painting on that, and only that, wall, the room would be complete, perfect. He had to be made to see how the colors of the Sam echoed and reflected the shifting tints and shadows of the natural world outside. The shadows were never the same, always changing. She tucked her legs beneath her tailor-fashion and stared fixedly at the Sam, thinking.

I am a clever woman, she thought. I have even been called a genius. It took brains, and it took taste, to last as long as I have lasted as the editor-in-chief of *Mode*. It took brains and guts and determination to bring the book's paid circulation up to the magical five-million mark without special-discount offers, without coupons, contests, or other expensive gimmicks—circulation, after all, could be bought. It took foxiness, inventiveness, and spirit to do what I have done. Then certainly I am clever enough to persuade Mel Jorgenson that he must buy this painting, to convince him that I am right—I, an acknowledged expert on color and design—and that he is wrong. Why is he wrong? The room is just too damned white! It cries for a splash of color. It is *screaming* for the Sam! Why, to do what this painting will do for this room, for the entire house, fifteen thousand dollars was *cheap!*

"I'll win this one," she said aloud.

When he came back from his swim, he would shower off the sand and saltiness in the outdoor shower, but his mouth would still taste salty when they made love. And after that . . .

He had called her mean-spirited.

And why must he buy this painting, this and no other? Because, as even he would be the first to admit, an appreciation of important art was not his strong suit, and why should it be? A Brooklyn tailor's son. She wanted her man to own this painting because she wanted his house to be perfect, she wanted everything about him to be perfect, as perfect as his Australian crawl, as perfect as his tennis serve, as perfect as his Italian seat on horseback, and she wanted all his friends to admire him for his perfect taste. She wanted him to be *praised*, for heaven's sake! Was that selfish? Was that mean-spirited? Surely, she thought, there was a clever way to win this particular battle. Surely, if she was clever enough, she would find a way. After they made love, and he was in that lovely, acquiescent mood . . .

But why do I want to win? she asked herself. Because everything I have ever got in life I have fought for, and I have always fought to win. It was as simple as that.

But why do I want to change him? Why do I want to change his life, his house, and the way his friends think of him? Simple enough. Because I love him, and the change will be for the better.

Or, she asked herself again, is it something else? Is it because I am an editor, and feel I can edit this man's life? An editor always changes. That is what an editor is for: changes. Change the layout, change the lead, change the headline, change the copy block, do something different with the cover for a change. Vivify it, give it an extra twist, crank the story up a notch or two. Change the girl's earrings, change her hair, give her a little more fox and flair. That rhymes, she thought; I have written a couplet. But a person was not a product, like a magazine. Probably a person could never be changed, never be vivified, twisted up a couple of notches, redone like a layout. And Mel was a person, a man who had told her he loved her, and whom she had told she loved.

The sound of the distant surf was a signal, and it seemed to match the sudden beating of her heart, and all at once there was the answer. Love had nothing to do with winning, did it? Love was the opposite. Love was loss. Love was surrender, love was sacrifice. Love was losing yourself in one other person. "You need to be needed," that first, painful love of hers had told her all those years ago, that lover who, when she thought of him, had left a thin splinter of ice in her heart. "No one needs you," he had said. But had he really needed her? In retrospect, not at all, and from that lack of need had grown the cold splinter of ice. Had Steven needed her? She had thought so at the time but, if he had, would he have done what he did? Then how did you get someone to need you? That answer was simple, too. To be needed, you needed to offer up, unbidden, some precious extra of yourself. Love was loss. Why had it taken her half a lifetime to discover this one small, pure fact?

In the excitement of this sudden discovery, this small epiphany, Alex sprang to her feet and began pacing the big glass room. Love is loss! If I am really going to win this one, I am going to have to lose myself, let go of myself, untwist myself, in love. She took a last, hard look at the painting leaning against the wall, and instantly decided: First thing Monday morning, I will telephone the David Findlay Gallery on Madison Avenue and tell them to take that painting back. How could I have been so stupid—stupid and selfish? I will give him back his wall, give him back his house.

But she knew that offering was not anywhere near enough. There must be more, much more. This was only a beginning. And—amazing how her mind worked this late at night—the pieces of their respective lives seemed to fall magically, symmetrically, into place.

Consider Mel. Mel was all about generosity, all about giving away pieces of himself. He gave of himself daily in all directions. He was generous to her, always giving her little gifts, like the Hermès silk scarf that she had bitchily tossed out the window of his car. He was generous to his parents, the retired tailor and his wife, and had bought them a lovely house in Westchester. He was generous to his two daughters, even though he rarely got to see them. He was wonderful to his dog. He was generous to his public, to his fans, all those people he would never know, answering every letter personally, even the crazy ones and the ones that wrote him asking for money. His generosity and his spirit shone from the television screen, which surely was why he was so popular. He had been generous to the two women stranded on the expressway with their flat tire. He had wanted Alex to have generous thoughts—was that too much to ask?—about Fiona. Even that dreadful woman in the tollbooth—what was her name?—he had treated generously, even leaving her ten dollars richer for her dreadfulness, enough for her dinner, as she had put it.

And Alex herself? She had spent the last few days full of anger, full of jealousy and resentment, thinking only of herself and her career. She had been angry at Herb, and had been busily plotting ways to bring him to his knees—ways to win! She had been jealous of Joel for growing up without asking her express permission. She had been rude to Marsha—that was it—Apfelbaum, rude and angry and imperious and, yes, bitchy. She had had jealous thoughts about Mel, jealous, unworthy, mean-spirited thoughts. She had bitchily suggested that Mel's interest in Fiona Fenton was more than friendly. She had found herself resenting Mel's fame, simply because his celebrity was more visible than hers, and because it inconvenienced her now and then, because his fans intruded on *her* space and made *her* feel

invisible, because they were not *her* fans as well. She had
even resented poor old Ho Rothman for becoming senile, too
old for her to manipulate any longer. Worst of all, she saw
herself turning into one of those hard-boiled, despotic boss-
lady executive types whom Joan Crawford used to play in
movies, who threw tantrums when they didn't get their way,
and hurled erasers at their secretaries when their morning
coffee wasn't hot enough. She was becoming a cliché, the
selfish, manipulative bitch-goddess.

Anger, resentment, jealousy—toward anyone who appeared
to stand in her way, who threatened to usurp any of her hard-
won power, who threatened her with any sort of loss. Where
was love in any of this? *Love was loss!*

She thought: I really am a genius! A genius, to have made
this great discovery which seemed, at the moment, greater
than anything discovered by Copernicus, Galileo, Columbus,
Newton, Einstein. There was a small, brown mole just below
Mel's navel, and suddenly she loved this mole with more
enormity and passion than anything she had ever loved in
her life, and the flush she felt in her face was sexual, and
it flooded through her body like that very first orgasm, the
one one never completely forgets.

Suddenly, outside the window, she heard a branch snap.
She knew, from having grown up in the country, that no
animal in nature, except a human, will step on a branch
that will not hold its own weight. And it couldn't be Mel
returning from the beach because the sound had come from
the side of the house that faced the highway. She turned, and
saw—or, for a fleeting second was certain she had just seen—
a white face pressed against the glass window-wall. Then it
was gone. Someone had been watching her!

They had grown used to intruders pressing their noses
against the walls of the glass house in daytime, hoping for
a glimpse of the famous anchorman, but, at one o'clock in
the morning, this was something else again. For a moment,
she stood frozen with fear.

Then she leaped across the thick-piled carpet to the small
kneehole desk where she knew Mel kept his pistol. He had
rarely needed to produce it, but there had been times when
the sight of it had helped send unwanted visitors on their
way. She pulled the gun from its drawer, ran to the sliding

glass door, and flung it open defiantly. "Who's there?" she demanded. But the dune seemed empty now in the moonlight, though she was certain she could hear the sound of running footsteps retreating in the sand. "Stop or I'll shoot!" she cried.

Briefly, she thought she saw an object move, low in the beach grass, and she aimed the gun low at that, her finger on the trigger. But then she saw that it was only the broken branch of a sea grape tree, dangling in the breeze. There had not been sufficient wind to break that branch. Whoever had broken it had fled off into the night. She stepped back into the house again, slid the door closed, and snapped the deadbolt lock.

"What the hell are you doing, Alex?" He stood there, still naked, but with a beach towel draped about his head and shoulders.

"We had a prowler. I heard someone, and I saw someone."

"Gone now?"

She nodded.

"Another member of my fan club, I suppose. Now put that thing away, Alex. It makes me nervous."

"I know how to handle a gun."

"I know. That's why it makes me nervous."

She returned the pistol to its drawer in the desk.

"Now, come here," he said, and opened his arms wide.

She flew—flew to him, as though wings had been provided—and buried herself in his embrace with a little happy sob.

When it was over—and it had been immensely, complexly satisfying for her tonight—she curled, like a nesting spoon, against the warm curve of his back, and thought about it. There was something different about making love with Mel, very different from making love with any other man she had ever known. She tried to define the difference, but it wasn't easy. What was it? It was more mature, perhaps, more grown-up, but that didn't quite explain it, for "mature" implied that they didn't do silly, sexy adolescent things with one another. They did. Tonight, for instance, she had been so excited that she whipped off her clothes in front of him, and let him lift her by her shoulders and let him enter her as he stood there, and she locked her arms and legs tightly around his back. He carried her, danced with her, really, like that, around the room before carrying her, locked to him, to the bed, where they fell, laughing at how they must look if someone were still looking at them through the glass, across the cool white sheets. Their lovemaking was adult in the sense of adults playing a childhood game, and she thought of the young men in their banana hammocks playing volleyball on the beach. Yes, their lovemaking was like a game in which no one really cared who won—the volleyball flew back and forth—it was all for the fun of it, the good times of being together, of being friends, and in love. In their lovemaking, there was no victor and no vanquished. Everybody won, when it was over . . .

It was so different from the way it had been with Steven, or that first one. When Mel made love to her, they laughed. They had little jokes. He had given her breasts names. Her left breast was Sarah, the right was Beatrice. He claimed to much prefer Beatrice to Sarah, but he tried to be fair. "Sarah is getting jealous," he said, after nibbling on Beatrice for a while, and he would let his tongue glide gently around Sarah's nipple.

"Sarah wants more than that," she would say, and they would both laugh, before getting serious again for a while.

And so she was revising her thoughts again. Love didn't have to be only loss, only sacrifice. It could be something even more complicated than that. It could be sharing—the first, and most difficult, thing that preschool children were taught to try to do, and how slow most children were to learn to share! Some of them never learned to do it. Probably most of them never learned to do it. And perhaps that was the special thing about Mel's and her lovemaking, perhaps that was why it seemed so mature, adult, grown-up. They were two children who had finally grown up and learned to share.

"I've been thinking," she whispered. "You are absolutely right about that painting. It doesn't belong there. That wall should be left absolutely bare."

"Mmm," he mumbled drowsily.

"I'm calling Findlay the first thing Monday morning to tell them to take it back."

He muttered something unintelligible. Then she heard him say, "It must have been one of the waiters," and she knew he was asleep.

But she wasn't thinking about Maggie Van Zuylen's waiters, or the women's purses. She was thinking now about poor old Ho Rothman, who had been her friend, but who had never learned to share. For most of his adult life, Ho Rothman had waged a pitched battle with his oldest son, knowing, intuitively perhaps, that one day Herbert would try to take over the company and that, when that happened, everything that Ho had created would be destroyed. Now that day appeared to have come, and Ho was too old and ill to know it was happening, the fall of the House of Rothman. . . .

The pale face she had fleetingly glimpsed at the window tonight seemed familiar. Where had she seen it before? As she drifted off to sleep, it became the face she had seen in her dream, her own face from the Bouché portrait, looking up from the spinning boat and calling for help.

The next morning, she slept late, as she often did on Sunday mornings. When she opened her eyes, there was no sign of Mel. She rose, put on a loose cotton robe, and opened the sliding parchment panel that separated the bedroom from the rest of the house.

The day was bright and sunny, and an easterly wind was raising whitecaps on the sea, and there was a heavy surf. From the top deck, she surveyed the beach, bridging her left hand across her eyes to shield them from the sun. There was still no sign of Mel. He was probably off somewhere, walking Cronkite. She stepped back inside the house.

That was when she saw it. The Sam painting had been hung on the white wall. He had driven a nail into the white wall, and hung it there. For a moment she thought her heart would break.

Then she burst into tears.

Chapter 20

Back in the spring and early summer of 1912, with his—
and the *Explorer*'s—new celebrity, Ho Rothman found himself flooded with new orders for subscriptions. Newsdealers
from across the Hudson, in Manhattan, Brooklyn, and the
Bronx, now begged to stock the weekly tabloid on their
stands. This put Ho in a unique position of power, and
he was quick to seize it. Newspapers were sold in those
days—and most are today—on a returnable basis. In other
words, newsdealers were able to return any unsold stock
to the publishers for credit. Ho informed the big-city dealers that, if they wished to stock *his* newspaper, the terms
would be cash, and no returns. There was considerable grum-
bling over this policy, but Ho was adamant. "Supply and
demand," he said, citing one of Sadye Rothman's capitalist
precepts. "You demand, I supply. No returns." This no-
returns policy continued to apply to Rothman newspapers
to this very day.

Handling this sudden spate of new business, needless to
say, presented serious distribution problems for the youthful
publisher, but Ho was still unwilling to take on any extra
paid hands. Fortunately, his new friend Sophie Litsky and
her family came to his rescue. The *Explorer* went to press
on Thursday evenings, and was distributed Friday mornings.
Early Friday morning, before school, Sophie herself took on
two of Ho's Newark routes, toting the papers up and down

the streets in a child's red express wagon. Her two-years-older brother, Morris, who had a bicycle, was able to cover a more extensive area. On Friday mornings, Mother Bella Litsky herself undid her apron and joined Ho on the ferry to Manhattan to help him make his deliveries in the city, and presently even Rabbi Litsky, caught up in the enthusiasm for the enterprise, abandoned his phylacteries and his Talmudic texts and, in his black hat and flowing side curls, joined his wife and Ho on the weekly cross-river treks to New York, where, on streetcars, the three fanned out in different directions across the metropolis and to the outer boroughs, carrying bundles of newspapers tied in twine. The rabbi's only condition was that he be home by sundown for *Shabbes*.

The reasons why the entire Litsky family were so eager to assist their young friend were not entirely altruistic. Privately, Bella and her husband had noted that this ambitious, hardworking young *mensch*—this national hero and celebrity-of-the-moment who had not only been the first to report the worst disaster in maritime history, but who had also forewarned that it could occur—might be an excellent choice as a husband for their Sophie, when the time came. Of course Ho had no such plans. But he did not discourage the Litskys from supposing that he might.

Still, even with the Litskys' help, Ho was getting only two or three hours' sleep out of twenty-four. And, on the short ferry crossings, it was not uncommon to see little Ho Rothman curled on one of the vessel's hard wicker benches, with a bale of *Explorer*s as a pillow, sleeping until roused by the bell that announced that the ferry had entered its slip.

Ho had followed his *Titanic* stories with a series of profiles of some of the great men who had gone down with the liner—Benjamin Guggenheim, Isidor Straus, the traction heir Harry Elkins Widener. Some of these stories paid off in interesting ways. For example, he had headlined one "JOHN JACOB ASTOR—AMERICAN HERO!" His account of Mr. Astor's heroism was a mixture of contemporary reports and certain fictional details that Ho invented himself. He wrote of how "Colonel" Astor assisted his pregnant wife into a lifeboat, and promised to follow her in a later boat, which was true enough. And he added that the colonel had then spent his final hours seeing to it that little children were warmly bundled up in caps, mittens, and mufflers before being lowered in boats into the icy sea, which Ho thought was a nice dramatic touch.

Not long after that story appeared, he received a letter from her private secretary saying that Colonel Astor's widow wished to see him.

In his best suit, he presented himself at the front door of the Astor mansion at 840 Fifth Avenue, where he was greeted by a butler in a black swallowtail coat and a gold-and-white-striped vest. Ho had reached out to shake the butler's hand, and the butler had accepted the handshake rather limply. Later, this would become one of the great stories he told around the dinner table at "Rothmere"—how he had shaken the hand of Mrs. Astor's butler.

The butler escorted him to the Venetian drawing room, where Madeleine Astor sat in a kind of throne—a small, delicate-looking young woman with a gold throw across her lap, which was intended to conceal her pregnancy. She extended her hand, and Ho bowed formally. "I just want to thank you for what you wrote about my husband," she said. "I always knew he was a hero, but I did not know that he spent his last hours seeing to the welfare of the little children. That was so like Jack, and I was very much moved by your account of it." Then she handed him a check for a thousand dollars.

At the same time, capitalizing on his fame as the newspaperman who had predicted the *Titanic* disaster, Ho added a regular feature called "The *Explorer's* Crystal Ball." The Crystal Ball department specialized in predicting other dire occurrences, and it was soon one of the best-read features in the paper.

It didn't matter that many of Ho's predictions did not come true. They made titillating reading. He predicted that the sixty-story Woolworth Building that was going up in downtown Manhattan—to become the tallest inhabitable structure in the world—would blow over in the first high wind. It is still standing to this day. He predicted that the New York Giants would defeat the Boston Red Sox in the World Series, but the Red Sox won. He predicted that the Leaning Tower of Pisa would fall down in six months' time. He predicted that President Theodore Roosevelt's split with the Republican party to form his own "Bull Moose" party would result in an overwhelming victory for William Howard Taft, but

it actually led to the victory of Woodrow Wilson. He predicted an earthquake in the heart of Paris that would topple
the Eiffel Tower. On the other hand, he did predict that a
massive volcano would erupt "somewhere west of the Mississippi," and when Mount Katmai conveniently erupted in
Alaska, burying Kodiak Island a hundred miles away under
three feet of ashes, Ho insisted editorially that this was the
volcano he had been talking about. Alaska was west of the
Mississippi, wasn't it?

As circulation climbed, so did orders for advertising pages.
One of his first important new advertisers was the Newark
Light & Power Company, and it struck Ho as a nice irony
that the company that was still unwittingly supplying him
with free electricity should also be paying him handsomely to advertise in his pages. For his advertisers, Ho began
employing a system he called "discounting." The idea was
simple. The more frequently a company advertised, the deeper was the discount that the company was given. This tactic is
widely used today, but Ho was the first to come up with it.

In the back of Ho's mind was already the notion that he
would expand the *Explorer* from a weekly to a daily operation. But, prudently, he decided to take his time. Wisely,
too, he decided to hold on to his job at Bamberger's, where,
instead of being fired for running off the job that April night,
he now found himself being treated as the store's fair-haired
boy. His reporting exploit, after all, had generated a great deal
of free publicity for the store. Now the suddenly benevolent
Mr. Gossage invited Ho Rothman to be his assistant furniture
buyer, at a salary of twenty-five dollars a week, and presently
Ho was helping Mr. Gossage prepare the same ads for spuri-
ous furniture sales that would end up appearing on the back
page of Ho's newspaper.

Though the hours involved were grueling, there were many
advantages to be had from holding down two jobs. For one
thing, as assistant furniture buyer, Ho now had a desk and a
typewriter. At his desk at the store, Ho was able to pound
out stories for his paper. If Mr. Gossage objected to this
use of the store's time, he did not say so. For another, the
store offered its employees discounts on its merchandise—
thirty percent off on items of personal clothing, and twenty
percent off on everything else. At his newspaper, all the furniture had been confiscated and sold at auction at the time

of the city's foreclosure. Gradually, Ho was able to refurnish his office there. He was also able to make private deals with some of the store's suppliers, and to buy, at wholesale, certain items not sold at the store—filing cabinets, for instance, to hold his paper's growing morgue. Suppliers also gave their buyers gifts—sometimes straight cash kickbacks for their orders, and sometimes merchandise that could be put right out on the floor and sold, for cash, which the buyer could simply pocket or, if he was like the kindly Eldridge Gossage, split with his assistant. Also, Ho was able to persuade Mr. Gossage to increase his advertising budget with the *Explorer*. In return, Ho was careful to make repeated favorable mentions of the store in his general copy. A racehorse, for example, was "as speedy as a Bamberger's delivery to a customer," and a hockey player was "as solidly built as a Bamberger's credenza." Later, Rothman newspapers would become famous for this sort of thing. It was called giving advertisers "editorial support."

But, most of all, Ho's Bamberger's experience taught Ho Rothman that there was really no difference between selling advertising space and selling furniture. It was all a question of persuading the customer that he was getting a bargain. Like Mr. Gossage, Ho offered his advertisers periodic "sales," and "one-day-only" special prices. By the end of May 1913, Ho Rothman had $7,145.84 in the bank. He began to think of himself as a rich man. Still, though he was always careful to see to it that his shirts were clean and his shoes were polished, he did not act or live as though he were a rich man. That came later.

It was an era of superlatives, of overstatement, of extravagance, exuberance, boastfulness, and baseless optimism, as the young century moved into its teens and early twenties. Everything that appeared was not only the newest but the biggest, the best, the tallest, the most opulent. Trains ran faster then, on rails of shining silver. Airplanes flew, but never crashed. Automobiles were replacing horses because they were easier to care for, cheaper to feed. Even the weather was better then, because the air was filled with hope and promise. Songs were more tuneful. Books and plays and films were more understandable, and even crimes were more perfect. You could get away with anything. The war in Europe was far away, and of little interest to Americans, and when America finally did become involved with it, the involvement was brief—just long enough to whip up a bit of excited patriotic fervor, and bring home a hero or two. Prohibition was exciting, because now Americans drank more than ever, and even women got roaring drunk in public places.

In this heady atmosphere, Ho Rothman *floruit*—Latin described it best: he flowered. People began to notice that, though Ho was small in stature, he was a damned good-looking fellow. There was a sparkle in his eyes as he strode down the street between his two places of business, and young women caught his eye and blushed from impure thoughts. What flowered was his self-confidence. He ruled the world, he straddled it like a Colossus, he could do no wrong, he was invincible, and the growing balance in his bank book proved it. He was master of all he surveyed, and by November of 1919 he was worth $29,176.42.

But that was when disaster struck. He received a letter from Newark's City Hall advising him that due to "an unfortunate clerical error," the city had been paying the electric bills on Ho's commercial property for the past half-dozen years. The city enclosed its bill for $14,987.60 for Ho's electric service. If he paid this, roughly half his savings would be wiped out in a single stroke. For the first time in his life, Ho found it necessary to consult a lawyer.

His lawyer, Mr. Waxman, took the position that, since the city admitted that it had committed an error, he saw no reason why his client, "a young immigrant, unfamiliar with the intricacies of the American property transferal process," should be penalized for the city's recordkeeping mistakes. It had been up to the city, Mr. Waxman maintained, to transfer the Newark Light & Power Company's account from its own name to that of Mr. H. O. Rothman. Having failed to do so, claimed Mr. Waxman, was tantamount to the city's acceptance of responsibility for the bill. To bolster his client's case, Mr. Waxman pointed to "the obvious good faith and esteem" in which the power company held Mr. Rothman, which it demonstrated by advertising regularly in his newspaper. The city was fortunate, Mr. Waxman added, that Mr. Rothman had graciously agreed to assume any charges for future electric service, and was willing to dismiss the possibility of legal action against the city, claiming that the city, having established this lengthy precedent, owed Mr. Rothman electrical service _in perpetuum_, as well as for his heirs and assigns forever, _in stirpes_. For good measure, Mr. Waxman threw in the assertion that, since the statute of limitations had long passed, "no civil tort, in fact, exists."

Back and forth the letters went between Mr. R. Jerome Waxman and Newark's City Hall. Particularly embarrassing to the city's casé was the fact that it could not seem to pinpoint the identity of the clerk in its Records Office, one J. D. Sasser, who had initially issued the directive to the power company. Mr. Waxman responded that he hoped the laxness of the city's recordkeeping would not be published in the press, in particular in his client's popular newspaper. "What would the taxpayers of Newark say if they learned that the elected officials of their City Government keep such shoddy records, and that the Government does not even know who its employees are?" asked Mr. Waxman, adding, "I can foresee a major scandal over this, with serious repercussions at the polls."

And so, finally, begrudgingly, the city relented, though it continued its search through personnel records for the elusive J. D. Sasser. It finally settled on a certain H. E. Sisson who, though he denied any knowledge of the matter, was reprimanded and transferred to the Sanitation Department, with a dock in pay.

Mr. R. Jerome Waxman sent Ho Rothman a small bill. He was more than happy to be compensated with a front-page story in the _Explorer_, headlined:

WILL BRILLIANT NEWARK LAWYER
R. JEROME WAXMAN BE
PRESIDENT WILSON'S NOMINEE
FOR THE U.S. SUPREME COURT?

Ho Rothman often wondered what President Wilson must have thought if he had seen this story.

Buried in the back of the same issue was a small story with the headline:

J. D. SASSER,
RETIRED CITY AIDE,
DIES

That tied up, Mr. Waxman explained, the only loose end, and ever since that episode Ho Rothman had found it wise to employ the services of good lawyers.

He had also been impressed by the phrase "heirs and assigns forever, *in stirpes*." He decided that it was high time that he began thinking about creating some heirs and assigns for his growing business. Sophie Litsky, sweet and hardworking though she was, did not appeal to him as the instrument through which to accomplish this mission. But someone would be found, and Ho began seriously looking around.

From Joel Rothman's journal:

Sunday 6/24/90
3.00 P.M.

I knew there had to be an explanation for why Fiona broke our dinner date Friday night, and she has just telephoned me, very apologetic, to tell me what happened. It seems her sister Brenda, who lives in Connecticut, was rushed to the hospital on Friday afternoon with a kidney stone, and Fiona had to rush up to Greenwich to sit with Brenda's kids. Of course she tried to call me, but I was out all afternoon doing dumb shopping errands! Anyway, her sister's kidney stone "passed," and Fiona's back in town, and she wants to see me tonight! Her place at 7:00 P.M., so I've made another reservation at Le Cirque for 9:30—same schedule I planned for Friday! . . . Meaningless phrases picked up from this A.M.'s Times, *mostly in ads in the Real Estate section. Keep coming across the phrase "world class." What does that mean? One apartment house has a "world class health club." Another has a dining room that serves "world class cuisine." Still another offers "round-the-clock world class doorman and concierge service." How about a world class parking lot? "World class" seems to be replacing "state-of-the-art," and means even less. Well, I'm getting a world class, state-of-the-art hard-on thinking about what Fiona and I will be doing about four hours from now!*

Now they were both lying naked on her pale blue satin sheets where they had just made love, and her telephone was

ringing. "I'd best get that," she said, reaching one pale arm
for the receiver. "It'll likely be my sister. Hullo?" she said.
"Oh, hullo, darling. . . . You're back from San Francisco?
But I didn't expect you back until *Tuesday.* . . . It went
well? . . . You're down*stairs?* No, you can't possibly come
up now—I wish you'd rung me first, darling, to tell me
you'd be getting back two days early. . . . No, I simply
can't. I've got the most bloody awful headache, and I'm
running a fever. I do hope it's not the flu. . . . No, I didn't
go to the Hamptons after all . . . my sister in Connecticut. . . .
No, I'm most frightfully sorry, darling, not tonight . . . I'm
feeling really so bloody punk, and I look a fright. In fact,
the doctor's with me now." She winked at Joel. "He's just
given me a great big injection." She winked at him again.
"And in a most indelicate place." Another wink. "Call me
tomorrow, darling, and if I'm feeling a bit more fit we'll
get together. Kiss, kiss. . . . Bye-eeeee." She replaced the
phone. "My friend Georgina from London," she said. "Most
inconsiderate girl. Never calls in advance. Just *appears*, and
expects you to drop everything."

Joel started to say that it had sounded like a man's voice,
and as though she had read his thoughts, she said, "Georgina
has this big, deep voice. Like this." She imitated it, and then
giggled. "Sometimes I wonder if Georgina is a Lesbian." She
was stroking his penis. "Oooh, look at Pinocchio!" she said.
"He must have told another lie. His nose is getting bigger
again." Then she said, "I think we're ready to try something
a little different tonight. . . ."

Chapter 21

Buy 'em sick, make 'em healthy—and if they don't get healthy quick enough, *sell* 'em!" That was the way Ho Rothman once described, to a journalist, how he had succeeded in amassing his communications empire, which, at the time, consisted of more than a hundred newspaper and magazine titles, along with radio and television stations, and was the third-largest in the nation. "And pipple don't have to be there to run a newspaper," he added, explaining how he acquired his reputation as "the absentee press lord." "You get other pipple to do that."

A publication's balance sheet told him all he needed to know, and otherwise his editors were permitted to print and publish pretty much whatever they chose. His was the Eldridge J. Gossage approach to journalism—if a story would sell papers, print it; if it wouldn't, don't. By then—this was the early 1970s—it was a well-known fact that Ho Rothman owned publications in cities where he never set foot, and ran everything from his huge thirtieth-floor office with its map of the United States covering one wall. By then, it mattered little to Ho whether his editors' opinions and philosophies coincided with his own. The name of H. O. Rothman might decorate the boardroom of B'nai B'rith, or the United Jewish Appeal, but he voiced no objections when the editor of his *Tampa Sentinel* published a series of thinly veiled anti-Semitic articles on "the invasion of Mediterranean-looking Miami

Beach types and rag-trade tycoons" coming to Florida's "traditionally more selective West Coast." A little anti-Semitism, it seemed, sold newspapers in Tampa.

But it was all quite different, back in 1921, when Ho was still the one-man proprietor of the weekly *Newark Explorer*. He was now twenty-four years old, and had run the paper for nine years. He had quit his job at Bamberger's two years earlier—retaining, naturally, Mr. Gossage's advertising account—but he still resisted the notion of taking on any employees. His paid circulation was now about fifteen thousand, which seemed to him spectacular, and he saw no reason to tamper with what was turning out to be a very good thing. He was also resisting the increasingly pointed suggestions from Sophie Litsky's father, the rabbi, that Ho could do worse things than taking young Sophie as his bride. In fact, Rabbi Litsky had lately been almost threatening, hinting that he, his wife, and his children could not be counted upon to toil for Ho's newspaper without wages indefinitely, unless matrimony lay somewhere down the road. Ho was able to hold the Litskys off by offering the family a small "profit share" from each week's receipts. But these pressures made Ho nervous. He had almost been forced into marriage once before, and he was handling his relationship with Sophie with extreme discretion, taking no chances and making no promises.

Then, out of the blue, a savior appeared on Ho's horizon who would remove him forever from the mounting pressures from the Litsky family.

The savior's name was Moe Markarian. Everyone knew who Moe Markarian was. Moe Markarian, they said, had made his entire fortune in fifteen minutes. That was the time it had taken him to recite his marriage vows to Mrs. Markarian. Mrs. Markarian was the daughter of wealthy Hymie Weiss, whose real name was Earl Wajchiechowski, who had gone out to Chicago a few years earlier and made his name, and millions, in the new and lucrative profession known as bootlegging. In fact, Midwest bootlegging was now controlled by four men—Hymie Weiss, Dion O'Banion, Johnny Torio, and another youthful Italian-American named Alphonse Capone. In time, of course, competition in the illegal liquor trade would eliminate all but one of the Four Horsemen, as they were called, but in 1921 the daughter of Hymie Weiss was considered quite a catch for Moe Markarian.

Using his wife's money, Moe Markarian had bought up several newspapers in Pennsylvania—in Wilkes-Barre, Pittsburgh, Lancaster, and Harrisburg, and a newspaper on Staten Island called the *Advocate*. The *Advocate* had become Markarian's only loser. In those days, Staten Island was a remote and sleepy place, consisting mostly of small farms. It had become a favored retirement place for minor New York bureaucrats, retired firemen, policemen, and other civil servants. In 1921, the population of Staten Island appeared to be shrinking, as the retired bureaucrats died off, and their sons and grandsons departed for more promising boroughs of the city. Rumor had it that Moe Markarian might be putting the *Advocate* up for sale. Meanwhile, the Markarians had built themselves two opulent residences—in Southampton and in Palm Beach—and were putting the finishing touches on a third in Westchester County. Markarian had also been watching with interest what Ho Rothman was doing with the *Explorer* in Newark. Moe Markarian wrote to Ho Rothman, suggesting that they meet.

Moe Markarian turned out to be a mountain of a man, built somewhat along the lines of President William Howard Taft, though where Taft sported handlebar mustaches, Mr. Markarian displayed luxuriant tufts of black hair in his nostrils. As he talked, he rolled an unlighted cigar between his massive fingers. He had brought his wife with him, and she, by contrast, was very skinny, with copper-colored hair, and was wearing many diamonds. Diamonds blazed icily from her throat, fingers, wrists, and ear lobes, and even, Ho noticed, from an ankle bracelet as she crossed her thin legs. Mrs. Markarian was the second rich woman Ho had met, the first being Mrs. Astor, and Ho was struck by the difference between them. Mrs. Astor had been pale and soft and almost childlike. Mrs. Markarian was all hard edges, and there was something about her that unsettled him.

"To me, your face is familiar, Mrs. Markarian," Ho said. "Is it possible we have mebbe met before?"

"I very highly doubt it," Mrs. Markarian said in her snooty, rich-person's voice. "I very highly doubt I know anyone in Jersey."

Mr. Markarian got right down to business. He was interested, he said, in adding the *Explorer* to his "chain."

"How much you offer me?" Ho asked.

Mr. Markarian glanced at his wife. "Fifty thousand," she snapped.

Both the Markarians must have noticed the gleam in Ho's eyes when she mentioned this figure. It was more money than he had ever had, at any one time, in his entire life. But Ho knew enough about the ways of American business to understand that a man's first offer was not necessarily his best. "I think about it," he said. "I let you know."

A week later, he telephoned Moe Markarian. "My price— one hundred thousand," he said.

"I'll have to consult certain business associates," said Markarian, meaning his wife. A little later, he called back to say, "Ho Rothman, we have a deal."

But when Moe Markarian arrived at Ho Rothman's office the next day and pushed a check across the top of Ho's desk with his large hand, Ho saw that the check was only for $75,000. "That's it," Markarian said. "My final offer. Cash on the barrelhead. Take it or leave it."

Ho relit his cigar, studying the check that lay on his desk. Then he lifted the check by one corner, and touched his lighted match to another. The check blazed up, and when the flames neared his fingertips, he dropped the ashes into his spittoon.

Moe Markarian pulled his huge frame out of the chair and marched angrily out of the room.

"Some pipple have a lot of brains. Some pipple have a lot of luck. I have both," Ho Rothman liked to say, years later, when he told of what happened next.

What happened next was this:

In Chicago, not many weeks later, Dion O'Banion—one of the Four Horsemen who controlled the Midwest bootleg trade, and who also ran a flower shop as a legitimate business—was working on a flower arrangement when two men walked into his shop. One shook O'Banion's hand, and the other gunned him down.

Now there were only three horsemen in charge of Chicago's liquor traffic, and none other than Hymie Weiss took over O'Banion's mob to challenge Johnny Torio and Al Capone for control of the Chicago market. Eventually, of course, both Weiss and Torio would suffer fates like Dion O'Banion's, and twenty-six-year-old Al Capone would rule supreme, adding gambling, prostitution, and the Chicago dance hall business to his list of profitable enterprises.

Meanwhile, Dion O'Banion's funeral was the talk of Chicago, and set new records for gaudy display. Ten thousand cymbidium orchids blanketed O'Banion's coffin, and in his eulogy the archbishop wept openly for the loss of this fine young Irishman. Outside the cathedral, an estimated one hundred thousand of the curious thronged, straining to catch glimpses of the celebrities as they made their way up the steps to attend the by-ticket-only High Requiem Mass. Police barricades had to be thrown up to hold back the surging crowd. Hymie Weiss was spotted among the famous mourners, but his arch-rivals, Torio and Capone, were conspicuously absent, and their whereabouts were the subject of much speculation.

An enterprising young reporter from the *Tribune*, however, had been able to track down Al Capone to a suite at the Palmer House. For five days, the reporter staked out the door to Capone's hotel suite. For five days, nothing much seemed to happen at the Capone suite, other than the arrival and departure of room service trays, which were accepted and returned by one or another of Capone's henchmen through the partway opened door. Then, on the sixth day, Capone emerged with a young woman on his arm. The reporter snapped their picture.

Now, for all this young reporter's enterprise, a photograph of the babyfaced Al Capone, who looked nothing at all like anyone's idea of a gangster, emerging from a doorway with an unidentified young woman did not represent great newsgathering, and the *Tribune*'s editor rejected it. So did other editors, when the reporter tried to peddle it elsewhere. "Who's the broad? Where's the story? Sorry," they all said.

But when the photograph reached Ho Rothman's desk, he immediately saw a story. He quickly picked up the telephone and called Moe Markarian. "I am ready to make a deal," he said.

When Markarian arrived at Ho's office, Ho slid the photograph across his desktop to him. Markarian looked at it, gasped, turned pale, and sat down hard in his chair. Then he grabbed the photograph as though to tear it up.

"Keep it," Ho said easily. "I have other copy."

"Would you publish this?"

"Might have to," Ho said.

"What would you say about it?"

"Say? Say that it seems very funny that, for Dion O'Banion's funeral, and for five days after that, Hymie Weiss's daughter, Mrs. Moe Markarian, spends living in hotel room with Hymie Weiss's enemy, Al Capone."

"You wouldn't dare!"

"Yes I would."

"I'd do anything to save my Rachel's honor!"

"I thought so," Ho said. And now of course he knew why Mrs. Markarian looked familiar. He did not say that he could also write that Mrs. Moe Markarian had once been a two-bit whore who had entertained her clients on a discarded mattress in a blind alley off Rivington Street, and that for some clients she had not even charged two bits. For him, she had done it for candy bars. He did not say any of this because, after all, Mrs. Markarian now had powerful friends and relatives, and Ho did not wish to push his luck too far.

Ho then outlined his terms. For $100,000, he would sell Mr. Markarian a forty-nine percent interest in the *Explorer*. Ho himself would retain fifty-one percent. In addition, he would also accept Mr. Markarian's *Staten Island Advocate*—a loser Markarian wouldn't mind parting with, anyway.

"And one more thing," Ho said.

"What's that?" Moe Markarian said, looking ill.

"You building house in Westchester."

"Yes . . ."

"I take that too."

And that was how Moe Markarian's spectacular house in Tarrytown became "Rothmere." The huge double M's that were emblazoned on the wrought-iron entrance gate were blowtorched off, and were replaced with graceful double R's, reversed, as:

ЯR

From the *New York Times* of October 10, 1921:

SOMNOLENT S.I. DAILY GETS ROTHMAN TREATMENT

When sleepy residents of Staten Island collected their morning papers from their stoops today, they discovered that the newspaper not only had a new name, but also a new look and a new editorial slant.

Under the stewardship of publisher H. O. Rothman of the *Newark Explorer*, the daily *Staten Island Advocate* today became officially the *Staten Island Adventurer*. And, in Mr. Rothman's now-familiar flamboyant muckraking style, the redesigned daily features "screamer" headlines reporting lurid events from all over the world—an editorial approach that did much to increase circulation and advertising revenue for Rothman's *Explorer*. The headline in today's edition in the *Adventurer*, for instance, announced: "MOTHER GIVES BIRTH TO THREE-HEADED BABY, Then Sells It to Circus for $1!" Buried deep within the story is the fact that the bizarre event did not, in fact, occur on Staten Island, nor even in recent history, but that something of the sort may have happened in Rumania in the early 19th century. Readers' reactions to the new format were mixed, ranging from "too ghoulish" to "makes for lively reading" and "Makes us Staten Islanders feel like we're part of the big, outside world."

Mr. Rothman, it may be remembered, early in 1912 forewarned his Newark readers that the S.S. *Titanic* might not be as "unsinkable" as her builders claimed, and was the first journalist to report the maritime disaster. . . .

After moving to Staten Island, Ho Rothman never saw the long-suffering Litsky family again. But, to his credit, when Sophie Litsky's marriage was announced two years later, he sent her a $59.95 Queen Anne–type chest-on-chest from Bamberger's as a wedding present. Even though Ho no longer worked for the store, Mr. Eldridge J. Gossage graciously gave him his employee's twenty percent discount on the piece. It stood proudly in Sophie's front hallway for many years, and her friends found it hard to believe her boast that it had been given to her by the great H. O. Rothman.

With his new acquisition came a full-time staff of six people—an editor, two reporters, a production manager, an advertising director, and a tiny, pretty sixteen-year-old

bookkeeper named Anna Lily Wise. Five years later, a staff
of forty-seven would be required to put out the *Staten Island
Adventurer.* By then, of course, Ho had acquired newspapers in Altoona, Bridgeport, Winston-Salem, Fort Wayne,
Akron, and Chattanooga. By then, too, Anna Lily Wise
had become Mrs. H. O. Rothman, and their son, Herbert
Joseph Rothman, had been born. And the phrase "the
Rothman Treatment" had entered the language of American publishing.

From Joel Rothman's journal:

> Sunday, 6/24/90
> 10:00 P.M.
> (2nd entry today)

*"I think we're ready to try something a little differ-
ent tonight," Fiona said and, Christ, I really blew it!
Literally. We'd had a really great first f---, and were
just warming up for another go-around, and she gave
me something to sniff in an inhaler. I've heard and
read a lot about "poppers," of course, but I've never
really tried one. Well, I guess I took too big a sniff,
because I really blacked out—completely! And when
I came to, I was suddenly really sick, couldn't control myself, and puked all over her bed! Christ! She
was furious. Her beautiful blue satin sheets and everything. They have to be specially cleaned and everything.
I tried to tell her how sorry I was. I told her I'd pay to
have the sheets cleaned and everything, and that even
made her madder. She said something like, "Just like
you Yanks—think you can fix everything with money!"
Then she told me to get out, she never wanted to see
me again. Christ! So I got dressed, and I kept telling
her how sorry I was, and I just begged her to give
me one more chance. And, just as I was leaving, she
said, "Well, perhaps." So maybe I'll have one more
chance. Keeee-rist, I really feel awful tonight! I love
her so, I really do! Why did I have to do something
stupid like this? What's the matter with me? This is
really the low point of my life. So ashamed. Blowing
the whole evening by puking all over her bed! She
said—and this is really the hardest part to put down—*

she said, "I knew I shouldn't have been fooling around with children."

I really feel like killing myself tonight.

She found him in the kitchen early Monday morning, listlessly spooning cornflakes from a bowl.

"Well, how was your weekend, darling?" she asked him. "Was it nice not having Otto around?"

"It was okay."

She sat opposite him on a kitchen stool. "Care to tell me about it?"

"Sure."

There was a silence. Then she said, "Well?"

"Well what?"

"You said you were going to tell me about your weekend, Joel."

"What's there to tell?"

"I guess you're not in the mood for talking," she said.

"Sure," he said, taking another spoonful of cornflakes.

"Well, I'm here, talking, and all I'm getting is monosyllables."

"I'm *talking*," he said. "There. I just said three syllables." His look was dark.

"Do you feel all right, Joel? You look a little pale. Do you think you could be running a fever?" She reached out and covered his forehead with her palm.

He threw down his spoon. "For Chrissakes, Mom, will you leave me *alone?*" he said. "Will you give me a little *air*, for Chrissakes? Will you give me a little *space?* First it was effing Otto, and now it's effing *you*. I feel like I'm suffocating here. I feel like I'm being effing smothered. I feel like everybody's trying to smother me, for Chrissakes, and if it's not one damn person it's another. And here's another thing. When I get to Harvard, will you please not effing call me on the phone every effing day, the way you've been doing for the last four years? Do you know the way the guys in the dorm used to kid me about that?" He did a mincing imitation. " '*Buster*—it's Mommie calling!' Because if you do that sort of thing to me at college, Mom, I swear to God I'll kill myself. I swear to God I will!" He jumped out of his chair and strode out of the room.

"Joel, don't you talk to me like that!" she cried.

But her only answer was the sound of his angry footsteps marching down the hall, and the slamming of his bedroom door.

The lovely eastern banks of the Hudson River were permanently scarred in the nineteenth century by the tracks of the Harlem Division of William H. Vanderbilt's New York Central Railroad. It was he who said, "The public be damned!" and the ribbons of ugly steel along the river's edge were proof that he meant what he was saying.

However, most owners of riverfront property here were given what were called riparian rights—rights of access to the river. At what was to become "Rothmere," Moe Markarian had built a boathouse on the river, and access to it was through a tunnel under Mr. Vanderbilt's railroad tracks. It had been Moe Markarian's plan, in the early 1920s, to buy an oceangoing yacht that would transport him between Tarrytown and his office in the city. Ho Rothman had toyed with the idea of a yacht, too. But his own vivid memories of that rough crossing of the Atlantic in the early 1900s deterred him. Also, he remembered only too well what had happened to the *Titanic*. The clincher was the fact that Ho had never learned to swim. Though, in later years, Ho Rothman flew fearlessly all over the world in his company's 727, he was always a nervous ocean traveler. And so, over the years, the boathouse at "Rothmere" remained empty and, for the most part, unused.

But the elegant boathouse at "Rothmere" was to become the scene of two separate, but related, family tragedies.

PART THREE

HIGH PRIESTESS

Chapter 22

THE FASHION SCENE
by
Mona

Well, kiddies, just as Mother Mona promised, here it is—my first exclusive interview with Fiona Fenton, the glamorous young Brit who's been taking N'Yawk by storm and who'll soon be sharing the tippy-top of *Mode*'s masthead with longtime fashion vet, Alexandra Rothman, and who'll soon be a fashion High Priestess herself, I betcha.

Fiona—or Lady Fiona to her chums back in Merrie Olde Englande—is the daughter of Viscount Hesketh, England's handsomest and richest peer, and she's a petite Size Six, with dark hair and eyes to die over. She received Mother Mona graciously in her glamorous East Side digs, wearing Chanel's hot pink lounging pajamas and a Nehru-type top, the height of chic. In person, she's a model of youthful pep and zip, something that *Mode* could use right now, and she outlined her unique fashion philosophy. "To me, fashion is basically *appropriateness*," she told Mother avidly. "I mean, one wouldn't go to a beach party in a floor-length sheath and three-inch spike heels, would one? Nor would one go to the Royal Garden Party in a T-shirt and jeans."

To which Mother avidly agreed.

So—move over, Alex! The British are coming, with lotsa youthful new ideas, just what publisher Herb Rothman is looking for! And how does Ageless Alex feel about sharing her crow's nest at the top of the mast with a much younger Brit? That's the burning question everybody's been asking Mother. And I'll tell y'all soon's I finds out, kiddies. Says Fabulous Fiona, "I do hope she and I can work things out together so we can share the responsibilities of running a big and important magazine. I know I'll have a lot to learn from her. After all, Alex Rothman will always be *the* High Priestess of American Fashion." Well, we'll just hafta see about that, won't we?

And speaking of beach parties, here's a few "grains of sand" for your mill. At a fab S'hampton bash Saturday nite, where so many veddy-veddy top names gathered to munch avidly on spit-roasted boar and goodies from a yummy clambake, and to have the thrill of watching a $35,000 sand castle created exclusively by Si Wells and Cliff Derr of Hampton Bays get washed out by the tide, including yours truly, something really fishy happened. To sport on the beach, lotsa the gals left their purses in the ladies' loo of the hostess's beach cabana. And while the guests dined & danced and sipped champagne, a cat burglar snuck in and emptied every last purse of cash, credit cards, etc., etc. Talk about a fishing expedition! Lotsa rich gals are feeling poorer today, I betcha.

At Mortimer's, Pussy McCutcheon and Molly Zumwalt were having lunch at one of the front tables. "Was *every* woman's purse emptied?" Molly Zumwalt asked.

"Every purse that was left in that room," Pussy said. "We were *all* ripped off."

Lenny Liebling strolled by. He often dropped into Mortimer's at lunchtime—rarely to eat, but to see who was there, visit the tables, and catch up on the latest news and gossip. A friendly waiter had just tucked a couple of luncheon receipts in Lenny's jacket pocket, which he would use later for his expense account. "Thank you, dear boy," he murmured. He approached Molly and Pussy's table, and was greeted effusively with air kisses.

"I assume that was Maggie Van Zuylen's party she was writing about," he said. "It was the only important party in the Hamptons Saturday night."

"You are absolutely correct," said Pussy McCutcheon with emphasis. "And every word of it is true."

"Who gave the item to Mona, I wonder?"

"Well, actually, I did," Pussy McCutcheon said. "I wasn't going to, at first. But then I decided that the publicity might help to catch the thief."

"Poor Maggie," Lenny murmured. "She must feel terribly, knowing that such a thing happened at her party."

"Maggie is absolutely *furious*. Maggie is absolutely ready to *kill* Mona! Mona mentioned her florist, and gave them a plug, but she didn't even mention Maggie's *name!*"

"And what about *you?*" said Molly Zumwalt, with a wicked look from beneath her famous false eyelashes. "How are you going to get along with this new young editor, Lenny?"

Lenny smiled a wan smile. "My dear, I am a survivor," he said. "I survived the Holocaust, and I shall survive this." He moved on, thinking: So much for these East Side Razor Blades.

Just across town, at Le Bernardin where Alex had suggested that they meet for lunch, Alex and Rodney McCulloch were being escorted to their table. Before taking his seat, Rodney McCulloch pulled off his suit jacket, slung it over the back of his chair, and loosened his signed Countess Mara necktie. Then he sat down. A captain hurried toward them. "Sir," he said, "we do request that gentlemen wear jackets in the dining room. And," he added almost in a whisper, "that they keep their ties fully tied."

McCulloch gave the captain a Don't-you-know-who-I-am? look, and Alex looked on with wry amusement.

"Sorry, our dress code, sir," the captain said, looking nervous.

Slowly, Rodney McCulloch rose and put on his jacket again, and straightened his tie. Then he sat down again. "What kind of a place is this, anyway?" he muttered.

"Four stars in the *New York Times*," Alex murmured.

Mr. McCulloch studied the menu. "Isn't there anything on this menu but fish?" he asked.

"We are exclusively a seafood restaurant, sir," the captain replied politely. "May I suggest the carpaccio of fresh tuna to start?"

Alex had heard and read a great deal about Rodney McCulloch, the brash young Canadian entrepreneur, recently down from Toronto and now fully prepared to take New York by storm. He turned out to be a brawny, thickset fellow, just forty-two years old, with salt-and-pepper hair that seemed to fly every whichway, twinkling blue eyes, and a smile that revealed teeth that were as every whichway as his hair. He had made his first fortune manufacturing babies' pacifiers. Then he made another with a chain of tanning salons. Then he got into North Slope Oil, and got out just before the market dropped, and made a third killing. Now he was becoming a force in publishing. He had started, as Ho Rothman had two generations earlier, buying up small newspapers—at first in provincial Canada, and later in the United States. It was widely rumored that he was now looking for something in New York City. Looking at him now, Alex was quite sure that shucking his jacket had been a calculated challenge to this fashionable restaurant, and that, back in Toronto, he might have got away with it. She had to admit that she rather liked his style.

This was the way *Time* magazine had described him in a recent Business story:

Big-boned, bushy-haired and snaggle-toothed, the gravel-voiced Media Tycoon McCulloch, 42, exudes a blustery charm and an air of down-home machismo which, those who have had dealings with him assert, can be misleading. Among his employees, the "Billionaire Bumpkin," as he is sometimes called, is known as the Father Confessor for his ability to involve himself with their problems, large or small.

"He's the most caring man I've ever known," says one. "I find myself telling Rodney things I wouldn't tell my parish priest." Learning that the wife of a reporter on his Brownsville paper had given birth to a baby with a clubfoot, McCulloch personally flew to Texas with a team of New York specialists who performed the necessary corrective surgery. Finding a secretary in one of his offices in tears, and learning that the diamond had fallen out of the setting of her new engagement ring, McCulloch crawled about her office floor on his hands and knees for half an hour until he located the tiny stone in the pile of her carpet.

At the same time, associates say, behind the good ole boy exterior lurks a tough-as-nails businessman who, in pursuit of a deal, will go after it with all the tact and finesse of a trained-to-kill pit bull terrier, straight for the jugular. . . .

For instance, in 1988, when McCulloch learned that Lorena Teasdale, the widow of Des Moines *Star* Publisher J. C. "Bud" Teasdale, was planning to wed Beverly Hills Designer Marc Collins while, at the same time, the *Star*'s typesetters were threatening to strike for increased benefits, McCulloch shrewdly decided that the widow Teasdale might be more interested in her future life in the movie capital than in Iowa newspapering. McCulloch made the widow what media experts call a "shockingly low" offer for her paper. It was promptly accepted, whereupon McCulloch notified the typesetters that if there were further threats of a walkout, he would fire the lot of them and computerize the entire operation.

Asked to comment on the Des Moines deal at the time, the Billionaire Bumpkin's comment was his trademark rapid-fire "Ha-ha-ha!"

The Rothmans might have been around publishing a lot longer, but Rodney McCulloch had already become someone to be reckoned with, and, before his most recent stroke at least, Ho Rothman had begun referring to Rodney McCulloch as "my enemy."

"Look, I know all about what that little shit Herb Rothman is trying to do to you," he said after they had ordered, pronouncing "about" in the Canadian fashion—"aboat." "Little shit's trying to force you out, and slide his little Brit tootsie in to take your place. You gonna let the little son-of-a-bitch get away with that?"

"Well, I—"

"Little son-of-a-bitch needs to have his ears pinned back. Little son-of-a-bitch has a Napoleon complex, if you ask me. Him *and* his brother Arthur."

She was noticing two things about Rodney McCulloch. He was a man who believed in getting down to business right away, with no beating around the bush, and when he asked a question he seldom waited for an answer.

"Both the little sons-of-bitches," he went on. "I see those little sons-of-bitches having lunch together all the time at the Four Seasons, which is why I said you and I would have lunch any place but there. Little sons-of-bitches with their heads together, making their little plans, swapping their little secrets. They pretend not to notice me, of course, but I know they know I'm there. Know what they remind me of? Couple of little ferrets. Two little ferrets with their heads together. Ha-ha-ha. We used to shoot ferrets down by the lake when I was a kid growing up in the backcountry in Manitoba." He raised his arms as though shouldering an imaginary shotgun, drew a bead on a passing waiter, and pulled an invisible trigger. "Ka-*pow*," he said. "Ka-*pow!* Ever have ferret stew? Polecat stew? It's even better than possum stew. It's sure better than Carpathian tuna fish, or whatever the hell this is we've ordered," and he laughed his big laugh, revealing that remarkably disorganized array of teeth, as his plate was set down before him.

From now on, he was talking between forkfuls. "Couple of little ferrets," he said. "Now listen to me. Their old man, old Ho Rothman, he may have been a bastard, and he may have been a crook. But at least he was a decent old bastard, and at least he was an honest crook. His ferret sons—that Herbert in particular—they're *mean* bastards, and they're crooked crooks, and believe me, there's a difference between an honest crook and a crooked one. So when are you going to tell that ferret outfit to go to hell? I think you should tell the ferrets to fuck themselves and the horse they rode in on, and come to work for me."

"What would I do for you, Mr. McCulloch?"

He swallowed a mouthful, and patted his mouth with a napkin. "Call me Rodney," he said. "Everybody does. I always hated the name, but that's what everybody calls me irregardless. Sounds like a sissy name—Rodney. I'd rather they called me Rod. Rod Serling. Rod McKuen, though I hear he's a pansy. Hot Rod. But Rod never stuck, and Rodney did. But to get back to that ha-ha-ha ferret. I mean, after all you've done for that magazine—Herb Rothman should be down on his knees, kissing the ground you walk on. Kissing your ass, not handing you shit. Five million circulation! That magazine would be nowhere if it hadn't been for you, everybody knows that. Knows *all* that. And that was a *great ad*—the whale spouting off—'Thar she blows!' I loved it. To hell with what the little ferret says. I also loved your June cover."

"Tell me something, Rodney," she said, taking a bite of tuna. "How did you know that Herb and I had a—slight disagreement—over the June cover and the whale ad?"

He hesitated. Then he said, "Ha-ha-ha. You got an office boy? Let's just say you got an office boy, and I've got an office boy. The office boys in this town all talk to the other office boys. This is a small town. Let's just say that. Ha-ha-ha. You ever heard of the Bay Street boys?"

"No, I can't say I—"

"The Bay Street boys're in Toronto, they're a kind of club. Hell, they *are* a club—it's called the Bay Street Club. They're the hoity-toity, elite types that call themselves the Canadian Establishment, the big bankers, and the Eatons that own the stores, and all those other elite types. They snoot me, and they snoot my wife, Maudie. They've never asked me to join the Bay Street Club, and you know why? You're Jewish, aren't you?"

"No, but my husband was."

"Well, I'm an Irish Catholic, and so is Maudie, and in Canada an Irish Catholic is worse than being a Frenchy, and being a Frenchy is considered pretty bad. Well, I'm out to show the Bay Street boys a thing or two. I'm going to show those Bay Street boys that they snooted the wrong Irish Catholics when they snooted Rodney and Maudie McCulloch. I'll show 'em before I'm through. I'm telling you all this because you need to know where I'm coming from, if we're going to be partners in this thing. What the hell is *that?*" he said, looking down at the new plate that had just been set in front of him.

"Your grilled sea bass, sir," the waiter said.

"Well," he said, staring balefully at the plate, "you got to die of one thing or another." He looked up at Alex. "Say," he said, "you're even better looking in the flesh than you are in pictures. Is that a compliment to a woman, or does that mean you take lousy pictures? Hell, I don't know, but I meant it as a compliment, anyway. Don't get me wrong.

I'm not trying to put the make on you. I'm a happily married man. Maudie and I have been happily married for eighteen years. Seven little kiddies. I guess you could say that I'm thoroughly domesticated at this particular point in time. Ha-ha-ha. But to get back to what we were talking about. How much of that little son-of-a-bitch ferret's shit are you going to take, anyway? You're not going to take that kind of shit laying down, are you?"

"Now wait a minute," she said. "Back up a bit. You mentioned partners. Partners in what?"

"You're supposed to be a tough broad," he said. "Lucy Withers tells me you're a tough broad."

She laughed. "Lucille is an old friend," she said.

"Now there's another tough broad," he said. "Lucy. She has the top modeling agency in Kansas City, but what kind of shit is that? If she'd of been just a little tougher, and moved her act to L.A. or the Big Apple, she'd have the top modeling agency in the country. But she wasn't quite tough enough to make the big move. You *were*. She also tells me you're a smart broad. You've also got credibility. You see, I know all about you—your background, Paradise, Missouri, and all that. I guess you'd hafta say that I've done my homework on you. Ha-ha-ha."

"Let's just say that I'm a little girl from the Missouri Corn Belt, without much in the way of formal education, and that everything I know about this business I've taught myself."

"That's what gives you your credibility. Now, what would you do if you were given all the money in the world to start your own magazine? I'm talking a whole new magazine. What would you do with it?"

She laughed again. "All the money in the *world?*"

He put down his fork. "That's what I'm offering you," he said. He held up his hand. "Don't interrupt, let me finish. I've been watching you, and I've watched what you've done with that magazine of yours. But to do what you've done you've had to fight the ferrets every inch of the way. What would you do in a ferretless world? Starting from scratch, with all the money in the world behind you. You'd create a magazine that would be even better than *Mode*, even more successful than *Mode*, wouldn't you? That's what I'm betting on. And I've got the money to put where my mouth is."

"Well," she said carefully, "that's quite an offer, Rodney."

"You bet it is. Now let's talk money. How much money would it take to start up a new magazine? To start it right, the way you'd like to do it, to your personal specifications. I'm talking a magazine that would bury *Mode*, circulation-wise and ad revenue–wise—a magazine that would send *Mode* limping off into the sunset, and that ferret Herb Rothman with it. What do you think? Fifty million? A hundred million? Hell, you tell me. I don't give a damn. I've got the dough."

"There's a lot more that has to go into a new magazine than just money. There's a lot of thought, a lot of research—"

"I'd leave that all up to you. I'd make you editor and publisher. You'd be your own boss. I'd let you toss your own party, and all I'd do is write out the checks."

"Well, as I say, that is quite an offer," she said.

"Damn right," he said. "Now let me tell you my plan. But first let me tell you what's going to happen to the Rothmans. Old Man Ho Rothman was a smart old bastard, but he made two mistakes that he's going to pay for now. A, he never delegated any authority to anybody else in the company. He always ran a one-man show. B, he never really believed in credit. He never really trusted banks. Most of everything he got that wasn't by hook or by crook, he got for cash. That was a mistake because a man is only as good as his credit line. A man is only worth as much as he can borrow. That's how I got rich, because I understand credit, I understand leverage. A man's credit is his credibility. Credit. Credibility. They mean the same thing. Now the old man's in trouble with the IRS because they're saying his whole damn empire was always a one-man show, and of course they're right, it was. And the IRS is going to win their case. This phony senile act he's pulling now isn't going to help him."

"Phony? What makes you say that?"

"Hell, Ho Rothman is about as senile as you or I. I know the guys in that Waxman firm that's working for him. Young Jerry Waxman is a worse shyster than his father. This senile act is all their idea. They want to take him down to Foley Square on a stretcher, and let him put on his cuckoo act for the IRS boys. They want to point at Ho and say, 'How can you accuse this poor old man, no longer in control of his faculties, of manipulating, et cetera, et cetera.' "

"Interesting," she said. "Very interesting."

"Why else won't they let anybody see him except his doctor and his nurses—and of course his wife? They'll get the doctor and the nurses to testify how sick he is."

"*Very* interesting," she said.

"Hell, you don't think it was real blood that Imelda Marcos coughed up in the courtroom, do you? It was ketchup that her lawyers gave her, and she coughed it up on cue, at just the right point in the trial. It worked for her. It turned the jury around, and they thought—Oh, this poor old sick widow, and all that shit, and they acquitted her. But the same sort of grandstand play isn't going to work for Ho, and you know why?"

"Why?"

"Because, A, there's too much money involved, and, B, because even though Ho's not senile, he's still ninety-something years old and he's gonna croak sometime soon. And if the IRS can establish that Ho's company has always been a one-man show, which it has, and which they will, the IRS can move in when he croaks and tax the entire company, the whole shebang, as his estate. So what's going to happen when Ho loses his case? The IRS is talking nine hundred mil—with interest and penalties, over a billion. We're talking big bucks here. A billion dollars is big bucks—I know, because I've got that much in a single brokerage account. So the company's gonna need cash, right? They got no credit. They're gonna have to raise that cash by selling off some properties, and one of the properties they're gonna be selling off is *Mode*."

"Why would they sell *Mode*?"

"Because I'm gonna make them an offer they can't refuse, that's why. I'm gonna buy it, and then I'm gonna fold it. Meanwhile, I'm gonna have you and your new magazine— right? And you and your magazine will have the field free and clear—no competition. That little ferret won't snoot me at the Four Seasons anymore. I'm gonna crush Herbert Rothman— crush him like a bug." He pressed his large thumb hard on the tablecloth as though crushing an ant, and then wiped off the imaginary offending matter on his trouser leg.

"So I'm faced with a kind of Hobson's choice," she said.

"Eh?"

"Either I let Herb Rothman destroy my magazine, or I join you and help you destroy it."

'That's the beauty of my plan," he said.

"But if you're going to buy *Mode*, why not put your money into *Mode*? Why spend it on the obviously very risky business of starting up a whole new magazine?"

"Yeah, I thought of that. The answer is, A, I like risk. I always have. And, B, *Mode* is an old product—I mean, *Mode* is something like a hundred and twenty years old. It's like fixing up an old car. It's like you can take an old Dusenberg or a Pierce-Arrow, or even a Model T, and fix it all up like new, and the result is pretty cute, pretty snappy. That's what you did with *Mode*. You restored a classic car. But what have you got when you're done? You've still got an old car. What I want to do is build something entirely new. I want to build a DeLorean, only even better. That's what I want to attach my name to in New York, something that's never been done before. And I want to attach your name to it, too—yours and mine. So what do you say? Are we partners? Is it a handshake? I've never done a deal in my life that wasn't done on a handshake."

"Let me think about this," she said.

"Don't think too long," he said. "We don't have too much time. The IRS trial's coming up. And if you do go along with me, there's only one thing I'd ask in return."

"Oho," she said with a little smile. "So there *is* a little string attached."

"Just a little quid pro quo. Isn't everything in business a little quid pro quo? It's a personal thing. It isn't much."

"Okay, Rodney. Tell me what it is."

He stared down at his plate, and he was definitely blushing. He seemed embarrassed to tell her what his condition was. Waiting for him to answer, she glanced around the restaurant to see if there were any familiar faces. She saw none, but that didn't matter, for she couldn't help but imagine what Herb Rothman's reaction would be when he learned—as he certainly would learn, in this small world that was New York, and in this even smaller world that was the magazine business—that she had lunched with the man the family considered its enemy, and when he found out—as he certainly would—what this man had just proposed to her.

She was still smiling, "Come on, Rodney," she said pleasantly. "Tell me what it is. I can assure you that after twenty years in this business nothing you say would surprise me.

You've made your proposal. Now give me the rest of the terms."

"It's—it's Maudie."

"Maudie?"

"My wife, Maudie. I just thought that—maybe—well, with the kind of people you know, the kind of people we read were at your party the other night, I thought maybe you could help Maudie get into New York high society."

"Oh," she said, sounding almost disappointed.

"These rich New York women, they've been snooting Maudie. They're just as bad as the boys at the Bay Street Club and their snooty wives. Worse, even. She's tried to do her best, to get them to like her, but they still snoot her. It hurts her—real bad. But I thought, with the kind of people you know, maybe you could introduce her around—to the people she reads about, Mrs. Peabody, Mrs. Buckley, Mrs. Astor, and this Mona—"

"Potter?"

"Is that her last name? The one that writes the column? Maudie loves that column. And it would mean everything in the world to Maudie if she could just see *her* name in this Mona's column."

"Is that *all?*"

"Could you help her? Is it too much to ask? Me, I don't give a shit. I know I'm no gent. But Maudie is a real *lady*. Like you. And I really love my Maudie."

Her smile was a little wistful now, thinking of the touching innocence and fatuity of Maudie's ambitions, and of her husband's sweet eagerness to help her fulfill them. And knowing that one of the great disillusioning disappointments of such aspirations was always the ridiculous ease with which they could be achieved.

"Lenny Liebling," she said slowly. "He could do it even more quickly and easily than I could. He knows all sorts of interesting people."

"But he couldn't do it and still work for Rothman, could he? If Herb Rothman knew Liebling was doing me favors, he'd can him just like that. Liebling's an old pansy. He needs the Rothmans. You don't."

"Yes, I suppose you're right."

"The ferret wouldn't stand for you working for me *and* him, either. So, you see, my two propositions to you sort of hinge on one another, don't they? That's the beauty of it."

"Well, let me think about all of this," Alex said at last. "You've got to admit you've given me a lot to think about."

"Do me one favor," he said. "Come by for a drink tomorrow night and meet Maudie. Get to know her a little bit. Then you can tell us what can be done with her."

"That would be very nice. I'd like that."

"Okay," he said gruffly, avoiding her eyes. "Six o'clock. We live at the Lombardy. And take your time thinking about my other proposition. I guess I didn't expect a yes-or-no answer today at lunch. But don't take too much time. Timing is everything in this business."

"There's just one thing I'm not too happy about," she said.

"Eh? What's that?"

"Your comparing my editing of *Mode* to driving a used car!"

"That's what it is, dammit! That book's been around the block more than a few times. It's sat on a lot of lots. It's had a lot of different people in the driver's seat, and they weren't just little old ladies who took it out once a week to go to church! It's had its odometer turned back more than once. Hell, you didn't *create Mode*. You inherited it from your husband. You took it over because your husband didn't know how to run it. He couldn't keep up the payments!"

"Correction. Steven edited *Mode* very well, but he just wasn't happy doing it. I was. Steven felt uncomfortable editing a woman's magazine, but his father—"

"What the hell. It was only a figure of speech. I'm giving you a chance to create something brand new, something nobody's ever seen before, something with your personal signature on it—yours and mine. Newness is everything in this game, lady. Wanna know how I made my first million? It was babies' pacifiers, yeah, and pacifiers had been around a long time, but my pacifiers had a difference. They had *flavors*. McCulloch's Yummies came in orange, strawberry, raspberry, apple, chocolate, marshmallow, and vanilla. Wild cherry and plum didn't sell, for some damn reason. But McCulloch's Yummies were *new*, and I knew they'd be a hit because I tested 'em on my own kiddies and my kiddies *loved* 'em. I paid that guy ten thousand for his patent, and made forty million! So let's send old *Mode* out to the used-car graveyard."

The image was so grotesque that she had to laugh. "All right," she said. "As I said, I'll think about all this."

"Take your time, but not too much time, and meanwhile give my regards to the ferret. Ha-ha-ha. And Maudie and me will see you tomorrow night."

Now he attacked what remained on his plate, managing a quick glance at the big gold Rolex watch on his wrist in the same motion. Rodney McCulloch's business-of-the-moment was completed. There was nothing left to do with the lunch now except to finish it. Now the fabled cuisine of Gilbert Coze, Le Bernardin's legendary chef, was just something to be packed away as quickly and efficiently as possible between now and his next appointment. For all the enjoyment he seemed to be getting from this meal, Alex thought, they could just as well have been eating at McDonald's.

"The tuna carpaccio was delicious," she said.

"Yeah, it was okay," he said with a shrug. "For fish."

She decided that Rodney McCulloch was one of the most extraordinary men she had ever met.

"Waiter!" he bellowed. "Lah-dee-shawn, see voo play!"

She also thought: I must find some way to get to Ho Rothman!

Chapter 23

"What's the matter?" Alexandra asked her mother. "What's wrong?"

"It's nothing . . . nothing." They had been about to order ice-cream cones at Mr. Standish's store on what was somewhat grandly called Main Street in Paradise. It was the only street in town and when residents of Paradise referred to Main Street it was always called "downstreet." "I'm going downstreet to the store," they would say when they needed something from Mr. Standish's, or "I'm going downstreet to the post office" when they needed to mail a letter. And, believe it or not, Mr. Standish's first name was Miles. "How was your trip on the *Mayflower*, Miles Standish?" her mother would sometimes joke with him. "Pretty rough, Mrs. Lane," he would answer. "Nothing but a buncha seasick Pilgrims."

That particular muggy afternoon in August, when Alex was eleven, her mother had said, "Let's go downstreet and get ourselves some ice-cream cones," and they had got into the black 1949 Plymouth coupe that her mother drove in those days, and headed for the little village, and Mr. Standish's. Alex had already decided on the flavor she wanted— a double scoop of chocolate chip—and they were standing at Mr. Standish's counter, waiting to be served, when suddenly a strange man, tall, with blond hair, turned from the magazine rack where he had been looking at paperbacks, and gave Alex and her mother a startled, questioning look. Then he started to move toward them, and the word *Lois* seemed to be forming on his lips. Alex could still remember the wide, appraising look in his blue eyes.

Her mother had immediately seized her elbow and whispered, "Quick! We've got to go!" Still clutching Alex's elbow, she had hurried Alex toward the door of the store, then out the door and down the steps and into the Plymouth.

"What's the matter, Mother? What's wrong?"

"Nothing . . . nothing."

She turned the key in the ignition, and they had sped away from Mr. Standish's, kicking up a fine spray of gravel behind them as they turned out of the parking space into Main Street.

"But what about my *ice cream?*" Alex had wailed.

"Never mind. Not now. We'll get that later. Or somewhere else." And she kept glancing in the rearview mirror, as though the strange blond man might be following them.

But there was no place else in town to buy ice-cream cones—no place between here and Kansas City, except for Mr. Standish's, and Alex knew that as well as her mother must have known it.

"It was that man, wasn't it? He acted like he knew us. He wanted to speak to us."

"What man?" her mother said. "I didn't see any man. I don't know what you're talking about." But her mother's face was pale, and her knuckles, gripping the steering wheel, were white, and they were driving toward home down the narrow country road, bouncing over potholes, much faster than her mother ever drove before.

"That man in the *store*," Alex said.

"Never mind. Never mind."

"Mother, who was that *man?* What did he *want?*"

"Mind your own business!" her mother had snapped. "Besides, there wasn't any man."

But of course there had been, and now, inexplicably, her mother was angry with her. They drove homeward in silence.

It was a strange experience, Alex often thought, growing up in the little town of Paradise, Missouri. She and Lenny often laughed about it, because the small-town background was something they had in common—she, with her memories of Paradise, and he, from farther south, really the Deep

South, with his tales of childhood in Onward, Mississippi.

"Onward was *worse*," he insisted.

"No. Nothing could have been worse than Paradise."

"We were the only Jewish family in town. We were considered *very* peculiar."

"We considered ourselves intellectuals. That made us even *more* peculiar."

Paradise—to the nineteenth-century settlers who founded the place, on a slight rise just east of the flood level of the Platte River, it may have seemed just that. In fact, it wasn't all that bad. Tall stands of sycamore and willow trees lined the riverbank. The river, as its name implied, flowed flat and smooth and pewter-colored in a graceful series of oxbow bends. Beyond the river, the land extended flat for as far as the eye could see, an infinite horizon. Widely spaced and neatly kept farmhouses, mostly of white-painted clapboard with dark green shutters, each flanked by its sturdy barn, stocky silo, and cluster of domed corncribs, dotted this endless prairie landscape, each farm seeming to comprise a little duchy of its own.

Here farmers raised principally feed corn, and by mid-July the cornfields became dangerous places for children to enter. Alex's mother had warned her never to walk into a field of tall corn, because a child could easily become lost between the rows, where there were no sights and sounds to guide you out, only the rustle of cornstalks whispering in the wind. The bodies of children lost in a cornfield were often not found until harvest-time. Later, Alex learned the rule: always follow a single row; every row of corn ended somewhere.

Other farmers raised oats and wheat and sorghum and soybeans and barley and tobacco. Still other farmers raised beef and dairy cattle, sheep and hogs and—at the bottom of the unwritten status scale—poultry. Deep beneath the fields of a few lucky farmers, another cash commodity had been discovered—natural gas.

But Alex's family house, out on Old State Road 27, was not like the others. It was not a farm, and it had no barn, silo, or corncribs. It stood on a mere acre and a half, surrounded on three sides by hundreds of acres of neighbors' cornfields. It was not built of white-painted clapboard, but of locally quarried stone. The Lanes, with the help of a G.I. loan, had built the house themselves in a style that would soon become known as California Ranch. The house looked out of place, and neighbors used it in giving directions: "You'll come to a funny-looking *modern* house on your left, and we're a mile and three-tenths after that, on the right."

The house had other peculiarities. It had an attached two-car garage, which none of the farmhouses had. Behind it, it had a patio, a foreign word in Paradise. The house was surrounded by hedges of ilex and yew, and Alex's mother had laid out perennial borders of iris, peonies, phlox, and chrysanthemums. No one else had perennial borders. There was also a carefully manicured lawn of zoysia grass, of which Alex's father was particularly proud. When Jeffrey Lane spoke of his zoysia grass, his neighbors and fellow townspeople looked puzzled. Zoysia was a crop that no one in Paradise had ever cultivated. "Looks just like plain old grass to me," they said.

"Zoysia is often used on putting greens," Jeffrey Lane explained. The neighbors scratched their heads. The Lanes, they said, gave themselves airs.

In those days, all the girls in the Paradise-Smithville Regional Elementary School had names like Mary, Jean, Betty, and Anne. There were also a few double names—Mary Lou, Betty Ann, Bobby Sue. There were fashions in girls' names, just as there were fashions in breeds of dogs. Later would come biblical names—Ruth, Naomi, Sarah, Hannah, and Deborah. And still later would come the fad for last names—Kimberley, Tiffany, Kelley, Kirby, Shelby, Ashley, and so on. But nobody at Paradise-Smithville R.E.S. had ever been named Alexandra, nor, most likely, had there been an Alexandra since.

"Where'd you get your funny name?" they asked her.

"I'm named after the last empress of Russia," she explained.

"Are you Russian?"

There were other differences that set the Lanes apart from their neighbors in Paradise. Alex's father did not go to work in coveralls, for instance, but in a pinstriped dark blue Brooks Brothers suit, white shirt, and tie, driving thirty miles each day to Kansas City, where he was a partner in an accounting firm, in his 1953 Oldsmobile Super "88." Alex's mother shopped for her good clothes and Alex's school clothes in faraway Kansas City, too, while the women from the

neighboring farms still shopped from the Sears and Roe-
buck catalogue. "You dress different," her schoolmates used
to say. When Alex asked them what they meant, their answers
were evasive. "You don't dress from *here*," they said. "You
dress from *away*." And when Alex asked her mother what
they meant by this, her mother's airy reply was, "It means
they're ignorant."

Alex would have done anything, during those preteen years,
not to be considered "different."

Behind every Paradise farmhouse, or so it seemed, was a
silver Airstream house trailer, not yet known as a mobile
home. Each winter the Airstream was tow-hitched to a pickup
truck, and the farmer and his family took off for a couple of
weeks in Florida or on the Gulf coast of Texas. In summer,
after spring planting was done, similar excursions might be
undertaken to the Ozarks, or to Sunrise Beach on the lake.
The Lanes owned no house trailer, and to the young Alex
this seemed a humiliating hardship. All her friends' families
had Airstreams. To the little girl, ownership of an Airstream
seemed the ultimate luxury. Her friends had shown her the
interiors of their parents' trailers—the narrow little bunk
beds that folded out of the walls, the little sofas that opened
to become more beds, the tiny kitchens with their miniature appliances, the chemical toilets. The trailers seemed to
her like dollhouses on wheels. Why, she begged her father,
couldn't they own a beautiful silver Airstream the way everyone else did? When she talked this way, her father merely
made a face and rolled his eyes.

But why, she often asked herself, had her parents chosen
Paradise, Missouri, to live and build their home and raise
their only child—a place they clearly viewed as inferior,
surrounded as they were by ignorant neighbors, and by dangerous fields of tall corn that sucked unsuspecting children
into their labyrinthine rows, where they might never be found
until corn-cutting time? That was always something of a mystery to her. Most of her parents' interests—the museums, the
symphony, the theater, the ballet, the library, the shopping—
were focused on the big city to the south. "Of course we can't
find that *here*," she would hear her mother say disparagingly.
"We'll have to go to Kansas City for *that*." Then why did they
live in such an insufficient place? Why had they carved out a
small corner of suburbia in the cornfields? It had something

to do, Alex was given to understand, with "good, clean country air," and it was true that, at the time, much of Kansas City was still shrouded by the stench of the stockyards.

Later, she realized that there were other reasons why the family had settled in Paradise. One of them was surely money, or the lack of it. Jeffrey Lane could never have afforded to build his house in one of the smart Kansas City suburbs such as Shawnee Mission or the Country Club district. There was an irony here. Their neighbors considered the Lanes not only snooty, but "rich folks." In fact, many of the neighboring farmers were far richer than the Lanes. A summer season's corn crop could be worth as much as a hundred thousand dollars.

But there was another reason why the Lanes had chosen Paradise. Alex's mother was trying to escape from an unhappy secret that she had tried to leave behind in Kansas City.

In the back of Alex's mind, from the time she was a little girl, grew the conviction that someday, somehow, she was going to get out of Paradise.

Her mother's attitude toward her farming neighbors, during Alex's growing-up years, was unrepentantly superior and condescending. "These *farm* people," she would hear her mother say. "Such hicks and hayseeds. The women's faces all look like apple pies."

As a little girl, Alex considered her mother the prettiest, most glamorous woman in the world. But she soon learned that, to the townsfolk of Paradise, her mother was thought to be almost dangerously unconventional. Instead of having her hair neatly permed or twisted into a bun in a hairnet, Lois let her long, straight, and shiny light brown hair hang straight down her back, where it nearly touched the base of her spine. Sometimes she ironed her long hair. At other times she caught it up with a ribbon into a ponytail, or plaited into a single long pigtail—hairstyles which, to Paradise, seemed unorthodoxy that bordered on heresy. Instead of wraparound house dresses, aprons, and smocks that the farm wives wore, Lois often wore tight jeans that flattered her slim figure and outlined the curve of her buttocks—or, in summer, short cutoffs with bare-shouldered, bare-midriffed halter tops—attire that was not considered entirely "proper" on the prairie. Often, at home, she went around the house barefoot, and was even known to drive her car barefoot—

had even been seen going downstreet and walking into Mr. Standish's store in her bare feet, bold as brass. "Get chiggers that way, Miz Lane," Mr. Standish had warned her, but she had just roared with laughter.

She chain-smoked many cork-tipped Herbert Tareyton cigarettes.

She had been seen, on the breezeway of her house, sitting in her cutoff jeans and halter top, barefoot, waiting for her husband to come home from work, with two martini cocktails and a shaker on a silver tray. "We voted Clay County dry for a reason," Alex had heard one woman say, "but that Lane woman drinks hard liquor right out in her front yard for the world to see!"

Her mother was "That Lane Woman."

She subscribed to *The New Yorker, Mode*, and a French magazine called *Mon Plaisir* that featured both male and female nudes. (This news came from Eulalia Staples, the postmistress of Paradise, who read all the postcards and flipped through all the magazines before putting them out for delivery.)

She walked her big dog on a long leash. People in Paradise let their dogs run free. "What'd you say the name of that breed of dog is again?" people would ask her.

"She's a borzoi bitch," Lois would say, and people would just shake their heads. The word *bitch* was bad enough, but all those words ending in vowels—borzoi, zoysia, patio, martini—branded the Lanes as foreign-speaking aliens. The dog was named Anna Karenina.

Needless to say, the family had not joined either of the two local churches, explaining that Lois and her husband were atheists.

There were some people in town who whispered that Lois was "a little fast," and they added, "Nobody knows what her real *back*ground is." In her bare feet, it was impossible not to notice Lois's brightly painted toenails. She also brewed strange, herbal teas. By the time she reached sixth grade, Alex had heard her mother described as "a weirdo."

Still, the little town had done its best—in the beginning, at least—to accommodate itself to the oddball Lanes, though Lois had made some initial political mistakes. Upon moving to Paradise, for instance, Lois had been invited to join the

Paradise Ladies' Benevolent Society. The Ladies' Benevolent Society was essentially a sewing circle of women who met, weekly, at one another's homes to hemstitch sheets and pillowslips for the Clay County Regional Hospital. Lois had politely declined the invitation. "These farm people," she said to her husband that night at the dinner table, with a dismissive wave of her hand. "That's all they care about—sewing, cooking, going to church, and having babies."

She had not realized that the Ladies' Benevolent Society had been founded, in 1862, by the unforgettable Mrs. A. Clement Mosby, after whom the whole *town* of Mosby—including Mosby Park, Mosby High School, and the Mathilda Belcher Mosby Memorial Library—had been named, and that to be invited to join the society was deemed a great honor, and that to turn the invitation down amounted to a slap in the face of Western Missouri History and Tradition.

Lois announced herself more interested in education. She often spoke scathingly of the local school system, including Paradise-Smithville Regional Elementary, which her daughter attended. "It's a school good enough for these farm people, I suppose," she said. But she made it very clear that, when the time came, Alex would be sent to a fine boarding school "in the East," and then on to an eastern college. "Not like these farm people, who quit school at sixteen."

In her one sally into local politics, Lois had run for election to the local school board under the campaign slogan of "Finer Schools for Paradise." She had been roundly defeated. Later, it turned out that Lois had lost the election in large part because of a whispering campaign that someone in the town had started to the effect that the Lanes were Communists. Somehow, from Lois's assertions that they were atheists, from their Russian wolfhound dog, and from their Russian-named daughter, the town had got the notion that they were Reds. It was proof, Lois said bitterly when she heard about these rumors, of how ignorant the townspeople were—if proof were needed.

Now Lois wrote plays, and later Alex would wonder whether Lois Lane, the playwright, as she often introduced herself, realized that she had the same name as Superman's girlfriend, and whether that knowledge would have deterred her mother from what would become an obsession: seeing her name in lights on Broadway. Again, none of Alex's schoolmates' mothers were playwrights. While the other mothers toiled in their kitchens preparing meals for their families, or sat in their sewing circles hemstitching sheets and pillowslips, Alex's mother sat at her Royal Standard typewriter in her "studio"— another foreign-sounding, vowel-ending word—which was what the spare bedroom was now called, and wrote her plays.

Oh, Mother, Mother, Alex sometimes thought, *why didn't I have the wisdom or the sensitivity to see that you were going mad, and that Paradise was driving you mad? Or perhaps, by then, we were all going a little mad, Mother, Father, and me, in Paradise.*

All the signs were there. When people spoke of her mother now, they tapped their fingers on their temples knowingly.

Perhaps her mother's plays were ever-revised versions of the same play. Alex was never sure. Sometimes, in the evenings, she would hear her mother reading scenes from her plays, or play, aloud to her father after dinner, over coffee. At least one of the plays was set in Imperial Russia, during the last days of the czars, and she could remember her mother's voice changing as she read the various characters' lines—characters that had names like Oleg and Alexis, Ivanov, Pavel, Dmitri, Anya, Natasha, Georgi, and Katia. "Katia," she could hear her mother's voice reading, "we must not think of our own love now. We must think of Mother Russia!"

So that her mother would not have to cook dinner for them, and could spend more time getting her plays in shape for the producers they would never find, her bewildered-seeming father brought home pizzas and Chinese food from Kansas City. That was another thing that was different about being the Lanes of Paradise, Missouri. They ate their dinners out of cardboard containers.

"Alexei, my heart is breaking!"

Meanwhile, as she entered her teens, Alex herself had become lost in a dream of her own. She had long since left Paradise, Missouri, and had gone off to New York, Paris, Madrid, and Rome, where she had become an internationally acclaimed designer of *haute couture*, along the lines of Gabrielle Chanel and Cristobal Balenciaga, who, at the time, she had no idea was a man.

"Cristobal, that dress you're wearing is divine," she said.

"It nowhere near matches the exquisiteness of your design, Alexandra," replied Cristobal.

She studied the fashions in her mother's magazines and, with pencils and sketchpads, she designed her clothes. Back in the first grade, her best friend had become a girl named Annie Merritt, whose family lived on a nearby farm. The girls caught the school bus at the same crossroads and, it turned out, Annie Merritt had become skillful at operating her mother's Singer electric sewing machine. Alex's mother had a low opinion of Annie Merritt and, indeed, of the entire Merritt family, whom she considered white trash. But, now that Lois Lane had become a playwright, she no longer paid much attention to her daughter's friendships, and the friendship lasted.

Together, using whatever fabrics could be salvaged from attic trunks, the two girls began running up some of Alex's designs and, in the process, Alex also learned how to operate the Singer. One day, Alex showed up at school in a black velvet bolero jacket and a black taffeta ballerina skirt of her own design, and of their joint manufacture. Looking back, Alex thought with a smile that she must have looked like a gypsy dancer. "What a weirdo get-up!" one of her classmates jeered and, pointing her index finger at her temple, drew circles in the air.

"You wouldn't know high fashion if you sat on it," Alex shot back.

By now, she knew she wasn't popular, and, by now, she didn't care.

She continued to bring home straight A's on her report card—which did nothing to add to her popularity—while the children of the farm people were for the most part content to coast along with C's and D's. All, that is, except for Annie Merritt. Annie Merritt, it seemed, was retarded. The kind word in Paradise for Annie Merritt was *simple*. The unkind word was *backward*. In Paradise, the word *backward* was always silently mouthed, not spoken, along with words like *cancer, Jewish, fairy*, and *Communist*. Annie had a sad little habit of reaching up and touching the back of her head, and Alex knew what this meant. Having heard people say that she was backward and, unable to see the back of her head in a mirror, she touched her head to see whether another face was growing there.

But, to Alex at least, her friend had a certain wisdom and understanding of the human condition that she was able to express, not so much in words, but through looks in her deep and expressive eyes. Sometimes, in those long looks at her friend, Annie could convey whole sentences and paragraphs of meaning and intensity that only Alex could comprehend. To Alex, Annie Merritt was a kind of genius.

Meanwhile, the town, and the school, grew used to the idea of Annie Merritt as a perennial first-grader, while the school waited patiently until Annie reached the age when the state of Missouri was no longer obligated to try to educate her. Year after year, Annie remained in first grade, struggling to memorize the English alphabet while Alex tried to coach her.

"Why am I backward?" Annie often asked her.

Alex composed a little rhyme for Annie to remember.

If your nose and your navel are on the same side,
You'll know you're not backward, and won't need to
   hide.

Annie Merritt's only visible talent remained her ability to operate a sewing machine. As the years went by, the first-grader's height and bulk increased, and presently she developed large and pendulous breasts. The town was even tolerant when Annie Merritt became the first pregnant first-grader in Clay County history. After all, Annie's mother was a member in good standing of the Ladies' Benevolent Society.

This happened when Alex was in the seventh grade, and, though she knew Annie faced some sort of ordeal, she remained loyal to her old friend who, by then, was known in the school as Annie Moron. As Annie's size increased, Alex tried to fit Annie out in styles that would be most flattering to her expanding girth. Sometimes, when they worked together, Annie would reach out and seize a piece of fabric from their worktable. "Oh, I just love the feel of cotton cloth!" she would cry, rubbing it between her fingers. And then, pressing it against her nose, "And oh, I just love the smell of cotton cloth!" And, pressing the cloth against Alex's nose, she would say, "Don't you just love the smell of cotton cloth? Don't you just love everything about a piece of cotton cloth?" And Alex would admit that, yes, there was something wonderful about the smell and feel of cotton cloth. But

their most communicative moments came when their heads
were bent silently together over Annie's mother's machine.
In Paradise, they had become two exotics, two weirdos who
would never quite fit in.

Her seventh-grade classmates tolerated her friendship with
Annie Merritt. After all, they had all started school together,
and Annie was still considered somehow one of them. But,
for some reason, the eighth-graders resented the friendship.
The eighth-graders were an arrogant, insolent lot, secure in
their superiority and knowledge that they would soon gradu-
ate and move on next year to that huge fortress out on the
four-lane that was known as Clay County Regional High
School.

There were eleven students in the eighth grade that year,
four boys and seven girls, and one boy, Dale Smith, was
something of a leader. Dale Smith had repeated two grades
and so, though he was still in the eighth grade, he was sixteen, bigger and better developed than his male classmates.
It was whispered that when Dale Smith took a girl in his
arms, she was powerless to resist his resonant sexuality. One
afternoon Dale Smith blocked Alex's path on the playground
and wanted to know, "How come you always hang around
with Annie Moron, smart-ass?"

The other eighth-graders quickly gathered around.

"Yeah, how come?" a girl named Maybelle Klotter
demanded.

"Think you're hot stuff, don'tcha?"

"Think you're the bee's knees, don'tcha?"

"Think you're hell on wheels!"

"Fancy clothes!"

"Stuck-up snot!"

"Weirdo!"

"Pinko-Commie!"

"Whore's daughter!"

"Who knocked up Annie Moron, smart-ass?"

"I bet she's not even a girl," she heard Dale Smith say. "I
bet she's a boy. I bet she's got a boy's pee-pee under them
stuck-up dresses."

"Let's hog-pile her!"

Alex knew what this meant, and she tried to run, but
Dale Smith was too big and too fast for her. She wore her
reddish-brown hair in pigtails in those days, and Dale Smith

grabbed her by the pigtails and threw her to the ground. The other children all threw themselves on top of her, while she struggled and screamed.

"Let's find out if she's a girl or not!" she heard Dale Smith say.

"Yeah!"

And she felt her skirts being pulled up by many hands, and her panties being pulled down around her knees.

"Aw, she's a girl," she heard Maybelle Klotter say disgustedly. "Let 'er go."

She sometimes wondered what the outcome of this episode might have been if the eighth-grade boys had not been outnumbered by the girls.

That afternoon, when she arrived home bruised and disheveled, and her mother wanted to know what had happened to her, she simply said, "Some big kids picked on me." After ascertaining that she was not seriously hurt, her mother simply shook her head and said, "Well, what can you expect from these farm people?" And returned to her typewriter.

Later, Alex walked across the field of cut corn to Annie Merritt's house. As they inserted a fold of cotton cloth into the presser-foot of the sewing machine, they said nothing. Annie Merritt knew what had happened on the playground. The whole school knew, except, of course, the teachers. Annie Merritt knew that she had been the cause of it, and Alex could read that knowledge in Annie's eyes. But there was no need to talk about it.

All at once, Annie put her work aside and reached into the drawer of her mother's sewing table. She withdrew an eight-inch-long old-fashioned hatpin and handed it wordlessly to Alex.

Alex knew immediately what she meant. Annie's eloquent eyes said everything. The boy who had got her pregnant was Dale Smith.

The next day she approached him on the playground, the long hatpin in her right hand.

"Get away from me!" he yelled.

"No." She pressed the hatpin into his chest, just hard enough so that a spot of blood appeared on the front of his white T-shirt. "Don't ever call my friend Annie Moron again," she said.

"Don't hurt me!" he sobbed. And then, "Help!" But his classmates kept their distance, their eyes downcast, their feet shuffling in the sandy soil, watching without watching, waiting.

She pricked him once more, and a second tiny spot of blood appeared. "Get down on your knees," she said.

He flung himself to his knees, and tears were streaming down his cheeks. The hatpin was now poised in front of his left eye.

"Raise your right hand," she said. He obeyed her, and she said, "Now repeat after me. 'I swear to God—I swear to God that I will never call Annie Merritt Annie Moron again.' "

"I swear to God . . . ," he repeated, and when he had finished she turned and walked away, leaving him kneeling and weeping on the sandy playground.

After that, she was not exactly popular, but then neither was Dale Smith.

A few weeks later, when Annie Merritt's condition could no longer be concealed, the entire Merritt family simply left town, trailing their silver Airstream behind them. They never returned, their farm was sold, and the town adjusted to that situation, too, and Alex never saw her friend again.

But she kept the hatpin.

Always follow a single row. Every whispering row in a cornfield had to end and come out somewhere.

There were other lessons to be learned in Paradise. There was the terror she had seen in her mother's eyes that muggy afternoon in 1955 when she had been hurried out of Mr. Standish's store without her double chocolate chip ice-cream cone. That terror had appeared in the form of a tall, fair-haired man who suddenly stepped toward them with a concerned, questioning look in his blue eyes. For years afterward, she would periodically dream of this man—the quick step forward, the eyes wide and startled as though he had seen a ghost, the word *Lois* half-formed on his lips.

It was not until a number of years later that she learned that that man had been her real father, and that the man she had always called Father was not her father at all.

That was the real reason why her family had moved to Paradise from Kansas City. She knew then that her mother had always lied to her—lied to her ever since that day in Mr. Standish's store when that fair-haired man had started to approach them, the man her mother had insisted wasn't even there.

"Mr. Henry Coker would like you to call him," Gregory said when she returned from her lunch with Rodney McCulloch.

"Good," she said. "See if you can get him now."

"I had a reasonably pleasant meeting with the Waxman, Holloway attorneys this morning," he said when she got him on the phone. "I explained that we intend to stick to the letter of your Rothman contract, under which you are *Mode*'s editor-in-chief until December thirty-first, nineteen ninety-two, and which makes no mention of shared responsibilities with a co-editor. In fact, the contract specifically rules it out. Your contract states, 'Alexandra Lane Rothman, and no other person, shall be et cetera, et cetera.' I'm treating the whole thing as though it was an unfortunate misunderstanding on Herbert Rothman's part, and I added that you and I both very much hoped it would not be necessary to institute breach of contract litigation over this matter. I think it's best to proceed politely at this point, and not bring out our big guns until we feel we really need to."

"I agree," Alex said.

"They're going to be back in touch with me, and I'll call you as soon as I hear anything. Now, as to the other matters we discussed . . ."

"Yes."

"I spoke with our financial department about your assets, and currently your equities, at today's market—stocks and bonds—total about half a million dollars, give or take a couple of thousand. Nice little nest egg, I thought."

"But not much by Rothman standards, is it?"

"No, but a nice little nest egg, in case you should be thinking about retiring."

"Which I'm not," she said.

"Of course not," he said quickly. "But now there is the rather puzzling matter of the so-called Steven Rothman Trust. The people at Waxman, Holloway agree that such a trust exists. At least they have heard of it. But no one there has actually seen a copy of the trust instrument, so it's hard to know what its provisions are. You see, it's all because of the rather special way Ho Rothman ran his business. So much of his business was in his own head."

"You think that's where the trust is, too?"

"I just don't know. I'm going to keep working on it. But I did learn who the two trustees are."

"Oh? Who are they?"

"One is Ho Rothman himself. The other is Steven Rothman's father, Herbert Rothman."

"I see," she said. "One is a man nobody can see anymore, and the other is—"

"—the man you may end up suing," he said. "That does impose some difficulties, Alex."

She said nothing.

"And lastly," he said, "I'm afraid I have a bit of bad news for you."

"There's more?" she said.

"Your apartment at Gracie Square. The apartment is owned by the Rothman Communications Company, Inc."

"*What*? But I've been paying—"

"That was the arrangement entered into by your late husband and the company. The tenant would pay the maintenance. But the actual shares of the cooperative apartment are owned by Rothman Communications. No one ever made that clear to you?"

"No."

"Most unfortunate," he said.

"In other words, they could kick me out whenever they feel like it."

"Well, technically, yes. But of course they wouldn't, unless—"

"Unless they happened to feel like it," she said.

"Well . . . yes," he said.

Now she picked up her private line and called Aunt Lily. "Lily," she said, "is there any way I could get to see Ho?"

"What? Oh, absolutely not, Alex. He can't see anyone. Doctor's orders. No visitors—no visitors at all. His blood pressure, you see."

"He's really that sick?"

"Oh, yes. And worse this week, it seems to me, than last. In fact"—and there was a little sob in her voice—

"I'm terribly afraid we may be losing him, Alex. He just lies there, a vegetable, almost in a coma. But I know what you're worried about, Alex, so just remember what I told you. *Don't resign.* If Herbie thinks he's going to have to fire you to get rid of you, he won't be able to, because he won't be able to afford that. Not at this point, anyway. And, in the meantime, I'm working on a little plan. . . ."

Alex replaced the receiver with a small sigh.

Chapter 24

Vladimir enters from stage left, and sees Natasha cowering on the Récamier loveseat, clutching her rosary. Vladimir holds the letter.

"Vladimir: 'What does this mean, Natasha?'"

"Natasha (visibly shaken): 'It means that Dmitri and I were lovers!' "

Alex's mother was reading to her father from her play-in-progress, and their voices floated from the living room through Alex's closed bedroom door.

"Vladimir: 'I forgive you, Natasha. I shall always forgive you. My forgiveness shall be your retribution!'"

"Natasha: 'Nay! My retribution shall be that I shall always love the man I killed!' (Coyly.) 'Will you still present me to the dowager empress tomorrow?'"

"Vladimir: 'Ods bodkins, it shall be done, Natasha! You have my solemn word upon it!'"

"He takes her in his arms, and she smiles mysteriously as the curtain slowly descends."

After a moment, she heard her mother say, "Well, what do you think? I want to get Katharine Cornell for Natasha. This will be the vehicle that brings her out of retirement."

"Hmm," he said at last. "But—'ods bodkins.' That seems a funny expression for him to use."

"Nonsense!" she said sharply. "That's the way they talked in the Imperial court."

"And are you sure that there really *was* a dowager empress at the time of Nicholas and Alexandra? It seems to me—"

"What difference does it make? I need the dowager empress because she's the only one who knows the secret."

"But if it's supposed to be historical—"

"You know nothing about dramatic values, do you!"

He changed the subject. "Where's *our* Alexandra?"

"How should I know? I've been working in my studio all afternoon." Her mother had not even heard her come home an hour ago.

"Do you *ever* pay any attention to that child anymore?"

"She's not a child. She's sixteen, and can take care of herself."

And they were quarreling again.

In the two years since Annie Merritt's departure, a number of things had changed. For one thing, there was no longer a Singer sewing machine available. For another, the family's financial picture appeared to have changed. Things were not going well, she gathered, at her father's accounting firm in the city, and there was no longer any talk of sending her to a fine boarding school in the East, and Alex was now a sophomore at Clay County Regional High School. Her mother no longer tended her perennial borders, which now grew tall with weeds, though her father continued to clip and manicure, edge and cultivate his precious zoysia lawn. Her father complained about her mother's housekeeping. "This place is a mess!" she would hear him roar. "Those dishes in the sink are from Thursday night's supper! And I'm tired of going to sleep in an unmade bed."

"I've been working on my *play*!" she cried. Everything, their entire future, now seemed to depend on the play. "The thing is, I've got to find an agent. It's hopeless to try to get anything on Broadway without an agent—everybody knows that!"

"What about getting somebody to clean up this pigsty of a house?"

"You know we can't afford a housekeeper! But when my play is produced—and if we can get Cornell—and it's a hit—or what do you think about Helen Hayes? Or is she too short?"

"Look at this table. A week ago, I took the tip of my finger and wrote the date in the dust. Look—it's still here! The date—in the dust!"

"And *you*," she said sneeringly. "*You* wouldn't lift *one* of your little fingers to help me—would you? Oh, *no*—that would be too much to ask. You and your damned lawn!"

"I pay the bills, don't I? I put the food on the table, don't I? I pay the bills for you and the girl."

When they talked like this, she lost her name. She became simply "the girl." When they argued like this, they seemed not to care whether Alex was in the house or not, or that the walls were thin and that their voices traveled. She pressed her fingers into her ears and tried to sleep against the sound of their angry voices. The next day he sarcastically brought home a carton full of housecleaning supplies. Cleaners. Bleaches. Polishes.

"Can I help you mow the grass, Daddy?"

"No . . . no. It has to be mowed in a certain way, in a certain pattern. It's too difficult to teach. . . ."

Absently, she began to pull large clumps of ragweed from her mother's abandoned perennial border.

"Did you notice that I dusted the living room and made the beds, Daddy?"

But he didn't seem to hear her.

She heard her father say, "When I agreed to marry you, Lois, and when I agreed to take on the girl, I didn't realize I was going to have to raise her myself—with no help from you!"

What did that mean—"agreed to raise the girl"?

"Why do you think I'm writing my play? To help you, to help her, to help all of us get out of this hellhole where you've made us live!"

"*I* made *you* live here? Moving out here was *your* idea, Lois—so he wouldn't try to follow you, and try to—"

"I'm talking about my *play*!"

"To hell with your play! I'm talking about—"

"All I need is the last act—the scene in the Winter Palace."

"I'm talking about that daughter of yours. Where does she go all day? You never—"

"She goes to school!"

"This is *July*, Lois. She's been on her summer vacation since the end of May. Where's she been all day? You pay no attention to her. You want her to grow up to be a slut like—"

"Like who, Jeffrey? Like who!"

"Never mind. What's for supper?"

"Didn't you bring home a pizza or something?"

"Dammit, Lois, today is *Saturday*. Don't you even know what fucking *day* it is, much less the month? I don't go to the office on Saturdays—remember? So where the hell would I pick up a fucking pizza, for Christ's sake? Isn't there anything in this fucking house to eat?"

"I could scramble some eggs, I guess. But we have to wait for Alex."

"Fuck her! If she can't get home in time for supper, fuck her!"

But I am home, she thought from her bedroom. You just haven't noticed me.

Now she heard the sound of her mother weeping and, as she often did when Alex's parents quarreled, Anna Karenina began to bark—sharp, anxious barks.

"Ah, don't cry," she heard her father pleading. "Please don't cry, Lois. You know I can't stand to see you cry. Please. . . . Where's my pretty girl? Let me see my pretty girl, Lois. Please be my pretty girl again."

"I want a divorce!"

Trapped in her bedroom, Alex knew that her parents mustn't know she had overheard any of this. There was only one solution. She slid open her window, lifted herself across the sill, and dropped softly onto a patch of zoysia grass below. Then she ran around to the front of the house and up the steps to the front door, and burst in, calling cheerfully, "I'm home, everybody! I'm home!"

"The Lunts!" she heard her mother cry. "The Lunts live in Genesee Depot, Wisconsin. That would be enough of an address to reach them, wouldn't it? Just Genesee Depot, Wisconsin? They're so well known, I mean! The post office will know how to find them. What if I sent the script to them there? Then, if they like it, they could take it to their producer! What do you think of that? Or what if I took the script up there personally? Wisconsin's not that far away, and I'm sure everybody in town knows their house, and I'm sure they'd like to meet the playwright who wrote the play. It would add a nice personal touch, don't you think? That's what I'll do! I'll drive up to Genesee Depot! What would you think of that? Then they could read it, we could discuss it scene by scene, and if they wanted any small dialogue changes, I'd be willing to—"

"Would you wash your hair first, before going calling on Mr. and Mrs. Lunt in Genesee Depot, Wisconsin? How long has it been since you've washed your hair? How long has it been since you've taken a bath? Look at the soles of your feet. The soles of your feet are black from walking around barefoot all day long. No wonder people call you a weirdo, no wonder they call you a Communist, walking around barefoot like a peasant—"

"I'm talking about getting my play produced!"

"Nobody's going to produce your play," she heard him say. "It's a lousy play, Lois. Your play stinks. What did all those agents say?"

"One of them said it needed rethinking, didn't he? And didn't I rethink it—right from the top?"

"It's still a lousy play."

"I know why you're saying that!" she cried. "It's because you don't want me to have any success! Because you're a failure! Because you weren't made a general partner! Because you were passed over in favor of a younger man. Failure!"

"You know why I was passed over? Because you wrote to Ed Meecham in the home office and asked him for a hundred thousand dollars to produce your play. That was a crazy thing to do, Lois—a really crazy thing to do behind my back."

"*Failure!* Failure-failure-failure-failure!"

That was when she heard her father hit her, heard her mother scream, and heard her fall back awkwardly against the kitchen table.

She pressed her pillows against her ears.

Later, she awoke to the sound of music playing. She tiptoed to her bedroom door, opened it a crack, and saw a strange light. A Strauss waltz was playing on the record-player, and they were dancing slowly about the living room, dipping, turning. Her father was wearing his tuxedo—it fitted him a little tightly, since he had probably not worn it since his high-school senior prom—and her mother was wearing a long, red, beaded strapless evening gown with a full skirt. She had washed and ironed her long light brown hair, and it swung smoothly against her back in the rhythm of the waltz. The waltz ended, and another record dropped on the turntable, and now their bodies moved together to the languorous, gliding, erotic tempo of the tango.

In the morning, she found her father sitting on the step of the breezeway. He had got his Toro lawnmower out, but had not started it up.

"Where's Mom?" she asked.

"She's gone," he said.

"Are you going to get a divorce, Daddy?" she asked him. "I've been thinking about it, and I think perhaps you should."

"No, it's too late for that," he said.

"Why?"

"She's gone," he said flatly.

"*Where?*" she asked, suddenly panicked.

"It's a place called the Menninger Clinic in Topeka, Kansas. Your mother's had a nervous breakdown, Alexandra."

"How long will she be gone?"

"A few weeks, perhaps. We really don't know, at this point. They came for her early this morning." He looked out across his lawn. "Look," he said, almost absently, and pointed.

At first she didn't see what he was pointing at. Then, as she moved out across the grass, she saw them—many livid yellow splotches across the dark green grass. There were more wherever she looked, in ugly, angry shapes and sizes—some large, some small, some in shapes suggesting orbiting planets, others streaked like the tails of comets. There had been a dispute about a neighbor's collie, who had been prone to relieving himself on Jeffrey Lane's lawn, leaving brown spots. But it would have taken an army of dogs to create this relentless pattern of yellowed blotches on the grass. "Daddy, what happened to your lawn?" she sobbed.

He pointed again, and she saw several empty white-and-blue Clorox bottles that had been tossed into the shrubbery.

"She did this," he said in a toneless voice. "She did this last night. I was holding her in my arms, trying to calm her. And she suddenly jumped out of bed and ran out naked into the night. And did this."

*   *   *

It was then, at that precise moment, she sometimes thought, that she decided that, somehow, she had to get away from that benighted household. The decision thrilled her with its stunning simplicity, its terrifyingness. Oh, seventeen was an awful age, the worst age for a girl who had been betrayed by her mother and who had lost her father to fecklessness and despair. It was a terrible age, and also the perfect age for her to be setting her sights on something huge and bright and dangerous and indefinable and far away. One thought's impulse later, and it would have been too late.

"I was born in the wrong century," her mother said to her once, many years later, when she had gone to visit her mother at one of the series of hospitals and sanatoriums that her mother would go into and out of for the rest of her life. This one was a particularly pretty place. It was set on a hilltop, surrounded by lawns dotted with big old shade trees, live oaks and elms, and there were many graveled walks and tanbark trails winding among the trees. The place had been designed to suggest a small New England college town, and the grounds were called its campus. Even her mother's room there was pretty, Alex had decided, though it was small and simple—a narrow bed, a comfortable chair, a chest of drawers, and a television set turned resolutely against the wall. Bright floral chintz curtains hung at the single window, and the only other decorative touches were a tall crucifix above her bed, and aquatints of Jesus and the Virgin Mary hung on either side. These were "my family," she explained to Alex. Since giving up playwriting, Lois had become very religious and, the nurses told Alex, much of her mother's time was spent alone in her room, kneeling by her bed in prayer, though she occasionally took walks outside, pausing to sit on one or another of the wooden benches that were placed wherever there happened to be a pleasing view.

"I should have been born in the nineteenth century, in Paris," her mother said, as they strolled, arm in arm, along one of the tanbark trails. "I should have been born into the world of Henri Bergson and Massenet, and Ibsen and Strindberg, Tchaikovsky and César Franck. Those were the sort of people who would have understood me. In the little cafés on the Left Bank, La Flore and Brasserie Lipp, or in the Latin Quarter, I would have been a beautiful bohemian, and I would have had many friends. At night, I would have joined the gypsy dancers in Montmartre, and clicked my ivory castanets with the flamencos of Andaluz. A dissolute duke would have made love to me, and praised my silky skin and Roman nose. I would have painted my eyelids with ocher and rouged my lips bright red, and have danced the night away. Then, when my play opened at Le Théâtre Français or L'Odéon—the play no one knew I was secretly writing—and the cries of *Auteur, Auteur!* rang out through the audience, I would have stepped out into the footlights of center stage, that perfect circle of light, and taken my bow, while the audience tossed roses onto the stage." She had smiled a small, wry smile. "But instead, I was born in nineteen twenty, and let myself be trapped in a squirrel cage by the banks of the Platte River. It was the river, and all those endless rows of corn, that made me crazy."

How had Alex spent her days that summer? Strange as it seemed, she had become a hitchhiker. She never talked much about that period in her life, probably because she didn't really understand it. On certain days she would leave the house, where there was nothing to do anyway, and walk down Old State Road 27 to where it met the four-lane, stick out her thumb, and hitch a ride to Kansas City. Why Kansas City? Simply because it was the nearest town of any size at all. It never occurred to her that there might be anything dangerous about this. Missouri was considered a safe place. No one had heard of drugs then. The Lanes' front door was never locked. Sometimes the people who picked her up were neighbors, on their way to the city to do some shopping, but just as often they were strangers. That was how she met Skipper.

"Hop in," he said, reaching across the seat of his yellow Corvette to open the door for her. He offered his hand. "Name's Jim Purdy," he said easily, "but call me Skipper. Everybody does."

For a moment she thought he was the same tall blond man she had seen with her mother in Mr. Standish's store years ago, grown only a little older. He was certainly tall and blond, with wide and curious blue eyes. Then she decided that he merely bore a strong resemblance to that man who had frightened her mother so, but, just in case, she asked him.

"Do you know Lois Lane?"

"No, can't say as I do," he said. "Should I?"

"She's a playwright in Paradise."

"A playwright in Paradise! Boy, that sounds like a nifty job!"

"Paradise is the name of this little town," she said. And she added, a little lamely, "She's my mom."

"Well, I can't say as I know your mom," he said. "I'm not from these parts. I'm just in K.C. for a two-week gig. Had the day off, and thought I'd see a bit of the countryside. But I like the sound of that—a playwright in Paradise." And as he drove along he began to sing. " 'Hold my ha-a-a-and, I'm a playwright in Paradise. . . . ' " He had a pleasant voice, soft and humorous. "Where you headed?"

"K.C.," she said, though she did not usually call it that. Local etiquette dictated that it was bad form to refer to Kansas City as K.C., just as it was vulgar to call St. Louis St. Louie.

"Take you all the way," he said. "That's where I'm headed back to. Got a gig tonight."

"What do you do, Mr. Purdy?"

"Call me Skipper, everybody does. I ride the circuit."

"The circuit?"

"The rodeo circuit. Bareback bronco busting, calf roping, steer wrestling—that sort of thing."

"You do all those things?"

"Well, not all at once," he said with a laugh. "But I can do all that stuff. What you do each night depends on the draw."

"The draw?"

"For each act, we draw out of the hat. It's all in the draw, what each guy gets to do each night, and the draw's important because some stunts pay better than others—the more dangerous ones. So you hope to get a good draw, but you never know until the draw."

"It sounds exciting."

"Exciting? Well, it's hard work, but the pay is good. It better be, because by the time you're forty you're a has-been. You ever been to the rodeo?"

"Never."

"Want to come tonight? Bring a friend? I get two free tickets for every show."

"I'm expected home for dinner tonight," she said.

"Well, if you can ever get your mom, the playwright in Paradise, to let you stay in town late, just call the arena and ask for Skipper Purdy, and I'll arrange it. We're here until the fourteenth. Then it's Wichita."

"Thank you—Skipper," she said. And then, "How did you get the name Skipper?"

He chuckled. "You really want to know?"

She nodded.

"Well, back in 'fifty-six, I was in Pueblo, Colorado, and that night my draw was to wrassle this big old Brahma bull. It was a real good draw, and I'm real happy. So—big bull comes roarin' out of the gate, see, and he's already fightin' mad because they'd gave him a little flick of the switch, see, just to spice things up for the customers. So big bull heads straight for me, see, and I grab him by the horns, see, to try to force his head down between his legs, like I always do. But all at once that big bull brings his head up—hard—under my chest, and that bull tosses me—up—up into the air—and I did a double somersault. Later, a buddy of mine said, 'That bull skipped you around the arena like he was skippin' a pebble across a pond.' That's where the name came from, and it sort of stuck."

"Goodness," she said. "Were you hurt?"

"Naw. Couple of busted ribs. Not enough to make me miss the next night's show, and of course the customers loved it."

As they entered the outskirts of the city, he said, "Let me know where you want me to drop you off."

"Oh—anywhere."

He gave her a quizzical look. "Anywhere?"

"Yes. It doesn't matter. I like to walk around. Sometimes I look at the stores. Sometimes I like to walk up on the bluff and look at the place where the two rivers meet."

They stopped for a traffic light, and she felt his blue eyes studying her intently, while she kept her gaze straightforward at the road ahead.

"Don't you ever get nervous, thumbing rides like this?" he said. "There's some dangerous characters on the road out here. Dangerous character could pick you up."

"Oh, there're no dangerous characters around here," she

said, even though she knew this was not entirely true. And she did not tell him that she kept an eight-inch hatpin in her purse.

The car moved forward again. "You don't look to me like the kind of girl who should be thumbing rides," he said. And then, "Can I buy you a cup of coffee?"

"That would be very nice."

Presently he pulled off the road into the parking lot of a Dairy Queen.

Inside, he ordered a black coffee, and she ordered a Coca-Cola. They sat opposite each other at one of the little tables, and she could still feel the blue eyes studying her over the rim of his coffee cup. "Funny," he said at last, "but you strike me as a young lady without a plan."

"Oh, I have a plan," she said, though she could not at that point have told him what it was.

"I have a theory about you," he said.

"Oh? What's that?"

"I have a theory that something big is on your mind. Something's holding you down, but you don't want to be held down. I think you could do with a bit of foxing up."

"Foxing up? What does that mean?"

"It's an expression we use on the circuit. You know what a mope is? You know what a kneeler is?"

"No."

"Well, a mope is mostly a bronco, and a kneeler is mostly a steer, but a mope can be either a bronco or a steer that won't perform for you. You know, when a cowboy jumps up on a bronco bareback, you expect him to give you a little action. That's what the crowd came to see, right—a little action? You may think the crowd's cheerin' for the cowboy, but they're also cheerin' for that bronco, hopin' to see that bronco knock that cowboy on his ass, pardon my French. Crowd came to see that bronco give your cowboy a good hard ride. But sometimes that bronco'll just stand there. We call him a mope. Same thing with a steer. When you're wrassling a steer, the crowd wants that steer to wrassle you back. When he won't, he's a mope, too. Or sometimes the old steer'll just kneel down in front of you, meek as a lamb. That's what we call a kneeler. When you've got an animal that won't give the crowd a good show for its money, when he's a mope or a kneeler, the guy like me has got to do something to give him some get up and go—fox him up, we call it."

"How do you do that, Skipper?"

"Well, with a mopey pony you can use your spurs. That'll usually get him going. With a mopey steer—well, that's a little different story."

"What do you do with a steer?"

He grinned and lowered his eyes. "Well, it's not exactly the sort of thing I'd tell a nice, well-brought-up young lady," he said.

"Tell me anyway."

"Well, if you think you got a steer who's gonna be a mope or a kneeler, there's a thing you can do just before he leaves the holding pen to fox him up. What you do is—" And his look now was humorous, but also sly. "Look," he said, "there's only one way to put it. What you do is, just before he leaves the holding pen, you lift up that steer's tail, and rub his ass with a little turpentine. That makes that steer go just about crazy. That really foxes him up. It's like a fox bit that old steer in the rear end. Back in the corral, we call a can of turpentine a can of fox. Now tell old Skipper what he can do to fox you up."

There was no particular innuendo in that unexpected invitation, and yet, in a way, there was, and she felt her cheeks grow hot and there was a ringing in her ears, and a sudden tingle of apprehension traveled from the back of her throat to the pit of her stomach. It was not quite a thrill of fear, though fear was a part of it. It was also a thrill of excitement, of danger, of somehow entering some new and unmapped territory of the unknown and perhaps unknowable. What does the paddler feel when he hears, just ahead of his kayak on the unexplored river, the first rumble of the approaching rapids? It was like that feeling, or as though she had all at once become lost in a field of tall corn, and must quickly decide which row to follow to find her way out. She took a deep breath, but no words would come out.

He tilted himself back in his tippy Dairy Queen chair, spread his legs, clasped his hands behind his head, and flexed his muscles, smiling at her in a lazy way through half-closed eyes. She stared at him, dumbstruck. He was not handsome in a conventional, movie-star sense, but his face had a kind of rugged, muscular beauty. Tilted back in his chair like that, he was all untamed muscle. His arm muscles swelled the light fabric of his checked cowboy shirt, and his leg muscles stretched the taut denim of his tight Levi's, and she was acutely aware of the bulge between his legs. Suddenly she was certain she could actually smell his sex—a hot, milky odor—though, looking back, it was probably just the normal odor of the Dairy Queen. Even to this day she could not pass a Dairy Queen without remembering that wild smell, that moment of violent confusion, and the inner shudder of animal arousal. Wasn't it strange, she sometimes thought, that a whole area of one's life could be polarized around some small, mundane image. Her first experience with sex would always be connected with that afternoon at the Dairy Queen, where everything seemed to happen at once, though nothing actually happened at all.

She began talking very rapidly, as though talking could cure the sudden dizziness she felt. She began talking about everything. She told him about Paradise, and the Ladies' Benevolent Society, and about Annie Merritt and her mother's sewing machine, and the clothes she designed and that they had made together, and she told him the little rhyme she had composed about Annie's backwardness. She told him about her father and his zoysia lawn, and about her mother running for the school board and losing, and about the man they had seen at Mr. Standish's store years ago, who looked in many ways like Skipper himself, though not really, and about her mother and her plays, and about how difficult it had been to find an agent, and about the Lunts of Genesee Depot, Wisconsin, who had returned her mother's playscript, unopened, just yesterday, with a stamp that said UNSOLICITED MERCHANDISE. She told him about her parents' quarrels over housekeeping, the play, and money. She told him about everything except the episode with Dale Smith and the hog-pile on the school playground, and the fact that her mother had been taken to a mental hospital in Topeka. And when she had told him everything but those two things, she stopped, out of breath.

He was still tilted back in his chair, smiling at her lazily through half-closed eyelids. "Yeah, I'd really like to fox you up," he said, and now there was no mistaking what he meant.

He leaned forward in his chair now, and touched the back of her hand with his fingertip and drew a careless zigzag pattern there, and Alex thought for a moment that she was going to faint.

"What are you doing?" she gasped.

"I'm putting my brand on you," he said. "That's an *S*, for Skipper. Now my brand's on you."

She looked at the back of her hand and, for an instant, saw, or thought she saw, the letter *S* rising from her skin as a great red welt and, even more terrifying, she felt a sudden wetness between her legs, and she heard herself utter a little cry.

"Look," he said easily, "it's almost five o'clock." She hadn't realized that they had been talking for nearly two hours. "My gig starts at eight, but I'm not going to have you standing out there on that highway with your thumb up after dark. I'll drive you back to that little town where you live—"

"Paradise!" It came out as a gasp.

"I'll drive you back to Paradise. I've got time to do that, and still get back in time for my gig. C'mon."

They drove home in silence, but she seemed to hear a kind of whirring, almost like an electric current, passing between them.

As he pulled up in front of her parents' house, he said, "Tomorrow. I could pick you up at the same time, same place. We'll go for a drive. I want you to show me that place where the two rivers meet."

"All right," she said.

He whistled softly. "Nice place you got here."

"That's our zoysia lawn," she said. "It's the only one in town." And she was grateful that it was getting dark, and he could not see the angry blotches that had turned from yellow, to brown, to dead white.

As she reached for the handle to the door, he suddenly seized her left hand, pressed the back of it hard against his mouth, and licked it with his tongue, and she thought she was going to faint again. "Gotta lick my brand," he said. "To make it heal real good." Then he said, "Tomorrow."

She stepped out of the car, and started up the front walk.

He leaned out the window. "Hey!" he called. "You didn't tell me your name."

She turned. "It's Alexandra," she said, and raised her hand.

He answered with a little jaunty wave that was almost a salute, and drove away.

She turned toward the house again, walked up the front steps, and let herself in the front door. She knew her father would be sitting alone in the kitchen, with an open bottle of beer, deep in the fathomless well of his own regrets. She went straight to her room, and lay down flat across her bed.

She knew what had happened. She had fallen in love. But she had never suspected that love would come with such thundering suddenness and terrifying force. It was more than the sudden spasm she had felt in her groin, sitting there in the Dairy Queen. Other parts of her body were involved as well. It came as that whirring in her eardrums, and a dull ache at the base of her skull. It came from the back of her throat, too, with a feeling of heaviness of her tongue, and a dryness at the roof of her mouth. But mostly it was a feeling deep behind her eyes, from wherever it was that tears sprang, and it blurred her vision. The lungs also seemed to be involved in the feeling too, for her breathing was rapid, and if she had tried to speak just then she could not have done so. Why had no one ever told her that this was what falling in love was like, that love made you feel so bruised and beaten? With her fingers she tried touching the parts of her body that hurt with love, thinking: I hurt here, and here. And here.

It was a feeling she had never had before or since. Wasn't it strange, she often thought, that a love so intense and raging, so violent and noisy and passionate as that first love had been, could have turned to hate?

"This is just great," Mel was saying, as he paced her library, a Scotch-and-water in his hand. "What an opportunity for you, Alex! What a way to tell that Rothman outfit to sweet fuckoff! McCulloch really *does* have all the money in the world. Just think—a whole new magazine that will be yours and yours alone!"

"Well, I don't know," she said from where she sat. "A whole new magazine sounds great, but you don't start a magazine by saying presto-chango, here's a whole new magazine. A magazine requires a *concept*, and I don't really have a new magazine concept."

"You'll come up with one, just like that." He snapped his fingers.

"Will I? I wish I felt that sure. And if I do come up with something, what if it—?"

"Fails? How can it fail? You're Alexandra Rothman, the best in the business. Where's the old self-confidence, darling?"

"But the thing is, I'm comfortable with *Mode*. It's home to me. It's—"

He turned on his heel, snapped his fingers again, and pointed at her. "And that," he said, "is the exact moment when it's time to move on to something new, darling! When the old job has become just a comfortable old routine, that's the time to take the giant step to the next big challenge, isn't it? So this couldn't have come at a better time for you."

"It couldn't?"

"Of course not. Go for the brass ring!"

She still looked dubious. "If I were still in my twenties, I wouldn't hesitate for a minute," she said. "If I were still in my twenties, I'd give it the old college try. But I'm not in my twenties, Mel. I'm forty-six. Do you know how long it takes to start up a new magazine, even when you've got a concept? At least a year—probably closer to two years. And then it's another two years before you know whether you've got a hit or not. Wouldn't I be better off fighting to hold on to what I've achieved already? If I take on this project of Rodney's, I'll be fifty before I know whether it's a success or a failure. That's the thing that worries me, Mel. Am I getting too old for this sort of thing?"

He stared at her in disbelief. "Don't tell me you're starting to believe Mona Potter's columns," he said.

"It's just a fact," she said discouragedly. "It's just arithmetic."

Chapter 25

"Tell me again, which river is which," he said.

"The one from the west is the Kansas River." She pointed. "The one from the north is the Missouri."

"Isn't that somethin'?" he said. They were sitting in his car on the bluff. "When two rivers meet like this, there's nothin' in the world can pull 'em apart. But people aren't like rivers. Sometimes people have to say goodbye."

She nodded. She knew what he meant. This was to be the last night of his gig in Kansas City.

"Tomorrow, Wichita," he said.

"I know," she said. "How far away is it?"

"Couple hundred miles as the crow flies. Four, five hours' drive."

She sighed. It seemed an enormous distance. "Any chance you'll be coming back?"

"Not real soon, at least. Coupla years, maybe. No telling, really, in this business. You see, in this business, when you hit thirty-five, you're on your way to being washed up. At forty, you're over the hill. New guys coming in who can do a lot of things you don't do so good anymore. So I've got to think of my future, 'cause I'm twenty-seven right now."

It was the first time he had mentioned his age, and the ten-year difference in their ages suddenly did not seem like much. "What will you do next?" she asked him.

"That's what I got to think about. I'm thinking about maybe buying a little business of my own. A bar, or a little café. I even got a name for it thought up—El Corral. What do you think of that?"

"I like it," she said.

"I'd hang a lot of pictures on the walls," he said, gesturing around him, turning the interior of the Corvette into the interior of an imaginary place called El Corral. "Like, over there, I'd hang some pictures of me bustin' broncos, and over there some pictures of me wrasslin' steers and cuttin' cattle. I got a slew of pictures from my career. I'd get 'em all framed, you see, and over there—well, over there—well, over there against that wall I'm thinking of putting an upright piano, so there could be music a coupla nights a week—maybe just Fridays and Saturdays. Music can make a place seem real homey. And over there, behind where the bar would be, I'd have stained-glass windows. Stained-glass windows, just to add a touch of class." And, as he described it, she could suddenly envision it all—El Corral, with lariats and chaps and ten-gallon Stetson hats, and spurs and stirrups hanging from the ceiling, photographs covering the walls, Western saddles for barstools, the glint from stained-glass windows behind the old-fashioned bar, the upright piano being played by a fat man in striped shirtsleeves, red suspenders, and a derby hat, a chewed-off cigar between his teeth, just like in the movies, and she could hear the lively honky-tonk music. And where was she in this picture? She was there, in a tight skirt, dancing with Skipper to the music.

"I could help you," she said.

"Help me?"

"I'm good at decorating. I'm good at sewing things. I could help you decorate El Corral."

"I got some money saved up to do this," he said. "How much money you reckon I got saved?"

"How much?"

"Thirty-two thousand dollars. Couple more years, if my luck holds out, I reckon I'll have close to forty."

She nodded, impressed. It seemed like a small fortune.

"And I've got it all right here," he said, patting his flat belly with the palm of his hand.

"Where?"

"Money belt. Don't trust banks. Men like me, who's always on the move, can't trust banks. So, will you come with me? I can take care of you."

"Come with you? Where?"

"To Wichita."

"Oh, I couldn't," she said.

"Why not?"

"Because—" But all at once she couldn't think of reasons why she couldn't go with him.

"Look," he said. "Look at it this way. Your mom's in the loony bin—you don't know how much longer." She had finally told him even that. "Your dad? Well, it sounds to me like he's got plenty on his mind already, without you to worry about. If you came with me, you'd almost be doing him a favor."

She closed her eyes. It was almost true. "But—" she began.

"I mean, I'm talkin' about takin' you along as my legal wife. If you say yes, I'll take you right down to City Hall tomorrow, and make you my legal wife. What do you say?"

She felt dizzy, almost ill. "But I haven't finished high school," she said. "I'm only seventeen."

"At City Hall, we'll say you're eighteen. Besides, you look eighteen."

"But don't you have to show some kind of proof?"

"Naw. They call Missouri the Show-Me State, but they never ask you to show them nothing. All it takes is five bucks for the license. I'll be your proof. Look at it this way. You got nobody on this God's green earth that gives a damn about you, or where you go or what you do. Except for me. You say you got a plan. Well, I could help you work that plan, 'cause I like a person who's got a plan. I admire that type of person." He patted his money belt. "What's mine would be half yours to help you work your plan, 'cause it won't take no forty thousand dollars to open the kind of little café I have in mind. Hell, don't think I'm trying to bribe you into marrying me. I'm just pointing out the advantages. Fact is, I like your style. You've got a lot of built-in fox in you. All you got to do is get out of that little old corral you're in with the loony playwright in Paradise, and that man who's in love with his lawn. Another fact is, it gets lonely on the circuit. I've got nobody much either, except a bunch of rodeo buddies—nobody who really gives a damn, and I think you're the kind who gives a damn about a person like me. And I'm off to Wichita tomorrow, irregardless, and if you don't go with me chances are I'll never lay my eyes on you again. I'm offering you an honest proposal. Take it or leave it. And that's the end of my proposal speech."

"But I've only known you for two weeks."

"What difference does how long you've known me make? I ain't gonna change, and what you see is what you get."

But there had to be more to it than that. Something, some potent key ingredient, was missing. She waited for him to supply it, but he did not. She felt suspended, dangling, awkward, a girl poised, on tiptoe, waiting for a kiss that hadn't come. "Do you love me, Skipper?" she asked at last.

His answer was a sigh. Then he said, "Let's take a walk." He pulled his lanky frame out of the driver's seat, and crossed in front of the car to help her out of the passenger side. They started along one of the rocky paths that followed the rim of the bluff.

The view from here was not particularly inspiring. To the right, below them, lay the Kansas City Municipal Airport, with its intersecting V's of runways, where a small plane was kicking up dust as it took off. To the left were the city's famous stockyards. Beyond the river, to the west on the horizon, lay the low shapes of what were called the Flint Hills. At this time of the year, late summer, and at this time of day, late afternoon, there was a yellowish haze in the air, and the air smelled of farming—livestock, wheat chaff, and flowering corn. As she walked with him along the path, she knew that if she did not say yes to him soon, she would never see him again, and her eyes blurred with tears. Whenever she thought of him she would remember the sweet, pungent smell in the air that day.

Suddenly he squatted on his haunches. "Look at this here dandelion," he said, poking the scrawny bloom with his fingertip. "Look how it can grow right in the crack of a rock. No soil, no water, all it needs is a crack in a rock. That's how I grew up," he said, "like this here wild dandelion, growing up in a little crack in a rock. They didn't talk about love where I grew up. They talked about death and hellfire and sin and damnation. My daddy was a Baptist minister. He knew what sin was, and sin was anything that felt good. I was called a sinner. I was called his bad boy. I was called the devil's tool. Seems like every day I was assigned to purgatory, and told I was going to roast on a spit in hell. And, yeah, I got in a fair amount of trouble as a kid—nothing serious, mostly mischief, kids' stuff, stealing candy or a pack of smokes from the grocery store, stuff like that. 'Down on your knees,' they told me. 'Pray for your eternal soul.' And then he beat me. Made me stretch face first across the bed, and came down on my back with the back of a chair." He stood up. "Want to see my scars?" he said; and pulled up his shirt to show her the welts across his back, shoulders, and stomach. "Some of those scars came from wrasslin' bulls and breakin' ponies, and some of them came from fighting men, and even a few from fighting women, but most of them came from my lovin' daddy. And I got other scars that I can't show you here." He tucked his shirt into his trousers again. "So I ran away from home when I was fourteen," he said. "Sometimes I don't know how I made it, but I made it, struggling up like that little old dandelion through a crack in the rock. And I won't lie to you—I've known a lot of women. But I've never been much of your Don Juan, Clark Gable type of loverboy. I never told a woman that I loved her. It wasn't just that I didn't want to be tied down, or fenced in, like the song goes. I was scared. I was scared of love. To me, love was like the Big Rock Candy Mountain—there just couldn't be such a thing. Love was like the God my daddy talked about—it didn't exist, not if someone like my daddy had been made God's messenger on earth. Anyone who talked about love was worse than a Goddamned fool. He was a Goddamned liar. One thing I did know, though. I knew that everybody sooner or later needs somebody else. Didn't want to admit I knew it, but I always knew it, knew I was always looking for someone to need—didn't know who it was, or where that person would turn up. Maybe needing somebody is even more important than loving somebody—could that be? And then one day, toolin' down the interstate in my 'Vette, I see this girl with her thumb up. It was her thumb up that got to me first. Her thumb was up, and so was her chin. In fact, everything about her looked up to me. She had the name of some fairy-tale Russian queen, and I thought right away maybe this is the one I've been looking for, looking to need. I still don't trust love, but I trust need. Seems like you and I have both been alone too long, is what I'm trying to say. Seems like you and I met, and flowed together just right, like those two rivers down there. If you get me, maybe you won't get much, but you'll get a man who needs you. Is that enough?" He held out his arms. "You need somebody. I need somebody. Maybe it's you and me," he said.

"Oh, Skipper, I love you so. Make love to me, Skipper. Now."

He held her at arm's length. "I told you I'd like to fox you up," he said. "I still would, and I'm going to—but only if you marry me. Because you're not like other girls. You're the kind of girl I want to fox up as my wife, and that makes you kind of special, see? But believe me, when I fox you up, it won't be something that either of us is going to forget real soon. So come with me. I don't care where we're going, so long as it's somewhere." She felt his arms fold around her shoulders, and he kissed her then, and she heard herself whispering, "Need . . . need," through her parted lips, and she found that she was weeping, weeping with both joy and terror.

"Dear Daddy," she wrote:

A friend of mine and I are going away on a trip, and I may not be back for a fairly long time. I hope you won't mind my doing this, but it has seemed to me for some time that, with Mother gone, I am more a hindrance than a help to you here. And you have so much on your mind right now that I'm sure you'll really be glad not to have me underfoot anymore, as just another one of your worries. I think that what I have decided to do is really the best thing for our family at this time. . . .

She started to write, "Life has become unbearable for me here," but decided that sounded too melodramatic, and instead wrote:

Please do not try to find me, for it will be very difficult to do, and as soon as I am settled I will drop you a line.

I hope the brown spots on the lawn will go away soon. Alben Sellers, who is supposed to be one of the best farmers around here, told me he has a good solution. He suggests mixing equal parts of potash, baking soda, lime, vinegar, and well-rotted cow manure, and spreading this mixture on top of each spot. Then keep the entire area flushed with fresh water. It sounds kind of nasty, but it's supposed to correct what is called the pH count in the soil. Of course I don't know if this will work, but it might be worth a try. Mr. Sellers says you will still probably have to reseed in the spring . . .

Give my love to Mother when you are able to go to see her.

> *Goodbye,*
> *Alexandra*

She left the letter on the kitchen table the next morning, after he had left for the office, placing it on top of the unopened manuscript from Genesee Depot.

Skipper had told her to pack very little—just her toothbrush, a change of underthings, a couple of nighties. Anything else she needed he would get for her when they got to Wichita. She stuffed everything quickly into a small suitcase. Then she carried it out onto the breezeway to wait for the yellow Corvette to appear around the bend in the road.

When it did, she ran to the end of the driveway, tossed her suitcase into the back seat, and jumped into the front seat beside him. "Let's go!" she cried.

"Aw, don't cry," he said. "I hate to see you cry. We're going to have a ball together, you and me. You'll see."

"I'm doing this," she sobbed. "*I'm really doing this!*" And she pounded both balled fists against the padded dashboard of the car.

"Damn right you're doing it, and it's a damn good thing you're doing, too. So don't cry. . . ."

She put her head back on the headrest of the seat, and squeezed out the last two tears as they drove toward Kansas City.

"You know," she said, a moment later, "I'm a pretty good seamstress. I design and make a lot of my clothes. Do you think, when we get to Wichita, I could get a sewing machine? It doesn't have to be a fancy one."

"Only rule is, if it'll fit in the trunk or back seat of this 'Vette, it's yours. When we're on the road, this 'Vette is our home away from home."

"A portable machine wouldn't take up too much room."

"Then that's what you'll get," he said.

"I could make things for you, too," she said. "I could make men's things. I could sew for you."

"Hey, I'd like that," he said. "I split out a couple of pairs of jeans a week in this job of mine."

At the Jackson County Court House, the ceremony was as swift and simple as he had said it would be. They filled out some forms, signed a register, and Alex subtracted a year from her actual birth date. Then they said the words, and the justice of the peace instructed Skipper to say, "—And with this ring, I thee wed," and Skipper, to her complete surprise, produced a thin gold wedding band. It wasn't much, as wedding bands went, but at the time she thought it the sweetest and dearest ring she had ever seen. Later, he would show her the inside of the band, where he had had engraved "*J.P.–A.L.*"

"I now pronounce you man and wife," the justice said and, turning to Skipper, said, "You may kiss the bride." It was the second time he had kissed her full on the mouth.

Then the justice of the peace filled out a very formal-looking certificate, signed it with a flourish, and affixed a gold paper seal. "Little lady looks a little sad," the justice said when it was over, and handed Skipper the certificate.

"Just nerves, I guess," Skipper said with a wink.

The date was August 20, 1961.

"Well, how's it feel to be Mrs. Skipper Purdy?" he said when they were back in the car, heading out of the city toward the interstate.

"I don't know. I'm still getting used to it," she said.

He patted her hand on the seat beside him.

Presently they passed a sign that said:

LEAVING MISSOURI
Y'all Come Back Real Soon, Y'Hear!

I've done it, Alex thought. I've run away from home and gotten married. I'm free. I have my own life now.

A few hundred feet farther on, another sign said:

WELCOME TO KANSAS
The Sunflower State

"This is the first time I've been outside the state of
Missouri," she said.

"You're going to see a lot more states," he said. "After
Wichita, the next stop's Omaha." He began to sing, "You
are my sunflower, my only sunflower, you make me happy
when skies are gray . . ."

She was laughing now.

"Oops!" Suddenly Skipper braked the car hard, and pulled
off to the side of the road. About a quarter of a mile ahead
of them on the interstate, just beyond a wide curve, there
appeared to be three or perhaps four police cars with orange
bubble lights flashing. Skipper made a quick U-turn, across
the grassy median divider, and headed back in the opposite
direction.

"What's the matter?"

"Smokey Bear," he said. "They like to ticket this yellow
'Vette of mine, 'cause they think it's flashy." He looked
quickly in his rearview mirror. "Didn't spot us," he said.
"Besides, with you being underage and all, and crossing state
lines—cops get funny about that, you know. And your daddy
might have put out some kind of alarm."

"My father won't get my letter until at least six o'clock
tonight."

"Best not to take any chances, if you see what I mean. So
we'll take back roads for a while, see some scenery. There's
more than one way to skin a cat, right?"

In a town called Lamont, they stopped at a diner for lunch.
Skipper seemed preoccupied, and didn't say much while they
ate. "Take us a little longer on these country roads," he said.
"But we're in no hurry, right? Gig doesn't start till tomorrow
night." But she sensed that something was worrying him.

It was nearly eleven o'clock at night when they got to
Wichita, and registered at the motel the rodeo people had
reserved for them. She watched him enter their names, "Mr.
and Mrs. James R. Purdy." She realized she didn't know what
the "R" stood for, but she was suddenly too shy to ask him.

The motel room enjoyed an expansive view of its own
parking lot and, in the room, they were both strangely qui-

et, quietly unpacking, opening and closing bureau drawers. Alex stepped into the bathroom first, undressed, and slipped into her nightie. Then she returned to the bedroom, opened the covers of one of the twin beds, and slid quickly inside it. Then he went into the bathroom, closed the door, and Alex turned out the light.

From the bathroom, she could hear water running. It seemed to run for the longest time. At last he stepped out and, from the corner of her eye, she could see the shape of his muscular frame, in his jockey shorts, silhouetted in the light from the bathroom door. His body, outlined in the light, seemed all flat planes, smooth edges. Then he turned off the bathroom light, and she heard him get into the other twin bed. The room was silent now, except for the sound of his even breathing, and a distant radio, from another room, playing country music. Lights from the parking lot flickered dimly through the drawn curtains, creating a pattern of light and shadow on the ceiling.

"Skipper?" she said at last.

"Uh-huh?"

"Are we going to—you know?"

She heard him raise himself on one elbow in the other bed. "D'you think?" he said. "I thought maybe we should wait, take it easy for a while, wait till we get to know each other a little better, wait till we get used to being alone together like this. Don't you think? After all, you're really just a kid."

"No. I want to," she whispered.

"Are you sure?"

"Yes."

"Have you ever—?"

"Never. But I want to. Now."

"Well, if you're sure."

"I'm sure." How to tell him she was aching with desire for him?

In the flickering light—and, again, from just the corner of her eye—she watched him as he put his long legs over the side of the bed, stood up, and slid out of his jockey shorts; they dropped noiselessly on the carpet, a small white pile. Then she felt him slide into bed beside her. "Skipper," she whispered, "I want to, but I'm a little frightened." With a fingertip she traced the scars on his back and shoulders, and the warm shapes of the welts were suddenly soft and exciting, and her lips flew to his.

"Hey," he said softly. "Not so fast. Take it easy. Relax. If this is your first time, everything's got to be very . . . very . . . slow. It's like a piece of music that starts out slow, then gets a little faster. . . ." He circled her moving fingers with his own.

And what happened next she could never really adequately describe to anyone, nor would she even try. Just as there is no real memory of pain, there is no real memory of ecstasy, either. It seemed as though for a long time he was simply teasing her, touching her lightly, deftly, with his lips and fingers here and there, while her breath came faster, more expectant. Slowly, he became more purposeful, whispering words of encouragement and flattery and pleasure, but when he first entered her it was only brief, and tentative, before he withdrew. Meanwhile something utterly new and unimaginable was happening inside her, a rush of billowing crimson that seemed to build with the sound of wind from a summer storm rushing across the cornfields. It had that sound, and a wet smell too, and when he finally whispered, "You're ready," she knew that she was ready, and he entered her completely, and she was answering each deep movement of his body with a deeper, more urgent movement of her own. It was as though they had become not just one body, but one soul, and with the feeling of billowing, of being blown across some landscape by some strange, hot wind, a wind that seemed to increase to an almost furious intensity until she felt it climax with a kind of explosion of white light in her brain, and she cried out with joy at the pinpricks of colored light that flew out from this white central core of light, like fireworks, bursting, and then bursting again, and then again. She clung to him, for if she had not she surely would have fallen off the edge of the earth just then. And for a long time it seemed as though they were both falling, falling together, limply, loosely, two parachutists, their cords intertangled, looking expectantly, confidently, for a soft place to land.

There was a small spot of blood when it was over—she had been told that there might be—but there was no memory of any hurt. And never, ever would there be lovemaking for her like that first night with Skipper Purdy when the earth fell away.

Chapter 26

Now it was Tuesday morning, and Coleman had just brought Alex's breakfast tray out to her on the terrace at 10 Gracie Square where, on good days, she liked to have her morning toast and coffee in the wrought-iron gazebo. With her breakfast tray were customarily four daily papers, the *Times*, the *Daily News*, the *Wall Street Journal*, and *Women's Wear Daily*. She was used to reading them in order—the *Times* first, for world news, then the *Daily News*, mostly to see what nonsense Mona Potter was reporting, the *Wall Street Journal*, which often had solid stories on the publishing business which, as usual, was in a state of uncertainty and change, and, finally, *Women's Wear*, to see which Seventh Avenue designer Johnnie Fairchild was pushing or punishing at the moment. *Women's Wear* wasn't really about fashion. It was about the garment industry.

She flipped quickly through the papers now. "Where're the *Times* and the *Journal?*" she asked Coleman.

Coleman's look was anxious. "There's an ad in both those papers this morning, Alex," he said. "And you're not going to like it."

"Well, let me see it, darlin'," she said.

"It's an ad placed by Mr. Herbert Rothman," he said.

"Then by all means let me see it. Who's afraid of the big bad wolf?"

"I just thought I should warn you." He stepped back into

the apartment, and returned with the newspapers, the *Times*
opened to a centerfold in the Business section, and placed
them beside her breakfast tray. She picked up her reading
glasses, and he started to withdraw again.

"No, stay," she said, and he hovered solicitously beside
her.

In the illustration, a man's hand extended from the upper
corner of the righthand page, pouring from a bottle of champagne. From the lower corner of the lefthand page, a woman's jeweled hand extended, holding a champagne glass into
which the bubbly liquid flowed. Across both pages, in 72-
point type, the headline proclaimed:

CONGRATULATIONS, ALEXANDRA ROTHMAN!

She set down her coffee cup quietly in its saucer, and
read:

Today, June 26, 1990, Alexandra Rothman begins her
eighteenth year as editor-in-chief of *Mode*. Incredibly,
she has occupied the top spot on *Mode*'s masthead
longer than any other person in the magazine's 116-year
history! Not even the legendary Consuelo Ferlinghetti,
Mode's editor for fourteen years, was able to demonstrate such editorial longevity!

When she came to *Mode* seventeen years ago yesterday, Alexandra was young . . . inexperienced . . . but
with a boundless supply of fresh ideas . . . enthusiasm . . . zest . . . energy that only the young can have.
Yet think how the world has changed since 1973! In
1973, the nation was just beginning to hear of a place
called Watergate. And now nearly all the figures in that
great scandal are dead!

Seventeen years later, those ideas . . . that youthful
enthusiasm . . . that energy have all paid off. She has
made *Mode* more than just a fashion magazine. *She
made it a magazine for the finished woman.* The proof:
Over 5,000,000 in paid circulation.*

But, wisely, Alexandra Rothman knows that a magazine can only stay young and fresh when there is a
constant infusion of young and fresh ideas. To insure
that this keeps happening, she has asked the youthful

British fashion expert, FIONA FENTON, to join her next month as *Mode*'s very first co-editor-in-chief.

So, congratulations, Alexandra, on a job well done, and may you enjoy a well-deserved rest! And hail to thee, blithe spirit, FIONA FENTON!

> HERBERT J. ROTHMAN
> President & Publisher
> Rothman Publications
> A division of
> Rothman Communications, Inc.

*SOURCE: Audit Bureau of Circulations

She put down the paper with a little sigh, and patted the ad with the flattened palm of her hand. "So," she said, "Fiona Fenton is now my idea. Very clever, isn't he, our little Herbert?"

Coleman still looked worried.

"It's a war of nerves, darlin'," she said. "He's trying to force me to resign. But he ain't about to, as we used to say back home—at least not on the terms he has in mind. But don't worry, darlin'. I still have a few more arrows in my quiver, and I intend to use 'em. If he wants to get rid of me, it's going to cost him. And a lot more than a double truck in the *New York Times*."

"And the *Wall Street Journal*."

"*And* the *Journal*."

"May I ask you one question, Alex?"

"Sure."

"It's none of my business, of course. But I know Mr. Herbert Rothman has always hated you. But—*why?*"

She looked at him candidly. "Actually, there're several reasons," she said. "For one thing, he had another woman in mind for my job, but his father voted him down. But the real reason is that a number of years ago he made a pass at me, and in a particularly unpleasant way. I'm afraid I laughed in his face. He never forgave me for that. Hell hath no fury like a Rothman scorned."

"I guessed it might be something like that," he said.

"You guessed correctly."

"And now that his father is ill—"

"Dying," she said. "I'm afraid Ho Rothman may be dying, or that's the way they're making it sound."

He nodded. "—the son is making his big power play."

"Exactly."

But now the telephone was ringing, and Coleman moved across the terrace to answer it. Alex picked up her coffee cup, and discovered that her coffee was cold.

Coleman returned with the telephone on its long cord. "Mr. McCulloch," he said.

"Good morning, Rodney," she said brightly, after picking up the receiver.

"Well, well, well!" he said. "Does this ad in the morning paper mean that you're mine, all mine? Ha-ha-ha."

"I really haven't had time to think about your proposal, Rodney," she said. "After all, it's been less than twenty-four—"

"*What?* You mean you haven't handed in your resignation letter *yet?* After being kissed off like that in the *New York Times* by the little ferret bastard?"

"*And* in the *Wall Street Journal.*"

"Damnedest piece of shit I ever read. I thought you'd of had your resignation letter sitting on the ferret's desk by now."

"It's quite clear that's what he wants. But there are certain contractual problems that have to be worked out. My lawyers are working on it now."

"Well, build a fire under your lawyers' asses. The more time you let a lawyer take, the bigger the bill they can run up on you. That's what lawyers call it. Billable hours. I know all about them billable hours. Meanwhile, you coming by to see Maudie and me tonight?"

"Yes. Six o'clock at the Lombardy."

"We want your absolute candy opinion about Maudie. Your completely candy opinion. We trust you, as a high priestess of fashion, to give us your totally candy opinion. . . ."

Downtown, in his office at 530 Fifth Avenue, Lenny Liebling's telephone was also ringing. Lenny lay on his back on the massage table, and Francisco, his young Ecuadorian masseur, who was working on his lower abdominal muscles and had noticed the bulge that was developing under the towel that lay across Lenny's middle, had just asked politely, "Would you like me to bring you off, Mr. Liebling?" Lenny considered this while the phone rang. "I'd better take this call first, Francisco," he said. His secretary had not yet arrived for the day.

"Maybe not be able to get you like that again, later," Francisco said, looking irritated.

Lenny reached for the telephone.

"Hello, sweetie, what's up?" he heard Mona Potter's voice say. "Has she quit yet?"

"I—uh—I haven't—*uh!*—heard anything yet, Mona," he said, gasping as Francisco's strong and agile fingers and knuckles kneaded and poked at his stomach and pectoral muscles.

"What's the matter? You sound like you're choking on a piece of steak. You need the Heimlich Maneuver or something, sweetie?"

"I'm—*uh!*—just having my morning massage," he said.

"So—you saw this morning's ad, of course."

"I—*uh!*—I did. But—"

"So when's she gonna quit? I need to know today, sweetie, 'cause I'm doing my whole tomorrow's column on it."

"I—uh—I just don't know, Mona. *Uh!* Not quite so hard, Francisco!" But Francisco, who seemed angry now that his best professional techniques were not being employed to his client's full advantage, was pummeling him harder than ever, his brown face grim.

"Think it's safe to say she'll be quitting some time today, sweetie? I gotta know for my column deadline."

"I don't know any—*uh!*—more than you do, Mona darling. *Uh! Please*, Francisco!" Francisco had just flipped him over on his stomach, and was furiously pounding his shoulders and upper arms. The telephone cord was now twisted around Lenny's neck and, with his free hand, he struggled to extricate himself from it.

"What's she cooking up with Rodney McCulloch?"

"Uh!—*who?*"

"Rodney McCulloch, sweetie. The two of them were having lunch yesterday at Le Bernardin. One of the waiters tipped me off. He said it looked like a heavy-duty meeting."

"I don't—*uh!*—don't know anything about that," he said, annoyed that she should have acquired a piece of news before he had.

"He said they were talking about money. Whaddaya think? Think he's offered her some kind of deal?"

"I just—*uh!*—I just don't know, Mona," Lenny said.

"Think it's safe to say they're cooking up some sort of deal? Everybody knows McCulloch's looking for a New York property. C'mon. Gimme a break, sweetie. I gotta have something for tomorrow's column."

"I—just—don't—know," he said again.

"Well, I think it's safe to say he's offered her a deal," she said. "Anyhoo, let me know the minute you hear anything. You know I never identify you. You're just 'a high-placed source at Rothman Publications.' Toodle-oo, sweetie."

"Toodle-oo," Lenny said.

Francisco flipped him over on his back again. "Okay, I make for you one more chance, Mr. Liebling," he said. "If this no work, my hour is up."

"Thank you, Francisco, dear," he said.

Alex strode down her office corridor that morning trying to exude her customary self-confidence, her chin up, her hands in the deep pockets of her Calvin Klein suit, her skirts swinging, her Chanel bag—stripped of its signature double-C's—slung jauntily over her shoulder, even though she was aware, as she passed each open office door, of the sudden and apprehensive little hush that seemed to fall, from within, as her Susan Bennis heels clicked by. This day, she promised herself, must not be permitted to seem any different from any other.

Gregory met her at her office door, and she immediately noticed another unusually tall stack of telephone message slips on her desk.

"Most of those are from the media," he said, "wanting to know about your future plans. Do you think we ought to prepare some sort of statement to give to the press?"

She tossed her bag in a chair. "I don't think so," she said. "I think we should leave all statements to Herbert Rothman for the time being. He seems to be very good at making statements."

"I agree," he said.

"If they call again, just say I'm unavailable, or in a meeting, or whatever."

"That's exactly what I've been saying."

"Don't even say, 'No comment.' I always think 'No comment' sounds snippy and defensive."

"There's one call here from Miss Lucille Withers in Kansas City. She just says, 'I've talked to the Canadian. Go for it.' She said you'd know what she meant."

"Yes," she said.

"And Mr. Mark Rinsky called. He'd like you to call him when you get a chance."

"Good. See if you can get him now."

Gregory glanced at his watch. "And we've got the Scaasi show at the St. Regis at eleven thirty," he said.

"Right," she said.

"Mark," she said, when she had him on the phone.

"Alex," he said, "do you think there's any chance your office phone might be bugged?"

"I doubt it," she said. "Do you think so?"

"Let's not take any chances," he said. "Things seem to be heating up over there. I've got a little scrambling device I can turn on. It'll scramble both ends of this conversation, and if this conversation is being recorded, both of us'll sound like chipmunks. It'll make my voice sound a little funny, but hold on while I turn it on." She waited. Then he said, "Hello? Okay, it's on. We can talk." His voice sounded as though he was talking in a wind tunnel.

"I've been talking with my operatives in London," he said. "A lot of what our friend has been telling people checks out, but a lot of it doesn't, and we keep hitting dead ends. To begin with, it seems she did work for a publication in England called *Lady Fair*. It wasn't much of a thing—just a little advertising giveaway, really, with fashion tips in it, and it was published out of a woman's basement in a house in Maida Vale. Woman named Jane Smiley. She and our friend Fiona put it out together, just the two of them. Anyway, *Lady Fair* went out of business two years ago, and Jane Smiley—who now works for a newspaper in North Wales—doesn't know what happened to Fiona Fenton. Doesn't have too much to say about her, either, except that she was a hard worker. Good at selling ad space, apparently. But the two women had some sort of falling out. My man wasn't able to get to the bottom of what it was about—the Smiley woman wasn't very forthcoming—except that it apparently had nothing to do with the little business they were in together. My man got the impression that the falling out was over some guy—some bloke, as my man in London puts it—that they were both involved with."

"Hmm," said Alex.

"Now, the next part of her story—about how she ran some ritzy little dress shop in Sloane Street, and sold clothes to the Princess of Wales—we've struck a complete dead end here. Nobody with a shop on Sloane Street seems to have heard of Fiona Fenton, or know anything about a shop she might have run. And Buckingham Palace just stonewalls questions like this. They refuse to say where the princess buys her clothes, except places that have so-called Royal Warrants, and all they'll give out is a list. So as far as the so-called dress shop is concerned, we've come up with zip."

"What about her family background? Anything there?"

"Another dead end, Alex. She claims that her father is the Earl of Hesketh, and there really is such a person. But it turns out he's a real looney-tune. Lives all by himself, with a single manservant, in a falling-down castle in Surrey, and hasn't set foot outside the place in years. Most of his neighbors haven't ever laid eyes on His Grace, though they know he's there because they see the manservant go in and out every week or so with groceries. The manservant won't speak to anyone. No one even knows his name. There's no telephone in the castle, and the entire place is guarded by big, fierce Doberman dogs. None of the people in the village know anything about the old earl's family, even if there ever was a wife or children."

"So, if Lady Fiona Fenton has picked a peer to be her fictitious father, she's picked the right one," Alex said.

"Exactly what I was thinking, Alex. My man did find one old lady in the village who claimed to know all about the Earl of Hesketh. She told him all sorts of stories, and the stories got weirder and weirder. She told him that the earl could change himself into a starling, and often came to feed at her bird-feeder. So—you guessed it. This old lady is the village crazy, who makes the Madwoman of Chaillot look like Margaret Mead. So I'm afraid, Alex, that this is all we've got and, as I said, it's not much."

"No, it really isn't, is it?" she said.

"But don't worry. We're going to keep digging. We're going to get to the bottom of this dress-shop thing, if there ever *was* a dress shop."

"Well, thank you, Mark."

There was a pause on the other end of the line. Then he said, "That was a shitty ad in this morning's paper, Alex."

She laughed softly. "Yes, it was a shitty ad," she said.

"Well, if someone's going to give you a shitty ad, maybe it's a comfort to know that it came from somebody everybody thinks is a first-class shit."

She whooped. "Yes! It is!"

Now Bob Shaw, her art director, was waiting for her in her outer office. He, too, was doing his best not to seem edgy and nervous. "I've got some more information for you on the sex life of the bees," he said. "I've been talking with a beekeeper out on Long Island, and it seems that it's tannic acid that attracts a swarm, which is why bees will usually swarm on the branches or the trunks of trees. This guy thinks that if we can put some tannic acid in the model's hair, and he can lead a few drones over to her from a crowded hive, he might be able to get the swarm to form in her hair."

Gregory beamed. "My mother had been swimming in the river. River water is often full of tannic acid."

"That is, if you still want to go ahead with this idea for the shoot," Bob Shaw said.

"Oh, I think it would be definitely worth a try, don't you?" Alex said.

"Well, I've been thinking about it," he said. "What's this shot supposed to *say?* What's it supposed to *mean?* I mean, bees swarming in a woman's hair could end up looking kind of *peculiar,* couldn't it? I just don't have a mental picture of what this shot's going to look like."

"You're right, of course," she said. "I've never seen bees swarming in a woman's hair, either. What *did* it look like, Gregory?"

"I thought it looked—beautiful," he said. "With her head tilted back, her long hair hanging down, and this living festoon cascading from it, like a waterfall."

"Yes, it could look beautiful," she agreed. "It could also look exciting, exotic—dangerous, even. Swarms last at least

twenty minutes, so we'd have time to get it from lots of different angles. Who were you thinking of for a photographer,
Bob?"

"Helmut Newton?"

"Perfect!" She clapped her hands.

He hesitated. "Or should we wait and see what Fiona
Fenton thinks about this?" he asked.

She gave him a quick look. "Miss Fenton hasn't even
joined the organization yet, Bob," she said.

He nodded, and looked down at the square of carpet
between his feet.

Now there was a telephone call from Miss Lincoln, Herbert
Rothman's secretary on the thirtieth floor. "I just wanted to
extend my personal best wishes to you, Mrs. Rothman," Miss
Lincoln said.

"Best wishes for what, Miss Lincoln?"

"All of us up here on thirty were so terribly sorry to hear
that you'll be leaving the magazine."

"Now wherever did you hear that?" Alex said.

"Oh . . . . But that's what we were given to understand,"
Miss Lincoln said.

"Not a word of truth in it, Miss Lincoln," Alex said, and
replaced the receiver in its cradle.

And now it was time to leave for the Scaasi show, and Gregory was waiting for her in the outer office with her briefcase.

In their taxi, on the way to the St. Regis, Alex said, "This
is Arnold's winter resort collection. So think picnics."

Gregory nodded.

All these fashion shows were somewhat alike, Alex
thought—the music, the lighting, the flowers, the parading,
skinny models, the often banal commentaries that no one
really listened to. Each collection opened with a few little
afternoon dresses, proceeded through evening dresses and
ball gowns, and closed, traditionally, with the kind of elaborate wedding dress that no one paid the slightest attention to,
much less considered buying. How many of these collections
had she attended over the years? Hundreds, easily. But she
attended them dutifully, always on the lookout for something

that might appeal to her readers, that might be new and different enough to include in the magazine. And whenever she saw that special dress or outfit that seemed to have *Mode*'s signature on it, she would touch Gregory's shoulder lightly, and whisper, "That one." And he would make a note.

But Arnold Scaasi always liked to add little expensive touches when he showed his collections, and that made them at least superficially different. Today, for instance, instead of lining up his audience in rows of little gilt chairs, the St. Regis Roof had been set up with round tables for ten, with pastel-colored cloths, and sandwiches were being served— turkey, Westphalian ham, thin-sliced filet of beef, and smoked Scotch salmon on the thinnest of white bread slices—while waiters passed champagne. Thus the first commercial showing of his winter resort collection—to his regular customers and to buyers from the stores—became more like an invitation-only luncheon. There were even engraved place cards, all examples of spending to put women in a spending mood. And, after all, Scaasi was one of the last surviving designers of American *haute couture*. Even he had been thought to be finished, until he was discovered by Barbara Bush. And the expensiveness of his presentation was justified because his were very expensive clothes, designed to be worn at expensive gatherings at expensive resorts where rich people went simply to enjoy being rich together. There were so few of these places left: Palm Beach, Acapulco, Lyford Cay, the Mill Reef Club . . .

There were other costly touches, Alex noted as she looked around the room. Tubs of plantain and bird-of-paradise trees and fishtail palms had been brought in to create the illusion of a tropical rain forest. Concealed pink spots illuminated the runway to suggest a moonlit tropic night. Instead of ordinary centerpieces, each round table was centered with a pot of white phalaenopsis orchids, from which also sprouted a cluster of transparent balloons, some of which had been magically filled with crumpled silver Mylar. ("Those balloons go for a hundred dollars a bunch," she heard someone comment.) Alex noticed that a number of the clear balloons had been partially filled with water, and that in these swam brightly colored tropical fish. ("A hundred and fifty with the fish," someone else said. "He's spent at least a hundred big ones today.") The collection opened with a simulated lightning flash, followed by the recorded roll of thunder, and a black model, wearing jaguar-printed chiffon beach pajamas, strode imperiously down the runway with a live jaguar on a leash. There were appreciative gasps, followed by applause, and the show was under way.

Still, for all the elaborateness of the presentation, the focus—thanks to the clever lighting of the runway—was always on the clothes. And, after each model did her turn on the runway, she had been instructed to step down from the stage and circulate among the tables so the women in the audience could reach out and touch the fabrics—a leisurely, and expensive, use of a model's time, Alex knew. Scaasi was showing a lot of chiffon today. Chiffon flowed in floating panels from wrists, elbows, waists, and plunging backlines. It had even been used, reinforced with invisible wiring, to create amusing artichoke and pumpkin-shaped capes in vivid greens and oranges. Suzette Bergerac, Scaasi's *directrice*, who was doing the commentary, was noting the preponderance of chiffon—"shee-foh," she pronounced it. "Pumpkin is definitely going to be this winter's *in* color," she advised her audience from the microphone. How did she know these things? How did even Arnold Scaasi know? Soft, lazy, vaguely Latin taped music played from hidden speakers, and the models paraded up and down the runway, did their turns and swirls, and then moved down into the audience to a sultry flamenco beat.

But was anyone really paying attention? Alex sometimes wondered. "Blaine Trump doesn't pay a penny for her clothes," someone near her was saying. "They're all loaned to her. The designers drop them off for her the afternoon before the party, and a messenger picks them up the next morning. How do I know? I live in her building, and the concierge told me."

"I make my cook use shallots. *Shallots*. That's the secret of perfect vichyssoise."

"This? It isn't real. All my good stuff's in the box."

Pussy McCutcheon was describing, to no one in particular, the recent incursions on her Visa card account. "Vuitton, Hermès, Giorgio, Baccarat," she was saying. "All on Fifty-*seventh* Street. What does that say to you? It says to me that Maggie's burglar had to be a *woman*. Those are places where women shop. Men don't shop on Fifty-seventh. They shop on Madison."

More little sandwiches were passed, and more champagne was poured. The tall, willowy models, wearing expressions ranging from indifference to insolence, moved one by one down the runway, paused to be admired, then moved between the tables to be touched and exclaimed over, before gliding backstage again where, Alex knew, the scene would be frantic and sweaty and not the least bit ladylike as the half-naked girls flung themselves out of one outfit and into the next. Zippers would jam, buttons would pop, pins would be applied. Shoes would be kicked off in every direction, and rat-tailed combs would attack errant hairdos. And there would be much profanity. Alex had stage-managed enough fashion shows to know what went on. "Who stole my fucking eyeliner?" "What the fuck am I supposed to do with this belt?" "Hook me up next, you black bitch! I go on before she does." "*Ouch!* You stuck that pin in my tit!" "Fucking zipper broke!" "That happens to be *my* hair spray, cunt!" Scaasi's wardrobe mistress would be busily logging accessories in and out, watching for pilferage, because runway models were notorious thieves. After every fashion show, you could count on certain missing items—scarves, belts, earrings, gloves, even pairs of shoes.

Meanwhile, in the wings and invisible from the audience, but able to observe everything, the designer himself would be tensely watching the show, groaning inaudibly at the occasional miscues—the girl whose panty hose were supposed to be taupe, but who stepped out on the runway wearing black—and hoping that the audience wouldn't notice. Scaasi would not make his appearance, and take his bow, until the show was over. At which point—he dared to hope—the room would burst into applause and cheers and blown kisses.

Suzette continued with her commentary:

"Yards and yards of shirred organza . . . perfect for a Palm Beach moonlit night . . . youthfully cut, with a peekaboo cutout at the base of the spine . . . the little black dress that every woman needs, whether for cocktails in the city, or on a terrace in the Hamptons, this time with a saucy little flared skirt . . . notice the embroidered detailing at the hemline . . . sheer, sexy silk pants, for a tropical evening . . . a jeweled belt . . . skinny little spaghetti shoulder straps, almost invisible, so young-looking. . . ."

Youthfulness was clearly a theme of today's collection, and there was a certain irony here, Alex thought, since most of the women who could afford Scaasi—and most of his audience here today—were no longer young. They were her age, at least.

When she came to Mode *seventeen years ago yesterday, Alexandra was young.* . . .

Across the table, a woman whose face she recognized, but whose name she didn't immediately recall, blew Alex an air kiss and mouthed the words, "My dear, I had no idea you'd been with *Mode* so *long!*"

Alex's answering smile was automatic.

. . . *inexperienced . . . but with a boundless supply of fresh ideas . . . enthusiasm . . . zest . . . energy that only the young can have*. All at once she was certain that Fiona had written that ad.

"A fresh idea for ripply moiré . . . slinky . . . youthful . . . sexy . . . blue, palest blue, the youngest color of the season . . . the youthful energy of crispy pleated cotton . . . golden tulle, reflecting Arnold's newest enthusiasm and energy when it comes to bold colors . . . new . . . young . . . vibrant . . . exciting . . . new . . . youthful . . . young . . . daisy-fresh . . . a new idea . . . forever young. . . ."

Beside her, Gregory touched Alex's shoulder, and looked at his boss questioningly. "That one?" he whispered. It was an evening gown of white tiered chiffon, slashed to the knee, with a heart-shaped bodice sewn with mirrored paillettes and tiny seed pearls.

Alex nodded, and Gregory made a note on his steno pad. From the wings where he was hidden, Arnold Scaasi saw this exchange and grinned with pleasure, for now he could see this dress not only in the pages of *Mode*, but also in Bergdorf-Goodman's window . . . in Neiman-Marcus's window . . . in I. Magnin's window. And he made a mental note to ask young Gregory Kittredge to lunch. And somehow Alex knew that all this was happening and, with a little shiver, she realized that, listening to Suzette's commentary, she had been paying no attention to the clothes at all, though it was supposed to be the other way around.

She asked herself: Was it possible that Herbert Rothman was winning his war of nerves?

* * *

Back at her office that afternoon, she found a stack of layouts for the October issue on her desk, awaiting her approval. But on top of the stack of layouts was something else, a folded card on which someone in the art department had drawn a single long-stemmed red rose. She unfolded the card and read:

Dear Alex,

This is just to tell you that, whatever happens, we love you, and always will.

Many signatures followed, and as she ran a fingertip down the list she saw that the card had been signed by all the one hundred and twenty-four members of her staff.

Her eyes blurred. "Gregory," she said, "was this your idea?"

He covered his heart with his right hand. "Swear to God it wasn't," he said. "It was Billy Greenfield's."

"Billy Greenfield? I don't think I know a Billy Greenfield."

"He's one of the mail-room boys," he said.

Chapter 27

There was a dream Alex sometimes had. It was a dream of a nightmare experience that actually happened, and it always began the same, with the sound of angry fists pounding on the door, and shouts of "Open up! Police!" With that, she inevitably awoke, and had trouble getting to sleep again, remembering how it happened. . . .

"Open up! Police!" There was a loud banging on the door. It was early in the morning of their second week at the motel in Wichita. Skipper leaped out of bed and pulled on his trousers without putting on his underpants. Alex sat up in bed and covered her bare shoulders with the bedclothes.

"Open up! Police!"

She watched him as he moved, shirtless, across the darkened room toward the door, and undid the chain latch. She reached out and turned on one of the two lamps. Two burly Kansas state troopers pushed into the room, their service revolvers drawn. "Okay, Johnson, this is it," one of them said. "You're under arrest." The other said, "Get your shirt and shoes on, Johnson. You're coming with us." Outside, in the early-morning light, she could see the yellow lights of their squad cars spinning and flashing.

"Stop!" she cried. "What are you doing? You're making a terrible mistake! His name's not Johnson!"

"You hear me?" the second officer said, ignoring her and waving his revolver at Skipper. "I said get your shoes and shirt on, Johnson. Fast!"

"Stop!" she cried again. "He hasn't done anything!" And she watched as he meekly put on and buttoned his shirt and tucked it into his trousers, then sat on the corner of the bed and pulled on his cowboy boots. He stood up, and the first officer seized his arms and quickly snapped handcuffs on his wrists from behind.

"But what's he *done?*" Alex sobbed.

"The charge is murder two," the first officer said.

Alex leaned forward across the bed, the bedsheet pulled around her. "But his name isn't Johnson!" she wept. "His name is Skipper Purdy!"

"Is that the name he's using now? Sorry, little lady."

"But he's my husband! I'm his wife! This is my husband, Skipper Purdy!"

The second officer threw a sideways glance at Skipper. "*Another* one?" he said. "Listen, little lady, this guy's got almost as many wives as he's got aliases. He's got wives from here to Pueblo, Colorado. Come on, Johnson, let's go."

"Wait . . . wait . . . !" she sobbed.

Standing tall and straight, and with as much dignity as possible, Skipper said, "Officer, may I please say goodbye to my wife?"

The two troopers exchanged questioning looks, and then briefly nodded.

Skipper stepped toward her, and kissed her awkwardly on the lips, not easy to do with his wrists manacled behind him. "It's all a mistake," he said in a low voice. "I'll explain it all later. You go home to your folks now. I'll be in touch with you there. I love you." Then, bending close to her ear, he whispered, "Under the mattress!"

"Oh, Skipper . . . Skipper . . ."

But then he was gone, marched out of their motel room between the two troopers, one at each elbow, and it was all over before she even knew what had happened.

She jumped out of bed and threw on her clothes, still weeping with fear and anger. Then she remembered: *Under the mattress.* She lifted one mattress, then the other. Under the second lay his money belt. She lifted it, and it was surprisingly heavy. She unzipped it, and emptied its contents on the bed. There were a great many tightly folded bills, most of them hundreds. She sat on the bed and began counting the money, soon realizing that it would be easiest to stack the bills in piles of a thousand dollars each. When she finally finished, she had counted a total of $34,974. This was even more than he had told her he had. She would need the money, of course, to use for his defense. Meanwhile, the motel bill had to be paid.

Outside, in the parking lot, the yellow Corvette was still parked, and the keys, she knew, were hidden under the floor mat. She found them there. In the glove compartment, she found the car's registration. It was registered in the name of William J. Cassidy, 314 Elm Street, Lafayette, Indiana. But the car, she noticed for the first time, bore Wisconsin license plates. None of it made any sense. *I will hear from him soon*, she thought. *He will write or call me soon.*

All sorts of guilty thoughts raced through her brain: Why hadn't I at least asked where they were taking him? Why didn't I find out under what name they were holding him? At the same time, even if I knew where he was, and were able to find him, would the fact that I'm a minor cause him even more trouble? In the end, there seemed to be nothing to do but what he had told her to do: Go home. And wait for some sort of word from him.

Alex knew how to drive a car, more or less. She had practiced driving her mother's car up and down the driveway at home, though the Corvette's stick shift would take some getting used to. But she had never driven on an open road, and she had no driver's license.

She drove home to Paradise that day very slowly and carefully. It was nearly dark when she reached the house with the ruined zoysia lawn, and, all the way, she had been thinking, *I will hear from him soon.*

Her father's car was in the driveway.

"Where the hell have you been?" he wanted to know. "Do you realize I've had the police in three states looking for you?"

So that may have been how the police located Skipper at the motel—looking for her. "I was spending a few days with a friend," she said.

"Whose car is that out front?"

"My friend's. He asked me to keep it for him for a while."

"You were off with some *man?*"

She nodded.

She heard him mutter, "Like mother, like daughter." Then he disappeared into the kitchen.

I will hear from him soon.

Her mother returned from the clinic in Topeka, and now there was no more talk of playwriting. Her mother had been placed on medication, and these pills were called "mood elevators." But they did not seem to elevate her mother's mood, exactly. Instead, they seemed to make her drowsy and forgetful, though she would occasionally burst into loud laughter, even when no one had said or done anything particularly funny. Her mother and father hardly spoke to one another.

I will hear from him today, she began assuring herself as each new day dawned. *Today I will hear from him. There will be a letter or a telephone call. Today.*

The days went by.

"How long is your friend's car going to be parked in our driveway, anyway?"

"He had to go out of town. He asked if he could park it there till he gets back."

"Where has he gone—to the moon?"

It began to seem that way.

"I tried to start it this morning. The battery's dead."

I will hear from him today. She told herself that on the day that the letter she had written to William J. Cassidy, 314 Elm Street, Lafayette, Indiana, was returned to her with a livid purple stamp in the shape of an accusatory, finger-pointing hand on the face of the envelope, and the message: "Addressee unknown. Return to sender."

"*I must hear something from him soon!*" she began telling herself aloud in the darkness of her bedroom. ⸗

But the days continued to go by. She went back to school, and she heard nothing.

At Clay County Regional High, a tall, thin woman named Lucille Withers, who ran the Lucille Withers Modeling Agency in Kansas City, came to talk to the girls about careers in modeling. After her lecture, Miss Withers stepped over to Alex. "I noticed you in the audience," she said. "I might be able to do something for you. You have a certain look."

"I've always thought my chin was too small."

"Mm—maybe. But a good model needs a good flaw. And I like the way you dress. That's a very smart-looking two-piece—clever, mixing checks and stripes. You have a sense of style. Here's my card. Look me up the next time you're in the city." And she handed Alex her business card.

"Any messages for me, Mother?"
"No, dear."
"No letter for me today?"
"No, dear."
I will never hear from him again, she decided. And, gradually, she felt that blindingly bright crimson light that had been beamed into her life that summer, and the great billow of hot wind that had seemed to fill her with its force and to give her head the airy lightness of an untethered balloon, beginning to fade. And in its place began to grow that thin, hard, cold and bitter sliver of ice in her heart.
To hell with him, she thought.

But it wasn't that easy. It was one thing to say to hell with him, but quite another to forget him. Does one ever really forget that first, great agonizing love? By October, she had the battery of the yellow Corvette recharged, and had begun practicing her driving seriously, spending an hour or so each day driving up and down country roads. By the end of the month, she decided she was ready to apply for her learner's permit. This allowed her to drive during daylight hours. She had driven to Kansas City and placed Skipper's money in a savings account where, she reasoned, it would at least earn interest. But, because he had promised her she could have one, she withheld enough money to buy herself a portable sewing machine, and she returned to designing and making her own clothes.

She drove to Topeka, the Kansas state capital, and found the state police headquarters. But no one there had any record of an arrest, the previous August, of anyone named James R. Purdy, or William J. Cassidy, or anyone named Johnson. The state police suggested that it might have been a matter involving the Wichita City Police Department. She drove to Wichita, where it was suggested that pertinent records might be found in Topeka; a sympathetic desk sergeant offered her two tickets to the Wichita Police Department's Annual

Thanksgiving Turkey Dinner for the Poor. The rodeo had long since left the Wichita Fairgrounds, and she telephoned Omaha, their next stop. But the rodeo had left Omaha as well, and no one had any idea where it might have been headed after that.

At the beginning of Christmas vacation, she drove to Kansas City again, and presented herself at the offices of the Lucille Withers Modeling Agency, and was pleased to find that Miss Withers remembered her.

"Stand up," said Miss Withers, who wore a pince-nez on a long silk cord and placed this instrument across the bridge of her thin, hawklike nose. "Now walk around, walk back and forth—that's right. Now turn. Try turning your toes outward just a little when you walk. Yes, like that, not too much." Lucille Withers was making notes on a long yellow pad as she talked. "Now turn again. Shoulders back a little. Chin up. That's it. Swing your hair—that's it. Try swinging your shoulders a little as you walk. Now take smaller steps. Turn on your heel. Let me see your hands. Good. Now put your hands in the pockets of your skirt. Try jutting out your hips a bit as you walk—tuck the fanny in. That's it. That's a pretty girl. Sexy Lexy."

No one had ever called her Lexy before, and she rather liked it.

"We're going to be partners, and we're going to be pals," Miss Withers said. "You're to call me Lulu. Only certain very special pals get to call me that. Now let me see you sit. Sit down *slowly*. Cross your legs. Age? . . . Weight? . . . Dress size? . . . Height? . . . Waist? . . . Bust? . . . Hips? . . . Shoe size? . . . Glove size?" Lulu Withers wrote all these numbers down. "Yes," she said at last, surveying Alex again from head to toe through the pince-nez. "You do have a certain style. And, as I said before, I like the way you dress. That skirt-and-sweater outfit—mixing plum with orange. Very *smart*, very snappy. Where do you buy your clothes, anyway? Certainly not in that hellhole called Paradise."

"Actually, I made the skirt myself."

"*Really?* Where do you get the patterns?"

"From my own designs."

"Really?" she said again, looking impressed. "That means you not only have a sense of *style*, you have a sense of

fashion. And that's rather rare, you know. Most of my girls
don't have that, I'm sorry to say. It's rare to find a fashion
model with a real sense of fashion. Most girls are simply
thinking in terms of what their precious bodies are doing
for the clothes they're wearing. They think from the inside
out. They don't think of what the clothes they're wearing
are doing for them, from the outside in. Fashion is cosmetics in cloth. Your feeling for clothes can help your modeling
career, and I'm pretty sure I can use you. There's a catalogue
job coming up at Stix's, and I'm going to push Lexy Baby
for the teen pages. But first I'm going to send you around to
a photographer pal of mine"—she jotted a name and address
on a slip of paper—"and have him do some shots of you.
Then we'll make up a composite for you, and take it from
there."

"How much do models make?" Alex asked.

"In this town, twenty-five an hour max for photography.
For runway work, less. We're not New York or L.A. or even
Chicago, I'm sorry to say. I might be able to start you off for
fifteen or twenty an hour. We'll see. But tell me something,
Sexy Lexy. What do you really want to be?"

"Be?"

"Uh-huh. Say, ten years from now. What do you want
to be?"

Alex looked at her new friend steadily. "I just want to be
the most famous, most successful woman in the world," she
said. "That's all."

Lucille Withers clapped her hands. "Good!" she said. "Yes,
Lexy honey, I really like your style."

Yes, to hell with him, she told herself again. May he roast
on a spit in hell, the way his preacher father said he would.
And at that exact moment she made a second solemn promise to herself. Dear God, she told herself—dear God, if there
is a God, I swear to You, dear God, that from this moment
onward, and for the rest of my life, the only person I will
ever trust to take care of me is *me.*

She was remembering that vow now as she stepped out
into the evening sunlight of Fifth Avenue. She had decided
to walk the few blocks to the Lombardy for her meeting with
Rodney McCulloch and his wife. Had she been so intent, over
the years, on taking care of herself that she had neglected to

care for others who had been entrusted to her care? Steven, for instance? Would he have done what he had done if she had been able to show him that she cared about him? Years ago, she had gone to see a famous Swiss psychiatrist, Dr. Richard—pronounced *Reekard*—Lenhardt, to try to find out what was troubling her marriage to Steven. "Why do you want so much control?" he had asked her. "You want to control your magazine. You also seem to want to control your husband. You even want to control the way he feels about you."

A couple of years ago, *Time* magazine published a profile of Alexandra Rothman under the headline "Fashion's High Priestess" in which the writer described her as an "icy-cool Olympian beauty." Olympian. Control. The Ice Goddess. She had not particularly cared for that description of herself, though the article was accurate enough:

Asked to describe her editorial philosophy, Style Arbiter Alex Rothman, 44, says, "I'm in show biz. I'm part of the entertainment industry. Fashion is entertainment. It's supposed to give the audience a little lift. So is a fashion magazine. I like to think of my readers coming away from my pages whistling, feeling a little better about themselves. Editing a magazine is like tossing a party for good friends. I want my readers to come away from each issue thinking, 'Wasn't that fun? Didn't we have a good time? Wasn't So-and-so charming? Wasn't So-and-so interesting?' But of course, every hostess knows that no party is ever *perfect*. There are always little flaws that maybe only the hostess notices. Even the best cooks sometimes complain that they can never really taste their food. They have to rely on what their guests say about it. And so, with each issue, I try to throw a better and better party. To do this, you have to keep stretching, honing, fine-tuning, experimenting with all the ingredients of party-giving at your disposal. The impossible goal is to completely captivate every one of your guests, and make them want to come back to your house again and again for more of what you have to offer. To make them want to come back to your house more often than to anyone else's. That's why my favorite editorial phrases are 'vivify' and 'fox it up.' "

Fox it up?

"It's a somewhat indelicate expression from the western rodeo circuit," says Rothman. "It means give it a
little extra twist, a little more bounce, a little more
spirit—the better to utterly captivate your audience, my
dear" . . .

Control. And the opposite of control was luck, and luck
was love, and love was sacrifice.

Mel had shown her what it was by hammering a nail into
a white wall, and hanging a painting he didn't really care for.
And yet, she realized, she hadn't heard from him all day. In
a kind of panic, she thought: Will I lose him, too, the way
I've lost all the others?

In his office on the thirtieth floor, Herbert J. Rothman
was talking on his speaker phone while a bootblack applied
cordovan polish to the tips of his Lob shoes. Using the
speaker phone left both of his hands free to attend to other
matters which, at the moment, involved depositing various
objects from the top of his desk—a sterling silver paperweight presented to him by the American Association of
Advertising Agencies, a silver desk calendar, a silver ruler
engraved H.J.R., a silver calculator, a silver water carafe,
a Steuben candy jar, various family photographs in silver
frames—into a series of packing boxes that lay about the
floor. Miss Lincoln, his secretary, had supervised the major
packing of his office earlier in the day, but had left the packing of the personal objects—such as the little black address
book in the back of his lefthand drawer, which she wasn't
supposed to know about, but did—to him.

"How is your headache tonight, my darling?" he asked the
speaker phone.

"No better, I'm afraid," came back the English-accented
woman's voice from the little box. "It's my nerves, I know.
My nerves are bad, Herbert, really bad. It's all this uncertainty and suspense. I don't know how much longer I can go on
like this, Herbert. I really don't. Not knowing—"

"Please be patient, my darling. Can I see you tonight?"

"I can't *believe* she's not resigned! After that ad in this
morning's paper. But you say she's not—"

"Not yet. Not a word. So please be—"

"I spoke with Mona Potter earlier today. She said that it seems absolutely incredible to her that she hasn't resigned. She simply doesn't understand it. She says the woman must have the hide of a rhinoceros. She says—"

"Mona Potter is on our team," he said.

"Yes, but how much *longer*, Herbert? How much longer must I be kept dangling, while that bloody bitch—?"

"It won't be long, my darling. Can I see you tonight?" He lowered his face to the speaker phone. "My cock can't wait to get in that hot little pussy of yours, darling. Is your hot little pussy panting?"

She laughed. "Of course it is. But my nerves are totally shot. What if you were simply to give her the sack? You said you could do that, Herbert. Why not just sack her?"

"I can't do that just now, darling," he said. "She's already spoken with her lawyers. They've brought up the matter of her contract. They're asking questions about certain trust funds. I can't afford another lawsuit at this point. I've told you about the IRS business, and our lawyers say that another lawsuit at this point in time would—"

"Then what *are* you going to do, pray tell?"

"I'm doing everything I can, within certain legal parameters that our lawyers have warned me about, to force her resignation."

"But it isn't bloody working, is it?"

"Darling, I am following the advice of legal counsel. They have recommended this psychological approach—the step-by-step withdrawal of her perquisites, for instance. I've already discontinued her limousine service. I've run the ad, exactly as you wrote it—"

"But nothing's bloody working! She hasn't bloody budged!"

A testy note was creeping into his voice. "Fiona, please don't nag," he said. "You're not pretty when you nag. You're not attractive when you nag. When you nag, you remind me of—"

"Your wife? Is that what you're trying to say? That I remind you of your wife? That wife you say you bloody hate?"

"Now, darling, I didn't say that," he said in a more soothing tone. "I would never say that. I'm simply saying that, on the advice of legal counsel, in light of the IRS situation, we are trying to wear her down to the point where she will be forced, if she is going to retain any sense of pride at all, to submit her—"

"Oh, fuck your bloody Inland Revenue, and fuck your lawyers, too," she said.

"It's you I need to fuck," he said. "Tonight?"

"Please don't make jokes. Just tell me what's supposed to happen next."

"Well," he said, looking around at the packing cartons that contained the contents of his office, "there are actually several further steps in our campaign to break this lady's will. Tomorrow morning, for instance, I'm moving into my father's old office. That should send a very strong signal to her that Ho Rothman's regime is over, and that a new regime has been established in its place."

"And if that doesn't work? And who's to say it will?"

"Next, I'm going to order painters into her office. The one they call her little jewel box, with all those magazine covers on the walls. I'm going to order all those covers stripped off, and the office repainted. By the way, is there any special color you'd like it repainted? Because that office will be yours one day soon, my darling."

"Chinese red," she said. "And her apartment, too. Don't forget you promised me I could have her apartment, too, and I'm getting bloody tired of living in a hotel."

"That will come *next*," he said. "I will have her evicted from ten Gracie. All these things I can do without violating the terms of her contract, and without fear of her taking legal action. You see, our plan is to wear her down, wear her down, bit by bit, day by day, until her spirit breaks, or her nerves snap."

"And it sounds like it's going to take bloody forever. I told you I wanted that terrace glassed in, didn't I? I can't stand a bloody open terrace."

"You shall have your glassed-in terrace, my darling," he said. "That is a promise. Just be patient. These things take time. Believe me, I'm as eager to get rid of her as you are."

Her tone remained petulant. "Why do they *need* to take so much time? You know, you told me once, Herbert, that you had enough evidence about her to send her back to that little village she came from in Ohio or wherever it is, with *nothing.* Evidence enough so she'd never be able to work in this business again. Evidence about that man she killed. Why not use that evidence? Now."

"Unfortunately, you misunderstood me, my darling. I didn't say evidence. I said suspicions. Strong suspicions. But no real evidence. Or, let me say, half a piece of evidence, which is inconclusive. The other half is missing."

"Then find it," she said.

"Easier said than done, my love."

"Evidence can be bought."

"But where? From whom?"

She was silent for a moment. Then she said, "What about Lenny Liebling? They say he knows where all the bodies are buried. Try him. Lenny Liebling can be bought."

He whistled softly. "You know," he said, "you may have something there. That happens to be a brilliant suggestion. That happens to be a suggestion bordering on genius, my darling. You've just given me another reason why I want you to be the next editor-in-chief of *Mode*, as well as the next Mrs. Herbert Rothman."

"Then get cracking on it," she said.

The bootblack took a final swipe with his polishing cloth across the tops of Herbert Rothman's shoes, and then tapped the tips of his toes with his fingertip to indicate that he was finished. Herb Rothman slid a five-dollar bill across the top of the desk in the bootblack's direction.

"Can I see you tonight, my darling?"

She seemed to hesitate. Then she said, "No. My nerves are just too shot tonight. Tomorrow night, perhaps. Ring me up and we'll see."

"Oh, my love . . . my love . . ."

"Ta."

The bootblack packed his tools inside his combination footrest—squat–box.

At that same moment, Alex Rothman stepped across a crack in the sidewalk with grass growing in it, looked up, and realized that she was lost. She was in a neighborhood she had never been in before. It was shabby and rundown. Overflowing cans of garbage lined the sidewalks. On the stoops of tenements, young men in sleeveless T-shirts sat drinking beer, and from a fire escape above, using an uncased pillow as an armrest, an enormously fat woman was having an unintelligible, but very loud, conversation with a friend in the apartment below. Out in the street, two unleashed dogs of no recognizable breed chased each other in endless circles. *Where am I*? she asked herself in terror. *Am I losing control of myself*? She had no idea where she was, and hurried toward the corner of the block, where surely there would be a street sign to help her get her bearings. "Hey, where's the party, sweetheart?" one of the undershirted men called to her from a stoop at the sight of this strange, fashionably dressed woman at dusk in his neighborhood. "Yeah," called another, lifting his beer can. "Wanna party here? Hey, sweetheart, what's your hurry? I got a party here, sweetheart," he said, patting his groin, and there followed a number of catcalls and wolf whistles at the woman who had dressed on Gracie Square that morning for Arnold Scaasi's winter resort collection at the St. Regis Roof, and was now walking through a slum.

"Aw, she's old enough to be your mother, Rico," she heard another voice say.

When she reached the corner, she saw that somehow, out of control, she had walked eleven blocks in the opposite direction from the Lombardy. She stepped into the street, her arm raised, praying for a taxi.

And for an awful moment—at least until she saw the reassuring yellow roof light of an approaching cab—she was back in the schoolyard in Paradise, with Dale Smith and the other eighth-graders about to hog-pile her.

"Ah, good evening, Wally!" Lenny said cheerfully as the black man entered his office and set down his box and began removing his tools and polishes. Lenny extended his left foot onto the footrest. "Now these are crocodile, Wally," he said. "So pay special attention to any dust that collects in the little ridges of the leather."

Wally wielded his brush. "Heard an inneresting conversation up on thirty, Mr. Liebling," Wally said.

"Ah," Lenny beamed. "Tell Uncle Lenny all. And don't forget that I'm remembering you handsomely in my will."

Chapter 28

"Forty-six separate coats of lacquer," Rodney McCulloch was saying almost defiantly. "Forty-six separate *coats*. That's what it took to get this effect. It looks like black mirror, doesn't it?"

"Extraordinary," Alex said. "Who did you say your decorator was?"

"Billy Yardley of Ottawa," he said. "Ours was the last job he did before he died of the AIDS. Faggot, of course. They all are."

This lugubrious piece of information added a sudden mortuary note to the McCullochs' living room, which, in Alex's opinion, needed no help in that direction.

"He also did Margaret Trudeau's new house," he added. "I guess that's a pretty good endorsement, ha-ha-ha."

The entire room—two stories high—was done in black and gold. The shimmering black walls, under their "forty-six separate coats" of lacquer, rose to the distant ceiling covered with more black lacquer, from the center of which descended a huge golden chandelier, necklaced with crystal prisms. Flanking the central fireplace, in which an artificial fire flickered behind a glass screen, were two sofas, each easily eighteen feet long, with ormolu gilt frames and covered in black toy plush. Along the buttoned backs of these pieces were arrayed a display of plush toss pillows, alternately black and gold. Between the sofas had been placed an equally long, low coffee table, with a gilded metal frame and a black onyx top. Throughout the room were scattered many—far too many—other pieces of furniture: tables, vitrines, prie-dieux, stiff little *Régence* chairs, cabinets, bombés, and chests, all of black and gold. On every flat surface in the room were arranged objects—clocks, boxes, pyramids, candlesticks, snuffboxes, inkwells, decorative vases, and statuettes of dancing nymphs and lyre-playing fauns—all of black onyx and vermeil. Four tall east-facing windows were draped with gold cut-velvet hangings tied back with wrist-thick black velvet ropes. The thick sculptured carpet was of a floral pattern of black and gold and, in the center of the long coffee table, was an enormous arrangement of black and gold silk flowers—roses, lupines, gladioli, tulips, hydrangeas, and hollyhocks.

"He's certainly been consistent with his color scheme, hasn't he?" Alex murmured.

"Sit down," Rodney McCulloch said, and she settled herself in one of the long black plush sofas, accepting the glass of wine he handed her, and he seated himself opposite her, briefly disappearing behind the bouquet of silk flowers. "Get these damn flowers out of the way," he said, pushing aside the vase and coming into view again. "Now, you know me. I don't like to beat around the bush. I like to get right down to brass tacks, and not waste time with any bullshit. We're doing this for Maudie, right? And we're going to do it *right*— right? No shortcuts. Now Maudie's a good-looking broad— hell, you'll see that when you meet her—but the thing is, she doesn't have a hell of a lot of class. I think that's why these fancy New York broads have been high-hatting her, giving her the snoot. Hell, I've seen the way some of 'em look at her. They look at her like they're looking at a plate of spoiled fish." He twisted his face into an exaggerated expression of disgust. "But, hell, why should she have any class? She grew up on a beet farm on the plains of Manitoba, where the nearest thing to a big town, Winnipeg, was six hundred miles away. Maudie's people were poor, dirt poor. Uneducated. Maudie never went past high school, not like you—"

"I'm a country girl myself, darlin'," Alex said. "And I never went beyond high school, either. Your wife and I should have a lot in common."

His eyes widened. "No kidding? I figured you for one of those finishing-school types. Well, I guess that just proves that what I want done for Maudie can be done, which gets back to Maudie's problem—no class. Hell, I know she's got no class, and I've told her she's got no class, and *she* knows she's got no class. But what the hell to do about it? That's what has us stumped. It's not that I don't let her spend money. Hell, Maudie spends a damn fortune on clothes, and I let her, but she still doesn't look quite right, and that's where you come in. When I bring Maudie down here, I want you to look her up and down and tell us just exactly what's wrong with her. Start at the top, with her hairdo. Then go to her jewelry"—he pronounced it *joolery*—"and then the dress she's wearing, the stockings, the shoes, the whole thing, top to bottom."

"Now wait a minute, Rodney," she said easily, taking a sip of wine. "Surely you don't expect me to let your nice wife walk in here and immediately begin telling her what's wrong with her—a woman I've just met."

He looked surprised. "Why not? That's what I've told her you're going to do. That's what she expects. Your candy opinion. Wasn't that part of our deal? You get my money to start a new magazine. I get you to class-up Maudie."

"To begin with, darlin', we don't have a deal. Not yet, anyway. For another thing, your wife is a human being, not a dressmaker's dummy. If I'm going to help her in any way, I'll need to get to know her. I'll need to get my eye in. That's an expression we use in the fashion business—'getting your eye in.' It means getting the feel of the person, her personality, her—"

"I told you the problem. She has no class. She has no personality."

"Come, come, Rodney. Everyone has a personality."

"Not her! I ought to know, I'm married to the broad. That's why we both want you to come right out and tell her, flat out, what's wrong with her. No bullshitting around the bush."

"And if Maudie doesn't like what I tell her?"

"She'll damn well like it! 'Cause that's what I've told her she's going to do. She's going to do what you tell her to do, and I've told her so! Maudie will do what she's told."

Alex wondered briefly if this was the sort of man—even for all the money in the world—she would ever want to back

her in a new magazine venture, a man who treated women
as though they were wind-up dolls. She pushed this thought
aside. "Do you want this makeover on your wife for *her*—
or for yourself, Rodney?" she asked him.

He cast his eyes downward. "My Maudie's not happy," he
said. "She's not happy in New York. She wants to go back to
Manitoba. I don't want to lose her, Alex. I don't think I could
stand it if I lost her. I love her. I want to make my Maudie
happy." And she thought she saw tears standing in his eyes.

"And you're sure this is the way to do it?"

"It's a way to try," he said.

"Very well. Then when do I get to meet the lady?"

He jumped to his feet and moved quickly to the gilt-
banistered, black-carpeted staircase that curved upward to
the floor above. "*Maudie!*" he bellowed. "You can come
down now. We're ready for you!"

Slowly, and with a certain amount of deliberation and
precision, Maude McCulloch began her descent down the
gilded staircase from where she had been waiting, perhaps
not entirely out of earshot, somewhere in the upper reaches
of the apartment. What Alex saw was a tall woman, slender but not thin, with fair skin and large dark eyes behind
tortoiseshell-rimmed glasses, and thick, curly chestnut hair
that was probably not its original color. As she descended
the staircase, looking neither to the right nor left, she wore a
shy but determined half-smile. She had dressed to match her
living room, in a gold cashmere sweater with a cowl neck, the
sleeves pushed up above her elbows to reveal many chunky
gold bracelets at her wrists, and a hip-hugging leather miniskirt in a zebra print. Alex's first thought was that, though
the miniskirt might have been a mistake, this was a woman
not without a certain chic. If you saw her for the first time,
in a crowd, you would take a second look.

"Rodney says you're going to do me over from scratch,"
Maude McCulloch said as she crossed the room. "Well, this
is scratch." She patted her zebra skirt smartly. "Or as close
to scratch as I can get unless I came down in my underwear."
She sat, crossing her long legs at the knee, and let one black
patent pump dangle from her toe. There was something a
little defensive in the way she presented herself, but Alex
decided to ignore this.

"I'm delighted to meet you, Mrs. McCulloch," she said.

"It's Maude," she said, and with her index finger she fished out a cigarette from a gold and crystal box on the onyx table, tapped it on the back of her wrist, and lighted it with a gold table lighter. Between pursed lips, she blew out a long, thin stream of smoke, her chin held high, her gaze fixed on some indeterminate point in space between the others in the room and the lacquered ceiling. Maude McCulloch was not a beautiful woman, but she was certainly handsome, with high cheekbones, and there was a certain resolute set to her jawline that suggested both fixity of purpose and repressed desire. As she held her cigarette to her lips, Alex could not help noticing that her fingernails had been bitten to the quick. Also, small pinched lines at the corners of her mouth and eyes indicated that her life had not been an entirely easy one. Certainly marriage to Rodney McCulloch had been no lotus land, and briefly Alex wondered whether Rodney had ever beaten his wife. Then she decided that he probably had not.

Yet there was something about Maude McCulloch that suggested that she had long ago struck a deal with this man and the life he offered her, difficult though it was, and that, to the best of her ability, she had kept her end of the bargain, through good times and disasters. Alex's first impression of Maude McCulloch was that she was a straight shooter. Her second impression was that she was a tough cookie— an unhappy tough cookie, but still a tough one.

"Look," Maude McCulloch said, slapping her skirt again, "I don't always dress like this. I don't even think I look good in miniskirts. I only wore this because Rodney—but never mind. In my closets upstairs, I've got clothes by all the top designers. He makes me buy them. I've got dresses by Chanel, Dior, Ungaro, Valentino, Adolfo, Lacroix—" She looked at her husband for the first time. "Rodney, why are we wasting this poor woman's time?" she asked.

"Hey, that's a swell idea," he said, hunching forward in the sofa. "Why don't you take Alex upstairs, and go through all your closets? She'll tell you which outfits are fashionable, and worth saving, and which can be tossed out. Easy! Ha-ha-ha."

"Oh, I don't think I need to do that," Alex murmured. "I'm sure Maude has many beautiful clothes." She turned to his wife. "Maude, suppose you tell me what it is you want—

what you think I might be able to do for you."

"She wants to be in Mona's column," he said. "She wants to meet the right people, and not have them look at her like she's a plate of spoiled fish." He made his spoiled-fish face again.

"Well, that part's easy," Alex said. "Mona's certainly aware of who you are. But I'll give you a little hint. As a newspaper-woman, Mona doesn't make a lot of money, and so the people Mona writes about supplement her income with little gifts."

"You mean you can *buy* your way into Mona's column?" Rodney said. "Why, that's like being a whore!"

"You said that, Rodney, not I," Alex said with a smile. "But Mona doesn't accept money. She'll accept gifts, though. A case of champagne. A pound of caviar. But Mona likes jewelry best, rubies in particular. She also likes to be taken out to lunch. All you need to do, Maude, is invite Mona to lunch at Mortimer's. Then follow it up with a little some-thing—nothing too lavish, just a little something from Van Cleef's or Cartier. That'll get you mentioned in Mona's col-umn at least once a week for the next six months. By then, it will be Christmas—time for another little gift. Simple."

"Make a note of that, Maudie," her husband said. "Mor-timer's. Van Cleef. Cartier. Something for the whore."

"But Maude," Alex said. "You still haven't told me what *you* want."

"She wants to be in fashion, she wants to be in style. She wants—"

"Rodney, will you please stop answering all her questions for me?" his wife said sharply. "You haven't let me get a word in edgewise, for Christ's sake!" He sat back, looking chagrined.

"She's right. Let's hear from Maude," Alex said.

"I told you what Maudie wants. She wants—" But Alex shushed him with a gesture.

"*What I want*," Maude said, taking a long drag on her cigarette, "isn't really a hell of a lot when you get right down to it. But there are a few things. I'd like to be taken a little bit seriously, for one thing. I'd like to be treated like a human being, for another. I'd like to be listened to from time to time. From time to time, I'd like a little attention to be paid. People pay attention to Rodney because he's made all this money. Because he's made all this money, they think he must be smart. Well, I happen to be smart, too. I may not have much formal education, but I happen to have a brain! Do you know that this so-called financial genius that I married can't do long division? Do you know that this so-called financial genius even has trouble with addition and subtraction? Do you know that he can't even balance his personal checkbook? I have to do that for him. There are other things I could tell you about this man I married. He says he made his first big money from inventing flavored pacifiers. He made his first big money as a butter salesman—selling fourteen-ounce pounds of butter off a truck. He doesn't tell *that* to the reporters from *Time* magazine. I've gotten used to all that. I'm used to his vulgarity and his boorishness and his crudity and his insensitivity and his cruelty, and his going 'Ha-ha-ha' every time he says something that isn't funny. He doesn't mind being called the Billionaire Bumpkin, because it happens to have the word *billionaire* in it, but all the bumpkin business is mostly an act, anyway. Do you know his dentist has begged him to let him straighten and cap his teeth? But he won't have it done because he thinks crooked teeth make him look sincere. Why do you think he combs his hair the way he does? Why does he insist on wearing suits that don't fit? So people will say he's a genius hayseed. But what am I supposed to be? His bumpkinette? What am I supposed to be noticed for? Meanwhile, I've raised his seven children for him. I've—"

"Wait," Alex said. "Tell me about the children. You've just given me an idea."

"Well, none of them are dopers, none of them are dropouts, none of them are in jail, if that's what you mean. The kids are all doing fine."

"What if Maude McCulloch were noticed in New York for *motherhood*? For being a superb mother."

"What's motherhood got to do with fashion?" her husband wanted to know.

"Nothing. That's just it. But it's something to be noticed for, which is what Maude wants. These so-called fashionable New York women aren't interested in being mothers. Pregnant is the last thing any of them wants to be. My friend Lenny Liebling calls them the Razor Blades."

"Nah, I don't like it," Rodney said.

"Shut up, Rodney," his wife said. "*I like it!*"

"But what about fashion? Clothes? Style? Class?"

"Fashion and style and class are more than just clothes,"
Alex said. "But I do believe that every smart woman who
wants to be taken seriously should have some sort of what
I call a fashion signature. It doesn't need to be much. This
triple strand of pearls I always wear, for instance. That happens to be mine. I don't know how it got to be, but it did."

"Okay, give Maudie a fashion signature, then. And make
it a good one."

"Rodney, will you please shut *up!*"

"Try something for me, Maude," Alex said. "Pull your
hair back away from your face." Maude McCulloch pulled
her hair back with both hands, and twisted it at the back of her
neck. "Yes, I like your hair that way. You have lovely skin,
and a lovely wide forehead. What if your fashion signature
were a little Chanel-type bow at the back of your head? You
could have different bows for different outfits."

"*What?* I'm talkin' fashion, and you're talkin' ribbon-
bows!"

"Rodney, I'm warning you! Put a lid on it!" his wife
said.

"It's a bit of an old-fashioned look," Alex said. "But it's
different, and it goes with you."

"*Old-fashioned?* We want Maudie to look fashionable, not
old-fashioned!"

"Maude is a nice, old-fashioned name," Alex said. "It's
distinctive. I don't think I know of another Maude in New
York."

"Okay, make a note of that hairdo style, Maudie," her husband said. "Tell whatsisname to do that to you, and get some
of those whatchamacallit-type bows."

His wife bared her teeth at him, and went, "*Grrrrrr!*"

"But what about dresses? All those designer dresses that
she's got. When're you going to tell us which ones she ought
to wear and which ones we're gonna throw out?"

"I usually recommend that a woman find one designer that
suits her," Alex said. "And then stick to that designer. And
the minute I saw Maude walk down that stair, I immediately
thought—Pauline Trigère."

"Make a note of that, Maudie. Pauline Trigère."

"Oh, for Christ's sake, Rodney! I've heard of Pauline
Trigère!"

"And all that stuff from those other faggots—out with the garbage. Down the incinerator."

"I could take you over to Pauline's workshop, if you'd like," Alex said. "Let her get her eye in with you, as they say. Sketch a few things for you."

"Yes! I'd like that!" Maude McCulloch said.

"Pauline's a bit out of fashion right now, but—"

"Out of *fashion!* But I thought we were going to put Maudie *into* fashion."

Alex smiled at him. "But Maude McCulloch is going to bring Pauline Trigère back into fashion, Rodney," she said.

Suddenly Maude McCulloch jumped to her feet and ran around the huge onyx coffee table to where Alex sat, hugged her, and kissed her noisily on both cheeks. "I love you!" she cried. Then, releasing her, she said, "I hate this apartment."

"*What?*" her husband shouted. "Do you know how much it cost me to do over this apartment? Do you know how much I shelled out to that Billy Yardley faggot?"

"Of course I know. I balance your checkbook, don't I? It cost too much. And what did we get for it? A place that looks like it belongs in Las Vegas. In a high-class whorehouse."

"*What?*" he cried again. "Alex, didn't you say you thought this apartment was beautiful?"

Alex hesitated. "I don't think I actually said that," she said. "I think I said something like 'extraordinary.' "

"Black and gold, black and gold—once he got off on black and gold, he couldn't stop," Maude McCulloch said. "My bathroom's got black sinks, a black toilet, a black Jacuzzi, and a black bidet. What kind of a woman would use a black bidet?"

"You *don't* think the apartment's beautiful, Alex?" Rodney McCulloch said.

"Let me put it this way," she said. "I think Maude McCulloch deserves better."

He let out a despairing howl. Then his chin sank to his chest and his shoulders sagged. "You're right," he said. "You know what I first said when I saw this room, Maudie? I said it looks like a faggot's wet dream. It still looks like a faggot's wet dream."

"I can give you the names of some excellent New York decorators, if you should decide to do it over," Alex said. She knew it was time to go.

* * *

Alone in the apartment with her husband, Maude McCulloch stood in front of one of the gilt-framed mirrors with her hair pulled back away from her face. "She's right," she said. "I do have nice skin for a woman my age. I have a good forehead, too." She removed her glasses. "I'm going to get contacts," she said.

"They'll make your eyes itch."

"Hmm," she said.

"Maudie," he said. "Those things you said about me when she was here. I know I'm a boor, but you used the word *cruelty*. Have I ever been cruel to you, Maudie?"

"Oh, I'm used to it," she said.

"I've never been unfaithful to you, Maudie."

"No, I don't expect you have. So. She's done this for you. What are you going to do for her? What's the quid pro quo? With you, there's always a quid pro quo."

"I'm going to let her develop her own new magazine."

"Really?" she said. She was still studying her reflection in the glass. "Why? She already has *Mode*."

"Not for long she won't. Herb Rothman's about to give her the ax."

"Really? Why?"

"There's a new Limey cunt wants her job. The Limey cunt's got him completely pussy-whipped. That's the scuttlebutt. The Limey cunt wants Alex canned, and whatever the Limey cunt wants from Herb, the Limey cunt gets, according to the scuttlebutt. As the Canucks say, *sher-shay la fame*. Anyway, I'm hoping Alex'll be canned soon."

"Oh? Why?"

" 'Cause the sooner she gets canned, the sooner she'll belong to me. And on my terms." Now he looked gloomily around the room. "Forty-six separate coats of lacquer," he said.

Not many blocks uptown from the Lombardy, the young woman with the helmet of dark hair was saying, "It was really terribly kind of you to come up here tonight, Mel. But I knew from the moment I met you that you were one of the kindest men I'd ever met. It's funny, but I have a sort of antenna about kind people. I recognize kind people right away. I can also recognize people who are not kind—cruel people. And I think I shall never forget what you said to me that night we met."

"Oh? I'm afraid I've forgotten. What was it?"

"Mel! How could you have forgotten? You said, 'Sometimes it helps to share your feelings with another person.' And it's so true. It helped me then, and it's helping me right now—to share my feelings with you. It helps so much."

"I'm glad, Fiona."

"And so the thing is, if you can just do something to get her to call off her lawyers. Once you bring barristers into a situation, it just makes things worse, it seems to me. It just makes things uglier."

"Believe me, I know all about lawyers," he said.

"Of course—that hideous divorce you went through! But in this situation, with her bringing in lawyers, it drives an even deeper wedge into an already deeply divided family. I know Herbert and Alex have never got on all that famously, but if she ends up suing Herbert, what will that do to the relationship between Herbert and his only grandson? Herbert adores Joel, and he wants Joel to succeed him one day as the head of the company. But a lawsuit could absolutely poison Joel's relationship with his grandfather. It could also poison Joel's relationship with dear old Aunt Lily. And it's really such a small family. To see it ripped apart by a lawsuit seems tragic to me."

"I know what you mean," he said.

"Of course you do! You've seen your own little family ripped apart by a lawsuit. And you can see my position— right in the middle. This trouble is all because of *me!* That's why I'd like to see this settled amicably, without bloody lawyers."

"Of course. But Alex's point is—"

"Herbert is a very determined man. He's determined to get me onto his masthead in some shape or form. He's already made a public announcement. He feels he *can't* back down at this point. If he did, it would be a terrible blow to his pride. If he did, he would suffer a terrible loss of face in the entire media community. People would say he'd been bested by his daughter-in-law. He'd be a laughingstock. So, given this situation, wouldn't it be better for all concerned if Alex Rothman and I could just sit down together and try to work out a solution where we could coexist in the company? I'd certainly be willing to listen to any suggestions she might have. I'm really an easy person to get on with, Mel."

"I'm sure you are, Fiona. But I just don't think you realize how much her magazine means to Alex. For the last twenty years, it's been the most important thing in her life."

"Oh, I'm sure it has. That's quite apparent from the wonderful success she's made of it. She's devoted nearly a third of her life to *Mode*, even at the expense, I suppose, of her own son—though I shouldn't say that, since I don't know her son. But I'm sure the magazine is the one true love of her life."

"She worked hard to get the terms of the contract she has now," he said. "And she feels—rightly, I think—that the terms of that contract should be honored."

"Oh, I do agree. But I think these things can be sorted out without bloody lawyers lining up on both sides, and driving a deeper wedge between members of the family. There are human ways to settle differences without bringing in barristers and their briefs. It's like national differences, isn't it? Isn't it better to solve national differences through diplomacy, rather than all-out war? It was a war that cost me my young husband's life."

"Well, I'll speak to her," he said. "I'll see what I can do. But I'm not sure anything I say will change Alex's mind. She's very angry at Herb Rothman. She feels Herb's trying to double-cross her, and I tend to agree."

"Oh, *would* you speak to her? That would be so kind. Even if it did no good, it couldn't hurt, could it—if she'd agree to let us settle this as human beings, without the lawyers? I'd be so grateful if you'd speak to her, because I'd do anything—anything—to see this bollix sorted out. I suppose I was naïve, but when I accepted Herbert's offer, I was so thrilled—I'd no *idea* of the kind of bollix I'd be walking into. These last few days have been terribly hard on me. You've no idea of the stress I've been under. The press have been hounding me. I've become a virtual prisoner in this hotel."

"I saw your interview in Mona Potter's column."

"That was the only interview Herbert wanted me to give, because Mona is his personal friend. And now, on top of everything else, all this publicity has meant that my father has found out where I am. He's threatening to send detectives after me. Everybody, it suddenly seems, is out to get me—including Alex Rothman, whom I've always admired so much. Mel, you've no idea what it's been like for me. It's been utter hell."

"Yes, I imagine it has been," he said.

"I'm not really frightened. I'm sure my father can't touch me in America. Still, it's worrisome—terribly worrisome. The thought of detectives after me. On top of everything else."

"Let me just ask you one question, Fiona."

"Yes?"

"If all this has turned into such a nightmare for you—"

"It has! It has!"

"Then why not just back out gracefully? Why not say it was all a misunderstanding on your part? That you had no idea of the complexity of the situation, but now you do, and so you gratefully decline Herb's offer. That way, Herb's famous pride would be intact, and you'd come out looking like a perfect lady. You could move on to something else."

"You mean go back to England? And the horrors that await me there?"

"Perhaps Herb Rothman could find something for you on one of his other magazines."

She hesitated. "There are several reasons why I can't do that," she said at last. "For one thing, I gave Herbert my word that I would take this job. This is the job Herb specifically wanted me to do, and I gave him my word that I would do it. And I am a woman of my word. Then there is the fact that I have always wanted to work for *Mode*. It has been my singleminded ambition—to work for the world's leading fashion magazine. This is an opportunity I have waited for all my life, and when Herbert offered it to me, I felt I simply could not turn it down. Then, aside from my personal ambition, there is my belief that I could bring a lot to *Mode*. I hope you won't mind my saying that I believe in my talent, and that *Mode* is the best—the only—place where I can use that talent. I think *Mode* is a wonderful magazine, but I believe I can make it even more wonderful, and Herbert believes that too. And I feel I can't in good conscience betray Herbert's belief and trust in me. But finally, of course, there is little Primrose."

"Little Primrose?"

"My daughter, Primrose. I deliberately didn't tell you about Primmy, because—because it's such a painful thing to tell about. But you see, when Eric was killed in the Falklands, I was six months pregnant. Primmy was born three months after that. Primmy is a sweet child, but she was born hopelessly retarded. The doctors blamed my shock at Eric's death. Primmy now goes to a special school in Switzerland. For years, nearly every sou I earned went for Primmy's care. But when Herbert Rothman offered me this post at *Mode*, I had very nearly run out of sous! That's why Herbert's offer seemed a gift from heaven! If it hadn't come when it did, I would have had to take her out of her special school. And the only alternative would have been to bring Primmy back to my father's house. And there—there—I would have always lived in terror that my father might have tried to do to little Primmy what he did to me." She brushed aside a tear. "And so—and so—that is why I need this job the most. For Primmy. I know you have two daughters, Mel. I think you understand. I need the money, Mel. I desperately need the money for Primmy's care."

His eyes moved around the Westbury Hotel suite, and she seemed to sense his question, for she said, "These glamorous digs are being rented for me by Rothman Publications. It was part of the arrangement when Herbert brought me over here. I wanted just a tiny basement flat, but Herbert insisted that I should live the way a glamorous fashion editor would, and Herbert is a very determined man. Oh, and I know all about the gossip, the rumors—that I'm Herbert's mistress, or something. Which is too ridiculous, since Herbert is even older than my father, and I personally don't find him physically at all attractive. But this was the way Herbert insisted on setting it up. And so here I am, sitting here, waiting for my first paycheck, because Primmy's tuition is already three weeks overdue." She dabbed at her eyes with a hanky.

She moved closer to him on the sofa now, and as she did so one thin shoulder strap of her long green chiffon hostess gown slipped from her shoulder, exposing a pale expanse of her upper breast, and it was a moment before she put it back in place. Once more, he was suddenly aware of the heavy odor of gardenia from her perfume. "I'm glad I told you about Primmy," she said. "I've told so few people about her. I've never even told Herbert Rothman about her. But you're different, Mel. Somehow I can tell you things I'd never tell another soul. I think it's because you're the kindest man I've ever met. And may I tell you that you are also one of the most attractive men I've ever known? And shall I tell you of the terribly naughty thing I did that night we met? That night you came to my rescue, and drove me home—the overdressed damsel in distress at the Van Zuylens' beach party?"

"What was that, Fiona?"

She laughed softly, and touched his sleeve. "It was really very naughty," she said. "And probably you'll think me quite mad. But after you dropped me off at the hotel, I suddenly had an overwhelming urge to see you again. Suddenly I desperately needed to see you again, and to talk to you again—the urge was overpowering. I called a taxi, and asked him if he knew where your house in Sagaponack was. It seems that everybody in the Hamptons knows Mel Jorgenson's house in Sagaponack! I took the taxi to your house, and told the driver to wait. I walked across the dunes to your house, but then—through the glass—I saw that she was there. I should have known that. So it was a totally crazy thing to do. But I had this absolutely uncontrollable desire to be with you, to talk to you, to have you hold me in your arms the whole night long, to have you make love to me." She lowered her cheek to his shoulder, and whispered, "Mel—I've never felt this way before. I felt I had to be honest with you. I felt I had to share my feelings with you. I can't help my feelings, can I?"

"No, Fiona. I suppose you can't help yourself." He started to rise.

"Please don't go, my darling," she said. "Let me freshen your drink."

"No, thanks," he said. "I'd really better go."

"Oh, please! I'm so alone!"

"Good night, Fiona."

"You won't forget your promise, will you?"

Chapter 29

When Ho Rothman purchased *Mode* in 1961, it was widely
assumed that his aim was to add status and respectability to
his family of publications which, at that time, had a somewhat tawdry reputation. "ROTHMAN SEEKS TO ERASE
SLEAZE IMAGE," said the *New York Times* at the time.
This was only partly true. Ho's son Herbert, then thirty-eight,
had just been given the title of president of the Publications
Division of Rothman Communications, Inc., and Herbert
Rothman and his wife Pegeen had hoped that the acquisition
of a magazine such as *Mode* would help them gain acceptance
and position in the social world of New York. Even more
important to Herbert and Pegeen was the notion that publishing a venerable fashion magazine like *Mode* would help them
attract a fashionable wife for their only son, Steven, who was
then a freshman at Princeton. Debutantes still left Foxcroft
and Porter to work in vaguely defined positions for insignificant salaries at *Mode*, where the magazine's headmistresslike
spinster editor, Consuelo Ferlinghetti, had announced that she
could tell how much a girl knew about fashion by the way she
tied a scarf.

Of course, if the family had not acquired *Mode*, Steven and
Alex would surely never have met. But Alexandra Lane was
not at all the Social Register sort of wife Herbert and Pegeen
had had in mind for Steven. By then, however, certain cir-

cumstances had caused Steven's parents to lower their sights considerably.

At the time, in addition to the string of small-city newspapers, Ho Rothman's Publications Division included *Homemaker*, a do-it-yourself magazine for young housewives; *Outdoors*, a sports magazine for men; *Teen*, a magazine, as the name implied, for teenage girls; *Teeing Off*, for golfers; *Your Wheels*, a magazine for car enthusiasts; *Dream House*, a shelter book on interior design, which had a sister publication called *Dream Garden*; a number of romance magazines variously titled *Strange Romance, Foreign Romance, Mature Romance* (for seniors), *Dark Romance* (for a black audience), *Illicit Romance*, and *Forbidden Romance;* and *Beefing It Up*, for bodybuilders. The company also published a Romance Comics series for young girls, Adventure Comics for boys, and a children's magazine called *Tiny Tots*. All these titles were extremely profitable.

Mode, on the other hand, had not shown any black ink for several years, which was why it had been put up for sale. Ho had originally opposed the purchase, though not necessarily for that reason. He disparaged the publication as "a little sissy fashion book. You want pipple to think we are a bunch of sissy pipple?" In fact, when the purchase was announced, one of Ho's lunchmates at the Harmonie Club greeted him with mincing gestures, uplifted pinky-fingers and lisping speech— which so infuriated Ho that he resigned from the club that afternoon and never set foot in it again.

Mode, however, had a long and distinguished history. It had been in existence since 1872, and had published exclusive pictures of every American First Lady's inaugural ball gown since that worn by Mrs. Rutherford B. Hayes. It had introduced American women to the vogue of the bustle. It had pioneered the lady's "duster" coat in the early era of the motor car. It had been first to publish the drawings of Charles Dana Gibson, and had thus launched the Gibson Girl look, which featured ruffled shirtwaists, and was therefore at least partly responsible for the Triangle Shirtwaist Company fire in 1911, where 146 young sweatshop seamstresses lost their lives. *Mode* had been first to present American women with Christian Dior's "New Look" in 1947.

But by the 1960s *Mode* had begun to seem largely irrelevant. Circulation and advertising revenues had fallen. Its readership was mostly in doctors' and dentists' offices, beauty parlors, and a few country clubs. As far as being a fashion force was concerned, the magazine had become a little like the Bible—nobody ever really read it, but it was considered a good idea to have a copy around the house, even if it was one of last year's issues.

Needless to say, the acquisition of a classic publication such as *Mode* by the raffish and upstart Rothmans was greeted with consternation by the men and women who then edited and staffed the magazine, including Consuelo Ferlinghetti, its editor-in-chief, who had for years proclaimed herself the unquestioned High Priestess of American Fashion. "I don't see how I can possibly edit a magazine for these peculiar people," Miss Ferlinghetti announced at the time. "They'll probably want to turn it into something called *Fashionable Romance*." Ho Rothman countered by repeatedly referring to *Mode* as "Mud," and to Miss Ferlinghetti as "Mrs. Spaghetti."

Consuelo Ferlinghetti's name led a petition signed by forty-nine of the magazine's other editors, staffers, and contributors protesting the sale, which read in part:

> We, the undersigned, find it intolerable to contemplate the sale of a magazine of *Mode*'s distinction and reputation to a publisher of sensational yellow journalism whose known disregard for editorial integrity flouts the very traditions and standards of excellence upon which *Mode* was founded.
> We unilaterally denounce . . .
> We unilaterally demand . . .

Of course the petition had no potency whatsoever, since the sale of the magazine was already an accomplished fact. But it was widely assumed that the much-publicized signing of it would be followed by a mass exodus of editors and staffers. In fact, there were no immediate defections. The editors and staffers stayed on, albeit grumblingly and complainingly, and Consuelo Ferlinghetti's famously painted eyebrows arched skyward, and she placed a lace hanky to her nostrils, as if gasping for smelling salts, whenever the Rothman name was mentioned in her presence.

But such was the outcry of indignation over the magazine's

sale that Herb Rothman felt it necessary to issue a statement to the press:

Both my father, H. O. Rothman, and I are getting a little tired of hearing Rothman Publications referred to as publishers of sensationalist journals, pulp magazines, and comic books.

True, we publish comic books, and we also publish a few magazine titles that might be described as pulps. But we also have two distinguished entries in the shelter field, *Dream House*, and *Dream Garden*, which are highly regarded by decidedly upscale audiences. It might be of interest to our detractors to know that both these magazines are personally subscribed to by First Lady Mrs. John F. Kennedy; that a subscription to our *Outdoors* goes to Prince Philip of England; and that our *Tiny Tots* recently received the distinguished Helen J. Pritzl Award for Outstanding Journalism for Juvenile Readers. . . .

We are an organization constantly expanding our publishing horizons, constantly on the lookout for products of higher and higher quality. When *Mode* was offered to us, we saw an opportunity to extend our outreach further into the field of high fashion.

Mode is a distinguished publication, with a long and proud history. We contemplate no changes at the magazine that will in any way tarnish, or alter, that reputation. In a series of meetings and conversations with Miss Ferlinghetti, we have assured her that she will continue to have complete editorial autonomy at the magazine, running it and producing it as she and only she may wish.

With the acquisition of *Mode*, the motive of cupidity has been ascribed to the Rothman family. Though the purchase price has not been disclosed, none other than the *New York Times* has asserted that we bought *Mode* "at a garage sale price." Let it be clearly stated that *Mode* is not now, nor has it been for many years, a money-maker. Nor do we expect it to become one in the future. With an expensive four-color printing process, it is a costly magazine to produce. Its editorial staff, and its contributors, are among the highest-salaried and highest-paid in America. Its circulation is small (less than 200,000) and select, and its advertising pages have been traditionally limited to ten percent of content.

We intend to respect and continue these long traditions and policies. We intend to continue to serve that small, select audience of readers, and that select group of advertisers. . . .

There was a certain amount of misinformation in Herbert's statement. *Mode*'s staff was far from high-salaried and, in fact, the staff, from Miss Ferlinghetti down, had recently agreed to a twenty percent salary cut in an effort to bring overhead down—a fact that had made the idea of buying the magazine much more attractive to Ho Rothman. As for contributors, there were none at the time of the purchase. They had all been notified that the magazine would henceforth be staff written, in another attempt to reduce costs. The ten percent advertising-to-editorial ratio was immediately abandoned by Ho in order to increase revenues. Regular advertisers in other Rothman publications were offered deep discounts if they would also advertise in *Mode*. And any advertiser who spent more than $100,000 a year in other Rothman publications was given four full-color pages in *Mode* a year, free, as a bonus—a ploy designed to make the magazine quickly look fatter, healthier, and more desirable—to readers, as well as to advertisers and their agencies. A word-of-mouth campaign quickly spread along Madison Avenue to the effect that any agency media director who was able to persuade a client to buy a full-page color ad in *Mode* could expect a two-week paid vacation for himself and his family in the Poconos, courtesy of Ho Rothman. A full-page black-and-white ad was worth one week. As for Jackie Kennedy and Prince Philip, both received free "comp" copies of the magazines mentioned, and could not honestly be called subscribers.

And as for Consuelo Ferlinghetti's tenure in the top editorial chair, she was then eighty-three years old, and Nature could probably be counted on to terminate her stewardship of the magazine. Indeed, four years later she walked out of her Fifth Avenue apartment, wearing a raincoat ("Well, after all, it *was* raining," someone commented at the time) and absolutely nothing else except a pair of Ferragamo slippers, and was arrested for exposing herself in front of a group of Buckley schoolboys near the Alice in Wonderland storytelling statue in Central Park. It was then that Herbert Rothman's son, Steven, just out of Princeton, was assigned the editor-in-chiefship of the magazine.

"The money is peanuts, I'm afraid," Lucille Withers said to her that day in the autumn of 1966. "All the Rothman publications are notoriously cheap. On the other hand, the exposure would be terrific, and it would look damn good on your résumé. Here, let me read you what their letter says."

They were sitting in Lulu Withers's office, and Lulu picked up the letter on her desk. " 'For a summer, 1967 feature on "That Fresh Midwestern Look," we are looking for a particular girl, age range eighteen through twenty-two, to model the designs of young Indiana-born designer Bill Blass. We are looking for a girl with a fresh, open face, preferably blonde, who will photograph well in Blass's sporty designs, as well as in his more sophisticated evening clothes, and we would prefer that this be a "new" face that has not appeared previously in a national publication. We will be shooting outdoor college campus shots as well as elegant interior shots, and so we want a girl who will look right at a fraternity-house party as well as at a formal, seated dinner. Send composites, et cetera, et cetera. With the right young lady, this could be a cover feature.' Anyway, I immediately thought of you, Lexy," Lucille said, putting down the letter.

"Midwestern Look," she said. "Do I have that?"

"That's a lot of garbage," Lucille said. "The Midwestern Look is no different from the Florida Look or the New England Look or the California Look. They've started doing these regional issues as a way of attracting regional advertisers who wouldn't otherwise come into the book. Advertising is what the Rothmans are all about. Anyway, I sent them your composite, and—are you ready for this, Lexy? You're one of ten finalists. Now they want an interview. I didn't tell you about any of this before because it seemed so pie-in-the-sky. They canvassed fifty different agencies in twenty Midwest cities, and I wasn't sure you had a chance. But now you've actually got a shot at it. Just think of it, Lexy. You've got a shot at the cover of *Mode*!"

Alex sat very still, letting it all sink in. For the past four

years, Lucille Withers had kept her quite busy, mostly posing
for local retail advertising. She had done a number of posters
for a local bank, and had done a certain amount of what was
called runway work, modeling at fashion shows put on by
such organizations as the Kansas City Junior League. She had
also done some radio and television commercials and voice-
overs for local advertisers and, since both her face and voice
had become reasonably well known in the area, she had filled
in as the girl who read the nightly weather report on television
when the regular girl went on vacation. Lucille Withers had
been gradually able to raise her modeling fees to thirty-five
dollars an hour for black-and-white and forty an hour for
color. She had taken a small apartment in Kansas City, and
was able to support herself quite comfortably without having to touch the savings account, which she still regarded as
Skipper's money.

"Anyway," Lucille went on, "they'll be in town on Monday, and I've scheduled your interview for two o'clock. Suite
four ten at the Alameda Plaza."

"They?"

"Some rather top brass, m'dear. The editor-in-chief himself, Steven Rothman. And the art director, whose name is
Sigourney Frye. Sigourney Frye's a woman, by the way. And
one of their photo editors."

"What sort of questions will they ask me, do you think?"

Lucille Withers laughed, and swung her pince-nez in a
wide arc. "My dear, your guess is as good as mine," she
said. "This is as close as I've ever come to getting a girl
into *Mode*. You're going to be on your own, because they
specifically asked that I not come with you. But if I were
you, there's just one word I'd think about between now and
then, because that's the one little word I'll bet they'll be
looking for."

"What's that, Lulu?"

"Poise," she said. "Between now and Monday, think
poise."

"What do you think I should wear?"

"I've thought about that. Why don't you wear something
you've designed yourself? What about that moss-green wool
suit with the covered buttons? I thought that looked pretty
snappy. And, during the interview, why not let it drop that
you design most of your own clothes? Who knows? They

might even shoot you in one of your own designs—along with the stuff by this Bill Blass, whoever he is."

"Oh, I've heard of him," Alex said. "He's new, and he's going to be big."

"Just don't get your hopes up too high," Lucille Withers said. "Remember there are nine other girls out there. They might not pick you."

"Oh, they'll pick me," Alex said with a smile. "Don't worry. They'll pick me."

"And one other thing. If they do pick you, there'll be something called a morals clause in the contract. That's standard for them. So—there's nothing in your personal life, which is to say your sex life, that could be potentially embarrassing to the magazine, is there?"

She hesitated. "No," she said.

"Good. Nothing to worry about there," Lucille Withers said. "And don't wear too much makeup. Just a light lipstick, and maybe a little blush. Don't do anything with the eyes. Remember, they're looking for a fresh, open face that says Kansas wheat fields on it."

"Maybe I'll run up a dress out of grain sacks."

"Now don't act smart," Lucille Withers said.

She had been doubtful about the wisdom of accepting his dinner invitation that night. Models often found themselves in awkward situations, and Lucille Withers had cautioned her about that. "Just a word to the wise," she had said. "I can't be a watchdog over my girls, but I can tell you to watch out for guys who offer to give you the big job if you'll just give them a little something *they* want." Several years earlier, Lucille had helped prepare a Miss Missouri for the Miss America pageant. The girl hadn't won the crown, or even been a runner-up, but when she came back from Atlantic City she told Lucille that several of the male judges had promised to vote for her—if. "Always the big if," Lucille said. "But putting out for the judges didn't get Miss Missouri bullets."

And so, when Steven Rothman asked her if she would join him for dinner that night in the hotel's restaurant, she had hesitated. But he had struck her immediately as a straightforward and decent young man. During the interview, his questions—about her hobbies, interests, likes, dislikes—had been intelligent and courteous. And he was extraordinarily good-looking—tall, slender, dark-haired and dark-eyed, with an almost imperceptible cleft in his chin, and a pleasant, slightly off-center smile. Later, she would learn that it had taken three generations for Rothman males to achieve any height; Steven was six-feet-two, and towered over his father and grandfather. Alex had liked Steven immediately, and he had also immediately made it clear that there was no big *if* involved—no *if* at all.

"You're the one," he said with his crooked grin as he folded his napkin in his lap at the dinner table. "You've got the job. You're exactly what we're looking for. Everybody agrees. We'll be notifying the other girls that we've made our choice. We'll be back to shoot the story next month. Well, how do you feel about all this?"

"Thrilled, of course."

"Mind you, I can't promise you the cover. That will depend on what we get from the shooting. And I can't promise you that we'll feature any of your own designs. Bear in mind that this is a Bill Blass story. It's got to be, because—but never mind the reasons why."

"Because you're trying to get Bill Blass as an advertiser?"

He gave her a quizzical look, and wrinkled his nose in distaste. "Now how did you know that?" he said. "Anyway, I will have a couple of my fashion editors look at your designs and tell me what they think. Me, I don't know anything about fashion. I was an economics major."

He also struck her as remarkably young to be editor-in-chief of a magazine like *Mode*. He was, in fact, only twenty-two—her own age. She had remarked on that.

He wrinkled his nose again. "I am a member of the Rothman family dynasty," he said with mock seriousness. "There are pluses and minuses to being a member of a dynasty, and remember you heard that here. The Rothman dynasty was started by my grandfather, H. O. Rothman, often called Ho. It is being carried on by my father, Herbert Rothman. I am next in line. When I got out of Princeton, it was essential that I be given some sort of position with Rothman Communications, and so I was given the lowliest position of all—editor-in-chief of *Mode*."

"The *lowliest?*"

"Oh, yes. Definitely. *Mode* has lots of prestige, but it

makes no money for us whatsoever. In fact, it's still losing
money. Grandpa Ho is trying to turn it around, but that hasn't
happened, not so far. That's why he wanted an economics
major for this job. I said to him, 'Gramps, I'm not an *editor*.'
He said, 'Any damn fool can edit a magazine like *Mode*.' So
I'm the damn fool he picked. I hate my job."

"Really?" She stared at him, astonished.

As they ordered and ate their dinner, he told her about it.

"Oh, yes," he said. "I really hate it. I'm just treading
water here, until the powers that be—my father and my
grandfather—decide I'm ready to move on to something
more important. You see, I'm not even interested in wom-
en's clothes. Oh, I can help someone like Sigourney choose
the right model for a fashion story. I'm certainly interested
in beautiful women. But *fashion?* A woman should edit a
women's fashion magazine, don't you think? Oh, of course
we have a few old biddies on the staff who claim they know
fashion. Me, I'd never even heard of this Bill Blass guy. In
fact, at first I thought his name was Bill *Bass*, and I thought
he was an Englishman. Turns out he's from Fort Wayne." His
dark eyes grew distant, almost wistful, for a moment. "It's a
sissy sort of a job for a man, isn't it? Running a magazine
about women's clothes? My grandfather thinks *Mode* is a
sissy magazine. So does my father. In fact, I sometimes
think they gave this job to me to punish me."

"Punish you? For what?"

He gave her a distant look again. "I don't know," he said.
"Maybe for not being smarter than I am."

"But what if you were able to make the magazine bigger
and more profitable?" She remembered asking him that naïve
question. That was how young she was.

He held up his hands. "Circulation can be bought," he
said. "There are all sorts of gimmicks—discounts, coupons,
special offers, even under-the-counter payoffs to newsdealers
to get them to display the magazine front and center at the
supermarket checkout counter. But nobody in the company
wants to spend the money—not until the magazine rakes
in enough money in ad revenues. That's essentially what I
am—a space salesman. I'm there to sell ad space, by hook
or by crook, and mostly by crook. Of course what I really
need, if we're ever going to make *Mode* a *good* magazine,
is a really good editorial assistant, a *woman* assistant, who

knows fashion, and who knows how to edit a magazine for women."

"Then why don't you hire one?" she asked innocently.

He rolled his eyes. "The money again. Nobody wants to spend any money on my poor little sissy magazine. Also, nobody really gives a damn what goes into the magazine editorially. Nobody gives a damn about the magazine's readers. Subscribers don't make money for a magazine. Only advertisers. In fact, if you get subscription-heavy, you find yourself losing money. So meanwhile, I'm treading water, waiting for the higher-ups in the Rothman dynasty to decide little Steven is ready for something better." His eyes had that wistful, faraway look again, and he said, "Do you know you're the first woman I've ever met who seemed even remotely interested in hearing about my job? When women hear that I'm the new editor of *Mode*, they come bubbling up to me and ask me what's new and exciting from Paris. When they find I don't know, and don't even care, they just walk off and find somebody else to talk to."

"If I were the editor of *Mode*, I'd want to make it the biggest, most beautiful, most important fashion magazine in the world. I'd keep foxing it up, and foxing it up."

He grinned. " 'Foxing it up'? What's that?"

"Just keep adding little new twists, little new surprises, with each issue—things that will keep the readers guessing, keep them on their toes, keep them turning the pages, keep them coming back for more."

"Fine," he said. "And how would you perform these little miracles?"

She thought for a moment. She was thinking of something she had noticed when modeling fashions for local stores. "I'm thinking of making *Mode*'s fashions more accessible to your readers," she said. "I read *Mode*, for instance, and I've often seen clothes there that I'd like to own, or at least try on. But then, shopping around the stores in town, I've found that nobody in Kansas City sells them. I've seen the line 'Available at Bergdorf-Goodman.' But Bergdorf-Goodman is hundreds and hundreds of miles away. This Bill Blass story—when it appears next summer, will women in Kansas City be able to buy his clothes in local stores?"

"We send out regular fliers to retailers, telling them what's coming up in future issues. But then it's up to the individual buyers to decide whether or not to stock the clothes. We can't control what the buyers order."

"You might, if you were to give a store—the leading fashion store in each major city—an exclusive right to sell *Mode*'s fashions. Then, the minute *Mode* came out, that store, and only that store, would put those clothes, and nobody else's, in their windows."

His eyes were bright. "Go on," he said.

"Then, if you picked Stix's here, for instance, women would know that the only place in Kansas City where they could buy *Mode*'s fashions was Stix's. Women would like it, the stores would like it, and I think advertisers would, too. Stix's would probably buy an ad."

"I've been trying to sell Stix's a page all week," he said. "It's been an uphill job."

"But what if you made Stix's *Mode*'s official Kansas City store?"

He was still staring at her intently. "What else would you do?"

"If you could make *Mode*'s fashions more accessible to women, you could also make the magazine itself harder to get."

"You mean raise the cover price?"

"Why not? A dollar-fifty seems cheap to me for a magazine like *Mode*. Double the price. Make it seem more exclusive, like the exclusive stores that would sell *Mode*'s clothes. It must be expensive to mail out all those subscriptions."

"Damn right. The most expensive, and least efficient, method of distributing any product is through the U.S. mail."

"What if there were no subscriptions? What if the only places in those cities where you could buy *Mode* were those special stores?"

He stared at her fixedly for a moment longer. "Your ideas are very clever, you know," he said at last. "You're a very clever lady. I was expecting to meet a pretty, empty-headed fashion model, but that's not you at all."

"Those special stores would promote *Mode*, and *Mode* would promote those special stores."

Then he tossed his dinner napkin in the air. It landed on the table. "But I can hear what my father and my grandfather would say," he said. "How much will it cost to try something like that? How much will it cost? The magazine can't afford it. No, your ideas are clever and original, but nobody's going to change a thing because there's nobody who really cares enough to make a change. Do you know the real reason why Pop wanted to buy *Mode?* Because Mom was complaining that she was the wife of a man who published *schlock.* She thought if he published a magazine like *Mode*, it would make her seem more *fashionable*, for God's sake. And Pop, for reasons of his own, would like to get Mom off his back right now. My parents are—well, that's another story. *Mode* is just window-dressing for them. That's all it is. Just something to improve their image, and make Pop's write-up in Who's Who look better."

"But shouldn't it be profitable window-dressing?"

"Sure. But my grandfather, who controls the money, doesn't believe in the magazine. Innovations like you're talking about involve risk capital, and my grandfather isn't willing to take the risks. First he wants black ink. 'Show me some black ink, Stevie, give me some black ink,' " he said, imitating Ho Rothman's Russian accent. "Until I give him that, *Mode* will just plod along the way it's always done. February is our Look-Ten-Years-Younger issue. March is our Diet issue. April is our French issue, May is Italian, and June is American designers. It's that way year after year. So be it. World without end. Amen. While I go up and down the street, trolling for advertisers, offering them deals—"

"But look," she said, leaning forward eagerly, "if you could first of all make the magazine exciting to readers, that would make it exciting to manufacturers, who are your national advertisers. The manufacturers would make it exciting to the retailers they sell to, and the retailers would help make it even more exciting to their customers, who are your readers." She made a circle with the thumbs and forefingers of both hands. "It's like a circle, isn't it? It would snowball. But you have to start with readers, don't you? I think your grandfather is approaching the whole thing from the wrong direction."

He sighed. "Try telling that to Gramps," he said.

"But if you were able to turn *Mode* into a huge success, wouldn't they stop punishing you—for whatever it is?"

He looked at her. "Would you help me?" he asked quickly.

"Help you? How could I help you?" And suddenly as he

looked at her, the air between them seemed to grow taut with
tension, thick and fibrous and heavy with unspoken thoughts
and unanswered questions, and she thought: The tip of the
iceberg; I have only glimpsed the tip of the iceberg with this
man; there is much more, very complicated, deep below. She
felt all at once shy with him, as though she had caught him
in a weak and shameful act. She lowered her eyes, and said,
"But I shouldn't be telling you how to run your business."

"Why not? Nobody else ever has." Then he said, "I don't
know how to tell you this, Alexandra. But I like you very
much. In my job, the people who work for me do what I
say, but I know that none of them have any respect for me.
I know they really hate me because I'm the boss's grandson,
and wouldn't be where I am if it wasn't for him. But you're
different. I think you care about me. I'm going back to New
York tomorrow, but do you think I could write or telephone
you from time to time—just to talk?"

"Of course," she said.

She had given him her address and telephone number. And
before she knew it, he was telephoning her nearly every day.
There was something about this sad and complicated young
man who claimed to hate his job, and yet felt chained to it
and imprisoned by it, that made her pity him, and want to help
him. Somehow, she felt he needed mothering. She already
had a vision of his cold, hard, brittle, and unloving parents—
a vision that would turn out to be remarkably accurate.

He telephoned her from New York the very next night,
and soon he was phoning her every night. The thing she
remembered most about those calls was that, for the most
part, he talked and she listened to him. But there was nothing
self-centered about this. Instead, she got the impression that
no one had ever listened to Steven Rothman, and that, for all
his family's wealth, he had never really had anyone to talk to.
He told her about his family's estate, called "Rothmere," up
on the Hudson River, where his parents, grandparents, and
uncle and aunt all lived together—"One big happy family,
except it isn't," he said.

"Why isn't it?" she asked him.

"You'll see," he said. "I'll bring you up here someday.
Happy families are all alike. Each unhappy family is unhappy in its own way."

"*Anna Karenina*," she said. "Of course in the translation I read, it was '*Every* unhappy family is unhappy in its own way'—small difference."

She could almost hear the surprise in the momentary silence from his end of the line, that a Missouri girl knew Tolstoy, and she wondered briefly whether he was perhaps one of those men who disliked smart women. She added, "My mother had sort of an obsession about Russian pre-Revolutionary history. We even had a dog named Anna Karenina, believe it or not."

He laughed, and the next day, by Special Delivery, came a copy of a new biography of Count Leo Tolstoy, inscribed, "*Every* Missouri girl is different in her own way."

So he did listen to the things she said, and he did like smart women.

He called to tell her about the opening night of a new musical he had attended. It was called *Cabaret*, and was based on Christopher Isherwood's stories of Berlin between the wars. He had loved it, but didn't think the *New York Times* had done it justice in its review.

She mentioned that she did not see the *New York Times* in Kansas City, and the next morning a subscription to the *Times* was on her doorstep. Shortly thereafter, he sent her the original cast album of the show. Then he called to ask her what she thought of it.

"I loved it," she said.

He loved music, both classical and popular. Sometimes he would play Beatles songs for her, on the telephone, on his guitar. He had once wanted to be a musician, but his family had put a stop to that idea.

He began sending her flowers. The first was a nosegay of violets. When she thanked him, he asked, "Did they match?"

"Match what?"

"Your eyes. I told them I wanted bluish-green flowers."

She laughed. "I have funny-colored eyes."

"Blue-green in some lights, hazel in others."

"You noticed that?"

"Oh yes . . ."

"Now what would have made you notice that?"

"I consider you my best friend," he said.

"But we've only met once."

"That doesn't matter. I've never really had a best friend,

you know." There was a note of elegant, sweet sadness in his voice. And of course she was flattered that this love-ly, polished young man from such a powerful background should have been attracted to her. She found herself looking forward eagerly to his nightly calls.

He came back to Kansas City in November to shoot the Bill Blass story, along with the art director, the photographer, the photographer's assistants, the lighting crew, the hair and makeup stylists, the designer himself, and the great wardrobe bags filled with clothes, shoes, and accessories—the entire, expensive crew for the weeklong shoot. She noticed that he began asking her opinions about the poses.

"Would you feel more comfortable holding your hand this way—or that way?" he would ask her.

She suspected that this annoyed the photographer, and she was certain that it annoyed Sigourney Frye, the art director.

"Who's art director on this shoot, anyway—me or her?" she heard Sigourney Frye ask him crossly.

"I just want Alex to look and feel comfortable in her poses," he said.

"And *I'd* just like Alice to pose according to the layout," Sigourney Frye snapped back. Sigourney Frye repeatedly called her "Alice," and Alex decided that she could never really like anyone whose name was Sigourney Frye. And, when she learned later that Sigourney Frye's name had origi-nally been Rose Freiberg, she decided that she liked her even less.

"I don't want to seem to be undermining Sigourney's authority," she said to him later.

"Don't worry. I'm still editor-in-chief," he said. "This job is an important step in your career. I want to be sure you look your best."

After one particularly long photo session, which had involved Alex, in sequined coveralls, standing on a step-ladder with a can of red paint in one hand and a paintbrush in the other, painting a ceiling—and, like so many too-archly clever picture ideas, this one ended up not being used—Alex had collapsed on the sofa in the trailer that they used as a dressing room. "Poor girl, you must be exhausted," he said to her. "Here, let me give you a back-rub." He knelt on the floor beside her, and began gently kneading and massaging the sore muscles of her shoulders, neck, upper arms, and lower back. "I'm famous for my back-rubs," he said.

"Mm, that feels good," she murmured. "How did you get to be famous for your back-rubs?"

"My mother has bad nerves," he said. "Whenever she has one of her attacks of nerves, she has me give her a back-rub."

Dreamily, under the smooth caressing touch of his expert fingers, she began to wonder whether his hands might begin to move to the front of her body, and what might happen then. She waited. But it did not happen.

They had dinner together every night in the dining room of the Alameda Plaza, where he was staying. On the last night of the shooting session, to celebrate, he ordered champagne. He touched his glass to hers. "To us," he said. She noticed that he was gazing at her intently, and had not touched his food. "You are so beautiful," he said, and she realized that Skipper had never told her she was beautiful. But then, Skipper had never told her that he loved her, either. Then Steven Rothman did that, too, almost whispered it: "I love you, Alex."

Then he reached into his jacket pocket, and produced a small blue box. In it was a Kashmiri sapphire ring with a girdle of diamonds. "To match your eyes," he said. That was when he asked her to marry him. He had fallen in love with her, he said, over the telephone.

"But do you love him, Lexy?" Lucille Withers asked her when Alex showed her the ring.

"It's called a Kashmiri sapphire," she said. "Sapphires are among the heaviest of all precious stones. Emeralds are among the lightest. Did you know that, Lulu? Steven told me that. He knows all sorts of strange and wonderful little things."

"You're not answering my question, Lexy," she said. "I asked you if you loved him. Or are you just in love with his money?"

"He's terribly sweet," Alex said. "He's one of the kindest, gentlest, most considerate men I've ever met. I like him very, very much."

"You're still not answering me."

Alex frowned. She knew what Lulu meant. She meant, did she love Steven *enough?* Well, how much was enough, anyway? Maybe it was not the same as with Skipper, but did it have to be? Perhaps that part would come later? Certainly that part would come later, after they were married, as it usually did in any marriage.

"So tell me. Is it him—or is it the Rothman money? They say his grandfather is worth two hundred million bucks." (Remember that this was in 1967, when two hundred million still seemed like a lot of money.)

"I've thought about that," she said carefully. "The trouble is, the Rothman money is a part of what Steven is. How can I separate the money from what Steven is? His money is just one aspect of the man I've grown terribly fond of. I've decided that the man I want to marry just happens to be rich, and there's not much I can do about that, is there? I mean, I think I'd still feel the same way about him if he happened to be poor. How can I separate my feelings from the facts that happen to go along with him?"

Lucille Withers shook her head. "I don't like this, Lexy," she said. "I don't like this one little bit. Of course I wouldn't give bullets who you married, if I didn't care a lot about you. . . ."

"She's totally unsuitable, totally unacceptable," Herbert Rothman said to his wife, Pegeen, as they sat in the living room of the apartment at River House that afternoon. "No, she won't do at all—some little adventuress fashion model from a little town in Missouri that nobody's ever heard of. She obviously thinks he's got a lot of money, even though he doesn't—yet. I've done a little checking on her, which Steven, in his haste to marry the first girl who'll say yes to him, clearly hasn't bothered to do. Her father is a small-time accountant who was passed over for a promotion in favor of a younger man in the firm. The family is not popular in the little town of Paradise, Missouri. Her parents are considered left-wing shirttail intellectuals—radicals, even Communists—by their neighbors. Her father drinks. Her mother is in and out of mental hospitals. The girl herself is considered fast. When she was in her teens, she was often seen hitchhiking out on the interstates around Kansas City, being picked up by God knows who. Imagine! A hitchhiker. She has no breeding, no education—nothing more than a diploma from a public high school. There are also rumors that the girl is illegitimate."

Pegeen Rothman was working on a needlepoint canvas of elaborate design, a butterfly landing in a field of brightly colored zinnias. She pulled a golden thread through the corner of her butterfly's wing. "Still, she's pretty," she said.

"My God," he roared, "is that all we want for our son's wife? Any little tramp, just so long as she's *pretty?*"

Pegeen Rothman drew another thread through the butterfly's wing, secured it, and knotted it. Then she spread the canvas on her lap, and studied it. "There's an old expression that might apply here," she said at last. " 'Any port in a storm.' "

Chapter 30

THE FASHION SCENE
by
Mona

What's black and white and gold all over? A "golden parachute" in the form of a two-page ad in the *New York Times*, that's what! That's just what long-time fashion maven Alex Rothman got from big boss publisher Herbert Rothman yesterday—an ad kissing her a sweet goodbye with thanks for all those long years of service, and making way for that adorable young newcomer from Merrie Olde Englande, Lady Fiona Hesketh-Fenton, who's expected to take over the reins of *Mode* most any day now, insiders say.

Alexandra Rothman is the li'l ole gal who, years 'n years ago, came down practically barefoot from the mountains of Iowa (or was it Indiana?) and married Herb Rothman's handsome son Steve—then quickly clawed her way to the top of *Mode*'s masthead. But you knew all that. And now it's all ancient history. Boo-hoo.

Meanwhile, it's been no secret that Herb Rothman's been on the lookout for a younger editor-in-chief, someone who can inject that old-time mag with fresh ideas and new approaches. And Fab Fiona is the gal he's settled on. Hooray! (Fiona, by the bye, is a very democratic gal, who doesn't like to be called Her Ladyship, even though she is one, and Mother Mona only mentions this to show that Herb's dealing with the Top Drawers.)

But wait. The plot thickens. Maybe it's a case of "Don't Cry For Me, Alexandra!" Just this past Monday, one of Mother Mona's most reliable little tattletales glimpsed the Ageless Alex having lunch at Le Bernardin with none other than Billionaire Bumpkin Rodney McCulloch, the crafty Canadian who, insiders say, would like nothing better than to make mincemeat out of the Rothman publishing pie. Mother's informants tell her that the Crafty One's and the Ageless One's heads were ever-so-close-together, and that the subject under discussion was Big Bucks. What are Alex and Rodney cooking up? Sounds like a Big Deal, Mother's informants say. Could be a counterattack, because Alex's well-worn claws are bared. . . . So stay tuned to Mona.

Meanwhile, 'member my story of the cat burglar who ransacked the purses of all the gals at Maggie Van Zuylen's beach party not long ago? Well, the bills are starting to come in from all the purr-r-r-loined credit cards, and they're all from shops like Martha, Hermès, Vuitton, and Sara Fredericks. Breakfast food heiress Pussy McCutcheon had a dozen Hermès scarves charged to her Amex Gold Card. Begins to sound as though the cat burglar was a cat burglaress, doesn't it? At least Pussy thinks so. Thanks for the tip, Pussy . . . Meow, meow! P.S. Alex Rothman was at the Van Zuylen bash, natch.

"I'd like to charge age discrimination in the complaint, as well as breach of contract," Henry Coker was saying. "In light of Mona's column this morning, with the repeated references to your age, and the fact that the Fenton woman is younger, I think a charge of ageism would add teeth to our complaint."

"Oh, Henry, do you really think so?" Alex said. "Age discrimination sounds so—defensive."

"But we have to take a strong defensive stand in this, Alex. Unfortunately, the other side is taking a very combative stance. We're forced to be defensive if we're going to fight back. We also have evidence that Mrs. Potter is being fed a lot of this material directly from Herbert Rothman. He's using her as his mouthpiece."

"That's more than likely," Alex said.

"Which brings me to another point about her column this morning. The repeated references to cats and claws and cat burglars. I come away with the distinct impression that Mona Potter is suggesting that *you* might be the cat burglar. That is definitely defamatory, and actionable, since you were at the Van Zuylen party. What would you think of a libel action against Mona Potter and the *News?*"

"I hate the idea of getting down and fighting on Mona Potter's level, Henry."

"I'd like to fight this on every level possible, Alex. And I'd like to neutralize Mona Potter, at least until this is settled. She's no help to us at all, and I'd like to see her neutralized. They're fighting dirty now, and I think we should fight just as dirty back." He paused. "Unless, of course, you decide to simply resign, and save yourself some legal bills," he said.

She replaced the phone. Gregory was standing at her office doorway. "Mr. Herbert Rothman would like to see you in his office," he said. "He says it's extremely urgent." She rose to go. "Incidentally, he's moved to room three thousand," Gregory said.

Room three thousand, of course, was Ho Rothman's old office.

It was a bit of a shock to see him sitting behind Ho's desk, in the huge office with the map of the United States, and its gold-starred Rothman cities, across one wall. He did not rise when she entered the room. The *News* was opened to Mona Potter's column and, without looking up at her, he tapped the newspaper with a fingertip and said, "This won't take a minute, Alex. Your lawyer has been talking to mine in terms of an alleged breach of contract. I would like to say just one thing on the subject of your contract. Your contract contains something called a loyalty clause. I gather from this story that you have lunched with Rodney McCulloch. Rodney McCulloch is my competitor. He is also my enemy. If, as Mona says, you are cooking up something with Rodney McCulloch, I shall consider that an act of extreme disloyalty to my company. If you enter into any sort of deal with McCulloch, you will have effectively breached your own contract. That would be grounds for dismissal, without accrued benefits, including profit sharing, et cetera, et cetera. That is all I have to say."

"The whole town knows you're trying to get rid of me, Herbert," she said. "Including Rodney McCulloch. Rodney McCulloch offered me a deal—a deal I have not accepted."

"Nor rejected?"

"Nor rejected."

"Then I'm warning you. Any further negotiations with my enemy I shall consider acts of extreme disloyalty, and grounds for your immediate dismissal from my company. Without benefits. I have discussed this with our own attorneys. They assure me that I will be acting within my legal rights, as specified in my contract with you. Good day." He turned his attention to other papers on the big desk, ruffling through them with his fingers.

Back in her office, Gregory Kittredge said, "Why not take the rest of the day off, Alex? Everyone on the staff would understand."

"Nonsense, darlin'. I've got work to do." She seated herself at her desk, and picked up a fashion layout that lay on top of a small pile. Pinned to the layout was the copy for the story, typed on yellow cap, indicating a first draft. She read the headline.

MINISKIRTS—YOU CAN'T PUT 'EM DOWN

She made a face, and quickly rewrote the head.

LET THEM EAT CHEESECAKE!

Then, just as quickly, she rewrote the lead.

We don't mean the eggy kind you get at Zabar's. We mean the leggy kind they keep sending us from Paris.

Then she penciled a quick note to Bob Shaw, her art director.

Bob—let's have some fun with this miniskirts-with-tights look. Only 5% of our readers can wear 'em, for God's sake! How about a small piece of artwork here? Marie Antoinette in a miniskirt & tights? Corny or cute?

A.L.R.

She pinned this note to the layout and revised copy sheets. Then she initialed the traffic-routing slip, and placed it all in her Out box.

Then she picked up the next layout.

Upstairs, in Suite 3000, Herbert Joseph Rothman was trying to reach Lenny Liebling.

"I'm sorry, Mr. Rothman, but Mr. Liebling is out of town this week," Lenny's secretary, who was new that week, was saying.

"Where the hell is he?"

"I believe he is at our printing plant in Paramus, New Jersey, Mr. Rothman," Lenny's secretary said.

"The *printing* plant? What the hell's he doing there?"

"Mr Liebling is our special projects editor," the secretary said. "I expect he is there working on a special project."

"Well, get in touch with him and tell him I want to see him."

"I'm sorry, Mr. Rothman, but Mr. Liebling left instructions that he was not to be disturbed."

"Now listen, you," he said. "You get ahold of Mr. Liebling, and tell him that Herbert J. Rothman wants to see him—right away!"

"I'll do what I can, Mr. Rothman," she said.

"Damn right you will!"

She did not add that, at the Rothmans' main printing plant in Paramus, which covered two hundred acres and employed twenty-five hundred people in twenty-six separate departments, she had no idea how to locate Lenny Liebling, whose presence there was unknown to all but one other Rothman employee.

"Joel, darling!" she cried, throwing her arms around him and suffusing him in the odor of her gardenia perfume. "It's so marvelous to see you, and I can just tell by the expression on your face that you're the bearer of good news for me."

He looked briefly confused. "I am?"

"You've spoken to your mother. She's called off her lawyers."

"Actually, I haven't done that yet," he said.

She moved away from him. "Then you've not kept your promise," she said.

"I'm going to do it, Fiona, but Mom's been awfully busy, and—"

"Yes, I daresay," she said in a chilly voice. "Busy plotting to get me shipped back to England, without a job, with no money—with nothing. And if I get shipped back to England, you know what that means. That's the end of you and me."

"I'm going to speak to her, Fiona. I really am."

"All I ask is that she call off her bloody lawyers. And let me try to explain my side of things. And end this bloody mess."

"I will. I promise you."

"Promise? You already promised once. You know what happens if you break a promise twice."

"No. What?"

"You'll see," she said darkly. Then, turning to him brightly again, she said, "But if that's a *real* promise, then I have a very special little treat for you tonight. Just for my darling Joel."

"Is it—?"

"You'll see," she said again with a wink. "But first let's get out of these silly clothes." She took him by the hand and led him toward her bedroom, and he could feel his erection swelling against the front of his doeskin pants. "I've missed you, Joel," she said.

"And . . . I . . . you . . . ," he muttered.

He sat naked on the edge of her bed, his swollen cock pulsating between his legs, while she removed her bra and panties. "I deliberately didn't offer you a drink," she said. "Because I think that's what made you sick the last time. The whiskey, plus the amyl nitrate. But this—this is going to make you feel quite different. Quite—heavenly, I promise you."

From her top dresser drawer, she removed a small round silver box and unscrewed the lid. Inside was a white powder.

"What is it?"

"Cocaine. I call it snow. It's very good, very pure. A chum of mine sent it to me from Bolivia. Have you not tried it, Joel?"

"No," he said, feeling ashamed.

"Well, you should. It will make you feel just dreamy. And don't worry. It's not the least bit dangerous, and, contrary to what they say, it's not the least bit habit-forming. Now here's the way we do it for the first time. . . ."

She dipped her forefinger into the powder, and then placed her finger in her vagina, rubbing it around. "Now it's your turn," she said, and with the same moist fingertip she spread more of the powder around the swollen head of his cock. "Feel it?" she said. "A tiny tingle?"

"Uh-huh."

"Now we're each going to take just a tiny sniff. Not a big snort, mind you—just a tiny sniff. Later, you're going to want a little more, but you just want a tiny sniff to start." She lifted her finger to one nostril, inhaled briefly, then offered the fingertip to him. He inhaled and, in a moment, he felt a swimming feeling in his head, behind his eyeballs, and his vision blurred. Then he sneezed.

"Now, silly, you've sneezed it all out," she said. "Try one more time. Just a sniff."

She offered him her fingertip once more, and he sniffed the powder again. "I love you, Fiona," he said in a sleepy voice.

"That's more like it," she said. "Now first I'm going to sit on you. Then I'm going to sit on your face."

But he was looking with dismay at the limp cock that now lay across his leg.

"What's the matter with you?" she asked sharply.

"I don't know . . . I'm sorry," he said groggily.

"What's wrong? It's supposed to make a man feel randy."

"I don't know . . . I just . . . maybe I just can't . . ."

"Oh, for mercy's sake!" she said, jumping to her feet. "You didn't sniff enough to turn on a canary."

"What's wrong with me, Fiona?" he asked miserably. "I really love you, but—"

"God knows what's wrong with you!" She was pacing up and down the room, a small, pale exclamation point of a woman in a helmet of dark hair. "All I know is that a girl expects more than that from a man—a real man, anyway."

"Please, Fiona. I'm sorry. Maybe I just can't handle—"

She pulled on a dark blue robe, and turned on her heel to face him. "Yes. Maybe you just can't handle a woman. Maybe that's what's wrong with you. It's what I suspected all along. You're an urning."

"An earning?"

"Urning. U-R-N-I-N-G," she spelled it out for him.

"What does that—?"

"You're supposed to be such a little expert in English," she snapped. "Go home and look it up in your dictionary. Now you can just put on your clothes and get out of here. I happen to have a dinner date tonight with a man. A *real* man."

"Please, Fiona—"

"Your father was one too, you know!"

"Was what?"

"An urning!" She spat out the word.

From Joel Rothman's journal:

6/27/90
6:00 P.M.

"Urning: a male homosexual."
   —Webster's Third
That's what Fiona called me.

An invert, a homo, a queer, a faggot, a fruit, a flit, a fairy, a pansy, a nance, a queen, a catamite . . . Like Lenny Liebling.

I feel like killing myself.

But I just can't seem to handle the drugs she gives me. They make me lose my hard-on. But she's right, most men, most real men, can handle a little coke. Why can't I? From everything I've read about the stuff, the high from coke is supposed to be really nice. A lot of guys at Exeter tried it, and really liked it. I probably could have tried it myself, plenty of times, if it hadn't been for old Otto. Damn Otto! At least I'd have known what to expect. What was the matter with me, then? I really wanted to try it with her tonight, but what the hell happened? Was I scared? Yes, maybe a little—I wanted so hard (!) to please her. Christ, I'm crazy about her, but now I'll probably never see her again, unless—unless I

*can get Mom to call off her lawyers, or whatever the hell
it is that Fiona is talking about. But how do I get Mom to
call off her lawyers? I don't even know what this whole
thing is all about. And what the hell is going on here,
anyway? Is Fiona just letting me f--- her and stuffing
coke up my nose because she wants me to help her get
something out of my mother? If so, F. is nothing but a
cunt—"koont," Otto would say—and the cunt is barking
up the wrong tree! Let's find out more about this whole
situation, now that I'm home for the summer. . . .*

*Mom's not home yet. Working late at the office,
Coleman says. My dinner on a tray. Then jacked off,
thinking of how it could have been tonight with Fiona. If I
hadn't f---ed up. Or am I just crazy f---ed-up myself?*

*Or am I an urning? God, what an awful word! Fiona
says my father was an urning, too. But I don't remember anything about my father. What was he like? Mom
doesn't talk about him much. Lenny Liebling would
know, but would he tell me?*

*From today's N.Y. Times: "Analysts say Keith
Lindner takes a different view of things than his
father. For one thing, Chiquita has a more conserva-
tive balance sheet than other Lindner properties."
Two misuses of "than"—instead of "from that of"—
in two successive sentences!*

From the entrance hall, he heard the front door to the
apartment open, then close. That would be his mother coming home. Quickly, Joel closed his journal. Then, standing
on his desk chair, he reached up and slid aside a square of
acoustical tile from his bedroom ceiling, the third tile from
the west wall, the sixth tile from the south. It was acoustical
tile his mother had insisted be installed when, as a kid, he
had briefly taken up the drums. He had discovered this one
loose tile and, in the airspace behind it, he stored his journals, in blue-bound notebooks, safe from all prying eyes. He
slipped his current journal behind the loose tile, replaced the
tile carefully, and hopped down from the chair.

His mother tapped on the door. "Are you decent, darling?"

"Come in!"

She kissed him on both cheeks, then held him at arm's
length. "Darling, you smell of gardenia!" she said. "Is that

your new after-shave? I don't think I much like it." Then she sat on the corner of his bed, and he thought he had never seen her looking prettier. "Joel," she said, "you've seemed so moody lately, so gloomy and down in the dumps. Is something troubling you? Is it a new girlfriend? Can we talk about it? Is there anything I can do?"

"You can call off your bloody lawyers."

There. He had done it. He had kept his promise.

"Hm? Oh, you mean Henry Coker? I didn't know you knew about any of that. It's just a little contract dispute I'm having with your grandfather, and in a situation like this it's usually better to let a lawyer handle it. I don't want you to worry your handsome head about any of that. I want to talk about *you*, Buster. Why do you seem so down in the dumps? I'll bet it's a girl."

"Goddammit, Mother, I told you not to call me Buster!" he shouted.

She just looked at him. Then she said, "I'm sorry. It just slipped out. But please tell me what's the matter."

"It's none of your effing business!"

Chapter 31

In the summer of 1971, Ho and Lily Rothman had thrown a famous party. The occasion was *Mode*'s one hundredth birthday.

There was a certain amount of hucksterism involved in this, of course. The first monthly issue of *Mode* had not appeared until November 1874, and so the magazine was at least three years shy of the century mark. On the other hand, Ho Rothman had learned that a small fashion quarterly called *A La Mode* had made a brief appearance in 1871. *A La Mode* had folded after two issues, but a few members of its disbanded staff had got together and been able to assemble, three years later, what became *Mode*. Thus Ho Rothman was able to rationalize that the "idea" for *Mode* had actually been born in 1871. Besides, he said, "Nobody counts."

Ho's original idea had been to produce a hundredth anniversary issue of the magazine. He was no doubt remembering the success of the yearly anniversary sales at Bamberger's, and his plan was to offer advertisers even deeper discounts than usual if they would buy space in the centennial issue.

The idea for the party, however, had been Alex's. She and Steven had at that point been married for four years, and she had been working with him closely at the magazine to try to produce the precious black ink that Steven's grandfather wanted to see on the magazine's balance sheet. The margin between red ink and black ink had narrowed considerably, but *Mode* was still failing to show a profit. And Alex's ideas for the anniversary party had grown out of an earlier idea—which was that the magazine run a monthly feature devoted to travel.

As usual, Ho Rothman had initially opposed the notion. "Travel?" he roared, pounding his fist on his desk. "We is a fashion magazine. What is travel to do with fashion?"

"Fashionable people travel, Ho," she said. "They need different fashions for different climates in different parts of the world."

"We is not foreigners. We is Americans!"

"And a monthly travel feature would help us attract travel advertisers—the airlines, automobile companies, hotels and resorts, luggage manufacturers—"

"No! Is not the point. Point is, fashionable people travel. Is why we need travel department, like I keep telling you."

"And instead of a hundredth birthday issue—or perhaps in addition to a hundredth birthday issue—what about a wonderful hundredth anniversary party? In Paris. Paris is still the fashion capital of the world."

"No! No French! No Froggies. Froggies said okay to Hitler in the war."

"But just think of the French advertisers we might be able to attract. We'd invite not only the heads of all the couture houses. We'd invite the heads of Air France, of Citroën, Peugeot—the French fabric makers, the perfumers, the milliners, the lacemakers, the wine and brandy makers. And don't forget, France was our main ally in the American Revolution. Lafayette—"

"The French is saints!" he said. "If not for French, we'd still pay taxes to King George. Which is why I say have this party in Paris. Is only place for it."

It was the only way to deal with him, and planning the hundredth birthday gala became Alex's principal project from that point on.

The party was held in June, in a huge red, white, and blue-striped tent set up in the gardens of the Palais de Chaillot, facing the Seine, and, inside the tent, forty tall ficus trees were decorated with eighty thousand twinkle lights. There were three orchestras, eight bars, and a thousand guests dined on baby lamb chops, Scotch salmon with Iranian caviar, fresh quail eggs, tiny ortolan and *fraises du bois* in *crème fraiche*, while consuming nearly a hundred cases of Dom Perignon champagne. Costumed mimes cavorted among the guests, gypsy fortune tellers circulated, reading palms. There were *tableaux vivants* and "living statues"—muscular young men clad only in dance belts and covered from head to toe in bronze, silver, and gold body paint, frozen in classic poses.

Naturally, all the Rothmans flew over for it—Steven and Alex, Ho and Lily, Herb and Pegeen and Herb's brother Arthur, his wife, Doris, and their two teenage daughters, Muffie and Nikki, and Lenny Liebling, who had by then firmly established himself as a member of the Rothman entourage—on the Rothman plane, and all the Paris couturiers sent their top models to provide a continuous fashion show all evening long. The designers themselves were there, of course—Yves Saint-Laurent in a black-sequined dinner jacket—along with the requisite number of Rothschilds, the Comte de Paris, and the international fashion press. Josephine Baker, in a tribute to Piaf, sang "La vie en rose," "Je ne regrette rien," and a winsome rendition of "Happy Birthday, *chère Mode*." Elsa Schiaparelli came out of retirement to make a dramatic entrance. And President and Mme. Georges Pompidou made a special appearance, and led a toast to *"La grande dame de la couture américaine."* Through it all, a beaming Ho Rothman circulated, taking all the credit. "Eight hundred bucks a guest," he told everybody. "So? What's a million dollars?"

Then it was midnight, and time for the giant birthday cake to be rolled in. The twinkle lights were dimmed, and Ho Rothman stepped to the microphone to say his welcoming words. "Our American fashion magazine could not exist today without the brilliant talents of the great couturiers of France," he said. With his Russian accent, he sounded almost like a Frenchman. Of course there were some who said that Steven Rothman, as *Mode*'s editor-in-chief, should have acted as master of ceremonies here, and that Alex Rothman's contributions should at least have been acknowledged. But that was not Ho's way.

Then, as the tall tapers on the cake were lighted one by one, Ho counted out the years of the magazine's life. "One . . . two . . . three . . . four . . ." as the twinkle lights were dimmed almost imperceptibly with each newly lighted candle. Presently, the twinkle lights in the ficus trees were extinguished altogether, and the only illumination in the tent came from the lighted candles on the great cake.

"Ninety-seven . . . ninety-eight . . . ninety-nine," Ho intoned.

But at that point it was noted that every candle on the cake had been lighted, and there was some uneasy whispering, and nervous laughter, among the guests sitting closest to the cake. That was Lenny Liebling's cue to stand up and say, "Oops! It looks as though you're one candle short, Ho!"

"Wait!" Ho replied. "*At-tendez!*" And he held up his hand, pointing skyward.

With that, the whole south-facing flank of the red, white, and blue tent flew open, and a single giant floodlight sprang upward from the top of the Eiffel Tower, directly across the river.

"One hundred!" cried Ho triumphantly, as the huge floodlight soared upward hundreds of feet and caught the clouds of the night sky.

The effect was breathtaking and, for a moment, the guests were speechless. Then the tent broke out with cheering, and everyone rose as the three orchestras launched into, first, the "Marseillaise," and then "The Star-Spangled Banner." Ho's hand went to his breast.

"Thank you, Paris," Ho said, stepping down when the music ended. "*Merci, Paris!*"

That last touch had been Ho's own idea, and it even took Alex Rothman by complete surprise. It had taken some doing to accomplish it. Ho had originally wanted fireworks—a giant Roman candle blazing upward from the top of the tower—but the city fathers of Paris had vetoed that idea as too much of a fire hazard to the rooftops of surrounding buildings. In fact, the final approval of the special floodlight had not come through until six o'clock that evening, and no doubt certain palms had had to be greased.

The Paris party was on the front page of *Women's Wear Daily* in New York the next day, under the headline:

MODE GALA DAZZLES PARIS!

Six pages of photographs were devoted to it inside the newspaper.

The *Times*, as usual, was more restrained, with the head-line:

NORMALLY BLASÉ PARISIANS
IMPRESSED BY FASHION PARTY

The party marked the turning point in *Mode*'s advertising fortunes. In the months that followed, new accounts poured into the book virtually unsolicited.

But meanwhile, backstage at the party, a very different scenario was playing itself out. It seemed that—perhaps because of the hasty, last-minute preparation for the climactic display of light—the switch controlling the floodlights on the tower had apparently been improperly grounded. As the young engineer, whose name was Jean-Claud Lautier, pulled the lever that sent fifty thousand watts of light into the night sky over Paris, he was instantly electrocuted, and his body was sent plunging nine hundred and eighty-five feet downward into the courtyard below.

When the news of the accident was whispered to Ho Rothman, an immediate family council of war was called in one of the small salons in the palace. Alex was excluded from this and, in fact, she knew nothing of the tragedy that befell M. Lautier that night for many months. At the time, she supposed she was excluded from this gathering because she was not a "real" Rothman and had no real title or position with the magazine. More likely, it was because Ho Rothman could not force himself to admit that the one detail of the party that she had not personally planned had gone tragically wrong. Steven Rothman merely told her that there was family business to discuss, and that he would meet her later back at the hotel. And so, in the early-morning hours at the Palais de Chaillot, grand portraits of assorted eighteenth-century Gallic courtiers and their ladies gazed sternly and imperiously down from the walls of the salon in gilded frames, while the various Rothmans screamed at one another.

"The only thing to do," said Steven, pacing up and down the Aubusson and puffing furiously on a cigarette, "is to issue a statement expressing our sympathy to the Lautier family, and offering to make any necessary reparations—"

"What?" Ho bellowed. "And take blame? You'se damn

fool, Steven. It was Frog's own fault."

"But the spotlight was *your* idea, Gramps. You insisted—"

"Why not blame the city of Paris?" Herb Rothman suggested. "It was their damned electricity that did it. They hooked it up. Crazy electricity system. I can't even get my electric shaver to work in my bathroom."

"And at the Ritz!" Pegeen interjected. "At the Ritz! My electric curlers won't work, either."

"Shavers! Curlers!" Ho roared. "You'se all damn fools. I spend million bucks tonight. And this I get for it!"

"Ho could be given the French Legion of Honor for having given this party," Aunt Lily said. "One of Pompidou's aides told me so."

"Damn right," Ho said, "Legion of Honor! Highest honor inna world." (Later on, in fact, he was given it.)

"But what about *me?*" Pegeen wailed. "This was to be the party of the century. This was to be my entree into society—not just New York society, but international society."

"Oh, shut up, Pegeen," her sister-in-law, Arthur Rothman's wife, said. "Nobody gives a damn about you."

"Herbert, are you going to let her talk that way to me?"

"Don't talk to my wife that way, Doris," Herb said.

"I was photographed tonight with the Baroness de Rothschild."

"Fuck the Baroness de Rothschild, Pegeen," Doris Rothman said.

"I'm *that close* to being invited onto the board of the Metropolitan."

"*You?*" said Aunt Lily. "You, on the board of the Metropolitan? That'll be the day."

"Herbert, are you going to sit there and let your mother talk to me that way?"

"Don't talk to my wife that way," he said. "Pegeen and I have a certain social position to uphold."

"I'll talk to her any damn way I feel like," Aunt Lily said. "Some social position."

"Bitch!"

"Social climber!"

"The point is, there must be no publicity," Herb Rothman said. "No publicity about this, is that clear?"

"But how can there be no publicity, Pop?" Steven said. "A man's been *killed.*"

"But I'm the publisher of *Mode*. If any publicity gets out on this, I'll be blamed. Actually, it's all Alex's fault. She planned everything."

"But how can you *say* that, Pop?" Steven said. "It was Gramps who wanted the floodlight. He wanted it to surprise Alex!"

"We could say she's young, inexperienced, uneducated. A little girl from the sticks—"

"Alex had nothing to *do* with the floodlight, Pop!"

"She wanted the party in Paris. Ho didn't want it in Paris— did you, Dad?"

"Damn right! I said no Frogs! Frogs said okay to Hitler— killed six million Jewish pipple!"

"You mean you've spent a million dollars on a party you didn't want to give?"

"Damn right!"

Steven shook his head in despair.

"Now, Ho, dear," Aunt Lily said, "you know that this party was your idea. You told me so."

"Damn right."

"Every important idea this company has ever had has come from you."

"Damn right."

"And you wanted to hold the party in Paris."

"Damn right. De Gaulle is hero. He stood up to Hitler. Saved millions of pipple's lives."

"*And you wanted the floodlight,*" Steven said.

"Damn right. Got it, too. Cost me a million bucks tonight. What happened was Frog's own fault. Frog who plays with Frog electric stuff should know better. If he doesn't, it's suicide."

"Could we say it was suicide?" Aunt Lily suggested.

"Look," Herb Rothman said, "what did we give this party for, anyway? For publicity—right? For *good* publicity, publicity that will attract advertisers. But can you imagine what the enemy press will do to us if they get hold of this story? Look what the enemy press is saying about us already. They're saying the Helen J. Pritzl Award for *Tiny Tots* is a fake."

"Helen Pritzl was fine woman! She taught me English language."

"But what if we were all just to stand up tall, and say we're sorry?" Steven said. "A terrible mistake was made—

by whom, we don't know, but a man's life was lost. We regret it deeply. Wouldn't that be good publicity?"

"Of course not, you horse's ass," his father said. "Haven't you even been following what the enemy press has been trying to do to us? They're even hinting that the loss of our Ingleside printing plant was an insurance fire, for God's sake!"

Steven Rothman looked sideways at his father. "Well," he said, "was it?"

"Shut up, you Goddamned horse's ass! *You* ought to know what the enemy press can do to us! What about what *Women's Wear* is saying about *you?* That you're nothing but your Goddamned wife's Goddamned errand boy—that's what they're saying. If you want to do something for this family, you can get your Goddamned wife pregnant, and give us an heir—that's what you can do."

"Damn right."

"Now, Ho, dear, they're *trying,*" Aunt Lily said gently.

"So what I been telling you all along?" Ho Rothman said. "Pay 'em off. Pay 'em all off—all the Frogs. Is all Nazis, anyway. Pay 'em off, and tell 'em to keep their traps shut. No publicity."

"Thanks, Dad," Herbert said. "That's what I was hoping to hear you say."

Ho Rothman shrugged, though he was clearly unhappy. "So what's another million?" he said.

"But don't pay them off too much," said Aunt Lily, ever the conscientious bookkeeper. "Keep your offers as low as possible. Don't let them get the idea we're rich Americans."

"Does anyone here speak French?" Herb Rothman asked.

"I do," said Steven miserably, and lighted another cigarette.

"So do I," said Lenny Liebling who, up to that point, had said nothing, but had been doing what he always did at gatherings like this one: listening, observing, making mental notes.

And so that was the team that was dispatched that night—Herb, Steven, and Lenny Liebling—to deal with Jean-Claud Lautier's family: his mother, whom he supported, his widow, and his four young children. Lenny and Steven handled the negotiations, while Herbert handled the checkbook. In their grief, as it turned out, the Lautiers' demands were modest;

in fact, the Lautier family seemed already to have resigned themselves to the fact that the young man's death was simply a work-related accident, and they seemed surprised that these strange Americans were approaching them with offers of money. But, most important in the waivers and release forms that they signed were statements to the effect that Jean-Claud's death bore no connection to the Rothman party and that, indeed, early that day, Jean-Claud had talked of committing suicide.

The cover-up operation did not cost Ho Rothman another million. It cost him only six thousand dollars—a thousand to each of Jean-Claud's heirs.

Alone in their suite at the Ritz, Alex Rothman lay wide awake, waiting for the sound of her husband's footsteps in the foyer. She had no idea where he might be, or what he might be doing. Here she was, in Paris, and as far as she knew then her party had been an unqualified success, the added touch of the floodlight a stroke of genius, the kind of genius she sometimes had to admit Ho Rothman had. Their suite was on the quiet side of the hotel, overlooking the Place Vendôme and the Espandon gardens, and the night was very still. But she was still on an adrenaline high from the excitement of the evening, and she could not sleep. She was thinking of her deep curtsy to President Georges Pompidou, and hoping that Steven had noticed it.

Here she was, in Paris, the City of Lights, the city of license, the city of sin, but she was certain that, wherever Steven was, he was not off in search of license or of sin. After four years of marriage to him, she had grown almost used to the fact that theirs was, as it was said, a marriage in name only. They were partners, they were friends, they enjoyed each other's company. They often made each other laugh. They told each other that they were good for one another. They told each other that they made each other happy. He told her that she made him enjoy his life, and his work, more than ever before. Their wedding present from Ho Rothman had been the apartment at 10 Gracie Square, with its magnificent terrace and sweeping river view, and Alex had spent nearly two years decorating it and designing the terrace plantings and gazebo. The black-and-white drawing room had a lustrous black walnut floor defined by thin lines

of brass inlay. The dining room was decorated entirely in a
pale gray-blue, with eighteenth-century English *faux marbre*
dining table and chairs. The library was painted a rich, dark
malachite green, and their newly acquired paintings were
illuminated with the latest Wendel lighting system—small
spotlights concealed in moldings and end tables and operated
by switches on a control panel. Alex and Steven entertained
often, and they were invited everywhere.

To all outward appearances, they were a dream couple—
bright, handsome, young, eager, and very much in love. They
were often in Mona Potter's column in those days, and Mona,
who had no reason to be jealous of Alex then, had christened
them the Ravishing Rothmans.

The Ravishing Rothmans entertained again Thursday
night at their fab-u-lous apartment high above the East
River—a gay dinner of sixteen in honor of the visiting
Sir Noel Coward. Alexandra and Steven Rothman are
the newest and no question the most beautiful of New
York's Beautiful People.

He is tall, dark and handsome, a young Rock Hudson
look-alike, the scion of the Rothman publishing fortune
and editor-in-chief of *Mode*. She's a willowy, creamy-
skinned beauty with hair the color of cornsilk from the
tall cornfields of Kansas, which was right where—you
guessed it, kiddies—Steven Rothman found her. (She
was last June's *Mode* cover girl.)

Steve Rothman says, "She's my new unpaid assistant
on the magazine." And, yes indeedy, that old-time mag
really *does* seem to be shedding some of the dowdy look
it was beginning to get under Connie Ferlinghetti. . . .
Editorially, there's a new sparkle . . . Now that the beau-
teous and talented Alex has a hand in things, I betcha we
can expect more changes. Remember, you heard it from
Mother, kiddies. . . .

They seemed a perfectly matched pair in every way.
Except . . .
In the quiet hotel room, her thoughts turned dark.

"There are some men who are simply asexual," Dr. Richard
Lenhardt had told her. "It's not common, but it's not unheard-

of. It isn't impotence. Sex simply doesn't interest them."

"But how can that be? Everybody talks about how much sex appeal he has. Women fall all over him. They—"

"Yes. Until they discover the asexual personality. There is often a psychogenesis. It may be due to some childhood trauma—the overpowering father and grandfather that you've told me about. It's really up to you, Alex, whether you decide to stay in this marriage that's without love—"

"Oh, there's love," she said. "I really love him very much. In some ways, we're crazy about each other. We never run out of things to talk about. We have wonderful times together, but—"

"I should have said without sex," he said. "The so-called white marriage. There have been other, quite successful white marriages like yours. There are asexual marriages."

"But—" she began. She realized that she was beginning to dislike Dr. Richard Lenhardt, and his repeated use of that term. In fact, this would be their last session together.

"But what, Alex?"

"I really hate talking about this," she said.

"But you must! It is important that you unlock these feelings, Alex."

"But there *is* sex. Sometimes. Not very often. And it's so— perfunctory. And quick. And he doesn't seem to enjoy it, and as a result I don't enjoy it. And I—"

"Yes?"

"And if there is sex, I have to initiate it. Which makes me feel—dirty, somehow. Whorish."

"The asexual personality," he said again. "A textbook case. So you must weigh your options. On the one hand, you have a husband who is very good to you. You have the excitement and glamour of working with an important fashion magazine, meeting and knowing famous and important people. You have the beautiful apartment in the city. You have the lovely estate in Tarrytown for weekends. You have the jewels he gives you, and I'm sure he gives you jewels in lieu of the sex he cannot give you. The jewels are his guilty offering. Each pearl on that triple strand you're wearing represents a drop of his manhood, a drop of his semen, if you will."

"Oh, come on!" she said.

"I'm quite serious. Those pearls are very symbolic, very talismanic. You also have more money than you ever had before. But, on the other hand, you also have the asexual, the white, marriage. Which means more to you? This is what you must decide for yourself—which means more to you, as you contemplate the future of this marriage?"

"But what about children?" she asked him. "The family has made it very clear that they expect us to produce an heir—a son, preferably, since Steven's Uncle Arthur has only the two girls."

"An heir for the Rothman dynasty. What about adoption?"

She shivered. "I don't think the family would stand for that," she said. "An adopted son wouldn't be a real Rothman."

"Have you thought of taking a lover? Certainly, under the circumstances, your husband could raise no objections to that."

"Oh, I couldn't do that," she said. "It would hurt Steven too much. You see, I'm really terribly fond of Steven. I do love him, you see, and I couldn't bear to hurt him."

"Do you miss the sexual side of the relationship that much?"

"Oh, yes," she admitted. "I suppose it's because—well, a man I fell in love with years ago was so—well, the sex was so wonderful that time, so deep, and passionate, and—fulfilling."

"But that is not to happen in this marriage."

"No. Apparently not."

He glanced at his watch, a signal that their hour was nearly over. "I think you want very much to stay in this marriage, Alex," he said.

She nodded. But there was one thing she could not bring herself to tell Dr. Richard Lenhardt. It was simply that she could not bear having her friend Lulu Withers discover that the marriage was not as perfect as Alex had pretended that it was, that Lulu's gloomy predictions had been right. "I told you so," Lulu would say.

Now she heard his key turn in the lock. It was nearly dawn, and sunlight was beginning to filter through the drawn drapes of her bedroom windows. She heard him open the door, and close it behind him. She heard his footsteps cross the thick carpet of the entrance foyer. Was it her imagination, or

did his footsteps sound tired and old? It was her imagination. She turned breathlessly on her side in the bed, and
bunched the big down pillows against her cheek. Now was
the time!

His silhouette appeared outside her open door. He was
still in his dinner jacket, and he paused in her doorway
and lighted a cigarette. They had separate bedrooms, in the
European style.

She sat up eagerly in bed. "Where've you been, darling?"
she asked him. "I was getting worried."

"Family crisis," he said. "But it's settled now."

"What's wrong?"

"It was nothing. I'll tell you about it later."

She patted the bedclothes beside her. "Come in, darling,"
she said. "Let's talk about the party. I've been so excited
I haven't been able to sleep a wink. Let's have one of our
famous postparty rehashes."

With a small sigh, he crossed the room and sat beside her
on the bed. She reached out and loosened his black tie.

When you have these postparty rehashes, Dr. Lenhardt
said, *you always begin by loosening his tie. Why, I wonder? Do the lobes of the black tie symbolize his testicles—
the black, sterile testicles?*

Now that's the silliest thing I ever heard!

I'm not so sure, Alex.

Are you saying I'm a castrating female?

You said that, Alex. Not I.

"Let's rehash everything from beginning to end, darling,"
she said. "There's chilled champagne in the sitting room.
Shall we split that? Oh, yes, let's!"

"No, thanks," he said. "I'm really pretty tired."

"What's the matter? Didn't you think everything went
perfectly?"

"Yes. Perfectly," he said in a dull voice.

*Your husband is subject to deep depressions. It's sympto-
matic of the asexual personality.*

*But he isn't! There's a cynical side to his personality, but
I've never seen him depressed.*

*Depressions are symptomatic of the asexual personality,
Alex.*

*Please stop using that word. It doesn't describe Steven at
all.*

Then perhaps he's bisexual.

Make up your mind, Doctor!

"I saw you dancing with the Princess de Polignac," she said. "What did she say?"

"She said it was a beautiful party."

"And I thought your toast to your grandfather was perfect, darling. Just perfect—giving him all the credit."

"I thought he might have given you some credit. After all, you did everything."

She laughed. "Oh, I'm used to that," she said. "It doesn't bother me, letting him take all the credit. He pays all the bills!"

He said nothing.

"You looked so handsome tonight," she said.

"Thank you."

"Did you see my curtsy to President Pompidou?"

"Yes. You did it beautifully."

"I practiced it long enough!"

"And the floodlight for the hundredth candle on the cake! I couldn't believe my eyes. How did Ho ever think of that? And what sort of strings he must have pulled to *arrange* it— I can't imagine. The Eiffel Tower! The very symbol of Paris! Sometimes I think your grandfather *is* a genius. Didn't you think that was spectacular?"

"Yes. Spectacular. But I don't want to talk about the party, Alex."

She was silent for a moment. Then she said, "What's the matter, darling? Didn't you think it was the most perfect party anyone's ever given—ever in the world?"

"Yes. It's just that I'm—awfully tired, Alex."

She touched his hand. "Spend the night in my bed, darling," she said.

"Night? The sun is up."

"Spend the day, then. We both deserve it, don't you think? After last night? Slip off your clothes, and slip into bed with me."

He lay back across the bed, still in his evening clothes, the tip of his cigarette a tiny pinprick of light in the dark, curtained bedroom. It glowed more brightly as he placed it to his lips and inhaled, and she saw that his eyes were closed.

"What's the matter, Steven?" she said. "What's wrong?"

"Nothing. I told you it was nothing, Alex. Nothing serious. Everything's straightened out now."

"I mean, what's wrong with us?" she said.

PART FOUR

TARRYTOWN, 1973

Chapter 32

"Was prison awful?" he asked the young man who lay naked across his bed as the afternoon sunlight filtered through the drawn drapes of the bedroom on Central Park South.

"Ah, it wasn't so bad," he said.

"Was it in prison that you learned to do all these things that you seem to do so *very* well?"

"Yeah, I guess so. Say, this is a nice place you got here. It's kind of like a museum—all this stuff."

"My friend and I like to collect things. We travel quite a bit."

"You got a regular friend?"

"Oh, yes."

"He live here with you?"

"Yes."

The younger man propped himself up on one elbow. "He apt to come back any minute? I better get myself outta here."

"Oh, no. He's off for the weekend visiting an auntie of his—an auntie he expects to leave him quite a lot of money, so it's an important visit. No, we have the afternoon to ourselves, my friend." Lenny stood up and threw on his red silk Sulka robe. Eyeing his visitor, he added, "Or the whole weekend, if you'd like."

The younger man considered this. "Well, I might just take you up on that," he said. "I got no place to go, and I'm just about flat-out broke."

"Then be my guest," Lenny said, with a little wink.

In those days, Lenny Liebling was not always one hundred percent faithful to Charlie Boxer, and this was in 1969, years before anyone had ever heard of AIDS, and there were times in those days—particularly when Charlie was out of town, tending to the cares of his dear old Aunt Jane—when Lenny strayed from the monogamous path of his union with Charlie, and this afternoon had been one of them. He had met this young man in an Eighth Avenue bar called the Silver Stud, and invited him home with him. And now here they were and, strangely enough, and against his better judgment, Lenny found himself powerfully drawn to this young hustler.

"This is quite ridiculous," Lenny said. "But I've quite forgotten your name."

"Johnny," the young man said. "Johnny Smith."

Lenny smiled. "Of course you don't have to tell me your real name," he said. "Johnny Smith will do."

"But I sure as hell know who you are," the younger man said. "You're that Lenny Liebling."

"Now how in the world did you know that?" Lenny asked him.

"Hell, man, you're famous. I saw your picture in the paper just the other day—in that column by the woman who signs herself Mona. That's how I recognized you at the Silver Stud, and decided to mosey over to the bar and talk to you. And now—hell, man, I've just fucked a real celebrity!"

Lenny lowered his eyelids modestly. "A very minor one, I assure you," he said.

"You work for that *Mode* magazine."

"That is correct."

"The one that's run by that Alexandra—"

"Alexandra Rothman, yes. Alex and her husband, Steven." The young man whistled. "My first celebrity," he said.

"But really, how extraordinary," Lenny said.

"What's extraordinary?"

"That someone like *you* would read Mona Potter's column."

"Hey, man, whatta you mean by that?" the young man said. "Someone like *me*." He reached out and snapped his finger gently against the front of Lenny's Sulka robe.

"Now, now," Lenny said soothingly, and stroked the

younger man's quite remarkable piece of sexual apparatus.
"I simply meant that I didn't realize that Mona's column had
such a wide—readership."

"Man, I can *read*," the young man said, and pulled Lenny
down beside him on the bed again. "I can read as well as I
can do other things."

And by the time that second little session was over, Lenny
realized that he was quite ridiculously, absurdly, mad about
this athletic young roughneck.

"And what do *you* do, Johnny Smith?" Lenny asked him.
"Besides what you so obviously do so *very* well?"

"Do? Oh, there's lots of things I can do," he said. "In
fact, there's not much of anything I can't do. The thing is,
man, I got to find myself a job. But weekends *are* bad for
job-hunting."

"Yes, I suppose weekends *are* bad for that," Lenny said
carefully.

"Those Rothmans," the young man said. "I guess they're
pretty rich."

"Oh, yes," Lenny said.

"And that Alexandra—you know her?"

"Certainly. She's a dear friend."

"Alexandra," he said. "It's not that common of a name. I
used to know a girl named Alexandra."

"Did you just?" Lenny said. "Well, well. You seem terribly
interested in the Rothmans."

"That H. O. Rothman owns the newspaper in the town I
come from out West."

"More than likely. He owns many newspapers."

"Not that anybody's ever laid eyes on the guy."

Lenny seated himself in a chair opposite the bed where the
young man lay, and just then a shaft of sunlight fell directly across the young man's face, a shaft of sunlight that was
almost like a pink key light falling from a proscenium onto
a stage, and when Lenny recalled that shaft of light—as he
often did—Lenny often thought that that light had marked the
beginning of what would become his inspiration and, later,
his obsession.

"You know, you're very beautiful," he said. "Except—"

"Yeah? Except what?"

"Well, I think you'd look much better with darker hair.
With black hair, you'd look rather like a young Valentino—

whom I happened to know, by the way, and who *was* gay."
Lenny had extended one finger in the air, as though sketching
a portrait on canvas. "And I'd have that small bump taken out
of your nose, and of course I'd have your teeth capped and
straightened."

"Yeah, but I can't afford to do all that."

"No, but I could," Lenny said.

The young man sat straight up in bed. "You mean you'd
do that for me—a guy you've just met?"

"Just thinking aloud," Lenny said. "Pygmalion and Galatea."

"Who?"

"Never mind. Have you ever thought of a career in the
theater? I might be able to help you. My friend Charlie and
I have lots of friends in the theater."

"You mean you think I could be an *actor?*" The young
man whistled. "Well, I guess I know a little bit about show
business."

"You *could*," Lenny said. "You have a good, strong voice.
It would take some work, of course. There would have to
be those little cosmetic changes I mentioned. There would
have to be elocution lessons, work with a drama coach, perhaps dance lessons, singing lessons, perhaps fencing lessons,
things like that."

"Yeah, but I could never afford things like that."

"Perhaps not, but I'm saying that *I* could."

"You'd do all that stuff for *me?*"

"I might," Lenny said with another wink, "if you promised
me you'd be a good pupil."

"Hell, man, you must be rich *too*."

"Let's just say moderately well-to-do," Lenny said. "But
what do you think of my idea?"

"Hell, man, I'll try anything—I'm just about desperate
at this point. If you really want to try it. But what about
your friend? What will he think? You know—about you
and me?"

"Charlie is very tolerant, very understanding. And knowing him as I do, I think he'll be amused by the challenge,"
Lenny said.

And so that was how the creation of the young man who
was to become Adam Amado was conceived.

"Man, you're really *nice*," the young man said. "I mean,

you're the first older guy I've been with who's turned out to be really nice."

Lenny laughed. Then he rose and sat on the young man's lap. "You are a true rough-cut diamond," he said. "Why do I so very much look forward to polishing you? Why do I find you so utterly enchanting, Mr. Johnny Smith? I think it's because you manage to radiate a certain sense of—menace. We're going to get you to radiate that sense of menace from behind the footlights."

The young man chuckled. "You ready for round three?" he asked.

What a fool I was twenty years ago, Lenny thought now. And now, not foolish, he was in Herbert Rothman's office in suite 3000 at 530 Fifth Avenue. "I see you've taken over Ho's old office," he said. "Very clever. Once again you've stolen the jump on brother Arthur. Congratulations, Herbert."

Herb ignored this. "Sit down, Lenny," he said.

Lenny seated himself in one of the big low leather chairs, the ones that, even with Lenny's height, placed the visitor's eyes at a considerably lower level than Herbert Rothman's eyes. They had been designed to do the same for Ho's. "Your map is out of date," Lenny said, glancing at the wall. "I don't see a gold star for Boise."

Herb Rothman waved his hand. "I'm having this entire office redecorated," he said. "The map is coming down."

"Pity," Lenny said. "I always found it so marvelously *daunting*. So symbolic of the Rothman power."

Herb Rothman changed the subject. "You've been unavailable all week," he said. "May I ask what you've been doing at our printing plant in Paramus?"

"Certainly. Alex is considering a story on how our magazine gets printed. I've been researching it for her."

"Stupid idea. Typical Alex. Who'd want to read a story like that?"

Lenny steepled his fingers. "Alex is my editor-in-chief," he said.

"Yes. For the time being. But let's get down to business, Lenny. Do you remember that incident in Tarrytown in September of nineteen seventy-three?"

"Of course. Tragic business. Best forgotten about, at this point."

"I am in possession of a photocopy of a certain letter. It offers a clue as to what may have happened there that afternoon. Unfortunately, it offers only half a clue. The other half is missing. You see, the letter which I have is clearly a response to an invitation to 'Rothmere.' What I am looking for is the invitation itself."

"Really, Herbert, I don't know what you're talking about. What invitation? What in the world are you suggesting?"

"That the alleged intruder and assailant was actually invited there. By Alex. And I have reason to believe that you may be in possession of that letter of invitation, Lenny."

Lenny's eyes widened innocently. "Why?" he said. "Why me?"

"It would seem likely, considering your—ah—relationship with the deceased."

"I really don't know what you're talking about, Herbert."

"If you have such a letter, Lenny, it would be worth a lot to me to have it."

Lenny's eyes narrowed. "Really? How much?"

Herbert hesitated. "Suppose you tell me how much you would ask for this letter?"

"Five million dollars," Lenny said. "Mind you, I'm not saying that I have such a letter. Since I assume this conversation is being recorded, I would like to place that fact on the record. I'm merely saying that *if* I had such a letter, which would presumably incriminate Alex, and destroy her career and life forever, I would ask five million dollars for it. That's all."

Herb's face reddened. "Too much," he said. "Out of the question. The company can't afford that kind of money. This IRS business is costing us—"

"The company's problems with the IRS are of no concern to me," Lenny said. "And I was not suggesting that company funds be expended for this. I am suggesting that, if you want such an important letter so badly, you should be willing to dip into your own pockets—pockets which, alas, have always been so much deeper than mine—to obtain such a letter. If, that is, such a letter exists."

"Two million five," Herb said. "But only after I've had a chance to examine the letter and determine its authenticity."

Lenny rose to his feet. "Five million seems cheap for a woman's life," he said. "It certainly seems cheap for a man as rich as you are. But I'll tell you something, Herbert. I've never liked dealing with you. I don't like dealing with you now. In fact, I've never liked one thing about you, nor, I dare say, do you have much love for me. We've been able to tolerate each other—just barely—over the years, for reasons that you and I both understand. As a matter of fact, I hate you, Herbert, and am in no mood to do any special favors for you and your friend Fiona. Steven, on the other hand, was quite another matter. I adored Steven—the son that you helped kill."

Herbert jumped to his feet. "Kike faggot bastard!"

"Good afternoon, Herbert," he said. "Let's stay in touch."

When Lenny had gone, Herbert Rothman reached for the telephone on his private line. "My darling?" he said when she answered. "I've got him on the hook. And you were right—I'm certain he has the letter."

"How much does he want for it?"

"Too much. But I'll work him down."

"Oh, pay him whatever he bloody wants, Herbert, and let's have done with the whole bloody mess."

"Now sweetheart, you never pay a man his first asking price. You offer him half, and settle somewhere in between. Just let me handle the negotiations, my darling. Lenny's hungry, and I know how to handle him. Can I see you tonight, my darling?"

She hesitated. "I suppose so. But I warn you, my bloody nerves are bloody shot from all of this."

"Not mine," he said. He lowered his voice. "In fact, now that we're getting close to the end of this, I'm feeling bloody horny."

She giggled. "Sevenish," she said.

From time to time, over the years, Lenny Liebling and Charlie Boxer dropped by the vault of the Manufacturers Hanover Trust to pay a call, as it were, on their letter. They slipped safe-deposit box number 369 out of its narrow slot, and withdrew with it into one of the small windowless rooms where there were a table and chairs, and a door that could be dead-bolted from the inside. Then they snapped open the box and checked its contents—their respective wills (each bequeathing whatever he had to the other), a few stock certificates and savings bonds, and the letter, along with that document from the Court House of Jackson County, Missouri.

Now, in the windowless room of the vault, Lenny removed the pale blue envelope and handed it to Charlie. "Your house in the Hamptons," he said.

"Not just a house. A showplace," Charlie said. "And this is the time to buy, you know. The real estate market is in a slump. There are 'For Sale' and 'Price Reduced' signs all over the South Shore."

"So I'm told," Lenny said.

"Will he really pay that much?"

"I'm quite sure he will. He faces a very expensive lawsuit if he doesn't. And apparently he has the letter that was written in response to this, which makes our letter much more valuable to him, doesn't it? Yes, ever so much more valuable."

"The two pieces to the puzzle," Charlie said.

"Rather like the two keys it takes to open a safe-deposit box, isn't it?" He smiled.

Charlie held the pale blue envelope by its corners, gingerly, between his fingertips. He pressed its slit open, just to be sure that the crested sheet of pale blue letterhead was still inside, along with the boxholder's note. There was no need to take out the letter and read it. Both Lenny and Charlie knew the words by heart, and the paper those words were written on was fragile, perishable, particularly if unfolded and refolded too often. "The postmark, everything," Charlie said. "Would her fingerprints still be on it, do you think?"

"Possibly," Lenny said. "After seventeen years, I don't know. But possibly. And it occurs to me, dovey, that probably you should not leave the apartment for the next few days, at least while we're negotiating."

"Oh? Why not?"

"Now that Herbert has guessed that we have this letter, it might occur to him to hire someone to do a little Watergate on us."

"My God! You're right!"

"Herbert's playing hardball now, dovey. And the Brit bitch is pushing him. My spies have been reporting to me."

Carefully, Charlie replaced the blue envelope in the box, and closed the lid.

Keeping the letter in the bank's vault had been Charlie's

idea. It was too dangerous to hide the letter, in, say, a desk drawer in the Gainsborough apartment. Apartments could be burglarized and, in New York these days, even apartments in the most secure buildings often were. Also, if a too-inquisitive guest at one of their famous Sunday soirees happened upon that letter, and grasped its significance, that would be the end of everything.

But the vault of the Manufacturers Hanover Trust was the newest, safest, most fireproof in the city. It was also Charlie's idea to keep the key to this particular safe-deposit box in another safe-deposit box, in a different bank—the Chase Manhattan, just down the street. Charlie knew that if one had a key, and knew another person's bank and box number, it was ridiculously easy to gain access to that person's box. The tellers rarely bothered to compare signatures on those little access slips they made you sign. Lord knows that he had gone into his dear Aunt Jane's safe-deposit box often enough, and no one ever questioned the fact that he was signing a woman's name.

Finally, it was Charlie's idea that both boxes be rented in his name only. After all, though Lenny never revealed his age, even he would admit that he was a few years older than Charlie, and probably would be the first to go. And both men had agreed never to have the letter Xeroxed, or copied in any way. It would be too dangerous if a copy of this letter ever fell into anyone else's hand. Possession of the original was everything. It was their insurance, for neither Lenny nor Charlie owned a penny's worth of life insurance. Lenny had always said that letter would be valuable someday, though he didn't know how, and now apparently that day was at hand.

There was also the document from the Jackson County Court House. That was a somewhat different situation, since other copies of it certainly existed. Anyone interested could easily go to the Bureau of Vital Statistics in Kansas City and obtain a copy for the asking. But the point was that, without the letter, that document was all but meaningless. Without the letter, the connection between the two pieces of paper would never be made. The letter was pivotal, and was worth much, much more—as they say—than its weight in gold.

"I was thinking," Charlie said now, "that if Herbert Rothman will pay that much for it, how much would Alex pay?"

"You mean put it up for auction? Sell it to the highest bidder?"

"Something like that."

Lenny ruffled what remained of his friend's thinning hair. "Now don't be greedy, dovey. I don't think Alex has that kind of money. Besides, other sources of income are on their way."

"Really? From where?"

"You'll see," said Lenny with a wink. "Irons are in the fire. All things come to him who waits."

"Voilà!" Lenny cried, unrolling the big rug across the parquet floor of the red-and-gold drawing room at 720 Park Avenue. "What do you think of your Isfahan, Aunt Lily dear? Isn't it gorgeous? And it wasn't gone too long."

Aunt Lily Rothman peered down at the rug. "It looks different," she said. "It looks new." She sniffed. "It even smells new."

"Of course!" he said. "Because it's *like* new! It's clean at last. Now you can see all the original colors, as they came from the weavers' looms."

She studied it some more. "It just doesn't look like the same rug," she said.

"Of course it doesn't, because it's been so long since you've seen it *clean*. How long has it been since it's been cleaned? Twenty years? Thirty years? You're seeing your rug with thirty years of filth and grime removed."

"My house isn't full of filth and grime."

"The cleaner did a really lovely job. And he only charged a thousand dollars. Can you imagine? I'm having the bill sent to you."

"Hmm. I don't think that's so cheap."

"It's an absolute steal, Lily dear. Now what about those two Boulle commodes?" he said. "Look at the way your stupid maids have chipped and barked and scratched their legs with their vacuum cleaners. As luck would have it, I have a little man who's a superb refinisher. Of course he'll have to have the pieces for a while. Refinishing fine furniture takes longer than cleaning a rug."

"No, I don't think so," she said. "Taking those out will leave big holes in the room."

"Only for a few weeks."

"No. I don't think so."

"But when you own fine furniture, Lily dear, you must not let it fall into disrepair. If you do, it's a sign of aging. And we can't have people think you're aging, can we, Lily? Letting things go?"

"Well, I'll think about it," she said, "But meanwhile, what about the other business?"

"Aha!" he said, reaching for his briefcase. "I have something for you. Hot off the presses." He opened his briefcase and withdrew a sheet of parchmentlike paper. "The first Rothman Communications stock certificate. I had it issued in your name—a thousand shares." He handed it to her, and she examined it closely.

"Notice the date," he said. "Nineteen twenty-two. You could say it was Ho's wedding present to you. Wouldn't that sound nice? I particularly like the Mercury symbol at the top—Mercury with his winged feet. Mercury was the messenger of the gods. Mercury—communications. See? And I also like the scroll and key design along the border. It's printed on something called distressed paper—new paper that looks old. Aren't I clever at making new things look old?" And he hoped, briefly, that she would not look down at the rug again. She did not.

"If you approve, I'll have more printed up," he said. "In different denominations, different people's names, different dates, as we discussed."

"What about the people at the plant? Does anyone know what we plan to do with this?"

He smiled. "Fortunately," he said, "I have found a pressman who is not too bright." He tapped his head. "He has been my sole accomplice."

"I don't like that word *accomplice*, Lenny."

"Assistant, then. Anyway, he thinks we're printing party favors."

She nodded. "Let me study this awhile," she said. "I'll call you in the morning."

When Lenny had gone, Aunt Lily walked quickly down the linenfold walnut-paneled hallway to her husband's room. "Why don't you take a coffee break, Mrs. Zabriskie?" she suggested. "I'll sit with Mr. Rothman for a while." Mrs. Zabriskie gathered up her needlework, and rose.

And when Mrs. Zabriskie had gone, Ho Rothman opened

his eyes and pushed himself up on his elbows in the hospital bed. "Damn bedpan," he said. "Damn pipple make me use this bedpan." He pushed the offending object out of his way. "Okay, whatta you got?" He pointed to the parchmentlike sheet of paper in her hand.

"I think we've just had a rug ripped off us," she said. "Now he's after my Boulle chests. How much more do we want to give him?"

"Chests, shmests," he said. "Let's see what the *schnorrer's* done for us," and he snatched at the sheet of paper.

"Three million," Herb Rothman's voice said into the telephone.

"Three million what?" Lenny said.

"Three million dollars. For the letter, you rubber asshole. That's my final offer."

"My dear fellow, I have no idea what you're talking about," Lenny said, and hung up the phone.

And at that moment, Alex was taking a telephone call from Rodney McCulloch. "I think we need to talk," he said. "Let's do another lunch. The fish place again? Ha-ha-ha."

She hesitated. "Our last meeting at the fish place got us written up in Mona Potter's column," she said. "If you think we need to meet again, maybe you'd better come to my house. But I ought to warn you, I haven't made any decision about your offer, Rodney."

"Look, you're fighting a losing battle," he said. "Everybody in this whole damn town knows you're fighting a losing battle now. Why fight a losing battle? Why not shake hands with Rothman and get out of the ring? Why wait till there's blood all over the floor?"

Chapter 33

"I usually try to read my so-called fan mail," Mel Jorgenson said. "But not the way things have been going this week. Luckily, one of the secretaries thought this letter might be of particular interest to me. I want you to read it." They were sitting in her dark green, book-lined library, and he reached in his jacket pocket, withdrew a letter, and handed it to her. She read:

Dear Mr. Jorgenson:
My name will mean nothing to you, but your name means a great deal to me. And since you performed a particularly kind service to me, I am writing not only to thank you for that, but also, I hope, to perform some equal service to you.
I don't know whether you will remember this, but at the outset of a recent week-end, my daughter and granddaughter and I were stranded on the median of the Long Island Expressway with a flattened tyre. Suddenly a mechanic's lorry appeared, and came to our rescue, and with his spanner the mechanic changed our tyre in a trice. When I offered to pay this gentleman his fee, he replied that there was "No charge," and explained that you, who had passed us on the motorway, had rung him by motorphone and described our plight and instructed him to send the bill to you. That was an extraordinarily

kind thing for you to do, and two helpless women, my daughter and myself—not to mention my infant grand-daughter, who was already wailing for her bottle (and in need of a nappy change, I might add!)—will always be extraordinarily grateful to you for that kindness. I am an Englishwoman, visiting in America, and everywhere I have gone I have been impressed by the extraordinary kindness and courtesy of Americans. But you, sir, are truly a Good Samaritan.

Which brings me to my second reason for writing to you. As I say, I am English, visiting my daughter and her husband, who live in New York, from my home in London to inspect the new grandchild. In reading American newspapers recently, I have run across the name and photograph—particularly in the Daily News column by a woman who signs herself "Mona"—of a young woman who styles herself Lady Fiona Hesketh-Fenton. I wonder if you are fully aware of who this woman is. To begin with, her given name is indeed Fiona, though I am not sure of the Fenton part. As my maiden name was Fenton, I can only say with surety that she is not a member of our own, rather small, Fenton clan. In England, I believe she used another surname, though I can't recall what it was, but I am quite sure that she does not bear the title "Lady." But what I am quite positive of is that she is not the daughter of Viscount Hesketh. Viscount Hesketh is, in fact, a distant cousin of mine (the Hesketh and Fenton families merged in the late seventeenth century) and a sometime neighbour, since he lives near Reigate, Surrey, where I keep a small week-end cottage, though I have never met him. The Viscount is one of our famous "English eccentrics," and something of a recluse and misanthrope.

But I have checked the Hesketh and Fenton family charts, and, as I was quite certain even before checking the "tree," Viscount Hesketh has no daughters, though there was a son who was killed in the Falklands War. Furthermore, if there were a daughter, she would normally style herself a Marchioness, which I suppose is neither here nor there since there are no daughters.

It is true that until rather recently this young woman worked in a dressmaker's shop in Knightsbridge, though *she was not the proprietress of it, as I have read in your news dailies, and it seems to me most unlikely, considering her position, that she ever designed or selected clothing for H.R.H. the Princess of Wales or the Duchess of York, or that she was the recipient of any sort of Royal Warrant, as I have also read. All that, I suspect, is a fiction.*

I should also tell you that when this young woman left England earlier this year, she left under a considerable cloud. In fact, it is my understanding that, should she return to England, she could face criminal charges as a result of certain financial peculations alleged to have taken place while she was employed at the dressmaker's shop. I confess not to have all the details of these, but it was alleged that she had embezzled or stolen sizable sums of money from the shop's till. The proprietress of the shop was a Mrs. Alcock, if memory serves.

I would not go into such exhaustive detail with you, dear Mr. Jorgenson, had I not also read in the American press that this young woman has recently been engaged as co-editor of the American magazine Mode, *whose other co-editor, Alexandra Rothman, is often mentioned in the press as a dear friend of yours, and sometimes as your fiancée. I felt it my duty to warn you and Miss Rothman that the woman who now calls herself Lady Fiona Hesketh-Fenton seems to be "flying under false colours" in America today.*

I hope that you and Miss Rothman will take this letter in the spirit in which it is intended, which is one of helpfulness—the kind of helpfulness which you so generously showed to me whilst my daughter and I were so ignominiously stranded on the motorway. I cannot thank you sufficiently for that.

> *Yours most sincerely,*
> *Elizabeth Fenton Hardinge*
> *(Mrs. John D.B.R.)*

Alex put the letter down. "She's a little vague, and fuzzy on some details," she said. "But I'll fax this over to Mark Rinsky in the morning. Maybe it'll give him a few more clues."

"I'm getting bad feelings about this girl, Alex. I'm getting the feeling that she's very bad news."

"Ha!" she said. "She's just about the worst news I've had in a long time."

"She told me she has a sister who lives in Australia. She told me she and her sister were both sexually abused by their father when they were little girls. She told me she had a husband who was killed in the Falklands War. She told me she has a daughter, who's retarded and lives in Switzerland. Suddenly I don't believe any of that crap."

"I didn't realize you'd gotten to know her so well, Mel!"

"I guess I felt sorry for her that night I took her home from the Van Zuylens'. But I'll tell you something else."

"What's that?"

"I wasn't going to tell you this, but I will. She tried to put the make on me."

"She *didn't!* That night?"

"A couple of days later. She asked me for a drink at her place at the Westbury. She wanted me to try to get you to call off your lawyers. She said she wanted me to help her make her peace with you. Then she tried to put the make on me. Literally."

"And what did you—?"

"Got up and left, of course. I sensed then that she was a phony, but . . ."

"A *phony!* The word begins with 'b' and rhymes with rich!"

"And remember that night after the Van Zuylens' party? When we got back to Sagaponack, and I went for a swim? And you thought you saw a prowler?"

"Of course."

"That was her. She came to the house in a taxi, thinking I'd be alone and feel like bedding her down. Then she saw you through the glass, and ran off."

"Oh, Mel!" she cried. "This is just getting to be too *much!* Fix me a drink, darling." She jumped to her feet, and found herself facing the René Bouché portrait.

From where he stood at the drinks cart, Mel said, "There's just one more thing I want to tell you, Alex. I know you're going through hell with this right now. But, whichever way it turns out, I don't want you to worry about your future. I don't want you to worry about where Steven's trust is, or whether

you're going to lose your job, or whether this apartment will
be taken away from you, because I'll always take care of you.
Just as soon as this mess is settled, I'm going to marry you,
and your future is going to be our future. Together. That's
all I have to say."

"But you don't think I'm going to *lose* this, do you, Mel?
Not now—when I'm suddenly, and for the first time since all
this started—when I'm all at once beginning to *enjoy* this?"

It was a second or two before she realized that he had just
asked her to marry him and, in his own way, set the date.

She ran across the room to him and hugged him as he
poured whiskey into their glasses. "Oh, Mel, what a dear,
sweet, wonderful thing to say," she said.

"Let's see if we can nail the bitch," he said gruffly.

"So that's Alexandra Rothman," Adam Amado said. It was
1971, and Adam had been with Lenny and Charlie for nearly
two years. Lenny was just home from Paris, and they were
going through the press clippings from *Mode*'s hundredth
anniversary gala the week before.

"Yes, that is she," Lenny said. "Lovely, isn't she?"

"Husband's good-looking, too."

"Yes, but unavailable, alas." Lenny sighed.

"Tall guy. Look at him standing next to his father."

"That's his grandfather, actually," Lenny said. "That's the
great Ho Rothman himself. But Steven's father is also a small
man. There's a picture of Ho and Herbert Rothman standing
together." He pointed to the clipping.

"Couple of midgets, compared with the son."

"Yes. Funny, isn't it? But I've noticed how the children
of the first really rich generation in a family seem to shoot
up in height. Better nutrition, I suppose, is what does it."

Adam turned back to the photograph of Alex curtsying
before President Georges Pompidou. "What was her maiden
name, d'you know?"

"Lane. Alexandra Lane."

"From a little midwestern town?"

"A little town called Paradise, Missouri, in fact. Can you
imagine?"

"She's come a long way, hasn't she? Meeting the king of
France."

"The *president* of France," Lenny corrected.

"Yeah," Adam said. "She's the girl I used to know. Wears her hair a little shorter now. But, if anything, she's even prettier than when I knew her."

Lenny looked up, startled. "You knew Alex Rothman?"

He nodded. "Back in Paradise."

"Well, if you're an old friend, why don't I get the two of you together?"

"Friend doesn't exactly describe it," Adam said.

"It would be easy enough to do. She and Steven don't come to our Sunday night salons because they spend their weekends up in Tarrytown. But I could ask them over for a drink on a weekday night, and you and she could have a Paradise reunion."

Adam laughed. "Nah, I don't think she'd be too happy to see me now. It would bring back too many unhappy memories."

"Oh?" Lenny said, all at once intensely interested. "What sort of unhappy memories, pray?"

"I don't want to get into any of that," Adam said. "Besides, she probably wouldn't even recognize me now—with my new black hair, my new nose, my new teeth, and my new, veddy fahncy speaking voice. No, don't tell her you know me, Lenny—that would be bad."

There was a twinkle in Lenny's eye. "When you first came to us, you said your name was Johnny Smith," he said. "I've heard Alex speak of a boy back in Paradise whose name was *Dale* Smith. I gather Dale Smith was something of the town bully. Alex hated him. Was that who you were, Adam?" He winked at him. "Were you the town bully, Adam? I'll bet you were. Peck's bad boy!"

"No, I don't know no Dale Smith."

"You don't know *any* Dale Smith," Lenny corrected.

"Right, Henry Higgins," Adam said, and grinned.

It was their little joke.

"Did you know Alex before or after you went to prison?" Charlie Boxer asked him a few days later.

"Before."

"You know, Adam, you've never told us what you went to prison *for*. Would it be rude to ask?"

"They tried to charge me with murder two, but they couldn't make it stick. It was reduced to involuntary manslaughter."

"You mean to say you killed a man?" Charlie said. "How exciting. How did it happen?"

Adam grinned a little sheepishly. "Barroom fight," he said. "A guy said something to me I didn't like. I slugged him. He cracked his skull on the bar rail. I didn't mean to kill him, but what the guy said really made me mad."

"Oh? What did he say?"

"I used to have a nickname—Skipper. This guy said that the reason why I was called Skipper was because I liked to skip around from one sex to the other—that I liked to have sex with both boys and girls. That really made me mad."

"Oh, my. Yes indeed, I can see how it would have."

"Anyway, that was in the old days. I'm a whole new person now, thanks to the two of you."

Lenny strolled into the room, a copy of *Casting Notes* in his hand. "There's an audition for the second male lead in a new Broadway musical tomorrow, Adam," he said. "I think you should get yourself over to it."

"Only the second lead? Not the lead?"

"Second lead is a very important part."

"I don't feel much like doing a musical," Adam said.

"Really, Adam," Lenny said with more than a touch of annoyance in his voice. "I *do* think you should apply yourself a little harder in terms of looking for work. The parts aren't going to come looking for you, you know. You've got to get out there and look for them."

Adam stood up and stretched. "Well, maybe I'll wander over there tomorrow," he said. "See what kind of a part it is."

Alex was lying beside the pool at "Rothmere," and Lucille Withers lay in the lounge chair next to her. Alex was wearing a red bikini, and the tall Lucille was wearing an old-fashioned, full-skirted suit. Lucille had arrived for one of her occasional, unannounced visits to New York, and Alex had persuaded her to come up to Tarrytown for the weekend. Lucille had agreed to come only after the inexpensive hotel where she was staying had promised not to charge her for the two nights she would not be using the room. Steven was on the tennis court, playing with his father.

"Yes, I can see he's made you very happy, Lexy," Lucille was saying as they watched the two men.

"Oh, yes," Alex said.

Lucille's eyes wandered across the pool, past the tennis court, to the gardens, and the great châteaulike house on the rise above them. "Well, it's certainly a far cry from Kansas City, isn't it?" she said. "A far cry . . ."

August, who was the family's majordomo in those days, appeared in his white mess jacket at the moon gate that led out to the pool area. "There's a telephone call for you, Mrs. Rothman," August said. "The gentleman won't give his name, but he says to tell you that he's an old friend from Paradise."

Alex frowned. "All right. I'll take it, August."

"Would you like me to bring the telephone down here, Mrs. Rothman?"

"No thanks. I'll take it in the house." She rose, knotted a white beach towel around her waist, and started up the garden walkway toward the house, with August following a few steps behind her.

Across from the living room at "Rothmere" was a small room called the telephone room. It was, as its name implied, a room designed just for placing and receiving telephone calls. It was furnished as a tiny, elegant office, with a loveseat, and a small, leather-topped table upon which reposed a pad of pink note paper, a slim pencil for doodling or taking notes, and a black telephone of the old-fashioned jonquil shape. The telephone room had a door that could be closed for privacy. Alex lifted the receiver. "Hello?" she said.

"Well, they finally put me through to you," a man's voice said.

"Who is this?"

"It's Skipper Purdy," he said.

When she returned to the pool several minutes later, Lulu Withers looked up at her questioningly. "My goodness," she said. "You look like you've just seen a ghost."

"Just spoke to one," she said. She unknotted her towel, spread it out on the lounge chair again, and lay down, facing the sun. Her eyes drifted off in the direction of the tennis game. "It was my old friend Annie Merritt," she said. "She just happened to be passing through."

Lulu's look remained questioning. Hadn't she just heard August say, *The gentleman won't give his name?*

But she said nothing.

Chapter 34

At Hobo's Luncheonette on West 44th Street, Lenny Liebling sat at the counter eating a tuna salad while having a small disagreement with Mr. Howard Bogardus, the eatery's proprietor, who, in turn, was trying to handle the orders from his lunchtime customers, barking the orders into a small microphone that was connected to the kitchen in the back.

"Scramble two. Side o' down."

"Pastrami rye. Extra mustard."

"Fry two, over easy."

"But you see, my good fellow," Lenny was saying, "we agreed that your invoice for last month's conference room lunches would be for twenty cheeseburgers, seventeen tuna melts, twenty-eight roast beefs, ten grilled cheese, and sixty turkey clubs. At eight ninety-five, the turkey club is your most expensive sandwich. But you have only billed for six turkey clubs. There's quite a difference between six and sixty. And the difference to me would amount to—"

"Rare cow. Side of French. . . . Sorry, Mr. Liebling, but that's what my records show."

"Four hundred and eighty-three dollars and thirty cents."

"Sorry, Mr. Liebling. . . . Egg salad on white down. Hold the mayo."

"I'm going to have to ask you to prepare a new invoice, Mr. Bogardus," Lenny said.

"Fry two, straight up. Side of down . . . medium cow, side of rings . . ."

"Yours is not the only coffee shop in town, Mr. Bogardus," Lenny reminded him.

"Rare cheese . . . pig 'n cheddar rye . . . stretch two . . . two blacks, two regular . . ."

"Did you hear what I said, Mr. Bogardus?"

"Look, whyntcha come back when I'm not so busy?" Mr. Bogardus said. "Maybe we can work something out. . . . Pig 'n Swiss on whole down . . ."

A woman seated herself on the stool next to Lenny, and suddenly the air around him was heavy with gardenia scent. He turned, and there she was.

"Why, Fiona, what a strange place for us to meet," he said.

"It's the nearest coffee shop to your office," she said. "I rather fancied you might come here for lunch."

"In fact, I usually don't. I usually have a hamburger sent over from 'Twenty-One.' But today I had some personal business to attend to."

"Then let's say I'm prescient," she said, and there was something sneering in the way she said *prescient*.

"What'll ya have, lady," Mr. Bogardus said.

"Just coffee, please."

"Five dollar minimum, twelve to two."

"That's all right."

"Black or regular?"

"Black, please."

"Draw one black!"

"Herbert tells me you're causing us some—difficulties," she said.

"Really? I wonder what Herbert means by that?"

"About a certain letter."

"A letter? What letter, I wonder?"

"A letter Alex wrote years ago. To a friend of yours."

"Well, Alex and I share a number of friends, and I'm sure Alex has written many letters in her lifetime, but I have no idea which letter, or which friend, you might be talking about."

"This friend is dead."

"Well, I'm reaching the age when many of my friends are dying," he said. "Alas, we are all mortal."

"I could cause some trouble for you," she said.

"Really? How?"

"Joel Rothman and I have become very close."

"Really? I was not aware of that."

"Oh, yes. Joel's mother has been so—preoccupied—these days that she hasn't had much time for him. And Joel's told me things—things that he would only tell a mother."

"What sort of things, pray?"

"That you have made sexual advances to him."

"But that is patently untrue," he said, eating his salad.

"But Herbert is very susceptible to things I tell him," she said. "And if I were to tell him that—that you have made sexual advances to his grandson, the last male Rothman heir—that wouldn't make Herbert very happy, would it? It could mean the end of your long, free ride with the Rothmans, couldn't it? You see, Herbert is quite madly in love with me."

"Oh, I'm quite aware of that," Lenny said. "That's been apparent ever since you appeared on the scene—from out of nowhere. It's quite apparent that you have Herbert Rothman in the palm of your hand."

"Herbert will do anything for me. He will believe anything I say. And if I were to tell him about you and Joel—on top of what he already knows about you and Joel's father—well, I think that would effectively end the career of Lenny Liebling, wouldn't it?"

"It might. But it wouldn't get him his precious letter, either, would it? Really, Fiona, you disappoint me. I'd expected you to come up with a more original threat than that."

Fiona glared angrily down at her untouched cup of coffee, and Lenny took another forkful of his tuna salad.

"Now let's talk about you for a moment," he said. "You say your father is the Earl of Hesketh. The one who styles himself Viscount Hesketh."

"That is correct," she said.

"Then your brother would have been Lord Moyne."

"Correct. My brother Alistair, yes."

"Alistair? I understood that Lord Moyne's given name was Percy."

"Percy, yes. But we've always called him Alistair. He hates his real name. He'll simply fly into an absolute rage if you call him Percy."

"Very curious," Lenny said, balancing his fork between

his thumb and forefinger. "DeBrett lists Viscount Hesketh
as having had only one child, a son named Percy Edward
George, Lord Moyne. Deceased several years ago. It's hard
to imagine him flying into rages now. DeBrett makes no mention of a daughter, or of any other issue, for that matter."

"I had myself taken out of DeBrett. I refuse to be listed
there. It's just a snob thing, you know."

"Really?" Lenny said. "I didn't know that one *could* have
oneself taken out of DeBrett, which is supposed to be the
official and complete compilation of the British peerage."

"Well, one can, and I did," she said.

"And can one also have oneself taken out of Burke's *Peerage*—where, incidentally, I can't find you either?"

"Absolutely. If you know the right people, it's easy. You
won't find me in the *Almanach da Gotha*, either. I refuse
to have my name appear in any of those snobby hereditary
listings."

"Interesting," Lenny said. "I didn't realize anything like
that was possible." Toying with what remained of his salad,
he changed the subject. "Your shop in Sloane Street. Where
was it exactly?"

She hesitated just briefly, but noticeably. "Number forty-
three," she said.

"Ah," he said. "That would be just down the street from
Harvey Nichols."

"Across the road," she said.

"And it was called?"

"My shop was called Fiona. What else?"

"And never listed in the telephone directory?"

"Never!"

"Pity I never noticed it. I've been going to London twice
a year for twenty years, and I thought I knew Sloane Street
like the back of my hand. But I never noticed a shop called
Fiona."

"There was no sign in front," she said. "It was that exclusive. You had to ring the bell for entry, and then take the
lift to the first floor. I never advertised. My clients were too
important. I was by appointment only."

"Oh, I'm sure," he said, and once more changed the subject. "As a Londoner," he said, "I'm sure you know my old
friend Nigel Dempster, the society columnist."

"Oh, dear me, yes. Everyone knows Nigel."

"Curious," he said. "I spoke to Nigel the other day, and he claims not to know you."

Her dark eyes flashed. "That," she said, "is for two reasons. Nigel is cross with me for refusing to share gossip with him about the Royal Family for his silly column. Nigel is spiteful. He's also cross with me for defecting from England, and coming to America. A lot of Brits are cross with me for that. Fergie is cross with me for that, too."

"Ah," Lenny said. "So that explains it. As you know, Nigel and Fergie are very thick. That would explain why Fergie claims she doesn't know you, either."

"Exactly," Fiona snapped. "Fergie is also cross with me because I told her she simply *had* to lose weight. I refused to fit her unless she lost at least a stone, and so she just flounced out of my shop. Typical Fergie. Typical Nigel, too. Typical Brit, if you ask me. Such snobs about Americans, whom I happen to admire."

"I don't suppose Nigel would have known you under another surname. After all, in England, the name Fiona is almost as common as Doris."

"Certainly not."

"Not as Fiona Stanfill?"

"*What?* What did you just—?"

"Fiona Stanfill."

"How did you—?"

He put down his fork. "At Alex's party the other night, on her terrace, after Herbert made his little speech and introduced you. You and Herbert were so busy dealing with the press and television cameras, and answering all their ridiculous questions. I happened to notice that you'd left your handbag by your place at the table. Quite a handsome bag, by the way—a Chanel, black alligator, with a long gold shoulder chain. I took the opportunity to open it, and found your passport. You see, you're not the only person who's clever at exploring the contents of women's handbags. Alex has a detective checking on your background. His name is Mark Rinsky. Mark's representatives in England haven't been able to come up with much in the way of background on Fiona Fenton. But they've been barking up the wrong tree. If they were looking into the background of Fiona Stanfill, they'd discover quite a little, wouldn't they? Yes, *quite* a little. I suppose one could tip them off. Yes, I can see why you're in such a hurry to get rid of Alex." He looked at his gold watch. "But I must get back to the office. Alex has a story meeting." He stood up, and dropped his paper napkin in his plate. "Just don't mess with Lenny, Miss Stanfill," he said. "Don't mess with dear old Lenny."

He walked out of the lunchroom and left her sitting at the counter in front of her untouched cup of cold, five-dollar coffee.

He also left behind his unpaid check. That would be for Howard Bogardus to deal with.

"I need to see you, Alex," he said.

With one hand she reached out and closed the door to the telephone room. "I have some money for you," she said. "The money from your money belt. I put it in a savings bank. I never touched it. With interest over the years, it's probably increased quite a bit. I'll mail you the passbook, wherever you are."

"I'm in New York. But it's not that. I don't care about the money, Alex, but I need to see you."

"I eventually sold the yellow Corvette. There was a little problem over the title to it, but I sold it. I added that money to the savings account."

"I don't care about any of that. I need to see you. When can I see you?"

"Are you in some other kind of trouble, Skipper?"

"No! Not at all. I have a great new life, a whole new career. Just tell me when I can see you."

"That's going to be difficult," she said. "Because I have a whole new life, too."

"I know. I know all about that. But I do need to see you. There are things I need to tell you. Things we need to talk about. It won't take long."

"It's been over ten years, Skipper."

"I know, I know, and you'll probably hardly recognize me now. But I do need to see you, Alex. Please. For old times' sake. For all the things we used to be to each other. For the afternoons on the bluff, where the two rivers meet. Please."

She felt her head spinning. "It would have to be on a weekday, when the rest of the family is in the city—you understand," she said.

"Of course. Just tell me when."

"Thursday," she said. "The servants here take Thursday afternoons off. Thursday at three. I'll meet you in the boathouse."

"Fine. Just tell me how to get there."

"When you come through the gates, don't take the drive to the right that leads up to the main house. Take the drive to the left, down the hill, past the pool and the tennis court. The drive ends in a circle, and you can park there. There's an underground walkway, under the railroad tracks, that leads to the boathouse."

He laughed. "Sounds like you live on a real estate," he said.

"Well, I do," she said. "It's called 'Rothmere.' You can't miss it. As you come up the Old Albany Post Road, just before the village of Tarrytown, there are big wrought-iron gates on your left—gates with big double-R's on them. I'll see that the gates are left open. . . ."

And now, nearly twenty years after all of that, whatever it all meant, she was sitting in the green library at 10 Gracie Square with Rodney McCulloch.

"Nineteen seventy-three," she said. He had just asked her the date of the Bouché portrait.

"Well, you haven't changed one bit," he said. "You're just as pretty as ever. Ha-ha-ha."

"I think I'm a little smarter now," she said.

He sat forward in his chair. "Now you know me," he said. "I don't like to beat around the bush. I've been thinking, Alex, and here's what I think. I think you should put up some of your own money into this project of ours."

She smiled. "You're changing the terms of your offer, Rodney," she said. "The last time we met, you offered to finance it with—'all the money in the world,' I think you said."

He scowled. "Figure of speech," he said. "But I was just thinking that you might feel better about this project of ours if you had a few million of your own in it. Psychologically speaking, I mean. It would give you the feeling that you were partways working for yourself, and not just for me. Besides, the market's down, and—"

"Do you mean the great Rodney McCulloch is feeling the great economic crunch of the nineties?"

"Not really, but—ha-ha-ha."

"A few million of my own? But I don't have that kind of money, Rodney—nothing of the sort that would be more than a drop in the bucket for what it would cost to start up a new magazine."

"Whadda ya *mean?* The Rothman millions?"

"I don't have the Rothman millions, Rodney. As far as anybody can figure out, the Rothman millions are pretty much all in the hands of Ho Rothman."

"But he's about to check out! He's a goner."

"That may be, but he isn't gone yet, and nobody's seen his will. There was supposed to be a trust fund set up for Joel and me, but nobody can seem to find it. That trust may all be in Ho Rothman's head."

"The head of a vegetable!"

"And since I last talked to you, I've learned that I don't even own this apartment. The company owns it. I could be kicked out at any time, I suppose." She spread her hands. "So, if you're thinking of me as an investor, you've come to the wrong woman."

He looked crestfallen.

"But look, Rodney," she said. "I've been thinking, too, about your offer. And—this is hard for me to say, because I like you, Rodney, and I also like your wife. And I hope she finds what she—what you both want for her, in terms of New York society. I was glad to help her in whatever small way I could, and I'll be happy to help any other way I can. But I just don't think I could ever work with you or for you, Rodney. Our personal styles and personalities don't mesh."

He jumped to his feet. "*What?*" he roared. "You're saying that you can work with a son-of-a-bitch like Herb Rothman, and you can't work for me?"

"I work for *Mode*," she said simply.

"Well, you're soon gonna be out of a job," he said. "You know that, don't you? Everybody on the street knows that. All the cards are stacked against you."

"Well, if I lose this one, Rodney, at least nobody can say that Alex Rothman went down without a fight," she said.

"Dammit, I am not fucking gay, Fiona," Joel was saying to her. "Please let me see you, and prove it to you."

"I think you're gay, but trying to deny it."

"But dammit, I'm in love with you, Fiona. I've fallen head over heels in love with you. How could I be in love with you if I were gay?"

"It's called compensation," she said.

"But, dammit, wasn't everything fine between us before you started shoving stuff up my nose? Wasn't everything fine before then?"

"Well, I guess so. It was all right, I suppose."

"I just don't get turned on by drugs, Fiona."

"Why not? Everybody else does."

"Maybe I'm not like everybody else, Fiona."

"Obviously not," she said.

"Please let me come up," he said. He was calling from the lobby of the Westbury.

"Not tonight," she said. "I'm busy tonight. Maybe some other time."

"And what you said about my father. That really hurt, Fiona. Saying he was gay, just because—"

"Everybody says he was gay, but trying to deny it. You know how he died, don't you?"

"He killed himself. But that doesn't mean—"

"But don't you know *how* he killed himself?"

"Yes! He hung himself in the boathouse at 'Rothmere'—in nineteen seventy-three! But, Christ, I was only sixteen months old, Fiona. I don't even remember—"

"But don't you know *how* he hung himself? The scandal?"

"What scandal?"

"Well, if you don't know about it, I'm certainly not going to be the first to tell you. It was in all the papers. Not the Rothman papers, of course—they tried to cover it up. But it was in all the other papers. You could look it up in the library—you're supposed to be such the little scholar. Look it up. I even remember hearing about it when I was a little girl in England. Look it up—and tell me he wasn't gay!"

"Fiona," he said miserably, "tell me what's wrong. We started out so—wonderfully. But now you seem so angry at me. What's wrong?"

"Well!" she said sharply. "It's funny you should ask! You ask me what's wrong. I'll tell you what's wrong. I let you seduce me, which was perhaps my first mistake. Then I let you come back—and come back again. I've let you treat me

like your personal toy—your personal sex kitten. Now you
think I'm at Joel Rothman's beck and call. All I am to you
is a convenient lay, an easy fuck. You're like every other
spoiled rich boy I've ever known—take, take, take, and give
nothing back. And meanwhile, what have you done for me?
Nothing! Nothing! And here I am—desperate! Desperate! In
a desperate situation here, in the middle of a horrible situation, with your mother coming after me with lawyers—with
detectives! Have you been any help to me at all? No! I
may have to go back to England, you know! I may be
forced to go back—by your mother! Back to my father's
wrath, back to the hell I knew there. But do you care?
No! Have you offered to help me? No! All you want is an
easy fuck! And you have the nerve—the bloody nerve—to
ask me why I'm angry with you! Because you're a bloody
selfish brat who thinks he can fuck me whenever he feels
like it, and give me nothing in return. Well, I'm just not that
kind of girl!"

"Fiona," he said, "I love you. I'll do anything I can to help
you—anything. Anything in the world, Fiona."

There was a brief pause on the line. "D'you mean that?"
she said, almost sweetly. "Even after I've just given you rud-
dy hell?"

"Of course I mean it. I promise you."

There was another brief silence. Then she said, "Lenny
Liebling. Is he your mother's friend?"

"Uncle Lenny? One of her oldest. He's been almost like
a father to me. When I was a kid, he used to tuck me into
bed at night."

"Hmm," she said. "Then maybe there is something you
could do for me."

"Just tell me what it is, Fiona, and I'll do it."

"You are sweet," she said. "I'd forgotten how sweet you
are. Will you forgive me for blowing off at you? I'm under
such a strain."

"Of course."

"Then come on up. I'll cancel my other plans."

When Alex entered the anteroom of her office the next
morning, Gregory sprang to his feet and blocked her path.
"Don't go in there, Alex," he said. "Please go home! Something awful has happened! Just go home! Don't go in that

office!" With shock, she saw that tears were streaming down his face.

"Gregory, what in the world—?"

"Please, Alex!"

She pushed him aside, and stepped to her office door. Painters were at work in there, and her furniture was draped with drop cloths. The antique *Mode* covers had been scraped from the walls and ceiling, and lay in damp curls and wads on her office floor. And her office was being painted in a bright Chinese red.

Chapter 35

When Moe Markarian built the boathouse at what later would become "Rothmere," his plan had been to acquire an ocean-worthy yacht, on which he would make the leisurely commute between his estate in Tarrytown and his office in Manhattan. He had envisioned inviting influential Westchester neighbors, such as the Rockefellers, to join him on these cruises. He had also planned on a yacht big enough to carry him and his wife down the Intercoastal Waterway for winter vacations in Florida, and sufficiently seaworthy for even longer voyages— across the Atlantic, into the Mediterranean and Aegean.

Of course none of this had ever come to be, but a channel had been dredged, and a berth had been dug deep enough to handle the future yacht's draw—both of these long since silted-in—and above the berth had been erected the boathouse.

But the building that rose above the yacht's berth was designed for more than dockage. It had been planned as a house to accommodate overflow guests. There were two full guest bedrooms on the upper floor, each with its own private sitting room, dressing room, and bath. On the lower floor, there was a fully equipped kitchen with a pass-through bar, a dining room, a powder room, and a long glassed-in living room, cantilevered out over the water, with a magnificent three-sided view of the river, upstream and down, and across to the Palisades and where they dipped at the Tappan

Zee. Though the rooms in the boathouse had been kept furnished, they had never, to Alexandra Rothman's knowledge, been used. Aunt Lily complained that the rooms in the boathouse, built over the water as they were, were always damp. Also, the Hudson River was still tidal at that point, and so there was often a brackish smell. Below, in what was to have been Mr. Markarian's yacht's berth, the largest vessel ever parked there was a somewhat leaky canoe, which now lay on its side on the dock.

Alex heard the sound of his tires on the gravel drive that afternoon, and went to the door to greet him.

"Alex," he said, and he started to take her in his arms, but she pushed him gently away.

"Come in," she said, and led him into the glass room. "Can I fix you a drink?"

"Okay," he said. "Vodka on the rocks?"

She fixed his drink at the bar, and then, though she didn't usually have a drink that early in the day, she fixed another for herself, thinking: *liquid courage*. She returned with their filled glasses, and they sat opposite each other on two Chippendale sofas in the great glass room. He lifted his drink, and smiled a little shyly at her. "Well, here's to old times," he said.

"Yes," she said.

"This is quite a place," he said, looking around. "It's a little like being on the prow of a ship."

"Yes. I believe that was the architect's intention," she said, and the words sounded stilted and formal. "In fact, on the plans, it's called the Deck Room."

"The Deck Room," he repeated carefully.

He had changed somewhat. His hair was darker than she remembered it, and his nose seemed straighter, but he was, if anything, even better looking than she remembered. And his speech seemed to have lost some of its western twang, but he was still the man she had once thought she would love forever. "Oh, here," she said quickly, reaching into the breast pocket of the pink Brooks Brothers shirt she had thrown on over white slacks. "Before I forget it—it's the passbook for the savings account I set up with your money. I haven't had the interest posted on it for several years, so the balance is going to be more than what shows there." She slid the bankbook across the coffee table to him.

"I don't want your money," he said, pushing it back to her. "That's not what I came for."

"But it's not my money. It's yours," she said, and for several moments they pushed the passbook back and forth across the tabletop between them until, with both their fingertips pressing against it, it seemed to become a sort of connective tissue. "It's from your money belt. I put it in a savings bank—even though you said you didn't believe in banks," she said.

"I left that for you, in case you needed anything while I was—away," he said.

"But I didn't. Oh, I did use a little of it to buy a small sewing machine, because you'd promised me I could. But otherwise—"

"You saved it for me. All these years."

"Yes. Because it was your money. You'd earned it. I saved it, even after I'd decided I'd never hear from you again. Please take it, Skipper. I didn't need it then, and I don't need it now."

He sighed, and picked up the passbook and placed it in his shirt pocket without opening it. "Who'da thunk it," he said.

Occasionally, she noticed, he still lapsed back into his more countrified way of speaking. But he was certainly better dressed now, with an air of casual elegance she had never noticed before, in gray flannel slacks, an open-collared white button-down shirt, a black V-necked cashmere pullover, and black Gucci loafers. He looked as though he had been doing well. He looked prosperous. The room was silent now, except for the sound of waves lapping against the concrete piers that supported the boathouse.

He sipped his drink. "You still sew?" he asked her.

"Hardly ever anymore. I'm too busy helping my husband edit his magazine."

"Your husband . . ."

"My husband, Steven Rothman. And what are you doing these days, Skipper?"

"Right now, I'm sort of between jobs. But I'm doing okay."

"Good."

"You know, I almost didn't come," he said. "I figured, why would you want to see me now? I almost didn't call last Saturday. I figured, why would you want to hear from me? But somehow—the more I thought about it—I had to call you. Alex, I had to come."

"Why?"

"Just thinking of the great times we had together—even as short as it was. The way I live now—well, it's not the greatest setup. I have a couple of roommates, a couple of gay boys. They're okay, but they bicker a lot, and—well, I guess thinking of the great times we had together, short as it was, I came wondering if you still feel the same."

She shook her head. "No. As I told you on the phone, I have a whole new life now."

"I came wondering if you'd ever take me back."

She shook her head again. "No. Too much time has gone by, Skipper. Perhaps, if you'd ever written to explain what happened. If you'd ever telephoned—"

His eyes widened. "But I wrote you! I wrote you every day! I explained everything. But when I didn't hear from you—"

"I never got any letters from you," she said.

He sat quickly forward. "But I wrote to you," he said. "I wrote to you that very day they arrested me, and the next day, and the next. Telephoning was harder because, from where I was, they made you call collect. But I did call—more than once. I got a woman's voice, not yours, who refused to accept the charges. And so I wrote more letters. For at least six months, I wrote you letters. But when you never answered them—"

"My mother," she whispered. "I suppose she—" She left the thought unfinished. She thought: Did my mother also open and read his letters? Probably. "I'm sorry, Skipper," she said, "but I never got your letters."

"If you had, would it have made a difference?"

"I don't know. You said your letters explained everything. What was the explanation for what happened that night in Wichita? I've never had a clue."

"Well, I don't suppose it matters now, but I'll tell you if you want to know."

"Naturally I'm curious. It isn't every young wife who has her motel room raided in the middle of the night by the police, and sees her husband carried off in handcuffs, and doesn't hear from him again until ten years later."

He stared at his fingernails, which were smooth and mani-cured now, not dirty and cracked as they often were when she first knew him, and she noticed beads of sweat on his fore-head, though the day was not warm. He took a quick swallow of his drink. "I was set up," he said. "It was a classic setup— I was accused of a crime I didn't commit. You see, there was this woman I was involved with in Brownsville, Texas, about a year before I met you. She was kind of a possessive type— wanted to run off with me on the rodeo circuit. But she was also married, and I didn't want to get involved any deeper than I already was with a married woman. So I told her that morning that I wanted to break the whole thing off. Well, she got real angry and said she was going to tell her husband all about the two of us—make it sound like I'd raped her, or some cockamamie thing. Now I knew her husband was a real mean son-of-a-bitch. He beat up on her a lot—she was really what you'd call a battered wife. But I figured I was leaving town early the next morning for my next gig, and I figured I'd be safe out of town by the time he got around to doing anything. But late that night I got a phone call from her. She was hysterical. She said, 'Please come quickly. I need your help. Something terrible has happened,' or something like that. So I got in my car and drove over to her house. Willa—that was her name—and her sister Loretta were in the living room, and they were both hysterical, but, my God, poor Willa was a mess. Her nose was bleeding, and she looked like it was broken, and there was blood coming from one of her eyes. A big hunk of her hair had been yanked out, and a couple of her front teeth had been knocked out. All over her face and arms were more cuts and bruises—he'd really let her have it that night."

"How awful," Alex said.

"Yeah. Well, it gets worse. I said, 'Did that son-of-a-bitch do this to you?' She said yes, and then she handed me this gun—a Smith and Wesson snubnose, I think it was. I said, 'You want me to kill him for you?' She was cry-ing so hard it was hard to tell what she was saying, but then I heard her say, 'No, I've already done that.' Then she took me into the bedroom, and there he was. She'd shot him right in the back of his head while he lay there drunk. I've never seen such a godawful sight, and I dropped the gun on the floor. I said, 'You better call the police,

Willa.' She said she was going to, but would I stay there with her till they came? I said, 'Hell, no—this is your problem, Willa. Just tell them you shot him in self-defense. One look at you, and they won't have any trouble believing you. I'm getting outta here.' And I did. I got outta that crazy house.

"Well, the next day I was in my car, drivin' to my next gig, which was in Waco, and I hear on the radio about this guy that's been murdered in Brownsville. But what I'm hearin' is that his wife is saying that *I* did it—that I did it when he tried to stop me from beatin' up on her. Her sister is sayin' that she saw me do it, and the neighbors, who heard the shots, are sayin' they saw my yellow 'Vette parked in her driveway. And there's my fingerprints all over the murder weapon!

"When I heard that, I panicked. I figured I had to get out of Texas. I thought of Mexico, but was scared I'd get stopped at the border. So I headed north—up through Oklahoma, Kansas, Iowa, Wisconsin. I got new plates for the car, and got it registered in a different name. You may have noticed—"

"I remember it well," she said. "William J. Cassidy, three fourteen Elm Street, Lafayette, Indiana. I wrote to that person."

He grinned sheepishly, and took another swallow of his drink. "No such person—probably even no such address. I made it up. When I went back on the rodeo circuit— 'course I never made it to the gig in Waco—I used a lot of different names. Hell, a lot of guys who ride the circuit do that, keep using different names. Most of 'em are runnin' away from somethin', hidin' from somethin'. Some-*thing* . . ."

"Was that a made-up name you were using when you met me?"

"Hell, no. James Robert Purdy is the name I was born with. I figured a seventeen-year-old girl out hitchhiking on the interstate wouldn't be working for the cops. Anyway, that was how I became what they call a fugitive from justice. I know I was a damn fool. I shouldn't have panicked. I should have gone straight to the police that morning and told them the truth about what happened. But by the time they caught up with me, I was a fugitive from justice, and nobody believed me. If I wasn't guilty, why was I running away all the time? Why was I using all these different names?"

"That night in Wichita, they kept calling you Johnson."

He nodded. "Yeah. One of the names I used. Willie Johnson."

"There's only one thing I don't understand," she said. "Why didn't the police ever contact me? After all, we'd been married—"

"I didn't want to get you involved with my problems, Alex. I didn't tell them anything about you. I told them you were just a girl I'd picked up in a bar that night. I told them I didn't even know your name."

"And the yellow Corvette? They never tried to—"

He looked at his fingernails again, and grinned. "Now that's a part I'm a little ashamed of," he said. "That night, when they took me out of the motel, they said, 'Okay, which is your car?' I pointed to a green Chevvy in the parking lot, and said, 'That one.' Next thing you know, they had that green Chevvy hitched up to a police wrecker, and hauled it away. I always felt kind of bad about that. Poor guy who owned that car, waking up in the morning, finding his car gone, reporting to the police that it was stolen, and finding out it was stolen by the police!" He chuckled softly. "In a way it's kind of funny," he said. "But still I keep thinking, maybe that guy had an important appointment the next morning. Or maybe it was a whole family, with kids, heading off on a vacation. Anyway, it was a long time ago, and it's all over now. And by the time the cops found out they had the wrong car, the 'Vette had vanished— vanished in Paradise, I guess, parked by a house with a zoysia lawn."

"Yes. And here you are," she said.

"And do you know something? I'm not bitter about anything that happened. I'm not even bitter about old Willa setting me up for a murder charge. My friends say I should be bitter about what Willa did, but I'm not. She probably panicked, too. She and Loretta probably had the whole scheme worked out before I got there. That's why she handed me the gun. Why would *she* want to face a murder rap? Well, I did, even though I didn't murder anybody. But I'm not bitter, because everything that happened was my own damn fault. It was my own damn fault to get involved with a married woman to begin with. So I paid the consequences. And, like

I say, I have a whole new life now. Maybe I learned something from the whole experience."

"Something about the duplicity of women," she said.

"Something about the duplicity of *one* woman. Not the woman I married." He rose and sat beside her on the sofa.

"No, no," she said. "I have another husband now."

"But you're my wife," he said. "I even have the marriage license to prove it."

"I don't think that piece of paper would hold much water now. I was underage. I lied—"

"That doesn't matter," he said. "You're still the woman I married. In prison, I used my time well. I read, I studied. I took correspondence courses. I even earned a college equivalency degree. I'm a different man now, Alex."

"And I'm a different woman."

"Not to me. After I got out, I tried to find you. I went back to Paradise, but your family had moved away, and no one knew where. Even the zoysia lawn was gone. There were ads I'd seen in the Kansas City papers—ads using a model that looked like you. I even traced the model to a modeling agent named Lucille Withers. She was real snippy. Wouldn't tell me your name, or anything. All she said was, 'I don't run a dating service, mister.' "

Alex smiled. "Dear old Lulu," she said. "That sounds like her."

"I never gave up. I kept on looking for you. Then, just the other day, I saw your picture in the *Daily News*. Alexandra Rothman, and the president of France was kissing your hand."

"Yes," she said. "But we can't turn back the clock, Skipper." The words sounded trite and foolish.

"I'll try, if you'll try. Let's try."

"No, no," she said again.

"What matters most is that of all the women I've ever loved—and there've been a few—no one ever made me feel the way you did, Alex. No one, before or since."

She started to move away from him, but he reached out and seized her hand. "Do you remember the idea I had for the little bar? You were going to help me decorate it."

"Oh, yes. It was going to have a piano player—a fat man in a derby hat and red suspenders . . . or was that just my imagination? There were going to be stained-glass windows.

You were going to call it El Corral."

"And do you know something? I got as far as buying the stained-glass windows. Oh, Alex, I've never felt about anyone the way I feel about you. Do you remember that first afternoon at the Dairy Queen?"

"Oh, yes," she said with a sudden shudder. "Look. I really don't want to cry. I'm not going to let you make me cry."

"I don't want to make you cry. I love you. Do you remember I said I wanted to fox you up?"

"Yes . . ."

"And I could have foxed you up that first day, couldn't I? I could tell it. I could feel it in the air. I could even smell it—that's how bad I knew you wanted me. But I didn't do it then, did I? I wanted to marry you first. That's how special you were to me. That's how much respect I had for you." He spread the fingers of her hand. "I wanted you to wear my wedding ring first. I gave you a ring. I see you have a new ring now. Do you still have my ring?"

She nodded mutely.

He studied the back of her hand. "But that was the day I put my brand on you," he said. Slowly, lazily, he drew the letter S on the back of her hand with his fingertip. "Look. It's still there." And suddenly she saw the scarlet welt fly up—S, for Skipper. "And then I licked it with my tongue, to make it heal real fast." He lifted her hand to his mouth, and licked the back of her hand.

"Skipper—it never healed!"

"I've never loved anyone the way I love you, Alex. No one's ever made me happier. I love you, Alex. I need you, Alex." And suddenly he was covering her mouth with urgent kisses, and unbuttoning her pink Brooks Brothers shirt, and it was happening to her all over again. "Take off his ring first," he commanded, and she twisted the sapphire from her finger and dropped it to the floor, where it landed with a soft plop on the rug, and then it was the way it happened that first night in the motel room in Wichita, with that noisy feeling of a tempest building inside her, with the dizzying sound of wind pounding in her ears, and a bright crimson light behind her eyes, and she was powerless again, and found herself returning his fierce, drinking, thirsty kisses, and heard herself cry out, "Oh, Skipper, why did you have to leave me? Oh, Skipper, love me . . . oh! . . . yes, do that . . .

and that . . . oh, fuck me . . . fuck me . . ."

When it was over, and they lay together breathlessly on the sofa in the boathouse, he said, "I've never made love to a woman wearing nothing but three strands of pearls. That's another first." He touched the pearls. "Beautiful," he said.

She laughed softly. "I guess I was in too much of a hurry to take them off."

"You're so lovely," he said. "Are you happy, Alex?"

"Oh, yes."

"Do you love him, Alex?"

"Yes."

"In the same way?"

"No," she admitted.

"Good," he said. "That's all I wanted to know."

"But—"

"But what?"

"But this is what I want to keep. What I have now."

"Because he's rich?"

"Perhaps that's part of it. There are other reasons, too."

He drew his fingertips across her lips. "You say you're happy, but there are little sad-lines around your mouth."

She laughed. "Just wrinkles," she said.

"And around your eyes—little sad-lines that weren't there before."

"More wrinkles."

"May I come back again?"

She raised herself on one elbow. "Please don't," she said. "If you really love me, please don't. Please don't complicate my life any more than it is already. If you really love me, promise me that. Please. It's important, Skipper."

"All right. I promise. But just tell me again that it's not the same for you with him—the same as it is with me."

"That's true. It's not," she said.

"And tell me that you've never loved anyone else the way you've loved me."

"It's true," she whispered. "And I'll never forget this afternoon, my darling . . ."

"I think you wanted this afternoon as much as I did."

"It's true," she said again.

"Perhaps he can give you pearls, but I can give you something better than that, can't I?"

"Yes," she said, and then they were making love again.

The boathouse was solidly constructed and reasonably soundproof, but now the building trembled. It was the 4:43 commuter express rattling its way out of Grand Central Station on its way to Harmon. That was another thing Aunt Lily Rothman disliked about the boathouse, the vibration from the trains that rumbled by night and day.

That fall and winter of 1971–72 had been one of their best times with Adam. For one thing, he seemed to have come into some money—just how, Lenny felt it unwise to ask. Adam bought himself a snappy green Mercedes 380-SL sports convertible, and he often drove Lenny and Charlie out for weekend junkets in Connecticut and Long Island. He bought himself a number of good-looking sport jackets and slacks and suits, and a drawerful of Turnbull & Asser shirts, and coordinated ties. He was becoming something of a fashion plate. He often took the boys out to dinner at expensive restaurants, and talked of taking them all on a spring cruise to Bermuda. Though he still liked his liquor, he now paid for his own cases of vodka, and had graduated from Popov to Smirnoff Blue Label. All in all, during this period, he was good fun to be with.

He was still not working, and where these funds were coming from was something of a mystery. Perhaps, Lenny decided, Adam had found himself a new patron, which was all right with Lenny, since Adam's new affluence eased the financial strain on the Liebling-Boxer household considerably. Whenever Lenny attempted to find out where the money was coming from, Adam merely shrugged and said, "Friend paid me some money he owed me."

But as the year 1972 drew to a close, the situation began to deteriorate again. The charges for Adam's vodka began appearing on Lenny's liquor store bills once more and, as had happened before, both Lenny and Charlie began to notice cash missing from their billfolds. On Christmas Eve that year, Adam was arrested for drunken driving, spent the night in jail, and had his driver's license suspended. After that, either Lenny or Charlie had to drive his Mercedes wherever they went.

By March of 1973, Lenny and Charlie had decided that it was time to have a heart-to-heart with Adam, and they had decided to emphasize the financial aspect of their relationship with the young man. They had decided not to say they were losing patience with him, which was beginning to be the case. And they had decided not to lecture him about his drinking, which only made him worse.

"Honestly, Adam, you have simply got to do something to find work," Lenny said to him. "If you're going to continue to live with us, you've got to contribute to our household expenses."

"What about all the dinners I took you out to?" he said.

"Those were fine, but that was nearly a year ago. Your situation seems to have changed. It's a matter of money, Adam. You know we love you, Adam, but Charlie and I simply can't afford to go on keeping you like this. Charlie has almost run through his inheritance from dear Aunt Jane, and I, of course, have only my salary. Last month, your liquor bills alone—"

"What about my liquor bills?"

"I hadn't meant to get into that, but last month the liquor bill alone came close to four hundred dollars. You've simply got to start contributing to this little *ménage* of ours."

"Broadway season's almost over. There won't be any casting until after Labor Day." His speech was a little slurred, and Lenny suspected that he was already a little drunk.

"What about summer stock? Have you thought about that? Actors are reading for summer stock all over town right now. I know the money's not much, and of course we'd miss you this summer. But summer stock gives you room and board, and a chance to be *seen*. The scouts from all the major studios tour the summer circuit, and—who knows? A job with summer stock could lead to something much, much bigger. An actor has to be *seen*, Adam—he has to be seen and heard performing. If you don't get seen, you might as well not exist as a performer. And you've never looked better, Adam," Lenny said, though he lied a little here. Adam was becoming a bit jowly, and had noticed this himself in the mirror, and had already suggested that the boys might be willing to spring for a face-lift for him. "You've simply got to do something, Adam," Lenny said. "It's a matter of money, pure and simple."

"Don't worry about me," Adam said. "Don't worry about me, good buddy."

"I don't think you think I'm serious," Lenny said sharply. "I am *quite* serious. If nothing else, you can get a job waiting on tables at the Stage Delicatessen—the way other out-of-work actors do."

"I ain't waiting on no tables!"

"I see," Lenny said icily, "that you can take the street hustler out of the street, but you can't take the street out of the hustler. May I remind you of what you were before I picked you up? You were a twenty-dollar trick, working the gay bars. But I thought you had a certain look, a charisma, a *presence* that only needed a little polish. For four years now, Charlie and I have tried to apply that polish. We have paid to have your nose fixed, your chin fixed, your teeth fixed. We have paid the hairstylists, we have bought you clothes, we have paid for acting lessons, singing lessons, dancing lessons, fencing lessons, elocution lessons, and karate lessons. We have also fed and housed you in our home. And what have we got in return for this investment? A man with a four-hundred-dollar-a-month drinking habit. The gravy train is over, dearie."

"You wouldn't dare throw me out!"

"Oh, wouldn't I just? Test me, Adam. Just test me. You'll see how fast I can throw you out. This apartment is leased to Charlie and me. Nowhere in our lease are we required to give you house room."

"Yeah, throw me out and have to admit to all your fancy friends that you were a miserable flop at turning me into something I never really wanted to be?"

"That's it, of course, isn't it? You never really wanted to be anything but what you are—a drunken bum."

"Don't call me no bum!"

"But that's what you are, sweetheart! And, on the contrary, our fancy friends, as you call them, would be very much relieved to see us throw you out. Most of them loathe you. You read what Mona Potter wrote about you in her column. If we threw you out, Adam, our friends would congratulate us for finally coming to our senses. They would throw a party for us to celebrate this blessed event. And when you go, where will you find yourself? Back on the street again as a piece of trade. And I lied a moment ago when I said you've never looked better. You're beginning to look *old*, darling. You're going to find it harder to turn those twenty-dollar tricks. At a rough guess right now, I'd say that most Johns wouldn't be willing to pay you more than five."

Adam started to rise, and Lenny reached for the house phone, and rested a finger against the red panic button that would set off the alarm downstairs. "Are you going to strike me?" he said coolly. "If you do, I'll have Peter the doorman up here so fast with the police that you won't know what happened, and you'll find yourself right back in jail on an attempted murder charge. With your record, it shouldn't be hard to make that stick, and I should imagine your jail sentence would be somewhat longer than the last time."

Adam sank back in his chair. "I wasn't going to hit you," he said. "I'm sorry, Lenny."

"That's more like it," Lenny said. "A little remorse is called for here. A little remorse, and a little gratitude."

"Just give me one more chance."

"All right," Lenny said. "One more chance. One *last* chance. And with this chance goes an ultimatum. We're giving you exactly six months, Adam, and I think that's very generous. Today is March twenty-fifth. That gives you until September twenty-fifth to find some work that will bring substantial money into this household. If nothing happens by that date, out you go. Is that quite clear, Adam?"

"You used to say you loved me, Lenny."

Lenny sighed. "Oh, we do, I suppose, in a way. But even love has its limits of endurance."

"Want me to give you a blow job, Lenny? Let me give you one of my nice blow jobs."

"Thanks, but I'm not in the mood. Six months. That is the final limit of our endurance. Six months."

March passed, and then April. "Five months," Lenny reminded him.

May passed, and June. "Three months," Lenny said.

Then July. "Two months."

"Don't worry. I'm already working on a deal."

"What sort of deal?"

"A big deal. You'll see."

"Money in it?"

"Big money. And if this deal goes through, and I think it's going to, none of us will ever have to work again. Get ready for our cruise to Bermuda in the spring."

Throughout the remainder of the summer, Adam continued
to refer to his "deal," though nothing much seemed to materi-
alize from it, and Lenny reminded him that it would not be
too long before Adam would have to find himself another
place to live. At least he had stopped drinking, which made
life a lot easier.

Then, in September, Adam announced that he was "going
out to wrap up my deal." That was when he handed Lenny
the long sealed manila envelope of "personal papers," with
the instruction: "Hold on to this—in case something happens
to me."

And, of course, something did happen to him, and the
man they had transformed into Adam Amado never came
home again.

From Joel Rothman's journal:

6/28/90
11.00 P.M.

    *Dear God, how did I ever get myself into this mess
I'm in? Dear God, I'm not even sure I believe in You—
You seem to take forever to do the things people ask
You to do. To hell with God, for Christ's sake, but I
just can't do what Fiona wants me to do. Not to Uncle
Lenny, who's been like a father to me, I can't do that.
I just can't, just can't, and she tells me I promised her
I'd do anything for her, and I did promise her that. Why
can't she see that I'd do anything in the world for her,
but not this? Not this! And now she says that all I ever
wanted to do was f--- her, that I never really loved her,
that I could never really love any woman because I'm a
gay, like Uncle Lenny, but a gay who's scared to come
out of the closet because I'm scared of Mom, and the
whole family, all the Rothmans. But I do love her with
all my heart and soul—and body, too!—and I tried to
tell her that. And I tried to tell her that, someday, when I
finish college, I was even thinking we might get married,
if she'll wait for me. But she says that if I really loved
her, I'd help her, and I want to help her! But not this
way. She say's she'll never—never!—see me again, if I
don't do this little thing for her. Little thing! Dear God,
my dilemma . . . why do so many dreadful words begin*

with D? Dreadful. Dilemma. Disaster. Destruction. Danger. Disappointment. Debris. Demons. Devil. Darkness. Decay. Dejection. Depression. Demolish. Depraved. Degenerate. Deranged. Desecration. Despair. Difficult. Dirty. Disarray. Dispirited. Dissolute. Disreputable. Distress. Dour. Doomed. Dragons. Downfall. Dungeon. Dope. Dorian Gray. Dreary. Dregs. Drunken. Drugged. Dreary. Drowning. Death. Disintegration.

How did Dad die? Dad. Die.

It will be a test of my manhood, she said.

Chapter 36

A few weeks later, she discovered that something far more serious had occurred in the boathouse that afternoon. Serious steps would have to be taken, and very soon.

That night, she slipped into Steven's bedroom. He looked up from the book he was reading, and lighted a cigarette. She sat on the corner of his bed. "Can we talk about something, darling?" she said. It was in October of 1971.

"Of course." He reached out and patted her hand.

"We've been married four years now," she said. "Your father keeps hinting that he wants us to produce an heir, and lately his hints have become a little bit—unpleasant. I know he's never really liked me, but perhaps if we could have a baby—perhaps—"

He smiled a little sadly. "I've never been much good to you in that department, have I?" he said.

"No. It's not that. But could we perhaps try a little harder? I know Ho wants us to have a baby, too. So could we try again? For my sake, Steven? It would make life for me so much easier in this family."

"What has my father said to you?"

"The other night he—he made a suggestion to me that was so awful I don't even want to repeat it to you. But it made me decide I could never spend the night under the same roof with him at 'Rothmere' again."

He sighed. "I can't control my father. Never could. Can't now."

"I know," she said. "And neither can I. But it's made me desperate, Steven. Desperate that I might lose you over this. I don't want him to destroy our marriage, Steven, but I'm frightened that he might try. So let's try to give him what he wants. Let's try again, and maybe if we succeed he'll treat us both a little better. Let's start trying now. I know you'll make a wonderful father, darling, if we can only have a child." She leaned forward and kissed him on the lips. "I'm ready to try, my darling," she said.

"I'm a little tired right now," he said.

"Let me try something," she said. Gently, she pulled aside the bedclothes, and lowered her face across his body.

Her son, whom they named Joel Steven Rothman, was born on June 29, 1972, under the sign of Cancer, a few weeks prematurely, it seemed.

She thought she had never seen Steven seem so happy.

And she had been right. Steven made a wonderful father.

Now it was the summer of 1973, and René Bouché's brush was poised above his easel as she sat for her portrait in the drawing room at "Rothmere." The little dog squirmed in her lap. Steven paused at the doorway with the toddler Joel by the hand. "We're going for a walk," Steven said. "Buster and I."

"Rock," said Joel.

"No, not rock, Buster. Walk."

"Mommy too?"

"No, Mommy's having her picture painted. Isn't Mommy pretty?"

"Pwet-ty," Joel said. "Pwet-ty Mommy."

"Why couldn't you paint me with my son?" she said to Bouché after they had gone. "It would make more sense than with a little dog that isn't even mine."

"Madonna and child? No, dear lady, that would be cliché, and nothing about you is cliché. No, Bonbon is perfect—all soft, fluffy loveliness, like yourself. Now please, look beautiful for me again. . . ."

She placed her fingertips against her cheek, as Bouché had instructed her to do. With her other hand, she tried to keep Bonbon still.

Now August appeared at the doorway. "You have a telephone call, Mrs. Rothman," he said.

"Who is it, August?"

"The gentleman won't give his name. But it sounds like the same gentleman who called you the summer before last. He said to tell you the same thing—that he's an old friend from Paradise."

She frowned. "I'd better take this, René," she said. "Will you excuse me?"

Lifting the skirts of the borrowed chiffon Poiret dress, she made her way to the telephone room and closed the door firmly behind her. She lifted the receiver.

"It's me," he said.

"Yes. You promised not to call here again, Skipper."

"Well," he said slowly, "I guess you would just hafta say I changed my mind." His speech sounded slightly slurred.

"What do you want?" she said, trying to keep her voice as cool as possible.

"You," he said.

"You know that's out of the question."

"Look," he said. "I've got myself in a little bit of trouble, Alex."

"Oh?" Her hand holding the receiver was shaking.

"I need some money, Alex."

"Oh? How much do you need?"

"I need a million bucks. If I can't have you, I want a million bucks."

"That's also out of the question. I don't have that kind of money."

"No, but I bet those fancy new in-laws of yours do. Rothmans spent a million bucks just on a party in Paris. I read that in the papers. I bet they can spare a million bucks for old Skipper."

"I'm sorry. I can't help you, Skipper."

"Oh? I think a million bucks is cheap for what I got. I got a valid marriage license from the Jackson County Court House, sayin' that you and me was legally made man and wife on August twenty, nineteen sixty-one. What would your fancy in-laws say to that? What would they say if they found out their son is married to a bigamist? What would the newspapers say to that one?"

"You're trying to blackmail me. You're not going to—"

"And here's another interesting little item. I read you had a baby born last year—born June twenty-nine, nineteen seventy-two. Counting back on my fingers, that makes just nine months after our last date. I kinda think that kid could be mine, don't you? Remember our last date? In the boathouse? The Deck Room? You see, I got all the details, Alex. I can prove I was there, describe the room—"

"You wouldn't dare do this to me," she whispered.

"Wouldn't I? Well, wait and see. A million bucks is all I want. Get the money for me, and you'll never hear from me again."

"You promised me that once before."

"Yeah, but this is an emergency. Oh, and by the way, I need the money by September twenty-fourth. That's my deadline, Alex. But it gives you a little time to scrape the dough together."

"How do I reach you?" she asked. "Give me your telephone number."

"No telephone number. But I'll give you an address." He gave her the number of a post office box in Manhattan, and she scribbled it on the pad of pink note paper on the telephone table.

"To think that I could have ever thought I loved you!" she said.

"Yeah. Well, them's the breaks," he said. "Be hearing from you, Alex. And don't forget my deadline. September twenty-fourth. And one other thing. I want the money in a cashier's check."

"My dear lady, what is wrong?" Bouché said when she returned to where he waited with his brushes and his easel. "I think something has very greatly upset you. You are white as a sheet, and trembling like a leaf!"

"Yes," she said. "Can we be finished for today, René? Something has come up. . . ."

"Of course, of course," he said, gathering up his tubes and brushes. "I just hope it is nothing serious, dear lady. . . ."

She knew that the only person who could help her now was Ho. Though they often argued and disagreed, he had become her friend. She found him in the library at "Rothmere" that he used as his weekend office, sitting in his high, thronelike antique Spanish chair that made him look like a king, monarch of all he surveyed.

"Ho, I need your help," she said. "Something terrible has happened."

He looked down from his lofty throne, and the sight of her, in the middle of the afternoon, in a pale pumpkin-colored Poiret ball gown must have signaled to him immediately that the matter was very urgent. "Sit down, Alex," he said. Then he said, "Woman problems. I think we get Lily in on this, no?"

"All right," she said.

He picked up the telephone. "Lily," he said. "Alex and I need to see you. In library."

Presently Lily joined them, and now two pairs of eyes stared at her as she sat there, her knees pressed tightly together, feeling like a guilty schoolgirl who had been caught doing something naughty in the playground, facing two stern principals. She began. "Years ago, I did something very foolish . . ."

" . . . and her little boy," Aunt Lily was saying when she finished. "Little Joel. How could something like that affect his future if the enemy press got hold of this?"

"Blackmailers," Ho said. "They is worst kind of pipple. They is cowards, stinkers, rats, worse than Communists. Give them anything, and they just come back for more. They keep coming back, keep coming back—for more, more, and more, for the rest of your life. Okay. You say this man has criminal record?"

Alex nodded miserably.

"Okay. Then here is what we going to do is . . ." Suddenly, in perfect and unaccented English, he outlined his plan.

In all fairness to Ho Rothman, in that late summer of 1973 he was feeling at the end of his tether, financially and personally, and so the solution he proposed at their little council of war that afternoon was perhaps harsher and more Draconian than it might have been had the problem arisen at any other point in his life or career. That summer, the universe of wealth and power that he had spent his whole life creating seemed in serious danger of falling apart.

On the national front, the energy crisis precipitated by the Arab nations' cutback of oil production, along with soaring grain prices, had created a world monetary crisis and then a worldwide economic recession that was felt to be the worst since the Great Depression of the 1930s. On a personal business level, the so-called Nixon Recession had caused advertisers to slash their budgets, and revenues from Ho's newspapers, magazines, and radio and television stations were lower than the year before. Newsstand and subscription sales of his publications were also sharply down.

There were other headaches. The experience of *Mode*'s hundredth anniversary gala in Paris two years before had taught Ho that fame, publicity, power, and money are all two-edged swords. The higher that the mighty rose, the more eager were the rivals of the mighty to see him brought to his knees. The splendid publicity that the Paris gala generated could have been destroyed altogether if it had become known that the highlight of the party had culminated with a young Frenchman's death. There were rival publishers who would no doubt have contended—loudly, in front-page headlines— that the Rothmans were responsible for that death.

Ho had managed to cover that one up, but other problems were proving harder to solve, and slower to go away. An investigative reporter from the enemy press was preparing a long story on the Rothman empire that would claim, among other things, that the Helen J. Pritzl Award for Editorial Excellence for *Tiny Tots* was a fake, and that Ho had never actually "predicted" the sinking of the *Titanic*, as he had long claimed. The reporter was pressing Ho for comments on these matters.

The company had also found itself the defendant in a number of petty lawsuits—petty, but also untidy. Ho's *Tampa Gazette*, for instance, had printed a story about a local clergyman who had been arrested for exposing himself to children in a local schoolyard. Knowing how Ho Rothman liked titillating headlines, the paper's overzealous editor had run the story under the headline "DEFROCKED PRIEST IS TAMPA FLASHER!" There was nothing wrong with the story itself, exactly. The crime was certainly an unsavory one, and there were reliable witnesses, including two teachers. There was only one detail that was in error: the wayward priest was not defrocked. His ecclesiastical frock firmly in place, he promptly sued Rothman Publications for defamation of character, asking fifty million dollars in punitive damages.

The Rothman lawyers recommended settlement, but an outraged Ho refused, shouting, "Now I'm rich, every pipple wants my money! Nothing to the pervert!" And so the case dragged expensively on.

An even more bizarre lawsuit had descended on the company. In Iowa, a woman named Reba Slobenska claimed that Ho's paper, the *Fort Dodge Clarion*, had libeled her by claiming that she had given birth to a three-headed baby and then had sold it to a circus for a dollar. The story, which several of Ho's tabloids ran every three or four years, in this instance somehow failed to include the fact that the alleged event had occurred in Rumania in 1801. And by a most unfortunate coincidence, the Iowa woman's name was the same as the Rumanian woman's—Reba Slobenska. Reba was asking for $100,000,000.

At the same time, union-organizing activity was in the air at Ho's newspapers, exacerbating his worries and problems. His employees were requesting, then demanding, all sorts of outrageous benefit plans, including coverage for dental care, membership in health clubs and spas, and—to Ho, the most outrageous demand of all—coverage of psychiatrists' fees. Ho had responded by announcing that he would fire all his employees and, if need be, shut down his entire operations, rather than accede to such demands.

And so, in light of all these pressures, it was perhaps not surprising that Ho Rothman's response to Skipper Purdy's demand was swift and brutal.

The small room, just to the left of "Rothmere"'s entrance hall—up a short flight of marble steps, past where the Augustus Saint-Gaudens bronze Daphne used to stand—was called the Gun Room. This was where Ho Rothman kept his collection of small firearms. He had started the collection in the early 1920s.

His first purchase had been a German carbine with a double wheel-lock, a handsome specimen, from circa 1585, and over the years the collection grew. It included a rare Indian matchlock from the fifteenth century; an early eighteenth-century musketoon that had belonged to one of Washington's officers in the Revolution; a breech-loader reputed to have belonged to Henry VIII, who was known to have owned at least three; an early Garand .30-caliber semiautomatic that was used to defend the Alamo; many vintage single-shot rifles by such English and American makers as Sharpe, Ballard, Remington, Winchester, Savage, and Colt; plus examples that showed the evolution of small arms—from antique Spanish hand-cannons through matchlock, snaphance, flintlock, percussion, and breech-loader automatic pistols.

The guns were kept in mint, working condition, though they were never loaded. At Aunt Lily's insistence, all the guns in the Gun Room were kept in locked glass cases where they could be displayed but not touched, and only Ho Rothman was supposed to know where the key was hidden. With two young boys growing up in the house, Lily Rothman was terrified that one of her sons might even touch the guns, much less play with them. But was it ever possible to hide anything from a pair of active, pre-teenage boys? Herbert and Arthur found the key's hiding place soon enough and, whenever they could, they would steal into the Gun Room, unlock the gun cases, and play the usual games, ambushing each other behind chairs and sofas and tables. ("Bang, bang! You're dead!" "Am not! You missed me!") Aunt Lily would have been horrified if she had known about this.

By the 1950s, Ho Rothman's gun collection had become quite valuable. An insurance appraiser had placed the collection's worth at $900,000. When the entire collection went under the hammer at Sotheby's in 1975, it brought $1,750,000 from a West German dealer.

That afternoon, the threesome moved from "Rothmere"'s library to the Gun Room, where it was decided that one of the small breech-loading pistols would be easiest for a woman to handle.

That night, Alex Rothman wrote the letter, on pale blue "Rothmere" letterhead, that would be mailed to the Manhattan post office box. In her distinctive, sharply pointed longhand, she wrote: *To think that I ever believed in you . . . that I ever believed I loved you . . . .*

In the Newspaper Room of the New York Public Library, Joel Rothman carried the spool of microfilm to an idle machine, and threaded the film on its appropriate sprockets and spindles. He adjusted the focus, and then fast-forwarded the film, and the events of the year 1973, as reported by the *New York Times*, flickered by on the viewer in front of him. When he got to September, he slowed the reel, and when he got to the date of October 14, he stopped the machine altogether, and began turning the machine with its handcrank. On page B17, he found it.

STEVEN J. ROTHMAN, 29;
PUBLISHING HEIR
A SUICIDE

TARRYTOWN, N.Y. OCT. 13. Steven Joseph Rothman, 29, an heir to the Rothman Publishing fortune, was found by his wife today, hanged in the boathouse of "Rothmere," the Rothman family estate in this affluent Westchester suburb. Mr. Rothman had apparently secured a noose to an overhead rafter of the boat dock, and then, standing in a canoe, had kicked the canoe out from under him. The canoe was found floating in the water a few yards away. A suicide note, addressed to his wife, directed her to the scene. The contents of the note were not revealed, but Mr. Rothman was said to be despondent over the downturn in revenues at *Mode*, the fashion magazine, of which he was editor-in-chief. *Mode* is one of many publications controlled by the Rothman family publishing group.

Mr. Rothman was born in New York City February 3, 1944. An honors student at Princeton, he joined *Mode* shortly after his graduation in 1965. In a bizarre coincidence, Mr. Rothman's death is the second to have occurred in "Rothmere" 's boathouse within the last month. On September 20, Mr. Rothman's wife, the former Alexandra Lane, was attacked by an assailant in the boathouse while reading manuscripts for her husband's magazine. After a violent struggle, Mrs. Rothman, who was not seriously injured, was able to shoot and kill her assailant, who demanded jewels and cash. The assailant was later identified as a 39-year-old ex-convict and drifter, wanted for parole violation in Kansas.

And in another bizarre touch to today's death, Mr. Rothman, when found, was wearing women's clothing.

A spokesman close to the Rothman family and company, who spoke only on the condition that he not be identified, explained the odd circumstances thusly: "Steven Rothman hated editing *Mode*. He had no interest in women's fashions, and hated the idea of working for a fashion magazine. But his father and grandfather insisted that he 'get his feet wet' and prove himself with one of the smaller magazines, such as *Mode*, before he could be promoted to a publication more suited to his disposition and liking. Dressing in women's clothes before taking his own life was Steven's final act of defiance to his father and grandfather. It was his way of telling them what he thought of how they had mismanaged his career. It was also an example of his black sense of humor. Steven was a wonderful man, and his loss is a great tragedy to all of us who knew and loved him."

In addition to his widow, Mr. Rothman is survived by a son, Joel Steven Rothman, age 16 months; his parents, Mr. and Mrs. Herbert J. Rothman; and his grandparents, Mr. and Mrs. H. O. Rothman, all of Tarrytown. There will be no funeral. A memorial service will be scheduled later this month.

Joel read the story through once more. Then he jumped to his feet, dashed to the men's room, and threw up in the toilet.

When he returned to the machine, his reel of film was still in it and, even though he had heard the story before, he turned the tape backward to September twenty-first. There he found it on page one.

EDITOR'S WIFE
SLAYS INTRUDER

TARRYTOWN, N.Y. SEPT. 20. Mrs. Steven Rothman, wife of the editor-in-chief of *Mode*, shot and killed an intruder and would-be assailant at the Rothman family's suburban estate today. The shooting, which occurred at approximately 3:20 P.M. (EDT) today, followed an attempt by the shooting victim to at first rob and then sexually assault the young Mrs. Rothman.

The victim's face was completely blown away by

a series of six gunshots, but he was later identified, through fingerprints, as Nils Johanssen, 39, an ex-convict and drifter, who had somehow managed to penetrate the normally heavily secured grounds of "Rothmere," the Rothman country residence. Police speculated that the burglar had first tried to enter the main house on the estate. Finding that locked and impenetrable, he made his way to the estate's boathouse, on the edge of the Hudson River, which was not locked, where he encountered Mrs. Rothman, 29, who was alone reading manuscripts for her husband's fashion magazine. Though the boathouse is rarely used by the family, Mrs. Rothman told police, "I often go there to read and be away from ringing phones."

"It was the maids' day off," Mrs. Rothman told police. "I was reading in the Deck Room of the boathouse. Suddenly this strange man appeared. He had a carving knife in one hand. He demanded cash and jewels. I told him I had no cash whatsoever, and the only jewelry I had was what I was wearing—a triple strand of pearls and my wedding ring. I offered him these. This made him very angry, and he said he was going to rape me. I ran to a table, and was able to get my hands on one of Ho Rothman's pistols. The man brandished the knife at me. I pulled the trigger."

H. O. "Ho" Rothman is Mrs. Rothman's husband's grandfather, president and chief executive officer of Rothman Communications, Inc., the publishing and broadcasting conglomerate which publishes *Mode*. The senior Mr. Rothman has a well-known collection of small firearms.

The carving knife was found near the victim's body, and was identified as having come from the kitchen of the Rothman boathouse, through which the intruder apparently gained entry.

Mrs. Rothman could not be reached for comment today, and was described by a family spokesman as "in a state of near-shock, and under sedation." . . .

There were only one or two faintly suspicious notes in the *Times* report.

Police officers, who gathered in the blood-spattered Deck Room—a large glassed-in room overlooking the river—of the Rothman boathouse, had come in response to an anonymous telephone call, presumably from someone within the Rothman organization. Police questioned why Mrs. Rothman did not immediately call the police following the shooting. Instead, she apparently telephoned Mr. H. O. Rothman at his Manhattan office, and had a 20-minute telephone conversation with him before police were notified. "I was hysterical," she replied. "Nothing like this has ever happened to me before. I didn't know what to do. I don't even remember what I did."

Police also questioned why Mrs. Rothman had found it necessary to empty all six chambers of the automatic weapon in order to ward off her assailant, when one shot would have sufficed to at least temporarily disarm him. "I was hysterical," she repeated. "I was terrified. I fired one shot, then another. I don't really remember how many shots I fired."

Another unanswered question is how Mrs. Rothman's assailant who, the *Times* learned, was also wanted for parole violation in the state of Kansas, planned to make his getaway, if burglary of the otherwise unoccupied Rothman estate was his intent. Johanssen apparently got off a northbound train, the 1:59 out of Grand Central, at the Tarrytown station, and took a taxi to the Rothman estate. Tarrytown taxi driver Carlos Flores recalls picking up a man of Johanssen's description at the station platform, and driving him to the entrance gates of "Rothmere," and dropping him there. "It seems a funny way to plan a big heist," said Tarrytown Police Chief Maurice Litwin, "to come in a taxi, and then walk away, in broad daylight, with the loot. It's a 3 ½ - mile walk back from the Rothman place to the station." A Rothman family spokesman, however, suggested that Johanssen may have had an accomplice waiting in a car outside the boathouse who, when the burglary plans went awry, drove away from the scene in haste.

This further suggested that, though no other persons were supposed to be on the premises at the time, other than Mrs. Rothman, the presumed accomplice may have been an "insider." This would explain how Johanssen passed so easily through "Rothmere" 's normally heavily guarded gates. Chief Litwin announced that the 27 members of "Rothmere" 's household and gardening staff would be questioned.

Joel turned off the machine, and the viewing screen went blank. He had never thought of it before, but it did seem strange that two men should have died in the boathouse within a month of each other. Could there possibly have been a connection? But what connection could there possibly have been? Then he thought: Where was I? My mother was supposed to have been all alone at "Rothmere" at the time. But I was only fifteen months old. So where was I?

The Rothman newspapers reported the event in even more lurid detail. They spoke of "the tiny, fragile, defenseless Alexandra Rothman, a new mother of an infant son," and of her "burly, hulking 6'3" sex-crazed assailant," who was a "hardened criminal with a long record of heinous offenses ranging from forgery to manslaughter, attempted rape, criminal trespass, burglary, petty larceny, and grand theft," who had "slipped through the holes of the American justice system," and who had come at Alexandra Rothman "wielding a nine-inch lethal blade with lust burning in his tiny, red-rimmed, piglike eyes, and a snarl on his moistened lips, intent on rape, robbery, and possibly even murder and mutilation." Alexandra Rothman, the Rothman newspapers claimed, had "with her quick thinking and doughty courage slain the monster who threatened to defile her innocence and sweet young motherhood," and had "performed an act of heroism hardly surpassed in history since Joan of Arc went off to fight for Christ" in ridding the world "of an unredeemable, unrepentant piece of human scum."

Alex Rothman, of course, remembered that afternoon quite differently.

"So you decided to betray me, after all," she said to him.

"I look at it in a different way," he said. "I figure you betrayed me—marrying another man without telling him you were already married to me. You really hurt me, Alex. Now you're going to have to pay me for that hurt. Where's the check?"

"Sit down, Skipper. Let's talk a minute."

"I think I'd rather stay standing up," he said.

"All right. But listen to me, Skipper. You meant a lot to me once. In some ways, you still mean a lot to me. You were an important part of my life, and in some ways you still are, and probably always will be. One doesn't easily forget the sort of thing we had between us. I never really wanted to hurt you, and I don't want to hurt you now. And I'm sorry you're in some sort of trouble, and I'd really like to help you out."

"It's my kid, isn't it?"

"I don't want to talk about that. I'm saying that I want to help you out of—whatever trouble it is you're in. But—a million dollars. I simply don't have access to funds like that. Being married to a rich man doesn't make me a rich woman. But what I've done—"

"You said a million bucks! You said it in your letter. You said 'all your demands will be met.' I got it in writing, Alex!"

"I just can't," she said. "I just can't get hold of that much. But what I did do was this. I went to a pawn shop. I pawned a rather nice triple strand of pearls with a diamond and sapphire clasp, that Steven gave me. I was able to get fifty thousand dollars for that, and I'd like to give that to you now, with the understanding that it's all I'll ever be able to give you, and with your promise that you'll never come back to ask me for anything more. I have the check right here—a certified check, as you asked for, payable to cash." She opened her purse, and withdrew the folded check. "Please take this, Skipper, and try to understand that this is the best I can do. Because I really did love you once."

He glared at the check. "You're double-crossing me, Alex. I'm going to your husband and tell him that the kid is mine!"

"Please, Skipper—"

He stepped toward her. "And I'm going to show him our marriage certificate. And I'm going to—"

That was when she reached in her purse and took out the pistol Ho had given her, and pointed it at him. "Very well," she said. "Then get out of here, Skipper. Get out of here right now. Get out of here, and don't come back—ever. Walk to that door right now, and don't ever come back. If you don't, I'll—"

With that, he struck her with a sharp karate chop across the side of her head and, with his toe, caught her simultaneously behind the knees, and she crashed to the hardwood floor, landing on her back, while the pistol flew out of her hand and slithered across the polished floor.

He stood above her with the heel of his Gucci loafer pressed hard against her throat. "Bitch!" he said. "Give me the money, or I'll break your fucking neck."

The sound of an express train rumbled by, and the foundations of the boathouse trembled. That was when the shooting started.

Chapter 37

"Herbert Rothman received service yesterday morning in his office at ten fifteen," Henry Coker was saying as he riffled through the papers in his briefcase on his lap. "And so now we are officially in litigation. Our lawsuit is a two-pronged affair. We are suing for breach of contract, which is fairly simple and cut-and-dried. We are also demanding to see a copy of the trust instrument—the so-called Steven trust—that is mentioned in your late husband's will, and we are asking for a full and complete documentation of the contents of that trust. Of course, if the trust never existed, or if, over the years, it has been subsumed by, or otherwise disappeared within, the company's rather unusual and idiosyncratic—to say the least—method of keeping its books, then there will be very little we can do. But on the matter of breach of contract, there's no question in my mind but that we have him cold."

"He said something to me about a loyalty clause," she said.

"Yes, there is indeed a loyalty clause in your contract," he said. "But as far as I can see, he can't prove that you've done anything disloyal to the company. You haven't sold any company secrets, or anything like that, for God's sake. Your conversations with McCulloch were perfectly open-ended. He made you an offer, which you considered, and then declined. Talking with Rodney McCulloch about a job offer doesn't constitute disloyalty to the company. Every successful person receives new job offers all the time. On the other hand, if you were secretly plotting with Rodney McCulloch to take over Rothman Publications, that *would* constitute disloyalty. But that was not the case."

She smiled. "Of course that's what Rodney would like to do," she said. "He'd like to destroy Herb Rothman."

"So," Henry Coker said, "would a lot of other people. But in the meantime, with a breach of contract claim, I think we've got Herb Rothman by the balls, if you'll pardon the expression. Of course now we have to wait and see what kind of response we get from the people at Waxman, Holloway, but I don't see how they could possibly recommend that he fight this. He hasn't got a legal leg to stand on, to begin with. For another thing, if he decides to go to the mat with this, it's going to cost him a lot of money. He's already got a billion-dollar lawsuit on his hands from the IRS, and I don't think anybody in his right mind would recommend that he take on another case that he's bound to lose. At the very worst, he could offer to buy out the balance of your contract—which would also cost him a lot of money."

"Or he could fire me."

"Yes. But your Aunt Lily Rothman was right. Firing you would *also* cost him a lot of money because he'd have to pay out the full balance in your profit-sharing plan. Firing you is the last thing he's going to want to do. So don't worry, Alex—we're going to win this one. I'm very confident."

"But now, on this other matter—" She touched the letter that she had just shown him, that had arrived in her office mail that morning.

"Ah," he said with a sigh, "I'm really afraid there's nothing we can do about that, Alex. Alas, they are within their rights."

She picked up the letter again. It had been written by one of the company's in-house attorneys.

June 29, 1990

Dear Mrs. Rothman:
The apartment you presently occupy, to wit the North Penthouse of 10 Gracie Square, New York, N.Y. 10028, will be put to other Corporate use in future. Therefore, it

*will be necessary for you to vacate these premises within
sixty (60) days of the above date.*

We trust this will cause you no inconvenience.

*Sincerely yours,
Stuart A. Melnick*

"You know, I could even accept him having this office
repainted," she said, "though Chinese red is not my favorite
color. It was petty and mean, but it was typically Herbert.
And, after all, the company owns this building. But I really
never thought he'd do this—throw Joel and me out of our
home. His own grandson."

"Unfortunately, the company owns the apartment," he said.

" 'I'll send you back to that little town you came from so
fast you won't know what the hell hit you—without a pot to
piss in. And on a Greyhound bus.' "

"Hmm?"

"That's what he said to me."

"That was just sword-rattling, Alex. But this, unfortunately, is different. The shares in the co-op are held in the
Rothmans' corporate name."

"How could I have been so stupid, Henry? How could
I have lived in that apartment for more than twenty years
without knowing that I didn't own it—just because I paid
the maintenance?"

"You were probably too busy running the magazine to look
into details like that."

"Coleman telephoned. One of the building's engineers was
there this morning, measuring the terrace. It seems there's
been a petition to enclose the terrace with glass. My beautiful terrace! My beautiful roof garden!"

"I know," he said sadly. "I know exactly how you feel,
Alex."

"Oh, I really think I do hate him now," she said. "Up to
now, I just thought he was a mean, petty, stupid, miserable
little man who never had any real power, and saw a chance
to grab some now. I thought he was pathetic, more than anything else. But now I think I really *hate* him."

"You've got him angry now. He was served with a lawsuit
yesterday, and so he knows we were serious when we talked
about taking legal action. He's playing hardball now, and he's

playing it as dirty as he knows how. In a way, it's good that we've got him angry. When people get angry, they're seldom at their best, or at their most effective. So try to contain your hatred, Alex. Continue to play it cool."

"Have you heard what he's calling himself now? President and chief executive officer of Rothman Communications. He's had that printed on his stationery! That was *Ho's* title! Can he just *do* that, Henry?"

Henry Coker smiled faintly. "The fact is, he's just done it. Grabbed the title before his younger brother could, I guess. When a company and a family are the same thing, anything can happen. The prize belongs to the person who grabs it first. And don't forget there's his new ladyfriend in the picture. He's got to demonstrate and prove his new power and authority to her. Which is why, if he loses this lawsuit—as I think he will—it will be an even bitterer, more humiliating pill for him to swallow. Which is why I imagine we not only have him running angry now, but also a little scared."

She hesitated. "Let's go back to the trust fund for a minute," she said. "If the trust fund exists. Could the trust fund be affected—not just for me, but mostly for Joel—if it turned out that I had been married to someone previously to Steven, and that, for whatever reason, I had never actually been divorced from that other man?"

He gave her his most prim, buttoned-down look—a look that suggested a mild stomach distress rather than a frown. "I think I once told you," he said, "that a lawyer always tries to learn as little as possible about his clients' private lives. I still believe that. But, in this case, Alex, perhaps you'd better tell me just a little more. For instance, is this other man still living?"

"No."

"I'm considerably relieved to hear that," he said.

"But what if someone should come forward with a piece of paper—a marriage license or certificate, indicating a previous marriage? Would that be anything more than just a mild embarrassment to me?"

He steepled his fingers. "Let me just say that I would hope that no one would come forward with such a piece of paper," he said. "But if someone did . . ." He smiled grimly.

She sighed. "You love a fight, don't you, Henry? I suppose all lawyers love a fight. That's their job—fighting other people's battles for them."

His buttoned-down look now composed itself into a prim, self-congratulatory smile, his eyes downcast. "Yes, I guess you could say I love a fight," he said. "In school and college, I was the gawky, skinny, ninety-nine-pound weakling, whom the bigger boys bossed around. As a lawyer, I have learned that there are other, more satisfying ways of besting one's opponents."

She sat back in her chair and looked up at the newly lacquered Chinese red ceiling. "But I dunno about this one, darlin'," she said at last. "Is it really worth the candle? Is this little job really worth the fight I'm putting up? Maybe it's time for me to throw in the towel."

Outside, in the anteroom, Gregory Kittredge, who rarely missed a word, heard these words, and winced. And, in the office, Henry Coker's buttoned-down look transformed itself into one of thorough disapproval.

"I found something interesting in Alex's jewelry case," Pegeen Rothman said to her husband when she found him in the music room at "Rothmere." It was ten days after the shooting incident in 1973. In those days, Pegeen's figure had a certain roundness, though she was not plump. It was before years of dieting had given her a figure which, when she stood in a room at a cocktail party, was straight up and down in every direction, and, when she gestured with her hands and thin arms, she became all corners and sharp angles. It was before, in Lenny Liebling's phrase, she had become another East Side Razor Blade. Pegeen had never been technically a pretty girl but, in those days, she had a soft and pleasant face, before the face-lifts had frozen it into a permanent, almost feral smile.

"I wouldn't dream of asking you what you were doing rummaging around in Alex's jewelry case, dear," Herb Rothman said. "But what exactly did you find?"

"This, for one thing," she said, and she dropped a gold ring into his palm.

"A ring," he said.

"Yes. It looks like a wedding band, don't you think? And look how it's engraved inside."

He peered inside. "J.P.–A.L.," he said.

"A.L. would be Alexandra Lane. But who do you suppose J.P. was?"

"I've no idea. Some teenage crush, perhaps?"

"And I also found this," Pegeen said, and she handed him a folded sheet of lined yellow paper. He opened it. It was a note scrawled in a large, uneven hand, and it bore no date or salutation. It simply said:

> *I don't know why you say such things to hurt me in your letter, after all we were to one another. I just need your help right now. Well, anyways, I'll be there on the date and time you said to be there.*
>
> *J.P.*

"Well, what do you make of it?" she said when he had read it. "It's from J.P."

"I don't know," he said.

"It sounds like a letter from a lover, or a former lover, doesn't it? 'After all we were to one another.' "

"Well, perhaps. But how can we even be sure this letter was addressed to Alex?"

"Why would she keep it at the bottom of her jewelry case? Under all the shelves and little drawers."

"Ah," he said, "I see you've done a very thorough search, Pegeen."

"I'm thinking it could have been a letter from the man she shot. He wasn't an intruder at all. She was expecting him."

"Hm," he said. "But that man's name was Nils something."

"Johanssen. But the police said he used a lot of different aliases."

"True," he said.

"You know, I've never figured out what a gun was doing in the boathouse—in a drawer, she told the police. But it was a gun from Ho's collection, and all your father's guns have always been kept in the Gun Room, right here in this house. In locked cases. That's your father's rule."

"True," he said again. "But look, Pegeen, this letter in itself means nothing. The point is, that this letter is an answer to another letter that *she* wrote to this J.P. He speaks of a letter from her, you see. Now if we could ever get hold of that letter, the letter that tells him the date and time to be there, then—"

"Then what?"

"Then we'd have proof that she'd invited him here. That it wasn't an intruder that she shot."

"That it was an ex-lover."

"And that it was premeditated murder."

"Where would we find her letter?"

"A letter to a dead ex-convict? I've no idea. Let me think about this, Pegeen. Meanwhile, put her ring back exactly where you found it. I'll have a photocopy made of this, and then you can put this back where you found it, too."

"Let's get rid of her, Herbert," his wife said. "You've never liked her, and I've never really liked her, either. She's served her purpose. She's had the baby, and it's the boy you wanted. Let's dump her, Herbert. She was never anything but a gold-digger."

"Let me think about all this," he said. Then he chucked her playfully under the chin. "Meanwhile, good work," he said.

Later that day, he spoke to August, the majordomo. "Did young Mrs. Rothman ever entertain any visitors here who seemed out of the ordinary, August?" he asked him. "Visitors who seemed to come from outside the family's normal circle of friends?"

"No, sir, I don't think so," August said. "Oh, yes, there was one—the very tall lady, Miss Withers."

"I meant male visitors."

"No, sir."

"Any unusual telephone calls that you handled?"

"Well, sir, now that you mention it there was one who called a couple of times."

"Do you happen to recall his name?"

"No, sir. Very mysterious he was, sir. Wouldn't give his name. He just told me to tell Mrs. Rothman that he was an old friend of hers, from Paradise."

"Thank you, August," Herb Rothman said.

One or two discreet telephone calls and a bit of detective work led Herbert to the funeral home of Sturm & Weatherwax, where the deceased's remains had been sent, and which turned out to be in a rundown neighborhood in the Flatbush section of Brooklyn.

"Boy, do I remember that one!" said Mr. A. Fairleigh Weatherwax, when Herbert found the funeral director in a

small office that smelled of cigar smoke and some unidenti-
fiable chemical substance. "What a time we had prepping that
loved one for the Slumber Room! That loved one had been
shot in the face six times, and we had nothing to go on! No
photographs—nothing. Ended up looking real nice, though.
Looked just like he was asleep. He looked real lifelike."

"Who paid for the funeral arrangements, I wonder?"
Herbert asked him.

"The state of New York, that's who! We got that passed
into state law. Every stiff's entitled to a viewing and a funeral, even if he's going to be planted in Potter's Field. Every
stiff's entitled to a full makeup job, even if it's going to be
a closed casket, or what we call a c.c. And every stiff's got
to be embalmed and have a coffin, even if he's gonna be
creamed."

"Creamed?"

"Cremated. We got that all through the legislature. Thank
God for the FDA."

"I beg your pardon? You mean this is a rule of the Food
and Drug Administration?"

"Hell, no. Our Funeral Directors' Association. We finally
got something out of Albany for the taxes we pay."

"Tell me something," Herbert said. "Don't you usually
keep a little visitors' book, where people sign their names
when they come to view the deceased?"

"Yeah," said Mr. Weatherwax, looking pained. "We usually give that to the loved one's next of kin, or to his nearest
and dearest among the bereaved, once we finish a job. But
that loved one didn't seem to have no next of kin, nor even
any nearests or dearests. Do you believe it? All that work we
went to, and only maybe half a dozen bereaved showed up
for the viewing! Talk about a waste of time! I coulda easy
done a c.c., and billed the state for makeup anyway."

"Then you still have the little visitors' book? I wonder if
I might take a look at it."

"Yeah, I got it here somewheres," Mr. Weatherwax said,
poking through a particularly untidy-looking desk drawer.
"Lucky you came along when you did. I was just about to
pitch it." He handed Herbert a slim black volume.

Herbert glanced quickly through the short list of names.
Most of the names meant nothing to him, but two signatures
jumped out at him:

Leonard J. Liebling
Charles Edward Boxer III

Next to his signature, Lenny Liebling had written, "Good night, sweet prince!"

"Thank you very much, Mr. Weatherwax," Herbert Rothman said, and handed the black book back to him.

"Say, are you a florist, by any chance?"

"No, I'm not, actually," Herbert said.

"Funny, you kinda look like one. We're working with the Florists' Association to make P.O. illegal in New York State."

"P.O.?"

"Please Omit. What kinda funeral can you have without flowers, for Chrissakes?"

Herbert had approached his father with what he had learned thus far.

"Stop meddling in other pipple's business, Herbie!" Ho Rothman shouted. "Is none of your business!" He pounded his fist on the top of his desk. "Stop meddling, Herbie!"

"But, Pop—don't you see? It begins to look as though the man wasn't an intruder at all. It looks as though she was expecting him. It looks as though he may have been a lover, and Lenny Liebling had something to do with it. The gun—"

"Shut up!" his father said. "What I just tell you? Is none of your business. Is over, is finished, is done, is none of your business."

"But, Pop—"

"Who is boss here? You? Or me?"

"You, of course, Pop, but—"

"Then do what I say. Shut up. Stop meddling where you got no business. Now get out of here. Get back to work making money for this company. Magazine Division's figures are down this month." And he turned his attention back to some papers on his desk.

Several days later, after further consultations with Pegeen, Herbert decided it was time to confront his son. "So you see," he said, after telling Steven about the ring, and showing him the photocopy of the note that was signed "J.P.," "it looks

very much as though her alleged intruder and assailant wasn't
an intruder at all. She knew the man, and the boathouse was
where they had agreed to rendezvous. It was a lovers' tryst, as
that note makes quite clear—'after all we were to one another.' It was a lovers' meeting, and Lenny may have been their
go-between, but something went wrong, and she shot him.
I think you've got enough evidence here, plus the telephone
calls that August has reported, to file for a divorce and get full
custody of the child. I'll call Jerry Waxman in the morning
and get him started on it."

Steven's face was a blank. "But I don't want a divorce,"
he said at last. "I love her."

"What?" his father shouted. "How could you say you love
that two-timing little slut? All she married you for was your
money to begin with, you know. Everybody knows that. Your
mother and I have known that all along. She couldn't have
married you for sex, could she? Not *you*. Knowing the problems you've had with women in the past—your problems
with impotence—it wouldn't surprise us in the least if that
lowlife, that ex-convict, was the father of that child you think
is yours!" Then he added, "That woman has fucked anything
that comes down the street—*including me*."

That last outburst, of course, turned out to be a tragic mis-
calculation on Steven's father's part. Because that was the
afternoon when Alex Rothman, changing her shoes in her
dressing room at "Rothmere," noticed the note that was
pinned to the skirts of her dressing table.

My darling—
    *You will find me in the boathouse. Please forgive me
for doing what I am going to do. And I forgive you for
anything you may or may not have done. I love you
always. My last picture will be of your tricolor eyes.
Don't hate me ever.*

Steven

It was nearly a mile from the main house to the boathouse,
and most people drove the distance. But by the time she got
to her car, she discovered that she had forgotten her keys,
and so she began running down the long gravel drive toward

the river in her bare feet, running blindly and praying. *Oh, Steven, Steven, give us one more chance, please, Steven, give me one more chance, let me try again, I'll try so hard this time, I promise you. It was a terrible thing I did to you, and I have no excuse except to say I'm sorry, sorry, sorry. Isn't being sorry for the rest of my life enough punishment for me, enough punishment for not loving you enough, or in the same way? Oh, Steven, please.*

By the time she reached the boathouse, her feet were bleeding. The covered yacht basin was open on three sides, embraced by two piers, and at first she saw nothing. Then she noticed that the old canoe, which normally lay on its belly on the pier, was floating, partially sunk, in the river. Then she saw him, and she knew that one of the most awful things that could ever happen to a woman had happened to her. The roar of a passing commuter express drowned her screams.

After that, needless to say, Herbert's and Pegeen's suspicions became something of a moot point.

"What did you say to him?" Pegeen demanded.

"*I said nothing to him.*"

"I think you did," she sobbed. "I think you did. I know you did."

Joel Rothman woke from his dream with a scream, and found his sheets soaked with sweat. Immediately, he reached for his journal.

6/30/90
3:45 A.M.

Just now I dreamed I saw him hanging there, and it woke me up. I saw the boathouse at "Rothmere," even though I can never remember being there. I saw the thick rafters overhead, and he'd tied the rope to one of them, and I saw the dark and murky water underneath, and I saw the canoe drifting in the water. His head was bowed, as though in prayer, his chin touching his chest, and the tips of his shoes were just an inch or two above the water's surface. But the tide was coming in. I've watched the tide turn in the Hudson River, when the river, which wants to flow from north to south like all the great rivers in the world—except the Nile—turns

*around and begins to flow from south to north. That was
happening in my dream, and I saw the river rising to
where it began to touch the tips of my father's toes,
and soon his toes were underwater, and then his feet,
and then his ankles, and I knew that if someone didn't
cut him down soon he would be underwater altogether,
but I was too far away to reach him. It was as though
my own feet were anchored in concrete, and I couldn't
move. Then I saw that my feet were actually stuck in
mud, in a kind of quicksand on the riverbank, and that
I was sinking too as the tide came in. I was crying,
"Stop! Stop!" I was trying to stop the tide. And there
was a breeze, and the breeze was spinning my father's
body in it, spinning him first one way, so his face was
toward me, and then the other way, so that all I could
see was the back of his head. And the wind was blowing the skirts of the long red dress he was wearing,
and now I know that we do dream in color, because
the dress he was wearing was a bright, bright red, the
color of blood, and now the water had reached the hem
of his skirts, staining them an even darker red that was
almost black, and that was when I knew we were both
drowning, my father in the red dress, and myself. And I
cried out, "Degenerate! Fairy!" Because it was all his
fault that this was happening to me. And then I woke
up. I saw something else today that wasn't a dream. I
saw Otto, and I know now that he is still following me,
and has been trying to follow me all along. It was on
Madison Avenue, not many blocks from Fiona's hotel,
where I'd made one last attempt to see her, to try to
explain my dilemma to her, that I just couldn't do what
she wants me to do with Uncle Lenny. But she wouldn't
see me. She says she never wants to see me again, and
if I try to call her from the lobby again she'll have her
number changed. She says I broke my promise to her,
and of course she's right, I did. Sometimes I think I've
let everybody down. But it's hard, very hard, on me to
know I've let her down. But anyway, there he was—
Otto. I was crossing 58th Street, and I just happened
to look back, and there he was, about ten steps behind
me. He tried to duck into a storefront so I wouldn't see
him, but I saw him, and I know he knows I saw him. So*

my mother didn't keep her promise to me after all. It was the only thing I asked for for my birthday, and she double-crossed me, just the way Fiona said she would. Perhaps Fiona's right. Perhaps I've always been too dependent on my mother, and that's what my trouble has always been. But without her to depend on, who is there left? My life seems to be full of broken promises now. Sometimes there seems to be nothing left for me to live for. I told that to Fiona, and I know I was crying like a baby, and she said, "Well, if that's the case, perhaps you should do what your father did." That's how little she cares for me. And I said, "Perhaps I will," and she said, "At least that would show that you can follow through on something," and then she hung up on me. And so perhaps I will. But if I did, would that show her anything at all? It's so hard, so hard. I feel that everybody has abandoned me now . . . Father . . . Mother . . . Fiona . . . everybody that ever mattered, or ever ought to matter. If I did that, would anybody really care? I just don't think so. It's so quiet in this house now, but I'm afraid to go back to sleep because I dreamed I saw my father hanging in a bright red dress . . . and I'm afraid I'll never be able to dream of anything else again.

Chapter 38

Lucille Withers sat at the table under the gazebo on Alex Rothman's terrace with her tableau of playing cards spread out in front of her, playing her favorite game of solitaire. Under her long and nimble fingers, order established itself, precedence and sequence, and the little symbols became integrated, correlated. The black seven on the red eight, then both of these on the black nine; aces went to the top of the board, but spaces were more important than aces, and queens were always bad news. Her hands moved back and forth quickly, as though across a keyboard, and the pattern grew.

She had come to New York as a chaperone for her young model named Melissa. She didn't usually perform this sort of service, but Melissa's mother had insisted and, after all, the girl was only sixteen and had never been to the big, wicked city before. It was an unusual assignment. They were going to try to make a hive of honeybees swarm in Melissa's long, blonde hair, and Alex, Melissa, the photographer and his crew, and Bob Shaw, Alex's art director, were all out at a beekeeper's farm on Long Island doing the shoot right now. Understandably, both Melissa and her mother had been apprehensive, but Alex had taken out extra insurance in case of any accident, and both a doctor and a nurse would be standing by. This shoot would be costing *Mode* a lot of money, and Lucille Withers was quite certain that Herbert Rothman knew nothing about it. Still, it would be interesting to see what came out of it.

On the long bus ride from Kansas City—at today's prices, Lulu Withers refused to fly—she had decided that Melissa's rear end wasn't all that bad. Perhaps the girl had begun to lose a little baby fat in that area. But anyway, this was to be essentially a head shot, as Lulu understood it. And the fact that there had been no telephone call from Long Island indicated either that the shoot was going smoothly, or that nothing at all was happening, that the bees had not yet decided to swarm. The black ten covered the red jack, and the two of spades covered the ace, leaving a space for the king. . . .

Out of the corner of her eye, she saw Alex's son step through the glass doors of the apartment and come out onto the terrace. He was wearing white pajamas and a blue terry cloth robe. She thought nothing of this, except that the boy should really be dressed by now; it was nearly noon. She continued to build the pattern with her cards.

He had not seen her, and he walked to the edge of the terrace and leaned across the wide stone parapet, looking down, and Lucille Withers had her first faint *frisson* of alarm. Now she watched as he hoisted himself up to the ledge of the parapet, sat straddling the parapet for a moment, then stood to his full height on the ledge. He was a tall young man, easily six feet, and the breeze blew the skirts of his blue bathrobe and ruffled his blond hair. An airplane passed overhead, on its final approach to La Guardia, and Joel looked up. Then he looked down. Lucille Withers put down her cards. There was no telephone in sight. She rose and stepped out of the gazebo. She moved a few steps toward him, then stopped. His back was to her. "May I help you, Joel?" she said in a quiet voice.

He looked, startled, over his shoulder, and saw her. "Get away from me," he said.

"Come down from there at once," she said. "You're frightening me."

"I'm going to jump," he said.

"No, you are not," she said firmly. "Now do as I say. Come down from there at once." She came two steps closer to him.

"Get away from me," he said again. "Don't come any closer!"

She advanced, deliberately, another step closer to him. "Obey me," she said. "Do as you're told, Joel. Come down from there this instant." She advanced another step.

"Don't try to stop me! Don't touch me! If you do, I'll—"

"*Do as I say!*" The parapet was at least four feet high, and Joel's head towered above her own. But Lucille Withers was a tall woman and, with a quick forward leap and upward lunge, she seized the cord of his bathrobe and pulled him toward her. He fell, and landed on the flagstone terrace on his hands and knees.

"Are you all right?" she said. "Well, I'll wager you're a damn sight better than if you'd landed in the East River." She still had him by the bathrobe cord. "Now stand up and explain yourself, young man!" She yanked him to his feet with the cord.

"Why did you stop me?" he sobbed.

"Get over here and sit down," she said, and led him by the cord to the gazebo and the table where her unfinished card game still lay. "Sit right *there*," she said, and pushed him by his shoulders into a chair. "Don't you dare make a single move, do you understand? And don't you ever dare try a thing like that again!" She seated herself in a chair opposite him. "Now tell me exactly what is going on with you, young man."

"Why didn't you let me do it, Aunt Lulu?" he whispered. "I wanted to."

"Why? I'll tell you exactly why. Because your mother is my friend, that's why, and that friendship is a very precious thing to me. I don't really give bullets what happens to your life, Joel. There are plenty of easy ways to waste a life. What's a life, after all? We're born. We live a little while. We die. But a friendship like your mother's and mine doesn't happen all that often, and when it does, you'll do anything to keep that friend from being hurt. I'd do anything to keep your mother from being hurt any more than she's been hurt already. By pulling you down from there, I was helping her, and by helping her I was probably also helping to lift up my own life a little. Do you play liar's poker?"

He nodded.

She gathered up the cards with her long, bony fingers, and shuffled them briskly three times. "Cut," she said.

He cut the deck, and she dealt them five cards apiece. "Any stakes?" she said.

"Whatever you say," he said.

"How about the winner gets to tell the loser what to do, and the loser has to do what the winner says?"

"Okay," he muttered.

They picked up their cards. "Well, what've you got?" she said.

"A pair of twos," he said.

"I have a pair of nines," she said.

"A pair of twos, and a pair of jacks."

"A pair of nines and three aces," she said.

"Liar!"

She laid down her cards: the ace of clubs, the ace of diamonds, and the ace of hearts; the nine of clubs, and the nine of diamonds. "Now tell me exactly how we're going to explain this morning's little episode to your mother," she said.

"I never want to see my mother again."

"Bullets. I won the hand. Now you're going to do what I say."

Lulu had always known how to handle a deck.

"What would make you even think of doing such a thing, Joel?" Alex said, trying to keep her voice calm. "Please tell me what it was. Whatever it was, I'll try to understand."

He lay on his bed in his darkened bedroom, still in his white pajamas and blue bathrobe. "I don't want to talk about it, Mother," he said.

"Mother? I used to be Mom, didn't I? We used to be pals, didn't we? Can't we be pals again? What's happened to us, Joel? You used to be my man of the house."

"I don't want to be the man of this house, Mother."

"But can't we at least be friends again?"

"I don't want to live here anymore, Mother."

"Oh, Buster—please—why can't we—?"

"I told you not to call me that!"

"Oh, Buster, Buster, Buster—" Her eyes were streaming now. "Why can't I call you Buster? You were always our little Buster. Why can't I have my Buster back?"

She reached out for him, but he turned his face to the wall.

"But what would make him want to do such a terrible thing, Lenny?" she said to him. "Do you have any sort of clue? I know I've been preoccupied with the situation here, and haven't spent as much time with him lately as I normally would have. I left him alone for an entire weekend when I went out to Sagaponack with Mel, but that was what he insisted he wanted. Could that be it? Or does he resent Mel? Could *that* be it? I always thought he liked Mel, but perhaps—"

"No, I don't think he resents Mel," Lenny said.

"Then what is it? He seems so angry at me, Lenny. He won't speak to me. He's angry at Lulu, he seems angry at himself. He seems angry at the whole world." They were sitting in her dark green library at 10 Gracie Square.

"I think it's a good idea to let him spend a few days at my house, until he simmers down," he said. "Charlie will keep an eye on him. Joel and Charlie have always gotten along. If anyone can get him out of this black mood, it's Charlie."

"Or did I leave something out of his life when he was growing up? I was always a working mother, and I suppose that might have had something to do with it. I didn't do all the things with him that other mothers did. But I always thought he knew that he was loved. Or maybe I smothered him with too much love. Maybe I was overly protective. Maybe because I grew up without too much in the way of a mother or a father, I hovered over him, fussed over him, *too* much. I just didn't want him to have the kind of childhood I had, and perhaps I gave him too much love. Perhaps that was all a terrible mistake."

"Don't blame yourself, Alex. You mustn't blame yourself."

"And of course after Steven—died—I tried to be both a mother and a father to him. Took him to ball games. Took him to museums. Talked business with him. Tried to treat him as a peer. Asked his advice on things. But perhaps that was all, all wrong."

"I don't think so, Alex."

"But I did worry over him, I know. Perhaps I worried too much. But he was all I had—my only real family, my only real flesh and blood. But I really thought he was growing up so well. I thought I was doing such a *good* job. Maybe I was so pleased with myself at the way he was growing up that I didn't look out for little signs, little signals, that I should have caught, but didn't. But he always did so well in school. He always seemed just a normal, bright, happy little boy. His teachers said so. But obviously something dark and terrible was going on with him that I had absolutely no idea about."

"Obviously," Lenny said.

"Or—I've been thinking about this—could it perhaps be some sort of genetic thing? My mother, you know, was a manic-depressive. She was later diagnosed a schizophrenic. Could some bad gene from her have popped out in him?"

"Don't blame your mother, either," he said.

"But what could have caused him even to *consider* doing such a terrible thing? If Lulu hadn't just happened to be there, he could have—"

"Look," he said, "I think there may be a quite obvious explanation for all this."

"Really?" she said. "Please, Lenny, please tell me what it is."

"There's a certain letter that was written years ago, at 'Rothmere.' Herbert Rothman would very much like to get his hands on that letter. So would Miss Fiona Fenton. They have both tried certain, ah, avenues of approach to obtain that letter. I happened to run into Fiona in a coffee shop the other day. She mentioned that she and Joel have become 'very close,' as she put it. I suspect that Fiona may have been trying to use Joel to learn the whereabouts of that letter. I suspect that Fiona may be the Afro-American in the woodpile."

"Letter? What sort of letter, Lenny?"

"The man who was shot in the boathouse years ago."

"Yes," she said with a little gasp.

" 'The intruder,' as he was described in nineteen seventy-three, in the press. It seems you wrote a letter prior to the, ah, intruder's visit, inviting him to 'Rothmere,' mentioning a specific date, time, and place for your meeting. Your intruder was expected, it would seem."

She touched her triple strand of pearls, and her eyes widened in a kind of fear, but she said nothing.

"If Herb and Fiona could gain possession of that letter, it would prove that your intruder was not an intruder, and that what happened that afternoon of September twentieth was not a self-defense shooting. It was murder, and, as you may know, there is no statute of limitations on murder cases. The case could be reopened at any time. If so, Herbert could presumably destroy your career forever, which, of course, Herbert and Fiona would very much like to do."

"He knocked me down," she whispered. "He had the heel of his shoe on my throat. He was going to break my neck. . . ."

"I happen to have that letter," he said. "Herb Rothman has already offered me a lot of money for it. But not enough."

"*You?* But how?"

"Do you remember a friend of ours named Adam Amado?"

"Some sort of actor, wasn't he, whom you were trying to promote? I remember you mentioning him, but I never met him."

"Actually, you did," he said. "Adam Amado was a stage name Charlie and I created for him. But Adam Amado was the same man you knew as James—Skipper—Purdy."

She covered her mouth with her hand.

"And so, you see, I bear a certain amount of responsibility for bringing Skipper Purdy back into your life. If I hadn't plucked him off the street one day, he might never have found out who and where you were. And my responsibility for what happened at the boathouse that afternoon goes even deeper, I'm afraid. In the months prior to what happened, Adam had become a considerable trial to Charlie and me. He wouldn't look for work, and he'd become a considerable financial drain on us. I gave him an ultimatum. I told him he had six months to find work or bring some money into the house. I gave him until September twenty-fifth, nineteen seventy-three. If he didn't come up with the money by then, I told him I'd throw him out on the street, which was where, alas, I had originally found him. That was obviously when he concocted his scheme of trying to blackmail you— which, of course, I knew nothing about. If I had, I would certainly have tried to stop him. I even bear responsibility for what happened in a third area. I paid for his lessons in karate, which, I gathered, he used when he threw you to the floor."

She shook her head. "No, I think he would have found me sooner or later," she said. "He'd been looking for me for a long time."

"Before he left the house that day, he left an envelope with me, saying I was to open it if anything happened to him. When I heard what happened, I opened it. In it were some personal papers—his will, a storage receipt for some stained-glass windows, your letter from 'Rothmere,' and your nine-teen sixty-one marriage certificate from the Jackson County Court House in Kansas City."

She sat there, twisting her pearls, looking stunned.

"I don't blame you for what you did," he said. "He was one of the most damnably physically attractive men I've ever known. There was a kind of magnetism about him—an almost animal magnetism, an aura of raw sexuality that we thought would project across the footlights. I was quite violently attracted to him myself, at one point. And of course he was hung like a bull, with a cock that should have been written up in the Guinness Book of Records, if you'll pardon my lapse into uncharacteristic vulgarity, Alex."

She nodded.

"But one thing I've always wondered, Alex. After he'd knocked you down on the floor with his karate chop, and had his heel on your throat in a classic karate victory stance, how were you able to retrieve the gun and shoot him?"

"I didn't shoot him," she said quietly. "It was Aunt Lily. She'd been hiding in the boathouse, in case something went wrong."

"Ah," he said. "I always suspected that."

"How?" she said. "Why?"

"Years ago, I mentioned to Ho Rothman that I was aware of a certain letter. He became very exercised, very angry and threatening. I figured he wouldn't become that angry just to protect *you*, Alex, fond though he was of you. There were only two people that he'd be that angry to protect—himself, or his wife."

She nodded mutely.

"Tell me something else," he said. "If you'd been able to, would you have shot him?"

She shook her head. "No," she said. "I know I couldn't have done it, and I suppose Ho and Aunt Lily knew it too, which was why she was there. I thought, with the gun, I could perhaps frighten him away, but—"

"And then, when it was over, why didn't you tell the police it was Aunt Lily? After all, she was the one who fired the shots."

"Three reasons. For one, Aunt Lily had saved my life—I had no money to give him. For another, it was my mess I'd gotten the family into, not Aunt Lily's mess, and it was up to me to get the family out of it. And for another, that was the way Ho wanted the story to go out. He said it was more appealing for a younger woman to be the attack victim, rather than an older woman—particularly a young woman with a young son. The story had all been prewritten for the press. Aunt Lily was supposed to be in New York, with Joel, who'd been taken there that morning by his nurse. Ho had worked out all the details, and it was too late to change them."

"So that was what the long telephone call to Ho's office in Manhattan was all about."

She nodded again. "To be sure that everybody's stories dovetailed. It was so horrible, Lenny. I've tried to drive it out of my mind, but sometimes I still have nightmares about it, even after all these years. Because, you see, even though I hated Skipper for what he was trying to do to me—and to my marriage—I didn't want to see him killed. In a strange way, I still loved him, Lenny. In some ways, I still do."

"Nor do I blame you, dear Alex," he said. "One never really recovers from one's first love, does one? The love to whom one sacrificed one's maidenhood. And he was a gorgeous man, even though there was something missing at the core. I loved him, too. I still miss him. We keep a little shrine to Adam Amado in our apartment, with his stained-glass windows."

"Those stained-glass windows," she said.

"You really must come to one of our Sunday-night salons one day. I'll show them to you. Tell me. Was Skipper Joel's father?"

She blinked quickly, and nodded once more.

"I always suspected that, too," he said. "There is a certain physical resemblance. The blond hair, something about the nose and jawline. Whereas Steven—"

"Yes," she said.

"Of course Steven was the great love of *my* life," he said. "Perhaps even greater and more poignant because it was unrequited. After all, there was a certain difference between Steven's and my ages—not much, perhaps, but enough to have made a relationship seem quite . . . inappropriate. When I first came to work for the Rothmans, as a mail-room boy, Steven had not yet been born. It was as a mail-room boy that I first caught Aunt Lily's eye—it was my beauty, I suppose—

and promotions followed. Later, after Steven was born, I was often invited to 'Rothmere,' and it was Aunt Lily's suggestion that I teach her five-year-old grandson to swim. Aunt Lily had learned that I was also a beautiful swimmer in my early youth. In fact, swimming was the only real talent I had when I was so rudely invited to leave Onward, Mississippi—I was the most beautiful swimmer. We used to swim, my friend and I, in the Deer Creek, and sometimes in the big river. That was the cause of my downfall in Onward—those late-night swimming outings. My friend's father was the town sheriff. It was swimming that gave me my golden tan. Did you know that when I first came to New York, people said I looked just like a jar of honey? It's quite true. And look at me now! I've dined at the White House with three U.S. presidents! I've emceed Bob Hope's birthday parties! I introduced Garbo to Dietrich, the woman dear Marlene most wanted to meet. I've had sex with Rudy Valentino! And most of all, no one has endured employment with the Rothmans longer than I. All because I was beautiful. But I'm wandering. Where was I?"

"Steven," she said. "Swimming. And the letter."

"Oh, yes. He was only five when Aunt Lily asked me to teach her young grandson to swim, and, needless to say, I have always done everything in my power to oblige dear Aunt Lily. That was when I first fell in love with that beautiful child. Not, as I say, that there was anything inappropriate in our relationship. I was never anything more than his dear old Uncle Lenny to him, alas. And it was thrilling to watch Steven grow into such a beautiful young man—quite different from Adam—tall and dark and slender, with a swimmer's build and smooth, long muscles in the arms and legs that I, in fact, used to have. And, different from Adam, Steven was all beauty and goodness on the inside as well. There was never anything physical between us, but, oh, dear, if there *had* been I'd have taught him a few more things than the Australian crawl! Herb always suspected that Steven and I had a sexual relationship, but we didn't. Herbert lived in terror that his only son was gay—it obsessed him—and he always suspected that I had some sort of evidence to prove that Steven was gay and, that if Herb didn't play his cards right with me, I'd spill the beans. Of course I had no evidence, but it didn't hurt to let Herb think I did. I don't think Steven was gay, unless everybody has a gay side, which is the impression one gets from reading Dr. Kinsey. If Steven had a gay side, he worked hard to suppress it—to please his father. Poor Steven. There was nothing he could do to please his father, though he tried so hard. I think his father had succeeded in destroying Steven, even before he destroyed himself. His father has a copy of another letter, the letter that Adam—Skipper—wrote in response to yours. That letter in itself proves nothing. But he showed it to Steven, implying that you and Skipper had been lovers. That was when he did what he did." His voice cracked, and he brushed a tear from his eye.

Alex closed her eyes. "And you have my letter," she said.

He cleared his throat. "The second half to the puzzle, the half that Herb has always wanted. I suppose you could say that this is a talent I developed under Rothman tutelage, collecting random pieces of puzzles and putting them together. That's been my genius, I suppose."

"That's why they say Lenny Liebling knows where certain bodies are buried."

"Dear me, yes. Lots of bodies. A body in Paris, and bodies here. All sorts of sordid little secrets. I call them my Rothman Retirement Insurance Policy. Herbert's penchant for little girls, for instance. Oh, Lordy, the irate mothers who've been paid off over the years! I know all their names. At least this new ladyfriend of his is over twelve years old!"

"And he's offered you money for my letter," she said.

"Oh, yes. Quite a lot, in fact. But don't worry, dear Alex. There's not enough money in the world to get me to give that letter to that dreadful man and his dreadful ladyfriend. That doesn't mean I don't enjoy playing a little cat and mouse game with him, of course. There's nothing I enjoy more than watching Herbert Rothman sweat. I've even thought of taking Herb's money, and giving him a totally bogus letter. But not now. Now that I know it was Aunt Lily who did the shooting, I think my little games with your letter have gone quite far enough. I rather like Aunt Lily, and I wouldn't want to see her name dragged in the mud at this point in her life. In fact, as soon as the dust has settled over all of this, I think you and I should have a letter-burning party. And a marriage-certificate-burning party. Should we invite Charlie to our little party? He'll feel left out if we don't. What do you think?"

"But I still don't see," she said, "how any of this explains what Joel tried to do this morning."

"Ah," he said. "Joel's little caper this morning proves to me that things have now gone quite, quite far enough. It is time to call in dear old Lenny to the rescue. Tell me something. Does Joel still hide his journals in the same place?"

"Journals? What journals?"

"He keeps a journal. Has been for several years. He's thinking of a writing career, you know, or of becoming a journalist. He says it's in his blood. He showed me some of his journals two or three years ago, to see if he had any talent. Quite frankly, I didn't think so, but what can you tell from the pubescent moonings of a fifteen-year-old? I didn't want to discourage him. I urged him to keep it up. Do you mind if I take a look in Joel's room?"

"Of course not."

He rose, and as he left the room she heard him mutter, "Third tile from the west wall, sixth from the south . . ."

He was gone a long time, and she sat curled in the green leather chair. Her portrait looked down at her from above the fireplace, and the expression that Bouché had painted on her face now looked accusatory.

When Lenny returned to the library, he had three blue-bound spiral notebooks in his hand. His face was grim. "I think," he said, "that we have found the answers you were looking for."

He handed her the notebooks.

"Mel?" she said when she reached him on the phone. "May I borrow Scarlett O'Hara for a few hours? There's something that I need from the house in Sagaponack."

"Are you all right?" he said. "You sound upset."

"No, I'm fine. But I need something from Sagaponack, and I need to dash out there and get it."

"Sure," he said. "You know where I garage the car. Just tell Harry to give you the keys."

She had no sooner hung up the phone than it rang again in her hand. It was Mark Rinsky, and he sounded jubilant. "Boy, have we got some great stuff for you from London!" he said. "It took us long enough, but it was worth the wait. Listen, she's—"

"I don't have time to talk now, Mark," she said. "Besides, I know everything I need to know about Fiona."

Miss Lincoln, Herbert Rothman's secretary, looked up from her desk and said, "Mr. Rothman will see you now, Mr. Liebling." As Lenny stepped toward the door, Miss Lincoln noticed that he had three blue-bound spiral notebooks under his arm. Before he closed the door, she heard her boss say, "So, Lenny. You've finally come to your senses and decided to accept my offer."

Outside, at her desk, Miss Lincoln continued what she had been doing, which was balancing Mr. Rothman's personal checkbook. She had worked for Herbert Rothman for so long that she was no longer astonished, or even mildly impressed, by the amounts of money that ran through this account. The fortune was so vast that the figures no longer meant anything to her. With hundreds of thousands of dollars running in and out of this account every month, it was simply a matter of placing the commas and decimal points in the right positions and the digits in their appropriate columns. Herbert Rothman's wealth, and style of living, were so far beyond her ken and understanding that she no longer bothered imagining what it must be like to be that rich, and besides, imagining what it must be like to be that rich was not part of her job description.

Like so many other spinster executive secretaries of Miss Lincoln's age and ilk, Miss Lincoln was secretly in love with her boss—secretly, and desperately, and passionately in love with him. He filled her daytime thoughts, and her nighttime dreams, when he often came to her and possessed her body with his own. There was no other man in her life. She had saved her virginity for him, and she would lay down her life for him—oh, yes. Even at home, alone, in Kew Gardens, while the cantor who lived on the floor above was singing, and when she was spooning condensed milk into her evening cup of tea, then holding out the spoon for Kitty, her Siamese cat, to lick before she stirred the tea, she imagined Herbert Rothman sitting on the sofa bed beside her, stroking Kitty's fur.

She knew all of Herbert Rothman's faults, and loved him all the more for them. She knew he was perennially unfaithful to his wife, and she approved of this. She knew of the series of girlfriends over the years, most of whom had treated him badly and cost him money. She only wished that just one of them had been able to make him happy. She knew of this new young Englishwoman, for whom he was renting the expensive apartment at the Westbury, and she knew that this was a passion more consuming than any he had ever experienced before. He called her constantly, begged to be with her day and night, but there was no jealousy on Miss Lincoln's part, just selflessness. She only hoped that this one would treat him better than the others had, and would help him fulfill himself in ways he had never been fulfilled before. She wished this Englishwoman happiness with all her heart.

Miss Lincoln knew all about Mr. Rothman's marriage, long gone sour, to the skinny, picky Pegeen, the wife who hadn't called her husband at his office in nearly twenty years, and whom Mr. Rothman never called at home. But even though Herbert and Pegeen Rothman no longer spoke to one another, the skinny, picky wife wouldn't give him a divorce. She could spend his money, though! Oh, yes, she could spend his money to a fare-thee-well! Look at the bills! There was $6,452.67 to Saks, $7,609.23 to Bendel's, $126,000 plus tax to Maximilian for the new floor-length Russian sable coat, $9,900.00 to Cartier for butterfly earclips of diamonds and rubies set in platinum! Not bad for a month of spending!

Miss Lincoln just hoped that this new love of his was of such immensity and fervor that he would at last take drastic measures to get a divorce from Pegeen, and at last find peace of mind with an understanding woman.

Miss Lincoln, unlike skinny Pegeen, was able to show her love for Herbert Rothman daily in all sorts of little, quiet ways. She saw to it that the pots of prize orchids on his windowsill were misted twice a day, watered once a week, and fed every fourteen days. She made sure that the candy jar on his desk was always filled with those little Italian caramels from Maison Glass that he liked to nibble on while he worked. She saw to it that his silver water carafe was refilled twice a day with fresh ice water. She saw to it that his refrigerator was always stocked with eight-ounce glass bottles—never plastic, never cans—of Coca-Cola Classic. Hard to find, those eight-ounce glass bottles, but Miss Lincoln managed to find them for him. She polished his silver picture frames—the Bachrach portrait of the skinny, picky, spendthrift wife, and the photograph of his late son, so handsome, in tennis whites, standing at the net with his racket, looking as though he had just aced a serve.

Hourly, she checked the angle of Mr. Rothman's venetian blinds so that the sun would not get in his eyes. At quarter to five each evening, she reminded him of the time, and again at ten to five, and again at five to five. At five o'clock, she was waiting for him outside his office door, with his briefcase packed, and with five crisp new ten-dollar bills—he hated used money—in case he should decide to take a taxi home rather than walk to River House, waiting to help him into his topcoat, hand him his hat, and be ready with an umbrella if it looked like rain. All this she did for him, and much, much more—a thousand little daily offerings for the man she loved.

Suddenly Lenny Liebling came bursting through the door. "Miss Lincoln!" he cried. "Call nine-one-one! I think Mr. Rothman may have had a stroke!"

"You are a dear to come and call on me this way," Fiona was saying. "I was certain we could sort things out between us without calling out all those barristers. Barristers are such a bore! Please do sit down, Alex. May I call you Alex?"

Alex seated herself in a small chair, and Fiona arranged herself on the big white sofa opposite her.

"That's a pretty Hermès scarf you're wearing, Fiona."

"Thank you!" She touched the scarf. "I have a passion for these, I'm afraid. I just can't have enough of them."

"Is it one you bought with one of Pussy McCutcheon's stolen credit cards?"

Fiona's dark eyes flashed. "I don't know what you're talking about," she said.

"I had five hundred dollars in my purse that night at Maggie's party," she said. "I suppose you took that, too."

"What on earth are you accusing me of? You're not making any sense to me at all. Scarves, money, credit cards—"

"I think you know what I'm talking about, Fiona."

"I thought you'd come here on a friendly visit. When you rang me up, I thought—"

"Well, now you know."

"I think you must be quite mad."

"Yes, Fiona, I think I am."

"Then I don't wish to talk to a crazy woman. I think I shall have to ask you to leave. I think I would like to terminate this conversation, under the circumstances. I have important matters to attend to."

"But I haven't finished what I have to say to you, Fiona. How much did you steal from that London dress shop?"

"Honestly, this is just too crazy-making." Fiona started to rise. "Really, I just don't—"

Alex lifted Mel's pistol from her purse. "Please don't move," she said, and pointed the pistol at her. Fiona let out a little scream, and sank back into the sofa. "That's not loaded!" she said.

"Yes, as a matter of fact it is."

"What are you going to do?" she whimpered.

"What I wish I could have done that night when you came prowling around Mel's house in Sagaponack. What I wish I'd done then. Shot the prowler."

"I don't know what you're talking about!"

"Of course you do."

"What do you want? Is it your five hundred dollars? I'll give it to you."

"That white sofa." Alex pointed. "Is that where you fucked my son the first time?"

"Please," she said. "I shouldn't have let him seduce me— I knew that. But he was so insistent—violent, almost! I was terrified he was going to rape me! He was crazed on drugs! I thought it was better to submit to him than—"

Alex flipped the safety catch open with a little snap.

"Oh, please," Fiona sobbed, cowering against the sofa. Tears streamed down her face. "I tried to help him. I thought I could help him with his addiction. You ought to know that Joel is hopelessly addicted to cocaine, and I thought perhaps—"

Alex leveled the pistol at her.

"Please . . . please don't . . . let me explain . . . I can explain everything . . ."

Alex studied the younger woman's face for a moment. Then she said, "Do you know something? I really was going to kill you. I really was. I drove all the way to Sagaponack to get this gun. But now I wonder if killing is too good for you."

"Please, I only wanted—"

"Wanting to destroy my career and get my job was one thing. But trying to destroy my son was another . . ."

Fiona's telephone rang, and she started to reach for it.

"Don't answer that," Alex said. "Let it ring."

The phone rang six or seven more times, then stopped.

"But now I wonder if you're even worth killing," she said. "I don't think you're even worth that. I think Herb Rothman is punishment enough for you. You and he deserve each other."

"Please . . . oh, please," the other woman said.

"But I warn you, if you ever come near my son again—"

"Please . . . I gave him his walking papers . . . I told him—"

"If you ever come near my son again—I warn you—I will kill you."

Now someone was knocking loudly on Fiona's door.

"Stay where you are. Don't answer that."

The knocking continued, and presently a man's voice called out. "Fiona—Alex—please open up. It's Mel."

"All right. Let him in," Alex said.

Fiona rushed to the door, and threw her arms around Mel. "Oh, thank God you've come, my darling," she sobbed. "She was going to kill me!"

He pushed her aside and walked straight to Alex, and picked up the pistol that now lay in her lap. "When Lenny told me about Joel's diaries, I knew immediately what you'd gone to get in Sagaponack," he said. "Thank God I got here before you did something crazy. Come on, let's get out of here." He took her by the elbow.

"Wait till I tell Herbert about this!" Fiona shouted. "She tried to kill me! Never mind about loyalty clauses and contracts! This was attempted murder! She could go to prison for this! Just wait till I tell Herbert!"

"I don't think Herb Rothman's going to be much use to you right now," Mel said. "He's in the intensive care unit at Roosevelt Hospital, on the critical list. He's had a massive stroke." He dropped the pistol in his jacket pocket. "Let's go," he said, and started to steer Alex by the elbow toward the door.

"But the bloody bitch tried to kill me!" Fiona screamed.

Alex stared at her. "Do you know something?" she said evenly. "I think I already have."

*   *   *

They sat at the table in the wrought-iron gazebo on her terrace with their drinks. The moon had just risen in the east. "They did a CAT scan on him this afternoon," Mel said. "They're talking major brain damage."

"I can't believe it," she said. "It's over. I ought to feel emotionally exhausted, shouldn't I? I ought to feel sorry for Herb, shouldn't I? I ought to feel drained. Why don't I? Why don't I feel any of those things? Why do I suddenly just feel so terribly excited, Mel? Can you explain it?"

"Because it isn't over. It's just beginning."

"That's right! And all at once there's so much to do! I've got to get Joel back, for one thing—but on a whole new basis. Not as the hovering little mother anymore, but as my friend, a friend who trusts me as an adult—a whole new relationship! That isn't going to be easy. That's going to be work, but I've got to do it, and I can't wait to start. And then— and then—"

"And before you know it, you're going to have a new husband to take care of." He touched his glass to hers.

"Yes! That, too! That's going to be work, too, and I can't wait to get to that, either!"

He smiled. "Neither can I," he said.

"And I've got a *magazine* to run, my very own magazine! At last! Deadlines to meet, assignments to give out—more work! But suddenly I can't wait till it's tomorrow, and I can start on all of it."

All at once he jumped to his feet. "Look," he said, and pointed.

"What is it?" she said, rising beside him, her eyes following his pointing finger, mystified by the pale arc of light that was now stretched across the night sky.

"It's a moonbow," he said. "It's a lunar rainbow. They're very rare. Atmospheric conditions have to be just right."

"But it has no colors."

"Moonlight is only a reflection of the sun's light," he said. "So moonlight can't refract the colors of the spectrum. Lunar rainbows are always white."

She laughed softly. "Where do you get your bits and pieces of arcane information, Mel? Lunar rainbows, tidal bores . . ."

"They generally last only a few seconds. Damn, I wish I had a TV crew here."

"I don't," she said. "I like to think we're the only two people in New York who've seen it. I hope we're the only two people in the world who've seen it! I think it's just for us. I think it means good luck." She took his hand. "Let's make a wish," she said.

He lifted his glass in a toast to the moonbow, even as it began to fade.

"What did you wish?" she asked him.

"Just a wish for a little girl from Paradise, who can't wait till it's tomorrow."

"Dots-a me," she said, with a laugh. "Dots-a me."

Epilogue

From the *New York Times:*

IRS DROPS
ROTHMAN SUIT

Courtroom Drama
Unfolds

By Irving Eichbaum

The Internal Revenue Service today withdrew all claims against Rothman Communications, Inc., the publishing-broadcasting giant, and its chief executive officer, Herbert Oscar "Ho" Rothman. The government had sought some $900,000,000 in back taxes from the company. With penalties and interest, if the government had been able to make its case, the total amount owed could have reached the billion-dollar mark, which would have been a record in such cases.

Essentially, the government had claimed that the senior Mr. Rothman, 94, had always run his company as a one-man operation, reserving all decisions for himself, and that therefore the entire earnings of the corporation should have been taxed as Mr. Rothman's personal income. Rothman attorneys had countered that, on the contrary, the private company had always been run on a

consensus developed among Rothman family members
and other shareholders, with each shareholder voting his
or her own interests.

Histrionic Outburst

As tensions built at the trial in the Federal Court-
house on Foley Square, witness after witness appeared
to testify in Mr. Rothman's defense, declaring that Mr.
Rothman's stewardship of the company had for years
been only honorary, and that no real decisions had been
made by Mr. Rothman since the mid-1970s. A series of
physicians and private-duty nurses who have attended
the ailing nonagenarian tycoon over the years testified
that Mr. Rothman was neither physically nor mentally able to exercise the kind of power and control the
government claimed he wielded. In a dramatic moment
in the proceedings today, an attorney from the firm
of Waxman, Holloway, Goldsmith & McCarthy, who
represent Mr. Rothman, arose and in a ringing voice
announced, "Ladies and gentlemen, may I present Mr.
H. O. Rothman!" The aged patriarch founder of the
company was then wheeled down the center aisle of
the courtroom in a hospital gurney, accompanied by
two male nurses, two female nurses, and two attend-
ing physicians, one of whom wore a stethoscope and
kept his fingers firmly pressed on Mr. Rothman's wrist
to check his pulse rate. Tubes from various life-support
systems were attached to Mr. Rothman's body.

Mr. Rothman was then asked just one question, which
had to be repeated several times before the witness
appeared to understand that he was being questioned.
"Mr. Rothman, will you please tell this court how
you run your business?" asked Jerome Waxman, 43,
Mr. Rothman's chief defense lawyer. When finally the
defendant's lips began to move in response to the question, a microphone had to be placed at his mouth in order
for the court to hear the response. The only intelligible
words from Mr. Rothman were, "The *Titanic* is going to
sink." This was an apparent reference to an early journalistic coup of the defendant's when, early in 1912,
Rothman's fledgling newspaper, the *Newark Explorer*,

suggested that the S.S. *Titanic* was not as seaworthy as its builders claimed, and "predicted" the famous maritime disaster. This coup launched the communications magnate's career, and became the cornerstone of his growing empire.

With the utterance of that last remark, Mr. Waxman turned dramatically to the members of the government's prosecution team, who were already looking unhappy, and declared, "And this, gentlemen, is the man you claim has single-handed control of Rothman Communications!"

This last provoked a histrionic outburst from Mrs. Anna Lily Rothman, 85, H. O. Rothman's wife, who was among the courtroom spectators. Pointing to the prosecution lawyers, Mrs. Rothman cried out, "You've done this to him! Does he deserve this at the end of a long and productive life? This case has almost killed my husband! It would serve you right if he died right here in this courtroom—murdered by the IRS!" Mrs. Rothman made various other slurring references to the "Infernal" Revenue Service before she was silenced by the judge and by nurses who rushed to her side to calm her.

More Surprises

Following Mrs. Rothman's outburst, Mr. Waxman then proceeded to introduce new evidence. In response to a hand signal, court wardens wheeled in a dozen portable file cabinets on dollies. These proved to contain hundreds of stock certificates, many of them dating from the first third of the century, indicating how shares of the family-owned company have been distributed over the years. This provided an intriguing glimpse of how ownership in a normally very secretive company has been divided over the nearly eight decades since its foundation.

The largest individual stockholder is indeed H. O. Rothman, but other family members also control large blocks of stock. These include Mr. and Mrs. Herbert J. Rothman, and Mr. and Mrs. Arthur R. Rothman, respectively H. O. Rothman's two sons and daughters-in-law. Another large stockholder turns out to be Mrs.

Alexandra Rothman, the widow of the H. J. Rothmans'
son, Steven, and the current editor-in-chief of *Mode*, the
Rothmans' fashion publication. Still another large block
of stock is controlled by the Steven Rothman Trust,
whose beneficiary is Joel Rothman, Mrs. Alexandra
Rothman's son, and a great-grandson of the founder,
with his mother as sole trustee and fiduciary officer until
her son reaches age 25. An eighth important stockholder,
to no one's surprise, turned out to be Mrs. Anna Lily
Rothman, who still serves as the company's treasurer.
Two other Rothman grandchildren own small amounts
of shares.

But the most surprising revelation in the courtroom
today was that a large and important block of Rothman
Communications is owned by Leonard J. Liebling,
the only nonfamily shareholder. Mr. Liebling, who
is thought to be in his seventies, has been a longtime
Rothman employee and family intimate.

Rudderless Arm

Meanwhile, though H. O. Rothman will retain the
honorific title of founding chairman for his lifetime,
the operational heads of the company and its various
divisions remained somewhat problematic and up in the
air. Arthur Rothman continues to head the Broadcast
Division and, until recently, Herbert Rothman headed
the Publishing Division. Herbert then, in light of his
father's incapacitation, briefly assumed the title of president and chief executive officer of the company, leaving
the publishing arm rudderless. But Herbert J. Rothman,
67, has recently become incapacitated as well. A massive stroke left his right side completely paralyzed, and
left him without the power of speech. The degree of
mental damage he may have suffered has not as yet
been fully assessed. He was in the courtroom today,
in his wheelchair, and appeared angered at the proceedings. Periodically, he tried to scribble messages to the
Rothman attorneys with his left hand which, the *Times*
learned, were unintelligible.

And so the questions remain as to who will take
overall operating charge of the corporation, as well as

who will take over the publishing arm. There has been
speculation that Leonard Liebling may be handed one or
another of these posts, but Mr. Liebling brushed aside
such speculation without comment.

Other Shifts Deferred

Other proposed shifts and staff realignments in the
company have been deferred, at least for the time
being. Earlier this year, for instance, Herbert Rothman
announced that his daughter-in-law, Alexandra Rothman, would thenceforth share her editor-in-chiefship
of *Mode* with Miss Fiona Fenton, an English fashion
expert. Mrs. Rothman was said to have been unhappy
with this arrangement, and this plan has apparently been
abandoned. Efforts of the *Times* to reach Miss Fenton
for comment were unsuccessful, since her telephone is
reported disconnected, with no forwarding number.

Meanwhile, faced with such overwhelming evidence
in the defense's favor, and even as the file boxes of stock
certificates were being marked for exhibit, the government attorneys for the IRS approached the bench and
announced that they were dropping their action against
the Rothmans. This drew a tart and caustic comment
from the presiding judge, Hon. Walter Liebmann, 57.
"The next time the IRS decides to bring a case of this
magnitude to court," Judge Liebmann said, "it should
try to have sufficient evidence to support its allegations.
This case has already cost American taxpayers in excess
of $200,000." Judge Liebmann's comment drew cheers
and applause from the Rothman side of the courtroom.

Mel Jorgenson and Alex Rothman were married in a quiet
ceremony not long after the trial. Joel Rothman served as his
new stepfather's best man.

Alex has moved out of the apartment at 10 Gracie Square,
and she and Mel now live in Mel's house on Beekman Place,
with Cronkite, of course, and the Bouché portrait moved with
her. Having discovered that she owned the apartment, or at
least a substantial share of the corporation which held the
title, she put the apartment up for sale. The asking price is
$2.9 million, but in today's soft real estate market there have

been few nibbles. Alex is in no hurry, however, now that her career future and her financial future are both secure.

Joel is now a freshman at Harvard where, from all reports, he is doing very well. But he has also fallen head over heels in love again, this time with the famous young model from Kansas City named Melissa Cogswell, who became an overnight sensation when the photograph of her was published with honey bees swarming in her long blonde hair. Melissa seems like a perfectly nice girl to me, if a bit empty-headed, and it is hard to know whether this romance will lead to anything at this point. Joel has had her up to Cambridge for several weekends. I suppose it is in the nature of eighteen-year-olds to fall head over heels in love several times a year. As for me, I choose not to remember what it was like to be eighteen years old.

Otto, Joel's former bodyguard, now drives a truck for United Parcel. He considers it a very important job because he gets to wear a beeper.

As I say, the bee-swarming photograph became a sensation when it was published. Wisely, I think, Alex chose not to put it on *Mode*'s cover where, she reasoned, it might too quickly become overexposed. Instead, she dropped the photograph almost casually in the middle of a sixteen-page spread on picnic fashions. For weeks after it appeared, it seemed, people could talk of nothing else but that photograph—at least in the circles I move in.

Helmut posed her in a one-piece swimsuit, sitting on a fallen log. There was a suggestion of mists, and forest sunlight, and water, in the background. Melissa sat, with her head thrown back, her long hair streaming down, and the swarming bees seemed to form a moving, gauzy glow around her, almost like a halo. But it was the expression on her face that was so extraordinary, a kind of flushed rapture that suggested sexual arousal. It was an enormously erotic photograph, for some reason, and someone quipped that it was the first time anyone had photographed a woman having an orgasm. The actual cause of the expression was no doubt sheer terror, and only a few people knew that it had taken five full days of posing, with the apiarist applying various chemicals to Melissa's hair, before the bees in the overcrowded hive decided to cooperate, and Helmut had exactly seventeen minutes to get his shot.

The photograph was taken up by serious art critics, one of whom wrote, "Newton's photograph becomes a metaphor for life itself—the throbbing need of wild creatures to establish new territory, a new resting place, a new leader, a Queen, and to propagate the species—the pulsating force that has driven nature since the dawn of time. And in the young woman's face is an image of not only life's nurturing joys and rewards, but also life's uncertainties, dangers, fears, and the dark certainty of death. Newton's photograph speaks eloquently of *en passant, ça va*, as poignantly and heartbreakingly as an Edith Piaf song." Oh, well . . .

The photograph has already won a number of important prizes and awards, including an award from the American Society of Magazine Editors, the industry's highest honor. The Pulitzer Prize Committee is very secretive, but my spies tell me that the picture has a good chance of winning the prize for feature photography. If it does, it will be the first time a magazine has won that particular Pulitzer since 1969, when it was won by a publication whose name I won't even deign to mention. Alex is often asked where she came up with the concept for that photograph. "It wasn't my concept at all," she replies. "The concept came from Gregory Kittredge, one of our bright young editors." Yes, Gregory has been promoted to assistant editor, quite a step up from being an editorial assistant. And Gregory is definitely a young man on the rise around here, something of the fair-haired boy, and if Alex ever decides to retire, there are those who say that Gregory will be her handpicked successor.

By the way, we had our little letter-burning party—just the three of us, Alex, Charlie, and I—not long after Herbert's stroke. We committed the letter to the flames of our fireplace at the Gainsborough, and the document from the Jackson County Court House met the same fate. During the cremation rite, I couldn't help noticing Alex's eyes traveling briefly to the pair of stained-glass windows. Then her eyes withdrew and, afterward, we went into another room and drank champagne, and got a little tiddly. I considered a toast to Skipper's memory, but then thought better of it.

With Melissa Cogswell—suddenly the hottest, and priciest, young model in the country—in her stable, you'd think that Lucille Withers would be doing very well. Still, to save money, she continues to take the bus when she comes to New

York from Kansas City, as she did for Alex's stylish little wedding.

Ho Rothman picked me to succeed Herbert as president of the Publishing Division of Rothman Communications. This was my reward, I suppose, for having saved the company nearly a billion dollars in taxes. But I also suspect that Ho realized that my talents were better suited to the business, rather than the editorial, side of publishing, that I am more of a financial person than an editor. The Publishing Division is doing well enough, though the late-1990 recession has caused our revenues to dip somewhat. *Mode* has felt the pinch, too, but whereas other magazines have suffered revenue losses of up to ten percent, *Mode* is down only three percent, so *Mode* is still ahead of the pack.

Also, now that she is freed of the constraints Herb Rothman placed upon her, Alex is able to have much more fun running her magazine. Already—subtly, gradually—she is introducing new themes and motifs into the book, changing it in ways Herb never would have approved of. I can't reveal the little surprises she is planning for the future, but the atmosphere on the fourteenth floor is suddenly exciting again. It is almost as though she had been given all the money in the world, and allowed to create her own new magazine—those are the sort of changes you'll be noticing in the months ahead. For instance, I can tell you that if Herb Rothman was scandalized by last June's cover, wait till you see the cover she has planned for this coming May! Even Ho, who is hard to scandalize, may raise his eyebrows at this one, though Ho never wails too loudly as long as the bottom line looks good.

As for Ho himself, he has made an astonishing recovery, just as Aunt Lily said he would, once the nightmare of the IRS suit was settled in our favor. As Aunt Lily says, it is shocking to think that a federal agency, such as the IRS, could come so close to destroying a man who has been a conscientious taxpayer for so many years. Though Ho no longer has the complete power that he once had, and must share his power with other stockholders, he is still very much in charge of things at the age of nearly ninety-five. He has moved back into his old squash-court-sized office on the thirtieth floor—the office with the huge map on the wall—and there is no question of who tells whom what to do. Ho's doctors say that they have never seen a case of what was diagnosed as advanced senility reverse itself so dramatically. It is as though the hardened arteries have thawed. Some physicians credit his comeback to his hardy, immigrant genes. One doctor has said that Ho was never senile at all, but was suffering from Post-Traumatic Stress Syndrome, rather like that suffered by veterans of the Vietnam War—in Ho's case, the IRS being the equivalent of the Vietnam experience.

But another doctor has decided that Ho was the victim of what this man calls "hysterical senility," brought on, again, by the IRS. Hysterical senility, this physician maintains, is like a hysterical pregnancy. Hysterical senility, of course, fits no known medical category, but this man is writing a scholarly paper on the subject.

Poor Herbert, on the other hand, has not been well, I am sorry to say. In the aftermath of his stroke, the right side of his once-almost-handsome face now sags rather horribly, making it difficult to look at him. To me, Herb Rothman's face calls to mind a sand castle that has been ravaged by the tide. Occasionally, he still tries to write company memos, if that's what they are, with his left hand, in a handwriting which, alas, no one can decipher. So, for the most part, he is reduced to a mute and angry, bitter glare from his wheelchair, as he watches the world pass him by.

But in the meantime, Herbert's illness has softened Pegeen considerably. It even seems to have saved their faltering marriage. In the process, Pegeen has lost her Razor Blade thinness, and has put on at least thirty pounds. Perhaps what Pegeen always needed was an invalid husband to care for, and Herbert's disability may have given her at last an opportunity to be splendid in a way she never knew how to be, or dared to be, before. Everyone comments on her obviously caring ministrations to her handicapped husband— the way she wheels him on daily outings in Central Park, and takes him to movies, plays, and concerts, activities he never enjoyed before. She has had all the doorknobs in the River House apartment lowered by six inches, so he can grasp them with his good hand from his chair. She has had an orthopedic toilet, with grab bars, installed in his bathroom. People have begun calling the new plump Pegeen Rothman a "saint," the way darling Marlene called Charlie and me saints. Thus beatified, Pegeen's personal star has risen consequentially in that fickle firmament known as New York Society.

But it has not risen to the extent that Maude McCulloch's has. Maude's rise has been meteoric. Let Mona Potter tell the story:

THE FASHION SCENE
by
Mona

Well, kiddies, now that autumn's here, you jes knew there'd be a buncha fashionable parties, dincha? Well, the most fashionable of 'em all was tossed last night by Magnificent Maude McCulloch in her smashingly redecorated East Side duplex, done all in white, with splashes of color provided ONLY by the Mirós, Picassos, Manets, Monets, and Gauguins on her walls, plus the Van Gogh her handsome hubby outbid the Japs for.

Magnificent Maude herself, who's never been skinnier, is singlehandedly putting my favorite sweetie, Pauline Trigère, back on the fashion map where she belongs. The wife of zillionaire Rodney McCulloch, her dark hair pulled back in a jeweled Channel bow, looked scrumptious in Trigère's hot pink evening pajamas as she greeted her guests who were everybody who was anybody. Anybody who wasn't somebody just wasn't there, kiddies. How does Magnificent Maude do it? Coming soon: My first exclusive interview with M.M., who's promised to tell Mother all her secrets. . . .

Et cetera, et cetera. I was at that party, of course. And I couldn't help noticing that Mona Potter was wearing a new pair of ruby chandelier earrings. They dangled beneath her birdcage of copper curls. From Mona's report it would be possible to guess that Maude McCulloch had transformed herself into just another East Side Razor Blade, right down to the death-rattle laugh. But I am pleased to say that, though she is fashionably thin, Maude has not gone quite that far. For one thing, she included her children at her party—as guests, and not just to pass hors d'oeuvres. A typical Razor Blade ships her children to the country when she entertains. There seem to be dozens of McCulloch children, though I actually counted only seven. They were quite astonishingly well behaved, as children go.

Mona also failed to mention that Maude McCulloch has inherited Coleman, Alex's former majordomo. Coleman had trouble adjusting to Alex's new husband, I understand. He told me that he considers Mel "not good enough for her." Ah, well. In Coleman's view, no one would be good enough for Alex.

Alex and Rodney McCulloch are still friendly—friendly rivals, you might say—for he still talks of wanting to develop a competitive publication to *Mode*. The trouble is that he has thus far been unable to find the right editor to steer the project for him.

As for Charlie and me, our new house in East Hampton is very pretty—a bit larger than we really needed, but very pretty. We really didn't need two tennis courts, for instance, one grass and one *en tout cas*, but I suppose they're nice to have. Our drop-in Sunday brunches are already becoming something of a social feature in this part of the South Shore. Drop in, next time you're in the area. Very casual. Drop in, that is, if you're comfortable with the sort of people we like to be around. Some people might find our guests a bit too high powered. Last week, for instance, Claudette Colbert *just suddenly appeared*. Guess what she was wearing. Hot pants. And a fisherman's vest. She looked divine.

As head of Rothman's publishing division, I find I can pretty much run things from the house out here, and don't need to be in the office in Manhattan all that much. In fact, where *Mode* is concerned, I pretty much leave business decisions up to Alex, and so, in effect, she is both editor and publisher of the magazine, a very nice arrangement for both of us. Though we keep the apartment at the Gainsborough as a *pied à terre*, our lives are pretty much out here nowadays. Even the canary seems happier out here. At the Gainsborough, Bridget hardly ever sang. Out here, she sings all day long!

We've moved the shrine to Adam out from the Gainsborough to East Hampton. I suspect this is why Mel and Alex haven't been over from Sagaponack for a visit, though they're only a hop and a skip away. She just doesn't want to see those stained-glass windows again.

I don't suppose Alex will ever get over Skipper. Her love for him was too bruising for her. I've thought a lot about the three men in Alex's life: Skipper, Steven, and Mel. There are many different kinds of love, of course, certainly more than Mr. Heinz's 57 Varieties, and perhaps more than there are stars in the sky. But when Skipper happened to her—and that is the right word, he *happened* to her, fell upon her like a hunter upon his prey—she was so young, and he was such a sexual animal. He even smelled of sex. When he was in a room with you, the smell in the air was so thick with sex that you could have cut it with a butter knife, sliced it off in great thick slabs and left them lying about the floor. In fact, that was probably the only thing poor Skipper . . . Adam . . . really ever had.

That afternoon of our little letter-burning party, I brought out one of our nude photographs of Adam, in a state of violent erection, which was really something to behold. I showed it to her. She looked at the picture briefly, then turned away with a shudder of revulsion. It could have been the revulsion of remembered lust.

Perhaps, at seventeen, she thought that was what all men were like. Alas, they are not. Perhaps, at seventeen, she thought that was what love was. Alas, it isn't.

Then came Steven. For all his sweetness and his gentleness and kindness—or perhaps because of these qualities—I am sure he was a passive lover, quite the opposite of Skipper. I know Steven loved her very much, and I'm sure she loved him, but it was just a different kind of love. She asked herself: Is this, then, what love is like?

Both men hurt her in different ways. Both men loved her in different ways. Both men abandoned her in different ways. Both men fulfilled her in different ways. Both men offered her a great deal. But both men robbed her of a great deal.

In Mel, I think, she has found the best of both at last, minus the worst of both. It would be trite and banal to say that Mel has made Alex happy at last. Alex is too smart and sophisticated a woman to think that anyone is happier, or unhappier, than anyone else. Or, to put it more accurately, no one is happier, or unhappier, than he or she decides to be. But, in some ways, marriage to Mel seems to have made Alex an even better editor—more willing to experiment, more willing to gamble, more willing to explore the untested and the risky. The untested and the risky certainly applies to her task of building a new relationship with Joel, too, and Mel is definitely a help to her there. The past is a great deal of heavy luggage for a person to carry about in life, and if there is one sure thing that Mel has done for Alex it has been to help her let go of the past. Is there any better kind of love than a love that makes one forget past loves? I think not.

I pray that this is true for her, because she deserves the very best of love.

You see, I love her too, in my own way.

And I think, in her own way, that she loves me. It's just another, different kind of love.

Sometimes I think that if love could be sold and bottled, its various formulas would fill an entire supermarket aisle.

Yesterday was my birthday—which one, I won't say, because at this point I really don't know, but it was one of them, one or another of them. I think age is the most boring statistic. Why are Americans so obsessed with age? Why does the *New York Times* insist on peppering its pages with the ages of the people in its news stories, when their ages have absolutely no relevance to the events being reported? It is a question I might pass along to Joel, in light of his proposed future journalistic career. If I were running things, I would like to see age done away with.

In any event, a huge UPS van backed into our drive, driven by, of all strange coincidences, that dreadful Otto Forsthoefel, whom I naturally pretended not to recognize. Her gift, she had said, was to be a combination birthday and housewarming present, and when we unpacked the large crates it turned out that they contained a lovely pair of matched Boulle commodes. They are perhaps not quite as fine as those Aunt Lily Rothman has, and they do not bear the hallmark of the Palais de Versailles. But they are signed, and they are in better condition than Aunt Lily's pieces, and they are very fine indeed. They look quite handsome where we have placed them, flanking the doorway to the room we call the Orangerie.

How did she know of my passion for Boulle cabinetry? I've no idea unless, as I suspect, she and Aunt Lily had put their heads together. The card was very simple. On it, she had drawn a slash through the word "old," and so the message looked like this:

FOR DEAR ~~OLD~~ YOUNG LENNY

XXXX

Alex and Mel

At first, we didn't open the drawers of either of the two cabinets. Then I opened the top drawer of one of them, marveling at how magnificently it was fitted and doweled, and Scotch-taped to the rosewood bottom of the drawer was the plain gold wedding band Skipper had given her. With the ring was another note that said, "I think you should have this now." I confess there were tears in my eyes.

And—oh, yes. Fiona. I rather imagine you are wondering what became of her. But I'm afraid the fact is that I have more or less lost track of her. After she was evicted from the Westbury for failure to pay her rent, I heard she went to Los Angeles, where in that fragile world of Hollywood society, and still posing as Lady Fiona Hesketh-Fenton, she did all right—for a while, at least—under the sponsorship of some producer whose last picture was made in 1971. Then I heard she was in Duluth. Why Duluth? I've no idea. I've never had the misfortune of visiting Duluth, and I suppose Duluthians (Duluthites?) feel fortunate in never having had me to entertain. The only thing I've ever heard about Duluth is that the Holiday Inn there closes up completely during the winter months because freezing spray, blowing off Lake Superior, encases the entire motel complex in a thick carapace of ice.

I've never known what kind of nasty scheme she was trying to cook up with Joel, which involved me somehow. It was no doubt something that she hoped would embarrass or frighten me, or put me in a blackmailable position. Needless to say, I've never asked Joel about this. I wouldn't want him to know that his mother and I had poked around in his private journals.

I've nothing personal against Fiona, actually. She was just a girl who'd botched up her life in London, and tried to reinvent herself in New York. Most people would like to reinvent themselves from time to time, it seems to me. Haven't you ever thought of chucking your old self aside, and starting fresh, someplace else, as someone else, with a